# A MOMENT OF SILENCE

## Also by Sister Souljah

*The Coldest Winter Ever*

*A Deeper Love Inside: The Porsche Santiaga Story*

*Life After Death: The Coldest Winter Ever II*

*Midnight: A Gangster Love Story*

*Midnight and The Meaning of Love*

*No Disrespect*

# A MOMENT OF SILENCE

## MIDNIGHT III

SISTER SOULJAH

EMILY BESTLER BOOKS

ATRIA

New York London Toronto Sydney New Delhi

EMILY BESTLER BOOKS

ATRIA

An Imprint of Simon & Schuster, Inc.
1230 Avenue of the Americas
New York, NY 10020

This book is a work of fiction. Any references to historical events, real people, or real places are used fictitiously. Other names, characters, places, and events are products of the author's imagination, and any resemblance to actual events or places or persons, living or dead, is entirely coincidental.



First Emily Bestler Books / Atria Paperback edition October 2016

EMILY BESTLER BOOKS/ATRIA PAPERBACK and colophons are trademarks of Simon & Schuster, Inc.

For information about special discounts for bulk purchases, please contact Simon & Schuster Special Sales at 1-866-506-1949 or business@simonandschuster.com.

Manufactured in the United States of America

15 17 19 20 18 16 14

Library of Congress Cataloging-in-Publication Data is available.

ISBN 978-1-4767-6598-3
ISBN 978-1-4767-6599-0 (pbk)
ISBN 978-1-4767-6600-3 (ebook)

# A MOMENT OF SILENCE

Some thing is in the water,
Some thing is in the food.
Some thing is in the atmosphere,
Some thing changed the mood.

Some one stole the feeling,
Some one flipped the beat.
There's meanness in the cold air,
And anger in the heat.

Now the souls are empty,
The strength gone from our stance.
Now most hearts are vacant,
And feet no longer dance.

Knees won't bend for prayer,
I can't breathe this air.
No one even cares,
Or remembers what was here.

Some thing is now nothing,
And ugly is extra bold.
Beauty has been stripped away
And only lies are told.

We need more than A Moment of Silence,
A year to just reflect
A time to become sincerely humble,
A truth worthy to live, believe and protect.

*By Sister Souljah*

# 1. MY SECOND WIFE

She is closer to me than my shadow. She's as precious as the sky. In my almost empty Brooklyn apartment, my second wife, Chiasa, aimed and then fired sharpened knives into the corked wall. I had taken everything out of this place, but the cork seemed permanent to my project bedroom. It had served as my target practice for seven years and unlike me and my family, it did not want to leave.

"Go stand over there for me," she said sweetly. As she locked her silver-gray eyes into mine, I looked at her and said nothing. My smile broke out naturally. "Don't smile at me," she said with a straight face. "Every time it's time for us to fight you flash that smile."

She must not have figured out that she brought that smile out of me, and so much more. It was because of my love for her that I held onto the keys to this place, where I wouldn't even allow my mother, Umma; my first wife, Akemi; or my sister, Naja to ever again step foot.

I walked to the corked wall like she wanted. I leaned back, my hands in my Girbaud jean pockets. She narrowed her eyes and hurled a knife at me. It cut through the still stale air that was typical in the projects and sliced through my fitted. I didn't flinch. She saw that, and inside of seven seconds she outlined my head and shoulders with eight knives rapidly fired by her quick and accurate combination of eyes and fingers.

"You going to kill me, with my own knives?" I asked her. She walked towards me slowly until only noses separated her and me. She pulled each knife down from the cork.

"Now you do me," she said, handing me the knives. Her breasts pressed against my chest, and her unusually long lashes brushed against mine. The last thing on my mind was taking aim at her with a weapon, and she knew it.

Chiasa, my second wife, is a badass, a flawless-skinned, pretty-faced, thick-haired, doe-eyed, ballerina-bodied, ninjutsu-trained warrior. Pretty and precise, she is disciplined to the extreme, same as me. Yet, she is the only one alive who could move me off point, cause me to temporarily lose my balance and have to check myself. The unusual combination of her deep fiery soul, her soft-spoken manner, her sharp mind, her vibrant energy and exquisite body, topped off by the intensity of her loyalty, moved me continuously and *I couldn't keep off of her.*

It had gotten to the point where she sometimes had me questioning things and matters I had never questioned myself about before. Boldly, she had become a Muslim woman at age sixteen. She accepted Islam on her own, without me asking her to do it or having to recite her any truths from the Holy Quran. She reads the Quran for herself, loves each *sura* she studies and each *ayat* she learns. She uses every word in the book to challenge herself to become more beautiful in her wisdom and her deeds. For her to love the faith like any Muslim born on Islamic land and raised with the Muslim example and lifestyle surrounding her made her irresistible to me.

When anyone in her family tried to reverse Chiasa's mind, she would politely and calmly reveal her angles of thought and her contentment. Once, one of her aunts said in front of her whole family, "A Muslim man can only have more than one wife if he can treat them all equally. No man can treat two, three, four women equally, so that means he can really only have one wife. You're supposed to be smart enough to figure it out. It's like a riddle," her aunt said.

Chiasa answered softly, correcting her aunt's interpretation . . .

"Treat us each 'fairly.' No woman wants to be treated 'equal' to another, because we are each different. We each enjoy our man in our own way. We each have our own thoughts, likes, dislikes, and hobbies. I don't want my husband to do the exact 'equal' thing he does with his first wife with me; or to give me the exact 'equal' gifts he gave her. Why would I want that? I just want him to love me how I, Chiasa, want to be loved. Us sharing the things that are unique to what we feel when we are together. I want us to enjoy and make each other feel good, because we believe the same things. I want us to learn, earn, and fight together, to be safe, secure, and happy. This is more than enough for me."

Those words she spoke shut her one aunt up for some time. And, I know she meant it. When we first settled into our new home in Queens, the house that Umma and I purchased with the money that we both earned through our company, Umma Designs, Chiasa chose the smallest bedroom for herself. She set her bedding on the floor, the way she was most comfortable. She lined up her books, mounted her swords, folded her clothes, set up her oils, potions, and creams, brushes, hairpins, and combs, and told me, "You are definitely welcome. Come whenever you want to see me. You know I'm from a military family. I am an expert at waiting."

Her words put me at ease. I was always one hundred that I could protect and provide for and love her. I never wavered on that. But she made me certain that although we have a teenage marriage and she is my second wife, who left behind her parents, her country, and her action-packed life of excitement, she had no regrets and that I made her happy. It felt good that even over time she had zero doubt.

Now she was touching my nine-millimeter. I had laid it on the kitchen counter away from both of us, and towards the wall. We were in my Brooklyn 'hood, my old apartment. So of course I kept it close. Her clear-polished, clipped, and curved nails and pretty fingers on the black steel aroused me. But the way she held it revealed she didn't have no experience with the piece. Chiasa is a bow-and-arrow kind of girl, not to be taken lightly. She could fire something into you, to rock you into a temporary sleep or send you all the way to heaven. Perfect vision, when she fires, she met her mark whether it was your brain, your heart, or your family jewels. And she wasn't above poisoning her arrow tip before positioning it just right in her target's jugular. Her target would be coughing up blood, his own veins exploding then choking him.

"How come you prefer guns?" she asked me, playfully. But I could tell she really wanted to know. She wanted to know and feel everything about me. And her inquiries were always subtle and sweet. The way she went about it would have me so open, I'd be telling her something I never shared with no one else. She mixed her curiosity and intellect with her seductions, and it was a powerful potion. I knew what she was really asking me, because I know her and her mind. She was thinking, to a ninjutsu warrior, a gun is a weakness, a type of excuse not to use your hands and mind to the furthest degree, to confront any enemy and solve the problem . . . any problem.

"The gun is the bottom line," I told her. "The Japanese don't need them." Japan is the country that my second wife is from. She's African and Japanese, an exotic combination. I plucked her from a pretty place, a popular park in Tokyo that was filled with green fields, flowers, and an alluring forest. In that forest there was only one house. Chiasa lived there with only her grandfather, the park ranger.

"There's peace in your neighborhood and in your country," I told her. "Brooklyn brings the noise. Over here there's certain times and situations where even the swiftest mind and hands move too slow."

"This block is not so bad looking. I like all the art on the bricks," she said, referring to the 'hood graffiti. "And it's kind of cool how they're setting up for that block party outside today. The music is loud but it sounds nice, and the people seem like they could become our friends," she said cheerfully. "I bet if you didn't suspect them," she said softly, "and trusted in them a little bit more . . ."

I interrupted her. "Don't sleep. These people will easily give a reasonable man a reason to use his trigger finger."

I know that men and women were both created by Allah from one same soul. Yet I also know that men and women are different. Chiasa, the woman, is friendly, loving, emotion filled, and hopeful. Besides, she's foreign to my Brooklyn 'hood, or any 'hood for that matter. She's a capable female fighter, but she's also innocent and naïve and likely to underestimate evil. She and I are married, similar in some ways and in deep love. But I am a man born and trained to observe, detect, and perceive all potential threats. To defend, guard, protect or attack, and eliminate all real enemies who don't understand any language other than the ratta-tat-tat or the boom of my "milly." I have killed before, for these same reasons. Chiasa has competed in sword fighting and martial arts and won. She has fought, poisoned, injured, and intercepted some enemies in real-life conflict, *but she has never killed.*

Now that she is my wife, she won't have to. I'm here for the sole purpose of protecting and providing for and loving my women, and in the future, for raising my sons to do the same for their women and families, *Insha'Allah.*

"Guns seem messy," she continued her soft expressions while caressing the steel. "They make too much noise." She held it now, with both hands. "The silent kill is superior," she said.

"I have a silencer," I told her. "I don't leave it lying around. If you get snagged with it, you do seven extra years—separate from gun possession charges."

"Seven years," she said. "That's too long . . . and separate from the other charges . . . that's too much." She retreated to silence for some seconds, returning the gun to its position on the counter and pulling back her palms. Then her eyes shifted from the gloom of that thought.

"You know what I want?" she asked, her eyes searching me now to see if I was giving her question real thought, and if I was sharp enough to guess. I was listening carefully now. I wanted to know all of her wants, everything she wanted right now and even in the future. I would be the one who was getting it for her, eliminating her need to *need* another human beside me, even her father.

"A crossbow, have you seen one? It's cleverly designed, a quiet, thorough, neater, cleaner weapon, but still super deadly . . ." She sounded like she was describing herself.

"What would you do with that?" I asked her.

"Run out into the woods," she said. Now she held her pretty arms in position as though she was firing her crossbow. "I'd climb a mountain, track down the bad guys, monsters and witches or avenge anyone who tried to take what I love."

She approached me, then pressed her thick, moist and warm lips onto mine.

My tongue moving over her tongue, our heads tilted, and there was only our breathing, sucking, and sincerity mixing with our silence. Her black silk *yukata* dress was easily released. She knew when she put it on this morning, as we trekked and trained over here to Brooklyn, what we came to do. My place in the projects was more of a hut than a palace. It definitely wasn't the nature-filled, beautifully blossoming gardens and forest where she had lived. This was an all cemented place that couldn't compare to the wilderness that she and I had traveled through together, or to eventually climbing over the mountains of Hokkaido, as we fell in love. I knew her soul still craved all of that adventure we had shared, but I also knew that my hut in the projects was where I am right now, and as long as I am anywhere she would willingly and voluntarily choose to be right beside me.

Bare backs and bare butts, we were both in the living room now on the warm hard floor, sitting in the spotlight from the powerful sun. Our sauna was natural. The living room windows were shut tight. Chiasa began gently rocking her pretty thighs from side to side, releasing her subtle scent. I watched, wanted to make her wait, while observing her dark brown nipples swelling on her golden breasts. I knew she wouldn't like me staying still and staring because this was her exclusive time with me alone and she cherished it. She started kicking me playfully. Only our feet fought. I cheated, grabbing hold of her right ankle and dragging her. She began laughing but still tried to leap up with her left. Off-balance, she fell. I broke her fall and now our bodies were entangled. I reached back and snatched from off the floor the cloth belt from her *yukata*.

"Oh no you don't!" She raised her voice playfully at what she smartly suspected she had coming. We tussled. I won. Her hands were now tied behind her back. She liked it. I flipped her, then licked her left nipple, then her right. I pulled back.

"Don't stop," she whispered. I knew her nipples were super sensitive. I began sucking one nipple and not the other. I moved my hand down her curves and rested it on her waist. "Stop playing," she begged. I moved my hand between her thighs and she moaned. I pushed my thickest finger inside and her pussy walls locked around it tightly and thumped rhythmically. When I began kissing her she was breathing hard but still tried to launch a sneak attack and flip me with her feet. I'm smiling.

"Don't smile at me!" she said, trying to mount me because I hadn't mounted her. We wrestled. My stiff-as-steel joint didn't give a fuck about the game I was playing. In moments I was deep inside of her, pushing and thrashing and the feeling was so extreme.

"I love you," her lips passionately pushed out causing me to fuck her the way I knew she needed to be fucked in that moment. We were moving, and feeling and changing positions and postures. Warmer than warm, our emotions were heavy like that and only our breathing was heavier.

Our mutual deep attraction, our mutual deep admiration, our mutual deep love, loyalty, and deep affection . . . our mutual faith, feelings, and friendship all exploded and I came pouring into her. She was quiet now, still shaking from her own eruption. She turned on her side to face me. So I faced her, watching her slide her slim finger in the sheen of my sweat.

"One of us should open that window," she said. Her silky Japanese hairstyle turned into a long, wild African bush, me digging it either way because it's all her. Checking her out I eased up, reminding her that "We are both naked." She sat up.

"I know," she said sweetly. I kissed her, just pushed my lips against hers. Her now relaxed nipples turned into Kalamata olives. In less than one second we were both swelling again and she leapt at me. Her hips spread in my lap and I touched her up until I was doing sit-ups between her thighs. Chiasa, my second wife, was no longer the unknowing virgin I had first met. She was swinging those hips, completely comfortable with our naked bodies. She craved that friction and would have an outburst when her feeling reached an unbearable high. Her voice echoed in my mostly empty apartment where she and I needed to be alone to get wild and dive all the way into our thing.

Her second shaking, and I was sure she wasn't done. Athletic and competitive, she has endurance. Yet in her eyes I saw a complete surrendering to me, from a sixteen-years-young feline fighter unaccustomed to surrendering.

"How come I love you so much?" she asked me intensely as if she needed to have an answer from herself. "I love you more than Konichi," she said.

Konichi is her American mare, a horse her father bought her, which she left behind in Japan after I married her.

"You love me more than your beast?" I smiled, saying it out loud so she could hear how it translated in my ear. She laughed a little too, then stopped smiling.

"I love you more than my mother," she said, pushing each word out from her heart. The air thickened and the room fell silent, even with the music from the streets thumping outside our closed windows. We both knew she meant it. She'd never say anything she didn't mean. And for words that strong and heavy, silence was my only response. She knew I couldn't wrap my mind around ever considering the depth of my love for my mother, Umma. Nor had I ever, or would I ever, or could I ever compare my love for Umma to my love for any other human.

Still, her magnetic confession moved me and I was making love to her now with an even deeper feeling than fucking. So deep it felt like a high-pitched sound. So high it could cause all eardrums to pop, then bleed. A feeling so meaningful it could push life into existence and hurl the two lovers ten years into the future within seconds. I tugged her clitoris and made her cum so hard she gasped and exhaled some sounds I had only ever heard in the jungle of South Sudan, word.

"Happy birthday," I said. Her seventeenth birthday was one week away, but she and I were celebrating it in the only time we had available to be alone. I wasn't big on birthdays, mine or anybody else's, but she was that special to me. She looked into me and said in her soft, slow, sultry way, "I love you more than my father."

Time stood still. I couldn't move. She couldn't move. Even our eyes couldn't blink. Even the boom of the 808 bass that shook the speakers on the outdoor sound system shut down. The turntable needle got stuck and could only repeat a piece of the beat. For a split second it seemed that even the fire-filled brilliant sun had blacked out.

Unique, her unusualness attracted me. Twelve clocks, ten phone cards, and a huge lighted spinning globe were the first purchases of my second wife, Chiasa Hiyoku Brown, as we moved into our new home in the borough of Queens, state of New York. I just took her to the stores where I knew the items she wanted to buy could be purchased, then watched as she walked around choosing carefully and intently. Of course I carried her choices, her boxes and bags, for her. She accumulated enough for me to go out and hail a cab and have the driver pop the trunk.

In her first-floor bedroom in our house, she lined her triple-A battery-operated clocks on the shelf after setting each one. They were all the same model, but she set each of them to a different time.

"Where do you want the globe?" I asked.

"One minute," she said as she began pulling books from a big box, rushing to stack and organize them on the floor.

"I should have bought you a table for this," I said as I realized she was using her books to build a stand.

"This is good enough. These are the books I've already read," she said. *She read them, but couldn't leave them behind*, I thought to myself. So I knew then how she felt about her books. I set the globe up on the book stand she built, plugged it in, and it glowed, colorfully outlining most of the territories on Earth. Helping her with these little things was a small task for me, yet like the moon, she glowed with a grateful smile.

On a short stack of same-sized encyclopedias sat her baby-blue-colored phone. Slim and feminine, it was curved nicely, with glow-in-the-dark push buttons. She called it her "blue phone." It was her own hard-line hotline, with a separate number from our house phone or our Umma Designs business phone. Only she could use her "blue phone," and that was on purpose.

"Daddy will call me tonight at eleven p.m. It will be the end of the night here in New York. It will be eleven in the morning over in Tokyo. It will be five a.m. in London, England, and eight p.m. in Los Angeles, California, and eight a.m. the next day in Riyadh, Saudi Arabia. It will be three a.m. in Antwerp, Belgium and in Zurich, Switzerland and six a.m. in Johannesburg, South Africa . . ." She pointed to each clock that she had set. "And in Antartica . . ." she said . . .

I smiled and repeated, "Antarctica . . ."

She laughed and said, "I was just checking to see if you were listening."

"So we bought twelve clocks, so you could know what time it is in all of these regions of the world," I said but it was more of an observation than a question.

"*Hai*!" she said softly in her energetic way, meaning, "yes" in her Japanese language.

"Daddy never says exactly where he is. But he will tell me which country he is in. I look the country up on the globe so I know where he is and exactly what's surrounding him, and what time zone it has. And if by chance he's gonna be in a certain place for more than one night, and if he is willing to give me his phone number, I can use these phone cards, and that way I won't run up a big phone bill. Then I can check these clocks to know exactly what time it is where Daddy is stationed. That way I won't accidentally wake him when he sleeps . . ." She exhaled, not being used to so much talking except when she is excited about her father.

I just looked at her, attracted to her passion, yet very aware of her anxious and deep love for her six-foot-eight black-skinned African-American brute of a father, a man of fifty faces who only showed his daughter one, and she believed that was the only face he had. She spoke about him with great affection as though he was her teddy bear, and her anchor, and her hero. "Daddy," who called her every other day, at any time he wanted to, with no consideration for our schedule or time zone, sometimes only had ten seconds of convo to share. He'd say, "I just wanted to hear your voice and be sure you're happy and okay." "Daddy," who has a serious weak spot for his daughter, who he could hardly ever see in person because of his work. So he filled the absence of his presence in her life with presents. Expensive gifts given on each of her birthdays and on selected Christian holidays. He gifted her anything she asked him for with only one rule. She couldn't ask him to come home on any particular day at any particular time. He would come on his schedule, unannounced and by his own choice. My wife marked time by her father's presence and presents and absences. The presents were gifts that no young husband who, although he is a hard worker and is steadily building his business, could match.

"Daddy," a general in the American military. "Daddy," who had declared war on me when he realized his daughter's heart had been swept away by a young Muslim man who was born on the other side of his world. "Daddy," who played deadly games with my life because he could. "Daddy," whose last words to me before I left Asia with his beautiful sixteen-years-young daughter who I wifed, were, "Take great care of my daughter or I'll find you and kill you."

Now his daughter, who is definitely my wife, lay naked on the hot floor beside me on her early seventeenth birthday party, stroking my joint with her pretty fingers, kissing me lightly with her pretty lips, hypnotizing me with her pretty eyes, and stroking my calves with her pretty toes. Saying she loved me more than him. My presence had outdistanced his presents. And our intimacy was an area where he naturally could never go. And our closeness was sealed . . . a bond never to be broken.

The metal tapping against the metal door unlocked time.

"Uh-uh, no . . ." Chiasa said, seductively.

No one was supposed to knock on my project apartment door. Even when my family lived here, no one did. And for the time that Chiasa and I had been coming here, no one else came, and no one else was invited. She licked my lips and her tongue fucking delighted me. Just as I moved to go in her, a voice within me ordered me to get up. Chiasa leapt up a fourth of a second after me and began collecting her clothes from the living room floor. I nodded for her to go into my bedroom. I stepped into my basketball shorts, then my jeans.

Easing up the metal shutter of the peephole, I saw hazel eyes, black lashes, and a red *hijab.* It was Sudana, a sixteen-years-young Sudanese girl who lives way out in the Bronx, but now she was standing alone on the other side of my door, in the dark, dangerous corridor of my Brooklyn project. Uninvited. I never gave her this address, and she had never, ever been here before. I felt a bad feeling as I quickly unlocked and yanked open the door.

"Umma," was all I said to her. She smiled calmly and said, "Your

Umi is perfectly fine. She's still at my house with my mom at the women's meeting."

Relieved that my sudden and dark intuition was wrong and that this was not an emergency, and that my mother was safe, as she should be, I turned my attention to Sudana, waiting to hear her reason for coming and what she wanted.

"Are you going to continue to block the entrance, or will you invite me in?" she asked. Actually, I wanted her to disappear, leave, so I could get back to my wife. I knew I had to be cautious though, and careful and courteous. Sudana and my mother are close. Sudana's father and I had done good business together. And for the time that I had recently been traveling in Asia, Sudana's whole family had taken care of my Umma and my sister Naja for more than a month. I owed her . . . to be grateful.

I saw her eyes moving over my chest, admiring my body. In haste, I was shirtless, unzipped and beltless, sockless . . . I stepped back from the door so she could enter. I locked it behind her, then quickly picked up my T-shirt and pulled it on. When I turned back to her, she was unwrapping her *hijab*, which in our faith, and in this situation was forbidden. There was no blood relation between us, and I was a man who could marry her, and she was an unmarried young woman. Her long hair was shining like she taxied over here fresh from the salon. She was watching for my reaction, now that she had showed me what I had never seen before. I gave off nothing. I knew she felt it. She moved her eyes slowly around the living room. First she looked back toward the front door. She paused on Chiasa's kicks, neatly placed against the wall. She turned again, her eyes landing on Chiasa's bangles lying on the counter next to the slingshot that she keeps strapped around her right thigh beneath the skirt of her *yukata*. She paused over the bento box Chiasa had packed and stacked with some foods for our "project picnic." Then Sudana stood staring at the only half-closed bedroom door. She twisted her body slightly and her gaze landed on my nine-millimeter, then eased back onto me. She had a serious stare now that she had surveyed everything. Her eyes were moving over me. The love that she was searching for in me wasn't there. My heart was full. And the scent of my wife's and my lovemaking still hung in the stagnant air.

Perceptive, Sudana switched from speaking the English she had been using to speaking only in Arabic. She realized Chiasa was here with me, and somewhere listening closely. She also knew that Chiasa could not speak or understand Arabic . . . but of course I could. Chiasa remained quiet and out of sight. Even that aroused me.

"I need to speak some private words just for your ears," she said in Arabic.

"You could've waited to tell me whatever you have to tell me when I pick Umma up from your house later on," I said in Arabic. "It's not smart or safe for you to just show up here." I walked over and picked up her *hijab.* "Put it on," I told her. Then I heard the shower splash on in my bathroom. My mind switched. I pictured Chiasa naked in the downpour. *Can you do that same thing to me that you did to me on our first time?* Chiasa had asked me.

"All this time I have been walking around believing that I was doing everything right and that these other nonbelieving girls were all wrong," Sudana said. I didn't like her referring to my second wife, who was not born into Islam, but who is Muslim by choice, as *kaffir*, meaning nonbeliever in Arabic.

Sudana continued in Arabic with soft but strong emphasis and attitude, "But I figured out, when you came back from Japan with *wife number two*, that these other girls must've been right all along—and I must've been wrong."

"Sudana . . ." I interrupted her.

"No, please let me finish," she said. "I've been wanting to say this for more than a month. I've been slowly getting up the nerve. I had been waiting for the opportunity where I could speak directly to you, just the two of us. But the chance never happened. We were always surrounded by so many.

"The whole time since you and I first met, I was doing everything you wanted and everything you asked me to do, and caring for your Umma as much as my own mother, even after you returned from Asia, *shocking me with this second wife*, acting all calm, cool, and casual."

Sudana's voice stayed in a controlled tone but her emotion was rising, so I let her get it all out. It didn't matter. If anything she was saying was against Chiasa as my second wife, she was walking down a dead end.

I met Chiasa in the sky, somewhere over the Siberian mountains. She was asleep on a flight, wearing her naturally long cornrows braided like streaks of lightning. Between her breasts was a gold first-place medal. When Chiasa and I stood face-to-face and eye-to-eye in Narita Airport processing through customs, the thought that came to me, and dropped directly into my mind about Chiasa, was *She seems like a gift from Allah.* And, if Allah had given me Chiasa, only Allah could take her away, *la kadar Allah* (God forbid). Sudana would have to chill and learn that she couldn't love me by force or keep a count or a scorecard somehow declaring herself the winner. True, I had always known Sudana is a beautiful Sudanese young woman who had feelings for me—but the timing between me and her was always off.

"You couldn't see me. When I was covered, you overlooked me. So I wanted to give you a chance to see me clearly," she said, holding the fabric of her *hijab* in one hand. "Take a look," she said, peeling off her light jacket, the one I'm sure she had to wear to get past her mother and father and brother's inspection and besides them, all of the Sudanese women at that meeting in the basement apartment of her house. Her red but sheer blouse showcased the cut of her satin bra and perfect figure. She spun around slowly, her jeans hugging her hips, her feet turning in her new red heels, which she wrongly and defiantly didn't remove when she walked in here.

"Oh these," she said, stepping out of those red heels. "Same as I stepped into them, I can step out of them." Her toes were revealed, red polish dusted with crystals. I eased my eyes up and away from her feet. Still, she stood posing and clutching her new red Coach saddlebag.

"Here I am, Sudana Salim Ahmed Ghazzahli, from *our country*. Speaking *our language*, from *our people*, a believer, a *muslimah* same as you, *mussulman*. There can't be anything wrong with any of that. I *know* those are things that you like; the same things that you love about your mother, Umma. The only thing left has to be that *you didn't see me*. Because I was always covered, you didn't notice that 'Ana ahla minaha' I'm prettier than her," she continued in Arabic, referring to Chiasa by shifting her eyes to the back room. Then Sudana uttered, "I'm more beautiful than both of them," referring also to my first wife, Akemi.

Chiasa came hurrying out the back bedroom in her black-laced bra and matching panties, her *yukata* half on, half off. In a frenzy she tied her black *yukata* and dove for her black Pumas.

"I saw Naja outside running . . ." Chiasa said, now down on one knee tying her laces.

"It couldn't be Naja. I left her downstairs, indoors with Ms. Marcy," Sudana said with confidence. "Naja told me that she missed Ms. Marcy," she added.

She was speaking to my back 'cause I was already out the door. It didn't matter what Sudana said. Chiasa has perfect vision. I was one hundred that whatever my wife said she saw, she saw. I had my little sister Naja in my first mind, my Nikes on my feet, my nine in my hand. I was on the stairwell. Bulbs were broken and it was darkened; I was headed down.

## 2. THE EXECUTION

Sometimes it's in the wind when men walk by one another, moving in opposite directions. I could feel it way back when—that I would murder him. It was just a matter of time, motivation, and just cause. I could sense that he would throw me a reason.

*Murder*, not kill. A person could be killed in a car accident, or in a storm, or a fire, or by choking on a fishbone. Murder is different. It's getting slaughtered with full intent. It's getting gritty and gruesome—hacked up. Eyes plucked, punched, or blown out of their sockets. Sliced open and skinned. Organs ripped out from their flesh frame. Hands twisted off at the wrists. Neck severed from the head. Head blown to bits and pieces.

There are men who deserve to be murdered. To kill 'em would be too compassionate.

Ninety-seven aggressive degrees outside same day, in the same place, my old Brooklyn block, except now it's 9 p.m. The sweltering orange sun refused to settle. The three-thousand-strong block party was officially over an hour ago. The fire department captain and the DJ were in an intense standoff. The captain had the authority, but the DJ had crowd control. Long as he was spinning the cuts, ain't nobody leaving the jam.

The Brooklyn crowd shouted and roared with a rapping rhythm, "Don't stop the music!" A suited public official over a megaphone kept reminding everyone of his name and status and crediting himself. He thanked everyone for coming to his "community event," and repeatedly asked the crowd to break up peacefully so the cleaning crew could do its job.

Police posed up their power, stepping out of their parked cruisers where they had been slacking and snacking in the air-conditioning. One po-po pulled the plug and the speaker system went dead after a screech. But they had interrupted Eric B for President while Rakim was rhyming and hundreds of 'hood heads performed Ra's rhyme in perfect sync, while others beat-boxed the beats.

From the wall where I was low-leaning, I peeped one cop who reached into his car to trigger the siren. He let the high-pitched sound leak a little, and then deaded it, but kept the red lights spinning. And now cops in other cruisers did the same, a chain reaction of lights and sound. Now there was movement. Now, even I was milling. My eyes speeding over grills and grimaces, T-shirts and kicks, jewels and scars, and watching all hands, all pockets, and all men moving—knowing, at least one of 'em was gonna get mercked, and die before midnight. The 'hood was all hip-hop. But, there was only one joint playing in my head, "In The Air Tonight," by Phil Collins. The truth of the track, the lyrics and the music, accelerated my anger, as it mixed with my usual calmness and precision. Anger overtook me and then turned to pure fury. My state of mind was explosive. It was burning hot outside. I'm hotheaded, but now my heart is ice cold.

Nigga, not ninja. 'Cause ninjas manage their emotions, eliminate rage, and deliver with ease the takedown of the target at the opportune time, and without leaving a trace.

But this was too personal to organize, calculate calmly or put off for a wiser plan or perfect opportunity, and definitely not for another day. No matter what, in these moments, I could not separate myself from my fury.

Suddenly the moon eclipsed the sun and darkness dropped down disguised as a subtle gray, then drifted into deep black. I didn't have my silencer on me, but my nine was tucked with one in the chamber. So heated out of my usual posture, I didn't give a fuck about the boom of my burner, only about the execution.

Shoulder to shoulder with many men moving like a stampede on the Sahara, a pack of 'hood-hyenas cut across the flow of the movement diagonally in front of me. Girls grouped up like desert foxes, wearing bleached-out jeans and fresh kicks, tight tees and hair gelled, followed close behind. A young mother held one baby in her left arm while walking a four-year-old with her right hand, who dropped a pacifier. Instinctively, I squatted to scoop it, handed it to her young son, and saw one lion moving behind her turn left and another lion turn right. And over the kid's shoulder, the approach of my target was revealed.

Sideways, he was the sidewinder type, a poisonous viper that usually sneaks around rapidly sliding sideways across the desert effortlessly. Closer now, he saw me squatted there with my milli in my grip. He froze. His own frightened feet were fucking him over. Shook, he was empty-handed and solo. The nasty shit he did, he had to do alone. He did it. He knew it. I knew it. He knew that I knew. In his eyes was fear. His left eye was bandaged where Chiasa's razor thin and lethally sharp blade had already cut him. I leaped. Punched him hard in his injury. He raised his fist in the aftershock. I punched him in his stomach. Big, slow, and stupid, he had left it unguarded. All those jail push-ups and that bench-pressing gave him the look but not the technique. His body buckled from the blow. His jaw dropped open. Speeding, I shoved my barrel in his mouth. Made him deep-throat it. He pushed back but couldn't move me. As he reached for me, he choked on my black steel. I squeezed off six in him to make sure only he swallowed the bullets and no one else in the crowd. I never want innocent blood on my hands.

Now his face was mangled and soaking in the blood of his brains. His whole body was jumping, shaking, in a jerking motion like a worm with its head cut off. His intestines were blown out of his sides. His blood was mixing with his pee and his shit, which splattered, and stained, and stunk. He wanted to be 'hood-famous. Now he was beyond recognition. Now, he would only be known for the last six seconds of his life. For peeing and shitting out of fear in his Guess jean shorts, and for getting hunted and slaughtered on the block like a beast.

More shots were fired. Not from me, but they sounded not too far away. Familiar, I figured young cubs was shooting into the air, just to fuck with the cops for shutting down the sound system. A bottle got thrown from the roof, smashed open, and caused a ripple in a crowd.

"Here come the jake!" someone hollered from the window ledge.

It was as though everybody out here had shot him dead 'cause some started running and bumping into others who already had been running since the split seconds that the six fatal shots got fired. Mamas were hanging out of opened project windows like curious monkeys.

Some 'hood-heads stayed still, chilling like they was huge elephants who owned the block, the building and the people, blocking the path of police on purpose while acting like they wasn't doing what they was doing. Another mother covered her young daughter's eyes with the palm of her hand so she wouldn't see what she would probably see many times more if they stayed living on my street. A small crowd surrounded the dead body like circling vultures. Talking, laughing, some shocked but nobody crying. Now the switched-on sirens were screaming, so no one in the crowd could hear themselves thinking or speaking or being spoken to. The stage crowd, politicians and performers, had scattered like rodents, nearly knocking one another over to escape the audience.

The police cruisers were deadlocked in the chaos of the party, and street exits and entrances were blocked off by them. So they charged like heavy-hooved wild pigs where they must've believed the body was stewing.

Searching for the shooter must've been crazy. Staring into a sea of faces that all "fit the description." Young, black—real black, armed and dangerous. For them, that's every man moving.

I lowered the hood of my black Champion sweatshirt.

*Don't react. You move the action. Make your enemy react to you*, I heard my father's voice in my head. I eased my right hand into my right pocket to remove my glove.

"Brownsville, never ran, never will," so I walked. My milli tucked till I could toss it, the burning-hot barrel feeling like it was branding my black skin blacker. I was walking casually, unloading my adrenaline, dismissing my doubts, regrets, and disappointment that I should have made his murder more brutal and even more painful for him. Maybe I should've stayed and skinned him alive, then hung his dead body from the streetlight to let regular niggas on the block know to stop letting foul men live—men who fuck with little girls who don't agree, don't have titties or periods, or even desires to be talked to, followed, chased, cornered, or touched.

*Persecution is worse than slaughter*, a line from a *sura* in the Holy Quran moved through my mind. *Maybe I should've tortured him.*

Now the police were surrounding the body, pushing the crowd back, and pulling out the chalk and yellow tape. A few of them dashed into the crowd in different directions.

Last look: the cluttered crowd was thinning. I wouldn't be looking back no more. Just facing forward, keeping an even pace as most scrambled. Now I was politely passing by the parked in the middle of the street police bus. The doors were flung open. Soon they would sweep and pile randomly cuffed-up, roughed-up prisoners in there and haul them off. I had already put distance between me and them.

Dropped down between two parallel parked cars two blocks over, I tossed my nine in the iron-slotted gutter after wiping it down with the white washcloth that I normally rocked in my back pocket. The cops would want the murder weapon. I wouldn't make it easy on them. I'd forced them to get low, crawl into the gutter with the fist-size water bugs and their rat rivals. The men in blue were already dirty. I'd make them get filthy, wade in the water, and inhale the stench of the project toilet shit.

"Police, stop!" I heard as I raised up. I didn't stop, didn't turn. Just walked swiftly to the nearest subway station. Shook ones turn when they hear those two words, afraid they'll get shot in the back by the Glock. I have zero fear; I believe that when it is my turn to return to Allah, I will. Fear was trained out of me from when I was young enough to walk on this earth. *Fear only Allah.*

Terror, not fear, had gripped me though, when I was out checking the whole length and width of my 'hood. Looking in the front, sides, and back of the buildings, searching down shortcuts and alleyways. Peering through car windows and parking lots, and even climbing up "the dumps" where trash is heaped up high.

The terror of hurting my Umma's heart, our mother. The terror of losing my little sister, oh Allah. The terror of her becoming ruined and raped and unprotected like too many fatherless American girls. The terror of her losing her honor, of me failing my father, my culture, and my faith.

Terror had soaked through my pores and seized me, when I had seen a body laid out and white-sheeted and being carried to the ambulance, only to overhear people saying, "It was some old lady from the building who caught a heatstroke and died."

As I looked everywhere and walked and searched in every direction from my Brooklyn building, my terror made my head get even hotter, and it felt like my own blood was boiling up my body organs. Yet, I have no fear of any man living and zero fear of my own death.

Frightened boys turn when they hear "Police, stop!" Ruled by their fears for their entire lives, both their bodies and their thoughts freeze up. If you stop when you hear those two words, you are revealing that you are the one they're looking for and that you know it. Especially when you're in the same street packed with plenty of people. The cops could be talking to anybody. Probably by now they were following four or five or fifty different niggas who "fit the description." I had already breezed by tens of youth snatched and lined up against the building with their hands in the air, the ones with the wildest reactions laid out on the pavement cuffed. I saw some soft-boiled boys, the type that would break and crack open like eggshells within minutes. Soon as they got in some private space they'd start snitching on their friends and even on family and would even tell on people the cops ain't even asked them about. Giving up information believing that it would somehow save them, and saving themselves would be all that mattered, because cowards can only think of saving themselves.

I reversed it on the cops, by acting and not reacting. Made the cops doubt their suspicion of me by never looking back or over my shoulders, and by remaining calm, detached, looking straight forward and keeping it moving.

As my feet moved down the subway stairs, I felt a second set of feet were stepping in my same rhythm directly behind me. On the subway platform I moved in and out of the outgoing crowd until the train stormed in. I stepped into the second-to-last car, with a group of random riders. Doors closed. Train pulled out. I was heading to the dirty door that connects one train car to the next, thinking that either way, I had achieved my objective: to move the action away from my Brooklyn block where I had lived for seven years. My 'hood, where I was often seen but never known. Where I had fought but never mixed or mingled. Investigate me! No one there had ever known my name. "Midnight" was the only name some could use or tell. My Umi, my sister, and both my wives lived safely elsewhere outside of the borough of Brooklyn, forwarding address unknown by even my closest, truest friends. *Insha'Allah.*

Looking through a backwards reflection cast on a dirty train door window, my eyes were scanning movements and faces. They paused on someone lovely, exotic, and familiar. My heart skipped half a beat before fast-forwarding. It was not time for love or longing, only for carrying out the plan to its completion. In this plan there are no comrades on purpose. I'm strictly solo.

"Hibernate the heart," my sensei had taught me. In extreme situations or in captivity, isolation or torture, only the hibernated heart will allow the fighter to prevail.

Again my eyes paused, then doubled back to confirm what I sensed. D-tec, undercover detectives, were only undercover to themselves. The street-trained eye could see them clearly. On my side of Brooklyn, they were usually black like us. But they were different from everyday street cats. They didn't have the swagger or the rhythm of the full-blown bold and ignorant niggas. They lacked style, wore the wrong fitteds and bogus jewels, which could only be wrong. Worn-too-long kicks is always dead wrong, because we either clean 'em or trash 'em when they get marks or specks on them. That's why we walk like we stepping on air when we sport 'em. Even our laces had to be flawless. The D's lacked ease. They were uncomfortable with themselves, uncomfortable with their jobs, and uncomfortable in our 'hoods, even if they came from 'em.

Train stopped, doors opened. I saw the D was still sitting, staring in my direction at the back of my head. Would he get off? He didn't. Seemed like he was waiting to see if I would. I didn't. He sat fingering his pager, looking into the slim screen. He stood up, one hand grabbing hold of the overhead strap while the train shook slightly as it moved forward while still pulling left to right. He was facing my direction. Took one step towards me, and then . . . *pop, pop, pop, pop, pop, pop, pop* . . . seven shots. Sounded like a 22-caliber. Nah, not a 22, it was firecrackers with the fuses connected to make them fire off rapidly and sound lethal. Then a stink bomb was let off. The smell and the smoke fogged the air and the train car lights went black for a half a second, as they often do. Fire flared up in the opposite corner from me.

"Remain calm," a male voice shouted excitedly as the riders

jeered and scrambled. Only one man seated and wearing headphones didn't panic. His head was bobbing rythmically to the music he must've been listening to. There was only one way to go, towards the dirty door that I was blocking. Glass broke and someone sprayed the extinguisher and another pulled the red wooden handle of the emergency stop rope. The train jerked hard and screeched and screamed to a halt. The crowd that was pressed against me fell backwards. Lights off again suddenly. In the coughing, cursing, and confusion, I opened and shot through the door past a pissy homeless man laid out on the seat, who I couldn't see but could smell. I dropped down from the last train car and onto the train tracks.

All New Yorkers know, pull the red emergency stop rope and the train gets stuck for a long time. Still they stay put, scared of getting electrocuted or suffocated out in the train tunnel where only the young wild wolves would venture. An A train recently got stuck and some Wall Street regulars got the shakedown: wallets, jewels, cash, coins, and even eyeglasses, shoes, and technology. They made them run it all and escaped through the tunnel. Now the subways in all five boroughs were crawling with police at every platform.

Walking through the darkness and cutting through the thick fumes that substituted for air in the underground, I was headed on foot to the next station, without the train, without the crowd, without the D-tec. There was one urgent thing that I had to do now, that I wasn't comfortable doing until after I had finalized the execution.

# 3. THE SILENCE

Thirty-six minutes after midnight and four nine-millimeters aimed at my head and my heart. Two police dogs, more like wolves or tigers trained on dark meat and human bones, were standing still and strong on long leather leashes. Three NYPD, one undercover, two transit police, and a small crowd collecting as six more NYPD came storming down the subway stairs. *Far too many cops*, I thought to myself, *to arrest one man for the murder of a nobody.* Everybody else is still. Still they shouted, "Don't move!"

"You are under arrest," a stern and stout uniformed cop barked at me, face-to-face as another patted me down asking me, "Do you have any weapons on you?" No response from me, so he picked up his speed searching my ankles, back and front pockets, and all the places where any man could conceal a weapon.

"Don't you hear an officer talking to you?" A solid, broad-backed policeman slammed me in the stomach with his nightstick, as the one searching me pulled my box cutter out of my side leg pocket.

"He's clean, nothing but a box cutter," the searching cop said. "And he only got six dollars on him."

"Impossible," the stern and stout arresting officer told him.

"Get down on your knees," the broad-backed nightstick cop ordered me. "And put your hands behind your head." Now he had both hands around his gun instead of his nightstick. The stick for when he thought I was guilty of possessing a concealed weapon. His gun drawn for after he was sure I was not carrying a weapon.

I stayed standing. A young looking, frightened rookie-type cop leaped over with a swiftness and stung me. A strong electric current ran through each of my veins. As my body overheated my legs began to buckle, and the broad-backed cop forced me down with his nightstick. His gun now in his left hand, the nightstick in his right, I was not on my knees, but was facedown on the pavement. He put his foot on my spine, using his heavy shoe and shifting his weight to press and hold me there. He pushed his nightstick against the back of my neck to be sure my face was mashed into the filth of the pissy subway cement. The stern and stout cop yanked my hands behind my back and cuffed me. The other officers began to huddle as the broad-backed nightstick cop shouted orders to disperse the small late-night crowd. He didn't want any witnesses as he attempted to crush me to death.

The two unleashed tigers approached me. In a haze, I watched the cops observing their canines' every action, eager for them to send even a slight signal. The police dogs sniffed me but didn't bark or growl or roar. They searched the area surrounding me. Disappointed, ninety seconds later, the cops called their loyal dogs back.

"You have the right to remain silent . . ." the stern arresting cop explained.

*Silence*, I thought to myself, in a flash of a second. I don't believe there is one American who knows what that is. They are a nation of chatterers, speaking even when there's nothing good, right, or true to say. Talking nonstop trash, and completely unfamiliar with the pause. Even when the greatest American tragedies occur, they can only reserve and observe a moment of silence.

Now the black leopard of Sudan will show them the true power and meaning of slience.

NYPD and transit cops and even the plainclothes detective argued over who caught me. *Caught me*, I thought to myself. Even after just having been electrocuted with the Taser, I was clear that I had walked right down into their nest on my own two feet, of my own free will. The fool who needed murdering, I had already murdered with full intent and zero regret. And the second and final deed I had to do had already been done. I had no plans to take down no cops, even though I could've waged war against them till the end. I could've run and hid myself away in any number of places. I have a house of love in Queens, where my women welcome me warmly, respect me, enjoy me, love me, and serve me. I have my two closest friends, Chris and Ameer, who would've both put me up till the heat was off me, or at least till it died down.

But a true man never leads a trail of pain or war to his own house or to the homes of his loved ones. Men fight. Men work. Men defend. Men murder. Ninja-trained warriors burn their trail and all traces that jeopardize their team, territory, or goals.

I know the deal. Now that I had done what had to be done, I'm like mercury or radiation to all who know and love me. I made a conscious and clear decision. I understood the seriousness. Now, I need all pain and punishment to fall only on my shoulders. I need for my sister and mother and wives to be untouched, unseen, uninterrupted and unknown to anyone who we, and they have not chosen to be a part of our world. I need family and friends to stay far away from me. Further, I need not even one of them to attempt to see, talk to, or even contact me, not even by letter. They each should deny that they ever knew me. Treat me like I'm dead and remain completely silent until I hit time served and my hands, mind, heart, and body are all free.

"Anything you say can and will be used against you in the court of law," the cop said. *The law*, I thought to myself. How can there be a law without trust between the lawmakers and the people? People don't ever expect to be protected by the law. People don't even expect their loved ones to ever be protected by the law. People don't expect justice from the law. People don't ever expect the lawmakers to obey the laws they made. So there is no law, just bandits with authority versus bandits without authority.

Now I was in the cruiser, not cruising, but cuffed and uncomfortable. One blue to my left, the same cop who first searched me; one blue to my right, the young frightened rookie. Nightstick blue was driving up front. The stern stout blue was riding shotgun. Loud police radio reports and orders coming in and out. No oxygen in the car, just heat. Serious-faced cops, even their body language and breathing was pure intimidation.

"How does it feel, asshole?" The nightstick cop broke the silence. I was blank-faced and facing front. "Can you believe this fucker?" the same cop, the driver, said. "He doesn't show us the respect of a response even though he's caught in our monkey trap." They all laughed.

"I think the nigger's deaf," the searching cop right beside me announced loud and clear in my ear. I didn't flinch.

"Must be," the arresting stern cop said. "We'll have to talk to him with our fists and guns. He'll understand that," he threatened, and the backseat cops chuckled.

"No, seriously, you know Officer Moldonado? The Spanish guy with the deaf sister who speaks only in grunts? He's sensitive about all the handicaps. He was on foot post, tailing this perpetrator right here, said he showed no signs that he could hear what was happening around him. Moldonado is supposed to apprehend this guy. He protects him instead. Lets the perp walk right out in front of him and disappear into thin air."

"Fucker might be deaf but he ain't blind. When I had my nine-mm pointed at his head and told him to get down, he dropped down like a prostitute," nightstick cop said. They all broke out in laughter. I didn't move.

Silence is discipline. Even while being provoked, lied to, lied on, insulted, and maligned.

"I just want to thank him for the overtime. I needed the dough. I'm ready to question him all night," the rookie blue said.

"Me too," the searching cop agreed.

I'm thinking these big white-boy cops ain't from Brooklyn. The way they're talking and their accents, they weren't from any close-by place. Probably poor white boys from upstate farms who caught a job that armed them, then paid them more than they could ever earn from their own intelligence.

Police cruiser I'm in, gets cut off by a speeding black Plymouth. All heads yanked forward then slammed backwards after the nightstick cop driver reacted to the shock and rammed the brakes, barely avoiding a collision.

"Fucking bastards!" he said as he jumped out of the cruiser at the same time as his front-seat partner.

"Don't fucking move," left blue in the backseat warned me with heated anxiety, "or you'll end up in the morgue." The crooked cruiser was paused right there in the middle of the street blocking all cars behind us. Both backseat cops remained seated on either side of me. The two trash-talking blues began barking on the two Plymouth pushers soon as they jumped out of their vehicle. They were all shouting and strapped.

*All cops, all four of them*, I thought while watching their every move through the cruiser windshield. Otherwise the uniformed cops would've popped and locked them two plainclothes ones easily for speeding through the red light, for cutting off the cop cruiser and causing the traffic foul-up, and even for getting out of their Plymouth, walking towards the uniformed cops, and looking them in their eyes and mouthing off. If the two Plymouth guys were not cops, if they were regular civilians, the cops would've killed them for that handful of violations. Killed them first and called it justifiable later.

Now the two blues beside me opened their back doors; each placed one foot on the ground but didn't get out. The rookie cop was on his walkie-talkie calling for backup. I observed that frightened cops are the most dangerous. Their fears and their imagination link up, and before you know it, there will be bodies everywhere. The uniformed blue who had arrested me was chest-to-chest with the plainclothes cop. "Hey! Back off! This is ours. We cuffed and collared him," his partner yelled as the four who had already been arguing were now shoving one another around and about to go to blows.

Some decorated captain showed up in a third vehicle, fucking up the already fucked-up traffic jam even further. A couple of drivers were forced to drive their otherwise deadlocked vehicles onto the sidewalk, to clear the way for the captain. Almost one in the morning; luckily there were no pedestrians. I knew it wasn't because no one was outside walking. Once late-night pedestrians peeped it was the po-po, they'd opt to take a detour on foot rather than encounter them.

The cop crew was out there for almost an hour before they made a decision. Left blue was out of the cruiser now, rerouting traffic around the cop beef. Right backseat blue, the rookie, was still beside me, inflating with anger as he watched the uniformed cops fighting and losing in the loud negotiation he could see clearly through the cruiser windshield.

"Get the fuck out the car!" The nightstick cop who had been driving and then arguing screamed on me. He had returned with the saltiness of an athlete who had just lost the NHL hockey championship game after an undefeated season, and by only one shot. When I did not move, the still seated rookie blue pushed me forcefully, then jumped out the cruiser himself. Now all uniforms were out of the car standing in the street, leaning in on all sides, ordering me to move. I didn't speak. I didn't move. Left blue had already said that if I moved one muscle, the next stop was the morgue.

Pushed and then pulled and dragged out of the car where everyone could see me, I balanced myself on my feet, hands still cuffed tightly behind me. I was turned over to the two detectives in plainclothes, who walked on either side of me, then mashed my head down until I was seated in the backseat of their Plymouth. Doors slammed shut and they screeched off at a high speed for a short distance.

Commotion at the 77th Precinct, I was cuffed and seated. A fat-fingered cop attempted to type, while another stood over me.

"Name?" the fat cop asked me. I stared ahead, blank-faced. "Name," he repeated, then paused, waiting for me to jump at his command. "Name, name, name, name?" The volume of his voice was steadily increasing, his fat head flushed now with a maroon color. "Jesus Christ!" he exclaimed.

"Maybe we should name him Jesus Christ," the standing officer said straight-faced, and other cops seated at their own desks dealing with their own matters laughed.

"*Cómo se llama*?" An officer from across the room stood up from his desk and walked over to where I was being held. He was serious-faced but even-tempered. Seemed like he really suspected that he was speaking a language that I understood. But I didn't.

"*De dónde eres*?" he questioned, attempting to look me in the eye. I continued to stare forward, still blank.

"He's obviously not Spanish!" the officer who had been standing over me the whole time said. "They ain't got no Spanish people that black! No offense, Officer Ruiz," they clowned the Spanish-speaking officer for trying.

Officer Ruiz didn't answer back to the ignorant cop. He probably knew what anyone with common sense knows. There are black-skinned people all over the world, speaking any and every language that has ever been spoken. Just then I recalled the Senegalese brothers whom I met in Tokyo. They spoke that Japanese fluently, like it was their father tongue. They could switch from speaking Japanese to Wolof, to Italian to even German, like it wasn't nothing, and they were black Africans, skin as black as mine.

"This asshole *won't* get the benefit of doubt from me. He hears and he understands and *he speaks English*. Let me walk him into a side room," the uniformed cop standing over me said. He wanted a reaction. Seemed to think I was supposed to start blabbering because he threatened to take me to the side room.

*That's all they could do*, I thought to myself. I had emptied my pockets of a slim stack of hundreds, a thick pile of twenties, and of all of my personal belongings. I also handed my gym bag, my cash, and identification to my second wife and told her to bury it in a place that only she knew, and where it could not be found. When she and I parted, I purposely had only my nine, three twenty-dollar bills, and one clean white washcloth on me.

"Address?" the obese typing cop asked me. Getting no response, he leaned back in his chair. "I'll give you one more chance before I hand you over for your private meeting, in a side room," he threatened. "Address?" he repeated. "Date of birth?" He switched his question. Completely frustrated, even though he had just got started, he pushed himself backwards and away from his desk, the chair wheels squeaking like they were alive and crying for mercy beneath his heavy weight. "Goddamn it, throw him in the holding cell till he talks," the fat-fingered cop concluded while blowing out a blast of hot air and rising up slowly, then wobbling away.

The cop left standing over me leaned in close to my ear. His breath was the odor of shit and his spit splashed out his venom.

"That guy right there is a good cop," he said, referring to the fat one. "The kind who gives knuckleheads like you a second chance. He cares whether you're a juvenile or not. That's why he wants your date of birth, for your own good. He even takes care of his kids. Why don't you cooperate with him? Tell him when that bitch you call momma dropped a fatherless son of a bitch like you out of her filthy fucking hole."

The fat cop looked back at the angry officer from across the room as though he wanted to know what the other had said to me. Then he disappeared.

"It's against the law to be outside without identification," the shit-breath cop said, now looking down on me. "And that's not the only charge you're facing . . . There's failure to stop and obey an officer's command, resisting arrest, fleeing from a crime scene . . ."

Then I knew. To hold me, they would grab at any charge. They would lie and make things up, and they did. I did not resist arrest. I did not defend myself. I had been silent and still. To me, that meant they were desperate and had not found the murder weapon yet, or an eyewitness to the murder, or any solid evidence. Instead, they needed me to incriminate myself, to make the major charges stick.

"Get up," the officer ordered. I stood.

Behind bars but no longer cuffed. It was crowded in their holding cell, dudes hugging the bench the same way they do on the block. Cool, I walked to the far right corner and squatted, my back against the wall, one of my usual thinking positions.

"What size you wear?" some nigga standing and staring at my Nike Jordans asked me. I stood up like I was about to cooperate. Halfway to standing with my back still against the wall, I kicked him and he flew backwards into the next man. He leapt up and now they were both glaring. I gave 'em the deadpan stare. Let's face it: we each knew we were all empty pockets and not holding. Hand-to-hand they would have no wins against me. Besides, I knew they didn't want none. I could see it in their eyes. They did what punks do. They backed down and went back to their nonsense. One of 'em picked a new vic; maybe that guy would believe him. I didn't.

Squatting again with my eyes wide open, I was traveling into my mind, setting and cleaning it up. First I had to empty out the anger and the fury and the rage. It was much less than before the murder no doubt, but even the amount remaining was a red fog that blocked me from precise, clear, and new thoughts. I was quietly inhaling and exhaling, shaking it off, lowering my blood pressure. At the same time, I was attempting to discipline my eyes not to keep checking the clock that was lodged into the wall outside the cell.

"While in captivity," my sensei had taught me in one of my many private ninjutsu lessons, "never obsess over time. It is a form of self-torture. Use your memories of the past. Relive them in your mind. Stretch each memory out, even the ones that only lasted a few minutes in real life, and relive each of those memories for days at a time. A man with no memories of happiness and pleasure, or family, friendship, and adventure, will be conquered by imprisonment, conquered by time, and conquered by his captors."

Faces and bodies in the holding cell kept changing. Some were released, others transferred to hospitals or central booking or wherever.

In the stench of blood, shit, and piss, my aim was to calm myself completely. I had considered whether this was a physical battle or a mental one. I concluded that it was both. It had to be physical, because I am confined. It had to be physical, because I had been nightsticked and dragged and electrocuted by the cops.

A mental battle, I had learned young, was tougher than a physical one. As I surveyed my surroundings, I was swiftly realizing that my mind, which was accustomed to being challenged, to learning and hearing various languages and actively solving problems and handling and conducting business and seeking out new and exciting things, was now imprisoned in a small and dirty place with small-minded, stupid, crazy, and backward men who could neither learn anything nor teach anything or even communicate effectively to one another in their own English language. Their vocabulary was limited to mumblings, curses, insults, screams, and corruption, and there was no light to be had from any of them, the police or the captured. I told myself that my mental battle would be to keep my mind strong, while being surrounded by the weak. I had to keep learning and growing day-to-day without any teachers or true examples. I had to remain active and increasing in knowledge. Moreover, I had to maneuver and outthink the cops. Even though I had considered owning up to the murder, I knew it mattered what I revealed and what I concealed, how much evidence I allowed them to collect and confirm. Yeah, I slaughtered the sucker, but the details of how that happened would determine how much time I would have to serve. The less time the better. Especially because I merked a joker who was a lesser man.

I know these Americans believe that "all men are created equal." I don't. I believe all men are created, *period.* And each man makes choices and takes action one way or another. What a man chooses to do or not to do is the only way to measure his worth. A man who chooses to love is not equal to a man who chooses not to love. A man who builds is not equal to a man who destroys. A man who protects is not equal to a man who offends and assaults women, children, and defenseless people. A man who thinks and solves problems is not equal to a thoughtless man who makes mischief and problems and who is himself a problem. Nah, not equal at all. How could a lazy man of excuses be equal to a hardworking man? How could an undisciplined man be equal to a man who is disciplined, who is straight, who resists temptation, addiction, and gluttony? He can't be equal. Those are my thoughts, my beliefs and my answer, and I'm one hundred percent certain. *So now that the lesser man is deceased,* I thought to myself, *I gotta accept my punishment for doing the murder deed, but that punishment should be equal to the worth of the man I slaughtered.* The more worthless he was, the less time I should serve. That's justice to me.

"You, let's go," a cop suddenly called me out. "Put your hands between the bars." He cuffed me and then opened the gate to let me out.

Escorted into a small room with a table, four chairs, and a video camera mounted on a tripod, I checked there was nothing but one blackened glass window, one same door to enter and exit, and no pictures or artwork or certificates or degrees displayed on the walls. There was a clock, though, embedded in the wall, large and circular and impossible not to notice or watch. Matter of fact, the precinct had clocks everywhere. *For the cops, time is money*, I thought to myself, recalling the rookie officer who was amped to be making overtime pay while dealing with my arrest and questioning in the dead of night. They love the clocks, 'cause with every tick-tock they was earning and no one else is making money while they're in here except them. To the prisoner the clock is a slow poisoning, a device that confirms a man's loss of control over himself, loss of control over his time. My sensei was correct. Staring at the clock just confirms the distance between a prisoner and his family and loved ones. Concentrating on that was a useless losing strategy.

New faces, one uniformed and two plainclothes cops, came in calculating, with their coffee cups in their hands. One of them threw a brown bag onto the table. The other cop opened it and pulled out a burger; I could tell from the smell. It was wrapped in white greasy paper and accompanied by a red-and-white paper dish filled with fries and a can of grape soda.

"Sit down," the uniformed cop ordered me. I sat. "We get that you ain't the talkative type. We got that you ain't got no name, because you're a nobody. We agree. *You are nobody.* We don't even want you here. But there's only one way out. Give us the name and location of your bosses. If you don't want to talk, just write it down."

He pulled out a small pad of paper and a half pencil with no eraser, laid them down on the table, then pushed them over to my side. I didn't reach for them, didn't move. We sat in silence. I didn't know what the fuck he was talking about anyway. My bosses?

"Holy shit, it's four a.m.," the uniformed cop said with intensity. "We can transfer you out to a place where no matter how sleepy you get, you'll be afraid to shut your eyes for fear of some nut crawling into your little dookey-hole." I didn't react. I didn't say anything or move one muscle in my face or body.

"Your silence is assuring us that you are guilty. You did something criminal and you know it," one plainclothes cop said. "There is a bunch of shit that we can pin on you. A busy Friday night in Brooklyn, a perp won't talk, got no name, no address, no identification, six dollars, no alibi, no defense. We could match you up with anything, from pickpocketing to murder one. But that's not what we're trying to do here. We want the truth, the name of the players. If I was you I'd start talking real fast and real soon," plainclothes number one said.

"I'll handle this," plainclothes number two said to number one. "You must be hungry," he said to me, pushing the burger towards me and moving the grape soda within my reach. Inside I was laughing. These were the type of cops my man Ameer had told me about, who would come around the high school asking students to participate in the police lineup in exchange for a lemonade and a baloney sandwich. Like a police lineup was some type of legitimate after-school job and the police were friendly neighborhood employers.

"So what'd you do?" I had asked Ameer.

"You know I had to fatten up the reward. Them other cats went for the free lunch. I talked 'em up to sixty bucks for each of my appearances."

"What if you would've got picked as the face that fit the crime?" I asked.

"Nah, the cop told all of us if you're not guilty, you got nothing to worry about and something to gain. Besides that, it's impossible. Ain't *nobody* got a handsome face like mine," Ameer joked.

Now this Brooklyn detective who must have thought he was better than the blue boys 'cause he got to wear his own cheap clothes to work was trying to buy me with a beef burger. Guess they thought the same shit worked on every man the same way. It didn't.

Mystery novels I have enjoyed reading taught me more than a few things about the American law. These cops had forty-eight hours to book me on charges and stand me before a judge. All of the charges they had mentioned so far were bullshit, although they were good enough for them to use falsely to book me. However, even they wanted more. I wanted them to hurry up and charge me and move me and get it over with. Still, I wasn't going to help them to do it.

"Not going to eat—we'll see how long that's going to last. Take one bite of this burger and you better be ready to give me something: names, bodies, drugs, weapons." He left. The others followed him out.

The door clicked closed when the last one exited. So what I was cuffed and locked in a side room. I wasn't sweating his burger or fries. I had already eaten after the murder and right before my arrest. The thought of my last meal threw my mind into rewind. I was alone, just me and my memories, and that was cool with me.

# 4. THE RED BAG • *A Reflection*

I had already eaten well in the few hours between the murder and my arrest. I had been crouched on the curb between two parallel-parked cars, a cream-colored Comet and a Ford pickup truck. I had two bags of purchases from the dollar store on the corner, in a Brooklyn neighborhood where I did not live, but where my family business had a few customers and where I had delivered clothing that Umma made for them. I was setting up to write Umma a letter, a task that had to be done with truth, intensity, and skill.

Seated in the middle of a darkened street underneath the radiant light pouring from a sign on a row of stores, it was the perfect spot for me to complete my second and final task of the night. Curbside, the vehicles shielded me from the view of the foot cop posted across the street on the corner, to my right. The pickup truck shielded me from the parked cop cruiser on the same side where I was seated but at the opposite corner from the foot cop, to my left. Behind me, a mailbox shielded me from the view of people walking by. As my second wife would say, "a strategic position."

Knowing that any of these vehicle owners could walk up at any moment to start their cars, drive off, and expose me to view didn't matter. There was no reason that any of these cops on this block in this neighborhood should be looking for me, other than the fact that police stay looking for young black males for the sport of their hunt.

The bright light made it possible for me to see enough to pen a letter to my Umma, the most serious letter I ever wrote in my lifetime, to the most important person in my young life. Sure, I could call her on the phone. Yet I couldn't call her. To call her would be to hear her voice, and her heart was always in her speech. And her expressions of love would cause me to unfreeze at the very time that I needed to remain ice cold, calculating, and calm.

Instead, I would mail her my words, thoughts, instructions, and feelings so that she could be absolutely certain. A letter would place enough distance between Umma and me that I could remain accurate and highly focused. I pulled out my newly purchased dollar-store gloves and put them on.

Unwrapping the six-piece stationery set, six pieces of pale mint paper and six matching envelopes, I placed the stamp on the right-hand corner of the envelope first. Pulling out my black ballpoint pen, I shook it to distribute and loosen up the ink. Instinctively I looked up into the sky as though I was asking the heavens to clear murder from my mind enough for my thoughts and words to flow perfectly, precisely, passionately. All I saw was blackness, a stingy moon, and a starless sky.

As I put the pen to paper, the radiant light from the store sign blackened, causing my area to darken and the block to become dim. What did it mean?

Placing the cap back onto the pen, I pushed all of my items back into the bag and eased up some to search my surroundings. The store three doors down was lit and open for business. The sign above it read MIDNIGHT WASH. It was a Laundromat. Reluctant to move away from the mailbox where I would post my letter, which was my most immediate concern, another idea swiftly came to mind.

Calmly, I walked diagonally and entered the place. It was empty at first glance. I moved three steps to my left and stood behind a paper sign taped in their window so no one could see me from the street. I glanced around. There were paper signs everywhere: WE

CLOSE AT MIDNIGHT was the first one I saw. *Good*, I thought to myself. It was 10:30 p.m. I calculated. I could come out of my murder wears, throw 'em in a twenty-five-minute wash and then a twenty-five-minute dry, and remove any evidence of the slaughter. The kind of evidence that the naked eye could not see but that might be on me. The kind of evidence that if erased, could cast doubt in any investigation, and in the mind of anyone in charge of deciding the term of my imprisonment. I could write the letter while the clothes washed and dried and be out of here no later than 11:30 and drop the letter into the mailbox. After that I wouldn't care what happened. Destiny would move me.

My thoughts were interrupted. I heard a female voice talking—not to me, but I didn't hear anyone answering her, either.

REMOVE YOUR CLOTHING IMMEDIATELY AFTER YOUR MACHINE STOPS was another sign on the wall. WE ARE NOT RESPONSIBLE FOR LOST OR STOLEN ITEMS. CHANGE MACHINE IN THE BACK. I headed to the back. That's when I saw her.

Bare feet, red hair like a fire hydrant. Dark eyes and sculpted black lips like a smoker. She had one leg cocked up like a flamingo as she held her phone to her face, talking. Her words flowed like music. Her accent came and went from 'hood chick to almost Jamaican. But the rhythm revealed that she was not Jamaican. She could do more than three things at one time. Deep in conversation with whoever was on the other end, even her hands were speaking as she gestured like a conductor leading an orchestra. All of that, and still, like a hawk she watched me as though I was food after a long starvation or drought.

Small waist, short legs with thick thighs and hips like they were created for continuous breeding. She was leaning lightly on the wall between a row of washers and the money machine that ate dollars and burped out quarters. I sized her up as no threat to me. She wouldn't run out into the streets and yell, "He's in here!" I could see that she was no joke either, serious, and brewing with secrets. She spoke in a lowered voice at first, but increased the volume as I approached. Moreover, on her long, black cobra-stitched lanyard key chain, which she wore on her tiny tight denim panty shorts, there dangled about twenty-one keys. So I figured she works here in the Laundromat; cool. I put my two dollar-store bags down on top of one machine. I pulled out my hoodie, a transit authority uniform shirt I had stuffed in one of the bags, and the matching cap that goes with it. Turning my back to her, I swiftly removed the murder black T-shirt and threw it all into an empty washing machine.

"Cutie on the run! As soon you said dat!" the redhead blurted out suddenly with slight laughter. I walked over to the vending machine and bought some detergent with bleach for colored clothes.

"I seen him around here before, just walking through," the redhead said.

I removed my belt and eased out of my sneakers, socks, and then my jeans. Underneath, I had on my black basketball shorts. I threw my jeans, the belt, and the socks into the machine with the clothes I already had in there.

"Him hold him head so high, you'd think him God's right-hand man." The redhead pushed each of those words out slowly with heavy accent and emphasis.

I poured two packs of liquid detergent over the clothes.

"Him don't give a girl a glance or a chance, like him too good for we," she said.

I closed the washing machine door, took out a ten-dollar bill, and inserted it into the change machine on the wall by where she was standing.

"Him body like artwork. I like ah lick him like a lime bomb-pop." She paused. "Yeah I know, dem thick Popsicles were red, white, and blue-colored. But, I love lime."

I pushed the quarters in and the machine started. I watched the suds form and rise up in the water.

"Me pull it gently with me lips, suck to the sugar come down like guava juice. Make he go crazy for I and relax a likkle," she said. "I swallow like it's sorrel. Soon him tell I, him love me."

I looked at her. Her eyes locked onto mine, still staring. She wouldn't lower her gaze, as though she expected me to look away first, as though she was the man instead of me.

"I fire up the cooking pots for he. Him too good for takeout. I prepare fresh roti with curry goat, or chicken curry rice and peas. Ya know I could do Guyanese or Jamaican ting." She said it as though she was making an offer to me, her eyes on me as she spoke to what had to be another woman on the phone. Then I knew . . . They sing their words in a different way from the Jamaicans. She was a Guyanese-born African with that Indian blood running all through her. I could see from her hair texture and length—natural, not a wig or weave, but the red color was just her style and spin on it. Still, the 'hood in her was the heaviest.

"Of course. Redverse is the only man for I. You don't hafta remind me, gal. Facing twenty-five years to life . . ." She grunted, ". . . is a long, long, long time. I hold it down for he, ayah. Me take care of every-ting for he. But I body is a nuther matter," she said as I headed to the bathroom, making good use of my time. The bathroom door was locked. The sign on it read, ASK THE ATTENDANT FOR KEY. BATHROOM IS FOR CUSTOMERS ONLY.

"Come December the sixth, mark two years I hold out. But on dis warm summer night me feel some-ting. Me see some-ting, I body want to own," she said without laughter and with a dramatic expression. Then she pulled the receiver a few inches from her face, where she had been hugging it. She looked at me standing there waiting for her to take a breath or break or to get off the phone.

"Him know me talk about he. But him pretend him don't know." She paused.

"Bathroom key." I said only those two words to her. She spun her hips around. Now her butt was facing me. A rectangular wooden paddle that said MENS was buried in her small butt pocket. She had stopped talking and stood staring again.

"Slide it," she said. "Take it!" she said. I pulled it out easy, not wanting to graze her body at all, even with my gloved fingers.

"No, I was talking to he," she said after pulling the phone back to her face and leaving it between her chin and shoulder as I walked away.

Bulb blew out in the bathroom as soon as I flipped the light switch on. Seemed like lights had been flickering, blacking out, or busted all around me all day and night long. I didn't have time to think about if there was a meaning in that. I felt around until I found the sink and the knobs for the water. I turned it on, removed one glove. Hot water worked. Cold water . . . nothing. I put my two plastic bags down on the floor and undressed completely. I didn't mind the temporary darkness. I needed the seclusion. I scrubbed my whole body like a surgeon does before surgery, even beneath each fingernail. Removing all blood, filth, germs, and yes, gunpowder and all other evidence.

Fifteen to twenty minutes seem to case by in seconds. I was wearing the new white T-shirt I'd purchased from the dollar store, not the quality I'm accustomed to, but clean and good enough for survival mode. Wearing new boxers and socks, I was standing and thinking about my Nike Jordans. I didn't have time to throw those in the machine or to wait the amount of time it would take for them to dry. I didn't have the idea or the willingness or the nerve to buy the bullshit men's skips when I was shopping in the dollar store (which was the only kind of sneakers they sold) to wear while my official joints were washing, either. And I didn't have the desire to stand barefooted in the Laundromat like the redheaded flamingo. With soap and tissue, and hot water that had increased so high in temperature that it felt like it was searing off my fingerprints, I cleaned my Jordans by hand, the tops and the soles. I pulled out the old laces and wove the new laces in the dark. Knew everything about kicks by heart. Didn't need my eyes or the light to get it right.

Done, I opened the bathroom door to catch some light to use to clean up behind myself. I pushed everything I needed to trash in one bag and placed everything remaining in the other. I wanted to burn my trash but didn't want to trigger any smoke or fire alarms.

My washer had stopped. I pulled out my jeans and threw them into the dryer, dropping in enough quarters for it to spin for twenty-five minutes. I tossed the plastic bag containing my trash, even my leftover bar of soap, into the washer with my basketball shorts and the rest of the clothes I purposely planned to leave behind. I fed the washer more quarters and rewashed the washed clothes and my trash, including the plastic bag.

The girl was gone. With only myself and my thoughts and the sound of the dryer drying my one pair of jeans, I was moved to make *salat*, a late-night prayer at the end of a day, weighted down by rapidly moving passions, pleasures, and tragedies. Events so serious they altered and rearranged and twisted the future of more than seven lives including mine . . . way more than seven, but only the seven is what I cared about most.

*I have missed three prayers today*, I thought to myself. I had the wall to my left and the machines to my right. There in the limited space between, I stood moving my mood and mind into prayer mode, then lifted my hands, then folded my right hand over my left hand at my chest, then bowed my body halfway and held my hands on my knees, then got on my knees, and bowed my head pressed to the ground.

"*A-Salaam*" was the last word of a heartfelt prayer. "Peace," even though this day was chaos. But prayer put me in the right frame of mind to write my Umma a letter. Once I did that and dropped it in the mailbox right outside the Laundromat, I would be ready to face anything no matter how harsh or horrible.

Between Umma and me, that's how it was, and that's how it is, and that's how it had been since our arrival in the United States of America at New York's JFK airport more than seven years ago. *We only trust one another.* To this day, because we know how outsiders, people, and politics can flip without notice, and circumstances change drastically, we keep our emergency suitcase packed so we can flash out in an instance. No one could tell me or teach me anything about my Umma. No one could tell Umma anything about me, either. We had agreed that urgent or important words had to come from her lips to my ears, and from my mouth to her heart—period. Even if there was an adult or elder speaking or saying anything about me, her son, it would not matter. Back home of course it would. Respect for elders and even a slightly older brother, sister, cousin, and of course for aunts and uncles and grandparents, was our way and beliefs. But in America, where the adults themselves are as confused as the children, afraid to grow up and embarrassed by aging, where it is a way of life not to believe, and where most adults are crafty liars, it would not.

Even though I had given Chiasa, my second wife and the last person in my family to see and touch and speak to me, my words and instructions, and even though Umma loves Chiasa, it would not matter. So both the murder and the letter go hand-in-hand—had to happen. Not one without the other.

*Bismillah* . . . In the name of Allah . . . *Allah isulik*, God is watching, hearing, so say only the truth. I wrote the letter exclusively in the beautiful language and lettering of Arabic. *Azeezti Umma*, I greeted her warmly.

Oddly, the dryer stopped at the same time that I heard a heavy gate slamming shut, resulting in a strange silence for a Laundromat. Leaving the space where I had been leaning and writing using their folding table, I could now see that the solid metal gate shielding the front door of the Laundromat was closed down and I could now hear someone rattling the padlock on the other side. My eyes shot towards the clock: 11:30 p.m. The front door entrance and exit was sealed shut, half an hour early.

Returning, I grabbed my jeans out of the dryer. I stepped out of my kicks, got fully dressed fast, and then stepped back in. Wearing a wool hat on my almost dry, washed hair and gloves on both hands, I pulled the few remaining bills out of my plastic bag. I pushed them into my right pocket. I then slid my box cutter into my slim side-leg pocket. Carefully, I signed the letter, folded it, and sealed it in the stamped envelope. Laying it down on the folding table, in neat English print, so that there would be no error or delay in Umma receiving it, I addressed it to my Queens home. I then pushed it into my back pocket along with the emptied and folded plastic bag. Now there were no bags to carry. Purposely hands-free, I pushed through the door marked EMERGENCY EXIT and walked right into the Red Flamingo.

"Ya sprinting out of 'ere on a hot summer night in your winter clothes?" she asked without smiling and looked down at the gloves I had been wearing to prevent myself from leaving a trail of fingerprints in this place or even on the letter, envelope, or pen I had been using.

"Open the door," I told her, referring to the door behind her that she was purposely blocking.

"Where's ya cleaned laundry?" she asked me. I moved her out of my way and opened the door. Instead of the door leading me out of Midnight Wash Laundromat and into a side alley, I was now standing in a tiny tight kitchen with two chairs, one table, a small stove, and a lighted glass fridge. Flames flared beneath three covered pots and one flat pan. The scent of ginger was good and it was trapped because there was no window. Instead there was an iron-grated vent. None of that mattered. I had no time and no reason to start playing house with her.

"Let me feed you some good ting," her eyes asked first, then her mouth said, "You seem hungry, but . . . more den dat, you seem thirsty." She was right. I was mad thirsty. But I didn't admit it . . . with words or gestures.

"Let me grab you a drink." She brushed by me, pressing her body against mine, and then opened the door of the glass cold case in the too-tight kitchen. "I want to give you a Guinness or Heineken or a Red Stripe. More den dat I want to give you what you want. So 'ere." She handed me a bottle of Poland Spring water. "I take you for da water type," she said staring.

I twisted the top. As soon as I heard the seal crack open, I downed it. Standing facing me and way too close, she handed me another. I cracked that one open and . . .

"That's how me and me man first met," she said. "It was back 'ere in dis small space. I went for a drink and rubs against him. He grabbed me hips and picks me up pon dis tabletop. Him tears open me shirt and cut off me jeans with him knife 'cause dey was dat tight tight tight on me body. Him buss my sweet cherry good. Make my body throb all over. Den him say to I . . .

"'Next time wear a dress so I could fuck you right.'" She smiled, remembering. "After dat me love he forever."

My mind wasn't on her. But then I also peeped that she was out of her denim booty shorts and wearing a colorful short dress that barely passed where her pussy was. I was grateful for the water. She had supplied me with the basic need. I also needed to eat. But I wasn't gonna eat her or sit and share a meal with her. And I definitely wasn't gonna fuck her. "It looks good but I'm not going to have any," I told her, stepping out of the tiny kitchen area and searching for the back door.

"The back door is locked and it's the other way, star," she said, reminding me of a Bed-Stuy, Brooklyn girl named Bangs who called me "Superstar" every time she saw me.

"The door that doesn't say exit is the exit. The door that says exit is not," she said, smiling and seeming to enjoy her own riddle. "But now is the wrong time for leaving. And if ya make a move now without carrying the red laundry bag, the cops on da other side of the door ah grab you soon as you step out," she said strangely, dramatically and seriously.

Thinking about what she was saying and why she was saying it had me still for some seconds. I didn't give a fuck about the cops. *I gotta mail the letter, though, uninterrupted*, I thought to myself. If I left through the side or the back door, I pictured in my head, "I would still have to walk around to the front to drop the letter in the mailbox without allowing them to take me. But was what she was saying true?

"You on my block. In 'my yard' as we say. So, listen good. Hear me now. In one hour and twenty minutes at one a.m. you can leave out the back door carrying the red laundry bag and no one, no man, no beast ah touch ya," she said, staring sternly. "Carry the red bag to da train, taxi, plane, or wherever. But once you clear three blocks from here in any direction you are good."

She could tell I didn't trust her. She seemed calm, like she expected me to automatically flow with her intimate dinner fantasy and her suspicious red-bag exit plan. She pulled one leg up back into her flamingo stance where she seemed most comfortable, causing her pussy dress to creep up even higher and shorter than before.

"You brought from da dollar store on da corner 'ere." She pointed towards the corner where I had actually shopped an hour or so ago. "You buy some wrong-ting," she said strangely. I knew I didn't buy anything illegal from the dollar store. Everything I bought was out in the open and for sale.

"You buy box cutter." She put up one finger like she was about to make a list. "You buy winter gloves and wool cap in a summer season." She put up two more fingers. "You buy soap and socks . . ." She continued until all ten of her fingers were spread. Somehow she knew all of my purchases. Yet she was definitely not in the dollar store when I was. I pay attention. She probably saw into my plastic bag when I set it on the machine, I swiftly considered. She placed her hands on her hips and stared into me, trying to demonstrate her seriousness, then continued, "Store manager over dere is dee informah."

"Dee informah," I repeated.

"The informer," she confirmed, turning off her accent. "Him tell da foot cop on da corner when people buy suspicious things. Gal gangs in our yard choose box cutter for a weapon. Any child, man, or woman buy box cutter is suspect." Sensing my doubt, she explained, "Box cutter, dem is not illegal for dee informah to sell, or fer you to buy. But police 'ere see it as a red flag. And dee informah tell all."

It didn't sound like something she was making up. But it didn't sound like a reason I needed to stay, either.

"Keys," I said suddenly at the same time both the thought and the observation dropped into my head.

"Don't have." She clapped her hands together and wiggled her fingers, then spun her body to show me that her cobra was no longer there and no keys were jingling on her. *But she had the cobra key chain on her panty shorts before, and the bathroom key in her back pocket*, I confirmed to myself.

"Go get 'em," I ordered.

"Me give 'em to da one who lock up the gate each night. Him open up again at one a.m., den safe," she said, returning to her serious stare.

My eyes searched the tiny kitchen, then my gloved hands pulled open one of two drawers. One contained laundry bags, neatly folded as though pressed. The other contained brown bags, foil, plastic bags, napkins, and straws.

Her arms were folded in front of her now, and both of her bare feet were on the floor. The tension tightened her up, when she'd been all laid-back and loose before. I knew I was on to something. She had to have hidden the keys somewhere. I yanked open the narrow spice cabinet on the sidewall beside the stove. There were no spices, but a tiny five-inch television was embedded into the wall. On the screen was an image of the Laundromat showing where all of the machines were, where I had just been. *A surveillance device*, I thought to myself. That was the reason she could leave her place of business unattended. She could watch and see all of her Laundromat customers as she chilled back here like she was at home. I looked up.

Pulling out one of the two metal chairs, I placed it on top of the table. When I climbed up and stepped onto the table, she got excited. Then the excited expression on her face evaporated as she caught on that I wasn't about to twist and bend her body in some mean-ass fucking position, but I had seen the lines on the ceiling in the shape of a square that seemed to lead to the second floor.

"You don't wanna do dat," she warned me.

She was wrong. I was already pushing on the square and climbing up. I lifted it only two inches at first, to see and listen if someone was up there. I figured she had a small bed for resting and a closet with a few changes of clothes. The keys were probably up there, where she had changed into her fuck-me dress. I wasn't gonna ask her again for them, or even trust any of her responses. *I know what she wants.* If there were no keys, plan B: I would leave from the rooftop, or at least use it to see for certain what and who was moving outside in the area. From the rooftop I could see clearly and then leap to or jump down to another connected building, or use the fire escapes. If the mailbox was too hot, from the rooftop I could spot another mailbox, then switch up my route.

I pulled my body weight up into a dusty room with no lights. As soon as I was in, I stood still to listen and check it out. I could hear the redhead pull the chair down from the table and drag and push it back in its place. *Good.* She understood, then, that I wasn't coming back.

No bed, no furniture, no clothing. I stepped lightly towards the room door. I heard a sound, looked down to be sure it wasn't coming from something being crushed beneath my feet. I scraped my left and right sneaker lightly on the floor. It wasn't me. It had to be somebody. Whoever it was had also purposely stopped moving so that they could not be heard. I stayed still. After a pause, I heard another sound. I leapt to the left side of the door, figuring the thump of one leap was better than several footsteps. Slowly the door pushed open. There was only the long black barrel of a shotgun. With both hands and without exposing myself concealed in the corner, I grabbed it tightly and forced it forward, using the butt of the gun to bang whoever was holding it. Now it was my shotgun and the barrel was pointed at his head.

"Blood clot," was all he said.

"Get up," I ordered him. He stood slowly, raising his hands.

"Lead the way to the roof," I told him. My thoughts were racing to organize my next move.

"What do you want?" he asked.

"To get the fuck out this building. That's it."

He walked with a cocky sway, even though he had a shotgun aimed at the back of his head and both hands up in the surrender position. He couldn't front. I could feel his fear.

"Put your hands down. I'm not the police," I told him. He hesitated. Just as he began pulling his hands down very slowly, as if he believed I might bang a bullet into his back, I warned him, "You don't want to die tonight," so he wouldn't make any sudden or dumb moves that forced my hand.

He dropped his hands all the way down to his sides. Within a few steps, he stopped walking and turned facing a door that did not look like an exit; it did not have an exit sign or any light coming from the narrow space below it. It was across from a door that did have an exit sign over it. Remembering the redhead's words, I figured the door with the exit sign should not be trusted. I tightened up on him, pressing the black steel barrel against his scalp so he could make the decision that would protect his life and keep me from spilling any blood without real reason. Slowly he turned the knob on the unmarked door.

I pushed his head with the barrel and his back with my foot. He needed to be the first man seen by anyone secretly posted behind that door, where it was so quiet, it was either empty or . . .

"Easy . . . ," my hostage said suddenly, as he broke his fall.

AK-47 on the left, nine-millimeter on the right, two men holding. There was light beneath the closed door that led to another room behind both of them. I could see feminine bare feet, about three sets, before the light coming from beneath the second door suddenly flicked off. Then I knew.

"I'm not the police," I said. "I'm a customer who wants to walk out the building like I was never here."

Nine-millimeter laughed.

"Shut your ras-clot mouth," my hostage warned him solemnly. Sounded like my hostage was in charge of them and not the other way around. All eyes were shifting, sizing up the situation. None of us were ready to die over some bullshit.

All of us had to be thinking how messy this scene could end. Bodies everywhere, and for what?

"Lay your weapons down," I said, nodding my head to the right corner. My hostage turned his head slightly, like he was turning to face me. His men didn't budge. Waiting for orders, I figured.

"Ne-go-ti-a-tion," my hostage said slowly, pushing out each piece of the word. I tightened up on him so he would stop moving to face me. He needed to negotiate with his men, not me.

"Respect! Him said him don't want no ting. Him's just a wanderer, a laundry customer who somehow get trapped in our building," my hostage said sarcastically to his men.

"He saw us," AK-47 said.

"We gon' kill he," the other one said and smirked.

"Kill him, he gon' kill I, Verse's bruddah," he warned them. "More den dat, one shot an' five-oh gwon rush our palace and we all gwon dead. Then dem get away with our product." My hostage was reasoning for his survival.

"He blew our spot," nine-millimeter said.

"We gwon let him walk. Uddahwise gwon turn graveyard ina ere," he told them. "Put your guns down," he ordered. They didn't. He raised his voice. "Now!" They did.

"Dere's only one way out alive for you," he said to me, speaking out of the side of his mouth but still facing his own men. I was hearing him but watching his men and calculating whether there were more men in the back room, or just the women whose feet I saw before the lights blacked out. *Are there other men anywhere else in the building?* I thought to myself, but I had no way of knowing.

"In my pocket is de key to the door for your freedom," he said with a serious tone, but I could tell he was a joker. I wasn't joking.

"Pull it out," I said. He did. "Tell your men to turn around and face the wall," I said. He nodded. Both mad as a motherfucker, they turned.

"Walk," I told my hostage.

"Slowly we turn . . . ," he said to me. We spun a 180, slow like Tai Chi, with the steel still pressed on him the whole time.

"Take tree giant steps," he said without laughter, but like me and him were playing a game. I wasn't playing. Through my peripheral vision, I was watching his men while watching him.

"I gwon reach and open dis door," he said, standing in front of the door across the hall with the exit sign. I pressed the steel against his back as he turned the key. The door opened to a darkened stairwell.

"Go down 'ere, 'n out the door at the bottom," he said.

"Step six steps to the side," I told him. He didn't obey.

"My shotty ayah," he said with a new confidence, requesting his gun back from me like it was some even trade.

"Nah. You can't call it," I said, reminding him who was in control. He wasn't.

"Bretheren," he said, as though he and I could somehow be brothers.

His two men made a dash for their weapons. I banged the hostage in the head, collapsing him, spun around, and shotty-whipped his boys before either of them could get a grip on the AK or the nine. Three men down, knocked out and bleeding without shots being fired.

I heard the voices of women reacting, gasping, whispering, chattering behind a closed door. They didn't open it. I grabbed the other two guns. I was headed down, hoping the exit door was the exit to the streets and that it was open and not bolted.

On the lower level, the Red Flamingo stepped out of the dark corner, interrupting my stride. Still wearing her "fuck me" minidress, her cobra keys now around her neck like a heavy necklace. She dragged a red laundry bag and was holding a small brown shopping bag in her other hand. I pushed past her, shoving open the exit door. It wouldn't open.

"Open the door," I told her, losing patience.

"Take dis. Believe me. You want to live, ya hafta carry out the red laundry bag. When the beast see dis red bag, dem no touch ya."

"And the other bag?" I asked.

"Your dinner." She smiled.

"Open the door," I told her again.

"Remember I," she said roughly, like it was an order. "Simanique is da name my mum gave me."

I put the weapons down, facing the opposite wall from where she stood. She was staring at the guns like she was somehow attracted to them. I looked in the red bag. There was folded laundry. It wasn't mine. I was rifling through it, a couple of sheets and pillowcases, inserting my hand searching for anything else hidden that I might not see at first glance.

"Me luv you, ayah," she said powerfully.

"Open the door," I told her. "You don't know me."

"I know three tings," she said, her hand resting on the door after setting the shopping bag down. "One." She pulled down one finger. Obviously she liked to count and list.

"I saw you praying that way. Me never see a man do dat before. Two, you write some lucky one a long letter; me want that for I. Tree, you went up in the hole." She pointed towards the ceiling. "And you come back out alive with all dem guns. No one wins over Redverse's brothers. You did. So you win I."

She turned the key in the lock. The heavy door creaked open. I pushed it with my gloved hands.

"The red bag," she insisted again. "You gwon live so I could love you." I took the red bag for one reason. If she was right, and if the police were outside her door, and if I could walk out past them, I could make it to the mailbox, which was my only goal. After that, I didn't give a fuck.

Outside it was still hot. Headed down the alley towards the front of the Laundromat, I could still hear the sounds of Brooklyn late-night street life. Looked left, looked right, without turning my head in either direction. New cop on the corner on foot, tall and slim. The one before him was short and slim. Cruiser still parked at the opposite corner. Now the mailbox was right in front of me. Walking out, calm 'n cool, I placed the red laundry bag on the ground beside the mailbox. I pulled the letter out of my pocket, pulled the handle, opening the mailbox, and dropped my letter inside.

Relieved, I checked inside the food bag before taking another step: two bottles of water, and food wrapped in foil. Walking and watching and being watched, I looked up. Man on the roof of the Laundromat. Dressed in all black, he blended in with the sky. But I could see the outline of his physique. I took him for one of "Verse's" men.

When an empty city bus rolled in slowly, my mind moved swiftly. Picking up my pace, I darted down the next alley while the foot cop's view of me was blocked by the bus. Squatted there, I took some seconds to get my mind right. I felt my hunger; I hadn't eaten since early afternoon. A minute later, I heard the voice of my second wife in my mind.

"So fucking cool," she would often say about me. "But sometimes," she had said softly, right before we last parted, "you have to throw cool away for a little while and do what's best to survive."

I ate.

# 5. TETRIS

Their side-room investigation pit was still empty, except for me in cuffs seated in the chair and the decaying burger on the table. The police detectives probably went to reshuffle their deck and would come storming back in here with a different approach. It didn't matter.

As I drifted off into a half-sleep, I suddenly realized that my mind had been measuring up the murder and the steps I took immediately afterward, as well as which tactics and strategies I should and shouldn't use now. So focused on that, I didn't focus on the reality, the impact or the results of my having entered Midnight Wash, that Laundromat. Now I reflected clearly. Now, I concluded that this investigation is not about the homicide I committed.

It was about the drug den that I'd unknowingly entered, to write a letter to Umma and to wash off the evidence of the murder. Unusually sharp usually, I didn't pick up on what my young life in Brooklyn had already schooled me on. Any empty business is a front for some illegal business, like a corner grocery store with very few groceries on the shelf and no everyday customers. Or a specialty shop whose window displays and decorations never changed because what's in their windows ain't what they selling. If I had lived in the neighborhood the Laundromat was in, I would have noticed. But I was just a man on a mission passing through. Now that I think about it, the three machines in a row that had a sign saying they were out of order could have had something big with high street value stashed inside—cash, drugs, guns, whatever. The whole switching of the exit signs and locking and bolting down the doors like that wasn't a crazy fucking fire hazard should've tipped me off. If one of their enemies set that place ablaze, they would all be trapped. And what about all that bullshit about the red bag? If carrying the red bag meant "no man, no beast ah touch ya," no street cats or cops in other words, would touch me, that had to mean that the cops and the dealers were working together and what they had in common was the red signal and the contents of the red bag.

What about the barefoot women who never opened the door even though they had to have heard the fight and the commotion? Were they also locked in? What else were they concealing and doing? Were there any men behind that door with them?

Now that I was alone in the room, I began to see some of the pieces of the setup. The Red Flamingo was their lookout girl. But she was a weak link in their chain. She was their untrained trusted girl soldier, although I didn't know why any man would have his woman as the face of his dangerous illegal business dealings, surrounded by other men, blood or no blood relation.

Glad I didn't fuck her. I didn't desire her or feel tempted by her. She wanted the dick-down so bad, if I was a weaker man she would've had me off guard and half naked. After the stroking, I'd be soaking in my own blood when her man's men came dropping down from the opening in the ceiling like spider assassins.

There is a difference between men who are believers and men who are not. Believing men don't take whatever is being offered just because it's available. The believers believe that there are three people in the room whenever any unmarried man and unmarried woman are in a room alone. The third one is the devil.

Believing men restrain first, and resist and select and take women as wives wisely, with all of their senses. Our reward is peace of mind, peace within our family, and also, Allah's mercy and protection.

There is a difference between niggas with weapons and trained fighters, armed or unarmed. No matter how much attitude or grimy looks or slick talk any untrained nigga has—and no matter if he is holding a stockpile of weapons and ammunition—a trained warrior will disarm and disable or dead him in seconds, and everything he has or had becomes mine . . . if I want it.

"It stinks." Hours later, the morning after the murder, two police in plain street clothes, wearing their badges like necklaces, entered the room. It was their beef stinking up their windowless side room. Now rotting meat mixed with the smell of their coffee and sugar doughnuts and the residue of their cigarettes, and a trace of alcohol on at least one of 'em. I had my head down on the table, not asleep anymore; my eyes were open and I was listening with my mind alert. Calm now, my thoughts dropping down rapidly, then shifting right into place like Tetris.

"Wake up! We don't sleep. You don't sleep, either," one of them said.

But of course I knew they had slept. Why else would they leave me sitting in the chair for eight hours? Seated straight now, I put my blank face back on.

"Get Officer Darby to escort this perp to the bathroom. It fucking stinks in here. Smells like he shitted in his diaper."

In the bathroom built with cement cinder blocks and no windows, I was about "to handle my business." First time in my life I'd ever been in a public bathroom with other men who were not there to handle their own business in their own stall or individual urinal. These cops were here to watch me.

"Bet you didn't know you have to ask every time you want to go to the potty and pee-pee," one of 'em joked.

"If you don't cooperate, you'll be doing this all day every day for the rest of your life." He exaggerated his threat. Still cuffed, I was standing, still adjusting. In a room where there was no way out except through the front door, in a heavily armed police precinct, where these two uniformed cops could've just posted at that front door and waited for me to finish, they chose to enter with me. One of them was walking in and out of each stall collecting the toilet paper.

"If you want tissue for your ass, you gotta open your fucking mouth and ask me for it," he said, juggling the rolls, dropping one or two and leaving them on the floor. I didn't reach down for it. "Oh yeah, I forgot. You don't have a name and you can't talk," he said sarcastically. "Go ahead. Take a dump. We ain't got all day."

He watched. Must've been some twisted pleasure for him to see if I could manage in the bathroom cuffed. As I walked in a stall he ordered, "Leave the door open." I pulled down my jeans and eased down my boxers. When I was done, I realized I couldn't wipe my ass while cuffed. He was standing in the stall with me now, laughing.

"Hey shitty ass," he said. "Need some help? Ask me for it." I didn't. He uncuffed me but stood in the stall immediately in front of me. "I'll let you wipe your ass if you ask me for the tissue," he smirked. I didn't ask. I stepped out of my jeans and removed my boxers and used them to wipe my ass. I threw the boxers in the toilet same as though they were toilet tissue. I flushed with my foot, and didn't pay attention to the toilet clogging as I climbed back into my jeans. Now me and him are face to face in the tight stall. "Don't you dare glare at me," he said. "Hands!" he ordered and cuffed me. I waited till he stepped back out. He did. I moved past the cop to use the sink to wash my hands, and even washed the shit off the cuffs.

"You should've emptied out the soap too," his partner said, laughing at his failed attempt to get me to break my silence.

Escorted out of the bathroom like a toddler, I listened with my brain and not my heart as they talked dumb shit.

"Fucking animal, I'd put a bullet between his eyes if he ever glanced at my wife," the cop who'd stood in the stall with me said to the other.

*He has a wife?* I thought to myself. I pity her. She probably respects her husband, the police officer. She probably believes he's out serving those who need help and protecting those who need to be rescued. She probably cooked him breakfast this morning admiring him and gave him a kiss and a lunch before he left, while not knowing he's just a fool who spent his morning on a black man's dick.

*This is how they break men*, I thought to myself. Being cuffed and trapped was expected. But what they kill you with is what no decent men would ever do, or ever expect to be done. It's the extra shit that has nothing to do with being questioned, or with being charged with a crime, or even with being sentenced or with serving time as a just punishment.

Inside the still stinking side room a detective spread some photos on the table. By now, I had observed that the detectives were more focused and serious than the regular uniformed cops. Yet all cops are cops to me.

*These are narcs*, I thought to myself. Drug detectives looking for drug dealers, drugs, and information leading them to a bust. I was clear now. *But one or more of them might be a drug dealer himself*, I thought. A dirty cop pretending to be a detective while dealing drugs on the low, or at least by protecting drug dealers on the low. Particularly, drug dealers on Redverse's team. *The ones carrying the red bag*, I said to myself.

"All that's required here are your fingers since your jaw is jammed shut. Point out which man or which men in these photos you recognize. Smartest thing you can do for yourself is to separate yourself from these guys. *Give them up. Cooperate with us*, and you can walk out of here a free man soon," he said.

In the photos were four different dreds, and one Caesar cut, all dark-skinned and Jamaican. I recognized two of them. The first was Shotgun; the other was AK-47. The other two I didn't know. I figured it was Redverse and one of his lieutenants, or maybe another one of his brothers or even his business partner. Neither me nor my face responded to the photos.

"You could move the photos around. Put 'em in the right order for us," the detective said. "The bigger the boss, the bigger the bang, the better the bargaining chip for you. Your freedom is based on this negotiation." I didn't speak. The officer who was trying to do all the convincing continued, as the other detective's face and body grew more and more impatient. He stood stiff, fingering his holster. The first detective threw a small pad and a piece of a pencil on the table.

"Give us some names. Write down the names of even one of the guys you know—his street name, name his momma gave him, whatever. But it better be right. Pull a fast one, and I'll have you serve all of their time put together. I can do that, you know." He was leaning on the table now where I was seated. His facial expression was serious, angry and frustrated. I knew the routine. He was playing "bad cop, good cop." I wasn't playing. The bad cop puts the fear in a prisoner and the good cop poses as a reasonable ally who the prisoner can mistakenly trust in and bargain with.

"Stand up!" the "bad detective" yelled, not giving a fuck about who could hear him. I stood. A tough guy, he took off his gun and handed it to his partner like he wanted me and him to shoot a fair one. There is no such thing as a fair one between a cop and his prisoner. The cop is hands-free and the prisoner is not. Even if I defeated the cop using only my trained feet, even if I knocked him out using the metal cuffs I was wearing as a weapon and banged him at a point on his body that I had already studied, even if I head-butted him into unconsciousness—and I could do all that—I knew if a man in custody, a prisoner, moves one muscle in his body, a cop is authorized to kill. And this detective wanted to kill somebody. He threw his best shots to my stomach, didn't like not seeing the look of pain on my face, and began slamming his fist into my sides. I felt it. I didn't react. His partner pulled him off me and pushed him outside the door. Now I was supposed to believe the "good cop" is my protection. I don't need it. I don't believe it. It was all a show to me.

Knowing they got no kind of charges they could stick on me, hadn't seen or caught me with any drugs, weapons, or even cash, I did a breathing routine I learned in my training, to shift the energy around in my body after the detective attacked me. The "good detective" stared at me. But all he could observe was my silence. He walked out saying, "I'll give you more time to think. Choose yourself, or choose them." He pointed to the photos.

Three detectives entered two hours later, two familiar, one not. One was carrying the Sunday edition of the *New York Daily News.*

"Where did you drop the package?" the unfamiliar detective asked me.

*I'm not no fucking mailman.* So, I didn't answer him. The unfamiliar cop laid his newspaper on the table. I took a good look at him. He was the same build as the foot cop I saw posted on the corner late last night. The same height and frame, I was sure. *He saw me exit the Laundromat carrying the red bag*, I told myself. He must've also seen me drop the letter in the mailbox. But he couldn't have seen me clearly from across the street where he was posted on the corner in the darkness of midnight.

"Was it the mailbox?" he asked with an urgent tone. Ignoring him, my eyes closed in on the *Daily News* headlines, one word in big bold black block letters: EXECUTION. One big photograph and it was me. I moved my eyes from it.

"Do you think we can't open the mailbox and look inside?" My mind is speeding. My face is blank. I'm thinking: he was definitely on the corner last night. I'm guessing he was the extra dirty cop in this setup. He saw me carrying the red bag, but he also saw me set it down, pull something from my back pocket, and drop something into the mailbox and then walk away without the red bag. If I would've held onto the bag like the Red Flamingo suggested, he would not have tipped off the cops who swarmed on me at the subway. Maybe I had confused him by both carrying the red bag and not carrying the bag till I got off the block. Maybe he thought *he fucked up* and lost the trail of the drugs.

My mind moved to the letter. Could they really open the mailbox? *The detective is bluffing*, I thought to myself. It was past noon. The mail had to have been collected already. They're looking for drugs, not mail. Maybe they had already opened the mailbox. If they did, they already knew there were no drugs dropped inside. At least, not dropped by me. Even if they opened it already, I told myself, the mail still would've got delivered. Long as Umma receives my letter, I'm good. *Oh, it's Sunday*, I reminded myself. Maybe they don't collect the mail on Sunday. It's America's day off. In the East, where I'm from, Friday is the day we go to mosque for Jummah prayer. Friday and Saturday is our weekend, and Sunday is our first day of the workweek.

"Answer the fucking questions, fuck face!" the bad detective screamed, playing his role. I sat silent. My eyes were back to the photo of myself executing the enemy last night on my Brooklyn block, a two-second hold, then my gaze was back onto the wall in front of me.

"What do you think those guys are going to do to you when they find out you handed the drugs to the government? The mail is federal property. What were you thinking? How much was in the package, a kilo? Two? Enough for you to pay with your whole life I bet. More money than your life is worth. These guys are gonna kill you. They'll put a price on your head and some crackhead on the street will blow you away for two rocks." The bad detective was leaning into my face and holding one of the photos up to try and extract fear in me.

The *Daily News* cover photo of me looked like it was shot from both behind and overhead. Maybe from a news helicopter. But I didn't see or hear no copter last night at the block party. *The stage!* The thought shouted on the inside of me. A photographer could've caught the shot from the stage, which stood high over the crowd. *Alhamdulillah*, the photo did not capture my face, only my back, my physical form and clothing, and my extended arm, my gloved hand holding my black milli. My barrel shoved in his mouth.

"Your loyalty to them is gonna backfire," the good detective said. "Cooperate with us. We can protect you. Give us the right info and we can even relocate you so that you'll never run into these guys again."

Funny, how he thought I was the dupe in this scenario. He thought I was protecting some drug syndicate because I didn't know any better. Actually, the good detective was the dupe, from how I see it. He was protecting the dirty detective who posed as a uniformed cop posted on that drug block—'cause he, the good detective, seemingly didn't know any better. The words the dirty D was saying revealed what his main focus was: Where are the missing drugs? He was concerned not because he needed to seize them and turn them in to the precinct. He was concerned because he was the real drug dealer, or the overseer and protector of a drug syndicate, who lost track of the package. Probably considered the worse possible fuck-up in their line of "work." Now nobody could get their payoff, at least not from last night's take, 'cause their drugs were missing. *Somehow, somebody g'd off*, I thought. Whether someone in Redverse's crew had the drugs and was acting like they didn't. Or someone who was supposed to deliver the drugs to them stole the product while pretending that they delivered it and that I stole it. Or even the cops could have one of their guys steal the product. I didn't know. I didn't give a fuck. I didn't have nothing to do with drugs, don't use 'em, don't sell 'em, but I could see now that I was somebody's come-up, somebody's fall guy and the diversion all in one.

"We'll take your fingerprints and match them with the package. Once we book you and you're in the pit with some of these other guys, you're done! Game over, finished!" the dirty cop threatened.

I knew there was no package in their possession. Not with my prints on it; that's why this bullshit boring-ass precinct interrogation was ongoing. They made a huge police scene in the train station last night. They thought they caught me red-handed. They made the mistake. Now, they had no evidence and no explanation. They needed me to do their job right now. They needed my mouth to snitch on the hustlers. They couldn't do their job; they weren't intelligent or clever or even capable of what they call good police work. And what about the fact that at least one of them in the room and probably a few of them in the precinct were part of the "red laundry bag crew"? They had to get some sucker and lock him up to cover up their own hands. They needed to make it seem like they wanted to stop the hustlers from hustling when they actually needed the hustlers to hustle to get their food, their cut, which I was sure had to be more than their little paychecks ever paid them.

"Smart-ass, you think we got nothing on you? We got your laundry bag that you left beside the mailbox . . ." he said. His hands were leaning on the tabletop. His fingers were pressing down hard and turning pale pink with stress. I knew the fact that they had the bag didn't mean shit. I was wearing gloves when I carried it that short distance. He couldn't see my black gloves on my black hands last night. And I had trashed the gloves in an outdoor trash can before I entered the lighted subway system immediately before my surprising arrest. There were no prints on the bag, at least not mine.

I saw the newspaper caption beneath the cover photo:

> Brooklyn youth executed in a crowd of hundreds. The bold assassin caught on film in the above photo. State senator outraged. Story on page 3.

Bad detective flipped the table, pushed me out the chair and onto the floor. I didn't resist. He swiftly grabbed the chair I had been seated in and got ready to crack it over my head. The dirty detective laughed. The good detective intervened, stopping the bad one by separating and distancing him from me. The dirty detective threw the chair into the wall. *Yeah, this is personal for him*, I thought. Maybe the missing drugs under his watch would catch him a bullet in the back of his head.

"Take a break," the good detective told the bad one and the dirty one. They both slammed out the door.

Good detective picked up the chair. "Sit down," he ordered me. I sat. Then he picked up the table. Next, he picked up the pad, pencil, and newspaper. Lastly, he placed all of the drug dealer photos back on the table.

"Last chance," he warned me. "I'm sure they're preparing to move you. I can stop them from putting you in that cell. I can even let the judge assigned to your case know just how helpful you were to us, if you make the smart choice. Think about it." He left.

Cuffed, I was still able to slide the Sunday paper over so I could read it:

> Senator Montgomery, a liberal Democrat who supports legislation for minority youth recreation, was rebuffed last night when an event he organized and sanctioned went haywire. It was a perfect day of sunshine and summer heat. A lineup of stellar performances and the excited crowd of thousands enjoying and cheering for hours ended in a chaotic and tragic melee. New York Police Department says groups of youth gangs began firing gunshots randomly into the air and others threw bricks and bottles at the police from the rooftops. In the confusion, one man focused and then executed another with a 9-millimeter, the same weapon used by the police department, and in the presence of the Housing Authority police, the NYPD and hundreds of spectators including the state senator. Despite the strong police presence, the assailant somehow managed to escape into thin air. The weapon used to murder Lance Polite, age 19, has not yet been found.

> The police conducted a full sweep, arrested 89 mostly juveniles, and the homicide investigation is ongoing. Community parents are outraged. However, only 18 parents showed up to protest in front of the 73rd Precinct late last night.
>
> Many parents interviewed last night say their children are minors being held and questioned without parents or attorneys present. The district attorney has issued a statement raising the capture of the murderer to top priority. He said, "The State of New York is populated by millions; 95 percent of them are law-abiding good citizens. We will never and have never tolerated murder, and we won't rest until the assailant is apprehended, tried and convicted of this violent, unconscionable heinous crime."

If I ripped the cover photo of myself out of the newspaper and laid it across my chest, or taped it to my forehead, it would probably be the only way the stupid cops and dumb detectives could "capture" me. I smiled.

Even though I was in the same room with them, and one of them actually had my photo in his hand on the cover of his newspaper, they were that slow and blind. I knew I could get away from these narcotics detectives. They had nothing drug related to hold me. They were betting I'd break down from their high-pressure performance and their bluff.

*I knew I might even get away with the murder that I had planned to take responsibility for, but . . .*

The good detective busted back into the room, interrupting my thoughts.

"Stand up!" he yelled. He was fired up about something. Now he had a style change. "Holy fucking . . ." He grabbed the Sunday *Daily News* off the table. He was staring at the front page. He took a quick look at me and began flipping the pages. I counted: one, two, three. He was reading. Then, he looked my way again. He walked towards the camera and stood in front of it like he was blocking it from capturing any images. He waved me to move toward the back corner. I did. He moved behind the camera, shouted, "What the fuck!" and kicked the camera from behind with full force. It didn't fly off the tripod but it did topple over. He kicked it again like it was a soccer ball, then picked it up from behind, pressed a button on the camera, and removed it from the tripod. He shot out through the door with it in his hands. I didn't know what was happening now. He left without giving me one of the commands they seemed to like to give. I was still standing in the corner. Before I could do anything else, he rushed back through the door without the camera.

Suddenly he grabbed the vacant chair from under the table and jammed it underneath the handle of the door. He yanked the table from its position and moved it to the side, away from the darkened window.

"Over there!" He pointed, speaking not aloud but only through gestures, ordering me to move. I did. He moved the chair I had been sitting in for hours to the side where he had placed the table. He struck the same pose as if he was the executioner in the *Daily News* photo. Then he nodded his head for me to do the same. I didn't. I just stood, my expression blank. I was realizing what was happening now. This idiot finally somehow put it together that it was me in the photo, or at least he suspected that it was me. He wanted me to pose so he could be sure. *I'm not no fucking model. I don't pose.* He was just staring at me now, not like he was actually looking at me, but was in some deep thought.

"Put your hands down!" he shouted aloud. But I was hands down and cuffed, still standing. He ordered me to sit by pointing to the chair that he moved into the corner. I sat. He scribbled on the notepad and handed me a piece of paper. I didn't reach to accept it. I looked down. He had written, "Don't talk." I read it, but didn't touch the note or react to his strange message. Why would he be instructing me not to talk, when I had not said one word since I was cuffed at the train station? He put his whole hand over his face and ran it through his hair and back over his face again. Crouching down suddenly, he removed his right shoe, stood, and smashed himself in the face with his shoe heel. After a pause, he snatched up the newspaper, folded it, and shoved it underneath his armpit. He began putting everything back where it had been moments ago—the table, the chairs, the photos, the pad, the pencil. He crumpled up his "don't talk," note and stuffed it in his pocket and left.

"Walk," he said to me when he returned. He led me out of the room down some corridor. I thought I was headed back to the holding cell. A few stray cops watched the path we were taking. None of them were the same ones from earlier today. A couple of them paused their own steps to observe us instead. One of them smirked at me. I figured they all suspected now that I am "the executioner" in the news photo, not the drug dealer they was thirst for. My face remained blank.

The good detective opened a door and nodded me in, then closed it behind us; there was nothing but walls—no table or chairs or cameras or windows or clocks or photos. He reached into his pocket. Out came tape and gauze. He began wrapping his own hands like a fighter does before he puts on his boxing gloves.

"You and I are on the same side," he said to me. "I gotta beat you to convince them that I'm a part of their team," he said strangely. So you stay still and let me fuck you up for show. *Don't you dare move*," he said forcefully through clenched teeth. "It's nothing personal." He punched me in the side of my head. Instant headache and a burning feeling, first time ever I let any man get at me like that. I had no idea what this had to do with the murder I committed or the punishment that I expected.

"There'll be some pain and a little blood, but you're my guy," he said, punching me full force in my ribs. "They got nothing on you. Believe me, it's better that I beat you than if I let *them* loose on you." He punched me in my jaw. "I'm not gonna hurt you. You and I are gonna do great things together." He landed one in my stomach.

I tasted blood in my mouth.

"You should've screamed. I wouldn't've had to make you bleed if you'd shown some fear and humility." He hit me again. I didn't scream. "Good enough," he said, unwrapping his hands and pushing the used gauze and tape back into his pockets. "Good boy! Good boy! Good boy!" he shouted. Yet he wasn't talking to me. I was right in front of him. Still silent. Still standing. He walked out.

I spit out the blood. Needed water. Wanted food, but didn't *need* it yet. Every few minutes the door would open but only enough for whoever to see in, and not for me to see out. Then it would close. I was leaning on the wall; felt the side of my head swelling and the tightening of my jaw.

Now we were in an unmarked car, just him and me. "You eat pizza?" he asked me. I didn't respond. He drove past a pizza joint, a regular dollar–dollar-fifty place. He didn't stop, just drove around the side and then zoomed down the back alley until he was in back of the store.

There was a heavy metal door, no knob or handle. Obviously it had to be pulled or pushed open from the inside. He did a rhythmic knock. The door eased open. "Yeah, yeah," he said to a fat guy wearing a greasy long apron. The guy didn't answer, turning his back and walking in the opposite direction of where the good detective was leading me.

Another back room with a table and four chairs, a tablecloth and no windows, some shelves packed with huge cans of tomato sauce, olive oil, jars of peppers, and sacks of onions and sleeves of garlic. There were crates stacked to the ceiling with bottled water, soda, and juices.

"Grape soda?" the detective asked me while reaching into the crate. I didn't answer. "Probably not. Everybody else your same kind chooses grape soda. So you probably don't want that. I told you—me and you are friends from now on. You should stop that silent-treatment bullshit and recognize who's on your side." He grabbed a can of Coke for himself, pulled the top, and gulped it. He let out a foul-odored burp. Then he set his can down and removed his gun from the holster.

"Easy, I'm not gonna shoot you." He used his gun to point out the small bathroom. "Go clean yourself up," he said, referring to the blood he punched out of me. I was still standing there.

"Oh, oh yeah. We're friends," he said, putting his hand to his head like he had forgotten. But his gun was still in his hand. "I'll uncuff you. You play nice," he said.

I went to the bathroom hands free. "Leave the door open," he said. I did. I take it they all like to watch, or at least hear the sound of a man pissing in the toilet or taking a dump.

Water going over my head and face, and water in my palms, naturally moves my mind to making prayer. However, I was bloody in an unclean space, a single-toilet bathroom, with the filth of men impossible to ignore. It was not a praying place. Still, I washed myself as much as I could. I was thinking, but couldn't predict what exactly was next.

Pizza, ziti, meatballs . . . the works were delivered to the back room without me ever seeing or hearing him request or calling in the order. The aroma of oil and vinegar, on a fresh green salad with olives and green peppers and a pile of onions, the scent of butter and oregano on Italian bread, and a small Italian feast was spread out on the table.

"Eat first—you gotta be hungry," he said. His gun was lying on the table where his fork would normally go, the barrel facing me. I waited for him to start eating, and then figured if the food was poisoned, he wouldn't be eating it. Besides, it did not seem like murdering me was his objective. He also did not make any threat over the food like the other cop did over the burger. Lastly, he seemed more worried about me trying to escape than anything else. He wasn't holding me into position by aiming his gun at my head. But he didn't know that whether he held me at gunpoint or kept his loaded weapon laying on the table facing me, I could easily relieve him of his gun and end his life. Murdering cops wasn't my objective. But he didn't know that, either.

Water first, plenty of water, and then I threw down the salad and next the pizza. I would have preferred peanut butter or chicken for protein and strength, but I was in survival mode. As he gobbled down the beef meatballs stuffed inside the thick white bread and smothered with mozzarella cheese over which he added Parmesan, I could see why most of these cops end up as sloppy fat-asses.

"Here's the deal. I don't know what you did earlier yesterday night." He let loose a loud burp. "But I do know you came out of the spot we've had under our surveillance for a good while. It's a major operation. Me, I'm a 'special cop.' I guess you could understand me if I say it that way. Internal Affairs—I watch over the officers in my precinct. So I got double duty, double the responsibility. I have to be the good narcotics detective who investigates all of the drug lords and teams, and then I gotta catch all of the cops and detectives who aren't good and who are not doing their jobs in the way I know they intended to do it at first." I noticed he described the dirty cops as though they were really good guys. He didn't call the dirty cops criminals.

He leaned back.

"I'm gonna let you walk out of here. I'm gonna pretend I didn't see that photo of you in the Sunday paper. I'm gonna do what no officer who wasn't a 'special cop' would ever do, or could ever do. I'm gonna let you get away with murder," he said, the wrinkles on his forehead deep and his face serious and stern.

"What you're gonna do for me is step right back into your crew, report to your bosses. Show 'em how I fucked up your face for remaining silent. Regain their trust and loyalty and work for me. It's a real job. You'll make real money. You'll collect information and feed it back to me," he said, staring into me for a reaction before chomping down on his meatball hero.

"I'm not looking for none of your little hand-to-hand friends.

I'm looking for three things: the top-level dealers, suppliers, distributors, and any officers—their faces, names, or better yet badge numbers—who you might notice along the way who are talking, meeting, or even arguing or fighting with anyone from your team," he said and then farted.

"What the fuck is that look?" he asked me. "That's the same smirk you made when you were reading the article about *the murder you did.* I saw you smirk," he said. "*That's how you told on yourself,*" he emphasized, getting more and more vexed. So now I knew that back at the precinct he must've been watching me reading the article in their interrogation room, through the darkened glass.

I didn't answer back. In my head I was thinking, This is fucking crazy. I didn't say one word to him or anyone else. This dude was trying to recruit me to be an "informah," on the crew I don't know, don't work for, and don't care shit about.

"There will be times where you'll wear a wire," he said, licking tomato sauce off his fingers. "No one will notice it. We'll put it on you nice the first few times. After that, you'll know how to wear it right on your own. This way, we can pick up on conversations, keep track of your location, and even save your life if you are in danger. That's what I mean when I say, 'I'm your friend. You're my guy.'" He leaned back on the two back legs of his chair.

I was solemn-faced. I wasn't responding. He brought his chair back forward. He grabbed a napkin and his gun. He was wiping his mouth with the napkin with the gun in his hand, giving me the understanding that it could "accidentally" go off at any moment. If it hit me, it was just a mistake, he would say. Or he would say that I lunged at him, tried to take it from him. He would say he was scared for his life. He would make people believe it. The authorities would back him up the same as if they were here in the room with only the two of us. I knew.

"It's a small stack of 'get out of jail free cards' for you. If you get picked up, since you're my guy, we'll let you walk. You might have to show up in court, go through the motions bam-bam-bam, but of course you'll walk. You're on my team and anything you do to further my goals was just that, you doing your job." He throws his hands up, clutching his piece still in his right. "You're not responsible."

*Done eating, I'm good now for at least twenty-four more hours*, I thought to myself.

"I know you make more money with your crew than you ever could with me." He brought both hands to his chest, gesturing. "But you're gonna accept this offer to beat twenty-five years to life for the murder you committed," he said, attempting to threaten me with the murder I was prepared to confess to when I entered the train station on my way to turn myself in.

Twenty-five years to life hit my head and my heart hard. Twenty-five years to life. *There's no way any judge would give me twenty-five years to life for merking a sucker like Lance Polite, the child molester, rapist*, I said to myself.

"You got a pretty little girlfriend tucked somewhere I'll bet. Right now, you make the money and she sucks your dick. Go to prison, you'll suck the dick and she'll make the money," he said.

I could tell he had used these words on many men before he tried them out on me. I'm sure nine times out of ten he broke them . . . all the way down.

"One call to the 73rd Precinct," he said, stone-faced, holding his Glock like it was a telephone, "where that murder occurred, and not only officers, but their captain, the district attorney, your state senator will be all over you." He stood. He began pacing around the table with his weapon on ready. He tried to make eye contact with me but I didn't allow it. He kept walking round, then he stopped right behind my back. I didn't turn, didn't flinch. I don't like dudes, civilians or cops or gangsters, who pull their piece and don't fire. I hate a dude who keeps speeching with a loaded weapon in his hand. I don't respect that. If I pull it, I fire it till the deed is done.

My silence, I know, caused the good detective's doubts and his threats and his offers to intensify.

"See, the thing about my offer . . ." He paused for effect. "Either you take it or you get locked up for so long, you'll forget what your mother looks like," he said, moving his talk from my "girlfriend" to my mother. He was searching hard for an opening, a vulnerability, a weakness in me.

"So what's it gonna be? You going to walk out of here a free man? Go home, get your dick sucked? Return to your crew, make money with them *while* making money with me, or, am I gonna throw you back in the Plymouth, take you back to my precinct, let you spend some time with some good officers who have the hots for you and want to throw you a nice farewell party? After they beat the Christ out of you, I'll let them in on our little secret about the murder you did. I'll get all of the credit for making that one call that charges you with the murder. Then, you'll be transferred to the 73rd precinct and the interrogation will begin all over again." He was standing with his arms folded now. He wasn't facing me. All I could see was his profile, but his barrel just happens to be pointed at my head.

Faith—not fear. I thought of Naja, eight years young, my father's daughter, my Umma's only girl, my sister, my reason.

If I were not a Muslim, a true believer, the good detective might've had me shook. If I was the average cat from the 'hood, he might have had me broken and wearing a wire and working for him. If I were not my grandfather's grandson and my father's son, he might have convinced me. But I am.

## 6. NAJA • *A Reflection*

"I found her. She's safe. I sent her home," Chiasa had said in the afternoon hours before the murder. She was in my Brooklyn apartment in her underwear, on her knees scrubbing the living room floor with an old cloth that had been stuck on top of an old bottle of Dettol beneath our kitchen sink. I was frozen by her words. I'd been outside for three hours looking for Naja and had checked everywhere in a six-block radius—every alley, each street, every car, parking lot, trash area, building, rooftop, and even down and into the subway and up and onto train station platforms.

"She's safe." I repeated out loud her words to me.

"She's fine, *alhamdulillah*," Chiasa said, but she was still scrubbing. "I walked her and Sudana to the taxi and spoke to the driver and all. I was gonna pay him. He demanded the money up front. But, Sudana insisted she wanted to pay. Seemed like she felt bad, so I let her."

"What time?" I asked her. "How long ago did you find my sister?"

"About three minutes after you and I both ran downstairs," she said calmly. Still scrubbing.

*Quick as lightning*, I thought to myself. My second wife had accomplished the task 180 minutes before I returned empty-handed to double-check what was happening back at my apartment.

"But we had to walk over seven streets to catch the cab because of the growing crowd, the road blocks, and the street party."

Relieved, I could only release and exhale about half of my tension from my body. No doubt I believed my second wife. Still, I had a strong feeling and wanted to at least hear my little sister's voice. But there was no phone at my Brooklyn apartment. I had shut it off a couple of weeks ago.

"I'll be back," I said to Chiasa and turned to leave.

"Wait for me," she said, picking up her scrubbing pace and finishing her last laps from corner to corner of cleaning the living room floor.

"A'ight," I told her, still feeling agitated and tight but unable to just tell her no, 'cause she is my shadow and my heart and my love. Waiting, I looked around. My almost empty apartment was completely empty now, no bento box or bangles, no knives, cloths, or clothing, and even the cork had been shaved and plucked off, each speck with patience. The living room window was open now; the heat rushed in and dried up everything that had been scrubbed and cleaned. The walls were glistening.

I eased out of my kicks and walked into my bedroom. It was all vacant and also scrubbed clean. In the bathroom, not even a drop of water remained on the sink or on the shower wall where Chiasa had showered earlier today. I'm accustomed to both of my wives' super-clean, Japanese cleaning techniques. Both of them cleaned the floors and walls as though they were tabletops used for serving foods. Their cleaning efforts did not leave room for error.

"Don't touch anything," Chiasa called out to me. The shower curtain was removed. *She must have burned everything in the incinerator*, I thought to myself. Even the empty trash can was gone. The tub was sparkling.

In Umma and Naja's rooms, all traces of their existence were gone. Even their scent had been completely removed and replaced by the strong smell of detergent.

"Chiasa." I was standing back in the living room, facing her. But she was in the kitchen facing the sink, washing her hands, splashing water over her face and neck and shoulders. The plastic Dettol bottle was inside the rubber glove she had been wearing moments ago. She had now placed it on the floor by the door. The second yellow glove was stuffed with the used soiled cloth she had been cleaning the floor with. She laid it by the sink where she was standing. She waved her hands to air dry them but still she did not turn around, although I was sure she could feel me watching her. I walked over to help her wrap up her untied *yukata.* Pressed against her back, I tied the garment from behind. It felt heavy.

"What's in here?" I asked her.

"Everything," she said coyly. "The keys to this apartment, our house keys, my slingshot and three rocks . . ." She began emptying her pockets, one by one. "My firecrackers." She laughed a little, placing them on the counter. "My 'stink bombs,' as you call them." I felt her smile slightly. "I have some twine and some matches . . ." I interrupted her. "You planning a kidnapping? I thought this was supposed to be your birthday picnic, just you and me?" I teased her.

"It is . . . Well . . . I know . . . you never know what might happen. So . . . I brought along some random things, just in case," she said softly. I preferred that she feel protected enough when she was with me that she didn't have to bring any weapons. She had carried that slingshot from when I first met her, and had always been an expert with wielding her knives and swords. So I just accepted that she is a fighter whether she's alone or we're together, wherever she goes.

Squatting, I felt her legs. They were soft, beautiful, and bare.

"Where are your stockings?" I asked her. Underneath her skirt or dresses, she normally rocks the thigh-highs with the ninja garter belt that holds her slingshot. She had those on when we first arrived here at my apartment, when the sound system outside was just beginning to be set up.

"It's so hot out. I packed most of our things into my bag and sent them home in the taxi," she said softly. But I could hear an unusual tremble in her voice.

"Turn around," I told her. She turned slowly. Our bodies pressed together, but her head was lowered.

"Lift your eyes," I told her. She lifted them and they were pretty as ever, silver-gray. Yet they seemed to be glazed.

"Did you cry?" I asked her.

"I missed you," she said and was already pressing her lips against mine. I fell for it, always fell for this clever, pure-hearted woman, and we were tonguing. That love was moving in me like a wave out on the ocean, slowly picking up momentum as it moved to crash and spill onto the shore. Her hand laid lightly on my shoulder, the other on the back of my neck. My mind went from heavy to lightness to blank. No more thinking, just feeling.

I was sucking her neck, palming her breast, just in love with the feel of them. Her skin was moist but not salty, as though the only liquid that oozed from her pores was natural spring water. Good for tasting or licking or sucking.

"No passion marks," she whispered. I pulled back and looked at her eyes. She smiled slightly. I smiled too, the first smile we'd shared since we were disturbed early today while making love.

"I'm just reminding you," she said. "You never put passion marks on my neck or face. They're always here." She placed her pretty fingers on top of the cloth of her dress and between her thighs. The gesture aroused me, and her observation was right.

"And here." She pointed to the back of her thighs and then her butt cheeks and laughed a little. Both of us recalling the feeling that night when I had passionately placed my lips there to her surprise and delight.

"I know why," she said softly, in almost a whisper. "I know why you don't put passion marks on my neck." But my hands were already all over her and untying her dress that I had just tied and stroking her panties, my fingers gliding on the soft silk in between the lips of her pussy.

"Ooh, don't do that," she moaned. That triggered me to pull out my nine and lay it on the counter on top of my white washcloth, away from us. I was quickly out of my jeans and T-shirt.

"Do that thing to me that you did the first time," she uttered. When she wanted to be sucked there, she always asked me to do "that thing." I pushed the fabric of her *yukata* off of her superbly sculpted shoulders. It glided down the curve of her body and fell to the floor. I rolled her panties off, over her pretty hips, and down her delicious thighs. Then, she sweetly stepped out of them. With both my hands on either side of her waist, I lifted her onto the kitchen countertop. She balanced there on her bare ballerina toes. I pulled open the freezer, pulled out one ice cube and placed it on my tongue. I unlocked her knees. Now they were spread open like the wings of a butterfly. Wide, like only a ballerina could do. I saw how she'd cut down her bush in her anticipation of this occasion. Her pussy looked like a peach. I sucked her clitoris, shocking it with a cold tongue and a small cube of ice. She gasped. Her fingers, now interlocked on the back of my head and pulling my face closer into her sweet pussy. I sucked and then licked it lightly while it was still pressed between my lips. Then I sucked the whole thing—the outer lips too. She exhaled wildly and then leaped up and jumped down onto me, wrapping her legs around my waist and hugging me warmly. I spun her around, leaned her against the counter, turned the faucet on, and splashed her with cold water. She laughed, wiggled and squirmed and screamed, and then smiled. Breathing hard, I could tell she was enjoying the intensity of our feelings. She fought to get loose from my grip. I let her go and she struck her martial arts fighting stance. But she was naked. I was erect. I kicked the back of her ankle, caught her and flipped her down to the floor, and went in her. In our naked sliding, using the moisture of her skin and the droplets of water and gushing around in the moisture of her pussy, I let off all of the tension and turmoil of the day into her. Her womb was a place of thick warmth, and the movement of her pussy muscles was a rapid massage for me, and a comfort; and after the terror, it was peace for me.

I was lying on my back now, and she was on her side, her face resting in her hand, balanced on her elbow. I turned to her. She turned away. Now her back was facing me. I was touching her soft skin, kissing from the back of her neck down her spine. She exhaled again seductively and softly asked, "If a woman loves her man, really, really, really a lot, a lot and very deeply . . ." She exhaled. "I mean like really loves him a little more than herself," she said, and I was listening, "and the woman knows something that her man does not know, but that he needs to know, but she also knows that if she tells him what he doesn't know, she'll probably lose him . . ." She paused.

I pulled her around to face me. There were tears in her eyes, welling up from her soul but not spilling.

"If she doesn't tell him, it's betrayal," Chiasa said, answering her own question. "I already know that's what it is." Her tears spilled out. "But if she tells him, she betrays herself and loses him, which is unbearable because she loves him more . . . than herself." Her tears were streaming.

Chiasa doesn't cry. Not tears of pain, only occasional tears of joy. She's always happy. That's all I've ever seen of her. And if anyone who she loves has a bad situation or problem, she goes straight to organizing and acting on the solution. She sacrifices herself, her time, her gifts for others. Chiasa is a problem solver, not a victim or a problem. This beautiful trait of hers is one of the many reasons why I love her . . . so deeply.

I was on my feet now, about to splash water on my face and clean my mouth and hands. Swiftly, she leapt up.

"Don't touch anything," she cautioned me with excitement, pulling some napkins from her *yukata* and placing one of them over the faucet to turn it on.

"Wash now," she said. Of course I knew something was wrong. I splashed water on my face and cleaned my hands and thoroughly rinsed my mouth. I stepped into my basketball shorts and then my jeans and pulled into my T-shirt. She was holding her panties tightly in her closed hand, picking up her *yukata* and putting it on. She pushed her panties into her inside skirt pocket. Then she washed her hands and face and pulled her *hijab* out of another pocket. As she wrapped it, I rewrapped her into her *yukata* and tied it nicely. We were both silent.

She was using her right foot to clean the area where we were just loving, right in front of the kitchen sink.

"That cloth is finished," I told her. I snatched it from beneath her foot and put it back inside the glove. "Tell me now," I said solemnly. I grabbed her with both hands by her waist and sat her back onto the other countertop. I turned the water on using the napkin that still lay on top of the faucet, and washed her feet starting with the right one, which she had used to clean the floor. I looked up at her while wiping the soles of her feet. I smiled at her, naturally.

"Oh Allah, that smile," she said, without laughter.

"I know Naja is safe," I said, looking into her eyes. "Because I know you would never lie to me."

"True," she said softly. "She's completely safe."

"So Naja is safe. That means Umma is happy," I said. "And Umma is happy, so I'm good. So what are we talking about?" I asked her with a true seriousness, because I could feel her true seriousness.

"The first thing I heard was a whistle. A subtle sound that should have been drowned out by the music but it wasn't." She looked up. "I found Naja in the basement of the other building." She pointed. My heart shook.

"It was the same direction she was running in when I first saw her from your bedroom window. When I reached the lobby of that building, I heard some screaming, but it was not human. It was a cat. I followed the sound down the stairs. It was getting dark the further down I went, and it seemed that someone had busted all of the light bulbs. I could feel the glass on the stairs cracking beneath my Pumas. Then I heard a male's voice say, 'If you don't do what I say, I'm gonna kill your cat.' His creepy voice froze me. By this time, I was paused on the bottom basement step.

"'You better mind your fucking business,' I heard him say forcefully as though he was talking to me, like he could hear that someone was approaching. It sounded like the animal was gagging. Then I heard Naja's voice say, 'I sure hope you won't kill my cat. But when my brother finds out what you did, he's surely gonna kill you.'

"Stepping down the last step lightly, I saw him and fired my knife through the darkness over Naja's head and into his left eye. He screamed in a way that I never heard a man scream in my life. He dropped the cat as soon as he grabbed his face. I could tell the cat was dead and Naja was stuck there from fright or grief. He looked like he didn't know what to do; my knife was just lodged there firmly and there was blood. I dashed in and grabbed her hand. But Naja tried to reach for her cat. Then he tried to grab Naja's hand, but I was swift. I yanked her and dashed out. I stopped on the bottom step and thought to go back and kick him, then yank my knife from his eye. I felt Naja's little fingers pulling me.

"'Come on, he's so stupid,' Naja said.

"That guy was spinning in circles like crazy. He seemed in shock. He was big and I didn't want to get close enough for him to grab me or to touch Naja. Soon as we dashed he started chasing us, but more like he was stumbling. I snatched open the heavy stairwell door that led back into the lobby. There were people in the lobby so we stopped running, and calmly walked through the lobby and outside. But Naja's hands were trembling. I couldn't believe that people were in the lobby but didn't come to help out when they heard the screaming noises. When we got halfway back to your building, I looked back through the concert crowd, but he wasn't coming out after us. From upstairs I saw him moving through the crowd with his hand cupped over his hurt eye. I didn't see the knife though. Strange; it was like no one stopped him or helped him. They had to see him bleeding." Chiasa exhaled.

"So what are you crying for?" I asked Chiasa, picking up my nine.

"Naja's safe, and I did get him back good. His eye was spilling blood. But I know . . ."

"You know what?" I asked her, putting on my belt.

"I know you . . ." she said, her eyes cast down. "Naja is right. You are going to kill him."

"Don't cry for him," I told Chiasa. I removed my wedding ring and began emptying my pockets.

"I'm not. Not for him," she said. "I'm crying because you and Naja both don't know that Ms. Marcy is dead. She had a heatstroke while she was outside, worried and searching for Naja."

# 7. HONOR

The closeness of men, a network of brothers, some related by blood, some related by word is bond, some related by faith, each of us related by action—I believe in that. Thought it should be automatic. Yet, I had operated as an army of one. Ninja style, it had worked for the eight years that I had lived in Brooklyn. Now I saw that what I had failed to consider strongly and to do was to build an army.

Now that I am sitting here with my hands cuffed, my feet cuffed, my hands chained to my feet and my feet chained to the next man who's also seated here with his hands and feet cuffed, I'm thinking. This is not the "closeness of men" I believe in. This is not "brotherhood." The one who is chained to me on one side is also chained to the man seated close to him on the other side. We are twelve men, hands and feet cuffed and legs chained one to the other.

Reviewing the path that led me to be in this unexpected position, I realized that what I had done wrong was that I had failed to build an army. I had created a business successfully, but not an army to protect the business or continue with the business when and if for any reason I ran into any serious trouble. I had not built an army, and therefore did not have the power to confront my enemies with any real force or threat or with lethal action or positive outcome. I could take down one enemy at a time, as I had already successfully done. Yet I could not defeat a system, an organized army of enemies or a rotten culture or attitude. Furthermore, I am here, mixed in and chained down with other men who had failed to do the same.

My mistake. I had been moving through life as an individual, believing that as long as I work hard and live right and respected limits, as long as I created businesses and stockpiled my paper and jewels, that was good enough. Now, I see that it's not only the hustlers and gangsters and politicians that need armies. Every man needs an army of brothers; every man, every family, every neighborhood needs an army of real men.

It's not just a numbers game, I'm thinking. It runs far deeper than that. A man could be a part of an army of one hundred, or one thousand or ten thousand or one hundred thousand or one million. But the value of that army or that team is in the value of each of the men it is made up of.

I looked to my left. Each man cuffed and chained together alongside me today—we look alike. We each speak English. Still, we don't share a common language. We know it too. So even though we are shoulder to shoulder, we don't speak. We don't say. We don't ask. In fact there is no "we," unless the chain gets yanked, or an order gets called out or the leash gets lashed. Then, reacting on impulse, we would either start or stop moving, we either sit or stand.

Locked down on my birthday, I'm thinking, *Now I have lived more years in Brooklyn than I lived at home in the African Sudan.* My body is here. My mindset is from the other side of the world.

My mistake. Muslim men are supposed to give *daa'wa. Daa'wa* is spreading light, teaching and/or introducing and/or inviting one or more people to an understanding of Islam, about Muslims and the Holy Quran. To give a man an understanding is to give him the keys to the universe. To hand a man a Quran is to give him the answer towards straightening himself, strengthening himself, and becoming useful to himself, his father, mother, family, and 'hood. I failed to do that. In fact I just watched quietly as men without understanding lived recklessly—some I knew, some I did not know. I just swerved around them, building and working and praying and being rewarded in so many ways.

Now I'm asking myself, what is the value of being one man who has a true faith, strength, family, and business trapped and surrounded by men who have none of that, who don't even want it or know that it is missing and who don't have any idea how it would feel or what it would be like if they did?

Inspiring other men to become believers, who are not perfect, but who are humbled and striving, is the starting point of building an army of men. Not just a band of niggers or a gang of fools or a heap of heedless heathens. I looked to my left at these men who are cuffed here, who I am cuffed to, and felt I knew for sure that the last thing they wanted to hear about was faith. They probably would figure I'm in the same cuffs, same as them, and in the same place, same as them. So, shut the fuck up.

Without an army of believing men I'm in a tight spot. There's no human to plead my case, who has an understanding.

In the East, where I hail from, men have honor. That doesn't mean that they are perfect. Yet they are better off than men over here, who have no honor at all.

Honor is honesty in action, fairness in action, and integrity in action. Integrity meaning a man has a set of guiding principles or beliefs that he bases his movements, decisions, and actions on. He doesn't trade those beliefs for anything. If he sees one man or a thousand men doing something that he does not believe in, he doesn't join them, isn't swayed by popularity but guided by principle or faith. I'm not certain if honor is something that can be taught to any random man, or if it is something that a man must be born into. I am certain, however, that in order for a man to have honor, he has to have seen other men living and acting with honor. Otherwise, he would not have a blackprint of or a feeling for what honor is or what the value of having honor means to him and to the men who surround him every day. Having friends and brothers and sons and fathers and grandfathers who are men of honor is peace. Having men without honor and without knowledge of the meaning of honor is chaos. Without honor, each man is an open enemy to the next man.

I could bond with men who are not Muslim if they were men of honor. I could bond with men who are Christians or Jews if they were men of honor. I could bond with men who had not yet chosen a faith if they were men of honor. However, I could not bond with any man who is dishonorable.

Back home across the globe, I could tell a million men about the day and the night of the execution. Not one of them would misunderstand the reason the deed had to be done. Each of them would know, without discussing or debating, that a man's women, his mother, wives, sisters, and daughters, are his honor. Back home, you couldn't and you wouldn't be a man chasing another man's little girl, filling her with fear and trapping her in a basement, unless you were ready to die, willing to be executed. Back home, even if you were a man filled with perverse feelings, you'd rather cut off your own hands or kill yourself than disgrace your parents by dishonoring yourself, them, or a neighbor. Back home, if by some stroke of chance or destiny you did dishonorable deeds, instead of you being left alone and accepted, you would become a target. The man whose honor you violated would be expected by all other honorable men to deal with you severely. Once he served you with death, he would be welcomed back into the brotherhood of men. Each man in the brotherhood would have done the same thing given the same or a similar situation. As a show of respect, they would never again mention the foul offender or his foul offense to the honorable man who murdered him. They would all know, without being reminded, that such unlikely violations can only be overcome through silence.

Over here in America, the dishonorable ones are accepted and sometimes even welcomed, and often are given authority over other people's lives, while the honorable ones are dealt with dishonorably. Despite my plan to make a confession and be judged based on my deed and punished based on justice, and to serve my punishment honorably, I am caught up in a snafu. Even if I explained, men over here would not understand. And even though I feel down today, jerked around on a chain, taking baby steps, part of a shameful parade, I still feel more sorry for them than I do for myself.

These men who are chained and seated beside me come from a culture without honor. I know. There's a thousand of them living in the Brooklyn projects where my family used to live. They don't even know what's wrong. They don't even know what's missing. They have no god and no father, no beliefs and no motivation to find out. Their worried and broken mothers and frightened girlfriends, baby mommas and sisters and daughters, were scurrying around the corridors of the Brooklyn court building talking to their enemies and captors, bartering for their sons', brothers', and boyfriends' lives. Their women, who are also without honor or husbands or protection, and who are also without standards or understanding, were willing to give up anything, say anything, do anything . . . oh Allah . . . to get their men out of bondage.

My mother, wives, sister, and unborns . . . I would never allow them to come in here, to see me this way, or to even be seen by my captors. I would never give my enemies the opportunity to lay eyes on them, to trade words with them, to take money from them, or to lay hands on them, *la kadar Allah* (God forbid). They would not have the chance to make their evil offers to my women, or take sacrifices from my mother or wives, or to question or interrogate my young sister, or to run my women ragged because of the desperation they feel because of me in cuffs and chains or behind bars.

I will keep my family separate from the heat. I feel good about that, could take anything and face any circumstance as long as they were protected, I told myself.

Yet, my failure to give *daa'wa*, to teach and to strive to create a brotherhood of men, to share what I know for sure, might be the cause of my temporary downfall. I know, if I am here, cuffed and chained and forced to be still and deep in thought and self-criticism, it meant that I am suppose to be. Allah is showing me something, teaching me something.

When a bad thing happens to a Muslim, we don't say, why did God do this to me? No, we say, what did I do wrong to earn this punishment? We believe that all that Allah does is perfect. We are the flawed ones.

We also believe that each of us will be tested, challenged, perhaps given a taste of evil. In these times, we don't move further away from Allah. We move closer.

Still, my failure to build an army even with the closest of my friends weighed heavily on my heart.

# 8. THE WALL • *A Reflection*

"Yo Chris," I said when he picked up the phone.

"You back? I thought you gave up on the BK and decided to chill in Japan."

"Nah, nothing like that," I said.

"Hope you shot some footage with that movie camera so we can check it out when we finally see you," he said. Then he asked me, "Why you calling from a pay phone?"

"It's summertime, man, you still on punishment?" I flipped it on him.

"Oh you got jokes. Nah, I'm good now," he said.

"Wanna work?" I asked.

"What's the job?"

"I got a home owner in Queens who wants to hire a crew to build a wall."

"A wall?" he repeated.

"Around his house," I explained.

"That's manual labor, my brother. How much is the pay? Not minimum wage that's like three dollars an hour," Chris said.

"The pay is good," I told him.

"What's that mean?" he asked me.

"It's good enough for me, and you know I'm about that paper," I said, and he laughed.

"Is Ameer working on it too?" he asked.

"Yeah, he's down."

"Then the money must be right," Chris said.

"Let's us three get up before dojo tonight. I'll kick y'all the numbers and the schedule then," I told him.

"A'ight," he agreed. "Let's meet at the Curry Shack at four then. That'll give us enough time."

"We all got blacker," Chris said. He was holding the door open as Ameer and I both rolled up at the same time, coming from opposite directions.

"Sun must've been sizzling in Japan. I didn't think this brother could get any blacker," Ameer said as he embraced me and gave me a pound.

I saw what Chris observed. We had each been in the sunlight, skin blackening. I checked Chris was out of his Air Force Ones and into some Stan Smiths. Those kicks were for tennis players. He was even rocking the green Izod instead of Polo.

"You been on the tennis court?" I asked him.

"Tennis!" Ameer repeated before Chris could answer, as though it was an illegitimate sport.

"My father signed me up for tennis lessons. I had to accept them if I wanted him to ease up and end my punishment," Chris said.

"Oh, it's part of the punishment," Ameer joked him.

"I thought of it that way at first, but it's an alright game. Try it. The girlies be out there playing in their miniskirts 'n shit, bending over chasing down balls." We all laughed.

"Let me get two beef patties," Ameer ordered. "And a ginger beer."

"Two more and I'll have the same," Chris said.

"Give me two chicken patties and a side of cabbage," I ordered. "And two bottles of water." We grabbed the last available table and waited. "Let's get down to business," I told them.

"Let's eat first," Chris said as he jumped up to pick up our tray from the register and pay the cashier from our group fund.

"Why you speeding?" Ameer asked me. "There's so much to talk about. We gotta update you on some real shit. And you need to tell us something about this fucking 'voyage' you went on." Then he lowered his voice some. "I got your joint," he said, referring to the burner that I let him hold while I was away traveling.

"Same as it was?" I asked him, meaning had he used the weapon for any reason. It was cool with me if he did, but I needed to know for sure.

"I flashed it on a few, but never fired," he said discreetly.

"Oh yeah," I told him. "We handle the cannon same as we handle the sword. Like Sensei taught us, 'Don't pull it out unless you're ready to use it.'"

"It worked for me. Next time, niggas that need to know, know," Ameer said confidently.

"What you gonna do next time you see 'em and you ain't got it?" I asked him. "That's why you don't flash it. Once they know you holding, they gon' go and get strapped and come looking for you. Then what?" I asked him seriously.

"What y'all talking about? Damn, I stepped away for a few seconds and missed something," Chris said, holding the tray with all of our orders on it. Neither me nor Ameer said a word. Chris caught on and didn't push it. He broke the tension like usual. "Grab your shit off the tray. Do I look like a waitress?" Chris barked, then laughed as we each reached in for our food and drink.

"It's not always serious like that," Ameer said solemnly after we were all paused and eating. I didn't follow up 'cause I meant what I said.

On a napkin, I drew a rough diagram of the dimensions of the wall. "The house is here," I said, drawing a small model to mark the placement of the house. "The wall goes like this . . . It's nine feet high all the way around. There are three sides: left, right, and back wall, and of course they all have to connect and line up perfectly."

"A brick wall, right?" Chris questioned.

"Cement blocks," I said swiftly.

"The owner must have something valuable inside that house. Good for us. He'll be ready to pay up," Ameer said.

"The pay is seven hundred dollars for each side. There's three sides and three of us, so that's seven hundred for each of us," I told them. "We get paid when it's completed."

"We gotta get him for a deposit. Just in case," Chris said, thinking aloud and sounding like his father, the Reverend Christian Broadman.

"Word up," Ameer said. "What if we build it and shit, and the cement dries, and for some reason he's talking about he don't like it. Ain't like we gonna knock it down and start over again." We were looking back and forth at one another as though we could see each other's thoughts.

"I'm sure I can talk him into that if I keep it reasonable. Say, one hundred for each of us as a deposit?" I checked their eyes.

"Cool," Ameer said, and Chris agreed a split second after him. "Seven hundred dollars, nice," Ameer continued. "It takes all summer to make seven hundred dollars working in that bullshit city summer work program around my way."

"My pops ain't gonna say no to seven hundred dollars in my hand. That's seven hundred less out of his pocket." Chris laughed.

"We start every morning at eight a.m.," I said.

"Damn," Ameer said.

"And we quit at two p.m. each day until the job is done," I added.

"Why can't we just bust it out all day long every day until it gets dark? We'll finish faster," Ameer proposed.

"No, he doesn't want none of us on his property before eight a.m. and he doesn't want none of us on his property after two p.m. each day. Those are his rules, nonnegotiable."

"Sounds crazy. How did you meet this guy anyway?" Chris asked.

"He got the idea in the hardware store where I was picking up a few things," I said, intentionally dodging.

"It's cool. Now that I think about it, if we finish two p.m., we got the whole rest of the day to get a pickup game or whatever else pays," Ameer said.

"Back to you, black man!" Chris joked me. "What about that footage?"

"Black is beautiful," I shot back calmly.

"Is that what your girlies tell you?" Ameer asked me, only half joking.

"My women," I corrected him.

"Whoa . . . that's right, 'wife'! Not 'wifey,'" Chris said. "I respect that," he added, straight-faced, and I could feel he was sincere.

"You come back flexing, huh? Showing off?" Ameer asked me. It didn't sound like he was joking, either.

"Nah, nothing like that," I said solemnly, and I meant it. Retreating into my thoughts, I was thinking that I wanted the opposite of showing off. I had not told either of my best friends that in addition to my first wife, Akemi, who they had each met one time only, at our unique and unplanned wedding at our dojo, I now have a second wife. In fact, I never planned to tell them about her, either. If Akemi had not come high-stepping into our dojo that day, unannounced, in her Manolo Blahnik sandals, causing each of the male fighters' jaws to drop down when they saw those pretty Egyptian cat eyes and thick lips. Black-haired Akemi, so sleek in her silence, her elite feminine fashions, unrivaled and extremely attractive, her walk mean and provocative, yet there was nothing loud about her except her feelings for me. If she had not showed up that day, I never would have introduced them to her. My wives are not showpieces to me. Both of them, when seen by any man capable of recognizing raw, natural, genuine beauty whether fully or partially covered, cause a man to react. So now they stay covered or out of most men's view, on purpose.

"When do we start?" Ameer broke my retreat.

"Tomorrow, eight a.m. Everything is in place: wheelbarrow, cement mix, the scaffold, the cement blocks, and all the tools we need.

Just wear some beat-up jeans 'n old Tims, long sleeves even though it's hot, and work gloves. He will supply the hard hats. Be ready to sweat and get dirty."

"Must've been some type of fence here before," Ameer observed, staring down into the soil. It was day one of our job building the wall.

"Probably," I said, looking into the deep line in the soil that ran across the perimeter of the backyard. "It's a good thing for us, though—it shows us exactly where the wall belongs."

"My pops said if we go even one inch into the neighbor's property, the neighbor could file a complaint and the city would investigate, then force the owner to knock the wall down."

"We'll be paid and long gone," Ameer said calmly.

"Most def," I said. "After we complete it, everything else is the owner's problem to handle. It won't happen, though. See these markers?" I pointed out the first of six iron stakes in the ground. I pulled out a thick white string and tied it securely onto the iron marker. I walked straight across and linked it tightly to the next marker, until the entire backyard perimeter was lined with a tight white string. "This string will be our most precise guide. Each block will be set evenly up against this line all the way around. With the iron markers from the land survey, and the indentation from the old fence, we'll get it right," I assured them.

"Damn, you sound like a real construction worker," Ameer said.

"Let's set this first block. Then we'll all three be real construction workers," I said, squatting to lift the first block and walk it right into position.

"My father said we are three underage, bootlegged, unlicensed, non-union laborers," Chris said, smiling.

"Right, but Reverend Broadman liked the sound of that seven-hundred-dollar salary," Ameer said, laughing. "So your ass is right here working with us at the crack of dawn. And this one-hundred-dollar deposit feels good in my pocket. So let's get busy." We all laughed.

"Word to mother," Chris said.

"Butter the block, then shave it evenly. Line up the joints," Ameer said, repeating what I had taught them earlier. "I like a lot of butter on my toast," he joked as he spread the cement over the block. Chris laughed. We were all three working, stepping back and checking our work, helping each other out. The atmosphere was warming up. From when we first began making the cement, 150-kilogram bags, sixty shovels of sand, three buckets of water, we had become closer as friends, I thought. Converting pounds to kilos caused Ameer some difficulty. Yet Chris was swift with mathematics and quick to teach everything he knew. Carrying the blocks set off a competition of strength and as time moved on we messed around, each trying to carry more than one at a time to see who could lift the most. Seemed like we did more talking and working in that afternoon than we had done in all of our time together combined. And it was only day one, with possibly almost two weeks remaining.

"You ain't ask me about the Hustler's League yesterday," Ameer said suddenly.

"You didn't speak on it," I said calmly, still looking at the blocks and filling the voids and checking the precision, then hammering them with the heavy rubber mallet. "So I know my team, 'the blacks,' stomped all over your red squad while I was away." I smiled, after having a look that was dead serious. Chris laughed.

"One point only!" Ameer shouted, dropping the block in his hand into the soil and then holding up one finger and raising then placing his foot on the block he had just dropped. I didn't react, just kept working.

"Losers always say it just like that," I said, rubbing it in. "'If we could've, if we would've,'" I said, straight-faced. Then I added the burn. "But the fact is you couldn't." Chris cracked up.

"What you laughing at?" Ameer barked at Chris. "You ain't even in the league no more!" he reminded Chris.

"I still get one-third of the purse whether the red team or the black team wins the tournament. I ain't mad at that," Chris fired back, and he was right. When Chris's father pulled him out of the Hustler's Junior League as a form of punishment, me and Ameer both agreed that same as when we each joined up for the league, if any of our three teams won, or if either of us three got most valuable player money, we would divide it three ways.

"You were gone more than a month. Your boys had to hustle like hell to keep the black team undefeated. They probably threw your ass out the league too," Ameer pushed back at me.

"We'll see," is all I said. I had called Coach Vega crazy long distance, using a phone card on a pay phone, while I was in Asia. As soon as I realized my trip was definitely going to take more than a week's time, like I had told him at first, I let him know I would be "missing in action" for a while 'cause my situation had gotten "a little hectic." That's all I told him. I cut the call before giving him a chance to think and ask me any follow-up questions that I was not gonna answer. I cut the call knowing that Coach had no idea where I was, and no option to call me back. Now that I was home, I had scheduled a face-to-face with the coach. He accepted the meet-up eagerly, telling me, "Yeah, face-to-face, that'll work. You're a little brief on the phone."

Chris, slathering the next cement block, looked up and smiled at Ameer, then said, "If both of us are kicked out of the league and you're still in, we'll need you to play real hard for us, brother. Get that cheddar and break both of us off our portion." We all laughed, even Ameer.

Break time, because we had to let the blocks we laid dry. I had learned that if we heaped them up too high while wet, the weight and the pressure would cause a shift and the wall would be lopsided by the next day of work. We cleaned up, put all of our materials and tools neatly in the corner of the backyard, on the inside of the low wall that we had built so far, and left.

As we walked down the block to get something to eat, Chris said to me, "You messed up the negotiation on this deal. We should have got the owner to get us a Porta-Potty. How's he going to have us working when we can't use the bathroom in his house?"

"Just take your dragon out and pee in the woods on the side of the house. Don't be so fucking spoiled," Ameer told him.

"I'm just saying, if I was setting this up, I would've negotiated for use of the bathroom and a big water cooler, 'cause it's damn sure hot. I would've even tried to get him for per diem," Chris said.

"Per diem?" Ameer asked.

"Yeah, like a small daily fee to cover our lunch expenses while he got us out here," Chris explained. "Hell, we ain't from Queens. Apparently he couldn't get any of these Queens cats to do the job for him. Still he's treating us like we ex-cons, locking up his house and confining us to his yard!" Chris said. I smiled. I agreed with Chris, but mostly I liked his business mind. I knew he was already calculating how much lunch would cost for each of us and multiplying it by however many days he figured the whole job would take, and then subtracting it from the seven-hundred-dollar payment that we would each get in the end. That's why he was tight.

"Fuck it, we can't negotiate after the deal was made, the deposit was paid, and the work has already gotten started," Ameer said. To-morrow, I'll bring my own lunch. Brown-bag it! Get one of my *women* to organize that for me!" Ameer emphasized, then looked toward me. I caught it. He was still uneasy because I'd corrected him to address my wives as women, not "girlies." Now he would call his girlies women too. I didn't say nothing back. He could call his girlies women if he wanted to, no problem. Yet we each knew that his were not wives, and that was the real big difference.

# 9. RIGHT TO AN ATTORNEY

Money-green eyes and pale skin, no cosmetics and nice lips, black lashes and black hair. No ring on her married finger and no jewels. A black embroidered bracelet on her left wrist almost completely covered a deep scar. She held her briefcase in her right hand. Slim, wearing a conservative well-tailored black suit, which she obviously spent good money on. She somehow chose to wear clogs on her feet confidently, but they didn't match the rest of her fashion. Birkenstocks—the tiny metal label on her clogs was the only obvious branding on her. I had to look very closely or I would have missed it.

She walked slowly, strolling past each of the twelve of us all cuffed and chained. She inspected us carefully with those eyes. When she reached the end of the line where I stood, she stopped and stared. Then she did a 180 and slowly walked back to the beginning of the line, opened her briefcase, fingered through some files, and pulled one out. She flipped through the few papers in the folder, held it open and started all over again walking back down the line. As she watched, I watched. She is after all, a woman in an evil space packed with evil men.

When she reached the end of the line the third time, she kept walking. Seconds later, she returned with a court officer. Approaching us again from the right side this time, she and the officer stopped where I stood.

"Unchain him, please," she said politely to the officer and without any emotion as she pointed her eyes towards me. He signaled a second officer. When he arrived she said, "I need a private room to counsel my client before his arraignment."

Unchained from the eleven, but hands and feet still cuffed and chained, I was only capable of small steps; still, I was grateful to be moving. One officer walked behind me and the other in front with her. Those two talked as though I had no ears to overhear them. But of course even with the commotion in the court corridor, I could hear clearly what they discussed.

"You should stop that guessing game you play," the officer said to her. His casual tone of speech let me know that he was familiar with her.

"Not playing, Officer Foley," she said dryly.

"I could've yanked that John Doe from the line, escorted him to the room, and had him chained to the chair and waiting for you while you enjoyed a nice cup of coffee," he said as though he had an interest in charming her.

"Not necessary; I even want to take a look at my coffee beans before they roast or grind 'em," she remarked.

"The pretty ones are always extra work," he joked, giving a short laugh. After a pause, he turned his failed flirtation back to the business at hand. "This guy here is no victim. Don't ask me to uncuff his hands in the counsel room. That's not gonna happen," he said sternly.

"Is that your decision or mine, Officer?" She pulled some type of rank on him.

"That's me looking out for your own good. That's me doing the same thing your father would want me to do." He emphasized this by stopping his walk and turning towards her. But she kept walking, leaving him behind.

"No thanks, Daddy," she said with calm sarcasm. "This troublesome, pretty little lawyer girl will make her own choices, and will take care of herself. That's what I learned to do in four years of university, three years of law school, and after passing the bar on the first go-round." She had shut him up and shut him down at the same time.

"Uncuff him," she said when we reached the room.

"Please have a seat," she said to me politely. I was reminding myself to not be off guard to her feminine manner. I sat down, hands uncuffed, unchained, but not my feet. It was a windowless, almost empty room with a solid door except for the slim rectangular glass, which revealed the court officer posted immediately outside it. There were no cameras visible. My eyes moved across the perimeter of the ceiling to check for small devices that I knew could easily have been planted there. I wasn't worried, but I was cautious, and more thoughtful about surveillance than I had ever been in my young life.

She remained standing. I was seated. She approached my chair slowly and pulled her face in close to mine and then walked around my back slowly. I didn't turn. I remained seated. She walked back to the front and squeezed herself in between the table and my seat, pushing the table back with only her backside. I did not know what she was doing. Neither did the officer on post who was now glaring through the glass on the door.

"Do you mind if I touch your face?" she asked me. I had one eye on him and one eye on her. I didn't answer. Couldn't call it. She stood up, still close in front of my chair. Him, still watching her back as she faced me.

"I like the whole silent thing. Brilliant," she said softly and without emotion. "However, you'll have to treat me differently than everyone outside of that door. Let's develop a system. I'll do my job my way. If you feel violated in any way, just tell me and I'll stop immediately." She was staring. "Let's get started then," she said touching my chin and the top of my head lightly with her fingers and moving it around gently. The door opened.

"What's going on?" Officer Foley barked as though the attorney was his woman.

"Attorney-client privilege—please close the door," she said calmly. He didn't. "Since you're still standing there, order me a car. I've got a hospital run. His head is injured."

"I'm sure it's nothing. Hard heads heal on their own," he said, aggravated. "You're just gonna make more work for yourself and more work for us. You know you have to get a court order to move him. Paperwork! You want to spend your whole day in the hospital?" he pressured her, but really he was telling her not to bother. She didn't respond to his advice, his commands, his words.

"Order the car. I'll run and get the judge's signature from the clerk. Will you take care of it for me, or shall I take care of both things for myself?" She checked him without even looking his way. The door closed. He left and less than three seconds later, another officer was posted outside the door. He was less curious. Obviously watching over her was less personal to him than for the other officer. He wasn't peering in, but he wasn't moving from his position, either. I could see the back of his head directly through the glass.

"I'm going to lift your shirt for a moment. I'm going to touch you," she said as she raised my T-shirt up. And placed her left hand over my heart and held it there to keep the shirt up. With her right hand she pressed her fingers lightly on my ribs, in addition to searching my stomach. "Turn around please if it's okay," she requested. I stood and turned as she dragged her hand from my heart to my back. Facing front again, she pressed my ribs again. "Does this hurt?" she asked me. I felt it, a slight pain that my mind had numbed a few days back. I didn't react. "I think it does," she said, disregarding my nonresponse and blank stare. "Please have a seat," she said softly, yet without emotion. I sat down and placed my uncuffed hands on the table.

She opened her briefcase. I could see in. The insides were covered with stickers, white backgrounds and colorful letters and slogans. I thought it was bugged out to decorate the inside of any carrier. Most people, especially travelers, post tags, labels, and bumper stickers and all kinds of things on the outside of their luggage, so they can identify it as it's being moved around the carousel after landing. But hers was reversed.

"Are you an adult?" she asked me casually, not like an interrogator. In a relaxed tone, she told me, "They have you listed as an adult and this courthouse is for adults. If you are not eighteen yet, it makes a difference in how you are handled, and a big difference in where you end up." I didn't respond. I was thinking. She was better than the rest of them. Just the fact that she was a woman lowered the volume of my hostility under these circumstances. I didn't feel any aggression towards or against her. She removed seven-eighths of the energy I normally burned up to restrain myself and to appear blank or neutral in the presence of the male authorities and their bullshit. Still, I didn't feel open or ready or at ease or certain yet that she was the one who would work my charges out with justice and to my benefit.

"It's to your advantage if you are a juvenile. If you are, I can keep them from photographing you any further. If you are a juvenile, it will impact which judge you're going to face, and in which court you are going to stand. I know you're silent and thoughtful. However, you'll need to present the facts so that you can be defended. I'll need time to investigate the history and quirks of the judge you are going to possibly face during trial. Each judge is different. The law grants them some boundaries, but they are tremendously powerful," she said calmly. I liked that she was planning to investigate the judge.

She leaned forward. "I represent you. So here's what we are going to do right this minute. If you are an adult, eighteen years or older, raise your right hand or wink your right eye, or simply say so. I'll give you ten seconds. Afterwards, I'm going to jot down in my file that you are a juvenile." She checked her watch, had her eyes dead on the movement of the second hand. Then softly, she said, "Go!"

She sounded confident, but I could tell on the matter of my age, she wasn't. She had seen and touched my body and it confused her. My body led her to believe that I'm an adult male, eighteen or older. Yet for some reason, she saw it to her legal benefit and mine for me to be underage. Or she had a hunch.

Clever, she was more skilled than any of the police and each of the detectives so far. She had gently turned my silence against me. Now, my not responding had become an actual response, according to how she twisted things. Maybe it was to my advantage to let her assume whatever she wanted to for a while. If I remained silent, whatever she wrote or reported about me was her assumption or her lucky or unlucky guess.

My silence so far had drawn out the demons that live in men. Each of them, the cops and the detectives, started off treating me with a certain stance and composure. The more silent I was, the less able they were to wear the masks they were wearing. In minutes for most, and even seconds for others, it became clear what kind of beasts they really were, whose side they were on, 'cause they were definitely not on the side of the law, and what exactly they were going after and what they were willing to do to carry out the threats they had made in the line of questioning me.

Because I did not cooperate with the good detective, his whole presentation flipped. I rejected his dirty offer with complete silence that night in the pizza shop. On the car ride back to his precinct, he threatened to kill me and call it self-defense if I discussed with anyone the content of the one-way conversation he'd had with me. The next morning, he reported that I had confessed to murder, despite me not opening my mouth and uttering one word to him. The following day, he had me transferred to the 73rd Precinct and the questioning began all over again. Everything I had already gone through with the narcotics detectives at the 77th Precinct somehow didn't count. The homicide detectives started the clock all over again. Consequently, for another forty-eight hours, I was jailed, interrogated, and subjected to all of that extra shit that they do and get away with. The whole time, I remained absolutely silent whether they were talking to me, shouting, or beating me. They tried to draw a murder confession out from me, spoken and written, or to have me confirm what the good detective had reported. I didn't. I knew he was trying to set me up for a twenty-five-years-to-life sentence. I definitely was going to do everything in my power to block that movement. That included not acknowledging anything to any of the cops, detectives, captains, or anyone on their team. I figured that the fact that I was now the main suspect for the murder, based only on the good detective's word and zero other evidence other than the faceless photo, the heat had been taken off the others who were swept up on my Brooklyn block and falsely accused. I could tell that based on the good detective's word, the blues and the homicide detectives felt sure that I was the murderer, although they couldn't prove it yet. I had stood in several lineups, and whatever "witnesses" they had on the other side of their one-way glass didn't pick me. Yet it seemed they didn't point out anyone else either. My mind stretched to even consider that the 'hood wanted that snake dead and was grateful somebody finally had the heart to merk him. It was hard for me to believe, but it seemed somehow that not pointing me out in the lineups and not cooperating with the police questionings had become the 'hood's way of looking out for me.

Back in the police cruiser and cuffed and on my way to Long Island College Hospital, located in downtown Brooklyn close enough to all of the courts, I had overheard that much on their walkie-talkies. The attorney had said she would meet me there at the hospital intake. She'd already warned me to prepare to be cuffed to the hospital bed and locked in a guarded hospital room. "Not to worry," she added. "I'm your attorney, and seeing as we don't have any parent's or guardian's name and contact information from you, I'll be the only one allowed in to see you, aside from selected hospital staff and of course the doctors."

Before she stood up to leave me back at the courthouse, she had asked me nonchalantly, and all of a sudden, "Do you like that name, 'John'? Are you okay with being known as 'John Doe'?" But I could tell she'd already perceived my answer. "That's what all your paperwork says, and of course eventually you'll be assigned a number." She waited, offering me a chance to react. I didn't.

"Let's come up with the truth. Or, a more suitable pseudonym," she'd said right before walking out. The last word of her sentence, *pseudonym*, was a test, I knew.

*Pseudonym.* I had read books in the past written by authors who used pseudonyms. They were made-up names that replaced the actual birth name of the author. Back then when I thought about it, I was curious if those authors just didn't approve of their real birth names, or if they felt they needed to hide their true identity because of what they had written in their books.

The 'hood was all about pseudonyms. Some cat would be born Mike Jones, but his mother would call him "Boo-Boo." Next thing you know, his brothers, sisters, and cousins were all calling him Boo-Boo, and then his friends. Boo-Boo would get into his first fight on the block. If he used a small knife to cut his enemy, the streets would rename him "Slash," or "Cutter." Yes, that's how it works. The narcotics detectives who investigated me also knew that's how it works. They asked me for names of the hustlers but told me they would even settle for their nicknames. They were studying the hustlers from a distance. In every police precinct I'm sure they keep a picture book of every arrested boy and man in the 'hood. Underneath each photo, it says Mike Jones, a.k.a. Boo-Boo, a.k.a. Slash . . . and so on.

Names have a deep meaning to me. So deep that even exposing your name is something heavy and special and sometimes even sacred. Since I was seven, I never spoke my name again to anyone outside of my family. I always thought revealing it would expose more than I wanted to share with any person who wasn't close enough to me to already know it. The 'hood gave me "Midnight," and I ran with it. It sounded strong to me and it somehow had depth and feeling. The men respected it, and women reacted like they wanted to get close to it.

Even for me to say someone else's name had meaning to me. Even if it's a dude, I'm not calling no young or grown man "Boo-Boo," even if everyone else does. I'm not calling the next man "Sugar," or "God," or any name that lets off some backward or wrong-meaning feeling. Nine times out of ten, I wouldn't be talking with no niggas like that. If I had to, for some unknown reason, I would talk without ever mentioning the pseudonym that didn't sit right with me or with my beliefs.

Both of my wives catch feelings, like a jolt of energy or a strong sensation, when I speak their names aloud. Even on an ordinary day, while doing ordinary things, or when I just came back into the house and called out for one of them, Akemi's hypnotic eyes would light up. Chiasa is in love with my voice, and more in love with my voice saying her name. I can't think about it the same way my wives do, but I know a man speaking a woman's name out loud arouses her, if she has love for him.

"You got nothing but time," the officer posted in the hospital waiting room with me said. He stood against the wall, close to me as I sat, hands and feet cuffed. The lawyer was very late arriving at the hospital. The place was packed with uncuffed patients, some obviously and extremely sick, some bloodied, some coughing, some leaned over, or lying down over three or four seats that were needed for others who were still arriving. No matter their conditions or aches and pains, they each took at least one glance at me cuffed and chained. It didn't matter.

The officer must've thought he was a mind reader. Every half hour or so, he would make some smart remark like, "You think you're the only client the lawyer has? She's got nine knuckleheads just like you at the courthouse waiting. You're all going to the same place. That's where you all belong."

None of that was on my mind. I was thinking about business. I was watching the sick people in this waiting area and their children and spouses, each getting up randomly and putting their coins and bills into the vending machines. Vending machines, that's my line of work. Being surrounded by them in here had me thinking back.

# 10. NEW BUSINESS • *A Reflection*

A truck rolled up to my Queens home, catching me off guard 'cause I didn't know when it would. Me, Ameer, and Chris were way out in the backyard building the wall.

"The owner got a delivery," Ameer said, peering. "Wonder what it is?"

"We'll see in a minute," Chris said.

"Let's stay focused," I told both of them.

Dilemma: if I ran to the front of the house to accept and sign for the delivery, then my friends would find out that I am the real owner of this house and that they were here building a wall, working for me. The job and the pay is legit. However, them finding out that I no longer lived in Brooklyn, and where I do actually live, was not part of my thought-out security plan. I did not want any men watching, mixing with, or lingering around my women. Even before I had taken two wives, I didn't invite Chris or Ameer to our Brooklyn apartment plain and simple because my mother and sister lived there. When I am outdoors with my women and they are each covered, no problem.

Naja, Akemi, and Umma were all at the Ghazzahlis. Only Chiasa was home. On the one hand, I knew she would see the truck out front because she tends to see everything. On the other hand, I knew she would also be in a dilemma because my wives and

I all agreed that they would not reveal themselves while "workmen" were anywhere on our property.

"What the fuck?" Ameer said, breaking our rhythm of laying the cement blocks. We each were now watching one guy carefully steering a gigantic nine-foot-by-six-foot box on a dolly. Then his man came out with a second huge box. Now I was surprised as well. I was only expecting one delivery.

"You think the owner's home?" Chris asked.

"I doubt it. He never comes outside while we're here and we never catch him coming or going," Ameer observed.

"It's a woman," Chris said. "Nice . . . ," he added.

Chiasa had emerged from the front door of our house wearing her Fila summer sweats and a thick wool hat that covered her hair, but her thick hair in the spring humidity made the hat lift and swell. She stood at the back of the truck, speaking briefly to the delivery man, signed the clipboard to acknowledge receipt, and then pointed to the backyard without turning around to face me or Ameer or Chris. She jogged back in the house.

"Is she the owner's wife, or his daughter?" Chris asked, looking like he was under a spell after a glimpse of only her profile.

"What?" I said calmly, but feeling tight while still working the wall as a way to get both of them back to work.

"I think I'mma try and talk to her," Chris said. "Word up. She looks good from a distance." He laughed. "Now, all I need is a close-up. I'm 'bout to ring the bell and ask for a glass of water."

"Use the water cooler right there. You know what's up," I told Chris calmly.

"Don't cock-block. The married men should let the single guys roam," Chris said, walking away from the wall where we were working and towards my house.

"I got dibs!" Ameer called out to Chris. "She'd pick me anyway," he said confidently. "She probably been watching me through her bedroom window the whole time we been back here working, *even if she is married!*" Ameer then tackled Chris before he could get too close to the house. Now the two martial arts guys were wrestling in the grass. Ameer is a fierce fighter no matter what style of fight he's using. But Chris is strong and underestimated, and I could see him using that strength to dominate over the underestimation.

The deliverymen were standing in the front of the backyard now. The presence of the strangers and the huge boxes being rolled in was the only thing that broke up Chris and Ameer's play fight.

"Where do you want them?" the buffed-up Italian dude asked us.

"Wherever she told you to leave it," I said. They wheeled both boxes to the side of the deck and skillfully removed their dollies. Both of them side glanced at the wall we were building before they turned and left.

"What would you have done if you went up and rang the house bell, and the owner answered the door with his shotgun?" I asked Chris as I was buttering a cement block.

"You know that she's his wife then?" Chris asked me.

"The shotgun if it's his wife, or the pistol if it's his daughter. Either way . . ." I said.

"You always gotta go extreme, man," Ameer said, leaping up from the ground.

"Word to mother," Chris agreed, then we all laughed at ourselves.

"How come there are two boxes here?" I asked Chiasa. This was after I'd wrapped up work and walked off the property with Chris and Ameer to the subway station and came back home. "I ordered one vending machine," I reminded her. She smiled.

"Let's make a *mudarabah*," Chiasa said. I smiled.

"How do you know that word?"

"I read it in a book," she said, smiling even more widely, her left eyebrow raised. I knew then that she was plotting something.

"*Mudarabah* meaning contract in Arabic, am I right?" she asked me.

"No," I said calmly. "*Agid.* Remember we wrote our wedding contract? It's called an *agid*, because in Arabic that is the word for contract."

"Oh, I see," she said, still smiling. "And *mudarabah* means . . . ?"

"Business partnership," I told her. She jumped up like she sometimes suddenly does.

"I ordered two!" she said excitedly, finally answering my first question about the two boxes. "So let's you and I make a *mudarabah* together, with your new vending machine and with my new vending machine." She was talking business and flirting with me through her eyes. I let the feeling move in me but stayed solemn on the outside, as though she was any businessman trying to make a deal with me.

"Let's check out what you ordered." We each drew our knives to slice the box open. When she saw mine, she put hers away. I sliced the first box, a nice clean cut straight down the line so I could close it back up properly. The box I cut led to a huge wooden box that looked like a portable closet. It had a combination lock built into it.

"Open the envelope," Chiasa pointed out. I did. Inside the envelope was a thick catalogue that was sealed in a thick plastic. I sliced it open with the tip of my blade to avoid damaging the pages. In the inside cover was the combination. I dialed it and the door swung open, like an actual precisely fitted door in a home would do.

Apparently it was the machine she ordered.

"It's a horsey ride." She smiled. "For children," she added. "It might inspire them to—" I cut her off.

"It might inspire them to give you fifty cents a spin," I said after swiftly sizing up the mechanics and finances of her machine.

"No, really—well yes, I would like the fifty cents per spin, but it might pique their interest in becoming equestrians," she said.

"Equestrians—what language is that?"

"It's English! Take me seriously! Don't play around!" She

laughed. "It means 'horseback riders,' or anything having to do with the world of horses," she explained.

"Okay." I folded my arms across my chest to make her feel like I was going to be difficult. I pointed to the iron lock box beneath her machine where the coins would drop down. "Your machine takes coins. The machine I ordered takes dollars. What would make me form a partnership with you, when my earnings are higher than yours? That doesn't sound like a reason to go fifty-fifty, does it?"

"True, your machine cost more than mine, and will probably earn more than mine, but that's not the point, is it?"

"That's my point," I said, still being serious just to fuck with her. Her face changed like now she was thinking much harder than during her light playful mood, and like this talk was much more difficult than she had anticipated. She walked up close on me, placing her ballerina fingers on my shoulder with one hand and the other hand behind my neck.

"You can't use your body as part of your business proposal," I told her.

"Yes I can." She smiled sweetly. "As long as it is only with my husband." And, she was right. She pressed herself against me, both of us standing in the yard. I was about to go for it but resisted her manipulations.

"I gotta go pick up my wife," I said to her.

"I *am* your wife," she said to me.

"My first wife," I said.

"Kiss me first," she said softly, like a whisper. *Fuck it.* I did. But the heat between me and her is too high. She often wanted to kiss and she could be content and delighted with just that. The momentum in me didn't work that way. For me, one touch led to another and then spread like wildfire. It was too strong. But Akemi and my Umma were waiting for me to come at the agreed time, so I would.

As I closed the wooden door and spun the lock, then taped up the box with the "horsey ride," in it, Chiasa came up behind me and wrapped her arms around me. My hands were way up high taping the top. She got on her tiptoes and was trying to reach up as high as my hands reach, which is impossible for her to do. Meanwhile, she was pressing against my back. Now she was trying to pull my hands down, massaging my chest and moving to tickle me. I was holding back my laughter and not showing her my smile 'cause I knew that's what she wanted. Feeling ignored, she squeezed herself in between me and the box.

"This is why I can't do business with you," I told Chiasa.

"We started off as business partners when we first met! How can you say that you can't do business with me now!?" she asked in her playful, flirty way.

"Because," I said.

"Because what?" she asked in a sexy voice.

"Because the situation is different now."

"Different how?" she asked. I paused.

"Because now, I've been in you. Every time we're close, I want to go in you. Every time I look in your eyes, I dream about how good it feels to be in you. That's why."

We were half an hour late, sitting side by side on the train quietly, our feelings thickening in the air. We got off in the Bronx and were walking together.

"The reason you should form a partnership with me," she said after seconds of us walking in silence, "is because my vending machine will make more money more swiftly, and it holds more money than yours because the lock box is at the bottom. It holds a thousand dollars in coins. And your machine is a merchandise machine and mine is not," she added confidently. "My machine is less trouble. You won't have to collect the revenue as often. The quarters will make the base of the machine so heavy it will be difficult for anyone to steal it. You won't have to stock it with any sodas, waters, chips, candies, products, or merchandise, which means that you won't have to restock it, either! The moms just put the coins in for their children and each child wants to ride over and over, or each mom has more than one child and voilà! I'm rich! You should take that into consideration and make a *mudarabah* with me." She had come up with all of her angles within minutes. Or maybe she already had all of her angles sealed beforehand and just slowly seduced me?

I had ordered the vending machine while I was in Asia. The Japanese company exported their machines to America and even had the U.S. dollar conversions factored into their mechanics and displays. Of course, the Japanese always make the most efficient, high-quality smart machinery. They always make it expensive yet easy to purchase and easy to utilize. They think long range instead of selling cheap shit and jerking their customers. They make a customer out of a buyer, *for life!* That's why I wanted to begin my business buying from them. I would test it out with my first machine just to be certain that it was a bankable option. Then if all was good, I planned to not only collect revenue from my one machine, but to reinvest and have many machines in ideal locations. Furthermore, I planned to sell the machines themselves. I paid $999 for one. On my next order I would buy in bulk and then resell the machines, placing a nice fee for my company on top of the actual cost. This was a business that would earn for me quietly, hardly ever required my presence, and didn't lock me into a mandatory schedule or location. Lastly, it was a business where only the owner—that's me—knows the count on my earnings. I liked that.

In Japan I had hired Chiasa as my translator. At the time that I hired her, she was not my wife or my love. She initiated and completed the vending machine transaction on my behalf. I paid the bill. Therefore, she knew all of the business details and followed through properly. I'm realizing now that mixed in her Japanese business conversation with the seller on my behalf was her business deal as well. I wasn't mad at her. I am not suspicious of her. I like her mind and I fucking adore her.

I didn't reply to her persuasions.

"Every time?" she said suddenly.

"Every time what?" I asked her.

"Every time that you look at me . . ."

"Every time." I confirmed the truth without looking at her. "That's why you and I are late."

Later that night at home, my second wife made her third attempt. This time, she was not using her sensual sexual powers to influence me. Instead she was brandishing her intellectual sword in a spiritual manner.

"You know, Khadijah was a wealthy woman when she met Muhammad," she began softly. And I already knew Chiasa's spiritual sword was her most powerful weapon in this battle to win me over and get her way.

" 'Prophet Muhammad, peace be upon him'—say that," I told her. "That's how Muslims say it whenever we are speaking the name of the Prophet."

"I know," she said sweetly, "but this story I am telling you begins when Muhammad was not the Prophet yet. He and Khadijah were not even married yet."

"Alright, I'm listening," I said. I watched her. She put on her *hijab* even though she and I were in her bedroom, just the two of us. Her mood and manner shifted as she continued to tell me a story.

"Muhammad's family worked as traders. They took goods and traveled in caravans long distance across the desert to sell the items they had for sale to various communities and customers. In business young Muhammad became known as an especially honest trader, a man who kept his words and promises, and as importantly, who treated everyone he encountered with truth and kindness. His reputation caused many to respect him and to request his trading services. Khadijah is one of the people who heard about Muhammad. She was a wealthy widow who also had inherited great wealth from her father. She became a careful, skillful, and successful businesswoman by investing her wealth wisely. Based on her hearing about Muhammad and a feeling that she had, she approached him to make a *mudarabah*. She offered Muhammad double the profit for his trading services to take her goods across Arabia to As Sham. Muhammad consulted with his uncle and soon agreed. And . . ." Chiasa took a breath.

"And what else?" I asked calmly.

"Well, you know, they did good business together. Muhammad sold her merchandise while on a long journey with other male traders. Eventually Muhammad and Khadijah married. Throughout their marriage Khadijah supported Muhammad in every possible way. And, before Muhammad became the Prophet, peace be upon him, he used to climb up the mountains alone to the Cave of Hira to think and listen and learn. Khadijah made him food to take with him to the cave. Sometimes she even climbed the mountain and sat outside the cave and waited for him. As Muhammad's trips to the cave lasted for longer and longer amounts of days and weeks, and even over a period of three years, Khadijah remained home and raised their children and waited. When Muhammad would finally return, she welcomed him warmly and presented him with a peaceful home. This is the kind of Muslim woman I strive to be. Like Khadijah, I want to make wise choices and investments. I want to be an active and useful and loyal wife. Sometimes, I'll want to climb the mountain and follow you to the cave and wait outside. The End," she said, with her eyes lowered.

I felt she was lowering her eyes because she wanted me to concentrate on the meaning of her story, and not the intimacy and yearnings we share. I understood. I had been concentrating. I enjoyed her true storytelling. I enjoyed even more, that she went about reading and researching our faith.

"You and I already have a *mudarabah*," I told her. "When I married you, we became partners in all things," I said. I showed her my heart and my truth, instead of teasing her or putting on a game face. She jumped up from her bed. Her smile was brighter than sunlight.

"I'm heading out now," I told her, letting her know I was going to Akemi.

"Okay," she said softly, but still beaming. "Good night!"

My second wife is like that, lovely and agreeable. Yet she is also clever and brilliant. When she and I are in the same space together, right before I am about to leave to go over, up, down, or out without her, she will say something or do something right before we part that makes me feel like she is still with me, even though she isn't. It feels as though we are both walking side by side up the stairs and into my first wife's bedroom. I always have to pause and shake it off before I enter the energy of my first wife. They are two different flowers, two separate blessings, two different comforts and pleasures, two different women, two different wives—to this one grateful man.

# 11. WEALTH, MY FIRST WIFE • *A Reflection*

She comes from wealth, my first wife. As soon as you see her, you'll know. Black hair, dark pretty eyes and thick lips. Slim and sleek, her walk is mean. Her beauty is evocative, making whoever is looking feel something. Her fashion is elite, feminine, and flawless. You can't imitate her. She's a Bergdorff Goodman kind of girl. Only the wealthy shop there. Even many of those who consider themselves fashionable have never even heard of it. It is so exclusive that it's too expensive a place to even window shop. My first wife, she's selective, extreme. It's all or nothing. She may go into a store with thousands of pieces in inventory and come out with only a scarf or a pair of stockings, or sunglasses or a badass hat. She doesn't care what's popular; she cares if it's the finest fabric that feels and looks good on her skin instead, and if it compliments her unique artistic sense of style. And she really loves if it's hand tailored, one of a kind, custom designed, almost impossible to find anywhere else. She'd rather search for hours, days, months, or even a year before she finds it. Her heels and her kicks are all incredible on her small feet. Nude, in only a pair of her six-thousand-dollar leather thigh-high boots, and I'm captured by her aerodynamics. She's a Ferrari.

Modest, quiet, mostly silent, she's foreign. She doesn't speak English but her emotions, body, and gestures speak my language. Lovable and sweet, there is no conceit in her and she gives in to me eagerly. She's not a fighter. She's not a pushover, either. Yet those few who know wonder why she agreed with my having a second wife who came along at the hottest temperature of her and my young-young marriage. But my first wife is moved by feelings—her feelings, my feelings—and she would give me anything I wanted even if she believed she would be slighting herself. I chose her. I love her. She's mine for life, no matter the storm that swirls around us. I'll work for her. I'll build for her. I'll protect her.

A motherless daughter, her mother returned to Allah when Akemi was only thirteen years young. She's vulnerable. Born in Kyoto, Japan, she embodies the best parts of their culture: calm, quiet, beautiful, well mannered, organized, intelligent, and highly capable. Yet in her veins boils the hot blood of Korea, which causes her to be deeply sensitive and very emotional, two traits that result in her being an ingenious soulful artist, who at her young age has been globally recognized and even had her award-winning art displayed at MoMA.

But for me, mostly she's soft, sensual, and sweet. The first woman I have ever loved in a different kind of way than the pure love I have for Umma, my mother. I protect her the same way I protect my mother. Her complicated family history gave me my first reason to travel to Asia and to fight to snatch her back from her father, who snatched her from me after our marriage was already in place, and after I spilled my seeds of life in her womb, repeatedly. My first wife was the reason to take down the fence that was already in place at our Queens house and to build the solid cement-block wall. Also for her, before leaving for Asia, in the backyard of our vacant new house, I planted a plum tree, which I expected to blossom over time, along with our love, and to represent how sweet her love is to me. I knew the new roots planted in the earth would be shaky at first, but then would go down deep, thicken, and spread and would give rise to a strong tree that would last longer than a human life and bear much fruit.

Her wealth, she gave it all up for me. Actually, her Japanese father cut it off as punishment for her choosing to be the sixteen-years-young wife of a young Muslim man born in Sudan, Land of the Blacks, who now resides in Brooklyn, New York. Her father tried everything to keep her to himself. In Japan, he owned houses and buildings and businesses and even a mountain. He gave her everything a father could give to his daughter—a private school education, chauffeured cars, cash flow and credit cards and free roam of the Earth. He even tried to give her the sky. Still, having fallen in love with me, she traded everything her father had ever provided for her, including his love and affection. In exchange she got a young husband, a young marriage, a mutual and true love, and twins in her womb, *alhamdulillah*.

Because of love, my first love, and because she is my wife, my first wife, I knew and I know just how hard I had to work, what I had to build and provide to convince myself that even though she is already my wife for life, I deserve her. I had never planned to be her father's enemy, had gone about loving her and marrying her the proper way. I felt good about that fact, but it stood out in my mind that I had not built or accumulated anything close to the wealth of her father, could not provide her with anything close in value to the items and surroundings she was accustomed to. Her father, on the other hand, was a wall of pride, and his pride was much stronger than his love. His pride caused him to refuse to face me man to man. To refuse to listen to his daughter's heart or her words and wants. His pride also caused him to lose. But I knew and I know, somehow, he will come again. I don't fear this, but I don't take it lightly, either.

Young, I'm just laying the foundation for our wealth. And, I know what true wealth is. Some men think if they have a heap of hundreds that they're doing it. Others need thousands to feel secure. Some men think that a hundred thousand means they're rich and set for life. Then there are the millionaires. Wealth is something different. It is what I am aiming for. True wealth is when a man has freedom of faith, high-quality loyal women, gold, land and property, and healthy, useful, grateful, and secure children. The money a man accumulates should be backed up by something precious, like gold. A man is not rich if spending what he has in his hand or carries in his pocket or wallet means he has gone broke. Or if he can't own his own land and house without fear of bankruptcy. A man is not rich if he has all the gold in the world and his wives are trash. Furthermore, a man is not wealthy if he has been warred on and somehow been stripped of all of his land, property, money, and gold, and has no faith to guide him in his battle, and no family to protect so that he will be inspired to build and come again. I learned these truths from my father. Because of him, wealth is not foreign to me. I was born into wealth, and even though I got separated from my wealth and had to start back at the beginning, wealth is not something I think is not within my reach. For me, becoming wealthy is expected, even though it's not automatic.

So I'm checking myself, taking inventory. I'm monitoring my pace so far and my process. Since my return from Asia, my mind had become even more clear. My standards were raised even higher.

Marrying the right women, planting my seeds, and securing my family—I achieved that. Yet I knew that securing a family is an ongoing everyday thing, an awesome responsibility, especially when I am the only male.

As a team, Umma and I had built our own business, Umma Designs. And even though we both have other jobs, we've worked at our jobs separately while running the business that we own together for seven years. We purchased our land and our house some months ago. We bought it in full, no mortgage. It's ours completely. We don't have to worry about missing a mortgage payment and having the bank that issued us the loan stepping in and taking over, becoming the actual owners of our house. Because of course, if you have a mortgage the bank is the actual owner of the house until you pay it off with interest over thirty years!

Our new Queens home is not in any way comparable to or even similar to the huge estate that my father built and owned and that we all lived in. Still, it is what I could manage so far. It is a blessing under the circumstances of our living in America, without our Sudanese wealth. We still have to pay property taxes, but the monthly amount is very small, especially when compared to the going monthly rent for any apartment in all five boroughs of New York. And of course when you are renting, you don't own shit. At any moment the real owners can decide to change your apartment into a condo and throw you out, or keep everything the same but raise the rent so high you gotta throw yourself out. When you rent, you always have to seek permission for things, like who and how many people can live there. Or how many people can share one room. And even simple things have to be requested, like changing the locks, or getting a new set of keys, or even permission to hammer or hang curtains or paint the walls. That's a constant reminder that the place where you live does not belong to you.

While I was away in Asia, my Umma and sister stayed in the basement apartment of the father of Sudana, Mr. Ghazzahli. I rented that space from him even though we had just purchased our new home. Our new home wasn't cleaned and sanitized, cleared out, repaired, painted, or furnished yet. It had no telephone or even power. All of that was my responsibility, but I had to move swiftly to Asia to get my first wife. So it made sense to provide a clean, organized, furnished apartment for my Umma, in a house owned by an Islamic Sudanese family where she and my sister were adored. The basement apartment was separate, with its own door and locks and phone, so I did not have to worry about anything improper. And Mr. Ghazzahli owned a taxi car service. So in addition to paying him rent for the month, I also paid him in advance of my leaving to drive my Umma to work and back home each day. This was the only way I could have peace of mind while traveling.

Now my liquid cash flow is tight. Umma and I had emptied our bank account in order to buy our new home. I was only able to travel to Asia because my father had given me, before we left Sudan and moved to Brooklyn, three diamonds to keep forever, or to use in case of emergency. The diamonds were valued at a minimum of fifteen thousand dollars for each one. Even though I did not want to sell them—they were heirlooms that I treasured and hoped to pass on to my future sons—I did sell one in order to have cash to set my Umma up properly before leaving, and to obtain my airline ticket and handle all travel expenses. A trip planned for one week turned into a necessary adventure that stretched over a month. Over there, I spent money and I made money, returning with ten thousand dollars remaining in my hand, plus the two diamonds I never sold and a second wife.

Ten thousand dollars is not a lot of money. Maybe it would be if I were not married or expecting, or had not just purchased a new home. Maybe if I just had to spend it on myself, I could coast and chill for a while. That wasn't the case. So I'm pressed, but not exactly under an unbearable pressure.

Umma has her own chest of precious jewels. Even though she had been relying on her small job salary until we were able to rebuild our treasury by working Umma Designs, she would not sell her jewels. They are each an intimate memory to her, and each one comes with an amazing story of my father and our Sudanese life and lifestyle. She had parted with only one of his memories. Right before I left for Asia, she handed me my father's Rolex. It was a Datejust with a cracked bezel that I had never known she had. It seemed like she wanted to part with it for her own reasons. Fortunately for me, while in Asia, I sold the Rolex to a Namibian jeweler in exchange for diamond bangles and a diamond ring, all the jewels I wanted, in order to propose properly to my second wife. I am aware that it was and is my father who gave me the means and the gifts that secured both of my wives. I want to be the same caliber of man that my father is to my future sons, *Insha'Allah.* And I am striving.

Building the wall had cost me two thousand dollars. Of course I didn't have to pay myself for working on it. All work and supplies were included in that sum. That was a big bite right there. There was also the furniture we purchased and the cost of the security gates I ordered for the ground-level windows. I settled my bill with Mr. Ghazzahli upon my return, so that while I scheduled to turn on the power and water and cleaned up and prepared the new house to make it good enough for Umma, she could stay on there. My first week back home, my wives enjoyed the overpriced hotel I checked us into upon our return from Asia. After all, Mr. Ghazzahli had two unmarried young but grown sons in his house. Although they were Muslim men, still I did not want them encountering my wives all of the time. Sometimes one or both of my wives would be visiting with Umma at the Ghazzahlis' basement apartment, or chilling with me in Queens for some hours as I prepared the house. I was working early morning to late night every day in the new house even before Ameer and Chris and I began building the wall, and before reporting back to my job in Chinatown.

My decision to ask Umma to give notice to her job at the textile factory was an expensive one, because her wages there covered my sister's private schooling and our family health care for many years. However, I had a plan to expand the business we owned, our products and services, and to free my mother of being a wage earner any longer. I wanted her to be able to work from home on her own schedule, to be comfortable and to just breathe and enjoy life, her new daughters-in-law, and of course her daughter, my sister, Naja. I had also decided that I was going to grow and expand my vending business and discontinue working my job as well. It was all a gamble, but I was betting on myself and planning on winning.

Down to $4,880, my first wife and I had an appointment at an obstetrician/gynecologist, a female Korean doctor recommended by her mother's side of her Korean family. I had no idea how much the doctor would charge for the safe medical delivery of our twins. With Akemi only three months pregnant at the time, I knew I had time to stack some paper. Although I was feeling the pressure, I was not a desperate man.

* * *

Somebody was working my spot in Chinatown at Cho's Fish Market. I expected that to happen when my trip to Asia had stretched to longer than a week. I had phoned Cho from overseas, not wanting to stick him. His weekend business began on Friday morning and was always packed with hard work to do and plenty of customers. That was my shift.

Early Saturday morning, June 14th, instead of giving some sort of explanation or excuse for my extended absence, I did the only thing the Chinaman respects: washed my hands, threw on my rubber apron and the welder's glasses I used for eye protection, and fell right into the rhythm of the work. I was carrying styrofoam crates filled with fish, shovels of crushed ice, empty barrels and tanks for the live fish, boxes of plain brown and waxed wrapping paper, and cartons of hundreds of plastic bags for the customers, and hosing down the prep tables. I was letting loose live eels in the tank, live scallops and clams and live crabs and lobsters, each in their own buckets and barrels. I was gutting and scaling sea bass, branzino, snappers, sea bream, rainbow trout, porgies, and whiting and a variety of types for the display.

The Chinese customers preferred to buy their fish fresh, as in still alive. The Americans were usually in a rush and wanted it fresh but dead, quickly cleaned and packaged and ready to go.

We worked like that till all of the customers were served, all of their choices prepared to all of their specifications—heads off, heads on, gutted, cleaned, split, sliced or filleted, and packaged and wrapped nicely for them to carry home without any leaking.

I worked that Saturday double shift for two reasons. One, I didn't work yesterday, which was Friday, the day I finished cleaning and setting up the empty house in Queens, to bring my family home. Two, because I wanted to speak with Cho after we closed up his shop. I wasn't charging him for my labor for the day. I wanted to make a new business relationship with him instead. My double-shift free labor was an investment in his ability to hear me out and consider what I was saying, while understanding and respecting my growth as a man.

He chose the spot for dinner. It was his regular spot. The Chinese did not dine in the same places or in the same manner or off the same menu as their tourist customers. So we were in a back room of a restaurant whose red canopy boasted bold Chinese letters, which I could not read. I could, however, read the English lettering in small print beneath the Chinese letters. It read CHUON TU CHIO JA. I learned from the restaurant business card that it meant Spring Restaurant. The room where we sat looked like a pig temple. There were pig heads and pig carcasses and even pig statues on mantels, and dead ducks with stretched-out necks, and damn, I did not want to be rude, but . . . I'm comfortable working with all kinds of seafood, but would not be comfortable working in a butcher's shop that was not halal and had pork displayed everywhere. Really, I did not want to consume anything in there, but I did not want to insult Cho, either. So my mind was swiftly putting together a plan where I could satisfy my faith and his culture without compromise.

I thought I was meeting with Cho for dinner. But when we arrived, there were ten other Chinamen standing in a huddle as though they were waiting for him. Cho and I joined them. I was just following and listening and watching. The ten men were looking at Cho as if to ask, "Who the fuck is he?" I heard Cho either introduce me or define me as "Jen Lu Li." Then he turned towards me, put his hand on my shoulder, and said in English, "Very hard worker." I knew then that was my name in those men's minds. At least it would be the description that separated me from whatever they thought based on my appearance and their prejudices. The Chinese don't call each other by names directly. The Sudanese and other Africans and Asians are the same on this issue. Most customers who were Chinese and regulars, if they were younger than Cho, called him "Shushu," meaning uncle.

When a twelfth Chinaman arrived, the eleven others greeted him with great excitement and respect. He was clearly older than all of the rest. His arrival inspired a chorus of "*Nee how ma*," which is the greeting our Chinese customers used every day, meaning "How are you." "*Nee how ma shushu*" was their way of showing him respect as a man older than each of them. The old Chinaman responded, "*Chen-how*," meaning "very well," but then he added "*Les-luh*," which I did not know the meaning of, but when he made a face and body gesture, I felt he was saying he was really tired. The other eleven Chinamen guided him to his seat, and not until he sat did the rest of us sit at the round table. I was the last to take a chair, and the youngest in our group.

The Chinese sit shoulder to shoulder even though our dinner table was wide and round. They don't waste space or air. It was an adjustment for me, having a business meeting at a table with twelve Chinamen who had nothing to do with the business I wanted to conduct with Cho. Each of them was either alone or with one or two others, but either way we were all together, each doing our own thing in our own language.

The food was placed on a small circular revolving table that was in the center of the huge round dinner table. One waiter came out and bowed to his guests, which was surprising because I'd never seen the Chinese bow. I always saw the Japanese and Koreans do so. I figured it was because he was a server. Right behind him came another Chinese male waiter carrying live fish in a clear plastic bag with water inside. I recognized the fish as sea bass. The men examined them from the sitting position and the elder gave the waiter the thumbs-up.

Chopsticks and no forks. I had been in this position many times in my Asian travels. I'm comfortable with chopsticks, even though I don't have the same ease in using them that the Chinese have. Now all of the food dishes, including *mee-fah* (rice), *pie gu tong* (spare rib soup), *hui gau jo* (pork belly), *ching jung uuer* (steamed sea bass), *Shang Hai cai* (bok choi), *sil gwa* (stir-fried vegetables), and *shi-gwa* (watermelon), had been placed in the center, and each of us had our own bowl for white rice. The elder *shushu* spun the table, serving himself what he wanted. He called out, "*Kuai-choo*!" which seemed to mean, "Let's eat." Everyone then took from the revolving table what they wanted. It was unique and interesting and a bit emotional watching each of the eleven Chinamen take some vegetable from their uneaten dish of food and place it into the bowl of the elder, as a show of both love and respect. In all of their actions, it was as though they were constantly conscious of distinguishing one man's age and position from the others', all the while remaining unified without a trace of envy, resentment, or competition.

I selected my foods last. I chose rice, steamed fish, and watermelon, but I left all of the soups and vegetables alone because of the pork I knew was inside or could be inside as a seasoning. And like all of the men at the table I drank *nu cha*, which is green tea.

Cho was straight-faced and slurping soup. I couldn't be sure, but I think he thought it was funny allowing me to follow him in here and fall in.

"Cho," I said. He grunted. "I have a new business," I told him.

"You work fish market? You no work fish market?" he asked me.

Instead of answering, I pulled out the neatly folded pamphlet, which contained photos of the vending machines. I had used a razor to perfectly slice out from the Japanese catalogue only the images I wanted to show, without revealing any Japanese letters or even English lettering or contact information.

"I would like to put this machine outside of your store," I said, handing him the photos. It was the same as though I had handed it to each of them at the table. All twenty-four Chinese eyes were on the paper, and it was then being passed around. Cho took it first, looked, flipped it backward and then forward. The next man took it from Cho and the paper made the rounds, around the round table.

"For what?" he asked me.

"For customers," I said, of course knowing that he didn't sell sodas or waters or any of the merchandise that my machine could offer for sale.

"How much?" he asked.

"I'll deliver the machine to the store tomorrow if you agree. Customers buy from the machine. I keep the machine restocked and I take the money," I said. I knew it was the best business scenario for me. I knew it was a long shot for him to just say yes and allow it, and then to allow me to keep all of the revenue, but I purposely pitched my offer at a starting point that was best for me; in case it got shaved back, I'd still make some profit.

Twelve Chinamen laughing, that's what I saw now. Even though we were not in the same conversation, and the men had arrived at separate times in varying numbers, we all seemed to be having the same conversation now. Then they erupted into the Chinese language among themselves, fingering the photo and passing it around the table to each man a second time.

"*Duo shao qian*?" most of them asked. I knew from working the fish store that meant, "How much money?" I wish I would've brought Akemi with me. My first wife speaks Mandarin Chinese. She could've sat quietly beside me and later translated these men's Chinese convo to Chiasa in Japanese. Chiasa would then translate it to me in English. Because of how complicated that sounds, is the reason I was seated alone. And of course because in the back room there were only men, I was satisfied that I was there without my wives.

It's funny how the gathered Chinamen spoke only in Chinese but could hear any and all money talk in English. Suddenly the eldest, who was the last man holding the photos of my vending machines, announced, "*Cho fong su.*"

"You pay rent," Cho said to me. I assumed that was what the elder had ordered him to say.

"How much?" I asked.

"*Ee bai qwah*," the eldest said.

"One hundred," Cho said. I guess that's what the elder suggested.

"One hundred dollars per year, good?" I said. Then, twelve Chinamen were laughing again. So I realized they wanted me to pay one hundred per month to be allowed to simply placc my machine outside of Cho's store.

"Fifty dollars per month," I counteroffered. "Or fifteen-hundred dollars for the horse ride machine and you keep it," I said to Cho, knowing he could either make six hundred dollars per year renting the space to me at fifty dollars per month or twelve thousand dollars a year owning the machine himself. If his customers gravitated towards it, even if he couldn't clear a thousand dollars a month worth of riders, if he took in half of that amount, he would still make six thousand dollars per year instead of six hundred dollars renting me the space. He had customers of all different backgrounds, including African Americans, who lined up and waited patiently for their orders to be prepared all of the time, and who often came with their children on the weekend, days and evenings.

"*Tai gwee la*," one of the men said, but he was not the elder. I knew what that meant. Chinese customers said those exact words when they thought their order was too expensive and they wanted the "We Chinese discount" at Cho's store. Now, twenty-two Chinese eyes were fixed on Cho, mine making twenty-four. They began speaking in Chinese again among themselves. I imagined that at least one of them was saying that he could make a horse ride vending machine easily for one hundred and eighty dollars total, parts and labor. The Chinese are smart like that. They could take anyone in the world's idea or product and duplicate it, even though they had not invented it or thought of it first. I anticipated the competition because I know when dealing with the Chinese, the angle is always that they can make absolutely anything that the human mind could imagine, and they could make it for cheap!

I knew that winning this offer that I was making to Cho depended on the fact that I am the first person he encountered making him such an offer, and that I had the machine available immediately. I already knew that whatever deal I might make with Cho, the deal would only last at maximum one year before he and they found a better, smarter, cheaper way to do it on their own. But that was cool. If I could draw in a year's worth of coins, or sell the machine outright, I was still making a real profit either way. In one year, I would have expanded and made new locations for my machines and new contacts and new customers also, just like the Chinese could and would.

"*Ee chien er*," the eldest said.

"Twelve hundred," Cho said to me in English. "I keep," he added. The eleven Chinamen began all speaking at one time. Then the speaking ceased and the oldest man was the only one speaking. The rest, including Cho, listening to him. When the eldest one was done, Cho replied in Chinese to him in a very respectful tone. I imagined he was saying, "Nah, this is my man here. He works at my shop. I can trust him." And of course he could. The eldest Chinaman stood and said in a low volume with his full vocal force, "*Kueee*," which for me meant the same as him saying, "Cool, let's do it!" I took it as an approval.

"Bring tomorrow, pay tomorrow," Cho said, sliding me my paperwork, which the elder had handed back to him. I pulled out a pen and handed it to Cho, as in asking him, "Sign." It was only the horse vending machine photo, which I knew was not a proper contract, but for me it was a gesture of his earnestness, as well as a way for me to fill out and complete his receipt and paperwork with his proper information. Up until then, Cho and I had no paperwork between us, yet I was embarrassed to ask him out loud, "What's your full name?" I knew that would be odd, since Cho and I had been together for a long time and he had made it clear that I was trustworthy to the other men at the table.

He signed in English, in large letters like it was his celebrity autograph. I was glad he did. He spells his Chinese name as *Zhou*. I had always had it spelled in my mind as *Cho*, which is how the word *Zhou* is pronounced. I also discovered that Zhou was his last name and his first name was Yong.

"*Shi-shi*," I said, speaking the one Chinese word that I was absolutely sure about. It means "thank you." And just my effort to speak that one word caused each of the men to nod their heads in approval.

Dessert was *tong yuan* (sticky rice balls) and *kong dou tong* (red bean soup). I passed on both, but completed my fish meal nicely, to show my gratitude, humility, comfort, character, and camaraderie.

Chiasa had paid seven hundred dollars for her "horsey ride." We grossed a five-hundred-dollar profit on it since I agreed to sell it to Zhou at $1,200. I made the decision without her. I hoped she would be pleased about it. If not, same as we ordered the first two machines together, we could order two more, and keep it moving.

I had another slick idea for my merchandise vending machine. It had everything to do with my first wife, Akemi. Amazed at vending machines in Japan selling kicks, I had envisioned owning one that sold Nikes. But I knew the Nike Corporation was a powerful monopoly. Getting a deal with them dispensing in America through a line of vending machines seemed unimaginable. Therefore, I came up with an alternative. The Chinese had the infamous "Chinese slippers." For African Americans, they would come into style for a brief moment and then the style would switch. For the Chinese, they were always in style. If a badass Chinese flick came out, the Chinese slipper would reappear again. I began thinking about how it didn't matter if a product was considered "cheap," as long as it was in demand. Something that sells for five dollars a pair is crazy paper if you sell one million pairs. And for the Chinese slipper that stays in use, I was sure there were way more than one million pairs being sold each year.

I wanted to create a trend for a product I had imagined naming "The New York Slipper," designed by my first wife. I had seen her dope off some customized Nikes with an airbrush. The couple of times that she rocked those kicks that she designed, with a mean-ass mini, before I put the ring on her finger, she caused everybody who knew high fashion to do a double-triple take. Now if I could get her to make a "New York Slipper," an exclusive design, and set up the vending machine for them at an exclusive location, for example at the Museum of Modern Art, where Akemi had business contacts. I could sell the slippers to tourists for a mean price, say fifty dollars a pair. If I purchased the white Chinese slippers in bulk in Chinatown and got Akemi to throw a crazy design on them, I could net forty-seven dollars profit on each pair, crazy!

If the idea tanked, and I only sold a low amount, say one hundred pairs, that's $4,700 profit for a poor showing. If I did a decent job and sold one thousand pairs, that's $47,000 for a decent take. If I did real good and sold ten thousand pairs, that would be $470,000, *damn*! If I hit the bull's-eye, so to speak, and sold one million pairs, that's $47 million. My idea, even if it tanked, was worth too much money not to venture into it. So I would. I could imagine wealthy tourists walking around Central Park with their noses in the air while wearing a cheap Chinese slipper, with a mean-ass New York design on it, that they had paid a ridiculous fifty dollars for, from a vending machine strategically placed, that they viewed as selling art, memorabilia, and even collector's items.

Mail was in my box even though my house was empty. I grabbed it, ran in, and showered and dressed. I was heading back to the hotel for our last night in the suite. Tomorrow was Sunday, family day for us. I would gather my wives and my mother and sister and bring them into our new home.

I was lying in the middle of the king-size hotel bed. Akemi was on my left, Chiasa was on my right. We were each fully clothed. I was opening the letter addressed to me from my man Black Sea, a Korean dude who is part of a break dance crew in Busan, Korea. We linked in Asia and formed a friendship that felt like it had been in place for a long time, even though it was only a few weeks. He calls me his "*chin-goo*," which is a hefty word in Korea for friendship. Korean friendship meant more to them than friendship seemed to mean in the USA. I must've felt close to him also, because I gave him my address, which I never do. I'm sure the fact that he lived overseas made it an easier choice for me, but I also know it was a little more than that. He seemed like a friend I would keep for a lifetime. That's how it felt.

Now, I was opening his letter. It was written in Korean except for his beginning introduction where he wrote "Mr. Manager." That's what he calls me, his "manager," even though he is a college student, a physics major, and I am younger than him. He continues in English, saying, "Please ask your Korean wife to read this letter to you." I handed the letter to Akemi. She read it to herself first. She then translated it into Japanese one line at a time and spoke it to Chiasa. Chiasa then translated it into English and spoke it out loud to me.

It went like this. Akemi said in Korean, *"Sarang hanin."* Then she said to Chiasa in Japanese, *"Sai ai."* Then Chiasa said to me in English, "My Dear Love." Then, Chiasa laughed. Then I laughed. Then Akemi laughed. Now we were all laughing. I said to Chiasa, "C'mon now, you know he didn't call me his dear love." Chiasa laughed and said, "He did so!" Akemi laughed. I put my hand on my head, ran it over my Caesar cut, and laughed at myself, and at my global situation.

That letter was the beginning of my fashion export business from New York to Busan, Korea, through one of Black Sea's uncle's friends, who lived out here in New York and who needed me to be a supplier. He would then send the clothes I chose and purchased and sold to him to Black Sea's uncle, who was opening a New York/Tokyo fashion boutique in Seoul, Korea. Black Sea admired my style and fashion so much when I was in Korea that he believed I could make his uncle, who had the connects and would handle the shipping, a rich guy. He said his uncle could not get rich on his own, 'cause he had no style and no eye for fashion, and no way to communicate properly in English to do business with English-speaking fashion wholesalers or retailers even though he was opening a high-fashion Western-style shop on a hunch. Black Sea said his uncle believed that he could get middle-income Koreans, whose fashion tastes were just becoming awakened, and who wanted highly fashionable high-priced clothing and accessories for discounted prices, to become his best customers. I was in.

## 12. COACH VEGA • *A Reflection*

A blacked-out, hand-built Maserati Royale, crazy—of course it caught my attention; most exotic things do. Made in Italy, and so pretty it couldn't be called "a car." *Car* is too bland of a word. This V-8 engine vehicle goes from standing still at zero to one hundred miles per hour in four seconds. At top speed, it's hitting almost two hundred miles per hour. I dig the selection because it's unique, and not the obvious choice. The designers only made about fifty-five models. Custom designed to limited order, not just anyone could cop it—mainly only kings, presidents, premiers, prime ministers, and princes, and for us in America, probably only big-money athletes, ballers and hustlers, or elite entertainers in the top-top level, top echelon. Yet it was parked curbside in Brooklyn in the exact spot where I agreed to meet up with Coach Vega. I was a hundred percent certain that he wasn't behind the wheel of that machine. And, if he was, I'd expect a SWAT team to drop down from the rooftops to surround, swallow, and arrest the community coach for impersonating a millionaire.

I was standing directly across the street and staring at it. Clutching my basketball in my right palm, I was paused at the red light. When it flashed green, I didn't move with the everyday walkers. *So many beautiful things*, I thought to myself. *Try not to lust them.*

A small mixed crowd was accumulating on the side of the car like they were waiting for autographs. Pedestrians passing by would jerk to a stop like they were suddenly shocked. And, in Brooklyn, "the borough of cool," where all knew not to look too hard at anyone or anything lest you get roughed up, razored, or robbed, everyone stood still staring. They weren't dazed enough to touch the vehicle, though, I know that's right.

I was looking around for Vega. He was late. I didn't see no floral shirts or smell no loud men's cologne, so I knew he wasn't in the area. The driver's-side window lowered a quarter of the way. A hand waved me over. I recognized the Rolex, a mean-ass alligator band on a Louis XIII joint. I signaled him to pull out and ride straight. His engine switched on, humming. I crossed, then walked past the vehicle. It was caught at the red light. Two blocks down, he pulled over to the corner where I stood. His passenger window eased down. He dipped his head. "Get in," he said.

"I got a meeting with Coach Vega," I said, my five fingers gripping my basketball.

"Is that why you left?" he asked me calmly. I didn't say nothing. Truth is I was mesmerized by the burnt-orange thick leather interior, the woodwork, the curves and figure, and the overall plushness of his ride. Now he was making a call. Never knew anyone who had a phone in their car, not even my father. He pushed a cobalt-blue Rolls-Royce, or I should say he owned one. His southern Sudanese homeboy driver chauffeured him around.

"Here." Ricky Santiaga handed me his phone. I was still standing outside.

"Young Money!" I heard Vega's voice say. "Congratulations, you got a face-to-face with the owner. I'm just the manager. Make me look good!" He hung up.

"Get in. It's business. Time is money, you know," Santiaga said.

"Basketball business?" I asked.

"That's the only kind of business you and me have right now," he said. I reached to open the door, didn't want to dirty up the detailing or even put my hand or fingerprints on it. I got in.

"Good choice," he said as he pulled off.

Speeding up the FDR Drive, the ride was immaculate. Only the hum of the powerful engine pierced the silence. Santiaga exited on the east end of 42nd Street, hugging the ramp at a high speed. Racing up 1st Avenue in the direction of the United Nations, I thought to myself, *Money-making Manhattan territory*. Of course I knew those streets and shops and fashions well. I reached 'em by train on the regular. I've walked down every block. From First Avenue all the way to the West Side Highway, the jewelers and boutiques low to the high end, I had been through them all.

It was clear that the car had a system, but he didn't play no radio, or no cuts from his personal music library. If he was waiting for me to say something, that wasn't going to happen. He must have had his reason for bumping Coach from our meet-up and placing himself in the driver seat instead.

"You don't talk much," he said. I didn't reply. Didn't think his observation needed a confirmation. He smiled, then made a sharp turn onto 47th Street, "the money block," and into a narrow driveway, which led down to a garage. He parked in a corner pocket spot marked reserved.

"Let's go," he said. We walked up to a private elevator that he used a key to control. Inside he pushed L for lobby. The door opened into a marbled-out, clean, chandeliered area. More importantly, it had two armed security guards, a reception desk, and a sign-in book on a marble podium. As he advanced, I stopped walking and stood to the side playing the wall. He looked back, smiled, and said, "I'll be right back." I nodded. He tapped the counter of the reception desk and the female attendant smiled at him. The guards acknowledged him and he pointed to me, then turned back to them and pointed to his chest, as though to say, "He's with me," then disappeared.

Twelve minutes later he came back through, walked right past me, and I followed. We were back in the Maserati moving up the FDR all over again. Soon as he exited down the Dyckman Street ramp, the sirens sounded and the lights started flashing. "Police, pull it over," they announced. He raised his eyes to his rearview mirror but looked calm and unaffected. Meanwhile, my nine was pressing on my spine where I had it tucked.

"Stay still," he said. A knock came to the driver's-side window, as I watched a second cop creeping up on my side through my side-view mirror. His weapon drawn, I knew I was in a dangerous situation. Not prone to panic, I remained calm. Santiaga lowered his window. The cop lowered his head to peer in as he said, "License, registration, and insurance card." Then the cop's grimace broke and he retreated. He stood up straight, saying to his partner whose finger was wiggling on the trigger, "Damn, it's Ricky."

His partner's tensed-up muscles relaxed and he broke out in admiration for the car.

"How's the family?" Santiaga asked the cop on his side.

"Better than ever," the cop said.

"Well then that's all that matters. I'mma let you check it out. I know you want to," Santiaga said to the cop and eased out of the vehicle. I looked to my right. The cop on my side had taken a step back. I got out also. We were four men. If three are standing, I'm not sitting. The cops were moving around the Maserati just sweatin' it as Santiaga reached in and popped the trunk. There was nothing in there but a jack and spare tire and a folded Maserati-branded car cover. It was obvious the vehicle was brand-new. Seemed like he drove it off the lot right before meeting up with me. Then, they were all three talking shit like old friends as they were looking beneath the hood of the car in awe. I wasn't up front and checking beneath the hood and chatting. I stayed standing on the passenger side. The cop who had crept up my way then had one eye under the hood and the other watching me.

"How's your man?" I heard him ask Santiaga, then he nodded his head in my direction. "Need me to run his license, fingerprints, check his record or his credit?" he said with a half smile. Santiaga's friendly tone and face switched to solemn.

"Don't talk like a rookie, Stubbs. If he's my man, he's good. You know the drill." The other cop laughed to break the tension and his partner forced out a chuckle. "He's a ball player. Put him up against one of any of your guys anytime. You want to make a wager?" he asked. "My team versus the PAL's best squad?"

"No, Ricky, the word is out. You win all the wagers!" The cop laughed and put his hand on the car. "This is the evidence," the cop said.

Back in the whip, Santiaga pulled off. As he did, he pressed a button and a compartment opened revealing his Smith & Wesson. "You wanna lay something in here?" he asked me.

"Nah," was all I said. He closed it.

On Dyckman he double-parked, got out, and entered a building. I got out when he did and just played the street corner, waiting. Four Spanish-looking dudes walked up, two from out of the building Santiaga entered and two who exited a building from across the street. Each of them posted up, seemingly securing all four corners of the Maserati. They were serious-faced, solid-looking older men. More than that, I didn't see any of them exchange any words with Santiaga, just automatically got on post.

I entered the corner store to buy a bottle of water. I was looking in the cold case. They had everything except water. A bunch of small cloudy plastic bottles filled with blue water, green water, yellow water, crazy cans of unfamiliar brands of sodas and flavors and drinks, but no real water. I closed the case. As I was walking up the aisle towards the register, the phone rang loud like a house phone.

"Take it," the man at the register said, extending the receiver to me. I walked out. Spinning the ball on my fingers, I was killing time, thinking whether or not I should jump on the train and head back to Brooklyn. Maybe this cat Ricky thought his time was money and mine ain't. Now the store man was out from behind his cash register and standing outside on the street beside me.

"Santiaga," he said to me like it was some kind of password. I didn't respond. Then, "Phone," he said, and pointed his thumb at the store, letting me know to come back inside to pick up a call.

"Don't leave. Give me seven more minutes," Santiaga's voice

said over the phone. I handed it back to the store man, who had returned to his place behind the register. I wondered how Santiaga knew I would leave.

I checked he had manners. Good for him. I take men who make other men wait selfishly or needlessly and without word or apology as disrespectful. I didn't like standing still in an unfamiliar territory. But I was clear that whatever the case, this was Santiaga's territory. I couldn't figure how a Brooklyn cat could have the reach of controlling some uptown Manhattan blocks, a couple of cops, some store owners, and even the dudes that stay hugging the block. I was thinking, it's interesting how a bunch of older dudes, like the ones guarding his car, who had plenty of time to come up and establish themselves, can have nothing. Instead, they were watching a cat like Santiaga, who was in his mid to late twenties, having everything. I'm at least ten years younger than Santiaga, I know. At the same time, in ten years I planned to have ten times more than what Santiaga had, not out of greed, but out of the fact that if I plan right, and work hard and live right, then the finest things in life should be what I have earned and secured and provided for my family.

He wasn't carrying anything visible when he got out of the car and entered the building. He wasn't carrying anything visible when he returned, either. We already got pulled over once. If it happened again, it might not go in his favor. So, I paid attention. I already knew we were riding dirty, got guns, his and mine. I could handle that. I wasn't game for drugs, though. Didn't want to be in a car with someone transporting. I didn't get that feeling from him at the start. And since he popped the trunk and it was empty, and nothing was in the car but him and me and my basketball and our burners, I'm straight.

"Let me keep these out." He placed his license and registration and insurance card on the dash. "These boys pull me over just to get a close look at the ride," he said. It sounded true.

"Last time I'm gonna ask you. Do you want to put your piece away before we hit the highway?" Behind the shade of the blackened windows, I pulled it out, wiped it down with a washcloth from my back pocket, hit the button I saw him hit the first time, and laid the nine in the compartment and shut it.

"Good choice," was all he said.

The East Harlem River was below me now. We crossed the George Washington Bridge into the state of New Jersey. I had been to Jersey before. My first wife's Japanese-American side of her family live there in Englewood Cliffs. I was studying the highway exit signs and mile markers along the way out of habit. When I travel in, I always need to know my way out. A man never knows which way a situation might flip. Yet a man should know his way out alone of anyplace he went into regardless of how many were with him at the start. Rely on no one else.

"'Bout to hit your exit," Santiaga said over his car phone. "Hold on!" he said to me, and his spaceship shot to 180 miles per hour. Suddenly, from a left side entrance, a Lamborghini sped out in front of us and almost went into a tailspin. Santiaga pulled to the right lane and overtook him until the Lam driver caught control and accelerated so rapidly it was like he was preparing for flight. Both vehicles sped down a two-lane highway marked Palisades Interstate Parkway. Neck to neck for a few miles, both cars battled and then curved off to the right and onto a one-lane winding highway of hills, Route 9W. Still the Maserati and the Lamborghini fought to ride side by side in one lane on a two-way highway that had oncoming traffic, outdistancing one another by inches off and on. The high-speed race was interrupted by random slow drivers, who slowed down even further to get a quick rearview glance of the exotic cars, only to be swerved around, dodged, and left in a fog. Weaving around same-lane drivers and oncoming traffic, we slowed to about 80 miles per hour and skidded to our right into a long, steep, and hidden driveway, Santiaga in the first position and the Lamborghini in second. In the intensity of the speed and gravity that pushed me back into the contour of the custom seats, all I had read clearly was a highway sign marked WELCOME TO NEW

YORK. I was thrown off by how we went from Brooklyn to Manhattan to New Jersey, rode past Englewood Cliffs and Alpine, and now within minutes, were back in New York again without making a U-turn. *But this ain't one of the five boroughs of New York*, I said to myself. It was a hidden place, a narrow route surrounded by beautiful trees and overlooking the water.

Santiaga jumped out. I hesitated. Should I push the button and grab my nine? Nah, it didn't seem like a beef. Seemed like a race me and Ameer might have had if we had our driver's licenses and could cop ourselves two exotic cars. I got out.

"How's business?" Santiaga said to the other driver. But he was still gasping from the adrenaline rush.

"You tried to kill me," the man said.

"Why would I do that?" Santiaga answered casually. "I can't run the shop." They laughed like friends.

"This is the man I told you about," Santiaga said and nodded toward me. "His name is Midnight. Midnight, meet Allastair."

"If I take you to the court right now, could you do it again?" Allastair asked me.

"Do what?" I asked. They laughed. I didn't.

"A humble Brooklyn dude, huh? That don't even go together," Allastair commented. But he still didn't tell me what he was talking about. If he wanted to get a game up, I was down for that. It seemed like they had money to burn. They definitely didn't give a fuck if they banged up two cars at $250,000 each.

"Shoot long with your eyes closed and let me see the ball swish in the net, no rim," Allastair said to me. Then, I remembered. That happened in the last game I had played for the Hustler's League the night before I caught a flight and headed out to Tokyo.

I smiled. "That was all momentum. I was feeling the heat, and I had the black team rocking on my side to get in that type of rhythm."

"You woke 'em up," Santiaga said to Allastair. "This cat wouldn't even get in my car until I said the magic word, 'basketball.' This cat didn't say one word from Brooklyn to Manhattan to Jersey to New York. He didn't even ask me where we are going. I hit 180 mph, this cat didn't blink, grip the handle, vomit, or tell me to slow down."

"That's the kind of cat who's good for the team, all heart," Allastair said. Then he pissed on his compliment to me by saying, "But this cat did disappear from the black team *for more than a few weeks.*" I didn't say nothing. His words were true.

"That silence lets me know he disappeared for something serious," Santiaga said.

"True," I confirmed.

"Well, is it all cleaned up?" Allastair asked with a stern stare.

"You got something to do with the black team?" I asked him since he was getting too comfortable in the conversation with me.

"Whoa! If you see a man standing beside me, that's my man, he's good," Santiaga told me.

"I know he got us to be undefeated, but this cat, in his eyes, he's undecided," Allastair warned Santiaga about me. I checked that this was Allastair's rhythm. He says something good, then he cancels it with something foul. It didn't matter to me. I didn't trust him or like him, either. It was just a sense that I had as soon as I met him, a feeling.

"You think so?" Santiaga asked him. But it seemed like they were both waiting for me to make some type of explanation or decision.

"Guns," Allastair said, pulling out a .357 Magnum. "Or basketball? Are you a gangster, a hustler, or an athlete? Can't be all three. Well actually you could, but it usually doesn't work out in the end."

"I'm a businessman who plays basketball. It's a game, but it doesn't come first," I said.

"I like that," Santiaga said. "What comes first?"

"A man shouldn't say what comes first. If it's in the first position, it's close to his heart. I don't know you dudes like that, to let you in close to my heart. I thought we were here to talk about if I'm in or out of the league, or to play basketball. Either way, I understand. And I appreciate the ride and the race. That was nice," I said, honestly. They laughed, and Allastair eased off of his aggressive path.

"You're in, but it's more than a game to us," Santiaga said. "We don't do any of our business halfway. Basketball is one of our smallest hustles. Still, it's important. Since you say you're a businessman, you should understand that too."

"So what are you saying?" I asked in an even tone, 'cause I really wanted to hear the bottom line.

"Can you function in a team?" Allastair asked me, strangely, I thought.

"How we run our business is like this: every man has to carry his weight. That means, every man has to come strong and stay strong. Every man has to show up. We're each interlocked into one another. If you don't show, or if one of you drops the ball so to speak, it means you are shifting your weight onto the next man's back. Now he has to carry himself and he has to carry you," Santiaga said.

"I carry myself. No one carries me," I said calmly.

"On a team, even if you are our starting star player, you're only good if you don't act like you're the star. If you can make each member struggle to play at your same level, and if you can keep up the morale of your men. Also, come on time, show up every time, play hard, win games," Santiaga said, then watched me. "If you can't agree to that, I understand, but let us know *now* so we can redistribute your weight for the playoffs coming up. If you can't guarantee that, there's no sense in coming back to the league. The team is just now successfully adjusted to your not being there," he concluded.

"You're right," I admitted. "One hundred percent. I love the game. I respect the team, and I'm grateful, Santiaga, that you have the league, word up."

"And your decision?" Allastair asked me.

"Let's give him some space. Some of my greatest thoughts occur when I'm driving alone on the open highway," Santiaga said.

"Yeah, in your Maserati," I said and smiled. He tossed me the keys. "Take it for a ride," he said to me.

"No license, no registration, no insurance," I said, mimicking the cop. "That's why I'm in the junior league," I reminded him.

"It's all on the dash. Use mine," he said. I looked at him. He was straight-faced and serious. I didn't think for one minute I could get away with using his ID if I got pulled over. I was tempted to drive anyway, yet I couldn't imagine making even a small mistake. I had only ever driven a motorcycle, and a car a few times at ages five and six seated in my father's lap. *That doesn't count as me* driving. *Is this a test?* I thought on it further. If it is a test, who's testing me? Is it only Santiaga and his man, or is it a bigger test from the Most High?

"Nah, I'm good. Good looking out, though," I said.

"Go ahead, it's yours anyway," Santiaga said, and his man was studying my reactions.

"You said you have a court, right? Let me get a game, me versus me. One game and I'll let you know where I stand. On the court is where some of my greatest thoughts occur," I told them.

"Right this way," Allastair said, leading both of us downhill on a steep driveway. The various sports cars parked in a line were more expensive than the house, a two-story joint with aluminum siding and shutters. I hate aluminum siding. It looks weak, flimsy, and temporary. If a strong wind came along . . . Our new home in Queens was all brick. Not brick face. That's why I bought it.

When Allastair opened his garage, a red Ferrari was unveiled. We each walked right by it like it was nothing. We each knew that it was something stunning, gorgeous, and official. They wanted me to see it. I saw it. They wanted to make an impression. They made it. We traveled through the garage and into the house, walked through a living room, dining room, and kitchen, and out a back door to a tarmac and a regulation-size court with rims and netted hoops. A short walk down, and we would be standing on a dock anchored but floating in the river. I couldn't front; I guess a man could have a small, modest, unimpressive house if he also had a lineup of dope cars and a basketball court and a dock and a row-boat, and a view of the New York City skyline.

I liked that they left me out there alone. I came out in my jeans. Had my sweats on beneath them even though it was spring warm. I had known that Coach Vega might make me do some drills solo. Or run a crazy amount of suicides, a hundred or so layups, and then tell me to take it back to the line and not leave until I hit fifty all net. So I was ready.

"So what's the score?" Allastair came out back to the court and asked me. Now he was out of his clothes and into his sweats. "Who's winning in the game of you versus you?" he asked. I guess he took it for a joke. I didn't.

"It's your court. You want to run one? Looks like you do," I said.

"Slow down, Junior," he said to me. I threw the ball to him and he caught it.

"Let's go," I said. He put his right hand up and placed his left hand horizontally over it.

"Time out," he said.

"How can you call time out and we just getting started?" I asked him.

"Okay, look, it's my partner who's big on you. I'm not. Like you said, I don't even know you like that. But how we get down is that if he wants to rock with you, I gotta put my stamp on it and vice versa. So just ease up. Like you said, you in the junior leagues. We in the major leagues, the big boys, understand?" He was giving me a stare, like he thought he was dominant. Santiaga came through the back door. Allastair softened his stance and switched topics.

"You call yourself a businessman. So what line of business are you in?" he asked.

"Vending machines," I said.

"You mean like bubble-gum balls and plastic toys 'n rings tucked inside those little-kid plastic cases for a *penny or a nickel or a quarter*?" he asked, talking down to me.

"I'm into the buying, selling, and placement of the machines. The product is up to whatever the purchaser wants to use it for," I told him.

"Is that right?" he said, looking like he was thinking.

"If you're done with your game and have made your decision, let's go grab something to eat," Santiaga suggested. "After that, I gotta bounce back to Brooklyn."

"A'ight, me too," I agreed.

"The steakhouse that we're going to requires all men to wear a suit jacket. Is that a problem for you?" Santiaga asked me.

"No, except I don't have one with me," I said. "Coach Vega don't require that," I added.

"Sharp tongue," Allastair said. I didn't say nothing back. I thought he was crazy, changing into his sweats and coming out here like he was gonna challenge me, and then backing down. Now he was game to jump right out of those sweats he just put on and into the suit jacket. I was thinking, *Yeah man, whatever.*

"We got you covered," Santiaga said as Allastair led us back inside.

*A hideout for superheroes or some shit like that*, I was thinking. This guy had one bedroom filled with dinner jackets, suits, and new dress shirts and packaged Hanes boxers, and a lineup of top-shelf men's shoes. I didn't see no women in here. If there was a woman, she would have offered me a glass of water or something. More than that, I didn't see no family photos or feminine touches.

"Another hard decision, huh?" Allastair said, as I stood looking at the suit jacket selections. I seen this cat was just gonna keep pushing.

"Nah, I just usually have my women lay out my clothes for me. I see you don't have no women though," I said extra calmly.

"You talk a lot of shit for a young nigga out with some real dudes. You carrying a basketball, I'm holding much more. Better wise up," he said.

"I was thinking the same thing about you. And you don't know what I'm carrying. You better watch out," I warned him. That was a courtesy I gave him out of respect for his partner Santiaga. Dude approached slowly, then swiftly tried to sucker-punch me. I caught his fist and used it to twist his arm. When he bent forward, I uppercut him in the eye, then I pushed him into the row of new dinner jackets.

"Don't flash your weapon if you ain't ready to fire it. Don't threaten me with your gun if you don't have it on you right then and there. Don't suit up for a game if you ain't up for a challenge. That's 'hood 101. You ain't no Brooklyn dude," I told him.

Santiaga laughed. He had crept in quietly. He was dressed up and ready to go. "I told you to stop fucking with him," Santiaga said to his partner. "We on the same team," Santiaga reminded him.

"He got it coming," Allastair said, straightening himself and embarrassed.

"Put it on hold. It's time for dinner. I'm hungry. Let's eat," Santiaga said.

In The River Palm Terrace restaurant we each ordered steaks. The filet mignon was tender, even though mine was well done. Allastair was still steaming, stabbing his steak with his fork and pressing down hard on his knife and ramming the bloodied steak down his throat, when maybe he should've laid the whole thing across his black eye. He must have felt like a sucker, sitting in a dimmed VIP-only restaurant—even though he drove up alone in his Ferrari and had the valet in awe, dancing around serving him and kissing his ass while he was wearing sunglasses indoors while eating and looking like an ass. He had to wear them. His black eye was swelling.

I was eating comfortably. We all had our guns. That's the way I like it. It evened out everything. When a man is among armed men unarmed, that's when shit gets deadly. That's when armed cowards start feeling themselves and posing and posturing. The fact that there's one unarmed man in the mix makes armed cowards feel powerful.

Besides, this guy had said he was Santiaga's partner, which had made me think they were fifty-fifty in business. Santiaga had described him only as "his man." But I could sense that Santiaga was also Allastair's boss. True, Allastair was pushing the Lamborghini and now the Ferrari. But Santiaga had tossed me the keys to his Maserati and said, "It's yours anyway." What did that mean? And maybe he had recently tossed the keys to his man Allastair also, and the jerk was just fronting like the lineup of elites were his whips, while Santiaga was the true owner. I was thinking. When we first arrived at the spot, Santiaga had remarked that he wasn't trying to kill Allastair because he needed him to run the business. Now I was confirmed in my mind. Allastair was just a manager, like Vega. He was running some exotic car business for Santiaga, same as Vega was running the team that Santiaga owned. So now I got it. The riverside ranch was Santiaga's too. He had to be the actual owner. Why would any man allow himself to get punched in the face at his own house like Allastair did? And then that same man sits down to eat dinner with the one who clocked him? Nah.

We were in the Maserati, Santiaga and I. Out of nowhere, he started laughing like he was caught up in a comical memory. I didn't say nothing. Let him have his moment.

"Did you really tell Allastair that he don't have no women?" he asked me, recovering from his laughter.

"I didn't see none," was all I said.

"You must be a ladies' man," Santiaga said. "I like that. I love the ladies too."

* * *

In a brownstone building that looked like a residential home, we entered a Cuban restaurant named "Azucar." I wasn't hungry. He couldn't be hungry, either. We both just ate. An older Cuban woman greeted us at the entrance and interacted with Santiaga like they were real familiar. We walked through the restaurant, which was almost full, with talkative diners speaking in low tones. We were led behind a red velvet curtain, and then through a door.

An attractive young woman removed his jacket and then mine. I tightened at first, at her touch. Santiaga smiled at that. I noticed he seemed to be observing every detail about me. She guided us up a few winding stairs, our eyes following behind her bouncing butt to a second level, where we were met by another young Latina woman who flipped open a box. He reached in and chose a couple of Montecristo cigars, ran them under his nose for the scent. She guided us to a room of expensive chairs and the aroma of cigars. The scent reminded me of my father. He was not an everyday smoker, but he enjoyed a cigar every now and then in the smoke house on our Sudan estate, especially when he was receiving guests or holding important business meetings. We sat. The young woman ran and carried back a footstool. Santiaga lifted his feet and placed them onto the red-carpeted top. He clipped the cigar at the bottom and handed me one and the clipper. I clipped mine. A pair of breasts appeared before me, 'cause that's all I could see. She leaned in and lit my cigar as another woman lit his. We puffed.

It was my first cigar. I smoked it imagining my father seated across from me smoking his. The first puff had a kick to it and I muffled back a cough, but I liked the scent of the smoke. I would do it just like my father, not take it for a habit, just on occasion or from time to time.

After a while, when his marble ashtray was filled and his cigar was shortened and hot, Santiaga pulled his feet down and leaned forward. He reached into his jacket pocket and pulled out a black envelope made from expensive paper. It was a quality stationary. The kind my first wife might select to use.

"This belongs to you," he said. I didn't reach for it. I placed my cigar on my tray. I still had a long way to go to finish it, unlike the expert seated across from me.

"Pick it up," he said. I looked to my left and then my right. The way our chairs were positioned, we were in a private space. The lady and the other set of breasts were serving other customers. There were six other men in the room, all engaged in their own private talks. Two of them were into a quiet chess game.

With my washcloth, I eased the envelope my way and held it between the cloth without placing my prints. Santiaga had one finger on his jaw and one on his forehead. He's watching me discreetly. Inside was a thick stack of crisp and clean hundreds. I looked at him.

"That's ten thousand," he said. "The other fifteen is in my glove compartment. That's yours too," he told me. Then he waited for my reaction.

"Nah, this can't be mine," I said. "Wish it was. But I missed too many games already. And the most valuable player won't be chosen until after the playoffs." I pushed the envelope back to his side of the table.

"I placed a wager on that game you played, the night that you closed your eyes and took the winning shot. It was a huge wager. I bet on you. I just had a feeling in my gut from the first time we met. I don't get that feeling often, but when I do, I listen to it. I got that feeling once when I was about to make a run. I had some money at stake on that run. I knew it was better to get it right then. If I waited it could have slipped out of my reach. Because of that feeling in my gut, I didn't chase that paper that night that was owed to me. I let it go. That shit burned. Next day, I found out, all the parties to that transaction got clapped up. That gut feeling saved my life even though I lost some money on the transaction. The second time I caught that feeling was the first time I saw my wife. She was fourteen. I was nineteen. End of story, I made it happen because of that feeling in my gut. Now she's my wife and the mother of my daughters. The third time I caught that feeling in my gut was when I met you. Don't get me wrong—I handpicked the black team, love my squad. But you stand out. You got that fire in your heart and a good head on your shoulders. You don't run your mouth and you don't seek attention. You're mean with that basketball and calm with your teammates, a quiet leader. I see big things for you in the future."

"If I recall, I only scored two points in that game. It was my worst performance for the whole stretch of the junior league," I said, and I meant it.

"That's where you're wrong. I watched the game. You fed your teammates, without worrying about yourself. You set up the right plays and the right picks. You rebounded. Played the whole game beautifully. And when the heat was up to its hottest point, and you had successfully misled your opponents to believe that you were not the man to watch, they left you open. You stepped out of the shadows, closed your eyes, and sank it, crazy! Couldn't've been better." He leaned back.

"I went into that wager with all the liquid cash I had on hand that night. The rest of my capital was all tied up in other ventures. Damn near all or nothing. You weren't the high score. But you were the man. Timing is everything. Knowing when to lay low and when to come up, when to step out of the light and when to come out of the shadows—perfect." He held his hands together, like a clap. He leaned forward.

"I came up so big it gave me the liquid capital that propelled me to the next level in my business. The twenty-five I'm giving you, you earned it. But because I see that you're into honesty, and I like that, I'mma let you know that twenty-five thousand is not even one-hundredth the amount I earned off of you." He gave me a serious stare so I would believe him.

"Cigars?" The breasts were back to refresh our smoke.

"We're good for now," Santiaga said. She was smiling widely. He pulled out his wallet and folded a clean one hundred once and slid it between her coconut-sized titties. She wiggled them, said a string of graciases, and asked if she could get him a drink, "or anything else?" He ordered a glass of Louis XIII. She left.

I was sitting, calculating. One hundred times twenty-five thousand. I was moving the commas over on the numbers. One mistake with a comma or a zero and my answer would be all wrong. I calculated it three times in my head. That's $2,500,000. My eyes widened. I calculated it one more time. That's the minimum amount he earned on the bet, that he won based on the shot that I made. On top of that, he had the balls to tell me calmly that what he was paying out to me wasn't even one percent of his prize. I leaned back. Some minutes slipped by.

"You said you are a businessman, right?" Santiaga said impatiently. It wasn't a question, I know. Leaning forward again, he checked his Rolex, letting me know we were running out of time.

Still, I paused for a minute or so, then said, "True, I made the shot, but I didn't make the wager, you did. I don't know nobody who could wager those kinds of numbers, or who could afford to lose that amount if their gut feeling turned out to be wrong. That means that all of the winnings are yours, not mine. You went all in with the money that you earned. I didn't help you earn a penny of it. 'Winner take all,' as they say. So you take all of it. But thank you, word," I added sincerely.

"How much are those vending machines you're selling?"

"Fifteen hundred dollars each," I said, thinking of the model I purchased, not the discounted seven-hundred-dollar "horsey ride." "But since we're being honest, I pocket five hundred dollars off of each sale," I confided.

"Give me seventeen of those at fifteen hundred each," he said. "I'll put them in my stores." I was calculating. Seventeen machines times fifteen hundred dollars each equals $25,500. *Damn*, he was swift with his numbers and figured out seventeen machines would get the deed done. He was determined to place $25,000 in my hand either way. Now he'd made me a straight-up business proposition, not a charitable donation or a gift, or a questionable payoff, all of which I could never accept.

"You're a young businessman, not a young fool, right, son?" he asked me with an even more serious look. "You either take the twenty-five I'm handing you as your earnings on the amazing shot you pulled off, or you sell me seventeen machines for twenty-five thousand. You drop the extra five hundred since I'm buying so many, and you pocket twelve thousand dollars profit since you'll have to pay for the machines, and you don't want to take twenty-five thousand no-strings-attached free dollars." He stood up. Because he stood, I stood.

He checked his Rolex again. "You got twenty-five seconds. Each second is worth a thousand dollars. Go!" he said.

"Deal," I said in less than a second. "You ordered seventeen machines at a cost of twenty-five thousand dollars total, a five-hundred-dollar discount. I pocket twelve thousand dollars," I said. He smiled.

"Now you and I are in business." He extended his hand to me.

"It's a clean sale. Once the machines are delivered to you, our deal is done, no strings attached. I don't owe you, you don't owe me nothing," I said. His smile evaporated.

"Deal," he said. "After tonight, I don't owe you nothing. You don't owe me nothing," he confirmed with a serious expression, mixed with a disappointed, angry, and almost sad look.

"I'll come play for the team. That's a separate matter, though. Treat me like every other player. If I miss one more game I disqualify myself from the possibility of earning the most valuable player purse," I said. "I'll be at every practice and every game barring an emergency."

He smiled brightly, and it seems his smile made the ladies, who were all looking in our direction since we had stood up, happy too. We gave each other a pound on it.

* * *

"You drive. I had a couple of drinks," Santiaga said, throwing me the keys. It was a test, I knew. I opened the driver's-side door. He got in the back. "If the cops pull us over, which I doubt, not twice in one day, we'll say I'm sick and you're driving me to the emergency room. If that don't work, we'll press some paper in his palms." He reclined and closed his eyes. I was thinking this cat either believed or knew for sure that money straightens out all matters. I hoped so. We were on River Road in Edgewater, New Jersey. I didn't think his arms reached all the way across the George Washington Bridge or through the Lincoln Tunnel, same as they reached across the Brooklyn Bridge to uptown Manhattan.

Sitting in the driver's seat in his Maserati, which my shot probably paid for, I was thinking about my father, and how he used to challenge me, just like how I was being challenged right then by this man. In both cases they were men who were much older than me, placing me in an unreasonable situation and challenging me to work my way through it and come out clean. I knew Santiaga was not drunk and that his one drink was not strong. Even if it was strong, it still wouldn't matter 'cause he only sipped it for show. He watched me. I watched him.

I accept the challenge from him, same as I accepted the challenges handed down by my father. In both cases they were not challenges to be turned down or avoided. They were tasks all about manhood, and of course they involved risks.

"I'm 'bout to turn the ignition. *Insha'Allah* . . ." was the most I could feel or think at the moment.

# 13. IDENTITY

"Uncuff him," the lawyer said to the guard posted outside my hospital room the second she arrived. He did. "Please excuse us." She dismissed him politely but with a tone that caused him to obey her. He exited, but went no farther than the front door, where he stood immediately outside. He was not the same officer who stood over me in the hospital waiting room this morning for three and a half hours. It was nighttime now and she was just arriving, looking hurried and slowly calming herself.

"We have the right to refuse medical treatment," she said to me strangely. She was the one who had requested the court order that I be checked into a hospital. Why was she saying this now? I didn't respond. "I want you to be aware of your rights," she said.

"You have some legitimate—I mean real—injuries, so it was within my power to insist that you be examined at a hospital. However, I also wanted to slow down the process and have you and me get organized. A lot of crucial legal decisions are made in a hurry, without regard for the truth," she said, and I understood. I took note of how she switched from using the word *legitimate* to her translation of the word into the simple *real.* Of course, I knew the word *legitimate* and did not need her to break it down for me. She didn't know that, because she didn't know me.

"Besides, believe it not, the food here is better than the jail food at Rikers Island, much better." She seemed sure, as though she had eaten at Rikers, or observed or overheard the opinions of others eating at Rikers. I had eaten a bland but decent meal here in the hospital, challenging myself to lower my standards regarding food so that I could endure imprisonment.

"Baked chicken, mashed potatoes, and string beans—that's what you ate—and orange juice and water," she said, making me aware that even when she is not present, she knows each of my actions and choices. "You didn't eat the slice of chocolate cake," she added and looked towards me as though she expected a reaction. It was nonsense to me, for her to care about such a small detail. I gave her no reaction. The truth is, I purposely didn't touch that cake because it's sugar. As I prepare to be locked away doing real time, I didn't want to be enslaved to any addictions, like salt, seasonings, sugar, or food prepared with love and quality ingredients like I enjoyed every day at home, whether it was prepared by my Umma or either of my wives. I didn't want to yearn for things. I would hold on to them in my memory, but not crave them. "Craving anything is a form of self-torture," my sensei had taught me. "Letting go of your desires is the key to self-control in captivity. Even in living life as a free man, it is necessary that you have the ability to control your desires."

She opened her briefcase, the one with the stickers plastered on the inside. It was fuller than it had been earlier in the day. She pulled out five thin books, more like pamphlets. "These are each books of names," she said. I looked as she spread them across the table. "In case you decide to choose a new one for yourself," she added. Her name books each had a different title: *Spanish Names*, *French Names*, *Christian Names*, *Jewish Names*, *Muslim Names*, *African Names*.

"It looks like you were hit in the head. Perhaps you don't remember your name?" She stared at me. In her eyes was feminine strength. I was thinking carefully. Was she suggesting that I should say that I can't remember because I was injured by the police? Was this some legal strategy that she needed me to follow, but that she wasn't allowed to tell me straight out?

"From here forward, your fingerprints, your blood and urine samples, everything will be linked directly with the name that we place on your legal papers, at least until your parents or guardians show up, or an authority discovers and confirms something different. Do you understand?" she asked.

I was sitting still, but my mind was spinning faster than the rotation of the Earth. I had not identified myself to them, but now, they were creating an identity for me through my body fluids and prints.

"And this information that the system collects and compiles will follow you for the rest of your life," she said. "Since you are a juvenile, or shall we say an adolescent," she paused and looked again into my eyes, "there are cases where minors can have their records expunged. Hardly ever in the case of murder, but even if your misdemeanor charges are successfully expunged, it's never actually erased." She had me now. I did not know the meaning of the word *expunged.* I didn't have access to a dictionary. I wouldn't ask her to define it for me, either.

"I'm going to grab a coffee and I'll be right back," she said, leaving her opened briefcase on the table. She grabbed some coins from her purse and left her wallet as well. Another test, I knew. She had only been here for six minutes and it seemed that she had set up six different tests for me through each of her words and gestures, questions and actions.

Everything I had accomplished and avoided in my young life was now coming into the open. I realized she was correct. What I had working for me, though, was that this was my first and only arrest. I had never been a part of their legal system, or their school system or even their employment system. Even my job at Zhou's fish market was a cash-only transaction. I got it when I was thirteen, from a Chinaman, who like most foreigners, such as myself, knew young people are capable and *need to work*, despite American ideas and laws forbidding it. I had never been hospitalized in America. There was no medical history for me. I had not been sick or even visited a hospital except for the time that Naja was born. Back then I didn't sign anything. They only asked questions of Umma, and required her signature. True, I had translated their questions so that Umma could understand them, but Umma and I do not share the same last name. We are Sudanese, from the "Land of Fathers." Each Sudanese person is identified through his or her father, grandfather, and great-grandfather. Umma's first name is Sana. The name of her father is Safieldin. The name of her grandfather is Al Salam. The name of her great-grandfather is Saif. So her true name is Sana Bint Safieldin Abd Al Salam Saif. And the meaning is deeper than any nonbeliever could or would ever imagine or know. Sana means "splendor," Safieldin means "pure religion," Al Salam means "peace," Saif means "sword." And Umma is the splendor of pure religion, and Umma brings peace, and the sword, well we know that is so necessary to guard peace. Not one of Umma's names, or the names of her fathers, is my name. My name is only the names of my fathers. On all documents that Umma ever signed in America, she used a combination of one of her four true names. Americans only require two names, first and last. Sometimes she was Sana Saif. Sometimes she was Sana Safieldin. Sometimes she was Sana Abd Al Salam. Sometimes she did not even use Sana, but a combination of the names of two of her fathers. We believed our true names, their meanings and depth, were wasted on Americans who couldn't seem to properly pronounce any name or thing that was not English. Americans whose names mostly had no meaning or depth. I found that out in casual conversation. Ask an American his or her name and follow up by asking the meaning . . . and there is no meaning, at least not one that any of them knows. Other than my friends Chris and Ameer, I knew better than to ask any African Americans about their father. It was considered some type of intrusion or insult, and it was a question they honestly could not answer.

*But there is Immigration!* That thought exploded like a bomb in my mind. Umma and I had recently obtained citizenship. They required a thumbprint from me. We had also obtained passports. My true name was definitely registered on my passport, and the name of my mother was required there as well. *They won't check that far or look that deeply*, I told myself. I desperately wanted to believe that. Yet, I knew now that it was my vulnerability, and it was a link that I had not considered.

*They'll see that my fingerprints don't match anything or anyone in their criminal system or criminal records, and they will stop right there!* I convinced myself. I reassured myself. I needed my thoughts to become facts. As long as there was no way for them to connect me to my Umma, I kept thinking and repeating that to myself.

*Fuck it, I'll choose a new name that cannot be traced back to my Umma, who I have to protect with my life.* I'll choose a name that completely separated me and severs any connection to my real life and true identity. I'll choose a name that will follow me for my remaining time living on American soil. The name I choose will be for them. For those who I am certain will only ever see me as a murderer. My true name will remain the name known and used only by those who love me loyally and deeply. My true name will remain the name of my fathers, and most importantly, the name of my soul.

Renaming myself took effort. Even though it would not be my real name, I did not want the name of a fool, a clown, or a sucker. I thought about African Americans and the types of names they had. I needed my false name to sound American so they wouldn't go searching through immigration records. Names of American entertainers and athletes kept circulating in my mind. Those were the things American blacks were known for.

"Michael Jordan," I said aloud as I sat alone in the guarded hospital room. He has a father. He's black-skinned like me. He plays ball like me. He's a man of action, not a trash talker like most. He went at that game with a concentration and an energy that was unlike any other player. I admired that, to the fullest. More than that, I admired how he gave the game his all, is a champion in his own right, even without his team. He seemed real, faced the same challenges that any and every regular everyday man faced. I remember the game he played this year on April 20. It was against the Boston Celtics, starring three-time MVP Larry Byrd. Me and Ameer checked that game on his television. I remember the announcer saying, "Can one man beat the Celtics?" Referring to Michael Jordan, who is young, only a sophomore in the league and coming off of a foot injury, but up against some hefty competition and seasoned players. That's how my life is. I'm just one young man up against some hefty circumstances and some dirty players, but I'm still pushing, working, fighting, and most of all believing solidly that I can win. Michael Jordan knew he couldn't win by being like every other player or by playing the game the same way his opponents did. He was even comfortable looking like himself, styling his kicks and basketball shorts the way he needed to rock 'em and then reversing it, causing everybody to want to be like him instead. In that game Jordan scored sixty-three points, crazy! He had them Boston boys frustrated, afraid they were gonna lose on their home court, which had not happened to them for a long stretch. At the free throw line, he forced the game into overtime with his accuracy and skill. I smiled. Then I laughed. I loved the way he made them sweat. I loved the fear he put in their eyes. I loved the way he made them hustle hard so that even if they won over him, they had to fucking earn it. I loved the way even though Boston won that game, all everybody was talking about was Michael Jordan and the spanking he gave Boston. A whipping so severe, it was clear that even though they won, he was a force to fear in the future. He would become a record breaker. Even though Jordan was not more than seven feet tall like the veteran Wilt Chamberlain, he was swift, skilled, and accurate enough to break Wilt's record-setting 100-point game. Young Michael Jordan was the future of absolute dominance. I smiled. That's the name I'll call myself, Jordan. I didn't dig the name Michael, so I'd drop that. Yes, he's a real man living a real life. He hit 63 points but still he didn't win. I could relate to that. In his mind was probably the same type of thoughts I had moving in my mind at this very moment. *Time to refresh, and reflect and strategize and train hard, and go hard, and hit 'em again.* Maybe Jordan was watching the film of his game and thinking to himself, even though I did a tremendous performance, I see a few flaws that I need to clean up and fortify.

I see some flaws in myself as well, as I'm reflecting, but my flaws were a lot less than my victories, *alhamdulillah.*

The lawyer returned before I had come up with a last name, like the "two-name Americans." The names of colors raced around my head. Jordan Black, Jordan Brown, Jordan Blue. Then adjectives started swirling in my thoughts: Jordan Strong, Jordan True, Jordan Power. She wasn't carrying her coffee cup. Instead she approached me with a newspaper folded and tucked beneath her armpit. She placed the paper on the table, then extended her hand and said, "Please allow me to formally introduce myself. I am Ayn Eliana Aaronson, your attorney. I'm on your side. And you are?" she asked calmly as though I was not a prisoner and she and I were just meeting in the bookstore. Still extending her hand as though she wanted us to shake hands, I extended my hand and answered, "Jordan." I paused and added, "Jordan Mann." She smiled. "Six days of silence—I'm honored, Jordan. Nice to meet you.

"Before we get started, I need to be certain that you are aware and that you are understanding me when I speak. It's really for your sake. A defendant is placed in a completely different category when he is not understanding his surroundings, or is not able to process and understand the words being spoken to him or the charges against him. So, I'll ask you a few questions. Please answer them as soon as the answers come to mind for you. What year is this?" she asked.

"1986," I answered calmly.

"Who is our president?"

"Ronald Reagan, and Vice President George Bush," I answered like a real proud American.

"Who is the mayor of New York?"

"Ed Koch," I said in an even tone. Everybody knew him. He is the mayor who rides the New York City subway.

"What's the name of the New York baseball team?" she asked.

"The New York Yankees, of course," I said.

"Okay, those were fairly easy questions, right?" she asked me. "Now, a few more, which are a bit more difficult.

"Who is Albert Einstein?"

"A genius," was all I responded. She smiled.

"Who is William Shakespeare?"

"An author, a writer, a poet," I said.

"Last one: Who is Holden Caulfield?" She looked at me like she had me stumped. She leaned back in her chair and waited as though she was sure she needed to give me extra time. Yet she looked like she knew that even with extra time to think, I would come up blank.

"A fool," I replied.

"A fool?" she repeated and asked at the same time.

"A fool who some fool wrote about, in a novel titled *Catcher in the Rye*," I said. She smiled again.

"So you enjoy books?" she stated happily at the same time as asking.

"I read books. I only enjoy the good ones," I replied. "Is that it?" I asked her.

"Now let's talk about Lance Polite," she said, swiftly switching her topic and casually dropping the name of the jackass I had murdered. She checked my face and opened her copy of the *Daily News* to page three.

"Who?" I asked calmly. She just looked at me.

"Very clever," was all she said, and she lowered her eyes back onto the article. I checked the headline. "Lance, Not So Polite," it read. And the caption below the headline said, "Man murdered in a public execution at a Brooklyn block party community concert was himself a convict, a repeat sexual offender and a public nuisance."

I didn't say anything. She went into her opened briefcase, her eyes taking note that her wallet was right where she left it and how she left it. Her name books still laid out exactly the way she laid them out and untouched by me. Even her Parker pen was in the same position. She pulled out some papers and began spreading them out before me. They were all clipped articles. She had some of the text in each of the articles highlighted with a yellow marker. What stood out to me was one headline that referred to me as "The Silent Killer." In each of the articles, there was only one photo. It was the same one of a faceless me with my nine in his mouth.

"If you'll look closely at this article, and this one too," she said, pointing, "they each suggest that this was a drug-related execution and that you are suspected to be a member of a gang of armed and dangerous men who specialize in robbing drug dealers." She was staring into my eyes. I was silent.

"I don't believe it," she said. "I think that's not at all who you are or what actually happened. I need you to confide in me so that I can defend you properly."

*Her to defend me . . .* It sounded strange in my head. My gaze was steady but inside I was getting heated. Not at her, but at the insult in one of the news articles. It is definitely not an honor to be branded a thief, even if I was "allegedly" robbing hustlers.

"I am not aware of exactly what crime I am being charged with, or the reason that I am being held," I suddenly told her. She revealed a half smile.

"You are right. You have not been arraigned yet, which is highly unusual after six days of being held, and I will certainly highlight that fact and challenge that process. Your arraignment is actually where you will hear the judge read the charges against you. I talked to the court today. They had you listed as an adult. And so far, it seems that you are definitely going to be charged with resisting arrest and assaulting a police officer. We can survive those charges and I will defend you against them. However, pending there is a police officer's affidavit stating that you confessed to having murdered Lance Polite," she said, straight-faced and searching me with her green eyes.

"Why don't you believe it?" I suddenly asked her.

"Believe what?" she said.

"That I am a part of an armed and dangerous gang that robs drug dealers."

She paused, adjusted her posture in her seat, and said very calmly and casually, "For a few different, very important, and very pivotal reasons, the first of which is because I sit across the table with armed robbers, drug dealers, and murderers every day. I know what it looks like. I know what it feels like."

I was silent.

"Look, I'm a court-appointed attorney. I'm not sure that you know what that means. I've been in court all day today and will do the same tomorrow. I have a caseload of 212 clients. Right now," she checked her watch, "I'm off duty. I'm not supposed to be here working, but I am. Tomorrow morning, I'll be scheduled to appear before five different judges all at the same time, nine a.m., which you and I and they all know is impossible. You are one of the appearances that I have to make out of the five at nine a.m. I plan to show up for you if you make it possible for me, by communicating with me and trusting that I am on your side."

"Why my case?" I asked. I wanted her to reveal her motivations. I had observed that each of the cops, detectives, and other authorities I had encountered so far would mention overtime pay, promotions, credits, benefits, receiving stars, stripes, or medals in relation to cornering and capturing and convicting me.

"Excuse me?" she stalled.

"Out of five cases at nine a.m., why take mine?" I asked her calmly. She wanted to know more about me. I needed to know more about her. She placed her right hand over her stomach and let it rest there.

"Gut feeling," she said firmly. "Besides, you have no idea what kind of charges they are cooking up for you at the arraignment or how many eyes are watching this case because the shooting allegedly took place in the presence or proximity of a New York state senator. There is major media hysteria, but let me tell you something: most reporters in particular and people in general have a short attention span. This will be a big story until the next big story comes along and buries it. The thing is, even though all may forget you and forget what happened, if your case is not handled properly, *you'll* never forget because the consequences are quite severe. I got your arraignment postponed today and it's a good thing I did. You got six stitches in your head and a couple of fractured ribs—good for you. The rest of your medical results will come back sometime tomorrow. I ran the information I received today over to the district attorney's office. They needed to know that some wonderful policeman beat you before you were ever booked and arraigned. Now I've got the medical record to back it up. And tomorrow's arraignment is our last chance to squeeze this matter in for this week. Tomorrow is Thursday. Friday will be motion day at the courthouse. The courts will be focused on something completely different. I don't see how they could possibly delay your arraignment any further, pushing it back until Monday. If they try, I'll know they're just buying time in addition to breaking the law, due to lack of evidence to even charge you with the felony crimes. Then I'll get them for unlawful imprisonment." She was thinking and speaking at the same time. She was revealing her passion. I liked that. I could see that she somehow enjoyed the fight. Maybe she even chose the most challenging situations on purpose.

"What if you're wrong? Your gut feeling?" I asked her.

"I'm hardly ever wrong. And I studied this case from the beginning, which is always good when a defendant's lawyer is brought onto the case early. The earlier an attorney gets involved in your defense, the better."

"Why were you studying the case from the beginning?" I pushed. It seemed like there was more to this woman than just me being one of her 212 open cases. After being questioned for more than four days, I knew not to accept just anything some official was saying. *Dig deeper*, I told myself.

She paused before responding, folded her arms in front of her, and exhaled deeply. Then she unfolded her arms and moved her hands beneath the table, almost as though trying to hide them. She began spinning her black embroidered bracelet around on her left wrist, like a nervous quirk. Finally, she leaned back in her chair.

"Do you like animals?" she asked me. I thought of camels and horses and giraffes, beautiful and amazing creatures that Allah created.

"Yes," I responded.

"Do you believe that animals have a soul?" she asked strangely. "That they can feel and cry and mourn and hurt, the same as human beings?" She sounded absolutely serious and emotional, after not being emotional at all. I paused, thinking. I knew how I would answer as the Muslim man that I am. It is a good answer that would take me some time to explain. But this situation required me to give her the answer that would most benefit me in this scenario, I could tell. I assembled my words carefully. Handpicked, they were also words that are true to me.

"Animals are living and breathing, seeing and hearing. They each make sounds that suggest that they communicate and express. So of course they can feel," I said, avoiding the soul part of her question. "But what does this have to do with you and me?"

"Lance Polite comes up on my list," she said.

"List?" I repeated. She paused.

"American Society for the Prevention of Cruelty to Animals. I've been a member since I was a teenager. We keep a list of offenders and pay close attention to repeat offenders," she said. I was lost. She seemed smart and sharp at first. Now I was debating whether or not she was crazy. What was she talking about?

"Lance Polite is a repeat offender, a guy who has been reported, accused, and convicted more than once for cruelly killing animals for no reason at all. It goes back to even before he became an adult. If this man was killing animals even when he was a kid, he must be a pretty sick creep. And it all goes together with his criminal past and convictions of molesting boys and girls. This is a guy who I peg as a sociopath. I'm a lawyer, not a doctor, but I feel that anyone who hurts animals or children . . ." She didn't finish her sentence.

"Anyone who kills animals or hurts children, you go after them," I stated. It wasn't really a question.

"On the day of the murder of Lance Polite, a cat was found choked to death on the floor of the basement of the building directly in front of the murder scene. It was reported to the ASPCA and we collected the body. Well, not me, our organization. We have investigators as well. So I've been thinking and putting things together in a way that the police department never would," she said thoughtfully.

I was alarmed, but my face was blank. I made an expression as though I didn't understand her talk or her direction. But I understood her now. Lance had killed Naja's cat. Her organization picked up the cat's body. And they must be extremely serious about animals if they came to my block and entered the basement in one of my buildings. But what alarmed me was what else they might have seen or picked up or reported about the basement of that building where he held Naja hostage. Did they snag the kunai knife that may have been on the basement floor? Or was the knife still sitting there waiting to be discovered possibly by the police if they were continuing their murder investigation? Or did the savage yank the knife out of his eye, panic at the pain and the site of his own blood, then run straight out to the ambulance that was parked at the concert? Did he take the knife with him? The knife would have Chiasa's prints on it for sure.

*But the ASPCA is an organization, not the police*, I thought to myself. She had said that they had their own investigators, but they didn't have police power, I assured myself. And the police had no reason to check the basement of that building. I slaughtered the sucker out in the open, outdoors on the block.

The lawyer interrupted my thinking. "I've confided something to you. I've answered your questions. Now you need to confide something to me and answer some of my questions about this crime and your role in it," she said, switching from her animal-lover personality back into the legal eagle.

"Were you defending a child or an animal from Lance Polite, the predator? The photo, which according to the police detective allegedly is you, looks emotional. It looks like a deep hatred being expressed through violence. If that is the case, then I understand. However, legally, this places you in the absolutely most vulnerable position to be sentenced to twenty-five years to life in prison. Meaning you either knew Lance Polite or you saw him do something disgusting and then you went after him. Meaning you thought about it, which makes it legally premeditated murder, and then you carried it out. To be convicted of this crime means that you'll be over forty before you will ever be unbarred, unchained, and uncuffed and free." She was emotional now, leaning forward and searching me for a reaction.

"Have you heard or read about this young lady who was sentenced to be put to death this summer? Her name is Paula Cooper. She's from the state of Indiana. Now, the laws from state to state vary. However, she was sentenced to death recently. The details of her case are completely different than yours, I suspect. But it might not be a bad idea for you to consider and know about her outcome on a similar charge. She's sixteen now, same as you," she said, guessing at my age again. Her points were clear to me though, and once again, the threat of twenty-five years to life was circulating in my chest.

"If you tell me that you were defending an animal or a child, I'll work my ass off to get you the best results, the least amount of time. Of course, if my gut is wrong and you turn out to be guilty of armed robbery or distribution of crack cocaine or anything of that nature, I can't guarantee you my best effort or the best outcome," she said.

"How long do I have?" I asked her. She checked her watch. "Well, it's almost nine p.m. I'd like to leave here no later than ten. I work in the system, so I know what goes on in this city, especially late at night. I prefer not to ride the train after eleven p.m."

"No husband?" I asked her. "No man would allow his woman to move around the city alone late night," I said, changing the topic from the heavy reality I faced.

"I'm not the kind of woman who would allow a husband to control me," she said sternly.

"I wasn't talking about controlling you. I was talking about loving you." Then, I just looked at her.

"Keep talking like that and I'll decide that you're an adult, not a juvenile or an adolescent," she said, flexing the power she believed she had to move my life in one direction or another. Then she held up both of her hands and wiggled her ten fingers, causing her bracelet to reveal more of the deep scar she used it to cover.

"No rings on my fingers." She smiled halfway. Then I knew. Someone had hurt this woman, and she had planned and trained to protect the hurt animals and hurt people. But in my case, she planned to protect the man who murdered the man who murdered animals and molested children. I thought about it. *She's glad he's dead.* So am I. We had the same understanding. We were on the same team, I decided.

"About court tomorrow: will all of this be decided on tomorrow in front of the judge?" I asked her.

"Oh no, tomorrow is simply the arraignment. It takes three minutes or less. They read you the charges against you. That's it. I don't believe they'll charge you with murder tomorrow, although you never know. My gut tells me aside from the detective's affidavit, they have not organized enough evidence. If there is a murder charge tomorrow, the prosecution gets two weeks to organize its investigation and bring you before a grand jury."

"Do they expect me to talk at this arraignment tomorrow?" I asked.

"No, I'm your attorney. I'll speak for you. They'll hold you in the bullpen until your case comes up, just like they did this morning. Then an officer will escort you out. You'll stand before the judge and hear the charges, and the judge will decide if he's going to set bail."

"I don't want bail," I said swiftly. She gave a surprised look, as though she normally knew what to expect, was used to following a certain procedure, and even knew beforehand what each person and side would say and do and how she needed to react, exactly.

"If I go directly to the jail where they're going to keep me, as soon as I get there, I've started serving down my time, right?" I asked her.

"Yes, that counts as time served, deductible against whatever you might be sentenced to," she confirmed. "But that's down the line," she added, and her face revealed a new suspicion. "And that's only if they get a conviction. Hopefully your refusal of bail is not a vote of no confidence in your attorney's ability to win this case."

"And you said the prosecution has two weeks to organize their case against me, right?"

"Exactly. They have two weeks after having arraigned you on murder to bring you before the grand jury seeking an indictment. During those two weeks I'll be communicating with them also."

"If I don't have to talk in the courtroom tomorrow, then why wait?" I asked her. She looked at me curiously. "You said that you're my lawyer. You can go hear the charges and tell me about it. I'll be locked up already," I said solemnly.

I don't like those hand- and footcuffs and the chain that connected them together and me to the others. Behind bars I would be confined, true, but I could still move around and work out, I believed. More importantly, behind bars I could make prayer, I believed. In the bullpen, in the courthouse, before the judge and prosecution, I was hemmed in and still protecting my true identity. I had been six days without prayer, like those American cats who were locked up with me. Of course I could pray within myself, silently, but I could not make the *salat* or press my head to the floor.

"Why wouldn't you want bail?" she asked me sternly.

"I'm alone in this world. I have no family. The guardian I do have, he has no money, no property. He's sick and won't be able to come to court or anything like that," I told her because that's what I wanted her to believe, and because it was also what anyone would believe about any African American: no family, no money, no property.

"Sick, how sick?" she asked me.

"He had a stroke, can't talk and can barely see," I told her, sealing her options or anyone else's of interviewing him. "Besides, if he knew I was here, it would kill him. I can't let him find out. I can't let that happen." She looked moved.

"Regarding the murder, the person you were protecting, was she or was he a friend, neighbor, or a relative? Was it a small boy or girl? Or were you protecting an animal?" she asked me. I paused. We stared at each other for some seconds.

I was curious if she caught on to me, the way I caught on to her. I was hoping my silence could convey to her that of course I was protecting people I know and love, my sister, a blood relation, and my wife who hurled the knife. Our Mrs. Marcy, who was our family's only loved senior in the USA. But at the same time, of course, I was never going to tell her or anyone else that aloud and have some dishonorable authority sentence me to twenty-five years to life, like the good detective wanted to do, over the slaughter of a lesser man. She and I both knew and understood that this particular murder had to be committed, I could tell.

"How much time could I get for 'resisting arrest'?" I asked her, overlooking all of her most serious questions.

"Six months to a year," she said. "It depends on how bad they want to keep you. And then there's the possibility of an 'assaulting a police officer' charge. There are a lot of variables. Maybe an officer or even the accusing detective will show up, and his presence in the courtroom may impact the judge in a particular way."

"Send me straight to Rikers. Let me hear back from you what the charges are. Meanwhile, I'll be working off the conviction for resisting arrest. I already know the outcome," I told her.

"How could you know the outcome? Are you saying you want to plead guilty to resisting arrest?" she asked. "And what about the other charges they may allege? Do you want to plead guilty to those? I have to enter a plea on your behalf. Once I do, I'd organize your defense."

"No, I did not resist arrest. I'm saying I already know the outcome because it's my word against theirs, and the police lie with authority."

"That's not true," she said swiftly. "Not all . . ." I cut her off.

"What is true is that I never resisted arrest. I never assaulted a police officer or a detective. I am not an armed robber or any kind of thief. I am not a drug dealer. I have never been in anybody's gang. Never liked none of these dudes enough to gang up with them. I never confessed to murder, although they are saying that I did confess. And, I agree with you that that guy in those news articles that you just showed me deserved to go," I said calmly.

"I never said that!" she exclaimed with guilt.

"Your lips didn't. Your heart did." My words somehow silenced her. She left for a few moments and returned with an orange juice for herself and a bottled water for me. Using my left hand, I wrote out a note for her to take with her.

"What is it?" she asked before accepting it.

"Read it," I told her. She took it.

"An IOU," she said, smiling.

"I'm no freeloader," I told her. "Whatever you spend on me, even if it's only your time, write it down. I'll pay you what I owe."

"I'm Legal Aid," she said. "The government pays me, not the client."

"I understand. How much was the water?" I asked.

"Just fifty cents."

"Write it down," I told her. She did.

Moments later, she slumped back in her chair and she just looked at me. "Thank you for saying that," she said.

"For saying what?"

"For confirming what I believed and what I felt. You did not resist arrest or attack a police officer. You were never in a gang or selling drugs. You did not commit armed robbery or confess to a murder. I needed to be able to trust myself. To trust my instincts and to believe that even though I sit down with hundreds of young men who stand accused, some of them are wrongly accused. Some of them are innocent," she exhaled.

"Remember this," I told her. "Babies are innocent. They are the only ones who are. When you sit down with any man, know that he is not innocent. Men are given evil options throughout each day. How each man responds to evil options and suggestions is the only way for you to determine if he is a good man. He may be good. But no man is innocent."

She stayed for a half hour longer. We talked, and I reminded her that she needed to leave so that she could get home before 11 p.m. and get up in time to appear in five courtrooms simultaneously.

"By the way, my sister thinks that you are guilty. She and I argued about it on my way over here to the hospital. My sister is usually right. Most of the time I listen to her. This time I decided to trust myself. If I am right after disagreeing with her, it will be the first time I won!" she said with a melancholy smile.

"Is your sister a lawyer also?" I asked her.

"No, she's dead. But we talk anyway. We are twins, she and I. I don't tell anyone about her. Somehow, you seem like a person who still has a heart and who would understand. And I know from working in this system that even if you told someone what I said, it wouldn't matter, because their prejudices would never allow them to believe you over me."

I just looked at her. She looked good, smart, and her eyes were clear.

"Memorize my number," she told me before she left, handing me a business card. "I don't think you really know what you're walking into. In a sense, that's a good thing. It means you don't have any experience with this kind of thing. Some of the young men I represent know the laws as well as I do, because they have been in the system for almost their entire lives. Rikers is a tough place. Remember you have a right to an attorney. If anything goes wrong before you see me, please give me a call. I'll be working on your behalf." She turned to leave.

"You have an unusual name," I said, staring down at her card. Her name wasn't Ann. It was Ayn. I'd never heard that name before.

"It's Hebrew," she said, as though just stating that fact would somehow turn me away.

"What does it mean?" She seemed surprised at even that simple question.

"It means 'prayer,'" she said.

"And Eliana?" I asked, reading her middle name off the business card.

"It means 'God has answered,'" she said, still looking at me as though wondering how I could be focused on her when I should be so weighed down by my own fears and problems.

"That's better than being my lawyer," I said.

"What?" she asked.

"I'd rather you be the answer to my prayers." She continued to look me in the eye.

"That's the name my parents gave me. As for me, I've seen a lot of ugly things. I'm undecided as to whether God even bothers with our prayers. If he does listen, how could horrible things happen to children? Why doesn't he protect them? And how could he let one die and not the other? Both of them would be just fine if they had either lived together or died together. That's compassion. Do you understand me?" she asked. I didn't respond. I knew something had happened to her. Her scar was on her wrist and probably even etched on her soul. People probably look at her every day and see the fight in her eyes, but not her sadness. I saw it almost immediately. Maybe that's why she gravitated towards me.

"Good night," she said softly and left.

She was smart. She was smarter than any and all of the detectives and definitely smarter than all of the police. She had figured out the case before it even became one. She had looked into the smallest details instead of jumping to the most typical and obvious conclusions. She had used her brain and her heart in her investigation. I peeped that she was warning me not to confess to murder for honor or any other reason. I peeped that she was gonna prove that I had been beaten by the cops. That their so-called unwritten, unrecorded "confession" was false! And that Jordan Mann, who had no documented history of violence or crime, was a falsely accused sixteen-year-old who like every good American boy had read *The Catcher in the Rye.* Yes, that would be her angle.

Alone now, I had more pieces to the puzzle than I had over the past week of my captivity. Neither the scenario nor the puzzle was completely clear yet. However, if I was correct in my thinking, the turn of events went like this. I murdered a man. Later that same night, I entered a Laundromat to wash off the evidence of the murder and to pen a letter to my Umma. The Laundromat was a front for some drug gang that was run, owned, operated, and/or protected by some dirty cops and some Jamaican gangsters. Somehow, some drugs went missing on the same night that I entered the Laundromat. Now the dirty cops and the Jamaican gang were looking for the drugs that either one of them, or both of them thought I stole. Either the dirty cops or the hustlers or both of them thought I was affiliated with some niggas who rob drug dealers. Either way, their drugs and/or their money is missing. They think I know where it's at. If I would've talked during the interrogation, which I did not, there would be one or two or three teams gunning for me: the dirty cops, the hustlers, or the stick-up kids. But the murder I committed and my silence had zero to do with any of that. What a fucking mess. I leaned back.

# 14. NIGHT NURSE

The cop that was guarding the hospital room door wasn't standing on point, I noticed. Was he to the left or right of the glass where I could not see the back of his head? Or had he stepped away for some reason as soon as the lawyer left my room? Did he follow my lawyer to question her because she had just become the only person I spoke to since they first cuffed me and began asking me questions a week ago? Maybe, but I doubted that the cops guarding the prisoners' rooms in the hospital knew anything about our case details. They were not the faces of any of the cops I had encountered during the interrogation so far. Fuck it, the hospital guard would definitely show back up to cuff my hands and feet, or chain me to the hospital bed.

Instinctively, I did a series of sit-ups, but I lost the count in my thoughts. The hospital door opened. A slim female nurse entered. Her face was stern and stained with a scowl, like she had been angry for years. She looked at me exercising, looked at my bedsheets and then left.

A new cop walked in moments later. "Hands," was all he said before he cuffed me. Now my hands and feet were cuffed, but I was still not chained to the bed. He stood post outside my door. I figured the nurse blew me up and went and got the cop to cuff me. *Too bad*, I thought. If I would've had a half hour more without cuffs, I would've undressed and washed the clothes I had worn for too many days. *It might be for the better*, was my second thought on the matter. By now, I realized I would never know when they would show up to move me. It would be crazy having to jump back into my clothes while they were still wet. At home my clothes were cleaned and sometimes ironed and laid out for me or hung in my closet, I remembered, but then canceled the thought, reminding myself not to crave home and not to desire or expect anything.

The same mean-faced nurse returned.

"Nurse," I said.

"I'm not a nurse," she said, in an even and dry tone. I looked at her. She was young but dry, like a raisin, I observed. She looked like she had not had a glass of water in weeks.

"What are you then?" I asked in an even tone also.

"Whatever I am, I'm not s'pose to be talking to you," she said.

"Cool, we don't have to talk," I said, not used to being shut down by any woman. She entered the little bathroom like she was making an inspection. Then she came right back out. I wondered why she seemed to be looking at or for something in particular but never asked me about it, said what it was, or changed anything she saw.

"I'll give you something. You give me something," I offered her.

"I hope you are not trying to get fresh with me. You ain't the only jailbird on my shift," she said. Her words cut through me, reminding me of my new identity and low status. It set me back some.

"Here." I handed her the slim packet of olive oil that was left on my hospital food tray. She looked at it like it was nothing. "Use this on your skin. After you wash your hands, put some in your palms and spread it around. You work with your hands. You should try and take care of them," I told her sincerely.

"And what do you want?" she asked suspiciously.

"A nail clip," I told her.

"You ain't gonna stab nobody with it, are you?"

"Nah." I smiled. She melted some. "I'm gonna take care of my hands too," I told her. She looked down at my hands.

"Yeah, you need 'em clipped. I'll be back." She slid the olive oil packet in her front scrub pocket. I knew she could probably go in some supply cabinet or even to the hospital cafeteria and get a hundred more packets just like the one I gave her. I also knew that the one I handed her would remain special to her. These angry 'hood chicks each looked different, with varying degrees of attractiveness. However, on the inside they were mostly all the same. They talked rough, some of them even looked rough, but if the right or even the wrong man showed them an ounce of attention or affection, he could get whatever he wanted real fast.

"If you make friends," my second wife would often say to me, "you won't have to work so hard, alone. Making friends helps you to get what you need." I remembered Chiasa's words. *She is an expert at making friends*, I smiled.

Where I'm from, women pay close attention to their cleanliness, their scent, and their hands. A woman whose hands are unkept, undecorated, or rough, ashy, and neglected like the nurse's hands were routinely considered by everyone to be unhappy, and unloved.

Feeling like I was being watched, once again, swiftly, I looked up and saw a dude dressed in street clothes looking into my room. The second he saw me see him, he vanished. A simple mistake? A lost patient? A detec in his street clothes?

Since arriving at the hospital, the thought never crossed my mind that anyone might try to hit me up or kill me while I was in here. Now my mind shifted. What was up with the guard who was supposed to be on post outside my door? Why did he keep appearing and disappearing? Needless to say, I didn't consider him my protection. At the same time, if I needed to move him into the category of an open enemy and prepare to deal with a random attack from him, or anybody else, my entire circumstance would become an entanglement that would keep me trapped in their legal system for the rest of my life.

The nurse returned what felt like an hour later.

"I can do it for you," she offered, easing the nail clip from her pocket. "Seems like it would be hard for you to do with them cuffs on. But I seen people do some crazy stuff while their hands were locked up like yours."

"I can manage," I told her.

"Just put your hands up here." She pulled over the tray.

Her hands were now oiled, and even her wrists and face and neck had some moisture and shine. *Hold up, she even switched her hair*, I observed. She began clipping.

"I don't do this for everybody," she said in her stern manner.

"Thank you," was my only reply. After that we both stayed quiet until the last fingernail was completed. "Good job," I told her. "I appreciate it," I added.

"You got good manners," she said, as she cleaned up the clippings. "How come you're not wearing your hospital gown? I see they got you in here till the morning. Ain't you gonna get some sleep?"

"Right," was all I said. She laid the gown over me.

"If you put it on, I'll wash and dry your clothes for you and bring them back," she offered.

"Bring 'em back when?" I asked.

"Soon as they dry."

"What if you don't? Then what? You want me to walk around in that hospital outfit?" I asked her. She laughed. It was the first smile I'd seen on a face that looked like it was in a permanent frown.

"I won't do you like dat. I thought you could tell I'm a good person."

"I can tell," I said.

"Well den?" she asked but was already reaching for my T-shirt, helping me out of it and yanking it over my head. She looked at my upper body, got stuck in a gaze for a second, then realized my T-shirt couldn't come all the way off and was now stuck wrapped around my wrists where I was cuffed. She laughed and reversed what she had done too eagerly.

"I'll be right back," she said.

She returned with the missing guard. He entered the room behind her, looking disturbed about being disturbed. "Hands," he said, then uncuffed first my hands and next my feet. He didn't leave. He stood staring and stuck like he planned to stay.

"Turn around," the "not a nurse" ordered him. He turned halfway and said to me, "Don't try anything stupid."

"Undress," she said to me in a friendlier tone. I did. She had ordered the guard to turn away, but she didn't turn or look away. She watched and waited, her eyes widening when she saw my jeans drop down. She grabbed the gown and rushed it over my head as if she was protecting me from her eyes seeing my bare body that she'd already seen and as though she somehow believed she was protecting me from the guard as well.

"Done," she said to the guard.

"Hands," he said to me. My hands and feet were cuffed again. He left. She stayed.

"You do me a favor. I'll do you a favor," she said oddly. "Just like we just did before with the olive oil and the nail clip." I just looked at her. "There's another nurse's assistant that works the overnight with me. Her name is Rhonda. She's a rotten egg. I hate her guts. Me and her the only two nurse's assistants who work this wing late night. The real nurses never do anything but sit on their butts at the nurses' station talking bad about people, even talking bad about the patients. Well, anyway, you don't talk to Rhonda. Just ig her. That's the favor." Her stare now was stern. "While I run your clothes down to our little staff laundry room." She exhaled like she was content with her offer and her request.

"What happened to the guard that was standing outside my room?" I flipped the topic from her nonsense girl gossip even though I could feel she was serious about it.

"He back at the nurses' station playing with the nurses like he do every night." Her explanation was helpful and lowered my suspicion some. "He not s'pose to do that. But he do," she added. "It's one of them nurses he likes for real, but both of them is married to someone else. So when they be at work, they act like they married to each other," she reported.

"How come you don't got no draws? That's nasty," she said.

"Draws?"

"Boxers or briefs or something to cover that thang up." She said it straight out like it wasn't an insult or an embarrassment for me, and as though she could still see something that she wasn't supposed to see, but already saw. "That's something else I can get for you," she said proudly.

"No thank you. I don't wear used boxers," I told her calmly.

"Beggars can't be choosers," she said. *From jailbird to beggar*, I thought to myself. She smiled and then laughed. "No psych!" she said like we had a joke between us. "I wouldn't bring you *no used draws*. That's filthy!" Then she turned serious.

"I'm clean," she said with emphasis. "Even though I gotta change dirty bedsheets and empty and clean bedpans and all the icky work, I wash my hands all the time. The hospital soap makes them ashy. That's why they were like dat before. But I gotta keep them clean. I don't want to catch no germs in here and bring some disease home to my family," she overexplained. But her mentioning her family made her more human to me.

"You're good now. Do the same thing tomorrow," I said, acknowledging her freshly oiled hands.

"You gon' be gone by tomorrow night when I get here. I already know dat." She said it as though she was sad about my leaving. Like she caught feelings in five minutes of meeting me. Then her face changed in an instant like she had a bright idea. "Why you asked me about that cop? You plan on escaping or something?"

"Nah," I said immediately. I didn't need her sounding no alarms.

"Good, 'cause I'll be right back with your clothes, and you would look real stupid hopping around the streets of Brooklyn in a hospital gown, no draws, and handcuffs." She laughed. I didn't.

"Watch out for Rhonda. She'll come around here 'cause she nosy and 'cause she s'pose to check on the patients like I do. She lightskinned-did. She look clean, but she the dirtiest one. Most of the patients get fooled by her. Thinks she's nice and I'm mean. Ha!

Really it's the other way around. She be charging the patients for every little thing they ask her for but can't get for themselves or ain't s'pose to have in the first place. She not s'pose to do dat. Don't you go asking her for no draws. I'll bring you some new ones free of charge. Rhonda don't do nothing for free. But she do *anything* for money, even put her mouth where it ain't s'pose to be for twenty dollars. And, for fifty dollars . . ."

"I need my clothes back—try and hurry." I interrupted her to stop her from gossiping to me like I'm one of her girlfriends, and to get her ass moving. She left.

The pretty nurse's assistant who looked clean but was "the dirtiest one" showed up. I heard her key turn in the keyhole of my locked but unguarded hospital room. I saw that she wasn't the ashy one. She was holding a metal bowl, which by the way she held it was filled up with some liquid.

"I came to change your bandages and wash your body," she said like it wasn't nothing. I wasn't supposed to speak to her, which I thought was nonsense, but I'd made an agreement so I didn't. She yanked the sheet that was over me as I was lying down on the hospital bed. My hospital gown had shifted, while I was asleep and my joint was out, and she was staring at it. I turned to my side to break her stare.

"We can start on the backside if you prefer," she said. Her hands were soft, not rough. She used both of them to gently push me into the facedown position. I cooperated because I like the touch of feminine fingers. Her fingertips grazed me as she cut the bandages from behind and let them fall to my side. The warm washcloth landed on the back of my neck first. In small circular motions, she washed my neck and eased down to my back, stroking with a bit more friction. The warm cloth and warm water felt good and more than that, I could hear her breathing while she worked on rubbing me clean. I could hear the cloth of her uniform. That aroused me, naturally. When she paused to soak the cloth and wring it out and then suds it again, she said, "You have a beautiful body, even from the back." I didn't say nothing. She returned with the warm cloth and was now washing my behind. With her bare hand, she cleaned the harder-to-reach area and accidentally touched the back of my balls. She withdrew her hand and walked away.

I liked the sound of the water. I could hear her emptying it into the small sink and refilling the metal bowl. She was back now, gently scrubbing my thighs and then my calves. When she cleaned the cloth again, she returned and scrubbed the soles of my feet. A sensation shot through my body and I got more solid than steel.

"Turn," she said softly. I wouldn't. Couldn't get my joint to lay down. She touched my sides to roll me over, like she was used to rolling patients and shifting their positions in the hospital bed all night. I turned myself slowly, knowing she couldn't turn me without my cooperation. As she saw my joint, I saw that she was topless. She put the cloth down. We were both staring at each other. She dipped her hands in the water and gently gripped on my joint. She got so aroused, instead of cleaning me with the washcloth, she was using her hand, caressing my joint with ease with the moisture of the water mixed with a few suds. She grabbed my balls, massaging them softly, and carefully, like a woman preparing meatballs, shaping them, touching them, holding them warmly.

She must have known I wasn't going to go in her. I reminded myself, *She's the dirtiest one.*

She leaned over, her titties dangling like dough. She put her two lips on the tip of my joint and began slowly swishing it around in her mouth. Oh it was warm, her lips moving down, my joint moving in her mouth. Then slowly she pulled her lips back up towards the tip. My joint, laying on her tongue, easing back and forth. Her hand caressing my balls. She began licking it, like it tasted good, then sucking it, like she could not get enough. When her lips were halfway down my joint, my tip touching the back of her throat, she began easing all the way up with great lip suction. Her titties were pressed against my leg and her butt was up in the air. When she pulled her lips back so that only the head remained in her mouth, she tightened her soft lips around it and then sucked real hard once. I busted off in her mouth. She swallowed it.

"What you doing on the floor?" the ashy nurse asked me. "And why did you switch off the lights if you were gonna be sitting on the floor? And why is this up against the door? I almost tripped on it when I came in. And why you got your pillow underneath the sheets like you was in your bed when you wasn't? You playing some kind of freaky game? I thought I could trust you." She said it like me and her had some type of real relationship going on.

I stood up from where I had been seated in the dark with my back pressed against the wall. I realized I must have fallen asleep in that position. I got down there to be ready to leap to attack if anyone showed up in my room besides one of the night nurses. I had seen the same strange black male face peering into my locked hospital room twice while she was gone.

*Damn!* I thought to myself. *That was a crazy dream.* I had it, enjoyed while I was in it, but didn't want to be responsible for it. *That was Jordan Mann, not me.* I smiled. Day seven in captivity, and I'm already having wet dreams like before I became a married man who has a beautiful and erotic wife and sexed and made love to her whenever I was moved to do so. A young man, who loved and married and lived with one, and then two beautiful badass women.

My hospital gown had a wet spot when I looked down. I played it off like it wasn't there. "You never slept on the floor?" was all I said to her interrogation.

"Only when I had to. Not when I had a bed right there just for me, like you do," she replied.

"Thank you for my clothes," I told her. She handed them to me. They were warm and cleaned, and below the short folded pile was a pair of new boxers, still wrapped in the plastic.

"I'm sorry," she said, handing them to me.

"For what?" I asked her.

"For taking so long," she said. "Did Rhonda come?" she asked, her voice more timid than before.

"Nah," I said.

"Good. You're my patient. I'll take care of you." She picked up the tray and left.

The second nurse's assistant showed up right before the break of dawn, this time not in a dream, but in real life. She wasn't topless. She was "lightskinned-did." She wasn't pretty. She didn't look clean to me. She looked ran through, slick and stupid at the same time. She was measuring me up while I was reading her.

"I got a note for you," she said. I could see the folded paper in her right palm.

"From who?" I asked.

"Don't know," she said. "Guy in the hallway been creeping around. I could've called security on him but that's not what I do. He been trying all night to get me for my key. I told him no 'cause that's just fucking up my business. He gon' get me fired."

"The note?" I asked her.

"Twenty dollars." She put a price on it and put her hand on her hip after announcing it.

"You can keep it. I wasn't expecting no mail in here. And you don't look like a mailman, either," I told her.

"I got slapped over this bullshit," she said.

"Slapped and paid," I said, letting her know I knew her hustle. She was trying to get paid twice off of the same errand. The door opened. The slim, previously ashy nurse entered.

"Rhonda, why you in here?"

"Why you asking!" she screeched on the ashy nurse. "Do you own him? Is this your room and your bed? Do you own the whole goddamned hospital?" She spit with venom.

"I took care of everything in here. There's more to do in the other rooms," the ashy nurse said in a scolding tone, opening the door and holding it open as though she had rank over Rhonda.

"You first," Rhonda told her.

"I'll be back," the slim nurse said to me. Rhonda exited the room, walking behind the slim ashy nurse. As she did, she flicked the note to the floor.

Seconds later I picked it up. I unfolded it. It said one word: REDVERSE.

I don't know if he was trying to strike some fear in my heart. If he was, he was wasting his time. I don't know him. I don't fear him. I don't fear those cops he's in business with. Fear only Allah.

I washed and prayed the Fajr prayer in cuffs. It took some maneuvering and double the amount of time that it normally takes. But, what a man wants to do, he finds a way to get it done and handles whatever discomforts may come along with it.

Sunrise, not sleeping, thinking sincerely. *I like my lawyer.* I had a feeling about her. I thank Allah for her. I respect her mind. Thought she was one of the smartest women I ever met. Together, last night, without either of us revealing openly what we were actually saying and doing, we plotted a course of action for my defense. She had allowed me to read each of the newspaper articles written about me without my input, interview, or cooperation. She taught me about the process, the meaning of each step, making it clear that each step was critical and crucial and life-altering. She was passionate about representing me. I knew it might include a boost for her career since my case seemed so important to the New York senator, the district attorney's office, and especially the press, the police, and other authorities. I didn't mind if legally defending me made her richer or more famous or whatever. Her presence was worth whatever earnings or notoriety she could squeeze out of it. She was willing to place herself in the center of all of this confusion, which she called a "fercockle," whatever that meant. She would fight against false accusations, police crimes, and filth for her own reasons. She was willing to write the judge, to stand up as my representative in the court at the arraignment. She wasn't worried about pissing off the cops, detectives, prosecution, politicians, and her co-workers in the legal system where she worked every day. She sent me to the hospital with the full intent to document the police brutalities. She was honest enough to tell me that she could not guarantee it would all work out her way or how much time it would take, but that however it worked out, it would be the absolute best option I would ever get. She confided in me that her father is a judge. She has two brothers, one doctor, one lawyer, but she's "closest" to her dead sister, who had been murdered at age six. She was angry that her father's position and prestige could not protect her sister and angry that she remained behind alive. She said her dead twin saved her life when she tried to join her by killing herself. Her sister promised her that if she stayed alive, she would stay with her even though it would be their secret, and no one else would understand.

I didn't try to figure it out. Her purpose for me was legal defense. Besides, I am a Muslim man who believes that believers will always be tested in this life. And, while being tested, no matter how difficult life gets, it is senseless to try and abandon faith. Allah is everywhere. At the same time, Allah is just. At the same time, Allah is above comprehension.

If I didn't know better, I would think that my life was in my lawyer's hands. But I know better. Whatever Allah wills, whatever Allah allows will be done, nothing more or less.

And whether Ayn Eliana Aaronson, Esquire, was assigned by her job or if she chose herself to represent me, I believe it was because that is what was supposed to happen. She might think it was all her idea. I believe otherwise.

Ayn had a calm and clever and scholarly way of speaking and questioning, signaling and profiling me without saying directly that that was what she was doing. Even her suggestions, strategies, and conclusions were not spoken aloud, plainly and straight out.

If I had not already met the most intelligent and cleverest

woman in the world, I might not have ever caught on to the double and triple meanings and behaviors and suggestions of my attorney. However, meeting my second wife's aunt prepared me in some necessary, peculiar, and urgent way for this difficult battle I face. Her name is Aunt Tasha.

# 15. AUNT TASHA • *A Reflection*

Her blue phone rang. We all heard it. It was impossible not to hear it. Chiasa had the ringer on maximum volume so that she would never miss her father's phone call, no matter which room she was in at our house, even if she was in the shower. We were each at the front door just about to leave and all very conscious of making good time.

Akemi, feeling impatient, was standing high in her Valentino Rockstud black sling-back pumps. The subtle tapping of the tip of her gorgeous heels was the only indication that she did not like that Chiasa was holding everyone up. My first wife had an appointment with the director of the Museum of Modern Art. He'd called her as a favor to a VIP donor to the museum. The donor wanted to meet the brilliant sixteen-years-young Akemi to discuss the possibility of privately commissioning her artwork that the museum had featured months ago. She wanted me to escort her. Of course I would, as well as carry her huge portfolio of original drawings and paintings.

Chiasa had dashed to her room and caught the call before there could be a third ring. "Daddy!" we could all hear her say in an excited tone. I smiled and Umma laughed. Akemi watched me closely with her shapely, expressive eyes. Those eyes were like sensors that captured images that her fingers would later sketch and draw from memory. But more than that, her eyes were sensors that recorded feelings as well. This is why her artwork has soul and movement.

You could look at it and feel like you saw her art breathing. Her drawings and paintings of nature seemed to capture the light of the sky and a glimpse of the beauty that Allah created in trees and flowers, mountains and oceans and waterfalls. Akemi was so highly skilled that she could draw something simple, like a chair. When you look at the drawing, you would feel as though you knew the last person who sat in that chair, their size and weight as well as what era the chair came from and how long it had been around.

She had her hair pulled back in a tight bun hidden beneath a mean black fedora. It was her style, and she knocked me out. I was content that she was covered. Her black summer linen skirt and beautiful white linen blouse made her look like a wealthy princess.

She exhaled, slid out of her heels and approached me in the living room where I now stood listening to Chiasa's phone call. Her black eyeliner, drawn on nicely, highlighted her sensual eyes. I hugged her and held her close in my embrace. Umma smiled. She had been smiling a lot lately, and a few times even laughed aloud out of nowhere, refusing to explain herself. My wives did not know why she did, but everyone loves smiles and laughter, so they let it pass. Besides, there was no common spoken language between my Umma and my wives. Umma only spoke Arabic and a few functional English words and sentences. Akemi could not speak in Arabic or English, but she also knew a handful of functional English words. She spoke Japanese, Korean, Chinese, and Thai. Chiasa could speak fluently, comfortably, and confidently in English, Japanese, and French. So my first and second wife shared only one common spoken language. I could speak fluent Arabic, and of course English. I knew a few functional words, phrases, and sentences in Japanese and Korean only because of my love for both wives. Love makes me learn.

I knew why Umma smiled and even why she laughed. She takes me seriously and believes in marriage as a requirement and the only relationship that can be shared between a male and a female that involves sex, babies, and family. At the same time, she thought there was some comedy in watching my wives and me, all teen years young, yet very global. She loved seeing me grow as a man as I attempted to balance two wives, which wasn't easy. Loving them both was easy, but balancing was a separate matter. Umma and my feelings were connected. She knew what I knew. I could not be in two separate places at one time, but I wanted to be. Umma would watch as I worked out the best and right thing to do in each situation. *Don't move too far from the front door. Don't follow Chiasa because I am curious as to what her father is saying now. Don't allow Chiasa to make Akemi and me late to her business meeting. Don't cause Akemi to feel that she is not my first priority. Don't leave Chiasa behind when we were all going out together. Don't forget Naja will be home soon and at the bus stop near our home, where at least one of us is supposed to be standing even before the bus pulls up and lets her off.* To be a son, husband, and brother and the only male in our household was more than a maneuver. A man could not pull it off, work hard, and also maintain peace and pleasure in his household if his love was not deep and genuine. The effort alone requires that.

"*Aafl lui*," Chiasa said—"forgive me" in Arabic—to Umma, using one of the ten Arabic words that Naja had taught her for good manners. Then to Akemi she turned and said, "*Sumimasen*," a Japanese apology. The two wives began speaking to one another in hurried hushed tones in Japanese. I did not interfere in their talk or question Chiasa directly in the presence of Umma or Akemi. I had learned how to handle these domestic situations. My wives had just recently made an agreement. Akemi told Chiasa not to translate between the first wife and her husband. Therefore, when Akemi had anything to convey to me, she would do it the same way she and I had always done it, through our eyes, facial gestures, and body language. Sometimes she would do it through her art, using a random sketch to get her point across, or by her putting my Japanese-to-English flash cards together to form an English sentence that expressed her meaning. Sometimes she would get frustrated and speak fluent Japanese to me, which I could not translate or understand. I could only react to her tones and my intuition. The truth was I loved my relationship with Akemi and the unusual way that we communicated with one another. It made me love her from the start, and that love only increased day by day. Making love to Akemi was like the conversations she and I never had, since we don't share a common spoken language. Making love to one another was one of the languages that both of us performed well, craved, understood, and felt deeply.

I opened the front door so both my wives would catch the message and walk out behind me. They did.

Very late that night, I entered our house. While removing my Nikes, I noticed that the aroma of the dinner we'd had earlier, which was prepared by Akemi on her night to cook, was wafted away by the purifying scent of eucalyptus that drifted from beneath Umma's upstairs bedroom door. Quietly I eased out of the shoulder straps of my North Face backpack, unzipped it, and lifted out two heavy bags of coins, which I had collected from one of my three vending machine locations, the only ones I had not sold off wholesale. I pulled out the money belt that I never wore around my waist, using it as padding in my knapsack instead to keep the coins from shifting around and jingling. My money belt was tightly stacked with dirty one-dollar bills. *Wish they were hundreds*, I thought to myself. *In time* . . . I reassured myself.

I stashed the earnings in the utility closet just for the remainder of the night. Before dawn I would bury half, and after dawn I would bank the other half. That was my method.

Washing off the grime of the streets, the filth of the money, and the soot of the subway in our first-floor half-bathroom, I was preparing myself for a late-night prayer. Cleaning my face, ears, neck, forearms, and calves, I finished by cleaning my feet. It occurred to me to ask Chiasa if she wanted to join me in the prayer. She was the only one in our house whose bedroom was on the first floor. Besides, I adore her.

I knocked; no answer. She must be asleep. I should have turned and headed straight to the living room to make the prayer alone as I had first intended, but other thoughts streamed in and invaded my right mind. I turned her knob, following my curiosity instead. She wasn't in her bed or even in her room. Yet the spring warmth was rushing through her opened window. I had told her when we first moved in not to leave it open or unlocked, even if she was only up chilling in Umma or Akemi or Naja's bedroom. I'd offered her an air conditioner, but she preferred a fan. Now her window was open, her fan was spinning, and she was gone.

As soon as I reached up to shut and lock it, I saw her outside, seated on the railing of our backyard deck. In the black night, at 1 a.m., she was reading a book with a small book light illuminating the words. I stepped out of her window, my feet landing on the deck. I reminded myself that it was just eleven more days until the decorative iron security window guards were installed, preventing any intruder from going in and out of her bedroom window with the ease that she and I had both done.

She smiled. I smiled. She clicked off her little book light and tossed her book, titled *Seven Pillars*, onto a small low outdoor table, which was situated next to where she sat up high. At times she liked speaking to me in the dark, I remembered. After we were first married she was shy about revealing certain feelings. Sometimes she would cover her face with her hand and say, "Don't look at me." Sometimes she would look away when I smiled at her. In the dark she would feel confident to speak and express her rawest emotions.

"I came to get you for the night prayer," I said. I was moving my mind back in a right direction.

"You don't need a reason," she said softly, and jumped over the railing and down into the grass. I walked over and looked. She was turning the metal knob to our garden water hose and rinsing her mouth, splashing her face, dousing her ears and nose.

"C'mon," she said excitedly as she rolled up each pant leg and used the hose to wash her calves and feet. She handed the hose over to me as she pulled out a long scarf that she had woven into her belt loops. She fanned out the wrinkles and quickly wrapped it into *hijab*, covering her hair, neck, and shoulders.

"I'm ready," she said. She's smart and swift. I never have to waste words with her. I rewashed using the hose. Felt I had to because since washing moments ago, my mind had wandered off where it should not have been focused at prayer time. The cold water cooled me down and set it right.

We made *salat*, she standing behind me, beneath the night sky and summer stars in our Queens backyard. Praying out of doors, and in the garden in Sudan, was something my father and I and our family and friends often did.

Many moments later, our prayers completed, Chiasa walked away towards the incomplete wall instead of back towards our house. I just watched her. Suddenly she stopped, turned facing me, and asked, "Could you go stand over there near the deck?" I didn't know what she was up to, but her hypnotic silver-gray eyes were sparkling in the moonlight. I did as she asked. She gestured with her hand and said, "Bend a little, please." The second I reached the squatting position like a wide receiver before the quarterback snapped the football, she ran towards me at top speed, jumped with both feet, and landed on my back, standing. She leaped from my back onto the rail of the deck and was then balancing herself like a tightrope walker as she walked the length of the railing, laughing lightly and covering her mouth to muffle her joy. Coming up the four short steps to walk beside her in case she caught a splinter or fell left or right, my smile broke out naturally, just thinking about her while asking myself the question, *What will she do next*?

"I have to do something," she said. "If you don't want to allow me into your dojo . . . I have to use the whole yard. I'll be out here late night with my sword." She was now gesturing as though she was holding her sword in her hand and using it to charge her rival.

Chiasa knows my heart. She knew I would never bring her into a dojo filled with men, even though she is an expert martial artist and trained ninjutsu fighter. She knew why. Still she had used the art of invisibility to follow me there one evening in her sunglasses and modest disguise. She almost had me blinded until we both ended up paused in a crowd of walkers, gathered on the corner waiting for a green light. Some old woman was crossing at the speed of an infant just learning his first few steps. She dropped one of her two bags and her grapefruits began rolling out. Everyone kept moving except the old lady and my second wife. Not a native New Yorker, she was the only one who eagerly grabbed up the grapefruits and helped the elder, who was still standing in the middle of the street when the green switched to red. Holding the elder's hand, she patiently walked her across, signaling drivers, who still honked and swerved around them. I watched her carefully and waited on the other side.

"Busted," I said to her when she reached safely, after she sent the senior on her way.

"That's not fair!" she said, startled because she was so focused on the woman she did not know her cover was blown.

"How was your day and how was your night? Tell me everything," Chiasa now said, jumping down from the railing and seating herself in her window. She wanted details. I wanted her.

"Everything is smooth," I said.

"So fucking cool," she said under her breath, not resisting or confronting me for ignoring her question. I sat on the floor of the deck, my back leaning against the railing, looking up at her.

"Your phone call?" I asked.

"Oh, Daddy," she said in almost a whisper. "He wants . . ." I was calm and cool in my demeanor, but anxiously waiting to hear what her father *wants now.*

"Two things," she said. "Daddy wants me to instead of doing the pilot's license program like I planned, which takes much less than a year, he wants me to get a bachelor of science degree in Aeronautical Science, which takes four years. He's convinced that I can earn it in three years since I completed four years of high school in three years. Daddy says the degree will give me much better business options." She paused and looked at me.

"And you?" I asked her.

"I just want to fly," she said, extending her arms like the wings of a small jet soaring through the sky. Since the day I met her, sixteen-year-young Chiasa had always made it clear that she planned to become a pilot. When I arrived in Japan, it was just weeks before she was set to begin her flight school training. We fell in love, married, and moved. Now she had spent all day today in the New York Public Library collecting information on flight schools here, so she could compare programs and schools, then select the best one and register and pursue the license here.

"And the second thing?" I asked her.

"I mentioned it before," she said softly. "We've all been so busy . . . But Daddy insists that I go to Harlem this weekend for dinner with Aunt Tasha."

We sat quietly for some time, her in the window, seated, facing out towards the backyard, me still leaning on the railing, facing her. I pulled off my T-shirt. I didn't have to call her over to me. I wanted to touch her. She wanted to be touched. She stepped down from her window seat and sat between my legs, her back leaning against my chest. She removed her *hijab*, her hair brushing against my skin. I touched her up gently, stroking her hair, touching her face and neck and easing my hand lightly over her breasts while her blouse was still on. She caught fever, and turned and began kissing my bare chest with her thick, pretty lips. I touched her chin lightly and her lips parted. Kissing her gently with my lips only at first, I could feel her body warming and her heart beginning to race.

I didn't know what exactly her father was pushing his daughter to do or to be for him. I do know that Chiasa is my wife and I'm about to go in her. If there is not a baby already in her womb, I'm about to give her one.

* * *

A malt-colored Jaguar with a deep chocolate-brown leather interior, the customized license plates said DR. TASHA. The vehicle matched the private brownstone she lived in.

"You didn't tell me your aunt is a doctor," I said to Chiasa.

"She's a psychiatrist," Chiasa answered, casually.

My eyes surveyed the impressive four-story fortress. It was the only home on the Harlem block that featured an American flag flying high on the rooftop. It was clean, untattered, properly mounted, and tilted on an iron flagpole.

Peeping a front and two side entrances, one on the east, the other on the west side of the building, I was figuring there was probably one in the rear as well. In my tradition, a man should approach the front door of the neighbor's house and greet the men of the house first. These were relatives I'd gained through marriage. So, I knew there would be serious differences in our culture. However, I planned to give them the gifts that my Umma and wives prepared, and that I carried in a shopping bag, and after greetings and gifts, I'd be laid-back and easy. *She is already my wife*, so this is not about gaining their approval. Yet, since Chiasa cares so much about Aunt Tasha, who she had been mentioning since the second day we met, I wanted our first meeting to go well, and for my wife to be content and at peace about it.

"She will probably be down in her office," Chiasa said. "That's the side door on the left." We walked around the building. Chiasa's fingers grazed mine and she folded them into my hand. I held her warmly. Our feelings were magnetic. Chiasa rang the bell with her left hand and leaned back into my body as we waited. Maybe she knew or maybe she didn't how her touches, even the lightest or most innocent ones, heated me up so crazy. She must not. Why would she want to get my mood moving in that direction as we stood underneath an arched and secluded deep brown brick entryway, alone? I kissed her neck on impulse. She looked up at me, smiling her beautiful smile. I kissed her lips. The door opened. We straightened up, but neither of us dropped hands.

"Don't allow me to interrupt," Aunt Tasha said, smiling widely. "I've been watching anyway and I see it very clearly. It's really quite powerful."

"Hi, Aunt Tasha!" Chiasa had an excited outburst. She jumped up and hugged her aunt with her left arm and remained holding hands with me with her right.

"Girl, let go of him for one second and embrace me." Chiasa, instead of letting go instantly, looked over and up to me. We stared at one another for some seconds. She pulled my hand, still in hers, and placed both our hands in Aunt Tasha's hand.

"My husband," Chiasa said. Aunt Tasha laughed heartily. It was a laughter laced with love.

"Husband, come in," she said, releasing our hands. I stepped forward and walked in first, Chiasa following behind me. I set the gifts down.

Her office was warm, walls painted in warm colors, a cranberry red in the first room we entered into and I could see a cantaloupe-colored room to the left and a sea-blue green room to the right. The feeling was intimate somehow and calming. Her degrees were mounted on the wall, all four of them. Each was set in an expensive frame, and on each frame there was a small spotlight that made the glass glisten and the black calligraphy of the degree stand out. Tasha Samantha Brown had an undergraduate degree from Florida Agricultural & Mechanical University and a Juris Doctor degree from Yale University; Tasha Samantha Moody, a degree in Medicine from Yeshiva University and one in Forensic Psychiatry from University of California at Los Angeles. I did a double take, rereading the wording of each degree again. It seemed unheard of. She was a doctor and a lawyer, a "super fox," I thought to myself, *a fox and an owl.*

She married after becoming an attorney, either during medical school or right before her forensics degree. I noted her name change. American women drop the last name of either their mother or father and replace it with the last name of their husband. So now I knew her husband's last name is Moody.

A brighter light suddenly switched on, and I turned towards it. The aunt was standing there looking at me. "Are you going to meet me formally?" Aunt Tasha asked me.

"Excuse me, I was meeting you by your degrees." I smiled.

"A million-dollar smile," she said. Then she turned towards Chiasa. "That's how you got stuck. You were trapped right there in his smile. Weren't you?"

"Aunt Tasha!" Chiasa shouted joyfully.

"I'm serious," Aunt Tasha said. "When your father told me that our Chiasa, the beautiful, young, trilingual, brilliant, talented, huge-hearted . . . sixteen-year-old," Aunt Tasha's voice grew louder, emphasizing *sixteen-year-old*, "got married! Oh my God, I thought he must be jesting. But now I see it. Step over here please, young man. Stand beneath this light," she ordered me. I took two side steps, feeling like an interrogated character in a Russian spy novel I had recently read.

"You're handsome enough to get away with murder," she said. Her words sent a wave of chill through me. I didn't know why.

"Aunt Tasha!" Chiasa said. She seemed to be stuck just calling out her favorite aunt's name over and over again.

"Very disarming . . ." Her aunt continued with her study of me. "Charming and ominously cool," she said, and her talk was without laughter, as though she was somehow analyzing me. It felt strange. She was speaking about my looks, but it felt like she was attempting to peer into my soul. I wasn't familiar with the word *ominous.* As soon as she took her attention off from me, I would look it up in the micro-dictionary I sometimes carried in my pocket. I remained calm, wasn't responding or reacting to her compliments. I was used to being admired by all types of women, although I already had a sense that she was unlike any woman I had ever met before.

"What do you know about this man, Chiasa, other than the fact that he's pulchritudinous?" she said, adding another word I'd never heard before in any conversation with any human being.

"I know he overtakes me," Chiasa said. "And whatever I am, he is more," she added. Aunt Tasha's jaw dropped and her right arm went up. She rested her hand on her waistline.

"Hmmm, *overtakes* you," she repeated. "And what else?"

"He makes me feel so good in every way. And . . . I love him . . ." And then Chiasa began speaking in her Japanese tongue, gesturing with her pretty fingers and eyes.

"What have we always told you about speaking Japanese in our house when you know so well that no one who lives here communicates in that language?"

"I'm sorry, Aunt Tasha, but I couldn't describe in English words that feeling I wanted you to feel and understand so well. I thought maybe if you listened to the Japanese expressions, even if you did not understand them literally, you could feel their meaning. That's what we do at home," Chiasa explained.

"At home?" her aunt repeated.

"Yes, where my husband and our family live."

"And where is that, because three months ago you lived in Tokyo!"

"Queens, New York," Chiasa shared.

"Your light is getting hot," I interjected.

"Pardon me?" Aunt Tasha asked.

"The lamp you have me standing under, the heat is intensifying," I said. She reached up and switched it off.

"And what do you know about our Chiasa?" she asked me. I smiled.

"Don't smile at Aunt Tasha!" Chiasa said playfully. "She's going to think that your smile is the only reason I wanted to marry you."

"Please take a seat," Aunt Tasha told me. I sat down in a majestic maroon chair made of thick leather and upholstered expertly. *A few thousand was dropped on that chair easy, maybe even ten*, I thought to myself as I tried to become comfortable being examined by a forensic psychiatrist in her office, on her turf, playing by her terms.

"Chiasa, you will know best what your husband likes. Please go upstairs and get him something cool to drink."

"Yes, Aunty," Chiasa complied. But first, she stooped to remove my Gucci loafers from my feet. "They don't, but we do," she whispered to me. I noted that she had already removed her shoes. She set mine at the side entrance. Then she dashed up the stairs and into the house. Now I was left alone with her aunt. She stepped to her doctor's desk, opened a drawer, and handed me some pages. I didn't look at what it was, just looked at her, a silent inquiry.

"It's like a Rubik's Cube," she said to me. "See what you can do with it." She handed me a pen. I looked it over, didn't feel pressed, and filled it out. Just a bunch of diagrams, math problems, and trick questions, but it didn't ask me for any of my personal information so I was cool with it. Soon as I was done I stood up and laid it on her desk, where she was seated looking at a magazine.

"Do you know how Chiasa likes her beef prepared?" her aunt asked me strangely, looking up and closing her magazine.

"Chiasa does not eat beef," I answered, and sat back down in her hot seat.

"Do you know Chiasa's favorite fruit?"

"An onion, which she eats like it's an apple," I said truthfully. Her aunt clapped.

"Do you know Chiasa's best friend?" She kept quizzing me.

"A horse, called Koinichi," I answered.

"Do you know Chiasa's best skill?"

"The sword," I said easily.

"Do you know what Chiasa hates the most?" she asked me. I leaned forward.

"Anyone who tries to stick their hand in someone's else love story and change the direction of her fate." I was quoting my wife. Aunt Tasha was taken aback by that point. I could see how her eyes widened a bit and she leaned forward.

"Even you did not know that one, did you?" I asked her calmly. She cleared her throat and did not answer my question. Yet, she continued questioning me.

"What does Chiasa fear the most?" she asked, growing more serious.

"Boredom," I said.

"Who does Chiasa love the most?" she asked.

"Her father," I said.

"What does Chiasa like the most?"

"It wouldn't be right for me to answer you truthfully about that," I said solemnly. And just the thought about the answer caused movement in me. Aunt Tasha gave me a half smile and said, "Is that so?" Her eyebrow lifted the same way my second wife's eyebrow lifts when she is thinking too hard about a complicated matter or surprised about something.

"One thing I see that is different from what I suspected is . . ." Aunt Tasha began, "Is that you are more deeply in love with our Chiasa than any of us would have imagined. It is not anything that you said to me right here and now. It's not even your responses to my inquiries. I could see it in your eyes even through my upstairs window and immediately thereafter, through my side-door peephole. We thought you had stolen only her heart, and that perhaps she had lost her mind and her way because of it. But I see that the two of you are thoroughly and deeply invested into each other. That's one huge plus on your side. And believe me, our family does not hand out stars easily." I didn't know what she meant by that.

"Is your husband home?" I asked her. "I'd feel more comfortable if I could greet him first."

"Clementine is on his way. He will be here shortly. And, you are right, perhaps I should save all of my questions and share each of my observations when our whole family is here for dinner. That would be better for you than repeating yourself to each of us separately," she said.

Chiasa walked down the stairs like a quiet feline, with a glass of pineapple juice in her hand. She looked at me, looked at her aunt, and then back at me.

"How would you like to be addressed? What should we call you?" Aunt Tasha asked me, breaking the awkward silence and almost pretending that she had not already asked me a series of personal questions.

"Midnight!" Chiasa said in an exasperated voice. "Let's start with that. He's comfortable with that name," Chiasa said, before I said my true name. My wife set the pineapple juice down on a coaster on the marble tabletop beside me. She unfolded a warmed cloth and wiped my hands clean with it, then handed me the glass. "Enjoy," she said softly.

I would do whatever Chiasa suggested. She never called me Midnight. When she first met me she discovered my true name. She had seen it on my passport as we both processed through customs, coming off the same flight. Yet she chose to call me by a Japanese name that she felt described me the way that she saw me. That name is Ryoshi, and in Japanese, the Kanji for that name means "the hunter." She must have had a reason to introduce me to her Japanese grandfather back then as "Ryoshi, the Hunter," and for introducing me now as Midnight. She and I are both ninjas, so I would go along with her lead with her family. I know she is smart and swift.

"Midnight it is," Aunt Tasha said. "An unusual name for a prodigious young man." That marked the third word I would need to look up—*ominous*, *pulchritudinous*, and now *prodigious.* I made a mental note of all three.

"Show him around the house, Chiasa, so that he can make himself at home until your cousins and uncle arrive for dinner on time, I hope."

"Do you want me to?" Chiasa asked me.

"I'm gonna chill right here until your uncle arrives. That's the best thing for me to do," I said.

Aunt Tasha smiled, and stood up and excused herself. Chiasa

walked over to me and sat down in my lap. Leaning her body against me, her face close to mine, she said softly, "Aunt Tasha is good. I know she asks a lot of questions, but she means well." She kissed my face.

"You want to get loved up in your aunt's office?" I was looking at her.

"You want the truth?" she asked me, smiling. We both laughed.

Her aunt's library was across from her office on the same floor, where she also had two "consultation rooms" for her psychiatry private practice.

"Your aunt brings mentally ill patients into the same house where her family lives?" I asked Chiasa.

"She used to, not anymore. But people with mental illnesses are not all serial killers," Chiasa defended.

"All you need is one serial killer in the house. If you let one in, it won't matter that all of the rest of her patients are very nice crazy people."

"Oh stop!" She hit me. "If one of her patients was a serial killer, Aunt Tasha would know it! She's really a smart lady. You saw all of her degrees."

"A lawyer and a doctor," I said. "And a forensic psychiatrist. Something big must have motivated her. Do you think she read all of the books in this library?" We were standing in the center of the room and each wall was covered from floor to ceiling with books neatly organized. Not paperback novels, mostly hard-covered thousand-page textbooks, and all was nonfiction.

"Yes, most of them. But some of them she probably just skimmed through and highlighted the important parts, like when you are studying for an exam," Chiasa explained. At that moment, I thought about how all of my exams had been in real-life challenges, in becoming strong, in dealing with these streets I walk on and travel through each day and night, in protecting Umma and Naja, in building and expanding our family business, and in maintaining my women and training my body. I read books, had always been a big reader since I was real young. However, I had never read books like the ones on her shelf. I had never even seen titles like the long scientific titles I was scanning now. Since leaving the Sudan, I had not been a formal student in a formal school. I had not obtained any certificates of completion or graduation in America.

I heard a truck pull up in the driveway.

"What are you thinking about?" Chiasa asked.

"Just checking it out," I said.

"Chee!" a male voice yelled out from upstairs. "We all here," he called out, sounding anxious. I could hear several sets of keys jingling.

Clementine Xavier Moody stood six foot one in height and had his four sons lined up in a row to meet me in what appeared to be their large living room. His wife, Aunt Tasha, wasn't in the lineup. She was leaning on the wall next to the fireplace behind the men, like an owl on its branch, observing, learning, and controlling all at once. I walked up the stairs from her office first. Chiasa was close behind me. I didn't like that I was in my socks and her uncle and his sons were all standing in their shoes indoors.

I walked past the sons directly to her uncle and introduced myself.

"Good evening, Mr. Moody, I'm Midnight." I shook his hand.

"My husband!" Chiasa burst out. The men all laughed tight laughs.

"Welcome, son," Mr. Moody said to me.

"He's Dr. Moody," Chiasa said. "Or Uncle Clem!" she corrected herself. "And these are my cousins: Junior, Marcus, Martin, and Xavier." I gave each of them a pound. They were Harlem dudes. The oldest one, Junior, was sizing me up. I took him to be about twenty-four or twenty-five. The youngest seemed about seventeen. Each of them was in good shape. The cat Marcus looked like he might be a boxer. I could see it in his physique and posture. I was in my Brooklyn stance, my martial arts frame of mind, just scheming out if I had to fight each one of them for any reason.

"Brooklyn, right?" Marcus asked me.

"You know," I said quietly.

"What's this kind of talk?" Aunt Tasha had intercepted the male mood. "I had some good help with dinner; let's all wash our hands and sit at the table like civilized folk," she issued her subtle order.

The dinner spread was a feast: peanut soup, salad, choices of steak or chicken or jumbo shrimp. There were plenty of sides—green beans, okra, macaroni and cheese, mashed potatoes, and stewed tomatoes. Biscuits were piled high, and gravy was available in a sterling silver server at each end of the table.

Dr. Moody sat at the head of the table and his wife at the opposite end. There were three seats on each side between them. I sat on one side next to Dr. Moody. His eldest son, Junior, sat across from me. Chiasa sat beside me and the other brothers fell in wherever they fit.

"Bless the table please, honey," Aunt Tasha said. Dr. Moody and his wife bowed their heads. Dr. Moody began the prayer. His sons watched me and I watched them. Chiasa nudged me. We both said, "*Bismillah*" over our food together at the same time.

"What does that mean, Chee?" Marcus asked my wife.

" 'In the name of Allah,' " I answered him.

"So Chee, are you really a Muslim now?"

"Yes," Chiasa said confidently.

"Where did you meet our Chiasa?" Aunt Tasha asked me.

"In the sky," was all I said. Chiasa smiled.

"On a flight to Japan," Chiasa explained.

"Were you part of the martial arts tournament Chee was in?" Xavier asked.

"Nah," I said. "I wasn't."

"What was your business in Japan?" Her uncle questioned me with a seriousness that went deeper than the seriousness that was already in the air. Chiasa's knee nudged me. She did not want us to start off by telling her family about my first wife, which was the only reason that I had traveled to Japan. She had requested that we get over the first few steps, which included meeting them, letting them get accustomed to the fact that we were married teens, and that she, who spent all of her time in America with her African-American Christian family, was now a Muslim. "That would be enough for the first visit," she had said. I told Chiasa, "I won't lie about Akemi. She is my first wife. But I can agree to not volunteer any information about her on our first visit. Afterwards, they're just going to have to accept her, or we will have to separate from them." Chiasa said, "I know, but it would be better for us all to be together as family and friends than to be separate. And on our next visit I will definitely invite Akemi and hope that she will come along." I agreed.

"I have a vending business that started in Japan," I said to Dr. Moody, avoiding a lie by stating a truth.

"Is that right. Why Japan?" he asked.

"Their vending machines are built superior and they distribute a greater variety of products through vending than here in America."

"So did your ticket happen to lead you to the seat right next to our Chiasa on the flight?" Aunt Tasha asked.

"No. She was seated up front in a different section with all of the females from her martial arts team," I said. I could feel that these people wanted and were fully prepared to press and squeeze me for the details.

"So don't tease us! Tell us how you first met. What did you say? What did she say?"

"I didn't say anything to her. She didn't say anything to me. But when I looked at her, I thought I saw *Jannat* in her eyes."

"*Jannat*?" Xavier repeated.

"Heaven," Chiasa translated softly. "It means 'heaven' in Arabic." Now they each stared at me. Aunt Tasha leaned back and exclaimed, "Oh my sweet Jesus!" Marcus looked at me like he wanted to go a few bare-knuckled, bare-fisted rounds with me. I was game.

"Dr. Moody, what's your business?" I asked him. Everyone turned even more quiet. I really wanted to know. I also was bent on changing the direction of the questioning and moving myself out of the focus.

"I'm a consultant," he said. Now he was being vague and secretive, same as me.

"What does a consultant do?" I pressed him. I really didn't know.

"Well, son, if you get a good education and study hard and master one or two areas of knowledge, you can become an expert. Once you reach a high level of expertise, instead of a standard or even an administrative job, major corporations, public and private business entities will come to you to license your expertise for a period of time. Depending on how good you are, you can set your fees at an astronomically high rate and charge these companies for your time, instead of being a salaried worker who's part of the daily nine-to-five rat race." He dipped his biscuit in his gravy and added, "And then you can afford all of this," waving one hand in the air as though to say that's why he can afford four sons, a wife, plenty of gravy, and a beautiful home. I also caught his unspoken questions to me. I believed he was inferring, "Can you afford our Chiasa? What kind of an education do you have? Are you an expert in anything? Can you house our Chiasa? Can you afford to finance children when you are so young and not yet fully established?" I caught it all.

"Are you a student?" Aunt Tasha asked me.

"I'm a businessman—vending, textiles, import and export," I said confidently.

"That's a good way to put it." Marcus laughed and his brothers snickered.

"Legal business exclusively," I said. It shut them down for a second. "How about you?" I reversed it.

"I'm at West Point Military Academy. September starts my senior year. My brother Junior graduated from Rensselaer Polytechnic Institute with his master's. He's a chemical engineer with the Dow

Chemical Corporation. Martin here just graduated from Princeton. He's about to head off to Georgetown Law School come September. And my little bro Xavier is planning to follow in Chee's footsteps and become a pilot." He looked at me like he thought he had just dropped a bomb on my head.

"Chiasa!" Marcus said in a tone with too much authority for a guy who was not her father or her husband. "You're still planning to fly, aren't you?" It was a question, but he actually said it like a demand. So, I interjected.

"Sounds good. By the time all of you fellas are through getting an education, I'll have more than enough capital. All four of you can come work for me," I said. Dr. Moody laughed a deep and hearty laugh and his wife began laughing also. Chiasa was smiling. I wasn't, and neither was Marcus or his brothers.

"But you do know that education is important, don't you?" Aunt Tasha asked me, as her laughter evaporated. "Part of our social adjustment is hinged on education. We've all read the classics, like the entire Shakespeare collection, Langston Hughes, Edgar Allan Poe's work, James Baldwin, and of course there are two must-read novels that come to mind: F. Scott Fitzgerald's *The Great Gatsby* and *Catcher in the Rye*, written by J.D. Salinger. Every American has to read those two in high school."

"This boy doesn't need Shakespeare. He just told us he saw *Jannat* in our Chiasa's eyes. He's a poet. Besides, Shakespeare's Juliet was only thirteen and Romeo not much older than her when they married after only knowing one another for one day. If he reads Shakespeare it might reinforce this boy's ideas," Dr. Moody said, half joking, half serious.

"Yes, but Romeo and Juliet committed suicide," Chiasa said. "Our love is not like theirs. We bypassed our obstacles. We are young and married already, and our love is awesome." She silenced them.

"I believe it is," Aunt Tasha said. "But that's not what we are discussing."

"What are we discussing?" I asked, and Aunt Tasha paused.

"I think we are all shocked. It is nothing against you at all. We held Chiasa in our arms when she was a newborn. She lived in Japan, but whenever she traveled to America, I raised her like she was my daughter and so did her uncle. My sons love Chiasa and grew up beside her over the years when she visited the States." She inhaled, then exhaled as though she had run a marathon. But she was just talking while seated. It obviously meant a lot to her.

"We saw her *just a couple of months ago* and she was the same girl she has always been, really beautiful, super intelligent, swift and joyful, and single."

"She still is," I said. "Really beautiful, super intelligent, swift and joyful. The only difference is, now, she is my wife, by choice. Not by force."

"But you are disregarding the elephant in the room," Aunt Tasha said. "This past Christmas, Chiasa and our entire family were guests at the Christmas Eve service in the Abyssinian Baptist Church, right here in Harlem. That was seven months ago. Now we are told that she is Muslim. All of these changes happened so dramatically, so swiftly, we are shocked, and I think we need to hear something moving and true to help each of us get comfortable with this idea." She exhaled.

"Your brother is Chiasa's father, true?" I asked Dr. Tasha.

"Absolutely!" she said.

"He handed his daughter to me."

"Fucking impossible," Marcus growled.

"I sincerely hope that's moving and true enough for you. A father has that right, doesn't he? Even her Japanese grandfather agreed," I said, shifting the weight onto the men in my wife's family, where in my tradition it belonged. A daughter goes from the hand of her father to the hand of her husband.

"That's moving enough for me," Dr. Moody said solemnly. "He made it out of Japan with the General's daughter. That couldn't have been easy." He chuckled, a sinister sound. "Matter of fact, I'm sure he's making it sound a lot easier than it was," he said, continuing his bass-tone sarcasm and laughter. "Besides, our Chiasa is wearing a clear, two-karat pear-shaped diamond wedding ring and seven diamond bracelets. She wasn't wearing those three months ago. That takes more than emotion. That takes commitment and capital. I think this young man is moving and serious," he said, downshifting me from "son," to "this boy" and then promoting me to "young man."

"I enjoyed the food," I complimented Aunt Tasha.

"It's catered by Copeland's, right here in Harlem," she said with a hint of frustration.

"Aunt Tasha," Chiasa said softly. "Remember how you guys used to tease me about how Japanese I was, and how I was so shy and subdued and wouldn't do the same things as you all did? Marcus spent a whole summer trying to teach me how to yell when I'm angry and what to say and how to curse people out when they deserved it."

Everyone laughed. They must have been remembering. "Well also, there were the times all of us would go to church, and you would ask me if I felt the spirit of Jesus and I would always say 'no,' and then apologize to you. Remember the lady who jumped up in the middle of the sermon and burst out in tears and began running back and forth in the aisles of the church and speaking some weird language, and you all told me she was 'speaking in tongues'? Then she broke out of her trance and collapsed! Does everybody remember?" Chiasa asked and a few of them mumbled, "Yes." Xavier laughed.

"Well, I think back then there was something missing inside of me. I don't know if it was missing because my mom and my grandparents and everyone on my mom's side is Japanese and they don't really have a religion, or for some other reason. But I knew it was missing. I desperately wanted to find that feeling. When Midnight and I first met, he was fasting from food and water. He told me that he was a Muslim. I could see that he was really handsome and beautiful and I liked that and all of that was obvious. But the idea that he was not having food and water for thirty days, each day until sunset and before sunrise, fascinated me. It wasn't a diet or a plan to grab first place in a competitive tournament or anything like that. It was a complete humbling. It was a way for him to express his thanks to the One who made his soul, not in simple words like thank you or *arigato gozaimas*, which we can all say even when we are not sincere, but through action and restraint and discipline and sacrifice. I loved that. I thought that was incredible. No one would do that in the blinding shine and intense heat of the Japanese sun that rises up so early. And I know it's scary to you guys, but I also know that it shouldn't be. Allah is the Maker of all of our souls, even the Maker of the souls of each of our prophets, including Jesus. The prophets were all human beings after all, right?" She glanced around the table. In her eyes was both her sincerity and her apprehension. She loved her family and didn't want to lose them. She really wanted them to understand.

"He didn't preach to me or ask me to do anything that he was doing. It was the beauty of the example he was setting for me by simply doing what he believed, that struck me," Chiasa said warmly.

"Now you know I love books. So I did some research and discovered the Holy Quran. I began reading it and I fell in love with the rhythm of the words, the meaning of the words, and what felt like the force behind the words. I'll admit, I began reading not at the beginning. I began with the chapter named 'The Women.' I thought it was great that it said 'Allah created man and woman from one soul.' That alone blew me away.

"And when I saw him pray, he went from standing upright to bowing slightly to going down on his knees and ultimately to pressing his forehead to the ground in what we call a full *sajdah.* Seeing that caused a shift inside of me and I could really honestly finally feel my soul move. The strongest feeling I experienced was that *this felt like the truth.* And more importantly, that it felt like what *I should be doing* also. Not for him, but for my soul." She looked around the table at her relatives to see if they could feel her words and how they would react. I knew it was very important to her that she say the truth without hurting any of her cherished relationships.

Everyone's reaction was the same—pure silence.

"Aunt Tasha, it was you who used to encourage me to read the Bible stories. Remember the story of Solomon and Sheba? Each of them had their own kingdoms, territories and riches and armies, and so on. They did not even know one another. Now I find that I am similar to Sheba. She came from a great land, was loved and had everything she wanted. But, she came from a people who worshipped the sun.

"Like Sheba, I came from a great land, Japan, a great language, a great culture of arts and literature and lifestyle, except Japanese people do not worship God. In Japan we can wake up each day for thousands of days and years and bow before family, friends, statues, and co workers, and even complete strangers, but never, ever bend our knees to say a prayer to the One who gave us life. When Solomon heard news of the powerful Queen Sheba who had everything, and who was a ruler in her own right, but that Sheba and her people did not worship Allah, he was saddened by it. How could any king or queen or nation or people not worship the One who created their souls, gave them life, and also created the sun and the moon and the stars and the skies and the heavens and the mountains and the oceans and the universe? Solomon sent Sheba a letter by a courier bird. The bird dropped the letter at the feet of Sheba. When she read the letter that Solomon wrote urging her and her people to worship only Allah, she did not know how to react. She had her pride and so did her advisors. The men in the council that surrounded her, whose opinions she respected, wanted her to go to war against Solomon for suggesting that such a great queen and her people of great wealth and prosperity should bow down. Sheba overruled these men. She said it was better to go take a look at and a listen to Solomon, and to then consider the truth and the weight of his words. She went. She saw. She bowed down, not to Solomon, but to Allah. My husband is my Solomon, so to speak. He delivered to me the message to bow down to Allah just by being himself. And a girl who thought she had everything before really does have everything now. And I have it in the right order, thankfully. Allah is One—my faith, my man, my family, and the community of everyone and anyone who is striving to live true."

"But you are not turned against us now that you believe that way, are you?" Xavier asked her.

"Of course not!" Chiasa smiled. "We will always be family. And goodness gracious, I humbled myself before God, and I got married, but I can still ride my horse and wield my sword, and fly my planes!" She was getting excited!

"And push your Kawasaki!" Marcus said.

"And come to the family celebration on July Fourth like every year," Martin said.

"And play the piano," Aunt Tasha added.

After dinner, I could sense by the way things were moving that they didn't want to let go of my wife. Her aunt was seated beside her on the piano bench in their piano room as Chiasa played and her family shouted out different songs they wanted to hear, from Beethoven to Joplin. Aunt Tasha's sister-in-law arrived with her grown daughter. Now there were four women and six men in the house, which made it less tense. Or maybe it just caused a delay in the confrontation of men.

"Dr. Moody, I'd like to make a phone call if you don't mind," I said.

"You can use my office. It'll be quiet in there," he said. I followed him out of the piano room and down a corridor. He unlocked his office with a key, I noted. He opened the door and pointed to the phone. "It's not long distance, is it, son?"

"No sir. If it was, I'd pay you for it up front." I smiled.

"Don't touch my papers," he said.

"No problem. Thank you."

I pulled out a phone card; I didn't want even the local call to appear on their bill. "Umma," I began speaking in Arabic. I was just checking on her and Naja. Afterwards, I asked to speak to my first wife.

"Akemi," I said.

"*Hai*," she said softly.

"You good?" I asked her.

"*Hai*," she said softly.

"What are you doing?"

"Music," she said softly. Then she exhaled. "I wait. You come," she said. I smiled.

"You wait, I'll definitely come home to you," I promised her, still smiling. When I looked up, Marcus was standing there in the office doorway. "Akemi, *aishiteru*," I said and hung up.

"Look like you want something," I said to Marcus because of his grimace.

"We gon' fight," he said. "But not in this house."

"Just you, or all four?" I asked him.

"Me first," he said.

"You first? You must already know you gonna lose," I told him and smiled.

"Think whatever you wanna think. I'll let my hands do the talking," he said.

"Yeah, money, whatever, wherever, whenever. You call it," I told him.

His father stepped up behind him. "You done, son?" he asked me.

"Yes sir," I responded. He put his hand on Marcus's shoulder and asked him, "Did you tell the young man we're headed to the club?"

"I was just about to," Marcus said.

"The men are all headed to the health club for a workout, swimming, basketball, racquetball, weight lifting, steam room, sauna—whatever your thing is. You're invited," Dr. Moody said, taking over what he had obviously sent Marcus to say and do. Marcus had taken it on himself to eavesdrop instead.

"In Harlem?" I asked. I had never seen no facility like that up here and I been through Harlem more than a few times and even check a barber out this way from time to time. Dr. Moody laughed.

"Harlem's got everything a man who can afford it needs. It's a private club. You can come in on our membership, VIP pass," he offered.

"I definitely want to. But the women got me out of my Nikes, and into my loafers for the night. Plus, I'm wearing a suit. I'm just not prepared. Maybe next time," I said, regretting not having my usual "ready for all sports, ready for war" wear. Marcus looked glad that I couldn't come, on one hand, and mad that he couldn't try and get at me, on the other. They both turned and walked out and I followed, shutting the door behind me. He better know I wasn't stalling on our battle, I thought. I'd fight him. I already knew I wouldn't hurt him bad and that he wouldn't hurt me, either. He's a son who does not want to disappoint his mother or his girl cousin. I am the same. Yet we are men, and sometimes we gotta rough each other up and knock each other out for no right reason. Just to prove who's dominant.

When the three of us men walked up into the den where the others were all gathered now, Chiasa stopped talking with the women and stared at me like she knew something. Aunt Tasha was staring at her husband, then at her son, then at me.

"What?" all three of us men said at the same time.

"The house is quiet now. Normally I would have gone to the club as well. It's a really relaxing end to an arduous workweek," Aunt Tasha said.

"Is the club for men and women?" I asked.

"Oh yes! They have something for everybody. I prefer a rough game of racquetball, a steam shower, and the massages. Chiasa, next time you and I will get massaged. But of course for children sixteen through eighteen, because you are not legally adults, I would have to sign a waiver and pay the membership visitors fee on your behalf. Under sixteen, you can't even get in."

I caught that she thinks that young people ages sixteen through eighteen are "children."

"I hope that you won't mind if I use this opportunity to steal my niece away from you for a while. I'd like to share a few words with her, 'girl talk,'" she said.

"What will he do?" Chiasa interjected swiftly. "I haven't even given him the tour of the house yet."

"For now, show him to the 'room of games.' He will probably like that. My sons love that room in particular. Then you and I can talk downstairs in my office," Aunt Tasha said to my wife.

"Your office, Aunt Tasha! I'm not a patient!" Chiasa protested sweetly.

"Don't worry about me. I'm good," I told my wife, to calm her.

"Do you play pool? You must like music," her aunt asked me.

"Actually, I'd like to take a closer look at some of the books you have in your library," I said to her aunt.

"Great then, I can show you 'the room of books.' It's our family library. That will keep you occupied for quite some time. Then, Chiasa and I can meet upstairs in my bedroom as we usually would," she said, making it clear that she didn't want me to be close to wherever her private meeting with my wife was taking place.

"It's there," she said, pointing me towards the family library as she led Chiasa up the stairs. But then, something began beeping. She lifted her blouse slightly, revealing the Metromedia pager on the waistband of her pants.

"Awful timing!" she said, sucking her teeth. "Don't leave," she told Chiasa. "I'll call in and come right back."

Chiasa stood midway up the stairs, looking me over. Her eyes lit up at our being left alone. In less than two and a half seconds, she was standing right beside me. "Unwrap me," she requested, her eyes sparkling. "There's no one here in the house except you and me and Aunt Tasha," she whispered. "And when Aunt Tasha's pager goes off, either she comes right back in three or so minutes or thirty minutes or three hours." I just looked at her, my mind already shifting and my heated heart heating higher. "You don't want to?" she asked me.

"I don't want to what?" I was watching her pretty lips move as she spoke, and her white teeth. And, I was warming her up by making her wait. Naïve at times, the look in her eyes changed as though she really believed that I somehow "didn't want to." She raised her hand to remove her *hijab.* The jingle of her bangles beneath the sleeves of her dress aroused me. I caught her arm, stopping her from removing her *hijab.*

"Now, it's three minutes," I said to her as I moved in closer and began to unwrap her. I felt her breathing. That aroused me more. *Hijab* removed, her two long braids holding her thick natural hair in place, I began to unwrap those too.

"That feels good," she said once her braids were free. She bent over and shook her loosened hair like a member of a crazy rock band. "Wait till Aunt Tasha sees this," she said, smiling. "She'll be insisting on cornrowing my hair. That would take forever." I didn't say nothing back. She looked like a she-lion with a majestic mane. Cornrowed, she'd look like an exotic lynx. Either way, I could feel that with her uncle and cousins gone, and her *hijab* removed, she felt even more comfortable and free. Purposely I watched her to see how she orchestrated her next move. She was staring at me, her eyes dancing.

"Come on, I'll show you around." She walked close to me, gently taking her *hijab* from my hand and placing it on the table. She linked her fingers with mine. Such a simple thing, but I could feel the electricity racing through my blood.

"This is the room of games," she said as we entered. "The family library is across the hall. But now that I'm here with you, you can play with me." She smiled. "Finish unwrapping me," she pleaded. I squatted down below the hem of her long skirt and raised it up to her hips. She gasped, but then covered up her sound. When my hands reached her pretty thighs, I rolled down her thigh-highs, slowly removing them both so her legs would be free. She sat down on the floor so I could pull them all the way off.

"The carpet in here feels nice," she said, her pretty unpolished toes wiggling in the fibers. I left her sitting there on the floor on purpose. I walked around, checking out the official-size pool table. It hogged up most of the space in the room. Still, there was enough space around the whole perimeter to angle for any kind of shot. Chiasa leaped up, picked up a pool stick from the wall mount. I didn't. I wasn't about to get into a game that wasn't my game with the sharpshooter, marksman's daughter who has perfect vision and works all the angles with her knives and swords and bamboo sticks. I was ignoring her. Instead, I was checking out the small-framed photos of her African-American family. Mostly males on the wall at different ages in their lives, and the flicks alternated from military uniforms to graduation gowns and funny flat hats. Aunt Tasha's sons appeared to have been in some kind of military-type uniform from when they were young boys. I took note of the fact that there was not one photo of Chiasa's father, "the General." Even in her house in Tokyo she had a wall of photos with no photos of her favorite person in the world. I wasn't in the mood to think deeply about him, even though it was obvious that their whole family had to have some reason that he was not to be photographed or displayed. He could be mentioned, acknowledged briefly, but not discussed.

In the corner was an arcade machine, the same kind that would be in a real arcade. It had Space Invaders, Pac-Man, Asteroids, and Centipede—a four-in-one.

"You don't have to put quarters in it to make it work," Chiasa said, squeezing herself in between me and the machine. I was just feeling the feeling. She pushed play for two players and the Pac-

Man theme music blasted on, and she began to wiggle the joystick around. I pressed up close on her from behind.

"That's cheating," she said, and turned around to face me.

"You're about to get eaten," I warned her. But she wouldn't turn back to her screen. I kissed her gently. As we both heard the withering sound of her man getting gobbled in the game, we laughed.

"Kiss me with your tongue," she asked softly. My blood boiling now, I smiled. This is what Chiasa likes most of all, deep tonguing and sucking, something that Aunt Tasha would never know. Neck and nipples, she was getting dragged in deep simply from my touch.

"You want me to stretch you out on your uncle's pool table?" I asked her. She didn't answer, but her eyes revealed that she thought that was a sensual idea. I was imagining her already lying there bare-assed with her pretty butt pressed on the plush green felt canvas. She began removing my suit jacket and laid it on the pool table, stuffing her thigh-highs in the inside jacket pocket. Then she began unbuttoning my white dress shirt. I smiled.

"Luckily you are not wearing a tie. I'd use it to tie you up and make you my hostage." She smiled, looking like she believed she could.

"I don't wear ties," I told her. "But if I knew you were gonna tie me up, I would've put one on."

"Come, let me show something." She linked two fingers into mine and led me out the room of games into the corridor and then into the family library. Standing in front of a wall of books she said, "Lift me up. I want to sit on your shoulders." I squatted down so she could climb on me. "Okay, stand up slowly," she said in her soft, excited voice. I leapt up fast and she shook and gripped me. "You never follow instructions!" She laughed, steadying her balance on my shoulders.

"Move closer," she requested.

"Closer to the bookshelf?" I asked, then stepped in. She reached up and grabbed a big hardcover book off the shelf. "I could've gotten that for you," I said. "Instead you're causing all this acrobatic . . ."

She leaned in and the wall of books opened up, revealing a slim entrance. She jumped down.

"Push the wall in." She pointed. I pushed. She hugged me from behind. We stepped into a dark corridor. "Sshh . . ." she said, but I wasn't speaking. She used her hand to feel around the wall. I thought she was searching for a light switch. But then I heard the sound of the bookshelf closing behind us. Now we were trapped in a narrow darkened space. I could feel her but couldn't see her. Then, I felt her energy walking away. I stepped forward to follow her energy, but stepped on something. I felt it out with my foot. It was fabric. I left it there and sped up my walk until I felt her presence, then reached out and grabbed her.

"Crazy girl." I kissed her. "You're naked," I said.

"Well then," she said softly. "Stop teasing me and fuck me right." Her dirty talk, the curses she didn't use to know and wouldn't ever say, she now used comfortably. We were tonguing. Her hands were moving all over my chest and arms, shirt long gone. I took her hands and raised them over her head and her body was pressed against the wall. The sound of our breathing was echoing in the empty narrow space and even the sound of the moisture of our kiss was amplified. I let one hand down and placed my hand over the silk of her panty. As I massaged that moist cloth over that warm, intimate space, I felt her fingers on my joint, her hand skillfully removing my belt and opening my pants. She wanted to feel skin, not the Armani fabric or the impression.

Her body was lifted in the air, pressed against the wall, and I was moving in and out of her. Her pussy muscles were gripping my joint, so warm and moist and tight that my joint was pulsating. It burst and shot up in her. Felt so good I lost my grip, and her body was sliding down the wall and hit the floor with a thump. I dropped down. We were both breathing like crazy, inhaling, exhaling, lying on the floor. She began laughing.

"Did that hurt?" I asked her.

"That felt so good," she said, then rolled around and climbed on top of me. My head so blown over this woman, she was kissing me with those thick lips all over my face and her whole body was oven warm. We were both completely naked in a dark space. I was loving the feeling but asking myself, *What are you doing in this woman's uncle's house*? Yet I could not stop, or shift back into discipline mode.

"You want some more?" I asked her, but I already knew. She was sucking my chest and her hands were roaming again. She didn't answer anything, just breathing. I flipped her sideways, palmed her titty and caught her nipple between two fingers. I brought my mouth over and sucked it. She wrapped her leg around me and began humping my leg. I knew she was using my thigh to rub her clitoris and liked the feeling of that friction. I lay her on her back and mounted her, pushing in hard, and she made a sensuous sound.

"Chiasa," her aunt called out. Her voice was faint, though. It could hardly be heard. "Don't stop," Chiasa whispered in my ear and squeezed my butt with both her hands. That ignited me. I pushed up in her again. She kept squeezing. I kept thrusting. Our breathing was so loud it seemed it had to be heard on the other side of the wall. I was moving over her. She was moving beneath me, until she cried out and her pussy muscles fluttered wildly. I didn't bust yet, I could hold it longer the second time around. So I sped up my grind, got overwhelmed by the sensation, until I exploded inside of her and collapsed over her body.

"I love you," she said softly. I pulled her hair, kissed her mouth, and said, "I love you too."

It wasn't until minutes later, when we eased out of the fog of our funk, that we both began to think clearly. We were seated side by side with our backs against the wall. Still couldn't see each other in the dark.

"Your aunt is looking for us."

"I know."

"This is a good hideout. But, she's gonna find the trail of your clothes from the striptease that you did to lure me in here," I said.

"Oh stop, I didn't." She slapped my knee.

"What is this place?" I asked her.

"It's the sealed servants' corridor," she said. "I found it when I was ten."

"A nosy little ninja . . ." I said.

"Yes, I guess so. Anyway, I found a book in the family library about these Harlem brownstone houses. And, it turns out that the people who owned these homes in this area all had servants. And they wanted their servants to be 'invisible.' So these houses were designed more than a century ago to have these interior corridors so servants could go up and down, in and out, serving the owners but not disturbing them."

"So you can get to any part of this house through these corridors?" I asked.

"Well, not the bathrooms or other places where it would be weird if someone could be there without you knowing it. Or if someone could suddenly come walking out of the wall."

"Any room in a house where the people living there can be observed without them knowing it is crazy," I said.

"Aunt Tasha would agree. That's why she had the servants' entrance sealed off," Chiasa said.

"But you still found it," I said.

"That's because she had it sealed off after I found it. So I knew all of the hiding spaces already."

"Get up," I told her. "We gotta find our clothes and get out of here before she panics and starts calling around, alarming everyone."

"Let's make a plan," she said, standing. "I'll go out first and find Aunt Tasha. I'll talk with her, just like she wanted to do. I'll tell her that you are in my bedroom waiting patiently for me."

"You have a bedroom in this house?" I asked her.

"Yes, Aunt Tasha made it for me a very long time ago. She doesn't allow anyone else to use it. I wanted to show you. Besides, Aunt Tasha did say it was okay for me to give you the tour. So, I'll tell her that was what I was doing," she plotted.

"That was a good tour." I laughed. She must have gone to swipe me the way she does whenever I joke her. Our bodies bumped into one another. I grabbed her waist. We both started swelling again. I could feel her nipples brush against my chest. "One of us has to be the first to stop," I said, stroking the moist skin of her pretty face.

"So who's it going to be?" she asked, playing in my pubic hairs. Now we were back to caressing, breathing hard, tonguing, and bumping.

"The other way," she said after we came down off the high of the third time.

"We came from the opposite direction," I reminded her.

"I know," she said. "But if we go out through the family library, Aunt Tasha, who is probably right there on the main floor, will hear the bookshelf drag open. We have to go through the upstairs." She grabbed my dick and said, "I'll take you there." I was thinking, *This girl is crazy, but I love it.* Of course, even though I couldn't see her, I was following her. She was holding my joint like a leash.

"Turn on the light," I told her. We were in her bedroom, where it was not nearly as dark as the servants' hidden path.

"Not yet," she said, pulling open a wooden chest. She rifled through some clothes, tossing everything up in the air. Each piece landed on the floor. There was a skylight window in the roof. The moon made her appear to be blue and her hair looked electric. "I found 'em," she said, waving around a pair of denim shorts. She put them on. She searched through the chest and found a particular tee she seemed to have been searching for. "Okay, you stay here—I'll be right back," she said, but everything about her look was a dead giveaway of what we had just done. She looked too sexy in her tiny tight shorts and tee. She wasn't wearing her bra. She had left it in the secret passageway somewhere in the dark on the floor. And even though there were no other males in this house at the moment, aside from me, I couldn't let her walk away like that. I wanted to grab her, go in her again.

"Hold on," I said. She turned around and looked at me. Her skin was glowing from a layer of sweat. Her eyes were wide. Her look was wild like a wildcat right after a satisfying session of sexing, screeching, and scratching in a secret alleyway.

"You smell like we've been fucking," I said to her calmly. Her look turned suddenly shy. She blushed, and then sniffed herself.

"I don't stink," she said softly, almost like a whisper. I smiled at her.

"Not stink, you smell like sex."

I picked up some sweats she had tossed onto the floor, and another tee. "Go to the shower first. Even if it's only suds and a three-minute hot splash, that's cool." I added, handing her the clothes.

"Okay," she surrendered softly. "But we are married. It's fine that we've been fucking, right?" she asked, then broke into a smile.

"It's definitely alright with me. And if you don't get moving, we'll be fucking again."

She paused. Her eyes were locked onto mine in a serious but seductive stare. Her love was a visible energy that surrounded her body and even framed her face. I could feel it. She fought herself, I could sense. Then, she turned and left.

As soon as my second wife was out of my atmosphere, I returned to my right mind. Naked in another man's house, I pushed right back through her hidden bedroom wall and into the dark corridor, moving quietly but swiftly down the interior steps and back to the place where I had left my clothes. With my shirt, boxers, and pants in one hand, I felt around the floor for my belt until I located it. Swiftly, I decided to get dressed in the corridor first.

Dressed, I purposely took another route through the servants' path. Instead of returning to her bedroom, where there was no sink or water to clean myself up with, I would search for a path through the kitchen, or a bedroom that had a bathroom in it. Either way, unfamiliar with the layout, I had to move slowly now through the darkness, keeping both hands on the walls as I walked, to locate an opening or a button or a switch, while listening carefully for voices, just in case. But I believed that Aunt Tasha and my wife would be in her bedroom. That was on the second floor. Therefore that was exactly where I wasn't headed.

I found a parallel crease in the wall. It wouldn't open or push in. I felt around for a button. There was none. I kept walking, still dragging my hands along the walls, trying to detect an opening. I found another one forty seconds later. It also did not open. *Strike two.* I would give one more try before I returned through the route to her bedroom. Walking through the dark, the path dropped down. It was a set of stairs. I took that route, hoping to get lucky. On the wall at the bottom of the steps, I felt around. My fingers felt a metal grate. It was a vent, but not a door. I crouched down and looked through and saw the cranberry-colored wall. I knew then it was Aunt Tasha's office. When I pressed my face close to peer through the vent, I saw my wife seated in the pretty ten-thousand-dollar chair, still wearing her tight denim shorts. She had her hands over her face and fingers woven into her thick hair. *She didn't get a chance to shower*, I realized. And she looked frustrated. Then Aunt Tasha walked in. I could see flashes of the white dress she had on earlier. My second wife removed her hands from her face.

"I don't think of a baby as someone who prevents his mother from living and learning, or even flying. You had four sons, Aunt Tasha, and look at all of those degrees you have on your wall."

I found myself in the middle of an emotional conversation between them.

"I had my first son, your cousin Junior, when I was twenty-nine. I had already completed all of my degrees and my residency," her aunt explained.

"But, what if you had met Uncle Clem when you were sixteen, and you were super sure that he was the man for you. Would you have told him no? Would you have asked him to wait thirteen years until you have enough degrees to feel comfortable enough to love and marry him?" Chiasa pleaded.

However, Aunt Tasha, the "forensics fox," seemed to be certain that she was the one who would ask all of the questions. She didn't answer my wife's sincere inquiries. Instead, she said, "And perhaps you have gone too far with this Muslim thing. I don't think you really understand the depth of it. You have some romantic view that only a young and naïve girl could have. And, the way you told that Solomon story was a little different than I remember it. I'll tell you what I do remember. Solomon had forty or more wives. What will you do when your young husband brings back another woman and says 'She is wife number two and three and four and so on?'" And then there was silence. I didn't move. I knew I shouldn't have come down here in the first place. Still, I wanted to hear for myself what my wife would say.

"I'm not greedy, Aunt Tasha. I'm so grateful to him. And he won't come home with wife number three. And I am already . . . wife number two."

Aunt Tasha screamed. She had an outburst. *Must run in the family*, I thought to myself. And in the pitch of her scream, I stayed stuck there.

Aunt Tasha began pushing the push buttons on her desk phone. I thought it was strange that she would make a call in the middle of her passionate conversation with her niece.

"Brother, I understand. You know I do," she said to the person on the other end of her call. Again, it seemed like the middle of a conversation she had already been having with the caller, not the beginning. There were no greetings or intro, which would be normal manners. The person on the other end must have been over talking. Dr. Tasha sat listening, her face a little tight. Then she spoke. "He has the chronological age of a young teen. He has the mental age of a twenty-five-year-old. I interpreted the Wechsler's. He zipped through it like it wasn't even a challenge to him. He has a tremendous intellectual capacity. But the drawback is, he is difficult to pin to one cluster. He's got a precarious mixture of personality types and I'm a profiler, so please believe me.

"This guy is incapable of functioning in a team. He's incredibly confident but not histrionic. He's introspective and resolute in his ideas and inextricable from his beliefs. He has this compelling beauty and implacable charm that triples his influence and capability, yet he doesn't exploit it. The most dangerous element here is that he reviles authority, abhors instructions, advice, or orders. He disregards conventional thought and actions and has zero group identity. His mind manufactures alternative routes to every desirable destination. He will never yield to a chain of command or relent before the hierarchy. And dear brother, your sweet daughter is absolutely in the palms of his hands."

Then I knew. She was speaking to the General, Chiasa's father, my father-in-law. The two of them together, I thought, formed a treacherous mountain for me to climb.

"Aunt Tasha, please allow me to speak to Daddy?" Chiasa requested. "It's so unfair for you to analyze my husband as though he's your patient."

I turned and left, back down the path I used to get there in the first place.

All cleaned up, I had used an upstairs bathroom comfortably since I knew they were engrossed in the basement. I had also collected my wife's panties, skirt, and blouse on my route back to her bedroom. Feeling better, I walked down the proper house staircase and into their family library. My wife still had not come up the stairs from her aunt's office, where both of our pairs of shoes were located and the shopping bag of gifts, I remembered.

In their family library, I was searching for a dictionary. I found one, a medical dictionary. I laid it on a long, wide table. There was a bin filled with scrap paper and a cup of blue Bic pens, and another cup filled with number two pencils. I imagined all of her sons seated in here studying for their exams under the pressure of matching the degrees their parents had already earned. I had seen Clementine Xavier Moody's degrees mounted in his private office. He'd completed the University of Pennsylvania's Wharton School of Business undergraduate and master's degrees. He earned a PhD in business at Harvard. I thought of my father. He is also a man of degrees, who graduated from the University of Khartoum in Sudan, from the Sorbonne University in Paris, France, and earned his PhD here in Harlem at Columbia University. I then thought of myself. Earning money setting businesses into motion would be my primary skill, focus, and accomplishment. Study would be my hobby, instead of the other way around.

Flipping pages, I looked up the definition of *forensics.* It said, "The art of argumentation." I paused and smiled. It sounded about right, fit Aunt Tasha perfectly. She has a degree in arguing and she would try to keep convincing my wife of her views no matter what because she was certified in arguments. I looked up the word *psychiatry.* It said "the practice of diagnosing mental disorders." Maybe she specialized in arguing with crazy people. I laughed. But when I looked up the two words together, *forensic psychiatry*, the profession became even more clear to me: It said "the intersection of law, the courts, and mental illness." Unlike the regular Webster's dictionary that I regularly used, the medical dictionary went into long descriptions and several paragraphs. I got drawn into reading about all the professional angles that a forensic psychiatrist could pursue. The most amazing one was that a forensic psychiatrist could be hired to reconstruct the mindset of someone who was already dead. I stopped there. I leaned back. My mind was questioning my soul about whether that was even possible. Could one human being, just because he or she was a psychiatrist, even construct the mindset of a living person? Wouldn't that involve the ability to read minds? Isn't that a space reserved only to Allah? Were educated humans just so arrogant that they felt they could confidently enter that space and accurately figure out the workings of another person's brain? And what about reconstructing the mind of someone whose soul had already returned to Allah? How smart would someone have to consider themself to be, to even agree to get paid to do that? I sat quietly.

Some minutes later I decided that it was not possible. It was guesswork being done by some people who studied so long and so much that no one could argue well enough with them to convince them that they were not capable of being right and exact or precise about these kinds of things. And if anyone tried to argue with them, they would have to have the same degrees to even be considered part of their discussion. And if they had earned the same degrees, they would just be another person agreeing with what the small group of "mind scientists" had already decided.

Aunt Tasha was a foxy owl for sure. But I think her belief that she could read people would end up as her weakness. That bedroom she set up for Chiasa in her home was a good example of a misunderstanding. The darkened pink room was filled with furry stuffed animals and dolls. There was a dollhouse with furniture, and the bed had a box spring below the mattress and sat up high in the wooden frame. It was covered with pink sheets and a white-laced quilt. Nothing I saw in there was a match for Chiasa, who sleeps on the floor on purpose and would have model airplanes and plastic soldiers and a spinning globe and a wall of knives before ever considering a stuffed animal. Chiasa, definitely not a girl who played with dolls, had been given a room that must have fit Aunt Tasha's designs and hopes and style and misinterpretations of the daughter she never had.

And I saw that she thought and felt she knew things about me that clearly she did not. I thought it was bold of her to think she could read me in less than four hours, as though she could summarize my life, thoughts, feelings, and even intentions, *la kadar Allah.* She had referred to me as *ominous.* I looked it up in their standard dictionary. It said, "Fateful. Either a good or evil omen." Quickly, I looked up *prodigious*, another word she had used on me. It said, "Having an extraordinary force." The third word that rolled off her tongue smoothly was *pulchritudinous.* I fumbled with the spelling for a few seconds. Then I located it. It said, "Physically beautiful."

So, she believed that I am a physically beautiful, extraordinary force for either good or evil. More importantly, that I am "fateful." I liked only that part. She needed to know that whatever the case, I am a part of her niece's fate.

I found the copy of *Catcher in the Rye* in their library. I just flipped through it, deciding I would buy my own and read it, since every American high school student should do the same, according to her.

"Let's walk to the train station," my second wife requested that night. "I'd like to show you some things in Harlem."

"You are going to show me around Harlem?" I smiled. I of course had been all through Harlem over my young years in this country.

"Sure." I agreed to let her guide me around because I wanted to be sure that she wasn't sad on the inside after her long talk with her aunt. I thought even though she has that beautiful smile, maybe she was covering up another feeling.

She chose to walk east, even though I knew we could catch the train on the west side where we had started out.

"I wanted to show you these two places," she said, pointing. "There is the Schomburg Library. Have you been there?" she asked.

"Never," I admitted.

"It's the library that has all of the books and films and research materials about the African and African-American experience in the world, and specifically America. I only know about this place because Aunt Tasha took me here when I was ten. It's not my favorite library, though. The best one is the main New York Public Library in midtown Manhattan, so awesome. The feng shui is so much better."

"The feng shui?" I repeated.

"The feeling, the atmosphere," she said. "In Chinese, *feng* means 'wind.' Shui means 'water.' And most Asians believe that the way a place is arranged adds to either a good healthy feeling or, if it is arranged poorly or is a cluttered place, causes a bad feeling," she explained.

"I see," was all I said, remembering that my African wife is half Asian. Her father and his sister, Aunt Tasha, and Uncle Clementine and their family are not half Asian, I reminded myself.

"And across the street is Harlem Hospital. Uncle Clem used to work there as an administrator, really high up," she said.

"And what happened?" I asked.

"Well, I was young when he left there, but I guess he wanted to do something where he owned his own business and would be in complete control of his capabilities. Uncle Clem is secretive. Aunt Tasha says that he's a genius and that even NASA recruited him as a consultant on a top secret project. When he completed it, NASA named it after him."

"NASA?" I repeated.

"The National Aeronautics and Space Administration," she explained. "It's the government."

"We can take this subway right here," I told her. It was right in front of the Schomburg.

"Can we walk over some more blocks?" she asked.

"Sure," I said. We began walking down from 135th Street and Seventh Avenue towards 125th Street. She stopped in front of another book place on 130th.

"This is Liberation Books," she announced. "There is a really nice lady who owns this bookstore. Her name is Una Mulzac. She's friends with Aunt Tasha. Aunt brought me here once. And this lady Una, her name sounds like Umma, right?" She paused and laughed. "Well anyway, this lady, when I met her for the first time, just kept talking about Africa and all of the problems in each of the countries. That's when I first had my idea that I would fight against the bad guys. I decided to become a mercenary and go fighting good causes everywhere in the world, solving problems wherever good people needed help."

"Now your family is disappointed because I married you, and that will no longer happen?" I asked, but didn't really need an answer. She stopped, turned, and looked at me.

"I saw you," she said.

"You saw me?" I asked.

"Through the vent. You know I have really good vision," she said casually, not like she was complimenting herself, but simply stating the truth. "And I hope that you know it does not matter what anyone says when it comes to you and me, and our faith and our marriage. Aunt Tasha thought I was debating with her and fighting to keep you. But the truth is, I was reasoning with her and fighting to keep *her.* Staying with you is permanent, and no human can alter that."

# 16. RIKERS ISLAND, THE KIDS' COMPLEX

A stampede, then bodies on top of bodies, fists flinging without precision. Feet kicking. Poles cracking heads open. Shank knives piercing flesh, randomly.

The rest of us still standing are moving around the perimeter of the pile-up; there is nowhere else to go. We are all locked in, and we were leery of standing still. So, we pace. Screaming from the top tiers, the cheering noise and commands being called out, turned this into an echo chamber. Down below where I am, there are grunts and cries:

"Get the fuck off of me."

"Move!"

"I can't breathe!"

"I'mma fuck you up."

I'm trying to figure out the formula. I just got here. We're all in our arrested street clothes. Couldn't tell who was down with who. A grown-up kid dragged a chair behind him, lifted it up, and prepared to swing it down on the pile-up. I snatched it from him midair and tossed it across the floor where no one was standing. It hit the wall and turned over. Now the kid was shouting out, "Hook!" Some of them boys buried in the pile-up tried to lift themselves up from the pile. Another man shouted, "Da Bridge!" A quarter of the bodies raised up, still fighting and fists still flinging in faces, and the pile shifted. But then they dived back onto the floor, scuffling for a shank that was just lying there in the open. One kid finally got ahold of it, but then his man pulled it away from him, slicing open both of his palms, the blood spilling everywhere. The chest of the kid left holding the shank was heaving. He pumped himself up and made a dash towards another kid who he caught sight of and pushed the shank through him. It wasn't enough. He pulled it, twisting it back and forth as he yanked it out from the kid's torso. The guy's body writhing and he was screaming at the top of his lungs. His boys came to help him too late. One took off his T-shirt and attempted to wrap it around the stabbed guy's stomach. The white tee was soaked red and the cut kid fell on the pile. Someone beneath him pushed him hard and he rolled off to the side and lay there looking lifeless.

But the one holding the shank on ready was still on the move. He was the one to watch. So I watched him. His arm raised in the air, he was setting up to slash down, and the bodies below his shank flipped and scrambled to get out the way of the blade. He was searching out his target.

"The Ville!" one of the kids that was on the bottom of the pile shouted as he leapfrogged up to his feet with a pair of Air Force 1's in his hands even though he had Jordans on his feet. "I got it." He yelled victory but didn't see the knife heading for his back. I did. I kicked the kid coming for him with full force. He flew over the pile before landing on the floor and dropped the shank. Another kid spit a razor at me. I leaned to the side and it lodged in some next man's neck. I snatched the kid from the Ville whose face I recognized, and two more from the heap. "Good-looking," one of them said, and his eyes checked me like he was taking a snapshot.

"Rasta Up!" one Jamaican kid shouted, and the Rastas rushed the pile-up and started kicking and smashing the others with their feet like they were smashing grapes or killing roaches or kicking soccer balls. The dropped shank hadn't surfaced yet, but the pile kept moving and shifting like footballers trying to pile up on a loose ball.

I was studying faces, weighing loyalties and allegiances, watching fingers, razored-up tongues, and facial gestures, even the ones from the Ville. I was checking who was left wearing shoes, who was without shoes, and what kind of kicks those wearing kicks were wearing. I just needed to distinguish the lions from the tigers, the wolves from the hyenas, the hippos from the elephants, and the rats from the snakes. And I needed to do it quick. It wasn't easy during a stampede or a riot, or where the fighting was random and ten or more guys who weren't ganged or boroughed up were just stray junkyard dogs in the mix.

I saw the shank, put my foot on it, and kicked it toward the wall with the pile pushing toward me. I was tackled and fought back, but got buried beneath the weight of bodies. Weight shift; someone must've got hold of the shank, and now he's the target. I was pulling up from the bottom.

Riot geared up and eighteen minutes too late, the special corrections officer squad opened the gate and came rushing in, while the two COs who had locked themselves in the booth and had been watching from the first fist flung laughed. Even though the riot-geared-up gorillas were charging, the threats were still being called out between the men fighting.

"Payback is a bitch!"

"There's nowhere to hide!"

*"Muerte a las mariconcitas!"*

"We run this motherfucker!"

One by one the riot squad took down all who didn't voluntarily lay down. Some got cracked with shields, hemmed in with knees buried in their chest and pinning them down. Some CO gorillas ganged up and threw their weight against a prisoner who they went at with a vengeance like there had been bad blood between them. I got the baton driven into my back and was pinned to the wall. Then I was cuffed, dragged down, and got a floor view of all of us who had been subdued. Along with the others who were still standing, we on the floor all began coughing and gagging. Someone had released a chemical in a room that had no open windows and no one had the energy, the clear vision, or the breath to fight or resist any further. *Good*, I thought to myself.

"Welcome to hell!" someone shouted through the slot on a closed and locked cell door. The CO unlocked the cell where we stood. He unchained and uncuffed my feet and pushed me inside, slamming the cell door shut and locking it.

"Hands!" he yelled through the slot. I pushed my hands through. He uncuffed me after he was sure he was safe on the other side of the locked cell door. I pulled my hands back, massaged each wrist, and exhaled. I was in the box, the bing, segregation, isolation, twenty-three-hour daily lockdown, doing ninety days. It was the most dreaded, most dangerous place for the most dreaded and dangerous inmates; only lawyer visits, no one else, no phone calls, no cell mate, no day room, no yard. Three minutes for supervised shower, fifty-seven minutes to go to the law library or move around in a fake tiny indoor yard, alone. Everyone on the Island called it hell or the black hole. It was exactly where I wanted to be.

"Welcome to hell." I heard it twice more. I just heard it shouted out again. *Business must be good*, I thought to myself. *They're bringing in another prisoner and pushing him into another box.*

I also heard it before I got up here, on the bus ride from the Tombs to Rikers Island. It was a packed bus, standing room only—only thing no one was allowed to stand. We were all seated, cuffed and chained. We started out in silence as the bus pulled into the busy New York streets. Most were looking around at each other, trying to get a read or a feel about who was the weakest, who was the strongest, who should be used, who should be joined, who should be avoided, and who should be feared. Me, I was playing the window seat, looking out and forbidding any eye contact. Strange, I'm sure ninety-nine percent of us speak English, but it was the same as though we each spoke a different language. No one wanted to break the ice that was frozen solid, dividing and freezing each of us into a separate cube, even though we were traveling in the heat of summer and even though we were all going to the same destination.

Seven minutes in, one dude started rhyming. It was hip-hop, but it was the blues. All about how hard life was for him. The one seated next to him started to click his cuffs together to the beat. Then one behind him began beat-boxing. Not everyone shared the same skill, but we were all black and young and we could each catch the beat with our hands, cuffs, chains, feet, or mouths. It was the only time I saw more than two or three young black males do anything together besides ball—football, baseball, basketball, or soccer. The hardest of the hard tried to ignore the pull of the a capella music. But even those few were either toe tapping or banging or stomping out to the beat. Dude in the middle made up a melody and started singing his own hook to our impromptu song. Somehow his deep voice was soothing, the way it laid back and laced the rhythm of the rhyme. When it was done, it was done. It was back to being frozen and hard-hearted and deaf and disconnected. The dude in front of me and the guy seated next to him were different, though. They broke the ice between them as we neared the Island. A few seconds of overhearing them and I knew that they already knew one another, which was why they were no longer frozen like the rest. One was older than the other, schooling him on the Island in a low tone. But there is no privacy in this circumstance, so I had to listen even if I didn't want to hear.

"Miz, we 'bout to arrive in hell. I know. This is my sixth time. You gon' be a target 'cause of what you got on. So let me get your chain and hold it for you. You too new to rock it without getting sliced up. Niggas are gon' test you for your kicks on your feet and for the shirt and pants off of your ass and back. Don't let 'em strip you no matter what. But if them niggas bum-rush you, four or five or six of them at a time, I'mma tell you now, *you gon' lose.* But fight them like you believe you can win. Hit 'em hard, fight dirty, bite a motherfucker if you have to. But show them you got heart and that you're willing to go for broke. That's the only way you can get some respect. If you don't fight, they gon' be 'maytagging' that ass. If you let them bitch you up like that there's no turning back; word travels faster than fire on the inside, and everybody will want a turn to get at you." The younger one leaned forward. The older one tried to remove the gold chain from his neck.

"When we get to intake, like when we first arrive, the CO's gonna talk a lot of shit about not fighting, not getting into no more trouble than you already in. Don't listen to shit that a CO has to say. It's fight or die. I was in your same position on my first trip up here. I had to lay a few kids down. They gave me a fifteen-second hearing, didn't hear a word I had to say about it. They threw my ass straight in the box. That shit was hell; twenty-three hours a day I was locked in for ninety days. Thought I was gonna lose my mind. I started seeing shit, word up, hearing shit, and talking to myself, banging my head on the walls in shit. Crazy! You don't want to go to the box. But believe me, when I got out of there, niggas started to show me some motherfucking respect."

I looked around. A quick glance was all it took to survey the limited space in my box. There was a sink. I went to it, turning on the water yet not expecting it to pour out. I wasn't expecting anything in fact. The water rushed out. I rinsed, then cupped my hands and began splashing water onto my face.

*This isn't hell*, I thought to myself. There is no sink or cool or cold water in hell. I know better. In the Quran, hell is described to us truthfully and clearly and in great detail. Nonbelievers wear "garments of fire" and hot boiling water is poured over their heads. Water so hot that what is in their bellies and even their skins will be melted. When those who have been "dragged to hell on their faces" try to escape, they are met by "whips of iron" and repeatedly pulled back in.

They cannot rid themselves of the feel and taste of constant burning. There is a tree in hell, known to Muslims as the Tree of Zaqqum. It bears no fruit; the only food it offers is thorns and snake heads.

*What this captivity is for me is a trial*, I told myself. In *sura* 25, *ayat* 29, the Quran says, "We make some of you a trial for others." And in *sura* 29, *ayat* 2 we are asked the question, "Do men think that they will be left alone on saying 'we believe' and will not be tried?"

In times of being tried, a true believer does not doubt or curse or abandon his faith. Allah can never be abandoned. We believe that Allah is closer to us than our "main vein." However, Allah can abandon whom he pleases, leave us in error if he pleases. So we humble ourselves in fear and in love of Allah that we might never be abandoned by the One who created us, gave us breath and light. We pray even more in times of difficulty. We are never disloyal. Those who are disloyal in faith are untrue and were untrue from the start. The Quran says:

> And among men is he who serves Allah on the verge, so that if good befalls him he is satisfied therewith, but if a trial afflicts him he turns back. He loses this world and the Hereafter. That is a manifest loss.—*Sura* 22, *Ayat* 11

It was hot in the box, but I was used to handling the heat. This was nothing compared to the heat of the desert, I remembered. And this was not the heat of hell. I took a few deep breaths, doused my entire self with water, cleaned even the soles of my feet, and made a prayer. Afterwards, I collapsed; my body was exhausted and my brain was on burn-out. *Sleep is a necessity not a desire*, I convinced myself. It was the only way for me to give in and let go.

Deep sleep, so deep there was no dreaming or memory of having dreamt. So deep there was no amount of cells slamming shut or men calling out that could rouse me. Deep, in a blanket of darkness so dark, there was no emotion in me, no desire to see, no fear of the unknown, no desires and no needs, not even yearnings, just sleep. This was the kind of sleep that could only be brought on by a week of interrogations and beatings, nearly two weeks of heavy suspicions and constant observing, and several days of carrying chains on hands and feet, taking baby steps and small motions, and of untangling lies that once untangled if pulled and stretched out in a straight line would run on for miles and miles and miles.

Fully awake and alert, feeling grateful to have finally slept. This was the blessing of "the box," solitude. Still there was a stench. *Ignore it*, I told myself. If I simply breathed in and out enough times, it would become like odorless oxygen. I smiled. But I was awake now and the action in me was fully awake as well. One towel, that's what I had been given, and one cup and one toothbrush and one bar of soap and one roll of tissue. On the metal slab that was my bed, on top of a cracker-thin mattress, I sat. Using my teeth, I loosened the threads of the towel until I could pull them out with my fingers. I ripped the towel into three portions and then each portion in half again until I had six washcloths. I began cleaning, a thorough cleaning without Dettol or detergents, but using the bar of soap that I was issued, and I was scrubbing each thing—the sink, the toilet, the walls, and even the floors—with a forceful hand and constant motion. "Allah loves those who purify themselves," I remember. I was washing off the saliva and tears and breath and residues of hundreds if not thousands of men. The stench made their presence here in the box obvious. If I didn't clean up, it would be like I was locked in a small space with all of the men who had ever been locked in this same space. With the soap and the cloths and the detailed scrubbing, I was creating a new start and a neutral scent, which was better than a foul one. With washcloth number four, I scrubbed even the slot where thousands of hands before mine had been pushed in and out, cuffed and released.

Eyes, a CO peering in. No privacy; I didn't expect any. I was being watched like a leopard in a cage.

Feminine fingers; I could tell even through the thin white gloves she wore. The dinner tray came. I didn't expect it. Didn't expect anything. It was pushed through the slot and I took it. "Thank you," I said through the cleaned slot. No response. Didn't expect one.

Eating now is just a function. The food is not connected to any emotional bonds, culture, or tradition. I would not savor it, anticipate it, or even taste it, yet I would eat it to survive.

After digestion was fully completed, I was weighing out my workout options. There was enough space for the usual dips and squats and thrusts and push-ups and sit-ups and so on. I didn't launch immediately into that formula. I was thinking and strategizing. My body was already cut and carved, solid and strong, flexible and fluid. Up against a wall of men, I realized that my most lethal weapon was my martial arts techniques. The Asian fighting arts were all about the art of the empty hands. Hands without guns, and sometimes without even poles or sticks or knives. And in learning those techniques, we are trained to fight more than one man at a time, sometimes five, ten, or fifteen. But there is a difference between men poised to engage in hand-to-hand and a mob, like the riot that landed me in the box.

The dilemma is that as a ninjutsu warrior, I am trained in the art of the kill. I can have an opponent that is a foot taller than me or a half foot wider than me, like some of these dudes up in here; I can have a rival who is a wall of muscle. Still, I could kill him through the technique of attacking his pressure points, joints, or his eyes, or by simply and swiftly catching him at the right angle, punching his flesh inside of his body and snatching back his organs. We are not trained in the "half kill." We are not defensive fighters. We are not martial arts exhibitionists or dancers. There is no cute choreography. We aim to eliminate swiftly and to not leave a trace.

I did not come here, however, to kill. I came here to serve my time until I am sentenced and sent elsewhere to serve more time, hopefully an amount of time comparable to the valuelessness of the deceased. The trick question or the trick situation for me, then, is, how can I serve my time without accumulating more time by eliminating enemies that simply appeared right in my face for no right reason when I get back into population after my ninety days in the box?

*Don't overthink it*, I told myself. I'd opt to change out of my street clothes and into the Department of Corrections–issued top and bottoms. While alone, I'd shadow fight, sharpening my techniques and accuracy, movement and speed, kicks and leaps.

While getting deep into the sparring, my peripheral vision was catching glimpses of eyes peering into my cell. Soon as I noticed this, I broke my momentum, not wanting to display my level to the officers for any reason, or to anyone who might be collecting information for my still-open case. I'm not under any impression that I know what side anyone I come across is on. They're all strangers to me. Give 'em a few minutes and something they say or do will reveal their hand.

After my extended shadow fight with a swift and elusive opponent, I wound down into dips and thrusts and squats and sit-ups and push-ups. Then I lay down on the floor, looking up at the rule book I had been given for this place. It was the only book I had so far. Should I read it when it was already crystal clear that no one on Rikers Island was following any rules anyway, not the inmates or the keepers?

I sat up and cracked it open. It was better for me to learn their official policy than to not learn it. This way, I would understand the consequences of each thing and how to possibly make moves in my own favor.

"An inmate shall obey all orders of Department of Corrections officers, personnel, and staff at all times and without argument." Now I knew that thinking was forbidden. I also knew that speaking was forbidden unless it was the normal nonsense.

"Good time for good behavior can reduce an inmate's sentence by one-third of the term." I paused right there. It sounded like a trick. Yet they were trying to give us the carrot to chase, something to strive for in a place where in order to survive, you would have to disobey at least a few rules and knock out at least a few men, if not kill them outright. So the one-third reduction was something available that couldn't actually be obtained.

Some of the rules did not match the nature of men. "No wrestling," or what they called "horseplay," and "no sparring." That was crazy to me. It actually meant that if we were fighting one another, it better be for real, and not because we are young men who are captives, rivals, or friends just doing what was normal for us to do. They labeled sparring and "play fighting" as assault, punishable by a trip to the box.

A conversation between two or more locked-up dudes, according to their rules, could catch an inmate a "conspiracy" charge. It is considered "forging an agreement to break the rules." So extreme, even if an inmate gives another inmate something, "with the intent to influence the person or benefit himself in any way," it's labeled bribery. I paused, thinking how the rules were worded and set in such a way that any inmate could be accused of anything at any time and he would be guilty, because what he was being accused of is normal everyday happenings. He would have no defense—although he would get a "hearing." What a joke. At the "hearing," once they charged the inmate with talking, or gathering together in a small group, or sharing a pack of ramen with the intent to influence another inmate to trade something he got, he would be found guilty. Even before reading their rule book I knew this system was a trap, not a place to expect or receive justice, not even if a man was honest and true about the unlawful actions he actually did commit. Not even if a man simply wanted to do what the facility was built for, serve his time . . . and nothing extra.

As a businessman, I understood this hustle. Each inmate was a "captive consumer." Out in the world, businessmen had to attract a customer by having an excellent product, or a very accessible product, or a very useful or popular well-advertised product, or a fairly priced affordable necessity product. But in here, according to their rule book everything an inmate buys *must be purchased* from the Department of Corrections "commissary." If an inmate buys or shares or trades anything, it is a violation that comes with a write-up and a punishment. It is illegal, and the thing that was purchased, shared, or traded they label "contraband." If an inmate got two Tylenols or Bayer aspirins and he gave one to his man who is sick, that's a violation. They wrote that in their rule book! Crazy.

I learned that in here you could buy food. The food is only legal if it is purchased from commissary. The food could only be stored in our cell if it was purchased from commissary. *That's a mean hustle*, I thought to myself. There was only one supplier providing products, setting prices, and controlling and monopolizing the market, which was definitely not a free market with competition at all.

There were other rules, of course, that were even stranger. Reading them typed out in a leaflet let me know what usually goes on in here. Rules like "No demonstration, boycotts, or work stoppages or interrupting the routine in any way." Same as saying "We know we're robbing you and fucking you over, but just let it happen." They even stated that no inmate can "resist" any correction officer or DOC staff member. They put in parentheses the word *physically*, but they already had stated that it was also wrong to "resist" by talking back.

"Inmates shall not make threats or take hostages." Now I was laughing to myself. They made the rules so ridiculous and so tight that it must be an everyday reality in here that shit explodes into the riot that I saw, or into inmates "taking hostages."

And the last and filthiest rule, one that should never have to be spoken or written down, is "No sex between inmates or anyone at Rikers. No exposing your private parts or asking or paying for sex." *An all-male facility*, I thought to myself. Why would there be any mention of sex between men? And what of the feminine fingers

I saw? Was the "no sex" rule put in place to protect whatever few women who were unloved and unprotected and therefore desperate enough and allowed to work in here surrounded and engulfed by filthy men including the male officials and the inmates?

The second part of that final rule, not to expose your private parts, was pure bullshit. I was part of a lineup of naked men, after having been stripped of my clothes at Rikers intake. Some of the same dudes that rode up on the same bus with me chained and cuffed together were there too. Men who were already humiliated prisoners became visibly insecure, embarrassed, and vexed enough to curse the guards out loud. I didn't say shit. I'm not shy. That's a feminine trait. Moreover, I'm not shy standing before men who although they are still in uniform, physically, have the same as me. I was not going to let these authorities raise any emotion in me, fear or otherwise, I told myself. Instead I pitied the corrections officers. Thought about just how miserable and desperate a loser a man would have to be to take a job staring at other men's dicks and balls and then asking them to bend over so you could take a look up their asshole. To take that job, a man would have to be a complete failure at business, which is the backbone of America. He'd have to be either too lazy or too dumb or too broken to have developed a product, opened a store, or dealt in trade, import or export. He would have to be a man whose father left him nothing—no land, no jewels, no gold, no cash. He'd have to be a man who had no other choice, was in debt everywhere, even to the mother of his children. So I was calm during the naked search. I felt despite my present situation that I was still above all of the men hired to do what they were doing right then.

In my Southern grandfather's village, there were times when men were naked and in groups. It could be while washing in the bathhouse or down at the water. It was no big deal. We would wash each other's backs. Men were solid. In our minds there was nothing a man wanted from another man besides true brotherhood and sincere friendship. In that village all men knew that we were bonded one to the other, as the protectors of our women, our land, our animals, and our culture and beliefs.

In the conclusion of their Rikers rule book, it was repeated in bold lettering that accused inmates have a right to an in-house jail hearing. But who would believe in receiving justice at a hearing, after reading the rules and therefore peeping both the hustle and the setup woven into the rules? I wouldn't.

That was one of about three urgent reasons why, in my riot hearing, which occurred before I was transferred to "the box," I said absolutely nothing.

Silence suits me. Solitude is my preference, and is also my premeditated plan.

## 17. NAJA'S WATCHING • *A Reflection*

"So which one do you love more, Akemi or Chiasa?" Naja asked me. We were standing outside our new home in Queens at her bus stop, waiting for the green minibus that picks her up and takes her to Khadija's Islamic School for Girls, where she just completed third grade and was now beginning her summer session.

"It's not a competition," I said calmly, looking down the block for her bus.

"I didn't say it was," she replied playfully. "But, everyone has favorites, even Umma," she said, catching my full attention.

"Did Umma say that she likes one of my wives more than the other?" I asked.

"Nope, she didn't. But you are Umma's favorite. She loves you more than she loves me," she answered with a seriousness, searching me for a real reaction.

"Sounds untrue. Don't feel like that." I hugged her with one arm around her shoulder. "I'm older. Umma has known me for more years. I'm a son, so I am responsible for a lot more," I reasoned with her. She stood staring up and into my eyes, her little bronze face framed by her pale pink hijab. "You know Umma loves you. If she heard what you were saying right now, she would feel disappointed," I cautioned her without a scolding tone.

"I know she loves me," Naja said confidently, pulling back her little shoulders in a proud little-girl stance. "Just like I know she loves you more." She laughed, feeling like she had won. "You even said it yourself. You said Umma knows you more, and that you are responsible for more. You used the word more two times! So *you* agree with me."

"Your bus is coming." I pointed.

"So which one is it? I know you love both of your wives, but which one do you love more?" She was determined.

*"Assalaam Alaikum,"* I greeted the woman who gets off from their bus, guides the children in, and walks back up the few steps right behind them.

"*Wa-Alaikum Salaam* brother," she responded pleasantly to me.

"Are you ever going to tell me the answer?" Naja asked me. "Or are you going to try and make me forget the way that adults do when they don't want little kids to know anything?" She and I and Akemi were all three walking in lower Manhattan, through the cobblestone back streets where the top vintage shops were tucked away. I was scouting out and purchasing the most fashionable items of clothes for resale in Asia. My first wife is a charm for my business. Her eyes know what suits Asian tastes and she could break it down country by country. She would hold something up and say, "Korea hai! Japan no!" She let me know that this would sell nicely in Korea, but not in Japan. Japan was all about designer kicks, and they would pay three to five more times the retail amount than we had already paid in America. Japan was all about the newest and latest trend. They had vintage shops, but the majority of Japanese wanted strictly new styles. Their tastes would switch rapidly, and they had the cash flow to keep up. At the time, Korea was behind fashion-forward Japan. But among the young Koreans, because of the products promoted by the music, television, and film media, there was a growing interest and market for anything that Koreans believed Americans thought was fashionable wear. However, they were not up on the shoe and sneaker game yet, and Black Sea and I were pushing to create that market among the teen and college student crowd. We were especially pumping it through the Korean entertainment circles, and break-dancing crews on their side. The vintage shops had the inventory that would sell in Korea at prices that they could afford and wear proudly. Even if an item was off-season or throwback, as long as it had the right brand name and Americans loved it, many Koreans would buy it, use it, keep it.

"Akemi won't know what we're talking about anyway." Naja was in sneaky mode. "So you can tell me which one you love more. Whisper if you have to!"

"Naja, Akemi does not speak English but she is not unaware of anything. I wouldn't speak about her the way that you are. You should stop," I said. She looked like her little feelings were hurt. That didn't matter. She needed to understand. "If you love Akemi like you say you do, you should help her to understand English instead of tricking her because she doesn't understand English."

"Sorry," she said softly. "Next time, I'll ask you when you and I are alone. And . . . I *do love Akemi more than Chiasa.* I knew Akemi first, same as Umma knew you first. And Akemi takes better care of me than 'the other one.' And, I do teach Akemi some English words sometimes. Like when you aren't home yet, but I'm still awake. Or like when you are on the first floor, when Umma and Akemi and I all live on the second." I just looked at her.

Naja's young, but she is not dumb. She's curious and watching everything that goes on in our home. I feel good that we are not showing her anything wrong or shameful. During this summer school session, she only has two courses: Classical Arabic and Islamic Studies. I knew that from her learning the Quran, she would begin to think and feel even more deeply than before, and also would be questioning and comparing everything she saw in her home, in school, and in the families of her and our friends.

Akemi turned in to a vintage boutique displaying last season's Laura Ashley summer collection. Naja and I walked in behind her. She eased by everything displayed up front, moving towards the back. Out ran a short, slim man dressed in lemon-colored everything, even suspenders.

"You're just gorgeous!" he said, placing the palms of his hands over his face, smudging the cosmetics that I just noticed that he was wearing. "And look at those baby-doll feet of yours! And those five-alarm fire-red Gucci sandals put Imelda Marcos to shame!" he said to Akemi. "While you're at it, name me the salon that painted those Picassos on your toenails? And why cover up that beautiful hair? Oh I know! Because beautiful hair on top of everything else you've got going on would be a crime!" He laughed joyously. Akemi stepped right beyond him.

"She does not speak English," I explained.

"Rude is the same in every language," he quipped. "And by the way, you are quite gorgeous too! Stop the bus! You're prettier than her!" he said, laughing. I thought he had a mental illness. But in business I've learned to interact with all types of characters until whatever deal I'm seeking is complete. He wasn't hurting nothing.

Akemi weaved in and out of the tables where wooden boxes were piled high with choices. She arrived at a back rack. Then I saw what she saw. High-fashion leather coats for the autumn season. She was thinking ahead. I liked that. She slipped one on to show me, and sat the black leather motorcycle hat over the Hermès scarf she wore to conceal her hair. "*Hai*!" I said to her, letting her know to pull it and anything else she found like that back there. I went to the wooden boxes. I started pulling T-shirts with brand names and bold English lettering. When I was in Japan, I was surprised to see how many teens were wearing T-shirts with English lettering on them. The illest thing though, was that they would be bootleg, with letters that didn't spell a word, or had a sentence that didn't make sense. The fashion for them was only the English lettering, I found out. So the English-lettered T-shirts that had the Coca-Cola brand stamped on them or Nike or Reebok or even Nintendo, I pulled all of them. I thought it was crazy. They manufacture all that over there, but would pay top dollar to buy it back in the form of fashion.

“Akemi is super pretty,” Naja said. Now we were in a nearby ice-cream parlor that both Akemi and Naja could not resist. While I was weighed down with bags, Akemi pointed to the toppings she wanted on her sundae.

“Yes, she is,” I agreed.

“She has nice eyes and her hair is long and perfect. Remember when she cut it? And now look it grew back even longer. I want my hair to be styled the same as hers,” Naja said softly, like she was making a wish. “But Umma said no. Umma says I am too young to go to the beauty parlor.”

“Whatever Umma says is what you should do, always,” I assured my little sister.

“Akemi does not treat me like a baby,” she boasted. “And she shares.”

“Shares what?” I asked.

“Well, she shares you first of all. And . . .” she continued, “she shares her lotions and creams with me. And she painted my face once. That was the best! And when I took a pair of her pretty heels out of her closet and put them on, I fell. Akemi picked me up. Then she showed me how to walk in heels until I got it right. And she even put a book on my head. I had to learn to walk in the heels without the book falling off. That was fun,” she said excitedly.

“Akemi’s bedroom is the only place where you can walk in heels, with a book on your head or not,” I said solemnly.

“I know,” she said, shrugging her little shoulders.

Our workshop is in the basement of our Queens home. Initially I thought it would be my space. In the interest of our varied family businesses, I opted to make it a place where each of us could organize whatever we were working on. I used a small corner table to take inventory of the items I had purchased and would be sending overseas. On the large table where Umma had her Umma Designs sewing machine and supplies, as well as a clean and smooth surface for measuring and cutting fabrics, she and Chiasa and Akemi sat. Naja considered herself a helper. She shuttled back and forth on any given night, choosing who she was going to work with on a whim.

Akemi and Chiasa were flowing in rapid, fluent, soft-spoken Japanese. Chiasa was describing to Akemi exactly how she wanted her clothing customized. Akemi was listening and imagining and sketching all at once the design that Chiasa was requesting. She would pause after a while and show the drawing to Chiasa for her approval or changes. Umma would then create a pattern for the design that Akemi sketched. Chiasa would choose her fabrics and Umma would make the new wardrobe. Once Umma had the pattern mastered, she could make those designs for sale to any customer if she chose to do so.

Naja was looking over the shoulders of my two wives as they worked. "Why do you want so many pockets?" she asked Chiasa.

"Pockets are for holding in place whatever I am carrying."

"But why are you asking Umma to put your pockets on the inside of the skirt instead of on the outside, like everybody else's?" Naja asked Chiasa, as she also began leaning on Akemi's shoulder.

"I like to keep my hands free," Chiasa said patiently. "And we are women. Sometimes we don't want everyone to know what we are carrying in our pockets."

"I have a quarter," Naja said, pulling it out from her jeans pocket. "No one knew I had it in my pocket."

"True," Chiasa said. "But, a quarter is a small coin. A bigger item might make an impression in the pocket. Then, some stranger could tell what it is."

"Then you should carry a pocketbook like Akemi. Her pocketbooks are beautiful, and she has a different one for every dress or outfit she wears and even matches them with her pretty shoes," Naja said, with one hand on her hip now.

Chiasa could feel what Naja wanted her to feel, I could tell. Yet, Chiasa was calm and cool and much more clever than my little sister, of course. "Naja, do you know any other little girl who is just like you?" she asked.

"Not exactly," Naja said.

"Probably not even close, right?"

"Nope," Naja said proudly.

"Right, because every girl and every woman is unique. There must be some things about you, Naja, that are special. Things that you like, or things that you do a certain way, or things that you say, that are unlike what anyone else likes or does or says? You do these things your way, not because you are a girl, but because you are Naja!" Chiasa said excitedly. Naja was thinking. For once she did not have the swift comeback. Seconds later she came up with something.

"At school, all of us girls dress the same way every day. We all speak in English, while we are each learning to speak Arabic better and better every day. We have the same classes all together. So I don't know," Naja admitted.

"Maybe we should find out," Chiasa said.

"Find out what?"

"Find out exactly what makes Naja special, different and unique, from others."

"Maybe," Naja said. She paused, then she blurted out to Chiasa, "But don't you think that you are a little too special? I mean, you don't eat lamb. Everybody else does. Even girls in my school who come from other places like Saudi Arabia and Malaysia and Nigeria all eat lamb! You don't eat beef . . ."

Chiasa interrupted her. "I don't eat any four-legged animals." Chiasa condensed it to stop Naja from listing all of the animals in the animal kingdom.

"That's strange . . . and every other day instead of eating three meals like everybody else, you only drink juices that only you have to make in your loud juicer. And you eat onions the same like they were apples—nobody in the whole world does that. You put coconut oil or olive oil on your skin instead of lotion like all of the ladies do. I saw you soaking your feet in cranberry juice and almost had a heart attack. I thought you were bleeding to death." Naja inhaled.

"I see you have really been watching me!" Chiasa smiled.

"And you read boring books. You should buy some new ones," Naja criticized.

"I read the books that I like to read. Books that teach me something that I don't already know about," Chiasa said softly. I was surprised she didn't lose the slightest bit of her cool. She's very sensitive about her books.

"And humans have two legs. Do you eat humans?" Naja asked sarcastically.

Later that night, after I delivered the clothes I had inventoried and packed tightly in two duffels to go overseas, I went straight up to the second floor to my first wife's bedroom. Quietly, I pushed her door open and looked inside, only to see Naja lying there on Akemi's stomach. Akemi's blouse was open. Naja's eyes were closed. Akemi placed one finger over her pretty lips as if to say Naja is asleep. I stepped right in and lifted my little sister and carried her to her own bedroom. I knew she was pretending. I could see her little eyeballs moving around beneath her closed eyelids. I laid her on her bed, her face landing softly on her pillow. As I walked out hitting the switch to turn the lights off, Naja began chattering again.

"Wait! I have two great reasons why you should love Akemi more." She sprung up to the sitting position.

"Good night, Naja," I said, closing the door.

"Please listen!" she said with enthusiastic desperation. I stood in the almost shut door not because I wanted to hear what she had to say, but because I did not want to hurt her little feelings even though I thought she was heading down a wrong path.

"One, remember when we first came to see this house? Like before you and Umma even bought it?" Naja asked.

"Of course," I said.

"Then you'll agree that it was a really stinky, messy place. Akemi changed this whole house and made it the most beautiful home. Not only her bedroom but every room. She even painted the whole Fatiha on our living room wall. How come she could make the Arabic letters look so perfect when she can't even speak or write in Arabic at all?" Naja asked innocently.

"No one has to convince me about my wife. I chose her. I married her. I love her. Good night, Naja," I said solemnly.

"And Akemi has three hearts!" Naja whispered loudly and quickly, holding her three fingers in the air and waving them.

"Three hearts?" I repeated.

"Yes, I had my face on her tummy. Her skin is so soft. I heard the babies' hearts. They're twins. That's two. And I heard Akemi's heart beating also. That's three."

I stood in the hallway with her bedroom door now all the way shut. I felt a little tight and a low-grade anger was building up in me. My head had been business all day and all evening, and business was real good. So, I didn't know why I felt stuck the way I did right then.

I could see the light glowing from beneath Umma's door. "Umma." I knocked lightly just in case she had fallen into sleep. When I heard her reply, I pushed her door open halfway. "About Naja," I said.

"I know," Umma said. "I know my daughter has been stirring up a storm in our home. Step in, I can see you have a question." Umma smiled and patted her bedspread inviting me to sit. Amazed, I loved the way she could possibly know the details of my thoughts and feelings before I expressed them.

Umma's bedroom was how I imagined an exclusive spa or club would be, although I had never been to a spa. But people seem to go there to relax, looking for a clean, good-smelling place to unwind and get massaged. Three walls, only one with a window, in Umma's room were lined with long, sheer, peach-colored curtains, which she kept open or closed based on her feeling. The moon pouring through the peach fabric would cast beams of colored light, creating the illusion of stars indoors. The fourth wall had wall-to-wall, floor-to-ceiling decorative wooden racks that held twenty test-tube-size designer glass vials in a row, and twenty shelves of rows of elixirs of perfumes, and oils and treatments that we packaged and sold. The natural scents created a scent that was pleasing and clean when you inhaled. She did not have or want a television, opting for a radio, which she had set on her favorite stations. The satin summer quilt that she made, and pillows from an array of fabrics, made her bed seem incredibly comfortable. Rather than get lost in Umma's atmosphere, her warm smile, or my admiration for her, I opted to sit on her floor and listen carefully to whatever advice she could offer.

"Do you think it matters if a man loves his wives fifty-fifty or not?" I asked her. She paused in thought.

"Fifty-fifty," she said with a soft confidence, "or any definite percentage would be impossible, I believe. And a fifty-fifty portion of your true love to each of your wives is not required in Islam. It is only required that a man treat them fairly. Because of course, the heart and love itself cannot be controlled or legislated by anyone else. Allah created each of us that way. Even you yourself cannot demand that your own heart obey you. You can want it to. You can ask it to, but in the end, the heart feels as it feels and does as it does," she said softly, and then smiled like she somehow could see directly into my thoughts, feelings, and concerns.

"Your father, before we married, had once said something to me that I had never considered in my own thoughts. I was young and in love with him and I listened and hung onto his every word, and he also clung to mine. As you know, I am from the north of Sudan and your father is from the south. He loved my talks to him about the Quran and my beliefs. I loved his talks to me about his childhood and growing up in the south and their beliefs. Well, your father said that being in love is not necessary to marry," Umma recalled with a melancholy smile. She had mentioned my father. She had my full attention. I raised my head to look into her eyes, not wanting her thoughts of my father, and his not being here, to cause her to cry.

"I said to your father that of course love is so necessary for marriage. Then I asked him, 'If I did not love you so deeply, what would be left over between us?'" Umma said and I smiled. I liked her question.

"Your father answered my question with a question," she explained. "He said, 'Sana, do you think every woman has the same kind of heart as yours? Do you think that each woman can love so deeply as you do?'" I smiled. I liked my father's questions also.

"'Some women want to marry with me because they think my father is a great man and they want to give birth to one of my father's grandchildren.'" Umma imitated the rhythm of my father's voice while speaking his words. "Your father told me that and I really laughed a lot at that idea. 'Some women want to marry me because of the amount of land I have and the size of the house I will build for her. One woman wants to marry me because I have traveled outside of the village and she dreams of one day traveling the world with me. One woman wants to marry because her father is the chief and her father wants me to work for him. If his daughter is able to marry me, he promises her great wealth in exchange for bringing him the "golden son in law." An even greater wealth than I myself can provide,' he explained."

"What did you say?" I asked Umma.

"It is what *he* said that matters. He said that he believes that marriage is a choice that a man and woman both make without force, and that was all that was necessary. He said there are so many different reasons to marry. There are marriages that are made to bring two certain families together in relation, marriage for tribe or nation, marriages that are made for money, land, gold, cattle, or fruits and vegetables. There are marriages that are made because a man took an oath to protect his brother or his friend's wife in the case that their soul returned to Allah and that woman and her children became widowed and alone, and even marriages that are made out of pure compassion," Umma explained.

"'What about love?' That's what I asked your father at that point. He said to me, 'The same as I just gave you a short list of reasons that two people want to marry one another, love is also another reason on that list. Different men and different women marry for different reasons. Their reasons lead them into marriage. But marriage is the bond. The reason is not as important as the bond. Bonds should not ever be taken as a trifle, or lightly, and easy to break or throw aside or away. That is why a man and a woman should clearly know each of their reasons for wanting to marry before forming that sacred bond.'"

"And what did you think about his words?" I asked.

"Honestly, after he told me all of the different reasons that different women and either their fathers or mothers or families or tribes wanted him as their son-in-law, I had counted about thirteen women all desiring to be his wife. Even though I felt I knew, I wanted to know what kind of marriage he believed he would have with me. What was his reason to form our bond?"

"Did you ask him?"

"Of course! Your father, in his sweet talk to me, said that our love exceeded the boundaries of north and south, of tribe and nation, and of even culture, soil, and family obligations and relations. He said that his marriage to me would be a marriage of the heart. He told me that I gave him Islam, and that he gave me his heart, and that we then shared the greatest love that could exist on the Earth."

"Did you believe his words? Or, does a woman worry about

comparing what type of bond a man has with his other wives and what each woman is receiving from the same man?" I asked my Umma. She smiled like the sun.

"What woman can hear such lovely words and not believe?" She laughed. "I believed him. We agreed to marry despite all of the opposition and challenges presented to our love and union. Your father chose me as his first wife. I knew there would be two others. I knew that his union and reasons to be with them were different, but that his bond with them and with me was the same. He gave each of us his word. His word was his bond. I did not worry at all about trying to figure out the percentages of his love. His love felt real to me every day whether he was with me or elsewhere. His love feels real to me even now. I did not feel cheated when he provided for them or spent time with either of them. I accepted them as co-wives and as family. I love him, so I love all that comes with loving him."

Umma's words silenced me, and for some moments she had even silenced herself.

"I agree with Naja. Your second wife is a bit complicated," Umma suddenly said to me, and my jaw tightened. "Yet she is quite heavenly," she added. My tightened jaw began to ease. "It's not that Naja and I don't love and accept your second wife. It is that Chiasa shines so brightly in every way that those closest to you, including your little sister, feel that you are only able to see her, when we are all living here closely in this one house." Umma lay across her bed now so that she could look over and see into my eyes.

"It's funny. You and your second wife are both quiet, yet your feelings for one another are so powerful and loud that in even complete silence, everyone around you can sense and feel them. The sea of emotions that swirls between you and Chiasa . . . What shall the rest of us do?" Umma asked me. I could tell she did not expect an answer. I also felt that she was speaking not about herself, but about Naja and my first wife's feelings. But as my mind sped, I was one hundred percent certain that Akemi had never said or mentioned or even insinuated a bad opinion or feeling or issue about Chiasa.

"Not to worry too much. I have never seen you doing anything *harom*. You have treated your first wife with an intensity and tenderness and with great attention and affection. You have provided for her, protected her, and it is so obvious that you love her."

I did not have a response. I never acknowledged or confirmed whether what Umma believed she had observed between Chiasa and me was accurate. I stood up. "*Shukran*," was all I could muster, thanking her in Arabic.

"*Afwan*," Umma said, Arabic for "you are welcome." I liked that she only said that one word, and did not ask me to speak on the feelings of my heart when it comes to my wives.

"Don't be too disappointed in your little sister. She's so young. It's easy for someone to pull her strings like a puppet. Especially if you and I don't set her straight," Umma said oddly. My hand was on the doorknob, poised to leave. My back was to my mother. I didn't move, still listening.

"It's not the first or the second wife pulling the strings. It's the one who feels left out and unloved. When a woman feels that way, she will draw closer and closer to the mother and siblings of the man she loves, even as he keeps his distance from her."

Then, I knew Sudana was the one dropping these thoughts and suggestions into my little sister's head and heart.

Paused in the hallway once again, I was facing the stairway that would lead me to Chiasa's room. I was four steps away from Akemi's door. The way I choose to flow with my wives is that usually if I have spent the entire day and evening with one, I would spend the night with the other. If I need to think, read, or plan, or just get into my own head, I chill solo right on the floor in the basement. I don't believe or feel that either of my wives are lonely.

I've observed that women need and like time to themselves. Akemi needed a good deal of time to create her artwork. Chiasa loves to read and research. And if my first or second wife were lonely, I know they would both take some kind of action to show me. When I was working hard on setting up this house before bringing them over, I'd return to the hotel we had been using, late at night. Both of them missed me. I'd wake up with one of them on each side. I felt like I was in paradise. I smiled.

Beneath Akemi's door was a purple light. In my rhythm, it was Chiasa's night. I had been moving with strictly Akemi for two back-to-back days and nights. But her purple pulled me. Akemi had a different color light bulb for every mood she felt at night, and an incredibly varied selection of music to match her nightly mode. In the upstairs hallway bathroom, I washed my face and hands, rinsed my mouth, and removed my T-shirt and belt. Back in the upstairs corridor as I stood completely still, the house was now silent. Umma's lights were off. Naja slept. I would never know if the ninja girl downstairs was asleep or awake unless I was lying beside her. It had always been like that since we first met. I headed down.

In the kitchen in the dark, I was purposely light on my feet. I lifted a clay dish from the cabinet that was filled with cleaned dishes without clanking it or making even one sound. Gently, I pulled open the refrigerator. I did a good job, but the appliance betrayed me and began humming. Hurrying, I assembled some foods on the dish and grabbed a couple of glasses.

When I pushed open her bedroom door, Akemi was in the midst of a yoga workout, the wicked scorpion pose. Topless, she had on only her black satin panties. Her arms were on the floor holding up the rest of her body. Her legs were curved over her head and dangling with the exact fluid look and feeling and manner in which a scorpion tail is shaped. She didn't move out of the posture or even glance my way. That's how she communicates, instead of speaking.

I placed the dish on the small wooden tray stand, where she kept a pitcher of fresh water each night. As I stepped out of my jeans and shorts, I asked, "Akemi, are you hungry?"

"*Sukoshi*," she said softly, meaning "a little."

"Akemi, why do you have my babies hanging upside down?"

"*Nani*?" she said, meaning, "What?"

"Akemi, do you love me?"

"*Mechya*," she said, meaning "a lot." I lay down beneath her, breaking her pose on purpose. She tried to ignore me and hold it. I saw her concealing her smile. But when I raised my lips to her nipples and sucked them, the good feeling caused her scorpion curve to unravel, and she was then lying flat on my chest.

"Were you busy? Did I interrupt you?" I kissed her. "Are you hot?" I began pouring the water from the pitcher over her body, which was already moist from her workout. She rolled off, laughing, but lay on her back so I could wet her breasts and belly. I poured the rest on her and moved the moisture around with my hand, massaging her. I put honey from the dish on her nipples. She put one finger on her nipple, swiped up the honey, and pushed her hand inside her panties, rubbing the honey on her clitoris. She wanted me to lick her there.

I was brick, my joint was doing its own pose. I was pulling down her panties and using them to rope her over. She was on top; I was thrusting her from the bottom. She raised up and threw her head back, but her hips were still swiveling and I was still pushing in her. We changed positions. Face-to-face, we were sitting and fucking. She moaned. I pushed my finger in her mouth, the one with the honey on it. She sucked it, a sensuous, quieter sound, as we bounced in the room next door to Umma. When she came, she did a lobster grip, hugging me tight as she could, scratching up my back and purring in my ear while I was sucking her neck.

She was sitting on my shoulders now, her pretty feet each pressed against one of my thighs, her purple Picasso nail design glowing in her lovely purple light. She leaned forward, her long black hair flowing in my face. She began speaking to me, softly and slowly, as though in conversation. Not in Japanese, but in Korean, the beautiful musical language that was itself like a moaning. I was listening to every word, understanding none but knowing this was some sweet talk she was saying. I flipped her over with one arm, caught and held her with the other.

"Let's eat," I told her. She smiled, still wanted me to eat her. I gave her a caramel instead, my answer to her sweet talk and her sweets cravings.

Our mouths tugged over one piece of sushi. We were laughing and spilling rice on the wooden floor, where it was already wet and slippery.

Last thing I saw, a view from her bedroom floor, was her exotic fish, beautiful designs that Allah created. Already glowing and swimming in the lighted water, her purple light made them look more amazing. I remembered buying her that huge tank and walking from place to place as she said no to hundreds of fish and would find just one here and one there, and another eventually, until she had the most beautiful collection of living sea creatures. Everything Akemi did looked beautiful, and that was very sexy to me.

Before dawn, my eyes opened. Akemi and I had fallen asleep on the floor. She still held my balls in her hand as she slept. It had been like that with each night that we shared. I would awaken with her body glued to mine or with her holding my balls like she suspected that I would somehow disappear. I would never leave her. She has me for life, and that's peace.

Showering, I was thinking of her, my first wife. Loving her, over the many months of our less-than-one-year, new marriage, it is actually her who disappears. Because she does not speak English or Arabic, she sometimes slips away through those silences and no one can blame her, especially not me. When Chiasa and I were half an hour late meeting her at the Ghazzalis', she was already gone when we arrived. Akemi has a way of sending a shock wave through me with her disappearances, enough to keep me focused on her and to keep her heavy on my mind. I'm never worried about her wanting or choosing anyone over me. She wouldn't ever. But she disappears through her silence and slips into her art. Her art is a magnet that draws every careful eye that recognizes the magnitude of her beauty, talent, and expressions. She is a diamond, my diamond. So of course, she is always in danger. So I guard her. Protection from a husband, father, or brother is a necessary thing. She has that in me. What she doesn't have yet is faith. She sleeps through the prayers and doesn't pray when she's awake. There is no sign of her worshipping anyone . . . but me. To be without spiritual protection is a highly vulnerable and lonely position, no matter how much your man stands beside you. Only Allah can be everywhere at the same time. Still, there is no compulsion in Islam. I don't force her. My prayer is that she will come along naturally on her own schedule, using her own feeling, thoughts, and will. I am one hundred percent certain, however, that she desires our children to be the same as me. They will be born Muslim, and will certainly be raised into the faith, *Insha'Allah*.

Dressed, I checked Umma before going downstairs to make prayer. She was not in her bedroom. Naja was not in her bedroom, either. Downstairs, Chiasa was not in her bedroom. I jumped into my kicks and pulled the front door open. It was unlocked, so I knew they went through the door. As soon as I stepped out, I saw Umma sitting on our front steps. She greeted me with a silent smile. I gave her a puzzled look. She pointed to the right. I looked. Chiasa and Naja were jogging in the dark, headed up the block towards our house. "Come on! Don't stop! Don't slow down! You can do it!" Chiasa was looking back, cheering Naja on to catch up to her.

"*Ohio gozaimas*!" Chiasa called out, waving and running towards Umma and me. Naja finally caught up and was standing there, huffing and puffing, her little brown face covered with sweat. "Drop down!" Chiasa said.

"The grass is wet," Naja complained.

"It's just dew," Chiasa said. "It won't hurt you. We're gonna stretch!" Naja slumped into the grass. Chiasa led her into some stretches. Umma looked up at me. I looked at my second wife. All I could do was smile.

"*Salaam*," Naja said, brushing by Umma and me. "She's crazy!" she muttered about Chiasa as she went back into the house. Umma followed her in.

"Are you next?" Chiasa asked, her eyes sparkling and her smile bright. "I can go for much more. Come on, catch me!" She ran off. I chased her. She wasn't jogging no more. She dashed like lightning around the whole block twice. On her third attempt, I sped up and passed her, then spun around and snatched her up and spun her around some more, her heart pounding. "You're making me dizzy. That's so unfair!" she said, laughing and falling. I grabbed her arm and pinned her against a tree.

When it was time for Naja to leave out for her school bus, Chiasa said, "I'll take her. I am going to school with her today anyway. We'll go together." As they walked out the door, Naja gave me a look. I didn't sympathize with her. I thought she should be grateful to have an amazing sister-in-law like Chiasa. Besides, she was getting to leave with my woman, who I was planning to take out with me for the day. Chiasa looked back and gave me her look. I gave her mine. Her eyes thanked me. She was always thanking me, as though I was doing her some favor.

"She gave Naja cucumber juice for breakfast," Umma said, smiling. "But she did pack her a lunch." Umma was leaning against the kitchen counter. I was just listening. "Maybe I'll go out exercising with them tomorrow morning," she said, stunning me. "Your second wife told Naja, 'Your *hijab* is not a prison or an excuse. Go out and live life!'" Umma recounted. "When Naja translated Chiasa's words to me, I felt something in my soul. You chose quite a powerful one. Her love for you is immense. And she is simply heavenly."

* * *

When Chiasa and I were up against the tree earlier, seconds before sunrise, she asked me, "Do you know what the secret is to understanding girls?"

"Can any man say that he does?" I asked her.

"In a girl's heart there is a desire for adventure. If she doesn't get it, she creates it. But of course there is a difference between adventure and mischief. Bored girls create mischief . . . because they are not experiencing adventure, and they don't know how to get it started. Some of the most evil, most jealous, and rudest girls in Tokyo were the bored ones. Those girls loved chaos, just sat around gossiping, lying, and commenting on the other girls who were actually living out their adventures.

"I want to make friends with Naja. I want to help her to discover who she is and what she really likes and wants to pursue. I want to help her to get her adventure started."

At the break of a pink dawn, standing beneath an ancient gingko biloba tree whose branches each pointed towards the sky and whose leaves dangled like beautiful emerald jewels, my second wife also told me, 'You and I have to keep our love a secret.'" I laughed some, but I was listening. I was thinking, *Is she saying that because the tree is in front of our house and Akemi or Umma or Naja could see us through any front-facing window, standing pressed against one another*?

"How can our love be a secret when I married you in a mosque in the presence of the Imam and the witnesses?" I asked her. "And both of our families already know it. And my first wife, she agreed to it and made it possible. Where's the secret in that?" I asked her.

"I mean," she said, "the secret is in the amount of our love, in the intensity of our love, and especially the expression of our love." She sounded sincere. Yet, I still wasn't clear where she was headed with it.

"It's funny—no, it's peculiar. Have you noticed that when two people love each other a lot, it makes the people around them feel bad on the inside?" she asked me. I never thought about it. Figured these were some feminine thoughts she was having.

"Almost everyone, because when a man and a woman love deeply, it seems others feel locked out of that love. And even if the others are people who the man and woman also love, they still feel cheated. Each person wants the same amount of love, it seems, even when their roles are different. Like Naja—she's your little sister, but because of the intensity of our love, she somehow feels locked out. Even my family, Aunt Tasha and Uncle Clem and their sons, who I really do love, seemed a bit irritated by the love that you and I share openly," she said, and then I could see her point clearly.

"Sometimes, I feel Umma's feelings . . ." Chiasa continued. I sat down at the roots of the tree, always alert when hearing my Umi mentioned by anyone, even her.

"She is a beautiful mother and she's young. Because I am a woman, I'm sometimes wondering if Umma feels lonely on the inside. Sometimes I don't want to laugh too much or let myself go when you are loving me. Like when I want to shout out in joy. But I restrain myself because I think Umma might hear. She *must* miss that feeling so much that your father must have given her. It's impossible not to miss that feeling once you have felt it even once," she said.

"I know all of this is a little strange sounding," she said softly. "And I just want you to think about it, but don't worry. I already know how we can solve this problem. First, we have to have a 'secret love,' like how the Japanese people conceal their feelings and even manage their facial expressions and gestures and body language." She was looking down towards me. I was looking up towards her.

"Next, we have to spread our love around more . . ."

"What? Spread our love around?" I cut her off. "You want us to hide it and spread it around?" I repeated to show her that maybe she was just having one of those emotional, confusion days that women have. She laughed.

"No! I mean yes! We hide ours and we spread more love around to the ones who we love. The ones who feel that you and I, or you or I, are not loving them enough. Get it?" she asked me, smiling.

"I see," I said.

"Then, when you and I are alone, I mean alone alone, really just you and I, that's when you'll feel me burst and explode and shout." She jumped up in the air like a cheerleader. Then she dropped down beside where I sat and leaned on me. I leaned on her too.

"So what are we doing now?" I asked her. "Are we hiding it, or are we spreading it around?" I hugged her. She liked it. She threw her leg over mine.

"I know it's really hard to hide all of these feelings, isn't it? But I want everyone around us to be as happy as we are, and to feel loved enough and comfortable. And . . . if I can conceal all of this love that I have for you, and improve the love between us and each of our family members, that would be a really good thing, Riyoshi," she said passionately.

"Don't hide too much," I told her. "Or else this hunter will do anything to track you down and drag out whatever you've been hiding that belongs to me." I touched her face. She leaped on me and we fell down, lying on the roots of the tree. We kissed.

"You're making it hard on me," she said.

"You're making it hard for me too." I smiled.

In the evening as Chiasa cleaned the kitchen and Naja helped, I overheard them.

"Are you planning to go to summer school with me every day?" Naja asked her.

"Why not? My college will not begin until September," Chiasa replied.

"Yes, but what for? Why are you following me around?" Naja asked.

"Because I'm your sister, and we should at least understand one another."

"Understand what?" Naja asked.

"Understand who you are, Naja, and who I am as well."

"You're my brother's second wife." Naja said it like it was an insult.

"We already know that, but each woman has an identity of her own. I have my own identity and my own reasons. Maybe if you knew my reasons, you might understand me and then we could love each other more," Chiasa pleaded.

"Love! I guess we better start off with 'like,' that's probably better," Naja said.

"Okay, 'like.' That's just fine," Chiasa said softly. "Let's start off with the onions that you asked me about?"

"Yes. Eating them like that makes your breath smell," Naja said.

"Have you ever smelled my breath?" Chiasa asked.

"Not really . . ." Naja said.

"It's really nice because I eat healthy. I love onions because they are a powerful vegetable. They're good for your heart and they cause your hair to grow really nicely. I happen to love them a little more than most people, who use them to season foods or thicken soups."

"Onions make everybody's hair grow?" Naja asked curiously.

"Of course, because onions are good for your heart, and if your heart is good, your blood will circulate nicely. You need great blood circulation for your body to be able to grow nice hair. What about my hair? Do you think it's nice?"

"Akemi's is better," Naja said nonchalantly.

"I used to think so too," Chiasa admitted. "But then, I realized that what a girl thinks about, and also what she thinks about her looks and her hair, is what makes her and her hair beautiful. I love my hair now. It's healthy. I keep it moisturized with coconut oil and olive oil. My hair is thick. It's long and I feel pretty. I think Akemi is beautiful. I don't compare my look to hers, though. She's unique and I'm unique."

"Sounds like you're making a salad on your head!" Naja mumbled.

"Oh, and the 'not eating four-legged animals,' that also helps me to be healthier on the inside. People who eat a lot of meat make themselves heavy, sometimes even sick, and you can smell the meats they eat through their pores when they sweat. Americans eat a lot of meat. So they have to use a lot of deodorant. So it's like they ruin their insides, then they clog the pores of their skin with a lot of chemical deodorants. I don't want that," Chiasa said thoughtfully.

"How do you know? Maybe everything you're saying is not all the way right?"

"Naja, I only know what I have learned from people who are older and who have lived longer and have already studied and figured a lot of things out. I'm a good student because I really want to learn and because I'm a good listener. I don't just always automatically block out everything that I hear. Besides, when I learn something, I experiment and I research it just to double-check that it's true."

"So you think that only old people know everything?" Naja asked.

"I think the wise ones among them know best. But I also learn from young people too, like you and the little girls in your school. I am learning some Arabic words from them and more about Islam. You all were born Muslim, so you've actually been training longer than I have. You should know more," Chiasa admitted.

"I do know more," Naja mumbled softly.

"I'm a fighter, Naja. I need to be smart and sharp. I also have to be healthy and light on my feet. And if I don't want to be detected, I don't want the smell of meat oozing from my pores," Chiasa explained.

"Detected," Naja repeated and then laughed. "Is somebody chasing you?" She laughed again.

"No." Chiasa laughed too. "Not that I know of, but you never know. I've been training since I was five, in martial arts. We don't train necessarily because we believe that someone is chasing us. We train because we should and because we want to be prepared for any and all situations that life might show us. I know you and I are girls, Naja. But, I believe that girls should be trained and ready and able to defend themselves. I don't have a big brother like you do. But even if I did, I would still train myself."

"I asked my brother to teach me how to fly. He didn't!"

"Fly?" Chiasa repeated with excitement.

"Yes, like he does in the dojo. I've been there before. Those guys leap up in the air like they're flying," my sister said, with amazement coming into her voice.

"I can teach you that, if you want to learn. I can definitely!" Chiasa smiled.

"I wanted *him* to teach me," Naja said softly.

"It's better if a girl teaches you."

"Why?"

"Because our bodies are made the same way and we just know more stuff about women than men know."

"Like what?" Naja challenged.

"Like the reason I soak my feet twice a week in cranberry juice."

"Oh, that . . ." Naja said, back to sarcasm.

"In martial arts we train most often without wearing shoes. We are walking and running, jumping and leaping. Sometimes we are inside of the dojo. A lot of times we are barefoot outdoors. That can make the soles of a girl's feet toughen and feel hard. But if you want your feet to be soft feeling, and to remove the germs from all of the places where you were barefooted, cranberry juice does that," Chiasa explained. "Would you like to see and touch my feet for proof?"

"No!" Naja raised her voice and almost dropped the teacup she was drying with the dish towel, but Chiasa caught it.

"Okay." Chiasa laughed. "They're really soft and I was just joking about you touching my feet."

"No you weren't!" Naja retorted.

"And about the books that I read . . ." Chiasa began.

"That's enough for today," Naja said. "I'm going up to my room to do my homework. Now that I know you're gonna follow me to school every day, I have to worry about you telling my brother if I don't complete my assignments."

"No, I'm not spying or telling on you. I'm just going for a few days each week, to help out and to get to know you better. I hope that you'll want to get to know me too."

## 18. FRIENDS • *A Reflection*

"We should autograph this wall," Ameer said.

"Man, straighten up your block," Chris criticized him. "We get paid to build the owner's wall. We almost done. Now you wanna tag it up, put your name on it! Damn, you could take the nigga out the 'hood, but can't take the 'hood out the nigga," Chris joked him. Me and him both laughed, but Ameer didn't.

"First this brother shows up in his Izod and Stan Smith kicks talking tennis. I can forgive him. He lives in Brooklyn Heights. Then today, you been talking about 'Let's go take horseback riding lessons.' How many New York cats you know riding around New York on a goddamn horse?" Ameer asked me.

"True," Chris jumped in. "The cops, some of them ride horses," he added.

"It's a skill," was all I said in reply to Ameer's complaints.

"Maybe, but what you gonna do with that skill? We ain't gon' be no cops. That's dead! So what else we riding horses for?" Ameer asked me.

"Maybe one day I'll buy a thousand acres of land, and we can ride horses out there on my land," I said casually.

"Fuck that. Me and you live in the Brooklyn projects. We about balling, Hustler's League. You in or out?" Ameer asked me, flipping topics.

"I'm in," I told him, laid-back like it wasn't nothing to me.

"Word!" Ameer got excited. "How'd you pull that off? I'm saying, shit just be going your way nice and smooth. No other cat could walk off the court for more than a month and just show up at playoff time six weeks later, except you."

"You don't want me to play?" I asked him straight-faced. "Scared?" I taunted him. "Can't take the heat?"

"Man, we can leave this wall now and run one," Ameer challenged me. "I been on the courts daily perfecting my game, lining my pockets, getting ready to take the League titles and eat up all da cash."

"Nah," I said. "Work first, play later. But I'll run one with you, why not?"

"That's not how we do it," Chris chimed in. "It's us against them, us against them. Not us against us."

"Whose 'them'?" Ameer asked.

"It don't matter," Chris said. "If you hitting the courts every day, we should be with you. As long as we us, them could be any fucking three guys. Long as we three stick together." He silenced us with those words. It felt real. Even Ameer had to flow with it. "And as far as the horseback riding lessons, I'm down. It's something new and different. How much does it cost?" Chris asked me.

"I got you," I told him. "I'm not gonna charge you nothing for going along with my idea."

"Aw that's sweet, you two going riding in them funny pants?" Ameer asked.

"We riding denim," I told him.

"Something tells me the girlies would like that shit," Chris said.

"What, a nigga on a horse?" Ameer asked.

"A young strong brother like myself on a horse. Ameer, you better get up on it," Chris challenged him.

"If you paying, I'll show up. But I'll only take lessons from a fly-ass female. I can't see two dudes sitting on one horse," Ameer said. We laughed. "And on Friday night y'all come through. I'm DJ-ing a party, my first gig."

"Where at?" I asked him.

"In the East of course, East New York projects, in the center."

"No thanks, that's gon' be a sausage party," Chris said.

"Nah, it's not!" Ameer said. "We got some badass shorties in my building."

"Yeah right, y'all so crazy in the East, everybody gon' be strapped, faces gon' be tight, scary niggas too cool to dance. Somebody gon' do something extra stupid. And the girls already know y'all, so they ain't gon' show up in the first place." Chris sounded sure.

"Everybody in the building know *it's my party.* I'm on the turntables. My pops gon' be there holding it down for me. The old heads will show him respect. And, I put together a little crew. The young ones will definitely show me respect. I'm pulling three hundred fifty in one night, one three-hour gig from ten p.m. till one a.m. That's half of what I earn here building the wall, and we been at it for almost two weeks!"

"Three hundred fifty for one night is good money," Chris admitted. "But not if it's the last night of your life."

"Come on, man, don't jinx it," Ameer said to Chris. "Why you so quiet?" Ameer turned to me.

"There's nothing to talk about. If it's your thing, I'm gon' rock with it," I said.

"Heard that, Chris? That's what you should be saying. You was just talking all that ying-yang about unity, and how we three gotta stick together," Ameer chided him.

"Only way I could come is if I lie to my father. I'm telling you. I won't even get the whole sentence out before Reverend Broadman shuts me down. Remember the last party we went to? I ended up in jail. Y'all ended up in church *checking to see if I was dead.* Me in jail, and y'all in church, everything that could've gone wrong went wrong that night." Chris made his point with intensity in his voice. I agreed with him. It didn't matter, though. If Ameer was gonna do it, I had to have his back. I remembered of course that he had already flashed my nine on some of them boys in the East. That was enough for me to know I needed to show up.

"Give him a pass," I said to Ameer. "Chris could sit this one out so he don't have to lie to his father. I can understand that."

"Alright, cool, we give Chris a pass on the party. Y'all give me a pass on the horses," Ameer bargained.

"That'll work," me and Chris both said at the same time.

"And there gon' be some girls there. It's a sweet sixteen party, for a girl from my building. She gave out invitations and the whole shit." Ameer wanted to get the last one in on Chris.

"It's the Globe Trotter!" Ameer's father greeted me. "We need to set up a separate thing just for me to hear about your trip." He wanted to know about Asia.

"He ain't gon' tell you. Don't take it personal, Pops. Me and Chris see him every day and he still ain't tell us shit."

"It's the silent man who has the best stories to tell. Give him time. It will flow out naturally when you least expect it. I'm sure it will be worth the wait." His father made me feel relieved. "And I see you got skills with the clippers. Thanks for using them," he said, about the clippers he gifted me before I left for Japan.

"I cut a few potholes in my head before I got it right," I said, joking.

Back in Ameer's room, chilling while he's getting ready.

"Fill me in," I told him.

"About what?"

"About this party. I'mma lay low. Still, I wanna know if you got beef, who you got beef with, and what the fuck is a 'sweet sixteen party,' anyway?" I asked.

"It's something the girls get all hyped about. It's like they young, but they really are women at sixteen. So on their sixteenth birthday they like to flash out," he said.

"Flash out?"

"Yeah, you know, like dress up and be the center of attention, and get gifts. It's like they could be bullshit the day before and bullshit the day after but for that one night, their sixteenth birthday, they in the spotlight center stage and shit."

"So how did you get involved?" I asked him.

"You asking if I'm fucking her and if that's the reason her mother hired me? You think I couldn't get my own business started up on the strength of my skills? I was practicing every day for two months, on the low. I got up a nice vinyl collection, one-third from my mom, another from pops, and the last third from Mitzie."

"Mitzie?" I had not heard him call her name even once before.

"She's the one turning sixteen. She got certain records she requested me to play for her birthday. I didn't have them. She gave me hers." Then he admitted, "Well yeah, I fucked her. Not really, though. I was supposed to, but something happened. Why does it matter anyway? I got the gig. Money is money, right?"

"I'm asking for one simple reason. Is there some nigga whose gonna be at this party gunning for you 'cause you fucked his girl? You gonna be cutting, scratching, and mixing records, watching the turntables, taking requests. I'll be on the lookout, holding you down," I said, and I meant it. He smiled.

"Good looking out, but this is my building. I got this. Word to mother," he said confidently. He sounded sincere.

"A lot of dudes do wanna get at Mitzie, though. She's a little sweet on me. I didn't even know until one day she invited me to check her, but asked me to come through at one a.m. when her moms and them would be asleep. So I'm like hell yeah, I know what she wants to do. I'm with it. So I comes through at one a.m. She opened the door and it was all dark and quiet. She had one finger over her lips like for me not to make no noise. Then she locked her fingers around mines so I could follow her. I never had been in her crib before. I couldn't see shit. I stepped on some toy that one of them little motherfuckers in her house left on the floor. The thing started screeching and lighting up. She pulled me into a room. It was dark in there too and there was two beds. Someone was asleep in the other bed. So she was like *sshh*, whispering in my ear and shit to be quiet. But then she starts doing all this sexy shit to me with her tongue. She's taking off my buckle, pulls me under her covers. Her titties is like warm water balloons. My hands is everywhere. I felt the nappy dug out and she was ready. Now I'm in my pockets trying to pull out the condom and shit. She jumps on top of me but we're still beneath the blankets. She starts crawling backwards over me. Next thing I know, she's giving me head. I mean like the juiciest, thickest lips ever. Shit felt so good she had me sounding like a bitch. I was making so much noise she put her hand over my mouth. I didn't give a fuck long as she didn't stop sucking. This girl fucked with me all night. Her pussy was crazy," Ameer said, seeming like he was trapped and dead set on going back for a few more rounds with her.

"I thought you said you didn't fuck her," I reminded him.

"I didn't fuck Mitzie. It was her sister who answered the door." I didn't say shit after he said that. In my mind, I had to regroup. Couldn't believe the backwards shit that happens right in front of me each time I come to East New York, or the crazy shit he's telling me that happened before I got there.

"The freaky fourteen-year-old sister named Mimi wore me out. I fell asleep in her bed and shit in the raw like it was her own apartment, not her momma's house.

"The one who invited me was standing over the bed early that morning. She looked mad. But I wasn't fully woke. So I'm tryn'a see her, you know, look at her and figure out who she is and where I was. Then I remembered. It was Mitzie. I wondered what she was doing standing out there in the cold when I had a warm body laying right next to me. I turned and looked and realized it was Mimi, the fourteen-year-old—not the fifteen-year-old sister who had invited me in the first place. I was like 'oh shit, my bad.' Mitzie took off her slipper and started hitting me with it," he said, ducking down like it was happening right then.

"She cried later on that night when she saw me outside. Soon as she felt her own tears she got mad at herself for crying and flipped it all into a mean act. Said she was gonna let me pop her cherry, but that I had *fucked up.* I apologized for making her feel bad, but man, her sister's pussy was good. So like I said, the one who's turning sixteen, Mitzie, whose party I'm doing, I didn't fuck her." Ameer's giving me a serious look now like there was anything right or good about the shit he just said.

"What about her father?" I asked. "You wasn't worried about him when you went creeping in her place at one in the morning?"

"Don't waste your time asking about people's father. She ain't got one. It's her, her moms Minerva, Mitzie, and her three sisters. Mimi, Mina, and Misha, five girls. Her moms looks like one of the daughters, though, definitely not a mother, so a nigga could easily get confused or tempted or say fuck it, I'll bend either one of you." He paused as though he was asking if I understood what he was meaning.

"So what made Mitzie ask you to do her party after you did all that?" I asked.

"C'mon, man. You know she still want it. I'm not sure if she still truly likes me like that, but I am sure that she just wants me to want her more than she wants me. And, she wants me to choose her over her mom and her three sisters so she could feel good about it. So she could feel she's better than them. You know girls compete like that, even if they blood-related." He said it like it was all strategy and game to him, no emotion, no love.

"Last round of questions," I said. "Does Mitzie have a man who wants to fight you?"

"Nah, it's nothing like that, I told you. She's a sixteen-year-old virgin. Or at least she was a fifteen-year-old virgin two months ago when she invited me up. So cats in the building got a wager going on who gonna get her cherry because she be playing high post and hard to get even though Mimi, Mina, and Misha and her moms is all slutted out," he said.

"You two get the crates—they in the back. You take one case. You take the other. You need to eat some food. Look like you can't carry nothing. Just grab my mixer, the headphones and wires. If you five little motherfuckers get robbed on the way to the center you know what's up. You gon' be broke *and* get fucked up and you'll still owe me! You'll be my slaves for the whole summer," Ameer threatened as he gave out the orders to his five-man crew of eleven- and twelve-year-olds. If I was listening without watching, I could've easily thought he was a sergeant in the army, but they were just a crew of boys who I'm sure had no other way to work themselves inside of the teen party without doing Ameer's bidding.

DJ Red Romeo on the wheels of steel was warming up the crowd. I don't know where Ameer pulled that name from. I figured it was because he was playing on the red team in the Hustler's Junior League, and because a lot of girls sweat him, he dubbed himself Romeo.

The cuts he selected was his way of introducing himself. That's the way it sounded to me. He led off with "Looking for the Perfect Beat" by Afrika Bambaataa, only let it play for seven seconds, then cut to the hook "Something Like a Phenomenon," from Grandmaster Flash's joint titled "White Lines." Then he killed it with The 20th Century Steel Band's joint titled "Heaven & Hell Is On Earth." He turned up the intensity in the community center dance hall with throwbacks like "Planet Rock" by Afrika Bambaataa and then "The Body Rock" by Treacherous Three and then "Rocking It" by the Fearless Four. I was watching the room fill up with dudes just like Chris predicted. All fifty of them was watching Ameer mixing, and all too cool to dance. Four or five cats pulled up too close to the side of the DJ table. Me and Ameer's father stood up to let them know to move the fuck back. Meanwhile on the sidelines, there were MCs try'na get the mic. Ameer saw, just smiled and flagged his father over. When he came back he told me, "He wants to charge ten dollars for every man who wants to rock the mic."

I told his father I didn't think it was a good idea security-wise. His father said, "Yeah, I told him that, but he said I could keep five off each head." I moved out of the way so his father could manage the money. Soon as they saw the first MC pay ten dollars, half of them fell back. Now the first MC was free-styling and the all-male crowd hung on the way he maneuvered his words. It was kind of dope the way the crowd was judging him on what he was saying and how he was saying it, instead of what gear and jewels he was rocking.

Thick beats in the cut titled "Apache" yanked one cool guy out of his spot and he began break-dancing in the center of the floor. He was the first dancer. Less than a second after him another break-dancer stepped out, and now this girls' "sweet sixteen party" was underway with only males. Mitzie wasn't even here. A couple of cats was moonwalking. The sausage party was under way.

The MCs who thought free-styling is supposed to be free, and who didn't want to pay up the ten dollars, looked like they was plotting something. The other tens of cats who were too cool to dance started getting restless and looking around, like, "Where the fuck the girls at?" Some of them started pacing around. My eyes were on them. Ameer peeped the vibe and answered them by throwing on "My Nine Millimeter Goes Bang," by KRS-One. The party tone and mood flipped to rowdy.

*I got my nine. I'm sure I'm not the only one*, I thought. This was a Brooklyn party.

Again, Ameer maneuvered the mood when it grew too hostile,

and threw on "La Di Da Di" by Doug E. Fresh and Slick Rick to throw it back into a playful mood. It worked.

"Women are always late," Ameer's pops said calmly. "They somewhere getting ready for us." I heard him, but I was watching these dudes.

Two front doors flew open and a gang of girls bum-rushed in. There were more girls than could fit through the doors at one time and the line buckled behind them, leading all the way outside. One girl had the crown on her head; *it must be her party*, I said to myself. Soon as Ameer clocked her he threw on "Ring the Alarm" by Tenor Saw and faded into "Nuff Respect," by Lady G. She started dancing in her pale blue chiffon mini and heels. Her body rock was mild and conservative as she wound to the Jamaican rhythm. I saw it was all for Ameer, but he was looking down at the turntables, watching his own fingers moving the switches on his mixer. A next girl stepped in front of her in a black chiffon dress, looking like she was wearing the same style—nah the exact same dress as the birthday girl, but the color was black. She started dancing a fuck-me slow wiggle like a caterpillar movement. Then all the girls beside and behind her began to dance too. The males closed in around them. Some girls had three males pushing up on them in the dance at the same time. Other girls had two. Everybody had somebody and the Carribbean rhythms changed what had been an explosive mood-swinging, all hip-hop party into a young sexual grind-out.

The sweet sixteener clawed her way out of the grinding mob and made a beeline towards the DJ table. She snatched the mic from the short stand on the table. She started saying something, but before she could get two syllables out her mouth, Ameer moved a switch that deaded the volume on the mic she was holding. She turned around and shot him a mean look. She came around to the back of the table, brushing by me and his father. She was close up on him, them exchanging words, lips separated by only a few inches. Her body language saying to him, "This is my birthday party."

She must've gotten her way and wanted to emphasize it. The

whole sexual feeling got washed away like someone threw a bucket of cold water, and now Janet Jackson's "What Have You Done for Me Lately" was spinning uninterrupted by looping or scratching. She gripped the mic like she had rocked it before. Ameer eased up the volume.

"Happy Birthday to me," she said calmly, smiling. "If I know you, you can stay. If I don't know you, you can step. If you didn't bring me a gift, you can get the fuck out. 'Cause I know everybody I invited brought me something, is that right?" She asked without yelling but with a thick, feminine Brooklyn-girl attitude. Then she began to laugh. "No, psych—we all came out here to celebrate me and to have fun, right? So we gon' get up a game of musical chairs. And the first-prize winner for the girls gets a date with the first-prize winner for the fellas, and we have a coupon for two for Red Lobster for him and her, a'ight? Let's have some fun. This ain't no party for the dead-heads and wallflowers. This is my night to remember."

I didn't know the game musical chairs, but I watched as they helped each other set up a line of thirteen chairs, every other one facing in the opposite direction. The girls in their minidresses and some in their skirts and some in just jeans began walking around the chairs as all the males watched. Each one of them put on her own version of a strut.

Ameer was spinning "Girls Just Want to Have Fun" by Cyndi Lauper, as all the males watched. Suddenly he switched the music off and each of the fourteen girls tried to sit in an empty chair before any other girl could get in it. But there were only thirteen chairs so one girl was left standing, as the others laughed at her. "You're out!" one of them told her. But she already knew and walked away into the crowd.

By the time there were only nine chairs remaining and ten girls, I was caught up in watching the game like all of the guys in the room. It was kind of funny. It sucked a lot of the hate and suspicion and fronting out of the air and out of the room.

"Word Up!" by Cameo was playing now and there were only four girls left. They were serious about these musical chairs and each kept darting their eyes towards Ameer 'cause he was controlling the music. Therefore he was controlling the game. He wasn't watching them, though; he would just cut the music when he wanted to. Sometimes immediately, and sometimes he'd let the jam play all the way out towards the end.

When the music stopped suddenly, two girls tried to sit in one chair. They were side to side in the seat. Hard to tell who was the loser, but then they both saw there was one open chair at the same time the fourth girl standing saw it. They all three dashed for the open chair. One of them lifted it up and the other two dashed back to the open chair they had both abandoned, and one of 'em got there first. The odd girl out stamped her foot hard and caught a tantrum.

"Move, bitch," one of the seated girls said, and then the crowd of girls who weren't playing in the game started chanting, "Move, bitch, move, bitch, move, bitch!" until she left. Now there were two chairs remaining and three girls. Ameer threw on "Bass Game" by Groove B Chill, featuring Finesse & Synquis. The crowd jerked, appreciating the return to hip-hop after a string of R&B joints. Each of the three girls were revolving around the two chairs, doing something they weren't doing before, touching the top of the chair the whole way around. When the music stopped, shorty—"the Black Caterpillar"—in the black chiffon dress was on the wrong side of the chair but she had her hand on it and flipped it around and jumped in it.

"Uh-un, uh-un . . . that's cheating," the girl still standing said.

"Move, bitch!" the crowd chanted until she went away.

One chair and two girls, both with crazy bodies and short minidresses, bare legs, and heels. The Black Caterpillar kicked off her heels, which amped up the crowd and had the men calling out. The one in the yellow chiffon mini kept her high heels on and walked around like she was on the runway in Milan.

Ameer threw on Salt-N-Pepa's "Push It" and the whole crowd got hyped. The two competing girls started dancing around the chairs and everybody cheered for their moves. Ameer cut the music almost immediately. The one in the yellow was directly in front of the seat. She jumped on the chair, standing up and claiming victory. The Black Caterpillar pulled the chair out from under the yellow-dress girl. The girl lost her balance and crashed to the floor, twisting her right ankle in her heels. The Black Caterpillar sat in the chair, crossing her legs, and her little dress crept up her thighs. "You supposed to sit, not stand," she told the yellow dress. The crowd started saying, "Move, bitch" repeatedly to the yellow-dress girl as soon as she pulled herself up from the floor.

The birthday girl in the pale blue chiffon mini jumped back on the mic. "Who you calling 'bitch'?" She had been watching the whole competition quietly, but now she was yelling at the people who came to her party. "That's my mother! Y'all better get civilized and show her some respect on my birthday! Come here, Mommy!" Her mother limped over in the yellow chiffon dress, took the mic from her daughter, and said "Happy Birthday, baby!" The crowd started singing "Happy Birthday" with the Stevie Wonder melody.

I couldn't believe it.

The Black Caterpillar didn't like the shift in attention. She stormed up and grabbed the mic, interrupting the birthday song, saying, "I won. I get to pick who I want to go to Red Lobster with."

"No you don't! It's my birthday, not yours," the birthday girl said, snatching back the mic. The one in the yellow tried to step in between their fight, but in seconds Ameer's pops touched her wrist and put his arm around her waist to help her walk, and she followed him off to the side. Pops dropped down and removed her heels and was massaging her foot.

Ameer threw "Push It" back on and let it rock since the crowd favored it. The Black Caterpillar dropped down and crawled underneath the DJ table and popped up beside Ameer. This wasn't the kind of attack I was set up to put down. The birthday girl walked around and stood on his other side. He took the mic from her, lowered the volume on the Salt-N-Pepa joint, and turned MC.

"Go Brooklyn, Go Brooklyn, Go Brooklyn!" he called out confidently, and the crowd joined as the whole place rocked to the chant. Moving the attention completely off of the girls that were on him to his left and his right, he was ruling and rocking the crowd.

"Ain't no party like a Brooklyn party and a Brooklyn party don't stop!" Ameer rhymed and the crowd repeated the rhyme. He had 'em all caught up. Another girl rushed under the table and was pulling the Black Caterpillar down by her ankles. The Black Caterpillar tried holding onto Ameer. He shook her off and threw on a cut called "Ego Trippin," by Ultramagnetic MC's. The crowd got swept into the beats and rhymes, ignoring what was happening up front.

A girl brawl broke out beneath the table and all the equipment was shaking. Ameer's eleven-and-twelve-year-old crew flew out the wings where they had been chilling in the dark, got on opposite sides of the table, and held it down steady, screaming, "Back up from the DJ table!" Some of them girls tried to stand up even though the table was above them.

Ameer's pops and the one in the yellow dress began tugging the girls from beneath the table, their clothes out of whack from fighting like alley cats and junkyard dogs. They each came crawling out or got dragged out and tried to straighten themselves and their clothes and hair.

"We gonna slow it down," Ameer announced. "So girls, take it easy. Us men are here for you. All the single ladies, come to the dance floor right here." He pointed. All of the single men over here." He pointed. "This is for you. Don't be shy. I'mma dance with this troublemaker right here," he said, pointing to the Black Caterpillar. "My pop's gonna hold the turntables down for me." His pops stepped up and nodded like a cool old dude and the crowd gave him props like they were all familiar with him. Then Ameer announced, "The birthday girl is gonna dance with my man Romeo

Black!" He nodded, and then pointed at me without waiting or checking for my reaction.

"I like it" by DeBarge was spinning. "I'm bringing the love back," his father said, all smoothed out like he was Frankie Crocker, one of them late-night radio announcers. The throwback record raised up the lust level in the young bodies. Now all teens were paired up and pressed together. Mitzie, the birthday girl, was standing alone, staring at me.

Ameer's pops was looking my way with a big smile on his face. Could be because the one in the yellow dress was right at his side, or because he knew his son had put me on the spot and in the spotlight, the place I hated the most.

I was thinking about the nine on my waist, the ring on my finger, my second wife in my heart, and the niggas in the room. I was looking at the sweet sixteen walking up on me.

"Hey Romeo, or should I call you Black?" she asked me

"Happy Birthday," was all I said. I put one hand on her waist but didn't let our bodies or our eyes connect.

"You not from around here," she said.

"Nah."

"But you are from Brooklyn, I can tell," she said. I didn't say nothing.

"You go to college?" she asked me.

"Nah," I said.

"You seem much calmer than some of these boys," she said. "Nice to meet you. Can I make you my birthday present?"

That was all before the finale. Ameer's pops threw on "Don't Look Any Further," by Dennis Edwards. That song was saying something and had the girls open. He let it rock uninterrupted and grabbed the hand of the one in the yellow dress, and they began dancing right in front of the DJ table. He was leaning her back and she was laying into him. Then he leaned her the other way and molded her body to his lead.

*She is the mother of four daughters, a grown woman.* I calculated the youngest actual age she could be was thirty. Yet she fit right into a sweet sixteen party, not as a chaperone or guardian, but like all the rest of the young ladies in the jam.

No one saw her walk into the party, but she did. I didn't see her until she was already beating the woman with the yellow dress's ass. The birthday girl flew to her mother's rescue. The Black Caterpillar and Ameer and two more girls ran off the dance floor and tried to stop the fight.

She was a vicious fighter, ripped the yellow dress off of the birthday girl's mother and dragged her by her hair naked all the way to the light switch and flipped it on. Ameer tried to stop her. She slapped him. She got away with it too, 'cause she was his moms.

"Chill in my room for four more hours," Ameer said to me, and he was dead serious. I had helped him lug all of his equipment and belongings back to his building and upstairs to his apartment, along with the five-man eleven-twelve crew. He gave each of them twenty dollars. "Damn, now I'm down a hundred," he said, muttering to himself.

"My moms, I understand that she's emotional, but she's getting worse. She fucked up the money on my first gig. If I hadn't listened to Chris talk about getting a deposit and per diem when we were setting up to build the wall, and shit like that, I would've got jerked for the whole 350 and still had to pay my young boys. Now, out of the 175 dollars up-front money, I only made 75 dollars off of this situation," he said.

"I'm gon' bounce back to my spot," I told him. It was two in the morning and I didn't want my wives to worry.

"You need to trust me on this. From twelve to six a.m. Pee Wee and them is downstairs sticking up anything moving. You won't even see them. They hang back in the shadows. And you ain't from around here," Ameer warned. "Them dudes is nasty. They'll take your steel and kill you with it." He sounded straight up.

"I'm not worried about Pee Wee, and them," I told Ameer.

"You not worried. I am. So do it for me," Ameer added with an emotion I didn't feel coming off of him ever. So I chilled, waiting on the sun.

"You asked me to show you how to make the prayer," I said, reminding him of what he had said the night before I went to Asia, when it was just me and him in my empty Brooklyn apartment.

"I remember," he admitted. "But after a party? Maybe not."

"What difference does it make?" I asked him, not to push, but to hear how he was thinking about it.

"I'm saying," he said and then paused. "If I'mma get serious, I wanna be serious, not sliding back and fourth. I'm not one hundred that I'm ready to get serious with it," he said.

"No pressure," I told him. Then I asked, "What are you serious about? The girl in the black dress?"

"Mimi? She's the freaky fourteen-year-old, Mitzie, the birthday girl's sister," Ameer confided.

My mind was blown and I stood still, putting it all together. The mother in the yellow dress purchased a Red Lobster coupon, dinner for two for the winner of the musical chairs game. And even though she was the mother and she brought the prize, she still participated in the game and jumped in the last chair remaining and declared herself the winner. Even though she is the Black Caterpillar's mother, her daughter still snatched the chair from under her and watched her crash down to the floor and twist her ankle, didn't help her up, but sat in the chair showcasing her legs and toes. Even though the Black Caterpillar is the sister to Mitzie, the birthday girl, she still upstaged her, and aggressively challenged her over Ameer.

"Who were the girls who were underneath the table fighting?" They were not the other two sisters, were they?" I asked, thinking and knowing it had to be impossible for all four sisters to be trying to give Ameer the panties.

"Nah, the other two sisters are older, seventeen and eighteen. They came to the party late with their boyfriends, so they were up under them. They all had on the same dress, different colors. You should've caught on from that. Their moms, Minerva, was in the yellow; Mitzie, the birthday girl, in the light blue; Mimi in the black; Mina in the red; and Misha in the green. Now, if they was some random chicks who just happened to be wearing the same dress on the same night at the same party, that right there would've set it off," he said.

*It was crazy,* I thought, him thinking anyone who didn't live in his building or live the way that he and these people think is normal could guess at some actions and happenings that were unimaginable, at least to me.

"The girls under the table were two girls that I talk to from time to time, and the third one was best friends with one of them." He broke it down for me.

"Why not choose the one you think is the one who you could chill with?" I asked him. I really wanted to know.

"None of them is the one," he said. "Maybe I'll import me something exotic like you did." I didn't say nothing back. I don't want anyone commenting on Akemi, my first wife, or on the second one either, but Ameer never met her.

"And don't throw me none of your girls no more. You know I don't like that shit," I said, referring to Mitzie the birthday girl who he said was sweet on him.

"I threw you a virgin. Something no one else can seem to get. I knew you would like that," he said. But he was wrong.

"Don't worry, brother," Ameer said. "I'mma get my weight up. I'll need three more years. When I'm eighteen, I'mma do the prayers same as you. I'mma have a badass wife like you do. I'mma have my business popping so I could be calm and cool like you. You so calm, so cool, you never even borrowed a dollar from me. Plus I'mma have clout and reputation, so I could walk in and out on the team anytime I feel like it, and still play in the playoffs."

"You still heated about that, huh?" I asked him, but it was really a statement.

"I'm more heated that you don't trust me enough to even fill me in on how you got put back on," he said.

"I made an appointment with the black team coach, Vega. Then bam, the owner, Ricky Santiaga, showed up instead of the coach. He wanted me to play. I wanted to play. So, I agreed," I said.

"That easy? The hustler, Ricky Santiaga, showed up for self, in person? I'm sure there was more to it. You secretive and stingy with your stories," he complained. "What was he pushing, that Black Ferrari 288 GTO you said he had the last time you saw him a couple of months ago?"

"Nah, a Maserati Royale," I said calmly.

"Damn! A Maserati *what*? Just a Maserati is crazy enough. A Maserati Royale, I never even heard of that. That's twice I missed out on seeing something mean like that. Did he let you ride in it?"

"He let me drive it," I said. "I'm telling you that 'cause I trust you enough to know you won't repeat it."

"That's something no one would believe if I told him. That's something a cat would have to see for himself," Ameer said. "You think he lets any of the other players on your black team ride in his whip like that and push it too? Nope! He got some kind of connection with you. You linked up with a major player. You think it's about basketball? He might want you on his real team, for real," Ameer said and we both seemed paused to consider it.

"Did he mention anything besides the junior basketball league?" Ameer asked curiously.

"He told me that he doesn't believe that there is any such thing as a bad man," I told Ameer truthfully about the conversation I had had with Ricky Santiaga. Probably I mentioned that one sentence to Ameer and left out a hundred others, because of how it had stood out in my mind. I began to recall it clearly.

Santiaga and I had been back in the parking garage below the upscale high-rise condominiums where he had stopped immediately after he first picked me up. It was nighttime. He had asked me to drive home from Edgewater, New Jersey. I did, but once I was about to round the bend and head into the Lincoln Tunnel, he told me to pull over. I did. He took over the driver's seat and I was back in passenger position.

When we reached the Manhattan condos, he asked me to come up with him.

"For what?" I asked.

"I have someone who wants to meet you," he said.

"Who?"

"A lady who I bragged so much to about that shot you made, that she wants to meet you in person," Santiaga said comfortably. But I was uncomfortable.

"Is she the only one upstairs where you're headed?" I asked him.

"Two," he said. "There are two women upstairs who want to meet you, and that's it." So I agreed and rode up on the elevator with him. He pulled out a small key with an unusual shape and placed it in an unusual-shaped slot on the elevator control panel.

"You seem not to trust no one," Santiaga said solemnly. Then he asked me, "Do you think you're the only trustworthy man and everyone else is below you?"

"Why would I think that?" I responded.

"Do you think there's 'good money' and 'bad money'?" Santiaga asked, ignoring my questioning of him. I understood. He was talking real calm but seemed tight all of a sudden because I did not take the $25,000 cash from him that he wanted me to take. Instead I made the vending-machine business deal with him. *Maybe he's feeling fucked up about it after we shook on it*, I thought.

"All money is good money. And there is no such thing as a bad man, so don't look down on the next man," he said oddly. I was thinking that he was the one with the elite exotic vehicle collection. Why was he now asking me not to look down on him? Or maybe he was tight because I thought his man Allastair is an ass and had punched him in the face. Maybe he thought that I looked down on Allastair. If so, then he was right.

Then he said again, "There's no such thing as bad men. There are only bad situations. And you, son, will never know if you yourself are a bad man, or if you would do the same things as a bad man, until you get caught up in a bad situation." He paused.

The elevator opened and were standing in an impressive living room in the sky. The beauty of it was in its spaciousness, and the placement of each of the few pieces of imported furniture. There was no do-it-yourself, build-it, borrow-it, or rent-it–type pieces in there and the huge, wide windows made the sky, moon, and stars seem like part of the penthouse.

The design of the marble floors was only matched by the design of the Persian rug that was perfectly placed in one area of the room. There were Tiffany lamps and tropical flowers, porcelain vases and expensive abstract paintings; even the media area could only be described as cinema and not television. An open air professional kitchen, two bedrooms, and a greenhouse. I was sure that this was a female place, paid for by man-made money. The type of place that a man would only provide and maintain for someone close to his heart, perhaps his mother, I thought.

"This way," Santiaga said, walking quietly in his leather Gucci driving shoes. He slid the heavy glass doors open and shut them as soon as we were both standing outside. On the terrace was a marble card table and four matching marble stools. On the table was a chessboard made of beautiful twenty-four-karat gold, with pure gold chess pieces; the king and queen pieces were detailed with genuine diamonds, and around the perimeter of the board were inlaid tiny princess cuts. It was an exquisite board, made with fucking passion and precision. It had to be conceived and designed by someone who loved the game, felt they'd mastered the game, and for whom the game had a deeper meaning than it carried for most. I got drawn to it.

"Do you know the game?" Santiaga asked me.

"Somewhat," I replied.

"Think you can beat me?" he asked casually.

"I think I can, but since you own that board, I think I'd have to let you win," I said. We laughed.

"Then one day we'll play in a broke-down little spot, on a cheap cardboard board with plastic pieces. On that day put all of your effort into it, so when I beat you, you won't front like you let me win," he said smoothly.

"A'ight, we'll do that." I put my word on it.

Facing the money-making Manhattan night lights and its unrivaled urban skyline, Santiaga said suddenly, "And if you are a good man in a bad situation who does something bad, you're still a good man, just fighting for your own survival, like all real men have to do."

"So what do you think about what Santiaga was saying?" Ameer asked me.

"I think if I don't take some sleep, I won't be able to figure nothing out," I told him, and put my head to rest on my knees in the sitting position on the floor in my best friend Ameer Nickerson's room. As I drifted off, I thought about how there was only silence coming from Ameer's parents' bedroom. His mother had got what she wanted, I figured: her husband, in her bed, every night. I thought of my wives, then my mind drifted back to the two women Santiaga had introduced me to in that plush penthouse. I considered what message he was relaying to me by introducing me to them at all. One thing I sensed and felt that I knew for sure was that the introduction and the manner in which he was dealing with me that day and night, like Ameer suggested, went beyond a teen's basketball league.

With blue eyes and blond hair elegantly wrapped into a flawless bun, the white-skinned woman in that expensive condo did not speak a word yet welcomed me warmly and was still very expressive. She approached with her eyes first, and then walked right over, reached out and touched my face with both of her palms, and opened both of my palms, then looked inside. She held my hands until the black-skinned woman, same complexion as myself, approached and took my hands from her.

Dark brown eyes. Dark brown was the lightest color on her. Her black hair was natural and each strand was twisted, instead of cornrowed, into a royal sculpture at the nape of her neck. She was thick, but not fat. Her clothing was fine fabric, her heels expensive and sturdy, not stylish. Unlike the white woman, whose hands were cold yet soft in a way that revealed she had never done a day's work, the African woman's hands were warm and worn like a worker's. Her heavy hands felt like the hands of a woman who had lived, really lived and loved deeply and strongly and continuously every second of her life. They were the hands of a mother, perhaps a cook and seamstress as well. Her voice was unusual and unexpected, high pitched.

"*Son coeur est pur. Il est fidele. Il porte le couronne. Il sauveru votre vie un jour*," she said, speaking in what I knew was French even though I do not speak any French. I tried to press her French words into my memory and store them long enough so I could speak them to my second wife and she would tell me their meaning. She is the only one whom I know who speaks the French language.

On the route back to Brooklyn in his speeding Porsche, which he hopped into after parking the Maserati at the private penthouse garage and protecting it with the car cover that concealed the beauty nicely, Santiaga said to me out of minutes of silence, "She has no tongue, the white one. Her husband cut it off."

*A warning to me maybe*, I thought. About the consequences of talking too much, or talking too much about him and his business in particular? But it was a warning I didn't need or fear. On my own, I am mindful.

Or maybe Santiaga was sharing a personal secret, or making a confession, or maybe, by introducing me to the women, he was just trying to show me another aspect of himself for some reason.

I was certain that these women were not women he was involved with intimately. They were both at least twenty years over his age. It crossed my mind that the black-skinned one might be his mother. If so, his father would have to be a white man, I thought. Santiaga's skin color was a degree away from white, not even close to tan without a long trip to a tropical island or even the desert, where the sun scorched and roasted anything and anyone who has a drop of melanin. I thought some more. Maybe the white woman was his mother and his father was a black man.

*Is there an African man who would cut off his wife's tongue?* I thought to myself. Each wife's tongue is so soothing and precious to a man, in my experience. The mouth itself, an opening so intimate, second only to the opening buried between her thighs.

Ameer was asleep now, and laid out on his bed in his party clothes, his red suede Pumas still on his feet. I was still seated on the floor, the wall behind my mattress. I gave up the fight between my mind and my body, and just let go.

"Something different," Chris said. He was talking about his riding instructor, Lila, a slim blonde of maybe nineteen years young, who had just mounted the horse where he was already seated. Now she sat closely behind him. "There are places in New York that the everyday New Yorker never even knew existed," he said, referring to the riding course that was hidden inside Van Cortlandt Park in Inwood, at the northern tip of Manhattan.

Lila reached her arms below his arms and grabbed the reins. She began touching his hands until she had them positioned how she wanted him to hold them. Then she placed the reins under his control. "Yes, now you are holding them the right way, your thumbs up," she said.

They were both seated in the saddle on top of a beautiful oil-black female horse named Medusa, with sculptured legs and a black mane of hair as long and soft and straight as the flowing human hair that lay on my first wife's back.

"Medusa? Like the one from Greek mythology who when you look at her, turns men into stones?" Chris asked her, flossing his school smarts.

"It depends how you look at it," Lila explained. "We call her Medusa because of her 'paralyzing beauty.' When anyone looks at her, they come to a complete standstill, almost as if they are under her spell." Her words seemed to place Chris under a spell.

"First, let's adjust your posture," she said to Chris. Then she turned to me seated solo on my speckled dirty white horse, whose skin pattern was more cow-like than anything else, and completely unimpressive. "Are you watching?" she asked me. I smiled at Chris. "Yeah, I'm watching," I answered her calmly.

"Balance out your weight so that you are not leaning more to the left or to the right," she said, touching Chris's sides with her fingertips. "Stay centered in the saddle." She pressed her body against his back. "Don't lean forward," she said after feeling his body's reaction to her body touching his. "Now, a careful review of what we have learned so far. You will have to remember it all for the times when you are riding alone. Approach her slowly and gently," she said, referring to the horse. "She senses your temperament. Only match yourself up with a horse that has similar energy to your own. If she becomes agitated, she's not the one for you. If she is calm and welcoming, sense that and touch her, petting her gently. Stand in front of her, never behind." Lila reviewed her previous instructions.

"And always mount her from her left side," Chris added. "And hold the reins firmly but not tight, keeping your hands in the right position." Chris demonstrated after summarizing.

"Good," Lila praised him.

"Now can we ride?" Chris asked.

"Patience," she said softly. "You are learning her slowly. Remember she is responding to your posture, your movements, no matter how slight or severe. Let's line up your body," she said, touching Chris's ear. "You ears should be aligned with your shoulders." She moved her hands to his shoulders as he continued to carefully hold the reins. "Your shoulders should be aligned with your hips," she said, now holding his hips from each side. "And your hips should be aligned with your heels." She tapped the back of his Beef & Broccoli Tims. "Don't push your feet too deeply into the stirrups," she advised him. "Balance on the balls of your feet. Got it? Do you think you could handle her alone?" she asked Chris.

"I can," he said thoughtfully. "But it would be better if you ride with me for today since it's my first lesson."

I was cracking up on the inside. She kicked the horse. She had told him to kick her. But Chris replied, "I don't want to hurt her."

"You are not hurting her. You are guiding her, so she will know what you want her to do," Lila said, and they were off. Medusa, walking like she wanted to evoke an emotion; Lila, both hands around Chris's waist. My horse rode beside theirs.

"Don't be too stiff. Move your hips with the rhythm of her body so she can move freely underneath your weight," Lila said. "Relax . . . She feels what you feel. If you're tense, she will panic and react. That's not good for you or for her. Now if you want her to trot, squeeze her with both legs and do this with the reins," she gestured, "and she will trot for you." Both of our walking horses merged into trotting.

The sound of the hoofs in the soil, the bounce of the beast, the trees seeming to revolve around me, and the motion and speed all moved me. The sun beaming down on my back massaged me as I was riding and imagining my second wife riding. She sparked me to do this, although she had no idea that she did, or of what I was doing at the moment or where I was doing it. I knew Chiasa had mastered horseback riding, and I wanted to make it possible for her to continue with it since she loved it. I didn't want her missing her horse or her country too much. I wanted her to want to be with me, to have whatever she wanted or was accustomed to, and to feel fully content. To do that, though, I had to catch up with her first, become fully capable in her hobby. When I take her riding, I'm gonna ride with her like I'd been doing it all my life, like I'm an expert. Like I am leading her. As a man, I had to do it just like that.

"Have you ever rode horseback? I'm sure you have," Chiasa had asked and said to me one late night as we lay between the sheets.

"I ride," I responded.

"Really!" she said super excited.

"A camel," I said.

"A camel!" she exclaimed and then laughed.

"Seriously. You know I'm from the desert. We raise, ride, race, and rely on camels," I told her.

"Oh," she giggled. "I never even considered that."

"Maybe you'll teach me how to ride camel? Take me to the desert where you're from," she said softly.

She wanted to go everywhere I've gone, and be every place I've been, and do or at least see everything I've done and seen.

"I was born in Khartoum, that's the city. My father has a second house in the countryside. Then we spent most summers in the south with my grandfather."

"Your grandfather! I want to meet him," she said, excited. "Let's write him a letter and plan a trip there." She was always about action, even when she was naked on her back, being caressed and her breathing was giving away her complete pleasure.

"He doesn't have an address," I told her.

"Everybody has an address," she said, laughing.

"Nah," I said, rubbing the inside of her thighs.

"Yes they do!" she said, exhaling.

"Uh-un, to find him you'd have to travel through the desert and then the jungle until you reach his village. There's no post office there and no mailbox," I told her truthfully.

"No mailbox . . . " she said softly.

"How do they get mail?" she asked.

"They don't want mail. Everybody they know and love is already in the village."

"No, not you and your father. Your grandfather must love both of you."

"He does. But he is the elder, so we have to go to him. My grandfather would say that if my father and I are not in the village where he is and where he has always been, we are in the wrong place."

"So fucking cool," she said. "The wrong place, huh? Well then, we'll go to him. After you make me feel good, please draw a map." She kissed me.

"A map?"

"From your house in Khartoum to your grandfather's village," she said sweetly. *Only if life was as simple as it is for her,* I thought.

I mounted her. No more words, just heated gentle kisses and deep, slow stroking. And, a lot of love and breathing. That's how I ended up taking horseback lessons, to keep up with my incredibly swift and curious second wife.

"There has to be more than one riding coach," Chris said to Lila. Our first lesson had ended and we were all three standing in the stables, where we had returned Medusa and my horse, named "Easy Does It."

"Of course—there are twelve instructors, to be exact. It all depends on your scheduling requests. Michelle was supposed to teach your friend, but he called in sick at the last moment, unfortunately," Lila said.

"He?" Chris and I both said at the same time.

"Yes, our apologies," she said to me. "And Michelle is a Frenchman. In their country, Michelle can be the name of a woman or a man—they're just spelled differently," she explained. "He is a student here in the U.S. and in any case, he is a great instructor, even better than myself."

"My friend here . . ." Chris began saying as I listened closely to how he was about to set this up. I knew he was attracted to Lila and had already decided that he did not want her body pressed up against my back or her fingers locked around my waist, even though she was an instructor and must do it all the time.

"My friend here will reschedule his lesson with Michelle," Chris said. Then he betrayed me with a sucker punch. "My friend here prefers a male instructor!" he said. I was straight-faced, but laughing hard on the inside.

"So you plan on becoming a serious equestrian?" Lila asked me.

"I'm serious," I confirmed. "And I want to sign up for the twelve-lesson package, pay up front, get the thirty percent discount and today's introductory lesson for free."

"I see you know your stuff!" Lila laughed. Before I could add anything to it, Chris jumped in. "I'm serious too. I want the same package, same time slot as today, and Lila as my instructor," he said, giving me a stern look. I didn't fight the challenge, it was unnecessary. I knew he was jocking for the girl. I also knew Lila was already his. I could hear her body talking to him. I knew she didn't have to get in the saddle with him to teach him to ride, same as she didn't have to get in to show me. And me, I was good, really good, in love with my women and all of my desires fulfilled in every way.

"Twelve lessons at fifty dollars each, that's six hundred," Chris said. "Thirty percent of six hundred dollars, that's a one-hundred-and-eighty-dollar discount. And today's lesson is free. That's four hundred and twenty dollars for each of us." Chris looked shocked at his own calculation of the cost, and at the sound of his own voice saying the numbers aloud.

I peeled off eight one-hundred-dollar bills and two twenties and paid for both of us. Good thing the payment went into the cashier's hand and not Lila's, 'cause her man Chris was at the front counter shrinking under the weight of the debt and his swift agreement without cost consideration. Now the numbers were dancing in his head. But he had also gotten Lila's phone number. I hoped that smoothed it out for him.

"I think I fucked up," Chris said. We were on the same train, headed to his house, at his request, even though I had mad shit to do at my house. "Now I owe you four hundred and twenty dollars. My father's going to kill me," he said, talking to himself really.

"Don't sweat it, man," I told him.

"That's easy for you to say. Thanks for coming back with me. It's a tactic. Your presence will cut the scolding I get from my father in half. He doesn't like to beat me down in front of a house guest." He let off a nervous laugh.

"You got six hundred more dollars coming your way as soon as we complete the wall," I reminded him.

"Man, you don't know the half . . ." Chris said. "My father oversees the management of my life. He says my money is his money, even if I went out and worked and earned it."

"How's that?" I asked.

"My father will pull out a spreadsheet of all of the money he spent on me since birth . . ." Chris began explaining, and we both had to laugh.

"Wait here," Chris said. We had just walked through the doors that lead into his Brooklyn brownstone.

"You can sit down you know, on the couch," his little sister said to me after I had been standing for ten minutes. I didn't sit though, wasn't comfortable taking up an offer from a young girl and getting comfortable in another man's house without first greeting Chris's father.

"Okay, well stand up if you wanna," she said, shrugging her shoulders and reminding me of Naja. "Would you like a glass of water?"

"No thank you, I'm good for now," I said to her.

"That's what you think. Daddy talks for a long time and Chris owes you money, so Daddy will be talking for even longer than before," she warned. Her mother came through the front door and paused when she saw me.

"Oh, hi!" How are you?" she asked me.

"Hello, Mrs. Broadman. I'm fine, thanks for asking," I said. "Let me help you with that bag." I reached for the bag of books she carried that looked like it felt heavy.

"No, I'm going to set them down right here. Taylor, why haven't you offered our guest something to drink?" she asked her daughter.

"She did offer me," I said swiftly.

"Oh, good. So Chris owes you some money, I understand?" his mother asked, though obviously she already knew. I heard Reverend Broadman approaching.

"Son, how are you?" he asked me. My natural smile came out.

"I'm good, Reverend Broadman," I said solidly.

"So what are you doing in my house talking to my wife?" he asked me with a stern stance and tone. I was stuck. Then he smiled and said, "Take it easy, fella. I hear my son owes you some money?" His smile evaporated. "Step into my office." He pointed for me to walk forward. I followed the direction of his finger.

He had a pipe and a pipe tray. Seemed all men smoked something. His office was neat, his files in perfect piles. He wrote with a Parker pen, but also had a fountain pen and ink well. I had not seen that in a long time. On his coat stand there were no coats, but there was one of the religious robes that I had seen him wear once before when Ameer and I visited his church. He had a hat stand with all types of hat choices. Most importantly, I figured, at least to him and his followers, he had a degree from Morehouse College, and one also from New York Theological Seminary.

"Since you are the man with the ideas, I want to talk to you one-on-one. I sent my son to his room. He's your admirer. I'm his father. I support him. Yet, he seems to follow your ideas," Reverend Broadman said, taking his seat in his black leather spinning chair with the high back.

"Chris speaks highly of you every time I see him," I said solemnly. "He teaches us the things that you teach him." The reverend leaned back and stared at me sternly. "My father is overseas. I listen to what you say to Chris, almost the same as if my father was saying it," I said, sincerely. I felt this man was about to hit me with a bunch of questions, so I wanted to impact the tone of this conversation. I wanted to say up front that I know Chris has his own mind and thoughts, even though we three are tight and influence one another in certain ways. I wanted to be cooperative with Mr. Broadman and his style of doing and saying things, but I have my own ways and certain things I would and wouldn't say.

"Like what? What have I taught Chris that you have listened to same as if your own father was saying it?" he asked, his two eyebrows merging into one.

"Your lesson about paying taxes, collecting receipts, and keeping good records. I listened to that and put it into practice in my own business dealings," I said.

"Is that right? What kind of business dealing does a teenager the same age as my son have?" he asked, as though he might think I was either exaggerating and doing nothing at all or doing something shady.

"I'm in the vending business. My mother and I also have a clothing design and tailoring company. If I had known I would be visiting your house today, I would have brought some complimentary samples."

"What kind of 'vending business'?" he asked suspiciously.

"I sell vending machines to business owners who want to expand their stream of revenue. I also own a machine and collect revenue from it as well," I said.

"Where do you get these machines from?" he asked, and he seemed interested, curious, and successfully distracted from whatever type of sermon he had planned on giving me.

"Of course from a vending distributor. I buy wholesale and sell retail," I said.

"And where do you store these heavy machines?" he asked.

"I don't have to store them. The distributor stores them at their warehouse. I have a pamphlet that displays the vending machines and product options. I show it to a business owner or potential customer. Once you make your choice and pay a deposit, I have the machine shipped directly to the location where you want it."

"What if it breaks?" he asked, trying to cover all of the angles.

"My machines are all brand-new, come with a warranty and a repair kit and instruction manual. Anyone can follow the instructions. It's user-friendly machinery."

"And what's the cut on the profits?"

"The cut?" I repeated. "Once you buy it, it's yours. You keep one hundred percent of the profit. In certain cases, where I own the machine and you own the establishment, you can give me a space in your place and we can agree to what percentage we want to share on profits, or the establishment can rent me the space at a small flat fee. I pay the rental fee and keep all of the profits."

"And when the machine is sold out, who's going to restock it?" he asked. I smiled.

"If you have purchased it, you restock it," I said. He leaned forward.

"Where are you getting these machines from?" he asked me, sounding more like an investigator than a potential customer.

"Which businessman reveals the details of his supplier?" I asked him swiftly. He flashed a rare smile.

"You said you have paperwork for these machines, son, am I correct?" he asked.

"Yes sir."

"Then I can just look at the paperwork and it should state clearly where the machine is coming from and how I go about securing my warranty," he asked like he had triumphantly finally cornered me into confessing some illegitimate or illegal affair.

"Yes, but if you are looking at the paperwork and at your warranty, it would mean that you had already purchased and ordered the machine from me. You would be my customer. So of course at that point, I would share all of my information with you," I said.

"How much per unit?" he asked me.

"Depends on what you order after reviewing the photos of the machinery. It also depends on which size and type of machine you chose, and what it dispenses. Could be soda, waters, chips, books, candies, hygiene products, toys, or even shoes."

"Good idea, son," he said, turning suddenly positive. "You're not the first one to have this idea though. I looked into it before. After some research, it seemed like a real rip-off. They wanted to charge me big money up front to buy the machine. Then I would place the machine in my church or business establishment. Then they said for me not to touch the machine. Their company had men who restock, men who repair, et cetera. Then they offered me ten percent of the profit. I told those con artists to stay clear of me before I report them to the Better Business Bureau. How do I pay for something, put it in my place of business, can't touch it, and they come into my place and take all of the money out the machine and give me a dog's share?"

"Was it an American vending company?" I asked.

"Of course! I buy American. I drive American cars. I support American workers. I am an American."

"Well, Reverend Broadman, I'll keep it one hundred with you. My machines are from overseas. My sales are 'clean sales.' Once money changes hands, it's yours. If you see me on your property after I've sold you a machine, I'm trespassing," I said. "This way we give you total control, one hundred percent profit, which is what you paid for."

"How did you come up with this idea, young man?" he asked, reminding me that he and I are not peers, and that I am only a teenager.

"I got the idea while traveling in Asia." I kept it brief.

"Oh yes, son, Chris told me that you were married to an Asian girl. I thought he was joking his old man. Typically a fella from your generation calls his girlfriend his wife," he said, chuckling.

"I am married. But I don't discuss my wives the way I discuss my business," I said. He looked at me, his elbows on his desktop now and his fingers interlocked in front of his face. "No disrespect, Reverend Broadman," I said, because it felt like I needed to say it just to keep things respectful and even. He stood up and left.

Returning with Chris close behind him, he cleared the way for his son to repay me. Chris counted it out. All of his bills were twenties and fifties.

"Thanks, man," I said. With the reverend hovering over him and me, I offered, "Would you like a receipt?"

"Son," the reverend said.

Chris answered him. "Yes?"

"Not you," the reverend scolded his son. "You are a debtor. Your friend is an earner, an asset. Your friend understands that his life is a corporation and he is making the best use of his time on Earth." Then he turned towards me.

"I don't know what you two are going to make out of horseback riding. When Chris first mentioned it, I thought it was a fine idea because he said 'one free lesson.' I agreed to it. After listening to you speak, son," he said to me, "I can see you have a lot of unique ideas, the art of influence, and great salesman skills. You'd fit right into the Baptist tradition. Come by tomorrow with your vending folder—you might have made a new customer out of me. But, I'll believe it when I see it. That's the difference between business and faith." He chuckled.

Outside on the step in front of Chris's brownstone, I told Chris, "I gotta get moving."

"About Lila," he said.

"I'm good. I'm married. I'm not cock-blocking," I said, putting my disclaimer on it.

"I know, I wasn't speaking on that," Chris said, and he seemed unusually serious. "She's a white girl. What do you think about that?"

"Women are women," I said, and I meant it.

"My mother would kill me," he said.

"Why?" I asked, and I didn't know the answer.

"Our family is on display. Everything the reverend's children do is a reflection on Christianity. That's how we are raised," he said.

"Does Christianity say that you can't marry a white girl?"

"Nah." He broke his solemn mood and laughed. "Jesus does not say so, but my mother says so, and up until now, I have not had no type of beef with Moms. We good," Chris said, folding his arms in front of himself.

"Do you plan to marry Lila?" I asked him.

"No, but I'd like to have the option to marry whichever girl I choose," he said.

"What does your father say?" I asked.

"He would offer me a negotiation and some type of compromise."

"What kind of compromise?" I asked.

"He would say I could date Lila, but not marry her."

"How you gonna do that?" I asked. "You think you could be riding around with that young lady and not go in her?"

"Yeah I know, that horseback riding is some real sexual shit, isn't it? She was driving me crazy on that horse." He laughed, reflecting.

"I know. I watched you flip on me, your friend of seven years, after seeing her for seven minutes," I joked him.

"Nah, I just know how you be hemming everything up in every situation you get into. I'm not as fast as you, so I had to make it clear that I had dibs on that." He laughed again, but his laughter shifted back into thought. "I could use a condom," he said suddenly. "Long as I don't get her pregnant, which would kill my moms, I'm good."

"So with Christians, you can go into the women without marriage?" I asked.

"You're not supposed to, but everyone does. It's not the fucking that upsets the church. It's the getting girls pregnant. That's a huge mistake, a total fuck-up," he said, and his words silenced me. As a Muslim, I could not understand him right then. I couldn't understand his faith. I couldn't understand parents that say yes to fucking and no to young marriage, or marriage based on race, or the worst, parents who say yes to fucking and no to babies, new life.

"I know you think that's crazy, right?" he asked, reading my mind or facial expression or something. I didn't answer him right away. I wanted to say true words that he could think about and consider and even do. I was pushing around the "street version" of my explanation, and the faith version of my explanation.

"I think men be thinking that taking a woman as a wife is taking a loss. But if a good man links with a good woman and they marry, he will see, feel, and be able to count up the benefits. For example, your father seemed surprised that a young man could build a business. I don't have to chase pussy, because I have a wife. Imagine how much time and aggravation that cuts out of my schedule. It leaves me with plenty of time to build my business."

"Yeah, but if you marry her, you're stuck with her. What if you change your mind or just get tired of her?"

"If you look at your wife as just pussy, then you went about it in a wrong way," I told him. "If you choose a good woman and you genuinely like her, like her thoughts and her jokes, and her beliefs and her conversation and expressions, and her talents and feelings, you develop a real love for her. You'll respect her and the scary thing is, once you have her, you need her. Then the love grows."

"I don't know," Chris said. "My mind tends to convert everything into math. Guess I got that from my father. If I get married at fifteen, by the time I'm twenty-five, I'll have been married for a whole decade! I might be a whole different dude by the time I hit twenty-five. Then I might look at my wife as an obstacle that I need to move out of my way."

"If you get married, nine months later, you'll become a father," I said, and paused and looked him in the eye. "So yeah, you will be a whole different dude. You'll be one of those 'responsible people' who your father talks about. On the other hand, you'll be so amazed at how loving your wife brought forth your son, and how your son looks like you and becomes your new challenge. That's where you get to prove what kind of man you are, by how you raise your son. Just think, you'll be in your father's position. Your son will be in the position that you are accustomed to right now."

"That's deep," Chris said, thinking. "I can't imagine being in my father's position. That's crazy. He controls everything: my mom, our house, my sister and brother, our family business, our place of worship, my studies, my money, everything, down to the last detail."

"And he will continue to control it for as long as you delay your manhood," I said.

"That's a fucked-up comment. What do you mean, 'delay my manhood.' I'm a man," Chris said forcefully.

"It doesn't matter what you say. It only matters what you do when it comes to manhood. As long as you are a dependent, you will be considered a boy without options. You will be ruled and loved, but not respected. Our parents respect us when we begin to put into action all of the lessons they took the time to teach us, and when what we put into action brings about real results," I said.

"Whoa! Hold up, I need to write that down," Chris said, shifting the mood into playful, something he definitely had a talent to do even when me and Ameer get into our disagreements.

"I didn't plan to get married," I told Chris as soon as the thought dropped into my mind. "I was about training my body for war, fighting, and working and building my mother's business. But then a diamond dropped down from the sky, right at my feet. As a man, and for any man, if you saw a diamond in the soil or on the curb or at your feet, could you just leave it alone, walk away and forget about it? Nah, instinctively you are going to pick it up, look around and see if anyone else saw you pick it up, or if it was someone else's diamond. Soon as you confirm that no one else saw, and that there was no previous owner, and that the diamond is just something extremely valuable and natural that the Maker made, and that it was your diamond, delivered by destiny, you're gonna pocket it, keep it, cherish it, protect it, love it."

"Nice metaphor," Chris said. "But what if five years down the line you find a second or third diamond?" He seemed to be preoccupied with the idea that one woman could not satisfy a man.

"As a Christian, *that's all you get* is one diamond. A Muslim man can have up to four, without sin," I said, feeling good about Islam and the way it flows smoothly with the natural science of man. Chris laughed.

"Damn, man, that's harsh. That might be the reason Christian men are all afraid to marry. Just one wife for life. Do you plan to have four wives at one time?" he asked me.

"I already told you, I didn't plan to have the first one. But the diamond was right there at my feet. I don't plan on leaving any diamonds behind that Allah allows me."

"Word up," Chris said. "Thanks, brother. That's a whole lot to think about."

"See you in morning at the wall." I bounced.

# 19. HUSTLER'S LEAGUE • *A Reflection*

"You was MIA," Machete said. "Where'd you bury the bodies?" he joked without a trace of laughter. I didn't laugh, either.

"I know you didn't show up empty-handed. You must got like a nickel bag for each of us. Some'um to hand off in exchange for being gone," a dude named Dolo said. He wasn't usually a starter. He wouldn't usually be saying nothing. Since I had been in Asia, he must've got some burn.

"We could do it favela style like back home. Give him forty licks for the forty days he been out. No face, no fight back, just body shots. Just take it, 'cause you owe us," Braz, the black-skinned Brazilian, said.

"Could be forty days was how long it took his people to get up the bail money. I been there before," Jaguar said.

"Four players times forty licks no fight back? That's 160 shots to the body. He'll be fucked up for the playoffs," Panama Black, the team captain, said.

"And what? We been winning without him," Big Mike, who played the center position, said, and everyone fell quiet.

"Winning by one point, two points, or one three-pointer or one layup. We bring him back to our team and we can sweep the playoffs," Panama strategized.

"True, but he gotta give up something," Machete said. "We want to smash the opposition like captain said, but at the same time, we each going for delf, setting up to win that twenty-five-thousand MVP cheddar. Only one of us can snatch that," Machete said, serious grilled, and everyone began looking around at one another like individuals instead of teammates.

"I'll be mad as a motherfucker if this cat makes a crazy comeback and grabs MVP. Word up, he won't make it home safe with that stack in his backpack," Big Mike said it and he meant it, but everybody laughed some about it.

"I say we keep 'em," Jaguar said. It's to our own benefit. And if our team wins, the starting five each pulls down ten thousand. That ain't the same as twenty-five thousand, but that ain't no joke, either. I didn't forget. Last game this man played, he fed the whole team, never hogged the ball, set each of us with some clever pics, good shots, and he rebounds. He only hit one shot in the whole game, but it was the shot that won it for us."

"But check, this cat ain't saying nothing," Dolo said. Then gave me the deadpan stare as I sat silently on my ball while they stood in a half huddle, hashing it out.

Coach Vega was leaning on the closed-up bleachers. He had given the black team of the junior division of the Hustler's League half an hour to debate, then make a decision whether Midnight is on or off the team. Clever, 'cause he and I both knew that Santiaga had already made that call and that decision. Business-wise that was all that mattered. Team-wise, I respected how Vega played it. He set the team up to think and believe that they had final say. That way bringing me back on wouldn't cause any player to resent him. Vega always knew how to keep himself looking good. It was also the only way for him as coach to protect the team spirit that moved, and was the key to, the unbreakable momentum of the undefeated squad.

All eyes were on me. I could feel that my silence was causing tension to spread out.

"I agree with my man Machete, and with Big Mike," I said

calmly. "I been gone too long to be a real contender for the MVP twenty-five stacks. So, I'll give that up. But Big Mike, if you win that and see me in the ski mask, don't get tight. Remember that was your idea," I added, and everyone laughed except him. "Braz, I'm moved, man. You was counting the days I was gone like one of my women. Thanks for missing me so much. I missed you too, man." And all cracked up, even Braz and Big Mike, and the tension was wiped out at least for now.

Dolo tried to turn it around. After the laughter, he said to Braz, "I thought y'all Brazilian boys was real men. What was you talking about, licks and body shots?"

"It's licks and body shots if we in the same gang. It's the Uzi if we not. Fall back," he warned Dolo.

"Time's up," Vega said, clapping his hands a few times. "What's the word?" he asked the team.

"We take him back. It costed him twenty-five thousand though. That is, *if he could have won MVP*," Panama Black said.

"So we all in agreement?" Vega pushed it, underlining that it was the whole team's choice.

Machete extended me his hand. I took it and stood. The team clapped, and Vega was clapping too. Only Dolo wasn't. He knew he just got knocked out of the starting position. In thirty minutes, he lost ten thousand dollars. Nobody spoke on it, but I pay attention. Dude had panic and fury in his eyes.

"That's some bullshit!" he hollered. "How we know if he even still got it? Dude could be rusty with the rock. Dude could be doo-doo," he said. The whole team was jeering.

"Hold up! We ain't gonna fall apart over this. Dolo held it down for a month," Panama shouted.

"But we already made the decision," Jaguar said.

"Take your Wiz gift certificate. Sit on the bench. Shut your mouth and be satisfied that we let you stand in, even though your game was never that nice," Braz said. The gym got quiet. Dolo was sizing up the situation. I could see that he knew he was outvoted, outmaneuvered, and outnumbered. Yet I knew this kid was gonna run out and run back in with either his heat or his street crew or both. I didn't feel to kill the kid. I even understood his point, but his style was crooked, unpolished, and wouldn't win him no friends or upgrades on the black team.

"Let's run one then. See how rusty I am with the rock," was all I said. Vega blew the whistle, excited by the athletic option more than by the potential bloodshed.

He announced, "Basketball is a team sport. We not gon' run a one-on-one at practice. Instead give me my top five versus the bottom five. Today, only for one day, I give any player on the bottom five the opportunity to replace a player on the top five for the whole stretch including the championship, not with your words or your temper, only with your skill. Show and prove. But the deal is, losers, whoever they are or whoever it is, handle the loss not on the streets, but as real sportsmen. Whoever loses, if you or y'all fail to handle it like men, it won't be you versus the player who defeated you. It will be you versus the league. And if you run to the streets breaking the league code of silence for any reason, no matter who you are, you will be dealt with, severely."

Me, Panama Black, Machete, Jaguar, and Big Mike teamed up, the top five. Braz, who gets play, Dolo and the four bench riders formed a huddle. They argued, pushed each other around, and fought at first. They couldn't start the game 'cause there were six of them and only five of 'em could play. Dolo dubbed himself their captain and told the sixth man to sit down with the same venom that Braz had told him to sit down and shut the fuck up. Vega watched them. So did I. My adrenaline was working. Panama was talking up a storm, getting Big Mike pumped on how he had to take down the center player from "the bottom five," named Tower.

The whistle blew. Big Mike and Tower jumped for it. Tower tapped it and the ball was moving in Dolo's direction. I jumped up and snatched it midair, passing it before landing back on my feet, to Machete in the left corner pocket. Machete took the shot, two points. Panama was smiling, his two gold-framed front teeth shining. He couldn't stop grinning. I didn't score the whole first half just to allow the bottom five to get cocky sloppy, while feeding my team. I just showcased my complete control handling the ball, faking them out, stripping them and leaving them with their hands in the air like they were still holding the ball, but I had already swiped it. I dribbled through legs and leaped up, snatching everything they shot right off the backboard. The second half I heated up. I started hitting those threes, "all net." I pulled down twenty-eight points in the second half before the clock ticked down. We ran the bottom five ruthlessly, without any respect. Sent Dolo home after dunking on him, with tears in his eyes.

"Good game," Vega had told him. "You might not want to hear it, but I'll tell you anyway. I learned in life to play my position. I'm not the top guy and I know it. But I'm good right here where I'm standing. You gotta get comfortable letting the top guys run the top. If not, you gotta find another arena to dominate in."

Vega grabbed all the black team players into a huddle, the top and the bottom five. Dolo didn't huddle, couldn't shake himself back into the team spirit. He became "the sixth man," 'cause he walked out.

"Don't worry about him," Vega said. No one did. Although I knew he would become a problem. In fact, the whole neighborhood where the black team practiced in a rented high school gym was a potential problem for me.

The night before I caught a flight to Japan, I had a confrontation in an alleyway in this 'hood. Uncertain of whether the dude I banged on was dead or alive was problem number one. As a rule, I never revisit a crime scene after the deed is done. So I wouldn't. Second problem was a girl called "Bangs." She lived in the 'hood where the black team practiced. She was the reason I had to take down the older man in the alleyway. But she is not my woman.

Bangs is a lively and pretty Brooklyn girl my same age, who chose me for herself, cheered for me, lusted me, and may have even loved me. Normally she showed up every time I had ball practice and at each game, wearing a bright white tight tee with midnight-blue letters plastered over her 36D's that said MIDNIGHT. I admit, I had an urge for her, but not strong enough to wife her. Still, I respected her enough not to go in her, for that same reason. She made it hard for me, but Islam made it easy. If she's not your wife, you don't go in her. If you want her, don't play with her. Marry her. Take care of her. Love and treat her good.

I expected that since I was back in her 'hood for the first time in forty days, she might not be at practice waiting on my arrival. She had no way of knowing where I had gone or when I would return. At the same time, I fully expected her to smell me somehow, and come running up in her tube top, wearing shorts tiny as Victoria's Secrets and no stockings or socks, body-rousing the beast in men the whole way.

I decided that from then on, when I ball for the black team, I'd go straight from the train to the gym or to the outdoor court behind the gym, whichever one we were using at that moment, and straight from the gym or outdoor court to the train. No familiar walk-throughs, visits, shortcuts, or dashes through the alleyways or side streets like before. Vega had given us the practice and game schedule. Fortunately, I only had one week of practices in this area. The rest were away games. The playoffs were scheduled for June 27 through July 4. I checked how the championship game was being held on the Fourth of July at noon. It was the earliest time slot for a game we ever played. I preferred the night games. When I asked Vega about the time, he informed the whole team that because we are the junior division, we had to rock with that early game, which is the championship game of our season but the first scrimmage of the "big boys," Hustler League's season. "The 'hood gon' come out in full force for the eighteen-and-up 'official' street ballers."

Panama Black said, "The 'hood gon' come out heavy for us too. We younger, stronger, quicker, and . . ."

"Undefeated," Braz said.

I wasn't hiding from Bangs. I know men control the action. The action should never control the man. However, my mind, my heart, and my hands were full. My business was booming. I knew one slip-up to the left or the right could smoke a blessing, ruin a reputation, and cause a setback it would take years to set straight. My sensei once taught me that "the best thinker is the one who can think ahead of the present time and set a strategy into motion that will best secure his future." I was making my best effort to do that.

On the train heading home, I thought of Marty Bookbinder. He owned a bookstore in that problematic 'hood where the black team practiced. Way back when, I took him for a friend, an older man who I ordered books from and played chess with. I smiled, thinking of how I came to be able to beat him at what he believed was his own game. I definitely wanted to check him. I even needed to put in time for a few games so I'd remain a sharp chess player. I believed that Santiaga was a man who would follow up on his challenge to me for a game of chess. When he does, I want to be lethal.

## 20. MARCUS

"It's for you," Chiasa said, handing me the blue phone. Our eyes locked. Her father had never requested to speak to me and he was the only one who called her on the blue phone. She felt me, then mouthed, "It's Marcus." I nodded for her to leave the room even though it's her bedroom. She left.

"Go," I said.

"It's Marcus," he said.

"What?"

"Are you ready?" he asked.

"Date, time, and place," I said.

"First things first, I hope you're not the type of dude who engages in pillow talk," he said. I didn't know what the fuck he was talking about, so I didn't say nothing, just waited for him to tell me when and where and at what time he wanted to fight. "No matter what happens," he began saying, "and no matter the outcome, you and me, we don't involve no mothers, aunts, or girl cousins in our beef," Marcus said.

"No women," I summed it up for him. Then I said, "What else would it be?" to let him know that's how I normally handle man-to-man conflict. Girls and guns, I keep 'em separate.

"Meet me tomorrow night at nine p.m. on 120th and Riverside Drive, the park between Riverside and the West Side Highway," he said.

"A'ight," I agreed. "Tomorrow at nine p.m. No women and no cops," I said.

"Definitely no cops, and no guns," he added on. I hung up.

Instinctively, while thinking about it, I started doing push-ups on Chiasa's bedroom floor. I was already in my basketball shorts from the early evening practice. Exercise never fails to speed up my thought process, brings me new ideas and strategies about anything on my mind at the time. Besides, exercise is daily; morning, afternoon, and night, second only to my prayers.

She knocked lightly. I didn't answer. I was keeping the count. She turned her knob and pushed in slightly. Now her face was in and her body was on the other side of her door. The whites of her eyes were shining like headlights set on high beam. She came in and dropped down beside me and began doing push-ups as well. Her being right next to me, and seeing her pretty arms and shoulders, diluted my concentration and fucked up the count.

"Sixty-eight, sixty-nine," she said, as she started counting for me from where I had left off. She was smiling at me, and I was getting drawn in by those long lashes.

"I'm breathing harder than you," she said. I didn't respond, just picked up the count where she'd stopped counting.

"Eighty-nine, ninety, ninety-one," I said, counting aloud. When I reached one hundred, she stopped pushing up. When I raised up on one hundred and two, she rolled over and beneath me. So, when I went down, she and I were pressed together.

"Tell me," is all she said, breathing hard and catching her breath. I raised up off of her and said, "One hundred and three." When I came down, she wrapped her arms around me and would not let go. I went up. "One hundred and four," I said. Now I was raised up and her body was clinging to me, adding enough weight onto a man who did a hundred a clip to cause me to come crashing down. We laughed.

"*Sshh,*" she said, and went into her "secret love mode" that she'd made up for us. "What did he want?" she whispered to me. She was curious about the convo I'd just had with Marcus. I was thinking, *At least she is smart enough not to say his name to me.* Even though he is her blood-related cousin, that would be too much.

"You slid beneath me," I said to her.

"Yeah, I did," she answered softly.

"So focus . . . *on what I want.*"

After the before-sunrise prayer, I was on Riverside Drive at the park, in my sweats, gripping my ball. I was checking it out. I had given Marcus some advantages I would never willingly give up to any other fighter, rival, or enemy. I allowed him to choose the location of our battle. So of course, he had chosen Harlem, his own territory. It would be familiar, almost second nature to him, and unfamiliar to me. I had also allowed him to choose the time. Of course he chose the cover of darkness, nighttime on his home territory. I allowed him to select the date. More than two weeks had elapsed since the first family dinner at Aunt Tasha's, his father and mother's house. Of course, he had been training his body every day since then, training and dreaming and scheming on how he could best get at me.

As I walked through this old park, I did a detailed survey of the area. I checked out the perimeter, the actual entrances and exits, the makeshift entrances and exits through the random holes in the fence as well as on the highway side.

Then I paused beneath the oak trees, looking at the bushes and scoping out possible hiding spaces where anyone could cover and spring out and attack. The fight between Marcus and me was supposed to be one-on-one. Still, I needed to consider that since we were on his territory, maybe he would have a crew laying in the cut in some of those hidden spaces. Ninjutsu training requires that one of my steps in a fight where I have time to plan must be to place myself into the mind of my opponent for my own good. If I could imagine his thoughts and strategies and moves, when he does actually make them, I have already eliminated the element of surprise, because I already saw those exact moves in my mind's eye and have already examined my options and choreographed my responses.

I spotted a big boulder and pressed my Tims against it to see if it moves. I was imagining throwing down an opponent, his head accidentally smashing open on that bolder. That wouldn't be good. I did not want murder, and did not have murder on my mind. I would put the hurt on him, though. I wanted him to feel the pain so the pain could be a reminder for him to stay in his lane . . . since we are family and I planned to love his cousin, my wife and second mother—to my first wife's children—*Insha'Allah* and first mother to her and my children, *Insha'Allah*, for as long as Allah gave me breath.

In the play area, I was scoping out the benches, the swings, the caves, and the monkey bars. It was a place made for children. At the same time at night when no children would be out here, all of these would become weapons, especially for a fighter who could leap, launch, and "fly," as my sister Naja called some of the moves in martial arts that she observed at my dojo.

I was moving past the handball court, onto the dirt of the volleyball area with the ripped-up net. I was envisioning my opponent being kicked down to the ground, then secretly coming up with a fistful of sand or soil to throw in my eyes and gain the advantage.

Right outside of that area is a small workout spot with three pull-up bars, all positioned at varying heights. It looked like a challenge to me. I leapt onto the highest one, banged out fifty pull-ups, before I lifted my legs, brought them towards my head, and then hung on the bar by my quads. I was experiencing now the feeling of reversing my blood circulation. Everything was upside down and my eyes were facing the sky. The promise of the sun was being delayed by hordes of crowded and busy black clouds. It felt like the clouds were having a massive meeting, where they were plotting a conspiracy to kill the sun. I smiled, knowing that the clouds, despite their numbers and movements, could delay but could never defeat the sun.

Arriving at their basketball court—rims, no nets, uneven and slightly shorter than regulation height—I thought, aloud. *Instead of a fight, He should've challenged me to a game on his court.* That way, no blood would be drawn and his defeat would be easier for his ego to manage. Then suddenly I heard my sensei's voice in my mind, the simple but true advice cautioning me to never underestimate my opponent. I smiled again, thinking to myself, *true dat.*

At the same time, though, I was also thinking, *What's this cat's motivation for this fight*? What did he stand to gain or to lose? He didn't attempt to place a wager on the outcome. There was no prize or reward in it for him. If we fought one-on-one as agreed, and no one else saw it, there was no glory in it for him. I reminded myself not to bang my brain on it. It was next to impossible for me to understand the African-American mindset. Most of them were mad at the things that should make them happy, I thought, and content and stagnant with the things that should make them make moves. Too many of them hated the exact things that they should love, I thought. Consequently, they loved the things that should be hated. It didn't seem to matter whether they were educated or uneducated; street cats or PhDs; rich or poor, or stuffed in between rich and poor. They all seemed to be comfortable with sex, yet fearful of love. Most of them seemed to be completely against marriage at any age, especially marriage before sex, or marriage between young adults.

The young females expected any guy who they found attractive to sex them, fuck them automatically, and to fuck them good, but at the same time, they humiliated and disrespected good guys who actually loved them, while they worshipped and chased and loved guys who ran through and abused them. They feared pregnancy and hated the thought of babies, and had already decided on abortions even before they conceived. How the hell was I supposed to understand people who thought and lived like that? To me it was all backwards.

Marcus hated that I had married his cousin, and his whole family appeared uncomfortable with how much she loved me and I loved her and that we were wedded and certain. Yet I had not disrespected his cousin, his parents' niece, my wife. I had not gone into her without marrying her first. I had not sexed her and abandoned her, or impregnated her and killed our baby. I had loved her and married her, and went into her only after marriage, and brought her to my home and protected and provided for her. Shouldn't that make them happy? Instead, this dude wanted to fight. My thoughts led me to the conclusion that he had a thing for my wife, even though she is his cousin. Now I'm heated and tight. Now I'm hanging, two hands on the rim that I'd just slam-dunked my ball through. It was on the ground rolling and I was just suspended in the air.

"Wanna get a game?" some Harlem dude asked me, after tracking down my ball. I dropped down, didn't even agree, but accepted.

"Check," he said, taking it back, and the one-on-one started. I was playing, but I was in my head heavy. I was stealing the ball, dribbling, pushing it back and forth through my legs while fancy footing it, spinning, and laying it up.

"Two," was all I said. *Fuck it*, now I was thinking of Marcus, the way a ninjutsu warrior thinks of his enemy. My mind was converting him from family into someone I wouldn't cease fighting until the deed was done.

In my mind's eye, I was seeing the metal trash cans. In this park, they were chained to the bench. I was planting a burner beneath it. I was burying and camouflaging my *kunai* knives in the soil, handle up so I could swiftly swoop down and grab them and fire them into his chest.

"Four," I said. I was seeing a human anatomy map in my mind, the one that sensei posted on the board in my private lessons. "Six," I said. I was deciding whether I was going to target his joints and break limbs, or just swipe a gentle cut through his brachial artery with my knife and let him bleed to death while he figured out that fighting me was a lose-lose situation for himself from the start. "Eight," I said. I was seeing him trying to fight dirty, wearing brass knuckles and banging the sharp metal against my temple. "Ten," I said. I was seeing him wearing a spiked ring and trying to gouge out one of my eyes and then drag the ring down, cutting open my face and trying to fuck up my look so my second wife could look at me differently than she does. "Twelve," I said. I was seeing him pulling out the four-pound after saying, "No guns," and then letting off.

"Fourteen," I said. I was seeing myself kick the gun out of his hands, both of us leaping to get it. "Sixteen," I said. Of course I got to it first. "Eighteen," I said. I didn't shoot; I whip him with it, just wanting to give him some natural cosmetics to wear for a couple of weeks. "Twenty," I said. I was seeing his cocky ass trying to explain why his face was all swolled up to his military friends and superiors. "Twenty-two," I said. My second wife's face popped up. "Don't hurt him," she asked me. "It's better if we can all be friends. We are family," she suggested softly. I slowed down my dribble. My bounce was slow. My eyes were on the hoop. With my right hand, I pushed the ball between my opponent's legs and palmed it from the other side and layed it up. Scoring, I said, "That's it."

"Damn," was all the guy said. He shouldn't said nothing. How could he invite me to a game and get shut out like that?

"I got winners," a next cat who rolled up courtside said. I looked at him.

"Nah," I replied. "I gotta go to work." I left the two of them standing there. It was 7:30 a.m. Never understood the dudes that show up to the court without a ball or a friend with a ball.

I hopped in a taxi back to Queens. I had twenty-five minutes to meet up on time with Chris and Ameer. Today would be our last day on the wall.

A light rain, more like a mist. It's nighttime. I'm headed to the train.

At 8:50 p.m., I climbed the last step that led me out of the subway and onto 115th Street in Harlem. I'm walking beneath a downpour. Had my wool hat on beneath my black hoodie. It was too warm out to wear it, but I wore it for war. Hotheaded, light-footed, heavy-hearted, I'm walking west. I don't have Marcus's phone number. I refuse to call my second wife to get it. I wouldn't give her swift mind even one clue. I could walk directly to his house to see if he stayed home due to the rainfall. But why show up there and tip off his moms? She's more clever than a fox and an owl, a forensic psychiatrist as aggressive as a pit bull or a bloodhound. Nah, I head straight over to the park, keeping my word to Marcus and assuming he would keep his word also and show up for the fight he wanted, undaunted by some heavy raindrops.

The park lights were off. The streets were wet and dark. The leaves on the trees were spilling ounces of cold water at a time. The park entrance on Riverside was chained shut. I kept walking, headed south 'cause I knew where the hole in the fence was located. On my way I saw cars, taxis, and vans speeding and splashing by, and a few people running into their Riverside Drive apartments, or beneath a canopy, or ducking into a doorway. Behind me I heard someone running, must be fucking up their kicks in the mud and puddles, I thought, but instinctively I turned to check. The knife that was about to stab me in my back stabbed me in my chest instead. I could feel the puncture, upper chest below my left shoulder but above my heart, and the knife was still in me like a stopper in a sink preventing the water from draining out. He leaned back, must have been more comfortable with his plan to backstab me and then breeze by like it wasn't him. But now we were face-to-face. I knew it was him. I flew my right fist and crashed it into his jaw. He stumbled to his left. Swiftly, I turned my back to him and kicked him down with half a left-footed roundhouse. He leaped right up, looked dizzy but caught his balance, raised his fists and lunged at me. I pulled the knife out of my chest and used it to back him down. He feared his own knife. As he backed up he tripped on a rock and fell backwards. I jammed the knife into the bark of a nearby tree. He was almost back on his feet when I kicked him in his chin forcefully and precisely like an NFL kicker. He was down again and bloody mouthed. I looked at him and said two words: "Stand up." As soon as he tried, I kicked him forcefully, crushing his kneecap, and broke his leg.

I pulled his dagger out from the tree bark. My second wife's image flashed before my eyes. When I had left the house for this fight, she was making a prayer. I wiped the bloody blade clean with the white washcloth in my back pocket, then stuck it down in the dirt next to him. He tried not to look me in the eye. He tried not to cry out in pain. But no matter how manly a man, no matter West Point military training or not, a crushed kneecap causes extreme pain.

A second thought came to me. I took two steps back where he lay squirming, and pulled his knife from the soil, and closed and pocketed it. As I walked away, I pressed the bloody cloth against my wound beneath my clothes to clog the blood that was leaking down my chest beneath my T shirt, which was beneath my hoodie.

I wasn't worried about him. His younger brother was across the street beneath a canopy, concealing his identity with an umbrella. *Good*, I thought to myself. He came to watch his big brother defeat the husband of the girl cousin who they were both in love with. Now he gets to try and carry his crippled big brother back home.

At my house, I headed upstairs to my Umma, the superb seamstress. I needed her to disinfect and stitch my wound. My second wife opened her first-floor bedroom door and saw me. She watched me move up the staircase. She said nothing. She never calls me back or follows me up these stairs that lead to the bedroom of my first wife. She is an expert at making friends, keeping friends, and not arousing jealousies or pissing anyone off. And she knew that once I take the first three steps up alone, towards my first wife, Akemi, I never turn back. Besides, once Umma disinfects and stitches me, Akemi is an expert at wrapping wounds without questioning, and at sensuously and silently soothing me. She'd done it a few times before. Like the difference between fire and water, tonight, I prefer her.

## 21. THE SHE-OFFICER

"Wrists," she said. I hesitated. All the other COs said, "Hands." I pushed my hands through the slot on my cell door. She cuffed me before unlocking the door and letting me out.

"Thank you," was all I said to her. I'm completing my first month of twenty-three-hour-a-day lockdown in the box. This is my one free hour of recreation alone. However, I requested a shower. She was here to escort me.

After a long pause, she said, "You're welcome." I wondered why she wore perfume to work in a jail surrounded by men whose minds and actions go from one extreme to the other. I could smell her perfume and her body lotion and even her hair spray and mouthwash. Of course I could. She is woman, the only woman I'd seen in four weeks. We're walking.

"You're quiet," she remarked. "You're *the quietest one*," she said with emphasis. "You have good manners. I hope you don't let this place destroy you." We continued the rest of our walk in silence. When we reached the shower stall, she watched me walk in. I knew the shower routine down pat. Before she could call it out, I put my cuffed hands through the slot. She uncuffed me.

"Three minutes," she said, like she regretted saying it but had to. She knew three minutes was not enough time.

"Please turn," I said to her, because she was still looking in.

"I have a son your age," she said.

"Impossible," I said at the same time that the water blasted on.

When my time was up, I swiftly toweled dry and dressed, and stood by the slot waiting to be cuffed again so she could open the door and escort me back. Instead of saying "hands" or "wrists," she put her face up to the slot.

"Why impossible?" she asked me. But my mind was elsewhere.

"Excuse me?" I said.

"I said I have a son your age. You said 'impossible.' Do I really look that young to you?" she asked, fishing for a compliment.

"No son my age would let his moms work in a place like this. He'd work two or three jobs if he had to, just to keep you out of here. That's why," I told her solemnly.

"Wrists," she said, and cuffed me. She and I walked back to the cell in silence same as we came, even as other inmates on lockdown shouted "Yo, CO!" or screamed or begged or rhymed, or cursed or cried. Agony hung in the air, agony and strife. The weight of being isolated and alone was crushing each of them one by one. I was not happy, but I was not crushed. For some of these guys, the last person they would want to be left alone with was themself. They reacted as though they were being tortured, but there was no one in the box with them but themselves.

My cell door locked behind me. I pushed my hands through the slot. The CO uncuffed me. I could hear her shoes on the floor as she walked away. *She normally works nights*, I said to myself. I would see eyes peering in or sometimes feel them paused on me when I wasn't looking. Or sometimes I would just smell her presence, or hear her breathing before I actually saw the pupils of her eyes. *That's her job*, I would tell myself. She was counting bodies and checking to see if I had hung myself same as the man three doors down did three days ago. It didn't matter to me how many times she checked or for how long she watched me standing or sitting still, or working out. Suicide is not my style, my reaction, or my option. I had love waiting for me.

Even-tempered, that's how I been, like a Zen warrior. I was

doing time. Time wasn't doing me. I cut each of my days in the box into fractions. Set and kept appointments same as a free man with a demanding, packed, and urgent schedule. Some were constant and at the same time every day, like my prayers, their count, my three-hour workouts, and their meal service. Already in mint condition before I murdered the one that had to be murdered, now I was becoming cut, carved stone and chiseled, a lean and solid force of steel.

Outside of the physical training, mind travel was my form of entertainment. It is better than an action flick, an awesome adventure movie, a comedy, a romantic film, and even an R-rated skin flick. It is more than and way beyond a great book or any magazine. Completely quiet and still I would leave my body seated on the floor or on the slab that was my bed, while my mind, heart, and soul escaped into one of my millions of memories. My memories are sharp, clear, vivid, and detailed. I could observe and feel more in a memory than I might have ever seen or felt during the moment that actually happened in real life. I could feel my wives breathing in my memories of them. I could hear my Umma's voice and feel the weight and wisdom and impact of her words. I could even see and feel the warmth in her smile. Through remembering, I sometimes found my shoulders shaking with laughter at something funny that I recalled. And, for the first time ever, I made love and had sex and even fucked through a memory. Sweetly and slowly it unfolded and spread out in my mind's eye. Wide awake, not dreaming, and fully conscious, I could see and feel my fingers gripping the tight waist of my second wife, my pinky finger grazing the roundness of her behind. I could see my own fingers massaging Akemi's clitoris, then pinching it slightly enough until her pussy walls quaked.

I could see nipples rising, feel lips and taste tongues. I loved being caught in the wind of my memories, sometimes inhaling the scent of my women. Akemi wore the scent of Sudan, perfume that Umma conceived, mixed and slow dripped into a beautiful crystal bottle shaped like an Arabic lantern and customized exclusively for her. In that bottle was the aroma that led to the creation of new lives in my first wife's womb. A concoction so powerful that through it, Umma's desire was born.

Chiasa's perfume was as unusual as herself. It was not perfume imagined, mixed, or personally and purposely gifted by Umma. She preferred pure fruit and vegetable oils with their natural scent. She always smelled like something edible, which instinctively made me lick, taste, and eat her like a delicacy. And she knew it. Doused from her scalp to the soles of her feet with pure oil from the coconut, or the olive, Chiasa was sensual and slippery. She would oil me after herself. Her nude and evocative body glided across a marble floor once, and I was sliding on her and in her, but that is a memory that I am savoring for a time when I might need it most.

The men in my memory are up close and sharp. My mind sees their fashions and styles of kicks and jeans and shirts and hats and jewels precisely. There is no fogginess and they are clearer to me in memory than they were in real life.

In my memories, I am able to go in slow motion, to rewind, to fast-forward, and even to use a zoom lens. Beyond my boys' styles, in my memory their strengths are amplified, and their flaws leap out as well. In my memory, there is no distance between myself and my male acquaintances, friends, or even the enemies I interacted with, as there was in real life. In my memory I study them all real hard. By studying them, I am also studying myself. In my memories of Chris and Ameer, I could still feel the energy of our friendship.

"Don't you sleep?" I asked the CO whose eyes were watching me when I raised my head from making the Isha night prayer.

"I'm doing a double-triple," she said. I didn't say nothing back. "I'm saving up. My son goes to an expensive private prep school in upstate New York. You probably never heard of it," she said proudly.

"You're probably right. I never did," I answered.

"I am right. It's you who is wrong," she said strangely. "My son does love me even though I'm a corrections officer who works in a place like Rikers Island."

"What's love?" I asked her nonchalantly.

She looked at me like it was a trick question. "For men and for women it's different," I explained to her. "A woman who loves comforts and serves. A man who loves protects and provides," I said, moving up closer to the slot. She was thinking about it. I could tell. "You are here unprotected," I told her and watched the thought move in her eyes. "You said your son is my age. Then he knows where you are, doesn't provide for you, but waits for you to work a double-triple in a dangerous place surrounded by dangerous men and then hand the money over to him, right or wrong?" She sucked her teeth hard and walked away.

"Get off his nuts and come get on mine!" an inmate shouted from the next cell over. He was the new body that replaced the dead body they had already removed.

Many nights came and went. Every night she worked, she came and stood on the other side of my locked cell door, speaking to me as quietly as anyone could speak in a space where you could not whisper and be heard unless your lips were pressed to an ear. So everyone yelled. I mostly listened to her private thoughts and experiences, in a space where there is no privacy. She talked the most, like her soul was vomiting, and I'd tell her the truth as I saw it about serious, everyday general topics and issues that she had spoken about. I never confided anything personal in her, or revealed anything to her about my case, background, or future. I never touched her or even flirted with her; still she came. She had no husband, she had told me casually, like it wasn't nothing. "Don't have one, don't need one," were her exact words. "Everything my son needs, I get it for him. He doesn't need his father either, just like I don't need no husband," she said passionately.

"His father is a real motherfucker, and he's a CO right up here on the Island making good money. But he's married already—that was the problem," she confessed.

On another night she admitted, "Yeah, I spoiled my son because I feel guilty that he was conceived in jail." Then she said with a slow, fierce force, "But if I don't do anything else right, I swear, I'll keep my son out of prison no matter what." She paused. Inside of her pause was only silence. Then she said without a smile and without any trace of laughter, "Now that's love!" She was confirming it aloud to herself, while days later, she was still trying to prove their mother-son love to me. I knew, however, that spoiling your son and loving your son are two different things.

For me as a young man who is a son and a husband, a woman protecting a man who fails to make a serious effort to protect her does not define love. She was protecting her son, financing her son, spoiling and serving her son. She admitted that he doesn't work and that she doesn't want him to work. Without him making a strong push, building a business or working a few jobs, whether she tells him to or not to, he is not a man to me, because he is sucking his mother's blood, absorbing all of her energy, eating up her time on Earth, stressing and strangling her emotions while allowing her to work for him in a place where she is jeopardizing and endangering her health and her self.

I understand that most mothers in the USA have to work, and that most African-American women have no husbands. It does matter, though, where they work and what they do, and whether or not they are safe. She was confusing love with guilt, I thought. She was punishing herself for her choices and deeds, and working herself into danger and death to reverse them. She was choked up by the guilt of having allowed a married co-worker to fuck her in a closet or in an empty cell, or atop or beneath a desk, or in a prison parking lot, on the ground or in a parked vehicle.

She would never understand that in my culture her son is a grown man. In America he's known as a "teenager," a man whose physique is that of a grown-up, who has already experienced puberty and has the ability to shoot and spill his seeds and bring forth life. In America, a teenage man is nothing but a burden, an overgrown child, a dependent, and sometimes even a parasite. This is the opposite of love.

"Say something," she asked me forcefully.

"Is that an order?" I asked her solemnly. She sucked her teeth.

"What could you possibly know about real love? I saw your paperwork. I saw how you requested no visitations from anyone. What is that about? What? You only love your lawyer? She's the only one allowed to see you besides the officers and the rest of the inmates?" She walked away cocky, like she had dropped a bomb on me.

I knew her regular work schedule minus the occasional double or triple shifts she would pull by working or trading off hours with her co-workers. I also knew that she would return to my cell the following night. She'd roll the book cart around and offer me books, encouraging me towards studying for my GED. She would hand me SAT study guides with complicated vocabulary words to learn and mathematics problems to solve. She would bring me gifts I did not ask for like extra towels, washcloths, and new socks or underwear, peanut butter or fruit, or a chicken breast sandwich. More than that she would tell me how things really go down at Rikers, not just in the box, but in the population or protective custody and in the hospital and on the yard. She wanted me to know how to stay alive, and just how nasty the "nastiest niggas" are. She wanted me to not trust anybody . . . except, of course, her. I listened 'cause I got common sense enough to learn and decipher.

I could tell that the older woman had developed a love for me even though I'm regarded as just a teenager. She talked to me like a woman talks to a man. She respected me like a woman respects a man after listening to his words and observing his conduct and actions. She looked at me like a woman looks at a man. She confided in me the most intimate of things, like a woman confides in her man. She lusted after me, like how a woman lusts after a man. Naturally, and instinctively, she even served me, like a woman serves a man whom her heart and her eyes and her mind have realized is not a child, is not her son, is not a dependent, a burden, or a parasite, in my case, despite being a prisoner.

# 22. THE EAGLE

She walked in bringing a breeze, the scent of summer, and a piece of the skylight. It was either that, or my mind had multiplied and magnified every tiny little thing after being in the box for fifty days, so far. She entered the meeting room, which was reserved for consultations between inmates and their attorneys.

Her green eyes pierced through the dim, stale air and lit up. She looked at me as though I was the light and as if she had just walked out of darkness. With her back to the guard who had escorted me from my cell to the meeting room, she smiled. I would have showed her my genuine gratitude by allowing my natural smile to reveal itself, but the guard was facing me and I was facing him. We both had to maintain the profile of the jailer and the jailed.

He left.

She skipped the greetings of "Peace," or "Shalom," or "Hello," or "Hi," or even "How are you doing?" Instead, she looked at me, placed her pocketbook and briefcase on the table, and then murmured, "Troublemaker." From her tone, I could tell that she didn't mean it.

"Thank you," I said to her.

"I haven't given you anything for you to thank me for as of yet," she said, reminding me of her sharpness.

"For wearing those heels," I said, glancing beneath the table at her Charles David pumps. "The heels beat the Birkenstocks," I added, and my smile broke through naturally.

"Your smile is misleading," she said. "It suggests to me that Rikers has been kind to you. My brain knows that's next to impossible, highly unlikely . . . and you just came from the box, not the beach. So wipe that beautiful smile off of your face."

"Yeah, I been in the box. But you chose to wear the dress and the heels. Did you expect me not to notice?"

"Today is my day off and I have a date *after* my meeting with you," she said.

"I must be your date since you always seem to come to see me when it's your 'free time.' Free time is reserved for what you want to do, not for what you have to do," I said. She smiled and swiftly and calmly spit her clever reply.

"The fact that you haven't grown a beard in fifty days confirms that you are in fact an adolescent, in which case I will refrain from engaging with you in a conversation about my date, my dress and my heels, or about your glowing skin and awesome physique." She had silenced me.

Finally she sat down. She wasn't wearing her black crocheted bracelet over her deep scar. Instead, she wore a silk ribbon, which she tied over the scar like a wrist ascot. The ribbon matched her summer dress nicely.

"Did anyone give you a hard time coming in here?" I asked her curiously.

"They know me here, and they know better," she said confidently. "And I should be directing that question at you."

"I'm chilling," I said.

"'Get me out of here.' That's supposed to be your line," she told me with a great seriousness, as her feminine eyes conducted a soul search on me, the opposite of the intrusive strip search that the guards enforced. After a pause, she searched her Donna Karan handbag and pulled out a folded document. She unfolded it and smoothed it out like it was a tablecloth. It was the IOU I had written out, promising to pay her for each expense that I generated as she worked on my behalf. I looked down on it, seeing that she had added some expenses and written in her own notes, and even added an additional sheet of paper to make space for more details. I was cool with it. I felt certain about repaying my debt.

"Good news, bad news, choices, and options. Which would you like to hear first?" she asked me.

"The worst first," I said.

"They found the murder weapon."

"What murder weapon?" I asked on purpose. She cracked a half smile.

"The nine-millimeter that killed Lance Polite." I didn't react. She waited, her eyes making note of my nonchalance. "It cleared, no fingerprints," she said, watching and waiting for me to celebrate the results. I remained still and solid.

"The autopsy results confirmed that the cause of death was the six bullets discharged into his mouth. It also indicates that Mr. Polite was stabbed in his right eye." She paused. I had the face of a listener, not a speaker. So I listened.

"The stabber and the shooter, I believe, are two different persons," she said. Her eyes revealed that she was becoming disappointed by my silence. "So maybe I have been giving the wrong person credit for defending the cat that was choked to death and avenging a murderous animal abuser?" She said it like it was a question and an accusation both at the same time.

"I see one thing changed," I said, cutting short the intensity that was building up in her and purposely ignoring all of the other issues and questions she raised in order to focus on the one thing that I knew touched her heart and for her meant the most. "You are now definite that the one who was murdered is also the same one who abused and murdered the cat," I observed aloud.

"He did, one hundred percent. Forensics identified cat hairs on the clothing of Lance Polite and he even had the poor animal's guts beneath his fingernails," she said bitterly.

"Crazy." That was my sincere one-word response.

"Maybe the stabber and the shooter are friends, relatives, or lovers who were offended by Polite. They were avenging the death of the cat and protecting each other and the neighborhood children from 'Lance the Predator,'" she said, seemingly with great thought and seriousness. "Our ASPCA investigator had his interns post flyers trying to locate the cat's owner. That was some free help that I thought and hoped would uncover some other useful evidence. I wanted it to perhaps lead us to locate the one who had the motive to murder Lance Polite. But no one came forward. No one called in. It's a very tough neighborhood, that area."

I didn't say anything, just listened. I thought it was crazy that she thought someone murdered that fool over the feline. No matter what she said to provoke me to feel or say something, I wouldn't. My strategy included timing and the skillful use of silence. Besides, I was certain that she was still thrilled that the serial abuser of animals and children was dead.

"Look," she said, leaning forward, her energy suddenly shifting. "I've had lunch and dinner meetings with some men, real schmucks and altercockers who I would never in my life get close enough to spit on, if it weren't for defending you. You ought to confide in me. I'm your attorney. We're on the same team. I have a professional obligation and requirement to keep whatever you tell me in strict confidence. I've been working tirelessly for you and you've been working against me."

"How?" I asked calmly as I noted that again she was using words I had never heard. Last meeting she had said *fercockle*, now *schmuck* and *altercocker*. I had long ago looked up fercockle in the dictionary I got off the library cart, but the word wasn't listed.

"At your arraignment, you were charged with resisting arrest, disorderly conduct, inciting a riot, and assaulting a police officer.

On your behalf, I entered a plea of not guilty on all charges. I believed you," she said.

"I know. I received the paperwork. Thank you," I said sincerely.

"So you know that your bail was denied just as you wanted?"

"Yes, I know. It was not what I wanted. It was what I expected," I clarified. "The police were using those minor charges to hold me, while they organized some major charges to sink me. So, I knew no matter what, they had no plans of releasing me."

"How did you know what they were up to?" she said, jumping right into what she thought was an opening up on my part.

"Easy," I said. "Because they made up the false resisting arrest, disorderly conduct, assaulting a police officer, and rioting charges in the first place. If they were desperate enough to make up those false charges, then I was sure that they wanted me locked up in a cell either way."

"You also are aware that a court date has been set concerning those 'minor charges'?"

"Yes, next Wednesday, September twenty-fourth at nine a.m. I received the paperwork from the court. The CO delivered it to me in the box," I confirmed.

"Jordan." She spoke my false name aloud like the jailers never did. In here I'm a number, a number in a count. "What are you expecting to happen?" she asked me, cleverly reshaping her strategy to open me up.

"My grandfather," I said with false emotion, "without my help, he has probably already passed away." I was playing on the identity I had invented for Jordan Mann. I did not want to say or do the typical things to my attorney that she was used to hearing and seeing from her hundreds of clients. I wouldn't beg her to get me released. I wouldn't pressure her to work on my behalf or seem too eager about anything in particular. The truth is, by now I was certain that Chiasa had done everything that I asked her to do regarding my Umma and my sister. And I was certain that Umma, having received my letter almost two months ago, cooperated with Chiasa. Therefore my women, all of them, were safe and out of the reach of interference from all police, investigators, and authorities *Insha'Allah*. So there was nothing left for me to do, other than to maneuver these legal situations and to win the smallest amount of time possible for the sentencing of whatever charges they managed to convict me of.

I wanted my lawyer, instead of trying to hear a confidential confession from me, to change her approach and lay out in front of me every single detail regarding my case to date. I wanted to know what was being said in these private conversations with these lawyers and judges and police and politicians. I wanted to know what they were insinuating or working towards charging me with. I wanted her to show me all of the news and/or magazine clippings where my case was mentioned or analyzed, the same way she did before when we met in the hospital. Yet even though I like her, I refused to ask her. I had grown uncomfortable in the victim-defendant position, and more uncomfortable with her cast as my savior. I knew she knew a lot more than she was saying. Instead of her trying to drag information out of me little by little, I wanted her to stop hiding what she already knew and lay it out clearly. I believed that was her purpose in interacting with me at all. I believed that was the reason Allah sent her to me.

She checked her Timex. "Detective Baldassari maintains to this day that you, Jordan, confessed to the murder of Lance Polite. He's got some connections and a pretty good reputation. He's been helping the prosecutor even though he's from a different precinct and not a homicide detective. I met with him and the prosecutor separately. Their investigation, however, has not uncovered any solid evidence to support or charge you with manslaughter or murder one. Astoundingly, to date, they have no witnesses to a murder that was committed in the presence of potentially thousands of people." She exhaled exasperation.

"So here's the 'worst first,' as you put it. The prosecutor still wants to charge you with the crime of murder." She leaned back, folded her arms before her, and searched me for an impulse—anger, fear, tears, an outburst, or even a slight shift in my body language. I didn't give her one, though.

"He has to deliver a culprit to satisfy the state senator," she said sternly, letting me know that even if it seemed unjust, it was likely to happen. "I had lunch with the state senator as well. I shared my file and all of the information I had gathered on Lance Polite with him. I wanted to convince him that Lance Polite was not the 'poster-boy violent crime victim,' that he, a state senator, should want to get behind. I let him know my exact sentiments, that he as a human being should not align himself with an offender like Lance even though I understand why this murderer has to be apprehended and charged," she said passionately.

"Now, I do and I can and I will represent you; however, you need to tell me and show me that you understand that this very serious matter could blow in either direction. It's an established, respected police detective's word against yours. There's a photograph of a faceless black male youth in a hoodie, committing the murder. They will stand you up, have you in a hoodie posing in the courtroom, and although you and every other well-built male your age would look the same in that pose, they will convince the jury that you are their guy. And I've seen and tried other cases where the prosecution had flimsy to no real evidence, but because of the climate of the country and the fears and mind state of the jury members, a conviction accompanied by a very severe sentencing was handed down." She paused.

"There are no words in English, Yiddish, or Hebrew to describe the look on the face of a defendant in such cases where it seemed obvious that there was little to no evidence, when the head juror stands up and says that one-million-ton word, *guilty*," she said, dropping her arms to her sides.

"You said that I was working against you. What did you mean by that?" I asked her.

"By withholding yourself from me, it hurts your case. You have not identified any of your friends who could and would be willing to say good things about you, or the names of a couple of schoolteachers who could testify to your good character and conduct. You haven't named a pastor who knows you and saw you in church even once on Easter! You say you have no relatives who could come forward and share with the court how loving and supportive you've been in the family. You have not even provided me with your home address or presented any neighbors who could testify on your behalf that they have lived next door to you, seen you coming and going, taking care of your grandfather and doing good things. Not one person who would say, 'this young man is not capable of committing this crime!'" She took a breath.

"And you are still not saying anything!" She gave me a deep stare. "I can feel that you are good because I am good at that sort of thing. But feelings and my masterful intuition are not admissible in a court of law. They mean nothing. They're meaningless," she said, exhaling again and throwing herself back into her chair, her arms flopping at her sides and her legs extended straight out.

"Maybe your sister was right about me being evil," I said, testing how certain my lawyer is about me, and measuring how much pressure she would take before breaking and turning on me. I knew her sister was closer to her than any human. I found it odd that she would go against the sister who she seemed to love more than her own life.

"My sister does not think that you are evil. She knows that you are good. She was the first to say so right after we both met you at the courthouse. It's just that my sister believes you are guilty. She can't forgive anyone for murder no matter the circumstance." Then Lawyer Ayn leaned forward and the volume of her voice dropped down very low. "She doesn't believe in revenge, but I do." She leaned back and straightened her posture into the chair.

"And I am the one who is a lawyer. Lawyers believe that everyone has the right to a defense, and that's what I am here to do for you. Please trust me."

Thick-skinned, I confirmed it, and was glad I asked her the

loaded question. My mind was speeding, my thoughts piling up in layers. Then I was asking myself, *but is an untaped and false confession admissible?* She didn't know how to interpret my silence. The more silent I was, the more she tried to convince me to talk. I caught the feeling that she planned to visit me today and give it her best, most passionate and honest shot, but that if it failed, she would bow out. I didn't want that to happen.

"I spent the first few days after we saw each other at the hospital trying to get those resisting arrest and all of those 'cover charges' dropped. I painted you as the misunderstood African-American youth for whom I had documented medical records that revealed that you had been abused and suffered injuries at the hands of the police, who held you for an illegal and inordinate six days of questioning without a parent, lawyer, or an arraignment. A young man whose urine was tested and clean, and whose eyes were clear. Then as soon as you got to Rikers, you end up in the box where the most unruly, violent, and difficult prisoners are held," she said. "What's with the fighting?"

"Men fight," I responded. I wasn't trying to be arrogant or ignorant. But I wasn't about to recount to her detail by detail who said what, who did what, and what I did and what exactly happened after my Rikers arrival.

"Why aren't you speaking up?" Why is someone so intelligent not using his voice at the most critical time in his life? Why aren't you confiding in me? Would you prefer that I leave?" Then she admitted, "I saw the tape."

"What tape?" I asked.

"The riot in the Robert N. Donovan Center here at Rikers was caught on camera."

*Everything is on secret camera*, I thought to myself. *If they could film it, why couldn't they prevent it from happening or stop it before the bleeding bodies began to pile up, before the beatings and the pepper spray had everybody gagging and choking?*

"You should have called me and told me what happened. I gave you my business card. If you have never in your life memorized a phone number, my number was the one to memorize! If you had called me, then perhaps I would not have been embarrassed painting you as an angel and a literate, scholarly, well-mannered person, and then hearing the prosecutor tell me, while cutting into the bloody steak he ordered, that you had an in-house hearing and had been convicted of a 'Tier Three' violation and had been confined to the box for three months, which is the maximum," she said with attitude.

"If you saw the tape, then you knew," I answered.

"No! I didn't know until the prosecutor told me. I got one-upped! Then I requested the footage to verify exactly what had happened. After weeks of red tape, an authority finally allowed me to view it. This is exactly what I mean when I say that you are working against me," she said softly, but powerfully proving her point.

"I could have used that tape at your in-house hearing. I could have convinced them not to send you into twenty-three-hour lockup." Then she paused to stare at me, like she was waiting for me to say a specific something. Straightening herself, she brought her face in towards me and quietly said, "You did good! I saw that your role in that riot was saving the lives of two or three fellow inmates, and moving the weapons out of reach before another violent crime could have been committed with a homemade knife and also with a chair. I will attempt to enter that footage as evidence at your trial to show the jury your active compassion.

"Jordan, you will have to appear before the grand jury. The murder charge in the violent death of Lance Polite will be handed down by the grand jury in court and added to your current cover charges. They are fighting to try you as an adult." She looked at me to measure if I felt the weight of the bad news.

"A trial date will be set. If you want me to continue to represent you, you will absolutely need to confide in me in great and specific detail. We must prepare for trial." Her words hit me hard. These were the words she should have said up front. This was the "first worst." This was the matter that could get me twenty-five to life.

"Jordan, if you want to plead the fifth and remain silent, you are perfectly within your rights to do so. At the murder trial, I can arrange so that you do not even have to testify. I'll keep you off the stand. But be silent with the court, with the prosecution, but not with me. Anything you say to me is said in confidence, by law—attorney-client privilege. I can't repeat what you confide in me," she said, pleading.

"And what do you think?" I asked her.

"I think if you and I don't work together closely, these guys are going to paint you as a monster, fan the flames of race, the fear of the young black male, and they are going to convince the grand jury, the trial jury, and the public that they need to be protected from you. I think the prosecution, the police, and the politicians are way too confident to be essentially empty-handed in terms of evidence. I think they have the nerve to offer you a plea deal when they have nothing but a fabricated confession that you deny ever having made and they cannot confirm or produce on paper or tape or film. It's an insult to you. And, it's a huge insult to me, your attorney!"

"A plea deal?" I repeated.

"Yes, it's ridiculous, I know."

"What exactly is it?" I asked calmly.

"The prosecutor says if you confess to manslaughter two, they'll drop all of the other charges against you and you'll serve five and a half to seven years. That's the offer."

My mind showed me a photo of the Rikers rule book. It was the section on good behavior cutting a third off of a prisoner's sentence. I heard my second wife's soft voice saying, "Seven years, that's too long." She had said that to me back in my Brooklyn apartment on the same day as the murder. But I calculated that if I copped to five and a half to seven, I could potentially get out in three years, or a little less.

"You're quiet again," my attorney said. "Are you actually interested in the plea deal? Why should you confess and accept the plea deal when you have maintained from the beginning that you never confessed to this crime?"

I knew she just wanted to hear everything in my own words, even the things I was sure she already knew the answers to, including my reasons.

"You said you saw the tape of the riot," I reminded her.

"What's that got to do with the plea deal?" she asked me swiftly. "Those are two separate matters. One was an in-jail hearing; this trial you're facing is in the official court of law."

"Either the authorities at Rikers saw the tape and ignored completely what they saw, or they did not even bother to watch the tape. Still, they tried me and convicted me and placed me in the box for the maximum. Not only me, they 'boxed' everybody who was there, no matter what they did and didn't do. And of course everybody was there. We were all locked in and could not have been anywhere else at the time. They just swept us up and boxed us. That means that in this new trial, which I understand is in a different building and separate courtroom, they could charge me with murder without having any real evidence. You said that yourself. Same as in my jail hearing, they could ignore what is revealed in the courtroom because of politics or fears, the same way the Rikers authorities ignored what they clearly saw on the tape. A jury could convict me of murder, even though they actually had serious doubts about it, no evidence, and like you told me before, they could convict me and then sentence me to twenty-five years to life, or execute me like they did the girl in Ohio. Only thing that we know for sure is they want a culprit and they have me, so I'm that guy. Mathematics say that five and a half to seven years is a better deal for me. If it's an offer and it's guaranteed in writing, and if it can't be altered or taken back and it's the only guarantee they're giving concerning the outcome, I'll take it," I said.

"You will confess to murder?" she asked me to be sure I understood.

"It's a 'forced false confession' because of the situation," I explained to her.

"Forced false confession . . ." she repeated. "You are absolutely correct! You shouldn't have to confess to murder. No one should be *forced to confess.* It goes against the whole idea of what the word *confession* means. A true confession should come from a person's soul voluntarily. You are brilliant!" she suddenly exclaimed to me. "Young man, you are absolutely right. Even your silence is right! If I'm worth anything as your attorney, I should never allow them to force and fabricate a confession out of you. *Nolo contendere*!" she said.

"Is that Hebrew?" I asked her.

"No, it's Latin!" she said excitedly. "I will get your plea deal done in writing. You will not confess to anything or break your silence to explain anything. You will not confess in writing or in speech. I will use United States Supreme Court Case *North Carolina versus Alford*, 400 U.S. 25. I'll enter the Alford plea and get the prosecutor and the judge to sign off on it." She said this aloud but she seemed to be speaking to herself, or working it out in her mind right then and there.

She stood up and began hurriedly packing away her papers and then closing and locking her briefcase. "I guess you were my date for today," she said. "I'm going to cancel my next appointment. Instead, I'm going to work out this plea deal, and make it even sweeter for you."

"And I guess you were the answer to my prayers," I said to her sincerely.

As she left, so did the summer breeze and the light, and her scent and the feeling and the beauty of the feminine.

I was back in my box, calm and cool, *alhamdulillah.*

## 23. TRUST • *A Reflection*

"Should there be secrets between two comrades, between two Muslims, husband and wife, between two ninjas, two friends who share a great love and a rare loyalty?" she asked me softly, speaking slowly and facing the fire. She had a small, quiet fire going in our backyard, as though she were camping in the woods. She was not camping or cooking, though. She was burning the bloody cloth and bandages and each item that had been placed in the trash can in the upstairs bathroom, one by one, including the T-shirt and hoodie I had worn. The nine foot wall was completed. It was dark out. Other than the stars in the sky and the allure of the crescent moon, we had complete privacy. The night was clear, as often happens after a heavy rain. All had been cleansed.

Her eyes were filled with truth serum. That's how it seemed. Look into them for more than a second, and her eyes would suck the truth out of my soul. This was our first time in more than twenty-four hours speaking face-to-face and alone. She had been busy and quiet all day as usual, but seemed strange if you knew her well. I know her well. She was waging her silent protest. Her lips were sealed, but her gestures were loud enough for me to feel and hear. It caused me to think hard all day as I carried out the various business tasks I was responsible for. Here's how it began.

My eyes opened before sunrise. My chest ached from the stab wound inflicted the night before. It felt sore and tight from both the stabbing and the stitches. Instead of a shower, I was thinking, I'd wash my body with a cloth so the stitches didn't get saturated and loosen. As I moved to turn sideways, I felt something. Akemi's erotic eyes opened at that exact moment. She looked at me, the way anyone would after first being awakened and needing a few seconds to really see clearly. She felt what I felt, I could tell. We sat up together. She swung aside the summer silk sheets. We looked down together. We looked at each other at the same time. We both looked perplexed. Then she smiled a curious smile.

Our ankles were cuffed together. It was her right leg and my left. Her smile led me to believe that she had done this. Yet it wasn't her style. She was into complete freedom. She wanted me to be with her because I love her and not because I'm caught in a cage, trapped in a promise, or going through the motions out of guilt or obligation. Even on our wedding day she had said to me, and my sensei had translated, "A beautiful leopard is not beautiful in a cage." So even though I know Akemi desires for me to be close to her, and glued to her body each night, and even though she falls asleep with her small hand wrapped around my balls, I knew handcuffs were the opposite of her way of love.

There was only one other ninja in our house besides me. That girl downstairs, who's wicked with the knives and bows and arrows. The one who is trained same as me, but fiercely feminine and immaculately designed like a flawless diamond. That same girl whose love is deeper than the crescent-shaped Marianas Trench, the deepest point in the deepest ocean on Earth. Although I did not understand her reasoning for cuffing us, she did it. I know.

Akemi placed her hand between her thighs. She had to pee. Pregnancy had her peeing more than before. We maneuvered out of the bed, wobbling as we stood cuffed together trying to balance. She laughed. I think she thought I'd cuffed her. Maybe she was enticed by it after all, since if she believed I had done it, it would probably also cause her to believe it was an expression of my love for her.

On the toilet we were side by side. Except, only she was on the actual seat. I was squatting beside her awkwardly, stuffed on an angle atop the bathtub. Her pee came splashing out at first. Then she must have clamped her pussy muscles in nervousness. A second later her pee trickled, stopped, and trickled once more until it dripped and was done. She looked at me. She and I had done all of the intimate things that sexual, sensual husbands and wives have done, yet we had never actually used the toilet together. Maybe we both thought that doing that would fuck up the fantasy a little. For us the fantasy is a constant enticement. So she didn't do anything more than pee. She held back, and I just hoped that it was not uncomfortable or hurtful to her in any way. Then I peed. In the sink she washed my hands and hers. Then she dried my hands and hers.

In the mirror, she used her fingers to comb her hair. Pregnancy made her hair grow like crazy. It is deep black and long and silky. Her pretty fingers were gathering each strand. Her long fingernails—pregnancy also made them grow—were manicured nicely. On each finger on each hand she had designed a small pyramid, and on top a clear coat of polish. I raised my hands to help her catch her hair and drop it into a slipknot, the way she likes to wear it in the morning. But when I reached, I could feel the ache on my left side and shoulder from the wound and the stitches. So I gave her one hand and she used one hand. Together we dropped the hair into a slipknot. She washed our bodies afterwards. It felt good.

In our closet we stood side by side. "Up," she said. I lifted her by her waist. The cuffs crept up and buried into my calf. She was as high as the cuffs would allow her to go. From the shelf, she grabbed a T-shirt for me to wear and a tee for herself. She put mine on me carefully. She put hers on herself. She didn't need a boost to get my sweats. They were placed on the hangers after she or Umma or Chiasa washed them. She handed them to me. Then we both laughed at the realization that it would be impossible for me to put on any boxers or basketball shorts or pants 'cause of the cuffs. With my right hand I chose a throwback miniskirt from her single days and gave it to her. She couldn't wear it outside unless she rocked jeans beneath it, but she could pull it over her head to put it on and wear it comfortably in our house.

In the hallway, we walked right into Umma, *hijabbed* up, dressed and ready to make the before-sunrise Fajr prayer. My Umi looked at me. Her eyes were questioning why my lower body was naked beneath only a bath towel that my first wife had wrapped around my waist. Then Umma's eyes dropped down to my feet. "*E' W'Allah*!" she said, finally observing the cuffs and the awkward way Akemi and I were standing stuck together. In Arabic, she began her questioning. Of course I never said what I knew, that Chiasa had done it. When Umma asked how I would make prayer like that, I invited her to make the prayer without me this time, and told her I was going downstairs to find the key for the lock. Instead of praying in the living room, she went back to her bedroom to make the prayer.

Now we were all three seated in the living room, Umma, Akemi, and I. Chiasa and Naja weren't home. We didn't panic, just waited. My second wife had been taking my little sister out for an early morning run every day, as though we lived in a harmless and safe city. Other than chasing Chiasa around a few blocks that surrounded our house, I didn't jog. Black men and running in the streets of New York wasn't it. Men know that. When the trigger-happy head hunters, also known as the NYPD, see any young black man running, they convict him in seconds of armed robbery in their minds and start gunning. To know that is not fear. It's common sense.

Chiasa pushed through the door full energy and then stopped short upon seeing Umma. "*A salaam alaikum*," she said to Umma, and "*Ohayou gozaimasu*," to Akemi, and nothing to me. Naja followed her in. Chiasa walked away and directly into her first-floor bedroom and closed the door behind her.

"I told you she was *waham*," Naja said to Umma and me in Arabic. Umma laughed. I listened. When Naja then saw that Akemi and my ankles were cuffed together, she laughed and said, "Yep! She got all that crazy stuff from The Spy Store last week."

"The Spy Store?" I repeated.

"Yep, I didn't even know that spies had a place to go to buy those kinds of things. And if they are spies, why does the store sign say Spy Store, like it's not supposed to be a secret? And the place is right next to other stores, so anyone can see you walk in there. So if you are supposed to be a secret agent or something, everybody is gonna know!" Naja said, shrugging her little shoulders. Umma looked at me.

"Your wife bought a whole bunch of sneaky stuff in there. She bought those handcuffs you and Akemi are wearing on your ankles and she bought a pen that writes but is really a tape recorder. And she must really want to record something, because she bought a second tape recorder that fits into the palm of her hand. Wait till you see her watch. Don't worry about asking her what time it is, 'cause that thing is really a camera! I know because the man in the store was teaching her how everything worked and, you know, they just acted like I wasn't standing right there listening. Then, at the cashier she bought like six more little sneaky things," Naja reported in Arabic. "One was a dog whistle. What did she buy that for? Only dogs and cats could hear it and we don't have any pets here. I asked her. She said she has really good hearing and could adjust the whistle slightly so that she could hear it like the cats and dogs do.

I looked at Akemi. She was always fascinated when Umma, Naja, and I were having a long convo in the Arabic language. She would be watching our lips and tongues and teeth and swooning over the melody of our language. Aside from that, Akemi is not dumb. I'm sure that even if she didn't catch one word of our Arabic, she did catch that Naja was repeatedly calling Chiasa's name out as she explained her after-school trip to the Spy Store.

Chiasa dashed out of her bedroom holding a towel, washcloth, and her small straw basket of girl's stuff and her clothes in her arms. In the downstairs bathroom, she closed the door behind herself.

"And that's not all . . ." Naja continued.

"You are going to be late for school. Go upstairs and shower and dress for the prayer," Umma said to her.

"Can I just tell you one more thing?" Naja asked politely, but I knew she was about to launch into some more mud-slinging.

"Make it quick," Umma told her.

"You know my brother's second wife has been following me to school four days a week, for two weeks? Well, yesterday she caused some trouble in the school. Chiasa asked this one Nigerian girl, and another girl from Somalia and the third one from Russia, how they could recite their prayers in Arabic without knowing how to speak Arabic at all. So they each told her that they are required to learn to recite the prayers and pronounce the Arabic words even though they do not understand them. Then your second wife told them, 'The meaning of the Arabic words is so much more important than reciting something that you don't know or understand. Reciting without understanding would have no meaning in your hearts or in your mind or soul,'" Naja mimicked. Umma's eyes widened.

"Then this is the part that really caused a lot of trouble. Your wife told these girls in my class that she wrote her own prayer in English and that at least once a day, out of her five prayers, she recites her own prayer and it gives her the best feeling in her soul," Naja said.

"What did the teacher say?" Umma asked.

"We were all at lunch, eating and talking. Chiasa was sitting with me and my friends, so the teacher did not know at first. But then the Somali girl agreed with Chiasa. Later, she even said her prayers in her own language that she learned at her mosque before her family moved to America, instead of Arabic like we all do. When the teacher insisted that she recite in Arabic, the Somali girl told the teacher in front of our whole class that her prayers feel better in the Somali language.

"When we were getting on the bus to come home, we saw the teacher speaking to the Somali girl's mother. When Chiasa and I walked by, the teacher grabbed Chiasa and told her that she couldn't come back anymore if she interfered with the lessons. The teacher told Chiasa that students at Khadijah's Islamic School for Girls will recite only in Arabic until they learn Arabic. Then she told Chiasa that she should learn to pray in Arabic also, and that for her to say the prayers in English is 'no good.'

"And she said if Chiasa said her prayers in English she would always have an excuse not to learn Arabic and that she would have no way of knowing if Allah accepted her prayers, because the Holy Quran was revealed in the Arabic language because it is the best and most perfect language. 'Arabic is not like any other language. It is not casual,' my teacher told your second wife." Then Naja was done telling and headed up the stairs, happy with herself.

When Chiasa emerged from the bathroom clean and dressed for the prayer, Akemi said something to her in Japanese. Chiasa responded softly. Then they were back and forth in their language. Seated beside Akemi, their dialogue looked friendly. But then again, the Japanese were the type who could say, "I'm going to break your fucking neck," softly and make it sound beautiful and polite. They were also the type who could maintain a game face through even the toughest confrontations. All I know is Chiasa ended up walking the tiny key over to Akemi and placing it into Akemi's palm without glancing my way.

After Fajr prayer, Chiasa was grinding out carrot juice in her juicer. "Carrot juice," Chiasa once told me, "is the best formula for vision." She explained that because carrots contain beta-carotene, she could drink a glass of it and feel the effects on her body in general and her eyesight in particular immediately. Perhaps that is the reason she always has perfect vision, and rarely overlooks even the smallest of things even if they were well hidden.

Whatever happened at Naja's school the day before, Chiasa left the house with Naja and boarded the school bus with her the same as though nothing had ever changed.

Akemi and Umma remained at home, working to complete orders for Umma's Designs. The customer base had expanded wildly and now included even some Asian customers. The designs that Akemi drew were added to the catalogue that Umma had already designed. Once Umma handmade all of the samples based on Akemi's new designs, a new market opened for us. At the same time, Umma had gotten a big account from a woman who had chronic allergies. She'd had to actually donate all of her store-bought clothes, which she'd accumulated over the years, and start her wardrobe from scratch using organic fabrics only. One hundred percent cottons and linens, no rayon, lycra, fake fillings, or chemically treated cloths. It was quite an expensive undertaking, with Umma Designs landing on the winning side. With her severe allergies, even the handling of the woman's fabrics mattered. She could not wear fabrics that had been stored in a drafty or contaminated factory, or thrown and transported into a soiled truck even though they were boxed and packaged, or a vehicle that had previously transported any chemicals or bleaches or toxic cargo. The woman and her husband both had six-figure salaries and spared no expense in commissioning new non-hypoallergenic clothing. She said no matter what amounts of cash she had to pay Umma to produce her new fashions, the cost for organic hand-tailored clothing would never be comparable to the astronomical medical bills that she would have to pay if she had not made the complete fabric and lifestyle change.

Out on the streets by 9 a.m., I made Umma Design deliveries. Afterwards, I went straight to scoring the right high-quality, low-cost vintage clothing, kicks, and accessories to package for resale in Korea and Japan.

On 23rd Street in lower Manhattan on the West Side, I looked up and saw on the theater marquee of The New York School of Visual Arts that they were featuring the following night an Arabic-language foreign film. Also, the actors for the film would join the audience after the screening in a question-and-answer session. I thought, *Alhamdulillah! I'll ask Umma for a date*, just she and I for a change, like it used to be. I'd dress up dapper like my father would for her, and she would dress up too. I'd take her out for dinner to show my appreciation to her, for her, and a great thanks that she did not panic when she saw my blood spilling out of my chest. She burned the tip of her needle and even sterilized the thread. Although she shed a few tears as she stitched, knowing that it caused me some pain, and was probably trapped inside of her thoughts wondering who hated her son enough to have done this to him. Further, she may have been thinking about what could have happened if the knife was pushed with greater force and the cut was three inches lower and into my heart, or dug inches deeper than it was. She stopped the blood, cleaned the wound, stitched it up like it was fine fabric instead of skin, and followed through until it was done.

I called home to let Umma know two things: one, I would miss family dinner tonight because I was going to basketball practice, and two, to ask her out on a date. I heard in her voice that the date idea made her feel happy. The call helped her to control any worried thoughts she was having over me. She remained quiet about the fact that I was still going to practice with the injury. I knew without words that she thought I should rest and heal before I raced back into athletic mode. However, I'd given my word on making my best effort to show up to all remaining practices and games. So I did.

I was excited to be back as a contender for the ten-thousand-dollar purse in the Hustler's League. Getting money playing ball, something that before marriage I would do every day for free, that was great for me. Business was sweet. I had sold in one month's time one machine to Zhou, two machines to Chris's father, and seventeen machines to Santiaga. For buying in bulk, I got three new machines for myself at a cut rate. When Chiasa called and placed the orders, the Japanese company was astounded at what we had accomplished in a short period of time as their new customers. A few days later, the company owner contacted Chiasa and requested to meet with "her boss." That, of course, was me. My second wife set an appointment to take place at a New York City office we never knew they had, since she first ordered the machines from their headquarters while we were still in Asia. I didn't want to be greedy but I had big plans and babies on the way, *Insha'Allah.* I also *had to* show up for every practice so my teammates would look favorably on me once again and get comfortable enough for us to sweep the playoffs.

As I approached my house at 11:15 p.m., I knew Akemi was awake and sketching. She had a bright white light shining through her curtains. The meaning was that she was drawing or sketching a masterpiece. Therefore, she preferred to be alone with her imagination, pencil, and paints. She and I signaled one another through her lighting choices. Red meant she had family matters happening, on either the Japanese or Korean side. Green meant she needed to talk to me right away about business. Yellow meant young Naja, Umma, or Chiasa was in our bedroom. Blue was any emergency or sad or sick feeling. Purple was the color of love. I liked the colored light bulb system, although both of us knew if either of us caught an urge or strong feeling, we could come to one another without hesitation. Akemi does not approach me, however, when I am in Chiasa's bedroom, or in Chiasa's energy, so to speak. She'll go in Chiasa's room if I'm not around and talk or read and chill with her, and Chiasa will go in Akemi's room just the same. I think Akemi does it that way for her own comfort.

Our front- and backyard are family spaces, especially on Sundays, which is our family day while living here in America. We all have something to do in the backyard, separately or together. Akemi lays facing the sky in her kaleidoscope-colored hand crocheted hammock that Umma stitched and I built for her. Naja plays with the pogo stick I purchased for her, or the Hula-Hoop Akemi gifted her, or jumps on the trampoline that Chiasa got her. Sometimes she swings in Akemi's swing or plants or picks or waters flowers with Umma. On the warm and loveliest days, Umma hangs washed sheets, silks, and linens on the clothing line I made for her. Or, sometimes she sits and enjoys being served fruits or juices prepared by her daughters-in-law, or her favorite well-seasoned meats from her son. I rock the barbeque grill. However, routinely, the backyard is Chiasa's territory, because her window is the only bedroom window that faces it, and also because she works out back there on a daily basis. While we were building the wall, when Chris and Ameer were not around, Chiasa would do her stretches, climb the scaffold, walk the deck railings, swing her sword, practice her martial arts, jump rope, do long jumps and leaps, and lie in the sun browning her body or reading her books. One night she was even out there on the deck placing her hundreds of toy soldiers on a wooden platform and using them to reenact military formations from one of her many books. How a pretty girl was so fascinated with fighting and wars was something I did not understand. She loved history and reading nonfiction. But when it came to her own flesh and blood, and the ones she held in her heart, she was soft, passionate, and protective. With the ones closest to her, she wanted peace. I knew that when I joined her at her little bonfire that night.

I walked out onto the deck. I leaned over the railing and watched her facing the fire. She looked up at me. Silenced, we were both just staring. My love for her gets caught in my throat, like I'm standing in nine feet of water, not floating or swimming, just standing and drowning. Her eyes reveal how she melts at my black silhouette against the dark night. Still, this time she wants me to come to her. I could resist, stay still and see how long it would take for her to be pulled and dragged by her own emotions right over to me. I give in because I'm so in love with her. Besides, I like the way the fire flickers across her face, the light dancing and illuminating pieces of her skin.

"Should there be secrets between two people who love each other deeply?" she asked me softly. She had a small, quiet fire going in our backyard, burning the evidence. Not knowing anything about the incident, but believing, as any ninja would, that evidence should be destroyed. The nine-foot wall was completed. It was dark. The night was clear, as often happens after a heavy rain. All had been cleansed.

Other than the stars in the sky and the allure of the crescent moon, we had complete privacy. She was uncovered in the spring heat, her hair wild and everywhere. I walked from the deck and into the yard and stood behind her. She did not turn. I pulled her hair back and braided it into two long, thick, rope-like braids.

"Can't let your hair catch fire," I said, the first words I'd spoken to her in twenty-seven and a half hours. I hugged her from behind, enjoying the hurt from my fresh injury. Rejecting it.

"When you do things like that, how do you want me to react?" she asked me.

"Like what?"

"Like, touch me like that so gently, and braid my hair."

I kissed her neck, and sucked it on a sensitive spot. My hands were traveling, caressing her shoulders and over her breasts, and brushing her raised nipples. I gripped her waist, slid my right hand between her thighs and held it there, touching lightly. "We have to get you to the doctor," I told her.

"Why?" she asked. "I'm so healthy."

"'Cause your pussy is fat," I said, squeezing it. I was smiling, but she couldn't see me because I was standing behind her.

"What!" she had an outburst.

"Seriously, your pussy is fatter than it was before, and sweeter than black cherries," I said matter-of-factly.

"I cannot believe you just said that," she said, bumping me backwards, then spinning around and fighting to hold in her laughter.

"So what's the doctor gonna do?" she asked.

"Well, you and I are going to go see her together. I'm going to tell her your symptoms. I'll say, 'Doctor, my wife's pussy is fatter, sweeter, and more juicy than anyone else's,'" I said in a serious tone. Finally Chiasa laughed.

"Oh my God," she said, bending over with laughter.

"Then the doctor will say to me, 'Sir, your wife is pregnant. Her pussy is going to get even fatter!'"

"Stop!" she fell out. I sat in the grass beside her. "Is that what you think?" she asked me. "You think I'm pregnant?"

"That's what I wish. Think I'm gonna have to go in you again to be sure it comes true." She kissed me, her thick lips pressing against mine. Soon she was smooching all over my face, her eyes closed and her breathing picking up intensity. We were tonguing and tugging at each other's clothes. My feeling towards her heated up so high, I pulled her out of her skirt, laid her down in the grass, rolled her panties down her thighs, and put both my lips over her pussy lips and pulled like I was sucking the inside of a lemon. When I caught her clitoris between my lips and sucked it gently, she let loose sounds of extreme pleasure. Both of us forgot about our "secret love," about being half nude in our backyard. Hotter than the fire she'd lit to burn the bandages, I was fucking her now, our bodies rolling in the grass and the soil. Her pretty thighs pumping, her hips swinging, her pretty fingers hugging me tightly. I was sucking her titties, making her so wild her braids were unraveling. We ended up more than a few feet away from where we started. She was sucking my throat until our bodies shook, erupted, and then collapsed comfortably on the earth. We were paused just soaking in the feeling that was still moving in our hearts.

"Let's wash up some and do it again," she said.

"I thought you were angry," I said, teasing her.

"I was, but I liked your apology. Oh Allah, what a feeling."

I love the way there was no fronting in her. If she feels good, she tells me and shows me. When she wants to kiss, she leaps on me. When she wants to fuck, she says "fuck me." When she feels hurt, she puts her words together nicely and says them softly. When anyone doubts her, she speaks her loyalty. Her heart is up-front and her thoughts, words, promises, and actions all match up. Truly, her humble brand of honesty knocks me off my feet.

I washed her with the water hose. She seems to think it's her personal shower. She spread her pretty thighs and smiled down at me, pointing. "Splash it here," she said. The water gushed in between her pussy lips, clearing out her juices and mine, tickling her with the water pressure. Her pretty thighs were trembling from the coldness of the water temperature. I liked washing her feet. I liked her washing me from head to mouth to toes even more. I liked how happy she was and how easy it was for me to make her happy, even after her angry feeling. I just love her.

"I've never seen you dance," I said to her when the thought just dropped into my head.

"When I'm swinging my sword, I'm dancing," she said.

"Nah, I mean like 'hood dancing, body grinding, riding the beat of the music. It's an African thing. All African people can do it, naturally."

"I was born in Japan, grew up there in the forest," she said, smiling, a pure, pretty smile.

"Then I'll have to teach you."

"Are you going to take me to a party?" she asked, excited.

"Yeah, right in your room. Me and you and some music."

"That's not the same thing!" she said, laughing.

"In Sudan, single college men and women can't even have a party. The police come in with sticks and whips and send everybody back to their families," I told her.

"Why!" she exclaimed like she couldn't believe it.

"It's an Islamic country. Islam is the wisest faith. It takes into account human nature and instinct in every instance," I explained.

"Meaning?"

"Meaning, if a group of young males and females meet up in the dark in a room where the music is playing, if the beat is powerful, naturally bodies start to bounce and move. If I see something I like, and a female sees something she likes, next thing you know, we're up on each other. And, if we are not married, we will most likely still end up fucking 'cause the mood is so intense and because it's a natural feeling. You already know, unmarried sex is forbidden in Islam."

"Hmmm," she said. "But whips and sticks? Do you think the same thing happens at every party just like that?"

"As long as there is one female or more, and one male or more, it happens, just like that," I assured her. "Just look at what happened between you and me when we first met. Soon as we saw each other, we caught feelings."

"True," she said softly. "We had feelings, but you didn't touch me. We didn't have sex."

"Right, but you kept trying to get me alone in a room," I said, teasing her with the truth.

"Oh!" she shouted excitedly. "I did not!"

"Yes, you came to my hotel room, didn't you? You were offering me translation services. I saw those big pretty eyes and thought I might lose my mind. It was hard every time it was just you and me in a room."

"But you resisted me," she said.

"Until I married you, I had to. Now look at me. I can't keep off of you. And if someone tried to keep me off of you now, they would need a stick and a whip and a pistol," I said. She laughed hard. I laughed too.

"Hope you know, it doesn't matter what anyone says about you, how weird or unique or different you are. You are right here," I told her, and placed my hand over my heart, then grabbed and hugged her up. "Come, let's go inside."

"What about the fire? What about our clothes?" she asked, a careful reminder. I scooped up two fistfuls of soil and suffocated the small fire. She swiftly picked up each of our pieces of clothing and we headed into the house.

"Your second wife will hand you your first son," she said. I was sitting on her bedroom floor with my back against the wall. She was sitting in my lap with her face against my chest, right over my stab wound. "Your first wife will have twin daughters."

"*Insha'Allah*," I said. Wild thoughts were streaming through my mind now. I know why any man would adore her, get obsessed and do some real stupid shit to win her. I know that any man that has the pleasure to see and speak to her, to look into her eyes or experience her smile, would fall for her. I know a man could lose his mind over her. I did. She felt so good to me, had me so open. I felt the heat of murder with the thought of anyone, anywhere, anytime trying to get at Chiasa. Word to mother, I feel murderous if any man even looks at her. I needed to admit that to myself. If I could lock her up and be the only one she talked to or ever saw, I would, but I know that's insane. *It's a strong feeling*, I told myself. *It's something you have to manage*, I told myself. *Get some discipline*, I scolded myself.

"What about the cuffs?" I finally asked her. She exhaled.

"I don't like when you leave the house without seeing me, even if it's only for a few seconds. And I don't like when you keep secrets from me," she said softly. "And I don't like when we pray separately. And I want to hear you call the *adhan.* I miss that," she confessed. "Remember in Itaewon?" she asked me, referring to a section of Seoul, Korea. "The mosque always had the call to prayer and we could hear it all around outside and in the open air. That was so nice," she said.

"You want me to say the call to prayer inside our house?" I asked.

"Yes," she said, "at least in the morning for Fajr and then the last prayer of the night. I never heard you sing before. But your speaking voice is so nice. I know it would sound beautiful, you calling the prayer. And I bet if Akemi could hear the call to prayer, it would bring her to her knees finally. That's what I love about our faith. It has everything anyone would need to hold their family together. And if we do what we are supposed to, the way we are supposed to do it, all of us will feel good."

"So you cuffed me to Akemi so that I wouldn't leave the house without you. But when I woke up, you were not in the house," I said.

"But *you knew* I was right around the corner with Naja," she said. "When you leave sometimes, I don't see you for a long time, the whole day, most of the night. And that's okay. I just want that whenever we part from one another, you say *ja mata* to me and then leave me with a nice *mazaj.*" I smiled.

"Mazaj," I repeated. "Where did you learn that word?"

"You know I listen carefully. I might know about thirty Arabic words by now. And in Naja's school there is this one teacher who every morning talks about her *mazaj* for the day. I love the sound of that word," she said.

"And *ja mata*?"

"That's Japanese. Just a cool way for young people to not say 'goodbye,' which sounds so final. Instead, it's '*ja mata*,' like, 'I'll see you later.'" She smiled.

"I can hold on to a good feeling for days and nights and even more days. I can wait for you. I'm good for that, however long it takes. But if you leave without saying anything, without letting me know what's going on and while keeping a whole bunch of secrets, that's no good for me. Then I'll be worrying the whole time. I need for you to take a few minutes and leave me with a good feeling before you go. Confide in me, so I can hold onto that."

"A whole bunch of secrets." I repeated what sounded like an exaggeration.

"Yes." She kissed me. "A whole bunch of secrets. Like what about your friends?"

"What friends?" I said.

"See! That's what I am talking about. You said those guys in our backyard every day were workmen building a wall. You told Umma and Naja and Akemi and me not to come outside when they were here and not to interact with them at all. *But it was obvious that they were your friends.* My window faces the yard. I could see how you were with them. I could see your smile. I saw you lifting weights with the cement blocks, challenging them. I saw the three of you talking together and laughing and joking. I can tell when you love somebody. I can see it and feel it right away," she said.

"And who do I love?" I asked her.

"Umma first of all, and Akemi and Naja and those two friends who helped you build the wall," she said. "Is there a reason you don't want your friends to know us?"

I was quiet, thinking about how to say the truth in a right way.

"You don't want me to train in your dojo?" she asked. "You won't tell me why my cousin Marcus called you? You went out in the night and came back with a stab wound. I would never have known if I didn't dig through the trash and see all of the bloody cotton, bandages, clothes, and used alcohol wipes. And even then, I still didn't know if it was you who got hurt. I worried about Akemi and the twins, and Umma and Naja. But I realized pretty quickly that it had to be you from examining your clothes. I wondered where exactly on your body you were hurt. Until I felt your chest, I had no way of knowing. Why won't you let me fight with you against your enemies? Why didn't you let me comfort you, clean your wounds? When we first met, I introduced myself to you the most natural way I could. I introduced myself as 'Chiasa, the whole woman, not a half.' So why not take all of me, instead of selected parts and pieces?" she asked me softly. "I am a woman. I like to love and fight and fuck and read, and learn and talk and earn and fly and ride and discover things. That's my adventure. Are there parts of me that you want to erase?"

I just hugged her and held her close for a while.

"I'm a Muslim man, living in a foreign land," I finally said, directly into her ear. "It's not my women who I don't trust. It's this place. Should I tell you what I would do if I just acted on my instincts and impulses? I wouldn't let you talk to any other men. I wouldn't let them see you. I wouldn't let you take pilot lessons with any other male students or teachers. I'd ask you to stay in the house when I go out and wait here till I get back. I wouldn't let you go anywhere, unless I escorted you. I wouldn't let you work for anything, but I'd give you everything you needed and everything you wanted. I know you are trained in martial arts, but I don't want you to fight. I get tight if I think that you think I need help to conquer my enemies. I'll protect you, provide for you, love you. How does that make you feel?" I asked her.

"It makes me feel really good. If that is your truth, I'm just happy you shared it with me," she said.

"And those two guys are my best friends. I do love them. But here is what you need to know about all men. If any man, relative, friend or foe, sees another man having something too precious, genuine, beautiful, rare, he wants it for himself. As a Muslim man, I want my friends and brothers and all men to have good and true and beautiful things for themselves too. But none of them can touch mine. Each man has to earn his own wealth, whether it's women, land, gold, or money. That's the struggle each man has to wage. There are men who want the gifts that Allah provides, but who are unwilling to humble themselves in faith to receive the rewards. Men unwilling to strive, sacrifice, or limit themselves, soon as they realize that there is some work or struggle involved, they turn away. But even after they turn away, they still want the wealth that Allah rewards to those who work and strive sincerely and who respect limits and walk the straight path. That's when there is war between men."

"*Arigato gozaimasu*," she said, thanking me in Japanese.

"For what?" I asked her.

"For answering my questions," she said. And then she was silent. I knew it was because I did not speak about the stabbing.

"Men fight. Expect that, and don't expect them to tell you about it. A real man keeps his women out of the realm of war. War is a brutal, man's space. If a woman, who a man really loves as deeply as I love you, comes into the realm of war, she will cause that man who loves to become distracted from his target. Instead of finishing his battle, he will become preoccupied with her. Just the fact that she's there will add more fuel to his fury. He may even kill, ignoring other options, because she is there. Her presence will make the war turn out differently than if it was just kept between men. If a man has to worry about protecting you, while confronting or being attacked by his enemies, it gives his enemies the advantage," I said. "You wouldn't want to be the reason your man gets merked, simply because you believed that you were trying to help him fight his battles, would you?" I asked her.

"Merked?" she repeated.

"Murdered," I clarified.

"No, not at all," she said. "Not murdered. That would be too harsh," she said softly.

"Don't worry about what Marcus said to me on the phone. Leave it between men."

"Even though I saw his *karambit* in your hiding space where you keep your guns? You want me to overlook it?" she asked slowly and sweetly.

"His *karambit*?" I repeated.

"It's a close-combat blade. The handle fits snug in a fighter's fist. It's easy to conceal and the blade itself is curved like this," she said, drawing the shape of the blade on my skin with her fingertip. "It's deadly. It belongs to Marcus. I've seen it in his collection before. But of course they make plenty of them, so maybe it's yours, although this was my first time seeing you with it."

Now I knew what I already knew. My second wife sees almost everything having anything to do with me. She went in the ditch I dug, the box I built and buried to stash my heat. And I'm sure checking my stash tonight was not her first time doing it. She knew so much about me that I didn't voluntarily tell or show her.

"Yeah, overlook it," I told her solemnly.

"Well, at least I know that it wasn't Marcus or Marcus's blade that cut you. The way that weapon is curved, if an enemy swung down properly, it would have not only sliced open your chest, the hook may have even snatched out your heart. The cut you have is not so deep," she said with the feeling of love streaming through her voice. "The cut you have looks like it was done by a halfhearted fighter."

"Halfhearted fighter?" I repeated.

"Yes, like a guy who wanted to make you hurt, but not enough to push the blade in forcefully. Like a fighter who was undecided, which is the worst kind of fighter. My sensei would say that this is a person who doesn't deserve the weapon he holds in his hand. My sensei would say that whoever did that had a weak mind. If his mind was strong, and if he was capable of making a decision and following through on what he decided, that guy would have never picked up the weapon in the first place. He would have figured out that he is afraid of the fight, he is afraid of killing and equally afraid of dying, and he lacks confidence in his victory. It would have been better for that kind of guy to just communicate and try to solve his disagreements with you. And Marcus has had military training. I don't think of him as a halfhearted fighter. Why would he fight you anyway?" she asked naïvely, but still poking around for details.

"Oh, and I decided that he probably called you to make sure that we all show up to the Martha's Vineyard July Fourth celebration."

"Vineyard?" I repeated.

"Martha's Vineyard, it's in Massachusetts. You must've heard of it before?" she asked softly.

"So you must have gone there before?"

"Twice," she said, smiling. "Once with Daddy; he was only able to come one time in the last ten years because he's always on duty. And the other time I went with Aunt Tasha and all of my cousins. Uncle Clementine owns a pretty huge house on the vineyard. We are invited to stay with them for the weekend, and this year July Fourth is on a Friday, so it's just perfect. If you'd like, we can go up on Thursday night and stay until Sunday, late afternoon." She looked up at me eagerly.

"Why would you think that I would know that place? Is it just because your aunt and uncle own property up there that I should've known about it?"

"No!" She laughed. "It's because it's a famous place for African-American families to vacation. Like especially the families of doctors and lawyers and judges and architects, engineers, executives, and you know . . . people who have professional practices and who own successful businesses."

I caressed her. I already knew I would be playing in the championship game in Brooklyn on July 4, not in a vineyard. I kissed her on her ear. I stroked her hair. I kissed her nose. I kissed her lips. I flipped her. I kissed her neck and caressed her butt checks. I fingered her from behind. She grinded on my finger. I mounted her from behind and entered her pussy. She pushed up onto her knees. Her breasts were dangling. I grabbed them. We were humping. I was aware that right then I was a little rough with her. As I was stroking her, I was convinced that I was right in my stance with her. She's a woman, one hundred percent emotion. She's naïve. She thinks her father and her male cousins are nice guys. She didn't realize she was inviting me to stay in a house with a man who'd tried to stab me in the back. So of course I should make all of the decisions and protect her. She is my love. I was caressing the back of her thighs. She was completely quiet except for her beautiful breathing. All of her curiosities and requests slipped away. As I pulled her into a new position so I could see her pretty face, her cheeks were flushed and her eyes were the eyes of a woman who would willingly obey. I was inhaling her scent, coconut skin and olive oil sweat, lavender hair and a clean-smelling pussy. Oh, *Allah.*

"And the dojo, the same thing. Stay out of my training space. Don't make me break somebody's neck," I warned her.

"Is there anything that women can do, in your mind?" she asked me softly, staring down at her own feet.

"Women can do everything," I said. "But women should do it among women, and men among men. If you want to be a doctor, be a doctor for hundreds of women. Do you think I would take you to a male gynecologist or male obstetrician? No," I told her. "I wouldn't. That's how it is back home. The men marry and love the women, protect and provide for their women and children. The men work and the women work also in separate realms, even the ones who have college degrees and powerful professions. Umma had her own business in Sudan, same as she has one here in America. She had many women working for her on our estate, but only women. She dressed so many women of the Sudan with her fabrics and fashions and designs. When she made clothing for men, she spoke to them through their wives, or their female servants."

"I like that," Chiasa said, surprising me. "I would think that it was really too much if you thought that women couldn't do anything. You are just saying that we should open businesses for other women and with other women, and not interact with men who are not our husbands or brothers or sons or cousins, like family, right?" She was right, but her cousin Marcus came to mind and that made me pause.

"Right," I said. "But you know in Sudan, some cousins can and do marry one another. It's the same in other Islamic countries as well."

"No way!" she said. I was glad to hear her feeling about it leap out like that.

"Seriously, sometimes two cousins have been promised to one another in marriage from early on. It could be an arrangement made by their parents or even between themselves, because they spent so much time together they just naturally became attracted."

"That would be weird. I couldn't imagine having to marry Marcus or Xavier, or any one of my cousins. I mean they all have known me since birth. We are related by blood. I don't look at them that way," she said.

"What way?" I asked.

"The way I look at you." She kissed me.

"There you go." I pulled back. "Trying to distract me with those pretty lips."

"I'm not!" She jumped back, smiling. I just looked at her.

"Don't stare at me like that," she said.

"Why not?" I asked her.

"It makes me crazy, gets me all turned on."

"Tell me *your secrets*," I said. I was hoping she didn't have any secrets. It was 2 a.m. then. We were naked beneath the sheets in her darkened room.

"I'm not going to lie and say that I don't have any secrets. But

I just hope that if I tell you mine, you won't get angry about any of them, and that you'll always trust me," she said softly.

"I won't get angry. I know you wouldn't do anything that you knew would make me angry."

"Well, my father has given me a bank account with twenty thousand American dollars in it," she said. "But, he says that it's not the birthday present for my birthday in a few weeks. He says it's for me to use for college in September, an education fund."

"Did you ask him for money?" I asked her.

"Not at all. He said he had been saving it up for me since birth, little by little and that he would provide a portion of it at the start of each college school year. I never knew anything about it. Right before you and I married, I always worked really hard to make money to pay for my flight courses. But now that Daddy wants me to go to a four-year college and to become an aeronautical engineer, not just attend a flight school, that's why he sent the money."

"Anything else?" I asked, avoiding reacting one way or the other.

"And Aunt Tasha scheduled an appointment for me at her gynecologist. She wanted me to get on birth control. I told her nicely that it was not what we wanted. She also offered me to use the ground-floor apartment in another brownstone she owns in Harlem," she said. I felt heated but remained quiet.

"But I told Aunt Tasha 'no thank you,' that I am happy living here with my husband and his family. So she said for my birthday she would gift me two memberships in their health club. It's really nice. I think you would like it, and that's a place where the male and female facility is separate. I can work out there and it wouldn't be so bad that I don't have an all-girl New York dojo to train in just yet."

"And what else?" I asked.

"Um, well, you know I've been going to the main New York Public Library, the really nice one, and I've been reading all of these books that I would never have been able to get, say, in a little local bookstore. Well, I've decided to write a book about my life."

"All sixteen years of it?" I asked her calmly.

"Come on, take me seriously, really. I'm about to turn seventeen."

"I definitely take you seriously."

"Okay, listen to my title," she said, excited. "The name of my book is *My Shahada*."

"I like that," I admitted.

"On my book cover there is going to be a sword, a star, and a crescent moon. Not just any kind; I'll ask Umma and Akemi to design it for me perfectly. And I came up with the idea because every book that I find about Islam, or about Prophet Muhammad, peace be upon him, or about the times when the Prophet was alive and among his friends and companions, they were always books written by men. I thought to myself, wouldn't it be awesome if Prophet Muhammad's wives would've authored books? I would love to have been able to read his first wife, Khadijah's, book. I've read two books about her so far. They were both written by men. It sounded and read and felt like they were written by men. I mean a woman would express things differently. And she wouldn't forget to include certain things like her true feelings. And men don't have the same thoughts and feelings and experiences as women do. What if Khadijah had written a book and inside of it, she also spoke about how she saw and experienced the Prophet, peace be upon him. That would be awesome. That would be something only she could do, a story only she could tell, because they shared a closeness that no other person shared, especially not with the Prophet. What do you think?" she asked me.

"Sounds good, even though you are not married to a prophet, but an ordinary Muslim man."

"Not a prophet, true, but definitely not ordinary. And *My Shahada* is not mainly about our marriage. It is about my adventure from young girl to young Muslim woman and all of the incredible places, things, people, and events that includes."

"Do it. You can write in the house or in a bookstore or library. I'll drop you off and pick you up when you are finished."

"Is that the only reason you agree, because you'll know where I am and it's work that I can also do at home?"

"Not the only reason, but definitely important reasons. Just remember, when you write about Islam you have to be very careful. Believers worldwide, we take it very seriously, and for most it's passionately personal. So give each word some thought before you write it on the paper. Do good research. I know you will.

"Naja told me what happened at her school about you writing your own prayer," I said.

"Do you think I was wrong?" she asked me.

"Nah . . . How could it be wrong for you to say a prayer in the language of your soul? And what human could judge the words you speak in prayer to Allah? I do think it is important for Muslims to learn Arabic, though. I also know that there is a definite way of making *salat*, and then there is a way to make supplication."

"Supplication?"

"Muslims all around the world, we make our prayers a specific way, with specific movements and in a specific language. But we can all also offer a prayer about a certain feeling or burden or desire or challenge or even a wrongdoing in the language of our heart, and from our soul or mind to Allah. That's called a supplication. When we do, we pray also that our supplication is accepted by Allah. Since Muslims believe that Allah is all-seeing and all-hearing and all-knowing, no one human can tell you that Allah doesn't understand your particular language or whether or not Allah accepts your supplication. That's between your soul and the One who created your soul, I believe."

"You are so good and so smart," she said in her sleepy voice, and then turned to face me. "That's what's so cool about you. Tomorrow, I'm going to write down my prayer and show it to you. And, I hope to record your voice calling the Azan. Is that okay?" she asked. "And is it okay that we speak about these kinds of things while we are like this . . . ?" she said, referring to our nudity.

"For Muslims, sex is not a dirty thing to feel guilty about. I'm your husband. You are my wife. We can speak about anything. And, I am supposed to go in you, repeatedly."

"Well, put me to sleep, then," she said, kissing my chest.

"From now on, I'll consider your *mazaj.* I'll check you before I go out and make sure you feel good so you can hold onto that feeling and wait till I come back to you."

We slept.

## Chiasa's Prayer

Dear ALLAH,
The Most High, The Most Gracious, The Most Compassionate.
Dear ALLAH
The Only, Forever Present. The Only, All Knowing. The Only, All Powerful.
Dear ALLAH
The only ONE who is Sufficient. The only ONE who is Above Need.
The only ONE whom every soul needs.

Dear ALLAH,
Creator of the sun and the moon and the stars,
Of the planets and the universe, within and beyond.

Dear ALLAH,
Creator and Painter of the sky.
Maker and Mover of the mountains,
Creator and Stirrer of the oceans,
Shaker of all worlds,
Bringer of the waterfalls.

Dear ALLAH,
The only Immaculate Expressor.
Creator of the heartbeat, the soul, and the breath of life.
Creator of the mind, the memory, and the imagination.

Dear ALLAH,
Creator of the earth, the sand, and the soil.
Creator of the seeds and the roots, the plants and the flowers,
The trees and the fruits.
The Supreme Healer.

Dear ALLAH,
The Life Giver, The Life Sustainer,
The Owner, The Maker, The Designer of all souls.
Dear ALLAH,
The One, to whom all souls must return,
To answer, for our living choices, actions, and deeds.

Dear ALLAH,
Above all.
Dear ALLAH,
Above any.
Dear ALLAH,
Who has no equals, no partners, and no children.

Dear ALLAH,
Maker of all souls, of all men, of all women, of all angels and all Prophets.
Dear ALLAH,
Author of the Book of the Right Hand.
Dear ALLAH,
Master of our fate, Master of our destiny.
Dear ALLAH,
Master of the day of Requittal.

There is no God but ALLAH.
None is worthy of worship but ALLAH.
ALLAH is the only One whom I worship.

Dear ALLAH, I want to be good and not evil.
Dear *Allah,* I want to be true and not false.
Dear ALLAH, I want to live right and not wrong.
Dear ALLAH, I hope to become pleasing to ALLAH,
Made pleasing by ALLAH, *Insha'ALLAH.*

# 24. IN POPULATION

Ninety days in the box. Wish I had ninety more, which gave niggas ninety-nine reasons not to test me. I went in as an "ayo." That's what they called "accused youth offenders."

Super-solid like steel, mind clear as spring water, my heated heart's temperature turned cold as ice. I'm doing my murder walk, to establish peace in my area. It didn't take nothing for me to figure out that in this jail world of reversals, the murderer gets top ranking. These dudes with lightweight charges had to play invisible, or either step aside or fall back.

Dorm style in the youth house I'm in now. No walls separating bed from bed. No individual cell doors to slam shut, no privacy. Zoo-style, one CO watched "the cage," through a thick Plexiglas command center. The second CO did the rounds, and of course he couldn't be everywhere at once. Besides our dorm area of sixty-six, there were many young prisoners jailed in individual cells in the Robert Donovan Youth building where overall, there are more than five hundred inmates. There were two corrections officers assigned to every group of a hundred.

"Get the fuck up! You on his bed," a Brooklyn dude who I never saw before said to some unknown cat lying on the cot I had used for one day only, before the riot jumped off in the day room and I got boxed. The cat, who was lying down, looked up at the dude barking on him. Then he glanced towards me. He stood up and stepped away from my cot. He looked around the overcrowded room like a homeless beggar with no place to go. The dude barking the orders kicked the stationary cubicle that was behind the bed. "Take all your shit with you. Don't nobody want your photos of your stank-ass momma," the barker said.

Now the dorm room of sixty-six males, side by side like sardines in a can, were all watching for him to pop. It's universally understood that a man who mentions any other man's mother in a foul way wants to fight. But the one who had been lying down, who was now standing up with his back to me, just squatted and cleared out his cubicle. I didn't know yet whether to give him props for discipline during a heated confrontation or to count him as coward. When he grabbed his notebook, his loose papers fell out and so did some photos. He nervously collected them. I saw one. The woman in the photo was a face that is known to me. Rapidly rewinding through my mental file of faces, I swiftly realized the woman in the photo was from my Brooklyn block. She was a chick known for fucking and fighting a nigga called "Mighty," which was short for Mighty Dollar. He was the leader of the Cash Crew, some brash and ignorant thieves that robbed the same people they lived on the block with. My eyes bounced back onto the dude who was clearing out of my spot. He wouldn't look up, over, or directly at me. I quickly noticed that he couldn't look any man in the eye. When he stood and turned I confirmed this. His fear was so strong it painted a black aura that framed his face, outlined his body, and shifted with every move that he made. *Yep,* I thought. *This is the humiliated young kid from my block.* The chick in the photo was the one the barker had called his "stank-ass mother." The kid was older now, obviously. He was taller, physique broader, but still his stance was weak and his eyes couldn't conceal his cowardice, same as from his childhood. When I once peeped it back on our Brooklyn block, I had handed him a flyer from my dojo, suggesting that he start training immediately.

I didn't say anything. Fear kept him staring at the floor. Instead, I was calculating how there would only be a few minutes or hours before the scared kid would be reclining and happen to notice that he'd seen me before. More importantly, he knew where I lived. Same place he used to live before he suddenly disappeared for a couple of years. And he had seen me with my Umma and my sister in the elevator and walking on and off the block from time to time. Crazy, how a man can get locked up in an alternative world where he thinks he can be anonymous among strangers, only to acknowledge what he already knew: that all the boys and men from his block check in and out of that same alternative world, like people check in and out of a cheap motel. Some for brief stays, some for long stays, some forever.

"Money, you good now . . ." the barking kid said to me now that my cot was cleared. "Hey, listen up!" he shouted to the sixty-five others like he was somehow boss over our dorm. "When ayo comes back from the box on a tier three, show him some respect," he ordered. Some inmates kept their heads down. Some nodded agreement. Most minded their business, but a random crew of familiar faces from the riot smirked at the barker and made subtle signals like they planned to get at him.

I walked away from the cleared cot towards one that was open in the corner. It would be hard for the CO to see that cot 'cause of how it was tucked beneath the radar of the command center. More importantly, I wasn't interested in sleeping with men side by side and above and beneath me. And I damn sure wasn't interested in no nigga preparing my bed for me like he was my bitch.

"Money, that's my spot." The barker called out his claim to me, but with no threat or force in his tone.

"Move, then," was all I said, calmly and straight-faced. Now he had sixty-five mouths laughing at him. Standing over the corner cot with my arms folded in front of me, I told him, "Pack it up."

"Get gully for it!" one of the smirking dudes called out to the barker. I could tell from the tone it was a challenge. I didn't say shit 'cause I didn't know what "get gully," meant. From how each inmate eased up and turned in my direction like they was about to watch a showdown, I figured out "get gully for it," meant to fight for something you wanted to keep.

"Nah, nah, nah . . ." the barker said, swiftly canceling the setup for a fight. "This man been sleeping on a hot steel slate all summer in the box. He deserves a good night rest," he nervously joked as he packed, turning from bully to clown. The sixty-five peeped his game, the smirkers signaling one another, acknowledging his defeat. A few laughing and some booing; even the frightened kid from my block, whose named dropped down into my head, had a hidden half smile. He was named Lavidacus.

Being solid, solemn, and a man of steel in the Rikers adolescent dorm worked well for me. First night back in population, I only spoke four words. The evidence in my stance eliminated the need for me to talk. The others backed down voluntarily. That was for the best. If anyone presented me with the opportunity to get back in the box, I would snatch it. But it had to be under the right circumstances. Now that I believed that we were always being filmed, taped, and recorded, I had to remain mostly silent and use my fighting skills only for self-defense. This way when my lawyer researched the reason for my second trip to isolation, she would see an ayo who was a good guy, not a predator. I understood my position. Until my manslaughter two plea deal was all worked out and signed off on, and until I understood fully how much time I would serve, I wouldn't let any of these ayos put me in jeopardy of an even more extended stay.

Young men moving in a line like lions, a fifth of them real lions, four-fifths of them lion's prey, and me, the black leopard. I was looking over my surroundings, scanning faces, monitoring movements, even the slightest gestures. I was at the front of the line from my dorm, leading the walk to the right of the line on the floor. I was the first to get searched. Therefore the first to get served and the first to be seated in the cafeteria as the CO shouted, "Twelve minutes, ladies! Shovel it in, clean up, and move out. Then we'll let the next group of girls eat! You know the routine. No time for talking or touching . . ." He called this out as he touched and talked nonstop. "Fight and you go straight to the box. Do not pass go. No commissary cookies, just tissue to wipe your ass . . . maybe!" He continued his rhythmless rude rhyme. Now I knew that Correction Officer Gordon liked to call men "ladies," and younger men, "girls." He liked the sound of his own voice. His strategy was to keep each man on guard and aggravated and uncomfortable even while eating. But to me, all that talking was a cover-up of his false pride mixing with his real fears. I knew he could count. Must wreck his nerves to try to manage a hundred men at a clip without him even having a young and fit physique, or more importantly, a Glock, like a real cop.

Three minutes in and eight trays hit the tabletop and eight youths dropped down and seated themselves beside and across from me. In a lowered voice one of them said, "This is the Murder-Mayhem-Money table." Now sixteen eyes were all on me. I didn't react. Then two more trays dropped down.

"Good looking out," one of 'em said to me. I knew him, and I had snatched him out of the pile-up during the riot and before he could get smashed with a chair or slashed with a shank. He was one of DeQuan's five brothers. Him and his brothers' names all sounded connected: DeQuan, DeRon, DeLeon, DeSean, and DeMon. The oldest one, DeQuan, was the gunrunner from my Brooklyn block. He also sold me my first two guns when I first arrived to America, a twenty-two and a nine-millimeter. Over the years I bought bullets from him and even a silencer. None of it was a favor to me. He sold guns. I needed them. I paid full price, cold cash for every piece I purchased, starting out when I was seven years young, determined and eager to protect my Umma and my newborn sister in a strange and dangerous neighborhood.

I was on my Brooklyn block one night about seven months ago, when DeQuan got caught red-handed and he and all of his five brothers' project apartment got raided. Weapons, weed, and sneaker inventory got seized and they each got cuffed and locked, even the fifth brother of his, whose name I never found out. DeQuan had later caught a murder charge on top of all them other charges. Now his youngest brother, DeSean, who was nine years young when I first fought him, was sixteen and seated at my table at the opposite end of me. He'd bulked up solid and got his grimace right so he could be safe among the lions and leopards and taken as true. When I didn't answer him, he stood up, grabbed his tray, and walked to where I was seated. He tapped the kid across from me with his tray and said, "Move down." The one he tapped seemed solid and strong also. Yet, he hesitated. A second of hesitation in a place like this causes a man to lose ground. But he flipped it. He stood up and ordered all the guys seated next to him to move over one, just to show he wasn't the low man in the crew. Each man shifted. Now DeSean was seated at the top of the table directly across from me.

"Yo! Move up!" He called his man from the other end of the table who he had been seated with to come over. This shit was reminding me of the gangster musical chairs in East New York at the party where Ameer was the DJ. "Sit right there," he told his man in a respectful tone as he stabbed his plastic fork into his powdered eggs. All inmates' utensils were small and made of plastic. All eggs were powdered. Most meat was "meat-looking," but was made from soy.

"This is my man Ramel, a.k.a. 'Slaughter,'" DeSean introduced us.

"I seen your face in the East before," he said to me. His head was tilted as though he believed someone could read his lips and he was preventing that from happening. "You rock with that kid turned DJ, Romeo Red. You Romeo Black," he said, like I was 'hood famous. "Word I remember. That was the last summer jam I went to before coming up here to Rikers," Slaughter said.

"Romeo Black?" DeSean repeated. He knew that wasn't my name.

"A Brooklyn brawler, Brownsville breed, and a ladies' man?" DeSean added as he downed his half a cup of sugared apple juice. It was the same apple juice each of us had on our tray. It was small and just enough to wash down a spoonful of powdered egg or a piece of hard bread that somehow got stuck in your throat. It was not enough to nourish any growing young man. But I didn't expect anything good, and no one should expect good food to come out of a place where there is no love, no relation, and no concern. My "sippy cup" of apple juice remained unopened on my tray. When anyone consumes a sugared drink, the result is an increased thirst and a deep dissatisfaction. So I don't touch it.

"'Romeo Black,' that's better than 'Lil Man'—that's what DeQuan used to call him," DeSean said to his man Slaughter as all eyes at the table hung on his every word. I looked at him hard so he would get the message to shut the fuck up. I know having five brothers up here pushed his weight up like crazy and that he would be reminding his crew all the time that he had brothers as a means of keeping them in check and bigging himself up. But still all the more reason he should know that this isn't the place for any man to be providing information on the next man, to the next man. His eyes acknowledged. Then he said, "You know my name and my man Slaughter right here. Let me introduce you to all the M3s."

"M3s," I repeated.

"Murder, Mayhem, and Money. That's us right here." He pointed with his head. "You sat at our table. Word on the streets is you caught a murder charge, so you down with us." Then he recited the names of the youth at the table. "Starting right here at the top," DeSean said in a lowered voice. He spoke always at a confidential volume. "I'm DeSean; you met my man Slaughter. This nigga right here is named Bobby, a.k.a. Ransom. Next to him is our man Craig, a.k.a. Ambush, and then that nigga Doug, a.k.a. Ditch, is in the greens 'cause he's been sentenced and 'bout to go up North. Next to him is a very serious brother from the Hook. His name is Nino, a.k.a. Narcotic. Coming up on your side is my man YesYesYall. He's a funny dude when you get to know him, classic case of being in the wrong place at the wrong time, but now that he's down with the M3's he's in the right place at the right time. My nigga Paul, a.k.a. One Punch; the god Jamar, the god Imperial, the god Mathematics and Puerto

Rican Paco. This my man Romeo Black, but you can just call him Black. Fuck Romeo, cause this place ain't no place for lovers." They all laughed. I nodded. "Seriously though, he did three in the box just like all of us. I got him and now we family," he announced.

"Come closer . . ." DeSean said to everyone at the table. They listened up, but there was no way we could get any closer. "From now on, me and my man Black head the table. We keep the seating arrangement like it is today every day till all of us get cut loose or sent up North. And as for that nigga Rory in our dorm, the one talking all that shit last night, the same one who did less than a month in the box although he was in the same fight we was all in that day, tonight we gon' roll him. Teach him how to keep his mouth shut and stay in his lane. After we take care of that, he gon' be known as 'Rory, Short Story.' He thought he could step into the power position while we was all locked down in the box," DeSean plotted.

In class, I'm down to study. But my mind was studying something different than what was on the blackboard. I was pressing names into my head and matching them with faces. I was scanning numbers on chests and watching seating arrangements, signals, and gestures. I was in the same frame of mind I was in eight years ago when I first arrived to the projects. *Same thing*, I thought to myself. A man has to learn his surroundings swiftly. A man has to study character and characteristics and names and faces and scars and jewels and kicks. Who's who? Knowing the answer to that question is the strategy and solution to survival. And of course a man can only know who's who and what's what by studying and watching over time. All of these youth I faced were going to say who they are, then show who they are through word and deed. I hear what they say. It's important for me to hear because then I'd know how they want to be perceived, how they see themselves, and what they want me to think about them. But, I would decide in each case who's who and what's what, through my own observances of their actions.

GED vocabulary "Top Ten Words of the Day" were listed on the board beneath the name of the teacher, Stephen Mack, and the date, November 2, 1986. I was tight that the date was on the board. Didn't like being reminded of time. Worse than that, the blackboard was lodged in the wall beneath a huge clock.

*Allude*, *aptitude*, *attitude*, *avarice*, *broker*, *condescend*, *cower*, *dominant*, *longitude*, *mandatory*, *moot*, and *opulent*; the GED words were easy and familiar, unlike the SAT vocabulary words I had already begun studying in the box.

"You know the drill, gentlemen," Teacher Mack said. "All of these words have to be used in complete sentences that reveal that you know and understand the definition," he said but the class of thirty black male youth was silent.

"Who wants to volunteer to go first?" he asked. No one answered. "As usual then, when I point to you, choose any word and use it in a complete sentence and if you are correct, we move on to the next gentleman."

Teacher Mack pointed to a youth up front. It was Imperial from the M3s. He sighed, leaned back, and stretched out his legs. "I'm dominant," he said. The class let out muffled laughter.

"That doesn't reveal to me that you understand the definition of the word," Teacher Mack said.

"It's a sentence, a subject, and a verb. That's what you said a few months ago." He stared at the teacher.

"Try to use the word *dominant* in another sentence that reveals that you know the meaning of the word," the teacher pressed.

"Everybody in here know the meaning of the word *dominant.* Everybody in here know what I meant in my sentence. Everybody except you."

"Problem is, Mr. Mack don't know the longitude of your aptitude, so he got a attitude," YesYesYall said, and everybody cracked up.

"Good, good, good, I like that," Teacher Mack said, breaking up the tension. Then he pointed to Doug Ditch. He started drumming on the table and rhyming:

Let me tell you lil story bout a bitch I know . . .
If you thinking what I'm thinking, you know she's a ho.
The bitch looked good, pretty and clean, sexiest young thing
you ever seen.
I pushed up on her and turned on my charm, knew I'mma
look good with that bitch on my arm.
She smiled like she liked me and agreed with my talk.
She laughed at my jokes 'n said she liked how I walked.
She was my girl and I was her man, so why that bitch had
my brother's dick in her hand?
Bitch said she was sorry, liked him all along.
Said she didn't mean to use me, an' knew she was wrong.
Said she liked him better, he was older and bolder,
More money in his pockets and his style was colder.
Bitch said yes to me, so she could get closer . . . to him.
My brother treated her foul, fucked her then beat her,
Said she wasn't worth shit, but bitch could suck up a dick.
He hurt her real bad so I went and got him.
He's my brother, my blood, but word to mother I shot him.
Now we both locked up. I'm thinking what the fuck is it?
The bitch that I loved, she only pays him a visit.
Bitch puts money on his books, buys him clothes and kicks.
I'm in the green jumper, bitch didn't bring me shit.
Called her collect, the bitch just hangs up.
Now I'm feeling like my brother and want to fuck the bitch up.
Smack her around put my dick in her butt.
I know one thing that's truer than true,
Don't be nice to a bitch, fuss an' fight for a bitch.
Bitch, Bitch, Bitch won't love you if you do.

Dudes were stomping their feet, clapping and cheering for Ditch's performance. Mr. Mack interrupted. "I like your enthusiasm," he said to Ditch. "I even like your creative approach. But what does your storytelling have to do with the assignment? You didn't use the vocabulary words in your rhyme."

"What my man Ditch was *alluding* to, Mr. Mack, was that the bitch was full of *avarice.* She didn't appreciate my hardworking man here 'cause he used to dig ditches at the graveyard for a honest living. She tried to *broker* a deal with his brother 'cause she loved that street hustle. My man Ditch here didn't have the *aptitude* to realize that most of these bitches love money over love and they respect a thorough smack-down from time to time. Naw what I mean?" YesYesYall said.

"In defense of women . . ." Mr. Mack said.

"Time's up, and it is *mandatory* that we travel to the next class," YesYesYall said, and everybody got up and walked out on his command.

"Write down your vocabulary word sentences and bring it in your notebooks tomorrow!" Mr. Mack shouted.

Lunch lineup after completing two morning classes and the count. I chose a table and sat. Two quiet cats, who looked like they were from a Spanish-speaking country, maybe Nicaragua, Guatemala, or El Salvador, walked up, looked at me, and sat down. I had peeped these two earlier, liked how they didn't do too much talking, figured they didn't speak English too comfortably and preferred to stay to themselves. I checked how during dorm time and down time, they stayed squatted low instead of standing, lying down, or sitting in chairs. Their silence and manner reminded me of my martial arts training and the martial arts frame of mind. I nodded my greeting. They each nodded back. We three were eating.

DeSean walked up, looked at the two cats. They stopped eating and started staring back at DeSean, whose crew strolled up behind him. The two cats got up and moved tables. DeSean dropped his tray across from mine. His M3s sat in the same order they had at breakfast this morning after the musical chairs without the music and the DJ, even though this was not the same M3 table.

"Same as it ever was," DeSean said to me. I didn't say nothing back. "You always was a quiet type of dude, mind your business, move alone, separate from the block. But that ain't how it is up in here," he said, staring down at his food and eating. "Quan told me to hold you down. That means I'm gon' do that. My whole crew is gonna do that 'cause Quan said so. I didn't ask you to look out for me, but you did. I know you didn't do it for me. You did it for Quan. But that's cool. You and him had that kind of relationship," DeSean said in his confidential tones.

The CO was focused on us. Maybe he was studying the movement of the inmates the same way I was. I didn't expect DeSean to follow me to a new table, not when he had just said this morning that the other table was the M3 table. Now I knew the young Murder, Mayhem, and Money crew in the adolescent lockup had decided to gang me up whether I wanted it or not. I wasn't gonna stress over it. Why should I? I moved. They followed me.

In the day room, where there were two televisions and one pay phone, I was seated with my back up against the wall calculating and writing out the answers to the math problems we were given in the second class before lunch. Same as the English GED class, the math assignment was elementary. It was long division and the teacher wanted us to show our work, even though it was much easier for me to do the calculations in my head and come up with a swift and accurate answer.

"Don't sit there," DeSean said to me. I looked up from my paper. "If you sit beside the phone, these other dudes are gonna be scared to step up and use it." I looked around. Across the room was a small huddle of boys that were looking towards our direction. I figured they were the ones scared to walk over and use the phone. "That's M3 clout. You sitting there. You M3, they figure you about to use it. All they can do in that case is wait. We run the house. We run the phones, the television, the whole day room, the dorm, and we run the yard," he said, giving me a firm look.

"If they scared to step up and use the phone, then they shouldn't use it," I said.

"That's cold-blooded," DeSean said.

"Tell 'em to step up then," I said.

"Ma, ma, ma, will you listen? Could you be quiet for a minute? Why you keep talking? I already knew that. I already said that. That's not what I said. I told you to bring me the high-tops. But the ones you bought was bootleg. I told you where to go. You can't buy them on the sidewalk. You gotta go to the store like I said. See, that's why you fucked up. 'Cause you don't listen. You still talking." He hung up. "Damn bitch never shuts the fuck up." He picked up the phone and banged it up against the wall. A next kid stepped up.

"Ma, yes I know. I'm sorry for calling collect again, but what can I do? Did you talk to the lawyer? How much? He's crazy. But did you get the money? Did you ask Vinny? How 'bout Steph, did you ask her? I told you Tony owes me that cash. Did you go by his apartment? How's work? Did you walk my dog? I know, Ma. I know you love me. I love you too." Then he whispered, "But please hurry." He hung up. Another kid stepped up.

"Momma, put Jozy on the phone quick. She ain't there? Where she at? I told the bitch I was gonna call and I told her what time. Did she come home last night? You saw her? Was she wearing that bracelet I gave her? She did? I told her to pawn it. What about Ralph? You seen him around the building? Did he come by and check on you? Have you seen Jozy talking to Ralph out on the bench or something? You did? Tell her I said she better bring her ass up here for visitation tomorrow.

If she don't come, just take back my key and throw the bitch out. Keep her out of my bedroom, okay? A'ight, thanks, Ma." He hung up.

"Mami, that's not what happened. Are you gonna talk or am I gonna talk? It's your money. You decide. Tell him I was in the car but I didn't know nothing. I didn't know what they was up to. How do you know he's not gonna believe that? You always have something negative to say. So what I did it once. That doesn't mean I did it this time. You should trust me. No, I ain't seen him. No, I ain't seen him, either. Why you always asking about them? You should be worried about me. So what we related. In here it's every man for himself. Do you remember what I told you to say? No I'm not. Uh-un. *No quiero rezar ahora*!" He hung up. Next cat strolled up nervously.

"Take the call, take the call, take the call, bitch! Take the call." He hung up.

"Give Marla the phone. (Pause) I told you to stop letting her answer our phone. You pick up! The bitch thinks she's the man of the house. I'm the man of the house. (Pause) How is she gonna tell you you can't work at the club because she's jealous of other bitches who like you? You gotta get that money! She's lucky I'm letting her eat you. She's just a freakin' stand in till I get back. She's try'na fuck up the money so I can't come home. (Pause) No she can stay long as you work at the club. Listen to me. Don't listen to her. No dicks in my apartment with my woman. Only dykes. And I'm the only dick. You got it?"

"Hi, it's me. I know you know my voice." He laughed quietly. "It's still the same. There's nothing you can do about it. You can't control them from there. It only matters who's in here at the time. I'm trying. But I already told you how it is. You know the ones. Just take care of yourself. I'm not gonna offer them that. They're not good guys. I told you, Ma, I'm the only good guy and I'm the only one who really loves you. Who's that? Tell me the truth. Why did you let him back in? You always do that. I'm hanging up," Lavidicus said. He left with his head hanging low.

Realizing that I should have gotten up and moved like DeSean had suggested, I did. The last caller before I walked away didn't say one word once his call connected. He just breathed and exhaled and cried. Maybe he spoke up after I left. I don't know.

He had a Muslim name. It caught my attention but didn't cause me any form of instant respect for him. A lot of African Americans have Muslim names that hold no real meaning, are not even the names of their fathers, and are not an indication that they have a faith or awareness of any kind. He was the teacher for the afternoon GED, history class, Karim Ali.

"Roots of Revolution," he wrote on the board. "Let's review for the eleven brothers who just returned to the class after being isolated for a few months and three completely new faces that have joined in. Peace and greetings first of all, and welcome back to some and welcome to others," he said.

Of course I took note that he called us "brothers," not "ladies" or "inmates" or "prisoners." He greeted us as though we had come to class voluntarily. He welcomed us instead of showcasing his false confidence, which I thought was normal for the men who are most afraid, especially the COs.

"Emilio, let the brothers know what revolution we are discussing," Teacher Ali said to a seated student.

"The American Revolution," Emilio answered. I realized now he was calling each male inmate by his given name.

"But the conditions for revolution can be the same in any land?" the teacher stated and asked.

"Word, wherever things is fucked up the condition for revolution exists," one student answered.

"Fucked up? Who can use a better, more detailed explanation than the words 'fucked up,' to be sure all of my students understand?" There was a murmur of laughter. I thought it was good and unique the way he didn't knock the youth for saying "fucked up," but challenged us to choose other words. I like words, the way they are spoken, the manner in which they are used, and even the way they are heard and interpreted.

Mathematics answered, "'Fucked up' is like when we standing down in front of the building that we living in, and the cops come rolling up and asking us questions, and telling us to turn our music down, or off. Then, making us put our hands on the police car and searching us for no reason except 'cause they want to. Even more fucked up is when they order us to lay facedown on the ground, or take the money in our pockets just 'cause they rather have it even though they didn't earn it. That's that fucked-up shit."

"Does everybody understand?" the teacher asked. The class broke out in reserved laughter.

"Who gon' understand 'fucked up' better than us?" Imperial asked, and the seriousness returned swiftly. "Fucked up is being in the box through the summer months feeling like your body is a piece of pork sizzling on a grill, can't hardly breathe, can't hardly think, can't hardly move."

"Can't get no visits from your old Earth or your wisdom," Jamar added.

"How can we describe that condition that the last three students spoke so well about? Condense it into a simple short sentence that every brother can understand?"

"A complete loss of freedom and control over your life," I answered.

"Beautiful," Teacher Ali remarked. "That's it. The brother hit the nail on the head. In the American Revolution, who was the enemy?" Teacher Ali questioned.

"The British empire, their army of soldiers," a student answered.

"And who were the victims?" Teacher Ali asked.

"The Americans, also known as the colonists," another student replied.

"And what were the specific conditions?" Teacher Ali asked. The class fell quiet. "What were the roots of the American colonists' complaints?"

"Strangers in the house," Lavidicus said oddly.

"Break it down for us, Lavidicus," Teacher Ali pressed.

"The British government took advantage because they had the power and the weapons. They would send soldiers out to certain areas and force the people to allow the soldiers to stay in their private houses, even though the people didn't know the soldiers, didn't invite them in, and didn't want them there," Lavidicus explained.

"Very good. Is that justified? Is it okay to force your way into another man's home and to take lodging in there?" Teacher Ali asked.

"Hell no. He comes into my house uninvited, he gon' get blown back out the door," Slaughter said.

"Word, let him try and eat my meat, put his legs up on my chair, or put his hands on my mother," Craig Ambush said, and his words unleashed a chorus of grunts.

"That's when there's gon' be some bodies, some hostages, and shit like what we locked up in here for in the first place," Bobby Ransom said.

"Well, hold up. Are the roots of the American Revolution the same roots as the conditions you students have described as being fucked up in your neighborhoods?" Teacher Ali asked, peering into each student's eyes one by one. It was silent in the room.

"Hell yeah it the same," Nino Narcotic said. "The cops be rushing up into our apartments, breaking down the door, destroying all our property, stealing our stash, cuffing us up, executing some of us, roughing up our moms, disrespecting our sisters. That's the same thing," he said. The class nodded, and some clapped two claps in agreement.

"So you are claiming that the cops are the same as the British soldiers and you are the same as the revolutionaries?" Teacher Ali asked. "By the way, what is a revolutionary? Could a man claim to be a revolutionary when if the cops weren't disrespecting the people, your momma and sisters, you yourself would be doing it? Is there any standard or firm definition for what a revolutionary man should and should not do?"

"A revolutionary is the man who gets the guns into the hands of the people so they can fire back and eliminate their enemies," DeSean said.

"What if I accepted your definition, DeSean? If the people in your neighborhood were all given guns to eliminate their enemies, who would they murder? Would it be the British soldiers, a.k.a. the police? Or would they rob, rape, and murder one another? And what is revolution really about? Is revolution the same thing as murder? And if enough people are murdered, would that mean the revolution was successful?" He looked around again.

"That's the assignment. Think about the American Revolution and the roots and conditions that caused it and compare it to your own lives and actions, and let's discuss it further tomorrow. There's no writing assignment on this topic for now. I'll give you a study sheet with the conditions for the American Revolution outlined on it. Make sure you read it. If you can't read, ask one of the brothers here to read it to you, and be sure to sign up for the reading course so you can learn to read. You know who you are. Take it seriously."

Walking to the right of the line down the corridor. "I don't know why, but every time I go to Ali's class I get heated, and want to hurt something," DeSean said. I was quiet and thinking. Teacher Ali was skillful with his words. He spoke them calmly, but they had a force behind them. I was weighing it out. What was that force behind his words? I had felt that kind of force before. But was it politics or was it Islam? A lot of African Americans talking politics say that it is the same as Islam and the people take them for Muslims. But politics is not the criteria for Islam. Islam is a straight path that is clear, that sets limits, guidelines, and requirements for the believers. Strong talk without prayer is not Islam, in my opinion. Heated truths, without submission to Allah, is not Islam. Even men who are legitimate victims of injustices, who do not humble themselves and restrain from the forbidden, are not Islamic, not striving, and not Muslim in my opinion. But I know it is not my place to say who is and who is not Muslim. It is my place, though, to make these judgments within myself so I can navigate myself around properly, as a man.

On the yard I'm facing the sky. Got my Jordans on my feet. I'm breathing in the open air, completely different than the stagnant air of confined men. Breathing first, then working out. That's the plan.

"Never thought I'd see you in here." Lavidicus walked up. "You was like my hero a couple of years back." I didn't respond. "I used to wish your mother was my mother," he said, and I dropped him.

Dinner, I chose a new table, sat, and began eating. DeSean walked up seconds later and sat across from me. Two Jamaicans rolled up, looked around like they was reminding themselves that it was their table. DeSean's M3s rolled up behind them. More Jamaicans rolled up behind DeSean's crew. They were all standing with their trays except DeSean and me. DeSean didn't turn or say nothing. The Jamaicans fell back. The M3s filed in and sat in the same order that they sat, no matter which table.

"The kid you knocked out on the yard, you don't get no points for that. He's sweet meat," DeSean said. "You remember him from the block? You might not remember him. I know you remember his moms. She was the stunt that was fucking with Mighty. Now Mighty upstate at Clinton. She works for us."

"His moms?" I asked automatically, when usually I wouldn't.

"Yeah, we told her we was gonna turn her son into her daughter. Now she's a mule, carries in our packages during visits. That kid so soft and so dumb, he don't even know his moms visits a bunch of us up in here. I can get you whatever you need. Just say it. She's only one of our mules. We run this money thing up in here," he said confidentially.

"Dude was already a girl anyway. DeQuan once caught him on the steps with Lance's dick in his mouth. You remember Lance, right?" he said without making eye contact with me. "Ha, if you don't remember him, I'm sure he remembers you. See what I mean? Lavidicus and you is opposites. He had Lance's dick in his mouth and you had your nine in Lance's mouth."

As I got ready to raise up, DeSean said to me, "There's no secrets up in here. We know who's constipated, who got diarrhea, who sucks dick, and who butt fucks, no matter if it's an inmate or a CO. We know what products are coming in, which ones are going out, and which COs are on our payroll and which COs know to look the other way. In here there's no secrets, just men powerful enough, or who got people and allies who are powerful enough, to make men do whatever they want whenever they want it done, keep their mouths shut, and mind their motherfucking business."

Lights out and I was sitting on my cot, deep in thought about new words I had learned, things I had experienced in one day, not as an isolated man, but as someone mixed into a strange environment. It was like the atmosphere of my Brooklyn block, but just that one block. I couldn't walk off and into a whole wide world, or learn and build anything elsewhere. I couldn't converse with anyone who had ever traveled off the block, or recline or interact with friends a few train stops away. I had to deal with and face the team that I wasn't interested in being on or contributing to or talking with or fighting for. In a full day of no prayer, a wide range of topics I didn't normally consider were racing through my head at the same time, like revolution and American history. Then there were the familiar thoughts about good and evil, right and wrong. Suddenly I heard the movement.

Rory got rolled, literally. Bobby Ransom pushed him off his bed and into a sheet held by Paul One Punch and Imperial. The white sheet rolled tight around his body turned bloody red as Slaughter and DeSean stabbed him up with sharpened wooden Popsicle sticks from the dinner dessert.

I'm sure everybody saw what happened. Rory, "Short Story," was either too hurt or too embarrassed or too frightened to try to fight back or get up. No one helped him, either. Either it was because the inmates had hated him already and wanted to see him suffer, or because they were paralyzed by their fear of helping out someone the M3s pegged as a snitch.

The ones who were supposed to help Rory the inmate didn't see what they get paid to see and not ignore. His body was lying there for almost an hour before the CO "discovered," and "rescued," and then moved him to the infirmary.

Once the body in the bloody sheet was cleared away, every youth who pretended to be asleep was wide-eyed and checking out three photos that were circulating around the room. All three were individual shots of girls our age in their tiny panties, ass cheeks facing the camera and a profile peek of their face and one breast and nipple.

"We gon' get up a game of hoops on the yard in a couple of days. Give y'all some time to get ready. Top three scorers on the winning or losing team gets a visit from one of these three. Highest score gets first pick and one option," Narcotic announced. The inmates were low-key on the offer but steady passing around the photos.

"You gotta tell 'em that none of these girls is your girls. Otherwise, they gon' be scared to fuck with them even though you offering," DeSean said to Nino.

"Nah, nah, nah, none of these is my girls. They just some good-looking bored 'hood chicks looking for some live niggas to talk to. They'll come up one time for the three high scorers of the game. If they like you, you got the option to see 'em again." Nino's laid-back explanation broke the ice and cats started looking eager about the possibilities. "It's a friendly service I provide," Nino added. "To keep the peace."

A mule is the offspring of a horse and a donkey fucking. A mule is a strong-bodied animal shaped like a horse. And of course a donkey is a jackass. DeSean said that Lavidicus's mother is just one of his mules carrying "whatever you need," in and out of Rikers. In my estimation, the three "fuckable" 'hood girls in the photos were part of Nino's stable. "Winning," a date with them was a setup for some gullible inmates who probably never got visits from pretty girls our age. Next thing you know, the gullible ones are caught up in the network, pawns in the M3s' import-export game.

Whatever the case, I was sorting out my thoughts and my movements from here forward. I knew my actions, reactions, or even inaction and any, and all of my choices and decisions in this particular circumstance, would tell and show me, and anybody watching, who I am.

# 25. LAVIDICUS

Seven hours later, I was awakened by a dream that I could feel but could not remember. My memory tried to chase down threads of blurred images that melted into nothing but a stream of colors. I heard only breathing interrupting the silence of the sixty-six sleepers. I sat up. Although my mind's eye now drew a black blank, my soul somehow recalled the instructions it had received through the dream. I stood up.

Looking through the glass of the COs' command center, I saw the one in charge of watching, asleep on the job. That meant the second officer was somewhere roaming. My eyes scanned the room. I counted two sleepers missing. Probably, they got picked up and moved in the middle of the night for stabbing up Rory, I speculated.

When I walked around to the only toilet washroom area in my section, I ran right into Slaughter hiding behind the wall. I kept moving like he wasn't there, but could not miss that the CO was standing there with him. I ignored them, peed, and washed up.

"What up, Black?" DeSean called out to me as I walked back to my cot. I nodded my acknowledgment. "We got a quick cypher before the count," he said, and I checked that a lot of heads that were down before were now up. I heard him but kept moving. In the slim space between my cot and the next one nearby, I spread my towel on the floor and stood for prayer. Closing my eyes, I eliminated my concern for my own security and my mental blueprint of where each youth was situated in my surroundings. I rested in my intention to submit my prayer and raised both of my hands to my ears, my palms facing forward. I began . . . *Bismillah, in the name of Allah.*

The noise of the movement to the count didn't reach my ears until my forehead was raised from the floor, my knees no longer on the ground, my feet now firmly in the standing position and my eyes wide open. I removed my towel, folded it, then stepped into my kicks and fell into the start of the count, very aware of the authorities' wasted menacing glares, the youths' curious eyes, and the M3s' looks moving from deciding if I'm crazy or "right and exact."

I was solid and sure. In my soul was the message for me to no longer conceal my Muslim identity in population. I would continue using the false name, but I am forbidden from false behavior or taking any action that doesn't line up with what a true Muslim man would do, as guided by the Holy Quran. In my soul was the message to make my prayers to Allah out in the open without concern for intervention or interruption by the lions, wolves, hyenas, or even the snakes. I thought it was a dangerous idea in an explosive environment. But, my duty to Allah is higher than any thought or fear that my mind might manufacture. The message in the dream was that if all of the other males were living foul and in chaos, naïvely and boldly and out in the open, and the Muslim males were concealing our Muslim demeanor, there would be no light in the darkness. The message was for me to be a light, a reminder, a warning to them and even a warning to myself. And to do it without fear. *Allah is your only protection.* So I'm doing it.

"I'm glad you chose our regular table this morning," DeSean said. "If you would've moved one table over from the one you chose last night, we would've ran head up with the Dominicanos. We been to war with them before, but it's bad for business."

"Fuck being boxed for the winter," Slaughter said. "Word," the other M3s' agreement with him came in a chorus.

"Where's Ditch?" I asked. DeSean smiled.

"Good looking out," he said. "But they snatched him in the middle of the night, sent him upstate. That's how they do it in here. The body snatchers grab a convicted 'yo' in the middle of the night and move them anywhere in America they want to move 'em to. But wherever it is, it's a fucked-up place. Jail and prison both fucked up but two different things, that's the word," DeSean said.

Ditch's rhyme in class yesterday had me thinking. I could feel his heart woven in the words of his story and thumping in his cadence and delivery. That was different. Wasn't used to feeling shit from these types of niggas. The whole day yesterday had my head bombed. Were these youth all sons of bitches? 'Bitch or bitches,' that's how they referred to their mothers and pretend wives and girlfriends and to all women. Is that what they really think and feel about them? Are their women just to be used as their workers and mules, fucked and abandoned? Are they familiar with the feeling and power of love? Are their women all scandalous, disloyal bitches, and their fathers, either unknown and absent or present and untrustworthy, motherfuckers that fucked the bitches they lusted after and then left them in the lurch? Maybe it's both. Their fathers are motherfuckers. Their mothers are bitches. Meanwhile they are the sons of bitches, the miserable bastards that resulted from sex, without marriage, love, or faith or any real and true intent or tight bond.

It is not that I was surprised. I grew up in it. However, if I wasn't forced to face it now, concentrate on it, study it, then I wouldn't. I was busy building my own world, loving my wives, enjoying my family, and handling my business guided by faith.

I learned from the few classes we shared that these cats had talents and were not dumb. They were clever with their words. At the same time, they were not smart, either. Same as in mathematics class, we are challenged to show our work and solve the problems with accurate precision. These cats could not do the math of life or solve their own problems. They were calculating, but performing the wrong functions, using the wrong formula, and coming up with the wrong answers. The fact that I'm in here same as them, interacting with them, is my hard reality.

Yesterday I looked up the word *revolution*. I realized I liked going to class from listening to the reasoning of Teacher Ali and the skillful way he dragged the cats into a convo they probably would normally not give a fuck about. I have good, strong, clear, warm, and useful memories of love of my friends, my teachers, my family, my women, my life. What happens, though, to young heads who have no memories or feelings or bonds or an uncorrupted sense of real love? Could men really be bonded by murder, money, and mayhem without anything else like love or truth mixed in and holding it together? When I was in the box, I realized the reason that isolation was torture to them and preferred by me. They were left in the box without memories of true love. What was revolving in their minds? Did they have only memories of the crimes they committed, or fucked-up families and dirty living? When they thought of their women did they only recall arguments, fights, and betrayals? Did only images of their disappointing and disappointed mothers flash through their thoughts? Did they only think of hate? Hatred of their mother's boyfriends or their disappeared deadbeat dads or hatred for themselves? What would I be like, what condition would I be in, if when boxed for three months, I could only recall the faces of dirty cops and detectives and racist judges and the abuses I had done and the abuses I had suffered?

*Revolution*, in my dictionary was defined as "an overthrow; a complete rejection and replacement of a government, or a system of control." I don't desire to be a politician or to replace the government of the USA or of Sudan. However, I realized in this situation where I was sleeping with sixty-six confined males who were obviously about taking action, but who were without the tradition or example of faith, respect, love, or discipline, that either I had to overthrow them, or they would naturally try and overthrow me.

* * *

*Dimension, facilitate, hypothesis, legislate, parameter, pause, psychology, scenario, subordinate, synthesis*; the GED English class vocabulary words were written on the blackboard.

"Gentlemen, open your notebooks," Teacher Mack said. We did. "I'll be walking down the line checking to see who took the time to write out the vocabulary word sentences. There will be a mock test next week on all of the vocabulary words I have assigned and you have studied since September. If you are behind, or if you just arrived, or whatever your attendance and circumstance, if you are here next week you will be tested. Ask any classmate for help or for notes. I also have a few copies of the complete list of all of the GED vocabulary words."

The classroom door opened and Lavidicus entered, escorted by a CO. His face was wrapped. The bandages went around the side of his face, over his hair, and underneath his chin.

"His jaw is broke. He won't be able to talk, Mr. Mack. So go easy on him," the CO said with a smirk.

"Luckily his hands are not broken. Long as he can write, he can participate," Teacher Mack said. "Take your seat."

All eyes followed Lavidicus to his seat. Imperial and One Punch shot me a look of praise.

"When is the real GED test?" a student asked.

"Two weeks after the mock test, the GED test will be available to those who are ready for it. If you blow the mock test, don't ask to sit for the GED. The State of New York has to pay for each applicant."

Teacher Mack pointed to YesYesYall to get the new vocabulary word sentences going for the day. YesYesYall looked around the room dramatically, like he believed he was a film star in a comedy flick.

"Mr. Mack, I'm sorry, man," he said, then inhaled, waiting to capture everyone's attention. "It seems like we need to pause and peep the scenario."

"What?" Mr. Mack asked him.

"It seems my classmate has been punched into another dimension. It's only my hypothesis, though," he said, pointing to Lavidicus and bringing the class to laughter. "That's four vocabulary words: *pause, scenario, dimension,* and *hypothesis,*" YesYesYall explained. "I'll take my extra credit."

Lavidicus could not laugh, move his mouth, or even speak.

After mathematics class Lavidicus was not in the lineup for lunch, where he normally would be. I ate my meal in silence as the M3s spoke confidentially about Rory. "He should thank us. I heard they're gonna hold him in the hospital for three days. We helped him get the fuck out of here. The hospital is like a vacation from this joint."

"He won't be back to our area. After his hospital stay he'll join the 'pussy club,'" Slaughter said.

"You right," DeSean added, "his snitching ass will switch right into protective custody."

"Lavidicus got the short end of the deal. No hospital stay for him and he gotta suck his food through a straw, applesauce and peas. Heard he'll be fucked up for six weeks," Puerto Rican Paco said.

"He's a good look for us," Imperial said. "Every time he shows his face, anybody looking knows to watch his mouth. I don't know what he said to Black, but whatever it was, he won't be saying that shit no more."

"He won't be saying nothing," DeSean said. "One of us is gonna have to make that call and calm his psycho-ass moms."

"That's you, god," Mathematics said to DeSean. "You the diplomat."

"Brother, are you okay?" Teacher Ali asked Lavidicus.

"He can't answer you," another student said.

"I see," Teacher said, and took a long pause to survey Lavidicus's face. "Deprived of your freedom of speech," Teacher remarked afterwards. The class responded with complete silence, including Lavidicus, who didn't shift his head, eyes, or body or react in any way.

"Yesterday, Brother Lavidicus identified one of the roots of revolution for our class. He said the forcing of strangers into homes of civilians was one cause. It may also be called the 'quartering of soldiers,' because the British government was forcing colonists to house soldiers in their private homes. From your handout, readings, and thoughts, let's discuss the additional causes."

"Plain and simple," Imperial said. "Them British dudes was tryn'a run the American 'hoods."

"The American colonies," Teacher Ali corrected.

"True dat—same thing, though. The British were sending in their troops dominating, shooting and killing. And them British boys had real cannons," Imperial said.

"The main thing is that the British were fucking up their money. That's gonna bring war into any territory," Nino said.

"Give me the details," Teacher Ali pushed.

"Too much taxes, closing down the seaports so ships couldn't bring in the product. Shit like dat," Nino answered.

"Perfect," Teacher said. "These were referred to as 'The Intolerable Acts.' Now, who can define what the word *intolerable* means?"

"It's like when you so used to shit happening a certain wrong way. You expect the cops to roll through, stop you, search you. That's everyday bullshit. But when they order you to lay facedown on the pavement, that shit is *intolerable*."

"Fuck that, when they bussing shots at your back when you are unarmed and standing still, that shit is *intolerable*."

"Nah, when they shoot your moms or your grandmoms, that shit is *intolerable*. Remember Grandma Eleanor Bumpurs? Two years ago the NYPD hit her up with a twelve-gauge shotgun 'cause she was late paying her rent. When they went with the fake-ass housing authority cops to evict her, Grandma wouldn't open up her door. She knew what time it was. NYPD executed her, an old lady. That was my BX 'hood," the kid from the Bronx said, and I remembered his face from the riot.

"Just to clarify, the NYPD did say that the old lady was crazy and threatening," Teacher Ali provoked.

The class laughed, a frustrated, angry laughter.

"They say that about all of us," YesYesYall said. "That don't give them the right to shoot us, though."

"C'mon, man, the cops don't give a fuck about anybody's rights. What you mean it doesn't 'give them the right'? They taking it!" Slaughter said.

"The cops are crazy and threatening. Maybe we should shoot them too," the kid from the Bronx fired back.

The sound of silence paralyzed the room. Even Teacher Ali didn't have his usually quick comeback. Then he said, "The circumstances that you brothers are describing right now were the roots of the American Revolution. You must remember, however, that these identical circumstances, happening anywhere on Earth where humans live, are the same causes of revolution." He looked around the room. There was a force behind his eyes.

"The American colonists, whether they were relatives, friends, or complete strangers to one another, were bonded together by their mutual interest, and in their mutual rejection of unreasonably high taxes, of murder, of unfair trials not by a jury of their neighbors or peers, of military force and might and poverty. The colonists were not secure in their livelihood or safe in their own homes. They effectively experienced the withdrawal of their core rights and freedoms," Teacher summarized, and then began writing one word on the blackboard: *contradiction.*

"What were the contradictions in the American Revolution? Let me back up. Who knows the meaning of the word *contradiction*? he asked all of us.

"A lie," Bobby Ransom called out.

"That's part of it," Teacher Ali said. "But not all of it."

"A hidden lie," the kid from the Bronx answered.

"Nice," Teacher said, and then repeated, "A hidden lie."

"A hidden lie by a liar who presented himself as the truth, but for his own benefit," I said.

"That's beautiful, brother, almost perfect! A contradiction is an inconsistency. In plain speech, however, we can summarize it as 'a hidden lie that doesn't match up with what a person, a group, or a government said they represented in the first place. In many cases, the contradiction may be the exact opposite of what a person said or pretended to represent or to have been pushing, politicking, and fighting for. We will end our discussion right there," Teacher Ali said. Then he added, "Your assignment for tonight is to think about this: what was the hidden lie of the American Revolution?"

"I already know it," Mathematics said calmly.

"Brother, it sounds like you need to say it right now rather than tomorrow," Teacher pointed out.

"The hidden lie was that all them white devils who were fighting for freedom were supporting slavery over the black man and woman at the same time. Meanwhile, the black man was helping them white devils win *their* freedom, and the first freedom fighter to get shot down was a black man."

"That's fireworks!" Teacher Ali said.

I had heard the breakdown of the "white man is the devil" philosophy. The Quran does not say that. I don't believe that way. True believers in Islam believe that all humans of any race are capable of both good and evil. Every soul is in a struggle to separate itself from niggardliness and evil. And it seemed to me that that war around the world is always about power, money, land, gold, and women.

Teacher Karim Ali pushed Mathematics to make himself clear. "But define the word you are using, *devils.*"

"The British were white devil people. The colonists were white devil people. That's white-on-white crime right there." The class laughed. "One set of whites wanted freedom from the other set of whites. So they called themselves freedom fighters. But the British, who were the dominant whites, wanted to keep profiting from the weaker white colonists while ignoring their complaints and demands and taxing and giving them hell and giving up next to nothing. The contradiction was that the British whites and the white American colonist freedom fighters both believed in, participated in, and profited from the enslavement of the black man and woman in Britain in the American colonies and all around the world," Mathematics said, summarizing his take on it.

"Outstanding! That definitely was an inconsistency, 'the hidden lie,' a disregarded and buried truth. Thus it was definitely one contradiction of the American colonists who dubbed themselves revolutionary freedom fighters. The assignment for tomorrow, then, is to . . ." The class groaned, interrupting Teacher. "The assignment is to write one paragraph and be prepared to discuss it in class tomorrow, answering the question, 'Are you a revolutionary or a contradiction?'"

"Lavidicus?" I called him over. He looked intimidated, lowered his gaze, then began to approach me slowly. "Look a man in his eyes when he's talking to you. That's what men do," I told him. His nervous pupils jumped around before he could straighten them to look at me.

"I apologize, man, for damaging your jaw. I'll back my apology up with a favor to you. Ask me for one thing. If it's within my reach, I'll grant it. If it's not, you can ask for something else that is. Something equal to the damage I did to you."

He was fidgeting. "Stop moving," I told him. "Straighten your two legs and make your stance firm in the ground." He began adjusting himself. "Breathe—you can't spend your whole life holding your breath. That's not what men do." He inhaled, exhaled, inhaled. "Calmly—be calm, not dramatic." Then, he began breathing normal. "Take some time and think about my offer. In as few words as possible, write down what favor you want. Hand it to me only in

Teacher Ali's class whenever you're clear. Understand?" He nodded painfully.

"Last thing," I said. "Mention my mother one more time anywhere, any place, any time to anybody, no matter who it is, even if it's only one word, one sentence, or even a compliment, I'll kill you."

Talking while locked up, the she-officer had already put me up on that. She said that the authorities would send you an inmate who is tagged an informant to them, and known as snitch to any prisoner. Their informant is a locked-up inmate, same as you, so your guard is down. He may tell you something about himself, then ask you something about yourself, your case, or some previous incident that occurred that you may or may not know anything about. "In casual conversation, you will say something that might result in new charges being added on to the ones you already have. In one word, or one sentence out of your own mouth to another inmate, you may be shocked when he suddenly appears testifying against you at your trial or could simply, with the information he gathered and you told him, be guaranteeing your own conviction." I thought it was hard to believe, doing an extra five, ten, fifteen years because of a conversation. But I thought about how even in my case, the number-one thing the detectives and prosecutor did not have was evidence and eyewitness testimony. I believed that they would easily plant someone beside me to collect information that they were incapable of gathering on me on their own and that I was never ever going to hand them.

Informants oftentimes are inmates who have a pending case. Since they face conviction, and as their trial date draws near, their fears stretch out and explode in them. They would trade another inmate's freedom to secure their own, even if they have to do dirty deeds, lie and invent details, or simply tell something that had been said, agreed to casually, or confided.

More than the murder I committed, any information that connected me to my Umma was what I intended to squash, avoid, eliminate. That reasoning led to my impulse to crash my fist into Lavidicus's face. I needed him and anybody else to know not to get casual or sloppy with me. Don't mention my mother or my women, or ask me any personal questions. Not one of these cats is a friend to me.

I'm not a man who makes threats. I execute. Whatever the truth is in my soul, heart, or mind, I take action over words. In my young life, I have never told any man, "If you do this or that, I'll kill you." However, the circumstances of this situation were different. I wasn't sorry that I silenced Lavidicus. I thought the hit he took would cause him to never mention Umma again. And in the extremely slim chance that he slipped up, to me that would mean that he was either stupid, or he was being used to gather or confirm information on me or my family. I meant what I said when I told him the consequences of that. So why did I apologize for smashing his face? Why did I agree to grant him a favor, especially not knowing his mind or what he would ask for?

I had to. In order to live with myself, to define myself, I had to apologize to Lavidicus. When I saw the M3s grouping me up with themselves and praising me for a deed well done, I knew I had done something that I wanted to do, but something that was wrong. I knew also that just admitting it to myself was cowardly. I could not accept myself as a coward. I hate that. I needed to apologize to him face-to-face, and I needed to back that apology up with something that I was willing to sacrifice, as a form of repayment for what I had done.

How did I decide that I had done wrong? Like in a math problem or an equation where we must show our work, our thinking through numbers, calculations, and answers and conclusions, I had to do the math of life. First, Lavidicus is a victim. The word *victim* has about three definitions. A victim is a person who suffers because of a destructive action. A victim is a person who is deceived or cheated by his own emotions or ignorance or by the dishonesty of others. A victim is also an animal served up as a sacrifice. Lavidicus was all three.

Lavidicus's mother had a legit job where she earned; I knew this because I used to see her wearing her work uniform. But she also carried herself like a whore. This caused her to participate in disrespectful arrangements and relationships with men. This meant that Lavidicus had been raised in the presence of men who didn't love or respect her, who also fought and beat her and consequently didn't love or respect him. He loved his mother. However, he was so young when the parade of her disrespectful boyfriends began, that he couldn't protect her or respect her from early on. I figured it must burn a continuous fire in his chest to love a mother he couldn't or didn't respect.

I used to see him around our Brooklyn block, looking embarrassed, vulnerable, and weak. For a few years I didn't see him at all. When I encountered him again here at Rikers, and he was grown and had the male physique, I did not know the details of what had happened to him. After I hit him was when DeSean told me that DeQuan caught Lavidicus on the back stairwell with Lance's dick in his mouth. Lance, the same trash who I murdered. As a man, I couldn't envision or fathom or accept or even imagine that. Only thing I knew was that Lance was at least three or four years older than Lavidicus. Still, Lavidicus was old enough at that time, eleven or twelve, to know better, to fight back and to retaliate. I can only assume that what Lance did to him was forced. Who would do that voluntarily? What I did know for certain was that Lance was a predator.

A predator is defined as someone or something that preys on others. The nastiest of all human predators use the nastiest tactics and prey on the weakest and most helpless among others. I know the laws of the jungle. I know every beast and every man has to eat. But I also know that there is a difference between men eating to live and men who have a perverse thirst to destroy and conquer and a love to kill. I have never been a predator. In my faith it is wrong to kill for sport, to satisfy a perverse desire or insatiable ego, or a heavy pride. However, in Islam we do have the right to defend our lives and loved ones from oppression and mischief and evildoers. Defense sometimes results in murder. I believe in that, solidly.

Yet, I had a need to define and distinguish and separate myself from any and all predators in my mind and in the mind of others, even though I already knew that only Allah is the judge and that Allah is the Best Knower. Once I saw Lavidicus all bandaged up, for a slight second, I felt like a predator. And even a slight second is too long for me to carry that feeling, especially when I am striving to be true.

I hit Lavidicus before I knew his mother was being used as a mule. Before I found out that Lavidicus did not know that she comes up here to see other men on visitations, not only him, her son. Before I knew that she delivered contraband, to prisoners. Before I knew he was an animal being sacrificed, a young man being cheated, a deceived victim. Once I knew, and once I saw the result of my hit, which added to his suffering, I felt guilty, wrong, and responsible. There was nothing left except for me to take responsibility for my part in that.

After all of that, why did I still say that I would kill him if he mentioned Umma in any way ever again? Because I would. Even if it was wrong, to protect Umma I would carry the burden, even the burden against my own soul. I also believed that I had done, *Insha'Allah*, enough good deeds and strivings in this life that Allah, the Most Compassionate, would forgive me for this immense love for my mother that caused me to protect her fervently.

Furthermore, since I apologized, I needed him and any onlookers to not see my apology as a weakness or an opportunity. I know these guys have no faith, no culture, no worthy traditions, and fuck it, no fathers. Therefore I knew that the streets, and these youth and many men, see and saw both prayers and apologies as soft.

In Islam, we have "tajweed," a requirement to strive to a level close to perfection. We have a consideration, a responsibility to think and rethink, to evaluate and weigh and make honest and careful decisions. We have a responsibility to pursue the truth, live the truth, be the truth, yet we know that we can never be perfect. We have a responsibility to remind and warn others. However, when we fall short we must seek atonement. Atonement is more than apologizing or feeling sad or sorry about a doubtful or wrong choice. Atonement involves reparation or a repayment to the victim of your wrongful choice, and in the case of death, to the victim's family. A spiritual atonement can be in the performance of a fast or sacrifice or several deeds of charity. In addition to that, a spiritual atonement involves a sincerity expressed from the soul of the wrongdoer to Allah. That sincerity is word and deed combined.

The favor I extended to Lavidicus was a portion of my repayment to him and of my striving for atonement.

Two words were written on the paper that Lavidicus dropped on my desk in Teacher Karim Ali's class the following day: "Teach me."

In the yard I called him over, knowing that he wouldn't approach my territory anymore unless I gave him permission.

"One for yes, two for no," I told him, at the same time holding up one, then two fingers to demonstrate.

"Do you believe in God?" I asked him. There was a pause. He didn't raise one or two fingers. Instead he started fidgeting again. "Stop moving. Stand still," I said calmly. He stopped rocking. I knew he had something to say but couldn't. "Do you pray?" He raised two fingers for no. I looked at him. The math in my mind was being sorted. A Muslim prays five times a day. If I have been praying five times a day since I was five years young, I had made almost twenty thousand prayers to Allah, and this guy, based on his answer, had made none. For me it meant that this guy was without spiritual protection other than the grace of Allah, because Allah does as He pleases. But seeing Lavidicus's condition, he had suffered a lot from his own unawareness. Subtract twenty thousand prayers and minus ten Ramadans, and minus one good father, as an example of a man. *Damn.*

"There is only One God," I told him. "And, it is not any man who ever hurt you, or any man you've ever met. It's not DeSean, Imperial, Jamar, or Mathematics, and it's definitely not me. Look at the sky." I pointed. "Look at the sun. The sky, the sun, the moon, and the stars were all created by the same One who created your soul. If you have never made a prayer to the One who created your soul, you are not only lost, you are ungrateful. But more importantly than that for you is that you are unprotected. Up to now, you have gotten on your knees for all the wrong reasons and for all of the wrong people. On your knees for filthy men, on your knees for the police, on your knees out of fear. Ungrateful and lost, never on your knees for the One who created your soul and gave you life, to say a prayer of appreciation, a prayer for guidance, a prayer for vision, a prayer for protection. Is that right?" I asked him. He held up one finger for yes.

"Having heard what I think, are you still asking me to teach you?" He raised one finger for yes. "Are you asking for help with your classwork or the GED or the SAT?" I asked, wanting to be clear. He raised two fingers for no. "Are you asking me to teach you how to fight?" He raised two fingers for no. "What do you want to learn? What do you want to be?" I asked him, already getting impatient. He pointed to me. I paused. "You want me to teach you how to be me?" He raised one finger for yes.

In the washroom before dawn, I was preparing for prayer. Lavidicus was standing over the sink beside me, doing what he saw me doing: washing my face, rinsing my mouth and cleaning my ears and nostrils, washing my hands and forearms, and washing my legs from the knees down and the tops and soles of my feet.

"You have to be yourself. You can never be another man. Starting today, I'll help you in the library for the next six weeks, to figure out who you are and who you can become once you strive for understanding. After the six weeks, your jaw should be healed and you will have all else that you need to guide yourself. I recommend that you make your first prayer with your eyes open and in complete silence. Watch me to learn and watch my back. Once you learn how it's done, you can begin to close your eyes and I'll watch your back."

# 26. LIGHT

"You fucking with that soft kid," DeSean said.

I looked up from my tray and locked eyes with him. "Each one, teach one. That's your belief, right?" I said.

He cracked a smile. So did Mathematics at the other end of the M3 table. I knew they were Five Percenters, same as my man Ameer and his father. Of course I had heard their talk. It wasn't my way, but some of the Fives claimed to be Muslim and others denied. Yet, I knew even the ones who denied felt a connection and a respect for Islam. They had to.

"You a teacher or a cold-blooded Murder Money soldier?" DeSean spit. "You cracked the soft boy's skull and then took him under your wing. That's cold, but it's smart. He definitely won't be diming you out in exchange for the protection."

"I'm just doing your job," I said.

"Non cypher, my job?" he repeated, and all the M3s were watching our convo closely.

"I'm the poor righteous teacher, civilizing the eighty-fiver. That's your job. Instead, you caked up and chilling with the ten percent," I said, and all the gods leaned back, mood moving from surprise to laughter to anger.

"Is that a challenge?" DeSean asked me.

"What would DeQuan say?" I replied, knowing he was heavily

invested in admiring and pleasing his oldest brother and living up to his brother's orders.

"You know the god DeQuan don't fuck with no soft motherfuckers," he said solemnly.

"DeQuan would say that you and me should fight a fair one. DeQuan would set it up, promote it, and be standing right there to watch it go down," I said. "It's either that, or DeQuan would appreciate you reporting to him that we got this whole dorm on lock. Let him know I'm soldiering for the eighty-five and you holding it down and running the industry and the paper."

"That's word," Jamar said. Slaughter grimaced.

"We should hold them down. They ain't doing nothing but praying to their mystery god," Mathematics said.

"And they ain't fucking up the business," Narcotic said.

"Word," Imperial said.

"Don't be quick to hop on his nuts," Slaughter warned. "Peep how he's raising up a little army. First it was him praying for delf. Now it's nine of them motherfuckers. And he got Karim Ali all on his tip. The COs ain't feeling none of that talk—how they be talking and the prayers they be making. That shit got COs on edge."

"The COs," I said. "Are they the ten percent or the eighty-five?" I asked, knowing Slaughter wasn't a Five Percenter, and dividing DeSean from his right-hand man. DeSean looked at me.

"We definitely don't give a fuck about what the COs think," DeSean said, feeling and knowing the importance of separating himself from the authorities. It was a mean game of chess I was playing with him. But, I wasn't playing. "Stay out of the way like you been doing. The M3s definitely gon' protect the poor righteous teacher," DeSean announced. *Checkmate*, I said to myself.

I had gotten Lavidicus to meet me in the library every other day, and the down days were for reading on his own. The Quran was his first and most important book. Lavidicus learned the short first chapter, "The Opening," by heart. It has seven *ayats.* The key was that once he understood and accepted that there is only one God, and that it's not none of these dudes, it helped to strengthen him and diminish his fears slowly as the days and weeks dragged by. At the same time, it helped him to learn not to worship his mother, hold her as his standard, or expect her to be his source of protection. His confusion over her began to clear up. It is important for fatherless sons to know that it is okay to love their broken mothers, but to separate that from what they should respect and view as an example. Otherwise their relationships would forever be fucked up. Confused sons would choose to love a woman who is a whore same as his mother. Or, confused sons who hate their mothers would hate women all together.

In his notebook, I had seen some random scribble that in tiny letters said, "I have loved you since I was twelve." I was happy to see that considering all he had been through and struck up a convo with him about girls.

"You have a girlfriend?" I asked him.

"No," he signaled.

"You liked her but didn't tell her?" I asked.

"No," he signaled, and opened up to a blank page and wrote, "I like you."

"That's cool. You can like me, but that's not what I'm talking about. I'm talking about girls." I flipped the pages and pointed to what he had scribbled. He wrote underneath his words, "I have loved you since I was twelve." I watched.

"You were my first and only love," he wrote.

"Who?" I asked.

"You," he wrote. I didn't break his jaw all over again. I was caught completely off guard and couldn't process or do the math on anything like what he was expressing.

"You hurt me, but I admire you as a man and feel love for you in my heart," he wrote to me. I looked at him. There he was, the same as his mother, with her same emotions. She wanted a man.

He did too. She loved men who hurt her. He did too. I told him, "Your confusion comes from your bad experiences. You admire me and that's okay. But as far as affection and intimacy, that's a man-woman thing. You have to move everything into its right and original category. Put everything back where it belongs and where it was *before* you got hurt and confused the first time," I told him.

"The Rikers counselor said I should just accept myself the way I am," he wrote.

"Think about it: for any other pain or illness or trauma, the doctor would give you medicine and treatment, to put things back the way they were before you got sick or hurt. Even with your broken jaw, the doctors worked hard to put your bones back into place, and have your face as it was before. How come, for this one thing that came from your being hurt and taken advantage of by dirty men, the counselor advises you not to try to fix it?" Lavidicus looked like he was thinking about something he had never thought of before.

"Did he try and touch you?" I asked Lavidicus. "Did the counselor put his hands on you?" Silence was his answer.

"Word is bond" is real for me. I stuck with Lavidicus because I said I would. I continued to teach him and read Quran with him and make the prayers with him because it was my word and my atonement. Besides, Lavidicus was no threat to me. I even got Teacher Karim Ali to organize a visitation between Lavidicus and a nice sixteen-years-young female who had recently become a believer, from his mosque. I wanted Lavidicus to be able to break the everyday routine of seeing and being surrounded by only male prisoners and guards, and just sit with her and talk and look and feel, which is all that could be done while locked up. I wanted to see how he would react to meeting not one of the three girls photographed topless in their panties whose pictures circulated around the jail dorm, but a female who had humbled herself and was striving, the same as he was. More importantly, I wanted him to see, feel, and explore for himself and for his healing. *Alhamdulillah*, slowly but surely, by the end of his six weeks of studying with me and being visited by her, he changed.

* * *

"You have a visitor," the CO said to me.

"No," was all I replied.

"You're not interested in the pretty girls?" he asked me, but more like he was trying to call me out in front of the other inmates. "Going once . . ." he counted down.

"What's her name?" DeSean called out.

"Strange name, exotic beauty," the CO said sarcastically, and my chest got tight. "Going twice . . ." I was one hundred that it wasn't one of my wives. They wouldn't overturn my order.

"Go meet her, man. What's the problem?" YesYesYall said. "You could send me by proxy—I'll give her a message. It's better than just leaving her hanging."

"Simanique, going three times, done!" The CO had called out her name and walked away.

"No visitors," I spoke up as he left, reminding him. I'm the inmate who wants zero visitors. Still, I was thinking how the Red Flamingo, aka Simanique, could have found me under the name Jordan Mann. Was it in the newspaper and she had peeped it all out? *No matter*, I told myself. *She definitely doesn't know my true name or my street name, Midnight.* She had my washed murder clothes that I left behind, but she wouldn't do or say anything. I was certain.

"You got a kite from 'His Majesty,'" Imperial said six days after the Red Flamingo had attempted to see me on a visit.

"Stop fucking around," I told him.

"Word to mother," he said, letting me know he was serious.

"That's his brother," DeSean said. "He's locked over in C-74, same as DeQuan." I took the kite. Couldn't believe Imperial's brother was named "His Majesty."

"I'm headed up North, same location as my man Verse. Before

he got sent up, he wanted me to relay to you his gratitude. Verse said 'You is the supreme soldier. You under his protection wherever his arms got reach,'" the note said.

*That's crazy*, I thought to myself. I never met this Redverse cat. Just walked into his Laundromat the night of the murder and somehow shit got turned upside down. I looked up.

"I already know what's in the letter. That's big," DeSean said. "Verse's operation is huge. Different territory and product, but larger network and greater influence and reach than my brother. That's what Quan told me."

"Puerto Rican Paco, you don't say much. But you speak Spanish. Is that right?" I asked him.

"Somewhat," he said.

"I noticed the Latin Kings speak Spanish and the Dominicans and the two dudes from Nicaragua. What's the deal? You all speaking Spanish but not speaking to one another? Just curious," I told him, but I had a plan more than a curiosity.

"The niggas is all speaking English but all 'hooded and ganged up and not speaking to each other. What's the deal with that?" he replied.

"True," I admitted. "I try and give the peace to each man, regardless. Thought I'd send a simple greeting to the Kings and the other Spanish-speaking brothers with your help."

"I can help you with that. But, just so you know, they all divided for different reasons but united about one thing," he said.

"What is it?"

"Jesus. So if you trying to get them on your prayer lineup, money it ain't gonna happen, even with your clout."

I smiled. "Muslims respect the Prophet Jesus, Peace Be Upon Him. I'm not at war with Jesus or the Christians. I'm planning to get up a soccer game, though, and want to invite all of them to play."

"Play soccer?"

"Something different for cats like us that been doing the same routine every day," I said.

"I'm a criminal. I'm your man, DeSean. I'm better than these other dudes. I'm not pretending to be God. I'm not poor. I'm not righteous. I don't give a fuck about teaching the next man shit. These niggas gotta teach theyself. I raised myself. On the streets, I prowl. I see what I want. I take it. 'Don't move!' I warn them. If they cooperate, I don't slit their throats or put a bullet in their head," Slaughter said.

"DeSean, I'm holding you down. But why are we holding this nigga down? He don't even put in no work. He wants to keep his hands clean. He's over there having picnics with the fucking foreigners and protecting the fucking faggots. Murder Money Mayhem never been about that. Him and his crew out here praying like a group of grandmas. What the fuck is up with that?" Slaughter was furious. He had been in a silent uproar ever since Teacher Ali had given the class definitions of the contradictions and differences between criminals and revolutionaries, and prisoners and political prisoners.

"I already stated my position. Long as him and his crew don't fuck up the money I ain't got no beef with him," Narcotics said. "But I agree with what Slaughter was saying about them foreign Spanish niggas. I never liked the way they hustle. They fair with their own kind but cheat niggas. They charge us more for the product and give us less on the cut. They always deal with niggas curbside on the block, don't even want you in the lobby of their building or up in their cribs, like we ain't all doing the same thing. They don't give a fuck when we exposed. Something goes down, them motherfuckers be all on their walkie-talkies speaking Spanish, warning their crew about the movement of the beast on the block. But once they got our money in their pocket, they don't give a fuck if the cops sweep us up. Sometimes I even wondered if they was letting the beast know which black guys was up in their area copping. Using us as a decoy. Sacrificing us to cover up their own dealings," Narcotic said.

"That's the Dominicans, not the Puerto Ricans," Puerto Rican Paco said. "I helped Black make the connection with them Spanish-speaking dudes 'cause it wasn't nothing to it. It was just a soccer game and that shit went off good. You know how it is. Usually we warring with them. It was nice to have a few days of peace. And it was good for business. They ain't got their hands in our pockets. We ain't preventing them from earning, either—all good. There's enough to go around," Paco said.

"Non cypher, Slaughter, if you had knowledge of self, you'd recognize the position you putting DeSean in. He can't flip on his brother's orders. He won't go against the gods. You shouldn't even be asking him to do that. If you got a beef with Black, just go head-up with him. If it's not one-on-one, this whole place gon' get turned out. We each gon' get boxed up," Jamar said.

"I'm not no motherfucking caveman. Fuck fighting with fists. Fuck face-to-face and head-up. I'm coming in the cover of darkness, cutting hearts out of chests, causing bloodshed. That's more respectful. I got one man in my scope. Y'all already know. I won't cross DeSean or fuck up the money. And I don't mind getting only my hands dirty," Slaughter said.

"Yeah, but that one man, if you hit him up, you got Murder Money Mayhem versus the Muslims. They def' gon' retaliate. The Latin Kings usually stay out of our business but like you said, since the soccer joint, they might try and jump in on his side. He got them other foreign dudes with him and cats from all the boroughs who he helped in them study groups," Mathematics said.

"You proving my point right there," Slaughter said. "He think he bigger than the M3s. He think he's bigger than us. He gotta go." No one gave a response. There was only silence. That was the exchange they had in the cypher before dawn, in the same space, at the same time, as the prayer.

That same day back then, I still ate my morning meal with the

M3s. It was the first meal we ever had in complete silence. In fact, there was a strange silence throughout that whole day. Teacher Mack peeped it when no one in the class would answer his questions no matter how he poked and provoked. When we got to Teacher Karim Ali's class, he wasn't there. Instead, there was a meek man whose presence was the opposite of Teacher Ali. Once he said he was our new teacher, the whole class went deaf, dumb, and blind. It was as though the same bodies were in the room, but each soul had slipped beneath the slim space at the bottom of the door and escaped down the corridor. Lunch was silent and the corrections officers had no clue. It was intriguing, how leery the silence made the COs. One of them was so stupid, he began barking orders at a time when everyone was following orders out of routine and without error.

On the yard there was no movement. Everyone was grouped up in their sections, no games being played. Just silent signaling and a few sharp weapons being passed off on the low and then concealed.

Dinnertime silence, same thing.

All males moving through the corridors close in the line but never touching. One line exiting the cafeteria area, while another entering from the opposite direction. Another CO was holding back a third line till the two lines moved through. Fourth line was paused on the stairs, guarded by their CO. I was heading my line as usual. There was a push from behind, men falling forward like dominoes, then balancing back up. "Keep your hands to your sides. Stay to your right. Keep the line moving, ladies," CO Gordon called out. I heard a scuffle. Turning, I saw Slaughter, who was in the middle of my line, moving like an offensive lineman but instantly being blocked by the men who stood in between me and him. "Ladies, step back into the line," the CO said. But my man immediately in front of Slaughter was bleeding. All eyes followed the trail of the blood and in less than a second, lines two and three jumped in, forming a mass that was no longer on the right of the line in either direction. The COs began pulling bodies back. But like an onion, the men were layered too deep, and the stabbing motions were swift and silent. The fourth line of inmates flooded through the doorway 'cause their CO left his position to clamp down on the fight. Fists were flying and bodies were piling up. The alarm went off on a day of silence. Riot patrol came blasting through the door. Their response so immediate it was as though they expected it. The pepper spray was let off and had inmates trying to cover their eyes, some coughing up dinner.

We were all facedown on the floor, hands tied behind our backs with tight, sharp, thick plastic cuffs, heavy knees and heavier boots pinned on our backs to hold us in position. Blood, shit, vomit, and piss on the floor. The medical team arrived, identifying the injured and moving them onto the gurneys to be transported out for treatment. Slaughter was laid out. He had a sharp shank lodged deep in his side like a skewer and his intestines oozing out like sauce. I smiled. He looked like shish kebab. He looked down at me from that hospital gurney with that Brooklyn dirty smirk. They moved him out. DeSean and me and all of the M3s were locked in that deadpan stare, from the floor. A CO had his heavy boot pressed down on the side of DeSean's face.

"You good?" DeSean asked me, from his uncomfortable position. I nodded.

I'm back in the box.

## 27. DOING TIME

"Three months in the box. Three months in population. Three months back in the box. Is that your plan? Thought you was a little smarter than that," the she-officer said. But I could hear the excitement in her tone. She was glad I was back under her control and on her tier.

"Relax," I told her. "I took care of the three things that you care most about."

"Three things?" she asked.

"I earned my GED. That test was easy. I took it before I had even completed their test preparation course. The SAT exam took more concentration, but the challenge was good. In between the chaos, I had nothing better to do than study," I said.

"What was your score? The perfect SAT score is 1600. I know that. My son studied for that test as well."

"I just sat for it before I ended up in here. Didn't get the scores back yet."

"I see. And what is the third thing that you took care of that I care about the most?" she asked, with a little wiggle in her tone.

"Myself," I said, opening my arms and striking a stance so she could see I studied but I also kept up my workout, and my warrior body was the evidence. And in a dark, dirty, dreary place, in the middle of the night, she laughed. Then she became unusually quiet.

"You did good with your studies, but I heard you fell in with them 'murder boys.' That's not so bright of a move."

"When I left the box the first time, I was already branded a 'murder boy.' You knew my charges."

"All the more reason to stay away from them and distinguish yourself."

"You think Rikers is the same as the boarding school where your son studies?" I asked her. "I'm a prisoner in a jail, shoulder to shoulder with every other prisoner locked and hemmed in the same space."

"I don't know why y'all boys have to fight each other. You're the same as the male inmates in the adult lockup areas. They should've beat those racist white boys' asses from Howard Beach who murdered that black boy from Bedford-Stuyvesant. If y'all was doing something like that, even my colleagues would've stepped out of your way. Every decent person in New York is heated over that shit. Meanwhile, our higher-ups are hammering the COs to protect them white-boy inmates, the murderers, from getting mobbed and hurt. Since y'all inmates are fighting each other every day anyway, y'all should've taken care of that." Then she gave me the grimy details of the Michael Griffith, Howard Beach case and how an angry white gang of neighbors attacked Griffith and his three companions after their car broke down and they entered a white neighborhood looking for help. The white gang, who outnumbered the four black men, beat and then chased twenty-three-year-old Griffith onto the highway, where he was killed by a vehicle being driven by a white police officer's son.

"He got killed by white thugs who terrorized him and then ran him down and left him like roadkill," the she-officer said.

I could tell that she thought her "colleagues," the other corrections officers at Rikers, had some sense of honor and allegiance. She believed that the COs would somehow link hands with the inmates and stand down while we thrashed the racist white boys for a racial attack and an unjust murder. Obviously that was not and is not the case. There is no honor among COs, same as there is no honor among thieves. And, if the COs link hands with some inmates, it would only be to bring drugs and other contraband, which they are supposed to keep out, in. And, if they ever stand down, it's to watch and allow and encourage a strategic hit being carried out against an inmate by another inmate who is a part of their dirty CO import-export drug ring. Like the hit that Slaughter tried but failed to carry out against me. I peeped over time how the COs like to maintain "their house." Keep the inmates fighting each other instead of them. Keep the inmates medicated so they didn't have the energy to resist. Choose a small group of inmates to be house leaders, and give them the space to crush and correct all the other inmates while they keep the crime circulating on the inside to supplement their income. The COs wanted desperately to chill like the hustlers they supposedly hated but secretly loved and admired and wanted to be like. They wanted to chill the way those hustlers chilled before their arrest. They wanted to get the same response from the women that the hustlers got, instead of being bossed by the angry bitches who they had fucked and fucked over and now owed a heap of child support. The COs were failures at business, failures as fathers, failures at family. The COs were desperate men.

Jail orientation had been over for me. Now I saw the setup clearly in great detail. However, I was not about to debate the topic with a woman. No matter how filthy a hole or a predicament is, a woman is still naïve in her mind, understanding of the schemes of men. No matter how low men might go, women can never fall as low as men or be as filthy as the filthiest man, because women are the wombs that carry, then push life into existence. That is the amazing difference that Allah originated between male and female, while at the same time creating man and woman from the same one soul.

At the internal jail hearing before I got convicted of another tier-three violation and boxed for another three months, I sat in complete silence. I'm not an actor. I already knew that the men in the room who had authority already knew what they planned as my outcome. Me stating my defense would've been nothing but theater. I already knew that even the one female authority in the room would agree with whatever the male authorities guided her to agree with. I had already discovered by then that one CO in our dorm was Slaughter's uncle on the low. The inmate nephew was dirty. The uncle CO was dirty. I do my research. Same as I studied faces, scars, jewels, and relations on my Brooklyn block when I first arrived in America, and the same as I matched the faces I studied with the apartments they lived in and cars they drove, the children they had and the habits and deeds they did, I did the same study in here.

At Rikers, I concluded, all of these inmates had brothers and cousins, uncles and fathers, and in some cases even grandfathers and mothers who were either inmates themselves or working as COs or administrative employees. It was against the jail rules for the COs to be working with inmates who were their friends and relatives. It was even a violation for the COs to be friendly, familiar, and casual with any inmate. But which man or woman from any of our 'hoods who had earned the well-sweated position of being a corrections officer was gonna forfeit their position, paycheck, or benefits by admitting they was born gang- and crime-related?

Ironically (one of those SAT vocabulary words), I was accused and convicted in the internal jail hearing of conspiring to create, organize, and run a gang that was disruptive to the day-to-day lawful standard and routine in the jail. Somehow, by making prayers and "causing" other inmates to gather and make prayers, by forming study groups and helping other inmates to study, by reading and teaching other inmates how to read and understand at least the letters they were receiving, and by working out in teams and organizing sports events that involved gangs, I had committed several code violations. The violation was not the praying itself, or the reading or the teaching or the working out, or basketball or soccer games. The crime was the organizing of males. Since I had been organizing, I must have been "conspiring." According to them, I had triggered a dangerous "day of silence" which had never happened at Rikers before. Now silence was a crime. Groups of silent men were a threat, a terror, a resistance.

The truth is, I had not organized men to be silent. Silence comes to men who after learning what they did not already know or understand become thoughtful. Thoughtfulness leads to consideration. Consideration leads to feelings. Feelings lead to brotherhood. Brotherhood leads to unity. Unity leads to defense against perceived and actual threats and injustices. I never once asked the male youth inmates to protect me. They chose to put their bodies in front of Slaughter once the rumor was out that he would take my life. They chose to move to protect me, I believe, because I had treated each youth not by race or language or the place of birth or territory they came from or claimed. And the same way I came to respect any male in my life who actually taught me something unique and useful that helped me to survive, build, and thrive, some of the inmates had come to respect me.

My father had taught me, when I was young enough to hear and consider, that language should never separate one good person from another. He said that any man could learn another man's language if he could shut up long enough to listen, and sit still long enough to study. All I had done was obey the words and lessons of my father, remain mostly silent and watchful, and learn the language of men, even the ones who were speaking the same language differently.

During my hearing as I sat silently, I was reminded of the words of YesYesYall. He once said to all of the M3s in the cypher, "Word up, by listening to what Teacher Karim Ali be teaching in class, or praying like Black, we gon' get in more heat and have more trouble than we already got for drugs, money, and murder." YesYesYall was sharp, but he usually hid his intelligence inside his jokes. In the end, he was right. Without me selling or buying any drugs or contraband, without me even having any money on my commissary or purchasing anything at all, without me making or having any weapons other than my hands and feet, or using any violence or waging any wars, I was pegged as a gang leader who had organized a prayer and study group that influenced and caused a deadly silence that incited a riot.

"Three years, it's a *shonda*, but, it's the best I could do," my green-eyed lawyer said.

"A *shonda*?" I repeated.

"Yes, a shame," she said. I smiled.

"I don't know what kind of math you are doing. But when we first met, you were talking twenty-five years to life, and even pointed out a case where someone my same age was convicted and sentenced to execution. Every time I see you, the number of years I might serve decreases. Now here you are with a deal signed and sealed saying three years. I'm almost done serving one. You did a good job," I told her.

"Three years would be great, and probably even impossible, if they had one shred of evidence against you. The fact is they do not and they have had ample time to gather it if it existed, and if they were capable," she said.

"Don't worry about it. It's spring all over again. You got a date, a fiancé, a husband?" I asked her.

"I probably would have all three if I wasn't out working for you!" she said, and laughed.

"You've had ample time to organize that," I said, flipping her words back. She smiled.

"Do you know what I think is really gracious about you, Jordan?" she suddenly asked me. I didn't answer. I felt choked by that fake name. After almost a full year of being locked up, "gracious" is not how I would describe myself. In fact, "the Most Gracious" is one way that all Muslims describe Allah. What I am honestly is striving and surviving.

"You have lost your grandfather. You have lost your freedom. You are convicted and about to lose three more years of your life, one at Rikers, although they could lawfully hold you here for up to two years, then one or two years at God only knows which prison, where God only knows which schmucks will be in charge. But you are still smiling," she said warmly to me.

"With good behavior I could knock off a year and only serve two years in full," I reminded her.

"You've been in the box twice on two tier-three violations. I don't want to piss on your optimism, but it's safe to say that you are a guy who can kiss your good-behavior relief goodbye," she said, and her words silenced me.

"And, if you don't stop praying and saving your peers' lives, and if you don't stop reading and forming study groups—*oy veh*—before they ship you out of here to another prison, who knows, you could end up back in the box again." She threw her hands up in frustration.

"That's funny, right?" I asked her with a straight face.

"Oh yeah, it's hilarious. If you would have called me about your second jailhouse hearing, and those bogus charges, I would've had the ACLU all over their asses for violation of freedom of religion, freedom of speech . . . I mean, these are basic freedoms. All Americans know that," she said.

"How is your sister?" I asked Ayn Aaronson, my peculiar, passionate, and precious lawyer about her deceased twin.

"She seems to be happier in her world than I am in mine."

Transferred from the box after ninety days to C-74, I was now wearing the green jail jumper reserved for convicts. Body more solid than steel. Side by side with other men who were also solid-bodied, regardless of their state of mind. A convict, I'm no longer an accused youth offender. I'm with the adult population, not the cubs, the kids, the youth, the adolescents, anymore. I'm in the adult facility at Rikers. I sleep in a cell, not bed-to-bed in a wide-open dorm. There's no blood or friendship between my young, "convicted as an adult," self and these men. But still, I am recognized as family. I'm a Muslim, moving in a space populated with many men who say they're Muslims. Upon arrival I was approached by a big man who recognized my *alamat sala*, a prayer mark that appears on the forehead of Muslim men from the continual pressing of the forehead to the ground during prayer. By him acknowledging my mark, which ninety-nine percent of others overlooked, he alleviated the tension that comes when any man approaches another man while incarcerated. I of course saw his mark as well, which caused me to consider that he might actually be a Muslim. I had met enough men claiming Islam who were without prayer. He ended up being a leader in the Muslim population on lockup. They claimed me, although I didn't ask to be claimed or protected or grouped or ganged up.

Meanwhile, I'm the "supreme soldier," so dubbed by Redverse and held down by his men, the Jamaicans who run "'nough shit in here" and got their own food ring going. They cared more about having fresh fruits and vegetables and "ital" foods than anyone else. They were heavy into commissary. Their women, outside of whatever else they might be bringing in and out on visits, kept them well fed. All cliqued up, the Jamaicans treated me good, like an ambassador, 'cause Redverse gave the order. One of 'em gave me enough fruits and vegetables to fit in a basket. It was a gift, same as gold to them. I had to accept it because I had rejected the weed they offered me, and to avoid causing insult.

It wasn't until I reached the C-74 adult building that I figured Redverse out. That's how many hours of rewinding, reviewing, and thinking I had to commit to the puzzle of the drug network I landed in. My hypothesis was that Redverse was linked with the dirty cops in the precinct in his area. They protected his spot and didn't arrest his soldiers or harass their posse. In exchange, they got a huge cut of the paper. But the paper was only guaranteed if the cops facilitated the drug deliveries coming and going. When I entered the spot unrelated and unknowingly, and once I exited the spot with the red bag, there was a confusion created. Redverse worked the confusion as though the cops failed to protect the product. No product, no paper for them till the next time. That's why they were furiously trying to link me to the package, and locate the package so that they could collect. Redverse double-crossed the cops. He held on to the product, sold it, doubled his take, and pinned the robbery on me and the blame on the dirty cops who never got paid on that particular take. He dubbed me the supreme soldier for three reasons. One, I could have killed his brother and his men. I didn't. Two, I could've identified his men, snitched, and recounted my encounter to the detectives. I didn't. But the most important reason was I could've fucked his girl in his building or welcomed her in on a visit and done anything to her. I didn't. What I had not considered back then, and even after my arrest, was that Redverse had a surveillance tape, a television recording everything. Maybe the Red Flamingo didn't realize it and thought it was just for her use to watch who came in and out of the laundry area and what they were doing while she wasn't in there. But I concluded that he was surveilling everything. He had her on tape and he had me on tape and could identify me. That's how they knew who I was. The Jamaicans, many of whom find Islam too strict and confining, owe a debt to the quality of men Islam produces. We know among other things that brotherhood is destroyed the second a man puts his hands on another man's woman.

I'm the poor righteous teacher, protected by the Five Percent because "Quan said so," and because DeQuan is also locked up in C-74 where I am. DeQuan was the same as he ever was on our Brooklyn block, with an added seriousness. He was solid from working out continuously. He had an army going at Rikers. It was not only about contraband for him. Some of his soldiers ran a newsletter that kept inmates informed about where men were being moved and what was happening at prisons all around the country, as reported by inmates who had been convicted and moved out of Rikers. DeQuan was like the king of communications, including if anyone needed to get a kite—a letter or message—to anyone using the network that he built. His man Butch, a.k.a. "Broadcast," was an old-timer whose first arrest had occurred in 1966. He was like a human computer. I peeped why DeQuan recruited him even though he was unlike anyone in the rest of his crew. During the workout, where men were trying to relieve their stress, Broadcast would give random reports, just speaking aloud casually, but in a loud volume with the authority of a news anchor.

"You young'uns better get ready. This is jail. Prison is something else. You think you don't like the COs up here at Rikers? You'd better get to loving them while the getting is good. Least they look like us and know where we come from 'cause they come from the same place. Once they ship you out of Rikers, you gon' encounter some big, ugly, hateful white boys. They gon' be everywhere, their arms as big as your legs. They Ku Klux Klan. They hate the black man. You gon' feel that hatred instantly. So thick you can choke on it. They don't only hate the blacks, they hate anybody with a drop of melanin, any kind of color in them. They shave your head with hatred. They'll grab your balls, shove their fingers in your mouth, choking you with hatred. Say they looking for something they ain't really looking for. They nasty, you gon' find out. They'll spread your cheeks and drill in your asshole 'cause they can, and 'cause they want to, and 'cause they hateful and jealous of you.

"How many prisons you think they got? Almost two thousand prisons in America, not including the federal ones and more than a million prisoners. Oh they got something for all of us. They got jails like this right here. Then they got transitional prisons. Then they got minimum-security prisons, low-minimum, high-minimum, medium, secure-medium, high-medium, maximum . . . Yeah, now they even got private prisons, run by some corporations for profit, or a group of greedy businessmen. One of them private prisons, the COs even got guns. They lawless. They can do anything to you. They got prison farms. Work you harder than a farm animal. They got medical prisons and psychiatric prisons—that feed you dope. They'll dope you up all night and all day.

"You better watch out. Even if you don't, it don't matter. They gon' do what they do regardless. Some states is worse than others. Watch out! Don't go to Texas. Soon as you cross the state line, if you black or Latino you under arrest. They got 116 prisons in that one state, not including the feds. Same as Florida. They got 125 prisons, then Georgia and North Carolina and good old New York. Those the top runners for locking us down brutally.

"Man, it's gonna be cold up North to the extreme. So cold you can't talk. And even if you could, you wouldn't. You got brain freeze. Even your thoughts are frozen. It's gon' be hot down South to the extreme. They'll have you burning in Louisiana. You wake up wet. Get confused, think you already showered but you stink. They'll bury you in their underground prison. Have you thinking there never was a sun. Make you question whether or not you exist. Make you rather be dead." And when he spoke like that, every man working out was grunting and lifting more than they ever thought they could. Broadcast got the respect because he was old and knowledgeable about the details of the world of prison. But his impromptu broadcasts tripled the anger, because most knew it was the truth.

I also got respect from the Spanish-speaking inmates from all over. I was the deep, dark black-skinned cat who knows a few key words and phrases in Spanish. Enough to give the greetings, and show respect and receive it back. When I'm around the Spanish-speaking inmates, I don't get tight when they speak their own language or envious like the African Americans do. I'm at ease.

Upon my arrival at the adult facility, the first one to lock glares with me was Tyriq. I recognized him immediately. He was only three seconds behind before he pinpointed and acknowledged who I am.

"Hustler's League, Junior Division. I recruited you to play ball. Brownsville, Brooklyn youth," he said.

"What's a big man doing in a small place?" I acknowledged.

"I was a 'bout to ask you the same thing," he said. "But, my peoples 'bout to bail me out. Anything you need I could get it sent in for you—talk quick. I'll be out of this small space by the morning."

"I'm good," I told him. He stared at me in my greens. He wasn't a convict, just an accused, still wearing his street clothes, looking fresh and fashionable.

"You good? Looks like they about to send you up North," he said, and it wasn't a question. "Man . . . ," he continued, "that tournament last summer was crazy. The junior division snatched the light and the hype from the adult league that year. Your skills were undeniable and impeccable. Caused a lot of argument among the judges. I thought you should have been the MVP."

Two weeks after Tyriq was bailed out, I received a visitor.

"Tiffany Kelly," CO Williams, an elder officer, who never referred to the inmates as "ladies," said to me. I realized then that I had not put in paperwork saying that I refuse all visits since I was moved to C-74. It didn't matter. I had not put in paperwork detailing my list of approved visitors, either.

"No visit," I said to him. He left. Before his shift ended he said to me, "Your visitor has a school identification that said she was eighteen. Now I done been around the block. I wouldn't usually comment. But since you refused her anyway I guess it's alright." He leaned into the bars that separated us. "Those big titties she has sat straight up. She's not a day older than fifteen. We catch a lot of young girls coming up here with fake IDs trying to visit grown men who ain't their daddys, if you know what I mean."

Bangs, a.k.a. Tiffany—I'm not even sure if her last name is Kelly, but I am sure that it was her grandmother's last name. She had that kind of effect on every male of every age. She was all beautiful body. In the spring and summer, she wore pants that fit like panties, had a mean camel toe, a tight waist, and 32D's that were filled with breast milk that she fed to her infant daughter. She was a runner with pretty thighs. Her legs were always naked. When she wasn't in her kicks or roller skates, she slid her pretty feet into tiny sandals that showcased her pretty toes. She was not suitable for me. Yet she loved me. Because of my faith, I didn't go in her. But the beast in me always wanted to.

Her visit, even though I denied her, caused my joint to swell, in a joint where I never wanted to be hard and swollen. Furthermore, her visit propelled me into a memory.

# 28. THE HUSTLER'S LEAGUE CHAMPIONSHIP • *A Reflection*

Beyond a doubt, the black team moved with the idea, energy, effort, and precision that we would be the champions of the junior division of the Hustler's League. Ricky Santiaga was so confident and certain that he prepared twenty-four-karat-gold championship rings for each of the eleven members of the team. The rings had never been mentioned at the start of the league with the other rewards being offered to the top players. None of us expected them. And, they were not ordinary rings that could be purchased from a catalogue, a retailer, or a trophy shop.

Coach Vega, one afternoon after another rigorous practice, let the whole team walk but held me back. Panama Black, the team captain, Machete, and each team member minus Dolo were used to Vega holding me back and then requiring me to put in extra time, extra laps, extra suicides, extra layups, extra squats, and extra dribbling and handling exercises, as though he was trying to force me to repay the team for the time and the practices I had missed while I was traveling. A few times, some of my teammates stayed back to watch him overwork me. Although my teammates showed me love and welcomed me back, I knew they were secretly satisfied that I was being punished and trained twice as hard as they were. I didn't mind.

On that particular afternoon the coach held me back, something out of the ordinary occurred. "Meet my boss tomorrow outside of Junior's Restaurant at noon," Vega told me.

"For what?" I asked.

"Don't ask. Just do it."

On the corner of Flatbush and Fulton, I waited in my sweats with my ball in my grip as usual. I didn't see him. It was 12:12. Caught off guard and slipping, I smiled when I finally recognized he had been there all along, seated in a ride that was the opposite of any whip I ever saw him push or even lean on. It was a 1972 Oldsmobile Delta 88. No rims, just wheels, not blacked out and customized but with the windows spray-painted black, like it was done by an amateur artist or a small child. His driver's-side window didn't ease down. It staggered, revealing that the driver was rolling it down manually.

"That's you," I said, not as in asking him if he was himself, but verifying if he was the same man I knew, pushing that piece-of-shit car where he was seated in the driver's position.

"Get in," he said. I did. "There's a time and place for everything," he said once I was seated on the ugly black velvet cushioned seats. He pulled off.

Moments later, on a fucked-up block in Bed-Stuy, he pulled over, then parked in front of an abandoned building. "First stop," he said, and we both got out.

"Hold up," I told him. "This ain't a ballpark. It's not the address you gave me for your vending machine delivery, either. Looks like there is no business between you and me right here," I said. He smiled.

"You gave your word," he said.

"Remind me," I said, but I was one hundred percent doubt.

"You owe me a game of chess on a broken-down board in a broken-down place. Now if you wanna back out, just let me know," he said calmly in his casual denim wear, and I noted it was my first time seeing him out of Gucci loafers or Tod's and into Air Force Ones.

*He's already playing chess*, I thought to myself. Between his jalopy and his clothes, this fucked-up block and the broke-down building he chose, it was his method of intimidation and mind control. That had to be the reason he didn't notify me in advance that today was game day. I'm sure he gave himself the time to prepare and sharpen his game and his psyche.

I had only managed to get in one session of practice with my man Marty Bookbinder. I had phoned him, placed an order for a book and a map, and then invited him to meet me in a Queens cafe I had carefully chosen one evening to deliver my purchase and play a couple of games of chess. He accepted eagerly.

"Let's go," I told him. We walked. *Everything with this dude is a test*, I thought.

Reverse aromatherapy, the place stunk of mildew and dog shit and some other odor I didn't recognize. Thought, *if he had to go through all of this, maybe his chess game is no good.* Then I warned myself not to underestimate him, because maybe that was part of what he wanted me to do, in his setup.

On a cardboard dollar-store board, on a rickety card table, in an empty room without walls, we both sat on cheap metal folding chairs. I could hear footsteps and movement above and below me. *He needs me to feel uncomfortable and surrounded and filled with fear of the unknown.* I had no fear. The championship games between the two top teams in the junior league were a week away. He had a vested interest in not doing anything to damage his investment. I took some deep breaths. On the tabletop he flipped the hourglass and it was on. He had the white pieces, the first move.

I was silent while he thought and even as he advanced his pawn. After a few minutes of play, I realized that he would say something each time it was my turn, just to throw me off. "Think on it," or "Careful now," or "Are you sure?" On my simplest moves he would even comment, "You give your pawns up too easy. You should appreciate them more." I checked how we would maneuver to hold onto his pawns, even allowing one move where he sacrificed his knight to save one of them.

Ultimately, I had lost each of my pawns except one, but held onto my queen, one knight, two bishops, and one rook. Half an hour later, I ate up his rook using my bishop. He devoured my bishop using his queen. But then, his king was left open except for the two pawns guarding him. I advanced my black knight and said "check." Soon as he got ready to move his pawn to gobble up my knight, he realized that once he did, his king would be exposed to checkmate. He chose to move his king to the left instead to avoid my knight, which was of course limited to L-shaped movements. I advanced my one remaining rook from the back of my side of the board, straight all the way to the back of Santiaga's side of the board. "Check," I said. As soon as he realized that the only way out for him was to use his queen to eat my rook and save his king, but that if he did, he would lose his queen with my follow-up move, he leaned back. He was paused so long that even the sand had run out of his favor. "Why don't you call?" he asked me.

"Take your time," I said just to mess with his head, and flipped the hourglass back over to emphasize it. He then moved his queen to gobble my rook. My one remaining bishop ate his queen.

"Game over," he said. But it wasn't rightfully over. He still had moves he could make.

"You have moves open—why quit?" I asked, using the word *quit* to push him to play on to the finish either way.

"Don't you know?" he asked me. "The game is always over once a player loses his queen."

"But one of your three pawns could become your queen," I said. But why was I helping my opponent?

"A pawn can only pretend to be a queen. But only a queen is a queen," he said. It sounded to me like this was his philosophy on life.

"You want to talk about life, or do you wanna play the game?" I baited him. Our first game ended in a stalemate.

"Rematch?" I asked him. He accepted and we began. But at a certain point, I purposely let him have it. He looked at me hard.

"Sloppy move," he said. "That's unlike you."

"Your move," was all I responded. I had decided I would lose the game. But in the real world I would play my position and somehow win in some other way. I was grateful to him for a few reasons. That was enough. He used the opening, dominated in the game until he called checkmate.

"Second stop," he said after his Oldsmobile plowed down the Brooklyn-Queens Expressway, not cruising but with great effort. Now we were in another beat-up neighborhood located in Queens, the opposite of the area I lived in, about to head into the side entrance of a brown brick three-story commercial building on a block of small businesses where any customer might think it was too risky to shop.

We got out. I didn't ask any more questions. I knew he knew by then what I was game for, and what I wasn't.

The front door was solid steel, no window or placard stating what they were selling or what a customer could expect. He pressed a buzzer. The loud buzz responded with an even louder buzzer. Santiaga opened the then unlocked door and we were one step inside, facing a gold gate from floor to ceiling, like cell bars that even a slim body couldn't slide between. It was locked and there was only a dim light, which revealed a set of stairs, the wall to the right lined with tall stalks of real sugarcane. Without our pressing a buzzer, a buzz sounded and the gate opened. We walked down. Each step was painted with a clean wide gold stripe.

In the basement, nothing was renovated or plush. The floor was made of some kind of rock and there was a huge tree stump, metal benches, and tables.

"My man Khan," Santiaga said, introducing me to a brown-skinned man who had a three-foot-long ponytail, longer than a horse's and beyond his backside. It almost concealed the long, thin scar that ran across the back of his neck that confirmed that someone had once tried to cut his head off. *He survived murder.* His hair was not manly, but his mannerisms were. His voice was rough, but he sang his words to an unfamiliar rhythm. Similar to Jamaican but not Jamaican, I could tell. He had to see the confusion in me as my mind tried to place him as having originated from either Pakistan, India, Bangladesh, or Kashmir. His name was Khan, and that is definitely a Muslim name.

"Guyana, Indian," he said without me asking, and he pointed to the small model flag of Guyana he had posted on a drink mixing stick and mounted on one of his tables. "But me grow up rough like dee African." He pushed his fist forward and bumped knuckles with Santiaga. When he withdrew his hand, I saw his fingers were worn and ragged and some of his fingertips burnt. Looked like he had either tried to seer off his fingerprints, or he had strangled a few men who all had thick muscular necks. Maybe one of them was the one who had tried to chop off his head.

"He's one of my champions," Santiaga told him, referring to me. "I'm gonna need eleven rings, twenty-four-karat dark gold. Size his finger," Santiaga told him. "Khan makes jewelry with the same kind of passion that you play ball," he said to me. The Indian pulled from his jeans buckle loop a set of about thirty steel rings and chose one out of all of them. It fit exactly on my finger.

"See what I mean?" Santiaga asked me. "Precision," then he reached into his denim shirt and pulled out a Zip Lock bag. My mind prepared for the worst because of what Ameer's father had once mentioned to us about the Hustler's League. I started suspecting and speculating that it was cocaine or crack in the Zip Lock, but it wasn't. "That's fifteen ounces of gold, 425.24 grams," Santiaga said, handing it to Khan. I checked it out. It looked like the light brown sugar my Umma used in some recipes. "Got it from your guy in the DD," Santiaga said to him.

" 'Ira the Jew,' or from Levi?" Khan asked.

"Ira—he's the more trustworthy of the two," Santiaga said. I knew then that DD stood for Diamond District. Of course I had been there in many of the shops, wholesalers and retailers in midtown Manhattan. And of course I recalled eagerly that Santiaga had an apartment on the east end of that money block that led straight to the diamond district.

Khan took the bag and hit an intercom button. A young girl, about Naja's age, quietly stepped down the stairs and without words rolled up Khan's ponytail and pinned it in place with a pure gold, uniquely crafted barrette that looked like it came from some royal family's treasure chest. It fit over the bulk of the wrapped-up ponytail and held it in position on his head like a crown. She handed him a red bandanna, then turned and left.

Khan went to a worktable that had a black stone top. He opened Santiaga's Zip Lock of pure gold and spread a thin line of it onto the stone. He dropped a few drops of a solution onto the gold, saying only two words, "Nitric acid." The line of gold did not dissolve in the acid. Then he chose another bottle and dropped another solution, saying, "Nitric acid plus hydrochloric acid." The gold disappeared. "Genuine, yes mon," he declared. Santiaga nodded his head in approval.

Khan was a chemist, a genius scientist in an urban laboratory customized especially for him. Unlike any jeweler I had ever encountered, Khan made his jewels by hand, from scratch, like a baker making a pineapple upside-down cake. Taking inventory now, in his space was a gas tank, and an oxygen tank, and a huge container plastered with a red warning sticker that said SULFURIC ACID. There seemed to be enough items down there that with one tiny mistake, the whole building would explode and be leveled. Santiaga observed me staring at the sulfuric acid and said suddenly, "It's lethal—burn the skin right off your body in twenty seconds or less. Some stupid stick-up kid tried to rush this spot. That acid got thrown in his face. Gave him a whole new look and a whole new outlook. That was before my man Khan got the steel door and gates installed with the camera and the buzzer locks."

There was a hammer—no, a mallet—that was lying on the tree stump. I picked it up as Khan worked his skill at his station. The handle was solid and the head was heavy as barbells and even heavier than an ax. In the corner of the room were some machines that looked like they came from the seventeenth century, with hand cranks and spinning metal wheels. He had metal saws and heavy sharp shears and every version of pliers, some thick enough to trim bushes or to pull fingers out of their sockets and some tiny enough to pick up the tiniest of diamonds. All of his tools could be converted into deadly weapons. I was imagining that he probably could make some wicked knives, better than a blacksmith. I envisioned designing a diamond-handled gold sword for my second wife, a weapon worthy of her caliber. Or maybe something more creative, tiny swords that could be worn as hair ornaments to hold her thick bun in place. When she needed them as a weapon she could just pull it from her hair and fire it into the eye of her enemy.

The intensity of the fire from his blowtorch captured my attention. "Don't look 'pon it directly. You can blind yerself," he warned. "Almost two thousand degrees," he said and I was amazed to see that the gold changed from powder to liquid gold, then poured inside of two molds that each sat inside two identical clay dishes filled with sand. He pressed the two clay dishes together. The liquid gold solidified into the shape of a ring. He dipped it into some solution. An hour and a half later, he handed me my gold championship ring. It was warm in my hand. He took it back and went to one of the antique machines, flipped a switch, and buffed and polished the ring lovely on a spinning cylinder lined with heavy brushes. "Dis is de prototype. Me can do 'nough tings to make it one of a kind. If you don't like, I torch it, it turn back to gold liquid in tree seconds. Maybe you want fer put a diamond pond dat?" he asked Santiaga. Santiaga reached into his denim shirt again and pulled out a smaller Zip Lock half filled with diamonds.

"Nice idea. I have the gems here, but these are for my queen. After you finish my ring orders, I'll order a separate piece for the wife. Just hit me up when the other ten rings are ready. First, let me show you my championship ring design and engravings so you can finish 'em off nice, perfectly." They hovered over a paper that Santiaga pulled out of his pocket with some designs drawn in pencil.

I was captivated. I thought it was incredible that this guy from Guyana, who felt like an everyday Brooklyn black man and was styled and street in his manner, but looked like an Indian straight from India, could do everything from start to finish. He could cook and mold and bang and shape and design and engrave the gold. He could create by hand the diamond settings and was even a diamond setter. He couldn't have been thirty years old yet, but he was a master of his trade. How could I not think so? I saw the gold powder in its rawest form and later held the handcrafted twenty-four-karat dark gold ring in my palm after watching him closely through every step, movement, and process. Besides, he had photos mounted of beautiful bangles and earrings and necklaces.

"Did you make all of the jewels in your photos?" I asked him.

"Every-ting come from my shop is original, handmade. You supply the gold or diamonds of your choice. I make it one of a kind."

"What about you?" Santiaga turned and asked me.

"What about me?" I said.

"You came into some paper. Want to place an order of your own?"

"How did you learn the trade?" I asked Khan. "If you don't mind," I added.

"I worked for some Indians that owned a shop in Guyana. They treated me like a little nigger. I was their runner, running from workstation to workstation. In one area they made bangles, in the other rings, in the other necklaces, in the other they made settings for diamonds, and in the other they set diamonds. I played dumb. The pay was dirt, yet the gold was a noble metal and the jewels I was handling were all precious and the Indian owner was filthy rich. I lived in the tenement he owned. I didn't complain. Kept me eyes open and me mouth closed. Learned everything, but me act like I know nothing. Seven years later me open me own shop so I could take care of me muddah."

"How much for a bar of gold?" I asked.

"Depends on the weight." Then, Santiaga and Khan spent the next half hour teaching me the weight system, about pennyweights and ounces and grams, karats and points on diamonds. It felt good. Any man not breaking down and humiliating the next man, but teaching him something priceless that he can use to his benefit for a lifetime, is the feeling of father to me.

"Once I tell you 'this is my man,' you can trust that you can show up at his shop, order what you want directly. He won't fuck with your gold or switch out your gems. There's a whole lot of goldsmith's and jewelers who will. He can make anything you can afford, anything. He made that chessboard for me. The 'real board,'" he said, referring to the twenty-four-karat gold board that no one would forget after seeing it once. The one with the princess cut diamond perimeter and the detailed handcrafted diamond and gold chess pieces. "And without my recommendation, you couldn't get past his steel door. This is a no-advertisement, by-word-of-VIP-mouth-only operation."

Without revealing my reasons or relations, I ordered two bars of gold, valued at five thousand dollars each, an heirloom for my twins, *Insha'Allah.* At the same time, I decided right there in that basement that as I earned, I would set aside stacks and convert them into gold bars to back up my paper money and secure my family's financial future.

Even though I was already in Queens, I let Santiaga drop me back in Brooklyn on Fulton Avenue. I would hop on the train. That's just my way. In the train car, I thought about how I appreciated him. At the same time, I thought about his attempts at mind control. He held onto the ring Khan made, but he made sure to place it in my hand without words or instructions to let me know I had to be pivotal in securing the black team championship. The ring, and allowing me to see what he did not allow others to see, was the incentive. Of course I understood the importance. Maybe he had another wager on the game. A bet so deep that if we won it for him, the price of 15 ounces of gold and the $25,000 for MVP and the $10,000 for the five starting champions would seem like nothing to him.

Before I had climbed out of his humorous Oldsmobile, Santiaga said to me, "I know you let me win the rematch. But what you don't know is that I allowed you to let me win. It showed me your character. You're a man who is capable of keeping your ego in check, and not showing your best hand when there's nothing in it for you. Great strategy, awesome timing—I like that. The next round we'll play for real after your tournament ends and I receive your machine shipment. At that time, there will be no courtesies or debts between us."

I appreciated that Santiaga didn't find it necessary to warn me not to tell the team about the rings, or not to discuss what I'd seen and where we went. I took that as the beginning of a trust. He did say to me, however, "The same way Khan tested the gold to confirm that it's genuine, men test men for the same reasons."

July Fourth in "Do or Die Bed-Stuy, Brooklyn on Kingston Ave. and Herkimer Street," the championship game. The stands were full, the park was packed, no standing room. Kicks covered every stretch of cement; kids climbed the fence, reached the top, and stayed, squatting there. Their friends were riddled in between, all the way down to the bottom. Fingers clenching the fence wiring and faces pressed to see in. It was only 11 a.m., but the 'hood was wide awake, cleaned up nice and fresh dressed for their holiday. Full families were out in anticipation of seeing their sons battle for the highest prize that wasn't money, but recognition. The red team entered the same way they had entered every game, a team of individuals only connected by the fact that they each wore something red. They didn't have uniforms. However that day, their coach, who was the opposite of Coach Vega, had gotten his shit together and had outfitted his top five players in red and white Nike Dunks and the rest in red Converse Weapons. His squad, known for being wildly disorganized and explosive, were also unpredictable. They were the only team in the league where one of their players turned around in the heat of a game and punched a member of his own team in the face for not passing the ball to him at the exact time he was open and had the shot. They were known for playing football-basketball, fouling and tackling, blocking and knocking opponents out. They'd rather take the personal or team foul, technical or otherwise, as long as they won the game. But that style got them through the playoffs and straight into the championship game as the only team that could face the undefeated black team.

Navy-blue Jordans with the metallic swoosh hugged all ten pairs of feet on the black team. Black starter jerseys with navy-blue numbers and all-black shorts—that's how we were doing it. The crowd was on our shit for our style, the girls mad excited and their mommas more excited. In the intensity of the adrenaline rush I was calm. I had sent my whole family to Martha's Vineyard. It wasn't my original plan, but my second wife had said some words that moved me. I also had figured out that I needed it to be only me and my ball and the hoop, in my mind.

"This is what we worked for. Think of everything you sacrificed: time, sweat, summer jobs, and even pussy, to bring you to this moment. Go out there and make me look good," Coach Vega said—his signature line. Team owner Ricky Santiaga was too charged to sit. He stood up front in his white tailored leisure suit and white crocodile Gucci loafers and Gucci sunglasses, surrounded by a few men who couldn't fuck with his look.

On the blacktop, the captain and starting red team guard, Ameer Nickerson, was my enemy and my best friend. He had fire in his eyes and the power of the charismatic underdog. He riled up the crowd to cheer for him, then turned to his teammates and threatened them. Familiar with his ways and watching his gestures, I knew.

Jump ball and I have thrown away all friendship and allegiance for the next two hours. Big Mike tapped the ball best, Panama swiped it, threw it to me, and I slam-dunked. It was psychological. Vega had said we needed our first two game points to be intimidating to deflate the reds' egos. Having watched the red team during the playoffs, he said they hustled hard, were skilled and physical, but not thinkers.

Their ball, the pass was in, and swift Machete stole it. He dribbled, passed it backward to Big Mike, and he hit from the foul line.

"Tighten the fuck up!" Ameer screamed at his teammates. He then caught the pass and was dribbling downcourt. He passed the ball to his forward tucked in the corner and he scored the shot. Now they were tightening defense, checking us hard. Ameer told the other point guard on his team, "I got him," and pulled up close on me. Hovering, he tried to strip me. I wasn't having it, and passed the ball through his legs to Panama. "Get on him!" Ameer told his man to check Panama, but then pushed his man out of the way and leaned on Panama himself. "Like this," he told his man, then stripped Panama and was heading back to his hoop. His man ran down long. Ameer passed the ball, and from the right corner, they tied the game, four to four.

Each step of the way it was neck-and-neck. Crazy watching Ameer play every position for his team, even center, even though he wasn't tall enough for that. Ameer was smacking Panama's shots and trying to check me at the same time. As I watched, I plotted to just run him, shake him down till he was out of breath. That's why there's a team. One man can't play every position and shouldn't have to.

The first quarter ended, 28 to 27. Panama complained that Ameer was riding him and we needed to switch it up. "Midnight, you and I will play forward position, give Machete and Jaguar the point guard position for a quarter, just to confuse them. Big Mike, I need you to smack their balls back like this is volleyball. Don't let 'em get near the hoop. Machete, you check that crazy red point guard, their captain."

Second quarter, Ameer went up, Machete smacked his shot. Loose ball; the red team snatched it up. They passed back to Ameer. He went up for the shot again, kicked Machete, and sank it. The crowd went wild. The coaches were out of their seats. The referee called the foul. The black team got possession of the ball. Ameer's shot did not count. Machete was tight. But Ameer was tight also.

"Hands in their faces!" Ameer yelled. Jaguar was dribbling, he cut left, then right, shaking the red man checking him and sinking the layup. Ameer went to his man and leaned on him. His finger was in his face and his man pushed him off. Their ball; his man passed it. Ameer dribbled, faked the pass. Machete went for the fake; Ameer was up in the air unguarded, sank the shot, and elbowed Machete on the way down. The crowd hollered. Machete's eye was fucked up. But the ref called the foul on Machete. The crowd was in an uproar. Vega called time out.

Coach and Panama tried to sit Machete down and send in a sub. Machete argued that he was good. Dolo, who somehow crept up to the bench even though he had been missing from all of the practices and playoff games since his blowup, said, "I told y'all niggas you was gonna need me. Look at the score. Y'all only beating them by two. What? I could've done that," he said and he was wearing a plain black T-shirt, not our team jersey, and a white pair of K-Swiss.

"Shut the fuck up!" Big Mike told Dolo.

"Yeah, I got your shut the fuck up. Don't even ask me to play until you show me some money," Dolo said. "No show, no go." Big Mike lunged toward him. Panama pulled him back. "Focus!" Vega yelled. "He's a nobody. Forget about him."

"Yeah, I'm a nobody. Forget about me. But y'all five ain't gonna get no burn. Fucking bench bums. Coach rather play a one-eyed point guard than any of you!" Dolo shouted. "Slide with me and we could work the crowd and get some money in our pockets," he offered the bottom five. But the crowd noise and excitement level was too high. Dolo, on edge, couldn't grab the spotlight.

Ameer's team, refreshed from the time-out, came back, doing some kind of crazy dance steps. My mind was divided. I was the ball player who planned on defeating the opposition, and the ninjutsu warrior who had a problem with Dolo, the loose cannon from my team. *Focus*, I told myself, then I hit long, a three-pointer. I snatched my point guard position back and checked Ameer to put a clamp on his thirty-two-point game, which was more than half of the points his team earned. Halftime, score was 57 to 54, in our favor.

Sweating hard, I was in the black bandanna, hustling like my life depended on it. I was on Ameer so rough, but we knew each other too well. We were both canceling one another out. Neither him nor me hit any points for six minutes into the third quarter because of the way we blocked, defended, and offended. It gave our teammates the opportunity to score. Ameer got his hands on thc ball somehow. I stripped him. Then he stripped me. The crowd was on their feet. I was back checking him. He passed the ball to his man. His man passed the ball to the red center. The red center passed the ball back to Ameer. He pumped, like he was going up for the shot. I jumped. He darted underneath me and hit the shot from an impossible, awkward angle. Now everyone was standing.

Our ball; Machete was dribbling downcourt. Ameer left his guard over me and pulled up on Machete. They were both in close, and talking shit to one another. "Fuck it, I'll give you the lane," Ameer said to Machete.

"I'll take it," Machete said, and headed for the layup. Ameer stripped him from behind and was on his way back down to his hoop. He passed the ball forward, then ran up full speed before the black team could get back and set up. His man passed him the ball and he layed it up. A herd of girls started calling for him, "Romeo Red, Romeo Red, Romeo Red!" It seemed like I could see his head swell too big for his neck. "That's right!" He pumped his fist and banged his chest. Still, the score was 79 to 76, our favor, at the end of the third quarter.

Our ball, and our bench was suddenly missing four players. I shot a look towards Panama. Panama shot a look towards the bench. Braz connected eyes with Panama and me and mouthed, "Dolo," and swiped his hand across his neck. The five starters, including myself, knew we had to be without error to win the game. I also knew we had an off-the-court problem. As I was dribbling downcourt, I saw Dolo maneuvering through the crowd. Kid had a twenty-two in his grip and his hand hidden at his side. Half a second away from approaching where Vega and Santiaga stood, I stopped and fired the basketball at him, hitting him in the head and causing him to lose balance. The gun hit the floor. The front-row crowd stood, saw the gun on the ground, and scrambled. Dolo tried to pick it up. But when he reached forward he got dragged backwards, out of the view of the players and the fans. As the rumor spread through the crowd to even the people who saw nothing, some started to make moves like bullets had been fired, when they hadn't.

"Play ball!" Ameer shouted. The referee threw in another basketball and gave it to the red team to check. He blew the whistle and it was back on. When the crowd cleared, Santiaga was still standing, chilling in his white leisure suit, no blood on his crocs or cloth. Not even looking over his shoulders one way or another. Dolo was gone like he had never been there in the first place.

End of the fourth quarter, the score was 98 to 95, in our favor. There were eleven seconds remaining on the clock. Ameer pulled up for the shot. Big Mike gummed it and forced Ameer down. Ameer landed on Big Mike's ankle. Big Mike was injured. He howled like a baby but drew the foul. He couldn't be subbed. Braz doesn't play center. Tower was gone. He shot from the line and missed, twice. Ameer sneered and grabbed the rebound. He passed the ball. His man hit the shot from the corner. It was 98 to 97, in our favor. Seven seconds left on the clock. We checked the ball. I had three reds guarding me and no opening. I bounced down the time clock. Jaguar was open. I passed the ball to him. The three reds flew towards him like flies smelling shit. He saw the tackle coming, jumped, and hit the three pointer, game over. The black team won.

In the heat of the victory, the crowd flooded the court. The ball players were mixed in the middle. The referees and coaches were all blowing their whistles. The red team lifted Ameer onto their shoulders and started a Brooklyn chant.

When the crowd was finally pushed back, the red team gave the black team no dap. They wouldn't line up to offer the black team that sportsmanship-like handshake. Instead, their center lit a blunt and started smoking it center court.

The red and black team owners came out half court, along with both coaches. Santiaga and the red team owner, both dressed to the nines and monied men, who I had never seen before, shook hands with no animosity. Then, both coaches shook hands. The emergence of the older men with the clout and the money and control over the purse brought both the crowd and the players to a hush. Ameer broke ranks and approached Santiaga for a handshake. Santiaga raised Ameer's hand and said, "MVP." The crowd cheered. The red team mobbed Ameer. Without a megaphone, Santiaga began speaking. The weight of his reputation caused a sudden silence. "Without a doubt, this youth right here got that Brooklyn struggle, hustle, and fight in his blood. Even though my squad, the black team, earned the victory," the crowd cheered at the mention of our team, "I feel good awarding this man the MVP title," Santiaga announced.

Ameer and I didn't acknowledge one another, like we had agreed for the whole playoffs and championship game. We kept our communication off court. We both played our best game. We both got what we wanted. Ameer had said to me when I first returned from Asia, "I'll be mad as a motherfucker if you come back after being gone for a month and win MVP." Now he had won and he was beaming about the bragging rights he had secured. He didn't even know that although he won the purse fair and square, I was never in the running for it. I had disqualified myself. I saw no reason to tell him. Both him and me were up. He was up $25,000 for MVP. I was up $10,000 for being champion top five. Together we pulled down $35,000. Divided three ways between Ameer, Chris, and me, we were all three up $11,667. That's friendship

Back in my sweats, after our on-the-court celebration, I ducked out. Everybody had to clear out anyway. The adult league was playing on that court in a few hours. And, other than Panama's house party, jumping off later that same night, nothing was up. The money-getting ceremony was top secret. Each starter trusted that we would get that call from Coach Vega right after the holiday weekend. As Vega put it, "You should be glad you don't know where the real celebration takes place and that the money gets handed over after all the hype dies down. Otherwise you would be a target. This is Brooklyn. Don't sleep."

Soon as I took one step towards leaving, Bangs, who was standing in the back of where the crowd wrapped around the black team, began moving in my same direction. I couldn't miss her. She was wearing the bright white tee with navy-blue letters that said MILK SHAKE. She tried to lock eyes with me. I wouldn't let her. Instead I moved swiftly, without looking back. I had to catch the LIRR to Penn Station and the 2:15 p.m. Amtrak train to Massachusetts, then hop on the ferry boat to link back with Umma, my wives, and sister.

Of course she followed me. She's a runner, more comfortable running than walking. She stepped onto the LIRR and said, "You wasn't running from me, right? I just wanted to see you and talk for a minute."

"What did I tell you about your clothes," I said.

"I was doing good for a long while, but you didn't come back," she said.

"So what happened?" I asked.

"If I was going to do it that way, I was only doing it for you. What's the sense in me dressing the way you like to see me, if I can't see you?" she said. I just looked at her. Her body was right but her mind was never ready.

"You look beautiful to me, Superstar," she said. I took off my black sweat jacket and put it on her. She had to cover up.

"Why 'Milk Shake'?" I asked her.

"'Cause it's thick and sweet like me and it jiggles a little," she said. I smiled, but not on purpose, naturally. I didn't want to encourage her. Yet she was so honest in her misunderstandings about herself. She hugged me. I didn't embrace her.

"And what do you want the men who see that you're thick and sweet and that you jiggle a little to do?" I asked her.

"Oh, they would know even if I didn't have 'Milk Shake' on my tee. You the only one who don't know," she said. "At least you don't act like it."

I zipped up my sweat jacket to cover her breasts. "How's your daughter?" I asked.

"I'm trying to get her off of my titties but she won't let me," she said, and my joint swelled.

"I missed you so much, Superstar. I see that you missed me too." She giggled. Then she got suddenly serious. "I was lonely no matter who else came around." She paused. "My grandmother died. It was so sad. And I didn't want to stay in that house anymore—it was too scary. And even though I got money from her insurance, I'm still feeling kind of, I don't know . . ." She was staring up at me.

"Where are you living now?" I asked her.

"At my girlfriend's mother's apartment in Fort Greene until my grandmother's house gets sold," she said sadly.

"How many males are living in the apartment with you?" I asked. She laughed.

"She doesn't have any brothers, just her moms and two sisters, her and me and my daughter," she said, not even mentioning a father because it was automatic that he wasn't there.

"Oh, and there's another serious thing I have to tell you, and one serious question that I have to ask you. But, not here," she said. Then her energy built right back up and she promised, "But I'mma hurry up now 'cause if I have my own place you'll come and see me, right?" she asked.

I didn't say nothing, wouldn't even look at her. In my head all I was thinking was, *Oh Allah.*

# 29. VINES • *A Reflection*

Unexpected, I was not a passenger on a passenger ferry with other passengers whose destination was the same as mine, Martha's Vineyard. Instead, I was on a pretty private yacht named *American Dream*, owned by its captain, Clementine Moody. The aerodynamics of the body were nice and sleek. However, it was the interior that was fully fine and fresh. Cherrywood floors, and the cockpit wooded out as well. White leather high-backed couches, a beautiful leather recliner with burgundy piping and stitching, and cherrywood cabinets and tabletops. Part of the Grand Banks Heritage Yacht Collection, the East Bay 55sx was a definite luxury item. Uncle Clem had the sound system on low volume, a nice Miles Davis jazz cut I did not recognize the title of but I liked the feeling of the groove.

*So many beautiful things; try not to lust them*, I reminded myself. Then I also reflected that I had been on yachts ten times the value of this expensive one, with my father on business with the caked-up Arabs, cruising in the deep Red Sea. Also, I reminded myself that no matter how beautiful a material thing is, nothing is more beautiful than the sunset sky that Allah created.

So I steadied myself for whatever it was that Clementine Moody wanted. Because of the fight I had with his son Marcus, I knew there could be anything on his mind. At the same time, I was hopeful that Marcus was not a coward who ran and called his father to finish the fight that he started and lost. If he did, I would lose any remaining respect I might have had for him as a man.

He returned to the plush sitting area where he had invited me to take a seat, still wearing his captain cap, but with a Winchester shotgun in one hand and a Kodamatic 980L Instant camera in the other. Donned in his pink Ralph Lauren shirt, white khaki shorts, and Sperry Top-Sider shoes, he didn't look threatening to me. However, my mind was swiftly calculating the possibilities of which way this scenario might move. Was he planning on getting Marcus's revenge by murdering me and taking photos of my corpse to show and then tell his son, "This is how it should be done"? Was he planning to hold me hostage and shoot photos of me to attach to his ransom note? Nah, who would he get ransom from? Was he planning to blow my head off and dump my body in waters that were unknown to me in a place where I had never been before and make it appear to my mother, sister, and wives that I had broken my promise to come join them and had abandoned them instead? Was Marcus sitting in another room in the boat, hoping his father would negotiate a truce?

"I'm going to have the bourbon," he said after setting down the camera, and prepared himself a drink. "Since you are underage, I'll offer you the drink my sons have had since they each turned twelve, a glass of Chicama wine made right here on the Vineyard."

"What's the shotgun for?" I got right to it.

"Ignore this thing. I use it when I go duck hunting," he said.

"Duck hunting on a boat?"

"With the Winchester, a man might have had one purpose for having it at first, but then a man and his gun get attached and somehow grow together. Next thing you know, you're carrying it everywhere 'cause you'll miss it if it's gone." He laughed two quick, insincere chuckles.

"If you have water, I'll have that," I said, overlooking his bullshitting.

"There's only me today because of the July Fourth holiday. My first mate and my secretary are both off celebrating with their own families. I'll be right back," he said, placing his glass on the built-in coaster on the wooden table. He took his shotgun with him, though.

"Take a look at these," he said, spreading some photos on the tabletop as soon as he returned. I looked down. The six photos were of Bangs and me in Penn Station just four hours ago. We had walked together. I stopped at a shop and bought her a jacket so I could take my Starter championship jacket back and she could cover herself. In one of the photos I was unzipping my jacket from her body. In the other she was smiling and trying on the jacket I purchased, which was nothing great, but it had long sleeves and was long enough for her to pull over her hips and to cover her ass. All of the photos seemed like they were snapped, not for the art of photography, but to confirm something the way a private investigator would confirm that two people had met.

"So?" I said, my face blank. Inside I was thinking of who could have snapped the shots and how could I have possibly overlooked a person following me. But Penn Station on 34th in Manhattan is a major thoroughfare and there are thousands of people passing through at all times of the day and night, every day.

"So," Clementine Moody repeated. "When it comes to men, 'too good to be true' is always an illusion. Isn't it?" he asked me.

"*Good* and *true* are the same thing, in my estimation. If a man is good and true, why would that be an illusion?" I asked, trying to follow his reasoning.

He smiled. "Slick talker, but there's only you and me here on the open waters. You can drop the whole religious routine. Save that for your wife," he said.

"Routine? How about you just get to your point. I didn't expect to see you on the Amtrak platform. You asked me to follow you here. Out of respect I did. I don't think we came here to discuss these photos. At least I hope not."

"You're right. These photos are just a precursor to let you know that I see you clearly, and that I have documentation of one of your secrets. All men have secrets. Isn't that right?" he asked. "And if any woman were to look at these photos of this pretty young thang wearing your jacket, the same one you have on right now, what would she think?" he asked, and gave a devious smile.

"If you were in these photos with a woman other than your wife, I guess based on your presentation today, it would be a problem for you. It would not be a problem for me. I answer to Allah, as each man and woman should. No woman controls my actions. I control my actions and my choices and only I am responsible for the consequences of each of my decisions," I said calmly.

"This is the first July Fourth in more than a decade where my whole family has not been together in the same place at the same time. In fact, my wife and your mother and family, all of the women, are up here at the Vineyard together. My sons, I had to hold them back, break a huge tradition, a family gathering that we have always looked forward to. I don't know what you are accustomed to because you and me are really strangers thus far. But I won't allow you to cause me any losses without collecting the debt," he said, sipping.

"Debt?" I repeated. "I understand numbers. Speak to me in numbers. That way, I can follow the conversation," I told him.

"You might be a good businessman like you say that you are. You might even be swift with numbers. But remember, son, you are too young to be wise. Wisdom comes very slowly through years of effort, of making mistakes, of feeling the pain, sometimes even the torture, of the reality of life. In business, wisdom comes after making some great decisions and then some foolish decisions and paying the price of your losses. Men who have gone bankrupt one time oftentimes become the wisest businessmen." He was holding his shotgun, leaning on it like it was a walking stick, while sitting not in the chair or on the couch or recliner, but on the countertop. I took it as him wanting to stay posed in a higher position than me, and reinforcing his pose with his weapon. I didn't have my nine. But I was confident that my skilled hands and feet were more than sufficient to handle this older man, to disarm him. It would only be self-defense. I had no plan to attack or injure him in any way. My second wife is in his family, loves him and his wife and sons a great deal, and I respect and adore her deeply.

"Even your arrogance is part of your youth. It's something you'll shed as life beats you up a little, drags you around, knocks you out a few times. If you were older and wiser, you would know that your arrogance is going to be a major setback, a pitfall, a ditch you dug for yourself," he said. "But you're not."

"The debt?" I repeated. "You seem to believe that I owe you something. I believe in settling all my debts fairly." I told him my truth.

"Some things are priceless," he said oddly. "Some debts you can never repay. Some debts can only be settled with your life."

"You want to kill me?" I asked him straight up.

"You would be worth more dead than alive," he said. All his smiles and fake chuckles turned solemn, serious, and dark. He was frowning now. The lines around his mouth seemed to suggest a permanent frown, that his face had done more frowning than smiling in his lifetime. It was something seeing a man with a family, four sons, and a few homes and properties and cars and a yacht appearing to be so grim, rather than grateful to the Most High.

No matter how many words he spoke, I couldn't wrap my mind around what his gripe was about. I couldn't decipher the ways of many of these Christian men. I couldn't even do the math of the debt he mentioned, or the reasoning of how he decided I was worth more dead than alive.

"So where does that leave us?" I asked him, thinking about my women, the hour and a half remaining before the light of the sky fell black and blue, and my hunger from the rigor of the battle of today's championship game.

"Have you ever known a person hanging on to life by a thread, waiting on a kidney, a liver, a heart?" he asked out of nowhere.

"No, I haven't."

"What do you think would be more valuable, my yacht or your kidney?"

"Don't know," I said.

"You're right. You don't know. That's exactly what I've been saying here. You don't know anything. You're too young to know anything. I could sell both of your kidneys, your heart, liver, eyes, and even your bone marrow. I could sell strips of that pretty black skin you have to a patient that understands the pain of fire because he or she has third-degree burns and needs skin grafting. I could sell your bones to a medical school that just happens to want bones to display for their anatomy course. I could sell every drop of your blood, and even your fingers and toenails, your tongue and intestines. Are you starting to understand why you are worth more dead than alive? If I snatched your heart out right now, and ordered a medical boat to come by and pick it up for delivery to the nearest hospital and to the next applicant on a long line of organ transplant patients, how much do you think I'd earn?" He smiled an evil smile.

Clementine Moody—his name was perfect. I reminded myself of his degrees from the University of Pennsylvania and Harvard School of Business, and that Chiasa had said that he had been a hospital administrator a long time ago. Now he was involved in some private venture that no one spoke about specifically.

"Is that what you do? You said before that you work as a high-priced consultant. Do you decide who is worth more dead than alive, and then kill them and snatch out their heart and other organs and sell them?"

"I'm no murderer. I have high ethics. So only a fraction of your answer is correct. And if you had lived a longer life than your young years, you'd know that there is no need to murder. The worst human vermin of the world are so good at self-destruction that a wise guy and businessman such as myself need only wait 'em out. I've encountered thousands of guys like yourself, who don't know and never understood the value of life."

"Thousands of men just like me?" I asked him.

"Oh no, the only thing they have in common with you is their ignorance of the value of life. The rest of the circus you have going on is a thousand percent rare and unique. But I can tell you for sure, same as I told my wife and my brother-in-law, you will be around for a long time. The only way to get you away from Chiasa is to kill you. I can see that. But since we're not in the killing business, we simply need to contain you and your recklessness," he sipped.

"It's a relief that you are not in the killing business. Point me to the bathroom, please," I said. He had talked too long. The Amtrak ride had been long, and the rocking of the boat on the waves. I was in need of a hot shower, some scented soaps, a thick fresh towel, and either of my wives.

"Down those stairs. Turn left. Let's see if you can follow instructions," he said oddly.

Down the few steps, as I made the left, I saw the door on the right move. It was already mostly closed, but someone had pushed it to shut it completely. In front of the bathroom, I smelled the scent of a woman. I went in, handled myself, washed up, and came out. I closed the bathroom door behind me and paused there in the small space for a few seconds. The door in front of me opened slightly. It was not Marcus waiting on a truce. It was a doe-eyed voluptuous woman with thick lips looking out.

Clementine Moody appeared at the top of the few steps with his shotgun.

"I told you not to come out," he said to the woman.

"I didn't," she lied.

"Come up here and prepare us some hors d'oeuvres now that you're out," he told her. "You come up first," he said to me. I understood. He didn't want me walking behind her ass, looking up her dress. Since he had already described me as a stranger, I knew he didn't know that I wouldn't. It wasn't my style.

"Aren't you gonna introduce us?" she asked him stupidly.

"Her name is 'Secret.' Now I know one of your secrets, and you know one of mine," he said. I just looked at him. Didn't bother to correct him about how Bangs was not my secret, not my woman, definitely not one of my wives, and I never went in her. "You interrupted my family holiday barbeque. Now you are interrupting my date," he said to me wrongly. "Now let's get down to the nuts and bolts of this thing so I can power this boat up, drop you off, and get on with my plans." He looked at her back, as she was putting together some sandwiches and chips and fruit. I had already turned my back to her so that he wouldn't get any more strange ideas than the ones he already had brewing.

"Even the superpowers need allies," he said strangely. "And the thing about allies is they don't have to love each other. They just need to have at least one mutual interest."

"Okay," I said, not agreeing but trying to draw out whatever he was getting at.

"Here's another secret, a big one, a bomb! It's in our mutual interest that you not ever repeat it," he said.

"So why tell me?" I asked.

"Because I have to stop you from killing even one of my sons. Literally killing, or messing up his life because he kills you," he said. Now I felt better. He was talking about Marcus, and all this other crap he was speaking was nothing.

"Here comes the bomb," he said solemnly. "Honey, pass me the notepad," he said to his woman. The notepad was embossed with the capital letters HWM. He wrote down only one thing: "Marcus." Then he leaned in and said quietly, "He's not my son." Then his woman brought the sandwiches over and set them on the table. By the time she reached us, he flipped his note over facedown.

"Honey, take this back. He's one of them Muzlems. He don't eat Virginia ham."

"Oh, sorry." She rushed over, leaned to pick up the plate and her cantaloupe-sized breasts were hanging dangerously close to my face. I lowered my gaze.

"Just bring him a fruit plate and some of those cheese and crackers," he said.

"I'm good," I told him, despite being mad hungry.

"What's your reason for telling me he's not yours?" I asked. "It doesn't add up."

"Oh, it adds up alright. Here comes the second bomb." He turned his note to face him and wrote, HE IS THE GENERAL'S SON. "The same man whose daughter you married," he said. "Now you've stolen away his daughter and crippled his son. Do you think you need an ally now?" he asked, and my mind was racing.

"If he's not your son, what's your interest in it?" I asked him.

"Listen here, you cold-blooded motherfucker," he said quietly through clenched teeth. "He is not my son, but Xavier is. Xavier loves Marcus even more than his other two blood brothers. I raised them all as brothers under one roof. Three of them are mine and my wife's sons. Marcus is the General's son. Your wife has no idea that Marcus is her real brother. I'm telling you so that you will understand that Marcus is not trying to sleep with your wife. Therefore, there was no need to bust his kneecap." He looked at me sternly, as though he thought I'd be shocked that he knew I was the one who crippled Marcus.

"The debt goes way beyond the medical bills, which are astronomical and include surgery, medical supplies, rehabilitation, and therapy. Or even the fact that you have probably permanently altered his career in the military, and as a fighter, and a boxer. The debt is that you are breaking up a respectable family that has been living together happily and peacefully. My wife needs to maintain her relationship with your wife. Not just because that's what her brother wants her to do, but because *it's what she wants as well.* Anybody who causes my wife any grief has made a headache for me. I do everything a man could possibly do to keep her happy and everything cool."

*Vineyard*, I had looked that word up when I was researching whether or not I would allow my Umma and sister and first wife to accompany my second wife up here. I had also ordered from Marty Bookbinder, a map of the island and a travel book that discussed it. Sitting in the exclusivity of a Grand Banks yacht, I felt like I was in the vineyard, covered with vines. Vines trail and creep and climb and wind themselves around a person, place, or thing. They clasp themselves on and hold tight, all connected. Vines are an entanglement.

"Sounds like you think Marcus is an innocent victim. Seems like you'd be wise enough to know better. I'm not going to say what Marcus did. I'll let him tell you himself. And since you are a wise elder and a businessman, you must know, and you must've raised him to know, that if men gamble, there are big and small risks involved and that you may suffer greatly. So there is no debt between you and me, Dr. Moody. You want peace for your wife. I want peace for my wife. As long as none of your sons don't offend me or my women, I'll be good to them like a brother. My religion is not a routine or a circus. My objective is family. And the young lady in the photo is not one of my wives. Any woman who is my woman is my wife. If she is not my wife, I don't go in her," I said to him man to man.

"Imagine if I told you that the woman here on my yacht," he said, nodding towards the curvaceous woman in the blue silk dress, "was not my woman." She turned around and smiled. "And that I never touched her or 'went in her,' as you say." Then he smiled at me.

"Darling, take your plate and wait for me downstairs. I won't be too long." He got rid of her. She shot him a look of boredom right before she left. I understood. I was even more bored with him than she was, I'm sure.

"See, that's the thing about wisdom. If you were older, you'd realize that the good, smart girl is the one you marry. The good-time girls are the ones you have a good time with for a few hours or days or weeks, or whenever it benefits you. Keep them hidden. Don't tell 'em or teach them nothing. Not even your home address or telephone number. Your wife is smart. You don't need the good-time girls to be smart. They just need to be ready to give you what you want, *a good time.*" He dragged out those last three words, like a drawl. "How you want it, and to do whatever you say. If you try and marry all of the women you lust, you'll give yourself a horrible migraine or a catastrophic heart attack. Shake off that arrogance. One wife is more than enough, and if you didn't go into this pretty young thang who's standing right next to you smiling in the photo, then you wouldn't be a man, now would you?"

I remained silent. My strategy was that if I did so, he would be content and he'd power up the boat and head to the island. He was eating his ham sandwich, cutting it into sections of four and dabbing his mouth with a napkin each time he finished a portion.

"Tomorrow, I'd like you to show up at the clubhouse for a men-only breakfast family meeting. My sons will drive up for it. We'll smash the beef, work it out, and all appear later in the afternoon to the barbeque, united."

"Marcus also?" I asked.

"Yes," he replied. "It's been weeks, but his knee is still in bad shape. He'll need to use the whole backseat of my son's truck just to make it up here. Xavier is already up here. He came up in the first-class car of the same train you arrived in today. This is his camera. He snapped these shots. Just happened to see you. Gave me a call and interrupted my plans for the day. But, he's my son so I had to show up. He's very angry. He loves Chiasa a lot and he thinks you are making a fool out of her."

"Is that right?" was all I said.

"He really doesn't want to lose Chiasa. You already injured Marcus, his hero. But Xavier is my son. I can control him."

"What do you expect to happen at this breakfast?" I asked him.

"My boys will listen to me, no matter what. I took the camera from Xavier and the photos. He won't have them to show them to your wife. He's young and doesn't understand that kind of thing. Marcus is enraged, but he's injured. He can't do anything right now. My older sons are established. They have their opinions, but they won't want to get involved in any of this. They know Marcus is a hothead." He paused.

"I need you to get in line. Lose that killer energy. Let go of some of that arrogance. Give me your word not to use violence ever again within the family, and definitely not in a family setting. You might not like it, but like I said, allies need only one mutual interest to appear standing side by side. And you and I, and my sons and Marcus, all have one: your wife."

Measuring Clementine Moody's words, I was quiet. I didn't want to head-butt with him. Definitely didn't want to be drawn into a continuous debate, either. Weighing it out, I knew I held the ace card. My second wife had already told me that she would walk away from all of them, although she didn't prefer to do so. Therefore, me working it out with the men in her family was something I could do as a consideration for her, and for no other reason.

I thought Uncle Clem, despite being paid, PhD'd-up, and "successful in his business," was a joke and an illusion. As he steered his yacht to Martha's Vineyard, I thought closely about how in my first encounter with him, his wife, Aunt Tasha, spoke passionately about church and Christianity. She spoke about how shocking and uncomfortable it made them each feel that Chiasa is now a Muslim. She said that she and her husband and entire family attend church and talked about how important the Christmas Eve worship was for them. Yet, Clementine Moody seemed to have very low regard for faith. That was burning me up.

Standing behind the captain's chair where he was seated, I asked him, "Is your Christian faith a routine?" He took his time. I hoped that meant he was giving it some honest thought.

"Religion is for women. For men who have families and who love their wives, we go to church to appease them. Our role in the church is the same as our role in the world—to handle the business."

Looking out over the new dark waters, I thought to myself, *No matter how long I remain in America, I'm a foreigner.* Men who don't worship the Maker of all souls, men who go to church only to shut their wives up, strange. Men who claim Christianity, but who are uncomfortable with the boundaries and limitations of Christianity, then disregard all of the rules about how a Christian should live life, strange. Married Christian men who say they love, honor, provide, and protect their one wife, but only if they have the option to disrespect, fuck, hide, and abort their seeds in the women who they desire to go into while being married, low and strange. Men who reach high positions in this country, and who enjoy the respect of hundreds, thousands, and even sometimes millions of people as they run amuck. And what about my second wife's father, the General? Why would he give his son up to another man to raise and claim? Why would he hide his seed and only claim his daughter? Strange, strange, strange was all I could come up with.

"Why did the General hand you his son?" I had to ask.

"Because Marcus was a mistake he made with a good-time girl. The girl showed up at our house one afternoon, nine months pregnant and had the baby on our front lawn before she could even reach the doorbell. My wife and the General are biological brother and sister. And, emotionally and in every possible way, they are closer than twins. My wife loved baby Marcus because he was her brother's son. And believe me, she verified it first. She's a doctor.

"I love my wife. She wanted to keep the baby. The General wanted a clean slate, a do-over. My wife wanted to make that possible for him. Soon as Tasha got attached to Marcus, his mother came and snatched him back, not because of love but because she needed to hold on to him to get that pitiful welfare check. But when Marcus turned ten years old, he put himself on a bus and showed up at our house looking for his father. We took him in and raised him as our son. He's had the same luxuries as our boys, but different DNA and personality. Even military school failed to change that. He's hot-tempered and short-sighted like his senseless mother. And he's got a heavy chip on his shoulder."

He knows who his real father is. His mother told him. The fact that the General didn't claim him and doesn't interact with him has been a thorn in his heart. Every crazy thing he ever did or may ever do in the future is just him acting out over his father.

A son who is a "mistake" is unheard of for me. A man grown enough to spill his seed in a womb, who wants a "do-over," *oh Allah.*

I washed and made a prayer on the deck of that yacht before leaving. As Muslims, we do not pray to be seen. At the onset of prayer, after we have cleansed ourselves, we clear our minds to set ourselves straight and to purify our intent. I'll admit, though, I wanted Clementine Moody to see the prayer. To see a man who makes the *sajdah*, brings his knees to the ground and presses his forehead to the earth in complete submission to Allah. I thought that perhaps if a man could understand that true-believing Muslim men submit only to Allah, they might rethink mistaking the way we carry ourselves, limit ourselves and what exactly we feel entitled to, as arrogance.

"Take a cab. The stand is to your right once you walk out. You never saw me today," Clementine Moody said as I left. "And you never rode with me on any yacht."

# 30. THE MEN

Criminal-minded I'm not, but the times were getting more-rougher. The projects were pouring into the prisons and the men were getting more-tougher. The crowded streets emptied the street crowd into the cells. Hotter than July, even the heat was getting more-meaner. More felons now than misdemeanors, and the mood was intensely tense in this city of men.

"You have a visitor," the CO called out, his gaze fell on me.

"Not me," I said, seated in the god 's cypher.

"Ricky Santiaga," the CO said, and the locked-up looked up, stood up, and paid close attention to the name of the man even the CO seemed to know. Paused in a squatting position, only my mind was moving swiftly.

"Do-or-Die Ricky Santiaga," one of DeQuan's captains named Walkie-Talkie said slyly. "Black, you better take that." I raised up for my own reasons, after reaching my own conclusions. I took my walk for the first time to visitation.

"My first time up here," Santiaga said.

"Mine too," I replied, my natural smile breaking out naturally. "What can I do for you?" I asked him. He smiled, then laughed a reluctant restricted but real laugh.

"What can you do for me?" he said, and we both sat in silence for some seconds.

"Did one of your machines break? You came all the way here

looking for a handyman? Couldn't find nobody else? The repair kit was in each box with the instruction manual," I joked purposely to lighten up what was already a heavy feeling in a tense atmosphere.

"Damn, that's more words right there than I ever heard you say," he said coolly.

"I must've been in here too long," I said.

"Two days in there is two days too long," he said.

"That's word," I agreed, the "locked lingo" all in me now.

"Less is more. What had to be done had to be done, I know," he said, and gave me a serious look. I read it. He wanted me to know that he knew I was no fool. I appreciated his words, the words he spoke and the ones he discreetly insinuated. He was the first one, the only man not to question my motives or my murder or whatever action had led me here. The first one to know, without knowing any of the details of my imprisonment, that a man who had all that I had earned, and that Allah had allowed me, would never just throw it all away without reason. I felt in my soul that more than any man, Ricky Santiaga knew I had murdered a lesser man, for the right reasons. At the same time, his facial expression expressed his regret that a lesser man had not pulled the trigger on my behalf, so that the deed that had to be done was done without getting any blood or dirt on my hands. However, when it is as personal as it was, I would have to be the only one to pull the trigger. Never would've handed that murder over to any other man.

"Did you come up here to check?" I asked him, and he smiled.

"Anything, anyone, any jewel that I want, choose, or that I plan to purchase, I pick it out myself. I test it myself. I pick it up myself. I verify myself. My man said it was you. Me, I had to see for myself," he said.

"How's the basketball going?" I said, purposely not to give any words or info away to any authority listening in.

"It's good as always, man, but no charm," he said.

"No charm," I repeated.

"Nothing to go all in on with complete confidence. Just something to watch." There was a pause. "How long?" was all he asked.

I had purposely not been counting time. Yet I knew in two weeks' time it would be my second birthday of being cuffed and confined. Then I reminded myself that I had been in the bullpen for my last birthday, which meant in two weeks it would mark one year of time served.

"Two years," I said, "if it goes well."

"Good man in a bad situation. So he never knows what he or they will do, right?" he stated. I didn't say nothing. There was no need. "I'll put money on your books. Check your commissary," he said.

"You know I don't like debt," I said. He didn't answer nothing back. There was no need to.

"Two years, drop me a line 'round release time. I'll have the limo down front," he pledged.

"Forget the limo. Park my Maserati and leave my key in the ignition. I'll drive myself."

"My man," he said, and left.

DeQuan, the Five Percenters, and their underlings all had their eyes plastered on my pace and my face when I walked back into the day room. It looked like they expected me to report back on my VIP visitor, "Do-or-Die" Ricky Santiaga. They had been huddled watching *Murder She Wrote*, like they usually did. They'd each try to solve the crime first. It was just one of DeQuan's several competitions, the kind that could be held and managed in a jail setting.

"Don't watch me," I told them. "Watch the TV."

The guy in the top bunk, I never referred to him as my cell mate or as my "celly," as many men do. The same way that Chris and Ameer and I built a nine-foot wall around my Queens home, I built an invisible but solid wall between me and him, even though we were both forced to share a sink, a toilet, and a very small space. He was a few years older than me, but in lockup, my solid-steel physique, reputation, and confidence outdistanced and outweighed his age. Soon as he arrived at my cell, after the last guy was evacuated, I read him my rules. "Don't look at me. Don't ask me any questions. Don't touch my things. Don't talk. Stay out of my way. Clean up behind yourself immediately." He obeyed.

"Check out your soldier." DeQuan handed me a copy of his newsletter, "Each One Teach One." It was only one page, with stories printed at the printshop on both front and back sides. I flipped it, scanning the two photos as well as the article titles.

"What am I looking for?" I asked him.

"Back page, bottom right-hand corner," he told me. I read it:

> "Sixteen-year-old adolescent petitions the Rikers Island jail administration for permission to marry and wins. For the first time ever, a youth in the Rikers Island, Robert Donovan Adolescent Jail, has gained permission to host a wedding and marry his eighteen-year-old girlfriend in a jail ceremony. The inmate, who is a minor and therefore cannot be named or photographed, waged a nine-month campaign to marry his girlfriend. His first hurdle was to win the permission from his mom, his legal guardian. Her signature was a requirement on the marriage license. "That was the part of the process that took the longest," according to Community Relations counselor Bryan Jones. The small ceremony will be hosted on Saturday, August 1, 1987.

I looked up. DeQuan had his arms folded in front of him.

"My soldier?" I repeated.

"The soft dude who you gave the knowledge, wisdom, and understanding. My brother said he did a one-eighty. You know DeSean don't respect or acknowledge a man who can't master himself."

"You taught him that," I said. Then, I was thinking about Lavidicus.

"Kid owe you his life. You're the father to his style," DeQuan declared.

*Alhamdulillah*, was all I thought. If a man strives with a good intent and all of his heart and mind to overcome his trauma and his challenges, there is a reward in it. Then I thought of how the article said the first "hurdle" was his mother. I could not imagine that she would have been against her son taking a wife, when before that ever happened, he was being abused and conquered and disrespected by men she brought around. I wondered if she preferred her son the way he was before, or if she admired the outcome of his efforts to overcome a very difficult situation and circumstance.

"Tell DeSean I said 'good looking out.'" I handed him back the newsletter.

"You keep it. Hand it to the next man," DeSean said. As I folded it, I noticed a black-and-white photo of a pretty female. Of course I would notice. She had clear eyes that shined and nice brown skin without cosmetics.

"Sister Lisa," DeQuan said. "She's coming up here to speak."

"Speak to who?" I asked.

"All of us, whoever signs up for the program. This is my joint. I got the Community Relations counselor to invite her up."

"For what?" I asked, not believing there was any reason to invite women into this filthy city of men.

"'Cause she's bad. She's young. She's smart. She's a poor righteous teacher and civilizer of the eighty-five. But most importantly, she runs these camps for the babies. Ask any god up here who got seeds. They all know her," he said.

"She's an Earth?" I asked. Earth was what "the gods" called their women. They called their mothers their "Old Earth," and their women their "Earth."

"Non cypher, she's not in the Five Percent, not in the Nation of Islam, not even a Muslim. I heard she works for the church. But she ain't no nun and she ain't no joke or nothing like that. Sign up, check her out. You'll only understand once you see her in person and hear her speak." I took a second look at the photo and read the article. I was curious. Besides, it broke up the regular rhythm and routine and I was part of a captive audience.

The mentioning, murmuring, maneuvering, and movement of men around the arrival of this one girl to Rikers Island was extraordinary to me. It was an unexpected, powerful momentum. Men jockeyed to be included, but the number of inmates who could attend topped off at 300. They raised it to 350. When an inmate got suddenly bailed out or moved out or had court appearances and trial dates, the next man would jump for the ticket that he vacated. I was calm and cool. Thought it was somehow funny. Couldn't guess what she would say or do that appealed to the beasts of the jungle.

Saturday finally arrived. Us prisoners were filed in and lined up, no chairs. I don't know what the authorities were expecting but I knew from experience, they get agitated whenever large groups of men are moving. Whenever large groups of men are united around anything, even if it is harmless and good for them. Whenever large groups of men are excited. In the gym were all of the COs we were accustomed to seeing, but doubled. Ones that usually worked the shift after the others were all here at the same time. Then there was the special forces all riot-geared up, their shields and chemical sprays and sticks and heavy boots and their fucked-up attitudes, postures, and dispositions. I was leery watching them watching us, and even more so, hearing 350 men speaking in hushed tones all at once.

The doors swung open. She was blocked from being seen by the COs who walked her in. Men were stretching their necks, inching sideways, trying to get a look. Then she walked out and away from the COs guarding her, in a manner like she didn't want them guarding her in the first place. She stood directly in the front, placed herself right in the center of the men where the aisle divided the crowd into halves. We were all looking at her. At the same time, she began looking at us, it seemed one by one, without skipping anyone. She surveyed until her eyes filled with tears. Watching her fill with natural emotion made some of the men emotional. They began clapping for her tears and stomping their feet. CO blew a whistle that was drowned by the sounds of applause. Then the thunder fell to absolute silence. She looked calm and comfortable. In her eyes was a force. They contained the calm of water and the fury of fire. I wondered how they occupied the same space. Her skin was pretty and clear. She was the opposite of "ran through." Her energy was clean. She looked eighteen years young and innocent. Either she was, or she was a fox with ninety-nine tails. That's more than Aunt Tasha has. I smiled at the thought.

"I love you," she said, and the men cheered as though it was their first time ever either hearing or believing those words, maybe both.

"I love you. Not because I am naive. Not because I lack intelligence. Not because I am unaware that some of you have done wrong on purpose, and others of you have done wrong by mistake. And still some have been wrongly accused. I love you because my soul has been missing you. My eyes have been searching for you. My heart has been wanting you, the fathers, the brothers, the sons of our hearts. We need you to be home," and the men went crazy cheering.

"We need you to be strong. We need you to be capable and above all to be true. We need you to be loving us, the women, as we work together with you, side by side.

"A person should always know who they are and what purpose they serve. A person should also know *who they are not*, and what they will and will not do or allow to be done with them or to them. So, I'll start off by telling you who I am not.

"I am not your bitch!" And the men threw their hands in the air, jumped up and down, and hollered like an unseen, unheard of exorcism.

"I am not a bitch. I am not that naked chick posed and pasted or taped or pinned to your wall while you jerk off." The men were high-fiving, some shocked, some shaking.

"I am not disrespectful. I am not disloyal. I am not the one who will disgrace you or who you will disgrace, slapping me in my face, punching me in my ribs, or shoving me down the stairs. I am not your bitch, your ho, your piece, your skeezer, or your baby's momma who called the police on you, dimed you out, fucked your friends, or aborted your seeds." The volume of the men's expression became so wild the riot guards eased off of their post and stood on either side of the girl facing the inmates with their shields raised up high.

"I am not the bitch who had your children, then hid them from you, placed a restraining order on you, dragged you into court, and sat silently while the judge ran your pockets. I am not your bitch who lied on you, who stole your money, or pawned your jewels. I am not that bitch you met in the dark, or fucked in your car or in the back of your building or on the stairwell." The men reacted as though the riot guards were absent, no threat at all.

"I am not the bitch who sucked your dick, without having your heart in my hand, your diamond on my ring finger, and my heart in your soul," she said, and the guards stepped up to the crowd.

"Calm down or we will shut it down," they threatened. She ignored them.

"I'm not your psychiatrist or your private eye. I am not your mother. I am not the police. I am not your parole officer. And you are not my hostage, my prisoner, or my slave. So don't be doing the running man when you see me. Look at me with love and affection," she said, placing her hands on her hips and twisted left, then right. Slight gestures that caused a frenzy among the caged.

"I am your sister. We are family. If someone fucks with you, they fuck with me." The crowd roared.

"I am a young woman. I am a fighter. I am known for four words, 'We are at war!'" The stomping began again. "Not because we want to be. Not because we ain't got nuthin' better to do. But just because we are. We have been set up! We've been sucker-punched! We've been southpawed. We've been stabbed from behind. We've been blindfolded. We've been gagged. We've been wronged. We've been wrong. We've been held down too low for too long." Now she was covered in a light sheen of summer sweat. She inhaled, then exhaled. She clenched her fingers and her face filled with ache.

"Brothers and sisters, we gotta get our hearts right. Love the right things. Hate the wrong things. Brothers, we gotta get our minds right. Read the right books. Write the right words. Rhyme the right lyrics. Sing the right songs. Speak the truth, Brothers! We gotta get our souls right. Praise the right God . . .'Cause if you are telling me that you are God, you better be the solution and not the problem." That was it. Her words tore the house down. No bodies were still. Even the guards looked shocked and somehow pleased with her and what she was saying and what she was evoking from the men, which they had never before seen.

"Only God is perfect. Men are not. Women are not. Praise God, not your self. Not your woman. Not your man. Fight your enemies. Not your friends. Not your family. Not your people.

"Handle your business! Every man knows that every man has to do that. Where my hustlers at?" she asked, and most of the men acknowledged, "We right here!" Then she stripped them. "You are loved. You got the right skills but the wrong product. You got the right look, young, fine, and fashionable. You got the cars, the jewels, and the women. You got the strong team, but the wrong target, made the wrong investment and created the wrong results. Men must build more than they destroy," and the Five Percent were cheering, even the ones who hustled.

"Where my pimps at?" she suddenly said, and the men who were normally good at game and sharp and slick failed to peep her next setup. They acknowledged, "We right here!" She turned a little and leaned forward. "You pimping her. Whose pimping you? You dress her up and throw her out on the block or the club or behind the building to spread her legs for paper. Now, whose dressing you up and forcing you to spread your legs for paper? The prison system in America, *cheap forced labor.* They dress you up in these odd striped jumpers, green jumpers, orange jumpers and orange hats. They make you spread your legs and raise your hands and shut your mouth and spread your cheeks and get out there and work the whole day for them every day. You earn less than a ho on the stroll." And the place exploded. Some COs broke their stance and laughed.

"The real pimps are in the government and the corporations. Sometimes, they're one in the same. They're collecting the money you earned and not giving you your cut. Check the labels. At least know whose getting paid off of you. Who got the contract to build these prisons? Who got the contract for the heavy machinery, the prison vehicles, the prison weapons, the prison furniture, the prison inventory? Who made those prison jumpers you're forced to wear? Who got the contract for the horrible food they serve you? Who made your bedsheets? Check the labels! See if I am lying to you.

"You were supposed to be our army! But the only ones you fighting is yourselves. Men divided by race, culture, faith, and language, all getting pimped by the same politicians, the same entities. All cooperating with the same scam. Look around the room." The men began checking their surroundings. "All blacks and Latinos, Latinos and blacks. All Africans and Latinos, Latinos and Africans. All African men!"

"Even the African and Latino COs are caught up in the color scheme," she said, and the room went to a hush. "They think you're the enemy. You think they're the enemy. They got the same problems you got. They think you're the product. They got the wrong product. But both groups are getting pimped by the same true pimps. CO can't pay his rent same as you." And the crowd cheered. "CO can't handle his women, same as you. CO can't afford his child support, same as you. CO can't afford the car he's driving, same as you. You're locked up now. CO is locked up in here, right with you!" It was fire on top of fire and it was spreading across the room, igniting everything. Then she softened her tone and dropped her convo back into the realm of the personal.

"I am nothing but a warner. I am nothing but a reminder, a woman. The same woman who will care for your babies. The same babies, not born from my womb. The same woman who will raise your daughters and sons to be better men and women than any of us have ever been. I don't hate your women. But I can teach them how to love you. How to get their minds and hearts right. How to see you in a better light. But, in order to do that, you have to be a better man. I love the black man, but I need a better product, a purer cut, a finer grain."

At that point, I observed cold-blooded killers, niggas who had two, three, four bodies on their charges. Men who got nabbed with kilos of cocaine and a truckload of weed. Men who ran guns and pimped women and committed armed robberies and even raped were on their feet with fists pumping in the air, with total loss of composure, and cheering like they were at the horse track or an auction or the strip club, but louder and stronger, and not from the groin but from their hearts.

"I'm calling for a complete humbling of every man and every woman. I am even calling for the humbling of myself. I am not your bitch! But, if I was, and even if I ever used to be, I am not anymore. And, I wouldn't be dumb enough to be bragging about it if I was. Arrogant and proud and flaunting it. I wouldn't be parading around standing in front of audiences, acting like I didn't know better, didn't plot and scheme to do it, and didn't get nothing out of it. Lying bitches. Fake bitches," and I saw a hard rock cry. "If I was your bitch before, I'd be correcting myself now.

"Work hard! Strive hard! Fight hard! Love hard! Man and woman, woman and man, let's build a nation where we can thrive. Where the police don't reign supreme and the slaughter of our children isn't sport. Where white is just one shade of skin without melanin, not to be worshipped or imitated or served.

"In the words of Marcus Garvey, 'One God, One Aim, One Destiny.' In the words of Malcolm X, 'By Any Means Necessary.' In the words of Harriet Tubman, 'Freedom or death.' Peace." She took a bow.

She tried to catch her breath as she and every man in the room recovered from something that couldn't be described. A bond that couldn't be broken. A woman who could never be forgotten. Words that would revolve around the minds of the oldest men, and even around the brains of the most ignorant men, and even within the youngest and darkest of souls. Young, I knew her words would stay with me. I felt I would somehow see her again, in another time, in a better place.

From the back row where I stood, I remained calm and still, even though I was moved. I see these men every day. I watched her instead. She was wearing jeans and a long-sleeve "in the summer" T-shirt that said LOVE. She was covered. It didn't matter, though. Her shape was crazy. She wore pumps, not kicks. She was camouflaged so well, she looked like she wasn't. She looked like a pretty 'hood chick without the glaze or glamour or attitude. Feminine feeling, without any confusion, she looked soft. Her teeth were white and her smile was warm, like she meant it.

Bold, her mouth was a machine gun. Her tongue, a machete. There was nothing about her physical look or her ordinary fashion that would give anyone a warning of what she would say or do. *She's a powerful bomb*, I thought. A bomb with a silencer, no tick or buzz or boom, no red light or alarm to alert people to stay away, don't touch or tease or insult her. She would detonate.

I asked myself, *what exactly is the feeling she caused me to feel*? It wasn't sexual, although she was lovely enough. It wasn't danger, although she was deadly enough. I wasn't challenged, although she was sharp enough. It was that even though she said she was not naïve, and even though she spoke as though she was not innocent, and even though she said she was a fighter, she was naïve enough to enter a filthy place, be surrounded by hundreds of men, and feel no fear or sense of personal threat. She wore those tight jeans as though she wasn't standing before a herd of hungry, starved beasts, and as though she would not possibly be looked upon as food or prey. She was still a woman to me, ruled by emotion. And I felt a strong feeling, and the urge to protect her.

They ushered her out. She looked like she wanted to stay. She reached her hand through the guards and touched the hand of every prisoner who was close enough to reach in. Soon as she was gone, all masks came off. The guards turned back into hate and the inmates turned back into the hated and vice versa.

In our darkened cells, men hugged and held the bars. Through the open spaces and the vents, the conversation began.

"Word to mother, I'm speechless."

"Yo, DeQuan, thanks for the hookup."

"We should have her speak at the Parliament."

"Nix that, she might influence the Earths."

"I hope she does."

"Might be better to leave it the way it is."

"Y'all scared of her."

"Non cypher."

"Yo, god Understanding, I seen you shed a tear."

"Who got her address? I'm 'bout to write her a letter."

"She got no time for that."

"Man, shut the fuck up."

"I'm 'bout to wife her."

"She don't want you."

"She got high standards."

"Yeah, but she ain't no gold digger. She's low maintenance."

"She's a soldier," DeQuan said. "The Minister put out a word of protection on her so the streets don't touch her. Go at her the wrong way, you lose your life."

"That's how it should be," I said.

"What minister?"

"You know, the only one who matters."

* * *

By the end of the week, the vibe flipped. The topic changed. Lavidicus's wedding in the youth house happened smoothly. However, his mom got arrested trying to bring in contraband. Now she's locked up in the Rose M. Singer Center, the Rikers maximum security jail for women. DeQuan lost a mule. Lavidicus lost a mother.

Bryan Jones, the Community Relations counselor who allowed DeQuan to plan events and host speakers, was gone. Word was he was fired, but no explanation was offered to the inmates he counseled or the community relations he formed. I believed he got fired for bringing that bomb into the jail and letting her detonate. Same as Teacher Karim Ali, mysteriously disappeared for teaching American history in a manner where students were actually interested and participating. Same as I was boxed for praying. It's crazy once you realize that even when you are trying to do good and be true, even when you are walking within the legal limits, you are still being stalked and hunted and fired upon. A number of COs got transferred to different houses and had to start all over again. Inmates got shifted and shipped out and cells changed. It was a shake-up that no one admitted was happening. The unspoken truth: no one wanted us to learn or grow or change. They needed us to remain in physical stagnation and bondage and in a criminal state of mind.

# 31. THE UNKNOWN

"Pack your things," an unfamiliar CO ordered me. Then he handed me a Department of Corrections–issued heavy coat, hat, and boots. So I knew I was going to a very cold place. It wasn't charity or concern for me that caused them to make it possible for me to dress warmly. I knew by now that to them, I am just a body, a number in their cheap labor system, which they fronted off as a network of facilities where men are "corrected." They need me to stay alive and healthy enough for them to capitalize off of me. The DOC uniform and winter wear was just a means to an end.

I was handed some folded paperwork. Just as I opened it to read, the unfamiliar CO said, "You have to move now. You will have plenty of time to read in the truck." He stood in my cell as I got dressed in the outerwear items he gave me.

I was suspicious, though. The maximum amount of time an inmate could remain at Rikers was two years. I had served seventeen months, seven of which was no longer as an accused youth offender, but as a convict. I was told that I'd be shipped, flown, or trucked out as soon as there was a bed available for me in the prison system. I wasn't in a hurry, but did notice that DeQuan and many of the men in his crew were moved out swiftly, immediately following their convictions.

Why were they moving me now, on New Year's Eve in 1987? In less than twenty-four hours, it would be 1988, *Insha'Allah.* Everyone in the world knows that New Year's Eve and New Year's Day is a huge holiday. Even the COs I was used to seeing on a daily basis were not working their usual evening shift. They were replaced by unfamiliar faces, COs who probably signed up to grab that overtime holiday paper, and do a double or double triple like the she-officer used to do.

I checked myself. No need to get suddenly sentimental. No reason to say goodbye to CO Williams, who made an effort to treat us decently or the other COs who would normally be cuffing and uncuffing us, escorting us around, rationing out small items we needed like towels and toilet paper, or forcing us down to the floor, spraying us with mace and then placing a heavy boot on our backs.

As I packed my few items, my mind switched. Tomorrow is my first wife's birthday. She will be eighteen years young. I began imagining and desiring and wondering. I shut it all down swiftly. I knew thoughts of the future are forbidden to me while incarcerated. For the sake of my sanity, I am only allowed memories, past or present tense. Thoughts of the future were a form of self-torture. I avoid it. I refuse it.

My few things were dropped into a cheap sack and tied at the top, including my heavy boots, I walked out wearing my Jordans, the same way I had arrived at Rikers at first. The fact that I still had them on my feet was a sign to every man locked and a sign to me also. I was cuffed and controlled, confined and commanded. However, no man could snatch me out of my kicks. In that Brooklyn way, I was undefeated.

My cell door slammed shut. The guy I shared the tiny space with said, "Fuck you, nigga. I hope your next cell mate is a six-hundred-pound faggot." I smiled. It was the first time he had the audacity to speak directly to me. Coward knew I wasn't ever coming back.

CO cuffed my wrists, cuffed my ankles, and dropped the chain that connected my hands to my feet. As I walked the tier, it felt like a trail of tears. Men who I was forced to know, who were forced to know me, men who I had made the prayer with before dawn and before the count, and during the holy month of Ramadan. Men who I had pumped weights with, worked out and shot hoops with, read books with, taught or learned from, shared words with, were at their locked cell doors calling through the slot.

"A'ight Black, stay strong!"

"See you on the other side."

"Respect."

"*Mantente fuerte.*"

"Happy New Year."

"Let us know where you at."

"*No dejes que te vengas abajo.*"

"Drop a line."

"Float a kite."

"Watch your back."

"Protect your neck."

"*Allah uh Akbar.*"

"*Hasta que nos encontremos de nuevo, mi amigo.*"

"*A luta continua.*"

"Brooklyn all day, motherfucker!"

A blast of cold air rushed my face when the heavy doors drew open. There were only twelve steps in between where I stood and the DOC truck. Still I was able to steal a glance into the night sky, which I had not seen from outdoors since being jailed. In the darkness of the winter early sunsets and long nights, the razor wire raised up high on the fencing was the only thing shining. Instead of stars, there was only the momentary sweeping of the searchlight surveilling any unauthorized movement. Snipers were in their towers. It seemed even the moon was hiding out. After a series of baby steps, I got in. On a steel bench I was chained and seated in the dark. The truck door slammed shut and was bolted, no windows. *Yeah right, plenty of time to read my paperwork.* It was pitch-black. I couldn't even see my own hand. I was the only man besides the driver who was gated up front in the vehicle. On the bus that first brought me up to Rikers, we were like a herd of cattle beefed up for slaughter. There had been many men, and windows we could see out of so that we were clear what we were missing, leaving behind and losing. I didn't trust the fact that now there was only me. If anything went wrong, there would be no witness. Or at least there would be no one to explain from my perspective. Whatever the driver alleged would be considered law. *It didn't matter*, I told myself. *I'm not planning to assault him or to escape.* I had no interest in becoming a man permanently on the run, a fugitive. Someone they gunned down on some deserted highway or tracked through some wooded area or swamp. I'd serve my time and be done with it. Just then, I heard the passenger door of the truck open and then slam shut. When the guard slid the slot open to check on me, I checked also, and confirmed that a second DOC driver was now riding shotgun. *Two of them, one of me*, I noted.

Riding off of the Rikers jail complex property, I could feel the truck pull over the bridge and the truck engine moan. What lay ahead was unknown to me.

Butch Broadcast's words began streaming through my mind. "They gon' do what they do regardless. Once they ship you out of Rikers, you gon' encounter some big, ugly, hateful white boys. They gone be everywhere, their arms as big as your legs. They Ku Klux Klan. They hate the black man. You gon' feel that hatred instantly. So thick you can choke on it. They don't only hate the blacks. They hate anybody with a drop of melanin, any kind of color in them. They shave your head with hatred. They'll grab your balls, shove their fingers in your mouth, choking you with hatred. Say they looking for something they ain't really looking for. They nasty. You gon' find out. They'll spread your cheeks and drill in your asshole with fingers, with mop sticks, with erect dicks 'cause they can, and 'cause they want to, and 'cause they hateful and jealous of you."

In a one-on-one conversation with him once on the yard, I

asked him if he minded if I asked him a question. He replied, "Go ahead. You so quiet, I thought maybe you knew everything already."

"Nah, that's not it. But I see from your jail number that you first got knocked a long time ago. I'm not asking you what they accused you of or convicted you for. I'm just curious, if a man does time in all of the prisons you say you done time in, what makes that man keep coming back?" He just looked at me.

"Every time I got arrested and tried and convicted, then served my time and got released, I said to myself and to anybody who would listen, 'I'm never coming back. Never gonna do time, never gonna get locked up again. But, turned out, everything I do is illegal. If I'm just sitting on my porch, cops roll by eyeballing me like there's something wrong with that. I'm like damn, this is my mother's house! Fuck it, if I stand up, they watching me 'cause according to them, I must be 'bout to do something wrong. If I walk down the street, the cruiser's slowly rolling up behind me. They lower the window, ask me a stupid question like, 'Butch, what you doing out here?' I turns arounds slowly, knowing if I turn too quick they gon' gun me down. I gives them the answer they already know: 'I live right there.' Seems my answer was illegal cause they calling me a smart-ass, jumping out the cop car telling me to spread my legs and put my hands on the car. Next thing I know, I'm in the back of the car with my hands cuffed behind my back for resisting arrest. I gets to the station, they booking and beating me. They release me after a while. I goes back home. My mother say, 'Butch, where you been?' She looking at me all suspicious. I calls my old lady, figure she'll help me to relax. She starts giving me the third degree. I hangs up. I go to sit in the garage. My father's already setting in there. He tells me, 'Boy when you gon' get a job?' But he ain't got no job and ain't had one in years. I wants to get a job, but I figure soon as I walk outside, the whole story starts at the beginning again, and it does. Small town works that way. I gets a job at the car wash, or washing and buffing cars at the local car dealer or the gas station. Here comes the police rolling through asking my boss, 'What you got Butch up here for?'

Boss starts looking at me sideways. I ain't done nothing but been wiping down cars all day for little tips. Couple of days later he finds a reason to fire me. I'm walking back home. Cops rolling up behind me, asking, 'What you got in your hand?' I don't say nothing. They could see it's my beer. 'You supposed to have that in a brown bag,' they says. 'It *is* in a brown bag,' I tell 'em. 'Then how come we can see it's a Colt 45 that you drinking?' Then I says, if you could see dat, why you ask me what I got in my hand?'" Butch threw his hands in the air. "That's how I became Butch Broadcast. Now instead of me waiting to be questioned by my mother, questioned by my old lady, my pops, the police, the judge, the parole officer, I just always say out loud what I'm doing, what I see, where I'm going, where I been, what's happening and what happened. People think I'm doing it for them. Really, I'm just reminding myself. I gotta remind myself. Otherwise, everybody will have me thinking and believing that I actually am a criminal, who did something wrong."

"So you not a New Yorker," I stated, but it wasn't really a question.

"Don't matter, son, it's the same everywhere. I been locked up everywhere. That's how I figured out that it's not just me. It's a conspiracy. Everything a black man say or do, even how we talk and walk or sit and chill, is considered a crime."

I didn't say anything in response to his story. I was thinking, though, that he had to be leaving something out. He couldn't have been locked up in all these places for complete innocence. And no man is innocent. I wasn't expecting a confession. At the same time, I'm young, but not slow or gullible.

"I know what you thinking. You thinking I had to have done something wrong to get locked up repeatedly." He smiled. "Well, you right. After while, I figured out if I didn't do crime, no one would respect me. Why should I live my life as a suspect for no reason? At least if I get out there and start making real moves and big money, I could live a little, feel a little freedom, before they do what they do, 'cause no matter what I do, they gon' do what they do regardless.

Man, when I switched it up on 'em and actually turned to a life of crime, my mother stopped treating me like a retarded toddler. I gave her money. You should've seen her smile. It was all good then. My father respected me once I got my guns, and even moved his shit out the garage so I could park my 1966 Mustang coupe once I took him for a ride to the liquor store in it. Fuck my old lady—I had chicks lined up on the corner acting like they wasn't lined up on the corner just waiting for me to drive up and choose one of them. Even the police showed me more respect for making them at least have to figure out my hustle, catch me red-handed, and get to take something from me of value once they finally caught up with me and made the arrest. 'Cause you know, they always steal something from the crime scene. You know that, right? All I can say, Young Black," which is what he called me, "once I played the role they obviously had casted me as maybe from birth, everyone around me was more satisfied than they ever was when I was honest and struggling. So I just kept running the hustles, no matter the territory. They kept locking me up no matter the territory. It was better than a slow, unjust death as a good guy who gets no respect, whose life is all lows and no highs."

I thanked him for his time and replayed his words. My take on it was that he believed based on his experiences in life that a black man, any black man, has no choice but to play a scripted inferior position as either the pauper or the gangster, nothing else. He saw the police and the government, their arms and their armies and their prisons and their prison keepers, as being all-powerful. So powerful that they could direct the destiny of men based on the complexion of a man's skin. I didn't take it lightly. I considered it. As a deadly martial artist whose hands and feet and mind are trained and powerful, in lockup I had been faced with some situations and had learned some things that as a free man I did not know, had not felt or even considered before. How does one man prevail in a physical battle when being inside of a wild mob or haphazard riot that is happening at the same time the mob itself is surrounded by men armed with shields, boots, and batons and chemical weapons? Furthermore, how does a confined and cuffed man, locked in a room with unconfined and uncuffed authorities bent on not fighting, but fucking violating his manhood, prevail? I wondered if what Broadcast said would happen in prison was the absolute truth, an excuse, an exaggerated fear, or just the way he sees it.

I could only remove the sting of Butch's words and experiences, and the threat of his predictions of what awaited me, and any man headed to any prison in the United States of America, with words of prayer. I recited the Fatiha. I also recited the 113th Sura of the Holy Quran, which is called "The Dawn" in English and Al-Falaq in Arabic. It is a prayer for protection from evil. Then I said to myself, *Only Allah is Everywhere. Only Allah is All Powerful.* Fear no one but Allah. I inhaled and exhaled, getting both my body and my mind right and ready, and hardening my heart even more than before. The girl was right. We are at war. Not because we want to be, just because we are.

The cold cut through the cloth of the DOC coat. The cold raised up and spread out through the steel bench I was seated and chained on for hours. It caused my bottom half to begin to freeze and then numb. The cold froze up the uninsulated truck walls. I began tapping my feet on the floor to get my blood circulating. The cold cuffs were scraping against my ankles. *At least I can feel that*, I said to myself. I knew when the cold became so intense that I couldn't feel anything, I'd suffer from frostbite, hypothermia, and even some kind of gangrene. Sensei had taught me many methods of torture, how the body reacts and what a ninja should and could do in those circumstances, especially when he could not immediately escape the conditions and causes. I was tapping my feet and clapping my hands together, tiny motions because of the cuffs. I couldn't warm my hands beneath my armpits to regain circulation in my fingers because of the cuffs. My face felt stiff. I needed the ski mask, not for no nefarious deed but to guard my face and ears from the freeze.

* * *

I could feel the truck angling, as though it was climbing a hill. It became clear that it was not simply one hill, and perhaps not a hill at all. We were climbing a mountain, I believed, and I could feel the effect of the elevation on the intensity of the cold and the air quality as I took deep breaths.

On an incline, the truck jerked, then slid and spun. Maybe there was snow or ice. I heard the driver's voice, alarmed but not a full scream. Maybe he just panicked. Now the truck was paused but shaking. I had never been in an earthquake, but the rocking of a vehicle that weighed a ton felt like how I imagined an earthquake might feel. The bench I was seated on was bolted to the floor. I was rocking like the motion of a seesaw in the children's playground. Chained, I couldn't get up. "Yo!" I called out to the driver. I was freezing, tapping and clapping, seesawing left to right and my body rocking forward for circulation. "Yo! CO!" I called out again, but nothing.

I heard at least one of the front doors open. *Good*, I thought. But then I didn't hear the door shut. I couldn't hear no talking. Three minutes lapsed. I was shifting for the few inches that the chain would allow, trying to get some circulation to my vital organs. I tried balancing my feet on my toes, and bouncing them a bit. Suddenly, I heard the guard unbolting the back door, *finally*.

Black snorkels, the hoods were zipped concealing their faces, all but the eyes. But I could see their broad shoulders and M16 assault rifles strapped on, which they held with both hands. A third man, unarmed, walked in my line of vision from around their right side. I was waiting for their order. I was chained to the bench freezing and now that the doors were unlocked, I'm even colder. But I could see the stars shining brightly in the night sky. It looked like a different sky than the one that loomed over Rikers, which was now hundreds of miles and hours behind where we were. The one who walked around back did a 180. No one was saying anything. He returned seconds later with some industrial tool shaped like pliers or branch clippers. He approached cautiously. I didn't know why. His team had the arsenal and his back. Instead of climbing up and getting in the truck where I was, he stood outside, leaned in to unlock the chains that strapped me to the bench, and snapped them with the clippers, which cut them like they were soft as butter. "Jump out!" he ordered. One armed guard waved me to come out as all three of them stood a few steps back like I had a hand grenade in my grip or something. I knew I was headed to a maximum-security prison and that I had committed a murder. It seemed to me, however, that they were expecting some violent reaction from a serial killer with superpowers, who could while frozen, cuffed, and chained, knock out three mountain-sized men, two holding heavy. My body creaked as I stood slowly, the cuffs iced around my ankles and wrists. I stood up. My feet were frozen and steady but the truck still rocked from side to side. It was painful to take one tiny step, but of course I did. I felt the truck falling. The unarmed man ran towards me and grabbed my chain and pulled me forward as the truck fell backward and made the noise of metal slamming against rock, crashing. As the truck tumbled, the unarmed guard reached down to the ground to help me to my feet, but the DOC-issued coat I was wearing was stuck to the slab of ice I was lying on. "Pull your arms out of the coat!" he ordered me. But my brain felt frozen and my movements were slow motion. He yanked me out of the coat and off the ground, using the dangling chain like a leash. Standing up, unable to control my shivering, I was in only the Rikers jail jumper and thin hat. The unarmed man forced his fingers into his front pocket. He drew out some keys and uncuffed my wrists and then my ankles, as one of the armed guards pulled around behind me, pointed the M16 to my back, and said, "Walk." I followed with one behind me and two in front, one slightly to the left the other to the right. We were inching up a slippery slope that led up a dark and overwhelming mountain. The iced wind was whipping me. Within seconds, I saw another armed guard inching down the slope towards us, with a prisoner of his own. My eyes began tearing up from the temperature, not the emotion. But my tears turned to ice in less than a second. I looked at the two as they passed by without turning right or left. I didn't want the big white boy guard's trigger finger to itch, pulse, or pull. Strangely, they didn't greet each other, the guards coming and going. They exchanged no words. Once we reached around the bend of what was an iced road in a mountain pass, there was another truck parked as close to the rocks and as far from the drop down the mountain as possible. There was no lettering or logo on that truck, not even the DOC insignia. The back door was already opened. The guard pressed a button and the ramp eased out. "Walk up," one of the armed guards told me. I did. He climbed in after me. There were two benches, one on the left side, one on the right. After retracting the ramp he sat across from where he signaled me to sit, with his weapon on ready. I saw a closed tool chest and an industrial-size stuffed black trash bag. I imagined it held body parts of a defiant prisoner. The unarmed guard slammed the door shut and I heard it lock. It was back to complete blackness. I heard someone climb in on the driver's side and the ignition started. I heard the heat switch on, even in the area where we were seated, unlike the unheated truck that drove me from Rikers. But of course I couldn't feel it yet. That was good. I knew it wouldn't be safe for me to go from extreme freeze to a forced-heated hot. We sat idling for more than ten minutes. It was true what Broadcast had said about brain freeze. My thoughts were not flowing like normal. I was unable to juggle the facts of what was happening in the moment, and unable to put them in a logical order backed up by reason, or at least a strong hypothesis.

Fifteen minutes in, I was just beginning to feel the presence of heat. I heard the armed guard seated across from me moving around a bit. Suddenly, he flashed a spotlight on my face that pierced through the darkness and caused my eyes to squint from the shock of switching from blackness to a powerful direct light. I knew then that he wanted to see me, and my facial features, but did not want me to be able to see him. It worked. All I could do was look away until my eyes could adjust. My unfrozen temperature tears were careening down my face. He probably thought I was crying. "Undress," was all he said. I heard some plastic rustling and a bag landed in my lap. "Put those on. Then, hand me your clothes," he ordered. He moved the spotlight from my face down to my feet. I assumed that was how he planned to monitor my movements. It was warming in the truck now. Warm enough for me to begin to feel my fingers and to use them to remove my clothing, and change into their prison uniform, and what felt like the same type of heavy snorkel they were wearing. I set my mind that, assault rifle or not, if this big guard tried to do anything filthy as I undressed and re-dressed, I was gonna kill him. I was fifty percent sure that he wouldn't. They had uncuffed me after all, and rescued me from becoming a fallen frozen fossil. However, without cuffed hands or ankles, in a minute or so I would be capable of disarming him, and without firing his weapon I would strike him into unconsciousness, then chill quietly. When the guards unlocked the back of the truck, they would be facing an armed, defrosted, ninjutsu warrior who did not want to take their lives, but would do whatever it took, *by any means necessary*, to survive. That was my plan. The girl was right. In the face of an attempt at a violation of my manhood, it would be *freedom or death*.

Swiftly undressed, the spotlight steadily aimed at my feet, I stepped into the prison jumper. It seemed to be black, although I wasn't certain because other than the spotlight on the floor, there was only darkness. There were wool socks, quality ones like I've seen in the stores that specialize in winter sports and winter wear for camping, mountain climbing, and a variety of seasonal activities. There were gloves, thick insulated ones. There was a real wool hat and heavy boots. I sat them on the floor where the spotlight was aimed. *Hi-Tecs or Vasque*, I thought. The boots were either brand. I speculated, but couldn't see or read any labels. I stared down at my Jordans. They were made for cement like on the streets of New York. They were for basketball courts, indoors or outdoors. For dribbling and faking players out. For shooting and jumping, and flying and dunking. Not for mountain climbing and sliding on sheets of ice or snow. That was precisely why I couldn't feel my toes. It only made sense for me to leave them to the side and step into the heavy boots. I already knew that once we reached prison intake, my Jordans would be confiscated. Rikers was jail. Things were allowed in jail that would never be allowed in prison. I picked up my Jordans, tied the laces from both kicks together, and retired them.

"Put them in the plastic bag," the armed guard ordered. I had dropped everything in there except my kicks. "The tennis shoes also," he said. I knew then that he wasn't from the state of New York. Who would refer to Jordans as "tennis shoes"? He had to be a down south farm dude, a countryside white boy. When I dropped my Jordans into the plastic bag, the guard ordered, "Take a seat." I sat down. He picked up the plastic bag, lifting the spotlight from his flashlight off my boots and back directly into my face. He walked backwards towards the driver, knocked three times on the gate. The passenger-side guard opened the slot and the plastic bag was handed off to him. Then he slid the slot closed and I heard the door up front open.

Twenty-one minutes in, as I tied my second bootlace, I heard a vehicle drive past the truck we were idling in. It was moving uphill. Seconds later, the truck that we were in pulled out, veering immediately to the left, reversing, and heading down the mountain. I thought it was strange that we were heading downhill when the first DOC truck I was being transported in spent a substantial amount of time easing up the mountain until it jammed, then skidded, spun, and dropped off the edge of a cliff. It had teetered and crashed downward the same second that I was yanked and dragged by the chain. My brain and my body were thawing now. I was questioning myself as to why the other guard was walking a prisoner downhill on New Year's Eve in the dark on an iced mountain slope. I knew from the sound of the accident of the first DOC truck that after it tumbled and crashed against the rocks, they could not have recovered that vehicle. Even if it could have been towed up the mountain on a powerful cable, there would still be no way to drive it in that condition and absolutely no way to tow it, repair it, and drive it in twenty-one minutes. Was it a random vehicle that drove past us just now while we were parked, that just happened to also be a diesel-engine truck out on a dark mountain road deep into the New Year's Eve night? Or was the guard who was walking down the icy slope with his prisoner walking toward a third vehicle, separate from the one that crashed and the one I was being transported in right now? And where were we? And *oh shit*, my few belongings went down with the first DOC truck and my paperwork was also in the sack. And how come these boots fit perfectly? Cancel the last question. The prison system knew all the medical and physical information about me from the day I was hospitalized, my blood and urine drawn and every aspect of my health tested. Even my weight and height were documented and my fingerprints taken. I reminded myself, Jordan Mann.

We rode in silence for about twenty-eight minutes. Oddly, as the truck rolled to a stop, someone up front turned on a radio that blasted out bad-sounding music. I could no longer hear if anyone was talking, if doors were opening or shutting, or nothing. After six minutes, much longer than the wait for a traffic light, yield or stop sign, we were rolling again, but very slowly. The truck would stop here and there. Now we were moving in a straight line, not turning left or right or reversing. The music was still a loud distraction up until the final point where it could no longer conceal or compete with the thunderous sound of a helicopter that had to be approaching us or was either already dangerously close. The back door of the truck was unbolted and then opened. It felt like a tornado was sucking us out of the truck. The ramp lowered and the two guards signaled us to come out. We followed them. I could see that we were on an airstrip. The iced wind came in waves, slapping our faces from all sides. The natural current and the force of what the propeller was propelling was powerful. We each rushed to hood up our snorkels. The Iroquois copter looked wicked in the night sky. The guard behind me, and the two beside me, broke into a slow trot. Of course I kept pace with them, believing that our destination must be the copter. The door opened. Without conversation, communication, or consideration, they signaled me and assisted me to board. As soon as I got in, the three guards fell back. The copter door shut. The pilot handed me a headset and motioned me to fasten my seat belt. I did.

The vehicle rose up into the sky. Unsettling, it felt like I was being shaken up like one of several popcorn kernels in a close-lidded pot, right before the oil and heat caused it to burst open. But there was no oil or heat. The intense pressure was in fact the unknown. *Am I being flown to a nearby prison?* Whatever the case, I was dry without water, which I was accustomed to being without, from lights-out until early morning breakfast. But I was also without sleep. At the same time, I was experiencing the rush of adrenaline that comes when being reduced to cuffs and chains and then faced with the uncertainty of correctional officers with M16s. Unarmed COs with shields and sticks, mace and an unlimited range of authority, was more than enough.

The headset I wore dulled the deafening sound of the copter, which was speeding at 150 miles per hour, but it did not eliminate it. Above the trees and tallest towers, between the few red lights that assisted the pilots' navigation, and way below heaven, my thoughts were suspended by my amazement. Of course I had flown on many commercial airlines, jumbo jets like 747s. I had traveled several thousand miles away and all around the globe. However, the helicopter was completely different. It was raw, like flying through the sky naked with only a jet pack strapped to my back. Feeling the force of the wind current and unprotected by the weight, size, and design of the aircrafts that frequent flyers are afforded.

In less than half an hour I saw that we were hovering over a particular area. The pilot was communicating with someone briefly and immediately after he began lowering the Iroquois, the craft swinging all the way down. We landed in snow-covered flatlands that were surrounded by the wilderness. He released my seat belt, then handed me a backpack. The copter door opened and he used his hand to nudge me out.

I high-stepped a distance to separate myself from the power of the helicopter as it took off, rising back up into the night sky. Once it was way above me and I was left below, I noticed the intense beauty of the starlit sky. The intense beauty of the whitest snow that made the ground glisten like sunlight. The cold whipped me into action. I opened the backpack. Inside and right on top of several items was a map. I pushed it to the side to examine the other contents. Each of them, I knew, would be my only clues, tools and means of survival, other than the mercy of Allah.

I pulled out a bottle of water. There was only one. I found a flashlight and immediately powered it on to see inside the pack and take inventory. I cracked the seal opening the water and drank half of it. It felt like my brain could immediately function better because of it. I pulled out beef jerky, then threw it back and snatched out a trail-mix power bar, opened it up, and consumed it. With the map open and the spotlight on the route it highlighted, I was relieved that the distance between myself and the building marked out as my destination was only a mile and a half away. *Alhamdulillah*, the copter had most likely landed as close to the place as possible. If I had a parachute, I could've been dropped right on target. That would've been crazy because I had never parachuted before and I had never been to the place where I presently stood, nor did I have any idea where it was, other than my hypothesis that I was up North, close to Canada. Raising my knees up high to take my first few steps in the two feet of snow, I thought, *a mile and a half is nothing on a warm or hot spring or summer day.* It's a trek in a below-freezing night. Holding the compass, I was headed in a northeastern direction. Shining the light on the snow, I checked for tracks of vehicles or even footprints. There were none. I wanted to run the short distance but I knew better. I paced myself so the temperature would not defeat me.

Half an hour in, I felt I had not gone anywhere, even though I had been trekking. However, the place was now within sight. I became charged with determination. After getting pumped up, I cautioned myself about becoming foolishly excited. Would my arrival at the place, where the authorities refused to face the winter conditions and come out to retrieve me, put me in a better circumstance, or worse? And what kind of fool had they caused me to become to be struggling to incarcerate myself? I looked back. It reinforced my need to forge ahead. The security of being indoors had to be better than what was behind me. Either way, indoors or outdoors, it would be dealing with wildlife, grizzlies and wolves and mountain lions, the four-legged or the two-legged ones.

It was a stone house, not a compound, complex, or single intake building. Fifty feet away, concealed behind a considerable pile of firewood that was beside a shed, I checked it out. Either there were people inside who had not come out of the place since their storm happened, or the cabin was empty. There were no tracks in the snow, which was hardened at the top. There were no lights on inside. It had to be almost four, four-thirty in the predawn morning. So of course the lights being off would be considered normal, I told myself. There was no smoke pouring out of the chimney, either. Still, I needed to announce myself rather than barge in like an intruder and end up getting clapped up, which would've been justified for whoever was either living there or stationed there. What if it was a military outpost?

I reached into the backpack and pulled back the one and only red apple that I had seen in there. I hurled it like Roger Clemens. It crashed into the front door before smashing open. I wanted the loud and sudden thud to draw someone, anyone, everyone, out.

Nothing happened, not even a hand separating the blinds or pulling back a curtain. Not even a barking dog or crowing rooster, or a howling wolf. I waited some minutes. I advanced to the shed and looked in. There was a snowmobile, a few shovels, an ice pick, an ax, a fifty-pound bag of salt, a toolbox, some flares, a horn—more than enough. I grabbed an ax. Then I began my approach. As I pushed down on the latch, the front door opened. I looked in before entering. There was no movement.

I stomped my feet to shake the snow off my boots. I brushed the snow off my clothes as well. I reached in, running my gloved hand along the wall, searching for a light switch. I found it, clicked, and a dim light illuminated a living room with an unlit fireplace. I walked along the perimeter, checking each room—two bedrooms, one bathroom, a living room and a kitchen. I was only looking for humans, before examining any of the details.

A loud noise, swiftly I turned. The front door had slammed shut from the force of the winter wind. A pile of snow had been blown inside. *If the loud bang of that heavy door didn't wake up any sleepers, there are no sleepers in here*, I thought. *Or maybe that is what someone wanted me to think*, I cautioned myself. The first floor is clear. I approached the staircase leading up. Removing my backpack, I pulled out a triple-A battery and threw it upstairs to provoke a sound, reaction, or any kind of movement from any living thing. No sound or movement, there couldn't be anyone here unless it was a calm and cool well-trained enemy, laying in the cut for a sneak attack.

Pressing one foot down on the first step, I checked to see if it would creak. It didn't. There was a rug runner lining each stair. I headed up. On the second floor landing, I walked right into a network of spider webs that spread across my face and somehow got in my mouth. I wiped it away. Now I was sure that there was absolutely no one here. Furthermore, that no one had been here for at least a few days. *Why was I dropped here by helicopter? What type of set up is this now?*

There was a master bedroom and two smaller bedrooms on either side, as well as a full bathroom. Hadn't seen a private bathroom and walk-in shower in a long time. Couldn't even imagine it. Heard COs voice in my ear giving me only three minutes to clean my entire body.

A ladder laid against the wall in one of the side bedrooms piqued my attention. I walked in, saw it was situated beneath an uncovered entrance on the ceiling, a third level. But there was no staircase that led up to a third floor. I dropped my backpack and removed my snorkel and hat and used the ladder to climb up, my hands still gloved.

Dark, but the moonlight and gleam from the white snow coming through the window gave it some visibility. It was a furnished bedroom, a loft style with slanted ceilings. Looked lived in but abandoned. I flipped the switch.

A mirage, that's what I thought it was.

When I was six years young, traveling through the desert with my father, I learned the meaning of that word. My father, who owned all of the finest luxury vehicles, had no qualms about leaving them parked on our estate undriven for days, and even up to a week. He is a walker. At times he walked long distances, because he is also the son of a walker.

My southern Sudanese grandfather would not ride in any vehicle. He believed that if there was a place that his legs could not get him to, he didn't need to be there. Southern Grandfather also believed that when a man does not constantly use his God given limbs, he is setting himself up for a downfall. So, things that other people saw as progress and advancement, like cars, trains, and planes, my grandfather saw as problematic. "Riding in cars, sitting in planes and trains, your legs are not moving," he would say. "Those foreigners with all of their inventions will die young," Southern Grandfather predicted. "But I will live on beyond a hundred years. Watch, you will see," he told the children of the village.

My father was Grandfather's nineteenth child. He loved science, technology, innovation, and inventions. The only thing he loved more than that was his father. So he found ways to please his father while pursuing his studies. In fact, pleasing his father while pleasing himself caused my father to become a skillful thinker and negotiator. An expert in the art of compromise. Ever since my father was young, he planned to leave the village and become part of the global movement towards progress. Before he left to travel to Khartoum to study at the university, he gifted his father an imported European race bike that the whole village admired. He said to Southern Grandfather, "Now you will ride, but your legs will be moving."

Southern Grandfather gave my father a warm smile and a great embrace. Then he gifted my father a pair of handmade shoes that he crafted himself. Southern Grandfather told father that if these shoes did not bring him back to the place where he started, he is lost, and in the wrong place.

Even though my father had his own mind and made his own miracles and achieved and built his own businesses and properties, every now and then, he would do as his father did. Not because his father ordered him to do so, but because he saw his father do it. So he did it. As a consequence, every few months or so, I would see my father preparing to walk and walk and walk. Because he is my father, I walked also. He didn't order me to join him. I followed because I saw him do it. He walked, so I walked. One time on a long journey through the desert, at six years young, I felt like we had walked a million kilometers. I tried to keep up with him, but I was way behind, could see him and our camel, but couldn't seem to catch up. I wondered why he did not turn around to see that I was far behind. Or why he had not invited me to ride the camel. But he also was not riding the camel, so I didn't ask. I didn't want to say that I couldn't keep up any longer. I didn't want to complain that this time the walk was too long or ask him to stop and wait or even take a break for a while. Thirsty, tired, and with an intense growing hunger, I remained silent and kept walking. When my mouth became so dry I couldn't taste my own saliva, I endured.

*Alhamdulillah*, I heard myself saying when I saw the river up ahead. I wanted to wash, swim, cool off. I dismissed my tiredness and ran until I caught up with my father and even passed him by. When I did, my father didn't order me to stop. He didn't say one word. I ran until my body just collapsed. With the side of my little face pressed into the heated sand, I could see my father, tall, calm, and cool, just strolling his long strides.

When my father reached where I was laid out unable to move, he squatted down to the earth and began laughing. His teeth were whiter than ivory. His white thobe glistening in the desert sun. "Son, why were you running so fast?" he asked me. "The river," I said, coughing a dry cough. "Water," I murmured and pointed. He laughed again. My father squeezed the canteen and water splashed all over my face before I took a drink.

"It was a mirage, you were only seeing what your eyes and your heart wanted to see. But son the river is not there. It never was." I sat up refreshed from the water he gave me. All I saw then was desert, no river, or trees, or shade from the power of the Sudan sun.

"Your father is not a mirage. I am right here. Trust your father. If you are tired, speak up and say so. If you are hungry or thirsty, say so. Don't allow your desire to please your father or your desire for anything at all cause you to rush into a place that is not safe. That is not real and cannot help you. Allah has given you a father as a guide and a protection until you are the age of man. Once you become a man, you will know then to always be prepared because anything can happen. And, you will know the difference between what is simply a deep desire, what is false and what is real."

In the attic loft I saw a cot on the floor with neat and clean white sheets, a folded neat pile of winter blankets, and there was a dresser drawer, a desk, and a chair. On the desk there was a typewriter and a lamp, a high stack of organized papers, and an opened Holy Quran on a carved wooden stand. I saw books lining the perimeter of the wall, no bookcase, shelf, or stand. I didn't see her. But I could feel her. Or was it a mirage? A deep desire? Something my eyes and heart wanted and even craved to see and believe. I felt guilty. I have so many loved ones. Is she my deepest desire? The one I wanted to see more than anyone else? A craving so deep that my mind was playing tricks on me?

I went to the closet and slid open the door. I began smelling the clothes that were hanging there. They were winter clothes. When I last saw her, it was summer. All of her clothes were summer wear. Coconut, traces of her scent in a thick beautifully woven sweater. I got excited.

*Expect nothing*, I reminded myself. *You are a prisoner. Think only of the past, powerful pleasant memories. For the next year and a half there is no future. I am not entitled to yearn.* I reminded myself. But then, there it was. I saw her blue phone. I stood staring at it.

I had to go grab it to be sure that it was real. I picked up the receiver. There was a dial tone. Impulsively I hung it up. Thoughts began racing. *Should I phone home, our Queens house? Nah, that would be creating a trace.* Maybe someone wanted me to do just that, someone other than her, perhaps an open enemy. I paused, couldn't get my mind right for some reason.

"*My Shahada.*" I was staring now at the top sheet of paper on the neat high stack. "Written by Chiasa Hiyoku Brown." I pulled the top page to the side. There was a table of contents. One hundred and fourteen chapters. *The same amount of suras in the Holy Quran*, I said to myself. I pulled out the last page, page 2,777. My mind swiftly began doing the math. She had written at least five pages for every single day that I was away from her. My cold heart began cracking. I flipped to the first page of her first chapter. Of course her long life story about her young life began with her father. The chapter was titled, "The General's Daughter."

My eyes began reading her opening sentence.

"What to do, Daddy? Even if you kill my husband, I will still be a Muslim woman. No honest person receives an understanding and a feeling in their soul and then turns back from it." I could hear her soft-spoken voice, her powerful words expressed so sweetly. And then there was her sharp threat to him. "Bring him home to me. Daddy, that is the only thing that you can do for me, and if you will not do that, I don't want anything more from you forever, not even words."

Then, I knew.

# 32. THE NEGOTIATION

Seated at the table, arranged as a feast in an Alaskan steak and seafood house, I am well rested and my mind is clear and sharp. This scene, however, reminded me of the time when I was seated in the back room of an Italian restaurant in Brooklyn with the "good" detective, a deceitful and filthy man who was up to no good and who wanted to enslave me to his agenda. Just like back then on that night, I am starved and concealing a ferocious hunger with a straight face.

Unlike that night, I am not arrested, cuffed, and beaten or bruised. However, I am surrounded by suited strangers, with the exception of one man. He is much wiser and slicker, more powerful and deadly than the good detective. He has a greater stature, and stronger stance and stamina, and he is a thousand times more passionate about his cause, for deeper, blood-related reasons. Most importantly, he is fully capable of carrying out and following up on his threats. He has the full authority of the United States military, and sees no reason to limit his actions when he is going after what he wants. He is my second wife's father.

It is January 1, 1988; however, I could not pinpoint the exact time. After a mysterious, uncomfortable, and dangerous trip from Rikers that ended in a cliff-hanger on a mountain in upstate Buffalo, NY, as well as a cold copter ride and a trek through the high snow, ice, and arctic cold, I had finally fallen asleep. I woke up once to the sound of my own voice calling the Azan, and in a sleepy haze I fell back asleep.

Through the attic window I could see that it was still dark outside and I figured I was dreaming or bugging because of exhaustion. I slept for what felt like several more hours, and finally awoke. It was still dark, so I imagined that I had not actually slept for long. It was only much later that I found out that the darkness was due to a storm that made it seem that the sun would not rise at all. So I had actually slept very well, through my normal routine times and prayer times and eating times. It ended up being about ten hours of rest.

I had fallen asleep with a growling belly while reading the first chapter of Chiasa's manuscript. Her words ripped off the armor I had layered my mind, body, and soul with for nearly two years. Her words demolished the freeze in my bones and they heated my cold-hardened heart. Her words had ignited my desires, the same deep desires that I had controlled, conquered, and canceled during my caging. Her words forced me into a deep sleep and an erotic dream. I woke up bricker than brick, my joint so solid and swollen, it wouldn't lay down for an extended amount of time. It would not settle for anything less than her touch, the pushing and plunging and pleasure of her pussy, a tight but warm and moist space where we expressed our mutual love.

I was fucked up, I knew. I needed to recover my discipline, restraint, and alertness. I needed to collect my composure and restore my warrior stance for the possible approaching threats and realities. After all, I was in an unknown space riddled with unanswered questions. The most severe ones were regarding my legal status. *Am I a prisoner? Or am I a fugitive? Is there a warrant for my arrest? Is there a manhunt underway for my capture?* As I had laid on my back on a mattress on the floor, dressed with sheets that carried her scent, in her room in a house made of stones, surrounded by nothing but snow and ice and the wilderness, I wondered. Was I rescued? Am I free? Could a daughter's subtle demand to the father who adored her actually cause a powerful man to deploy his trucks, helicopter, arsenal, and assassins? And if she was the trigger, what would happen next? How far would her father go, and how far had he gone so far, beyond what I could possibly see or know or imagine?

Before I could decode the past twenty-four hours, I heard the rumblings of a Hummer. I leapt up, then watched through the window. As soon as I confirmed that it was her father, the General, arriving alone in the vehicle, I dropped down from the secluded space where she had her clothes, blanket, and books, her bed, desk, and dresser, and her writings and hardly anything else. I securely closed the lid that sealed it, and removed the ladder, pushing it into a side room. I did not know if her father normally came here, or if he was aware of her manuscript. He was a man who their family was normally very discreet about, never mentioning his name or his title and ranking, or even taking or hanging his photographs.

But in the side room I saw men's clothing. Was it his? I didn't have time to check. I was in the washroom, washing my face and hands and rinsing my mouth. I saw a razor for shaving. My jaw and my chest got tight. I slipped out the blade and cleaned it off. Instinctively, I'd carry it on me. Then he knocked on the door with the heavy hand of the police or the military during a raid.

Grabbing the snorkel, which had my gloves and wool hat tucked in each coat pocket, I put it on over the black jumper that I had fallen asleep in. I stepped into my boots and headed outside. He had gotten back in the Hummer, and was seated behind the wheel. He lowered his window when he saw me approaching.

"We have an appointment. Let's go, son," was all he said casually, as though he had just chilled with me the day before. But, in reality, he had last seen me two years ago. I climbed in. "Jump in the back and get dressed." I did, surprised to see the dress clothes hanging in the rear on the hook. I was clean shaven head and face, but my body was not showered.

His Mickey Thompson Baja Claw tires were crushing everything in their path. Only the hum of his engine could drown out the rumble of my hunger. Fully dressed, I decided to remain seated in the back. Through the rearview mirror he locked eyes with me and said, "You are not naïve, son, are you? You know the rules of war."

I stayed still and silent, thinking. "Happy New Year," was all

I said to him. I knew better than to utter one word that could be used as a one-word agreement to any of his ideas, plans, or schemes then, now, or later on.

"So, you are the General's son. Pleased to meet you," a well-suited European woman in her thirties introduced as Urschla said as she sipped from her water glass. "I know fathers are demanding and rarely compliment their sons, so I'll have to say that your performance on the SATs was outstanding, almost perfect. They were above the scores of our average students, which is quite high, and equivalent to the scores of our top three students in a class of one hundred and twenty."

"Indeed," a dark-blue-suited white man who had been introduced as Roy said. "We are excited to have recruited you and are fully prepared for you to enter our academy next week after the holiday break. And because of the preeminence of your father, we have all assembled here on the great holiday. Fortunately for us it's late afternoon. Otherwise we may have had to disappoint your father after a night of cheers." They all laughed.

"You already look like a soldier," an older white man introduced as Tom, commented. "You are already as silent as an elite global soldier must be."

"So true," the dark-suited Roy said. "Normally such silence is achieved only after our specialized training. The fact that you are already silent has me feeling a little less necessary." They each laughed. "It's either that, or he has some ominous secret to hide," he added.

"Nonsense," the European woman said. "Look who his father is. He obviously has been in training for years." Then she turned towards me and said, "There is no need for you to feel burdened—only the top brass gathered around this table will know your roots. And we won't tell a soul," she promised. "We don't want the other students to feel that you're getting preferential treatment."

"He may be advanced in his training already, which is excellent since he is entering the academy in the second semester of our school year, which is rarely ever allowed. However, he won't be spared any of the workload that he has missed. Therefore he will have to forfeit his summer leave. He will also need to polish up on his social skills. He had to have suffered from being homeschooled, and studying for his SATs all alone and earning his GED in place of attending full classes with qualified instructors, and bonds of friendship and team spirit, and of course the godforsaken high school prom. Simply trying to get a date to that damn thing is a social experiment," Tom said, and they laughed.

"No worries," Urschla said. "Our school is coed and international, and Switzerland is quite lovely. Our host country is famous for chocolate. And you are a very handsome young lad, if you don't mind my saying so."

Back in the blacked-out black Hummer plowing through the storm-dark roads, he had his huge hand gripping the shift stick tightly. What I really wanted to ask him was the whereabouts of my wife. I knew that he knew that she is my great love and deep desire, also his only daughter, his ace card and the only reason me and him were together, and that I was riding shotgun with a military man. I knew he would attempt to convert my love and my desire for his daughter into my weakness. So I didn't mention her. I only asked, "Where are we headed?"

"You'll see."

We pulled up to a checkpoint, which ended up being the entrance to a military base. The signage said Fort Drum. Each soldier who encountered him saluted, shuffled, kowtowed, and all but bowed down. He was riding from building to building getting his holiday greetings, salutes, and reports, and showing me without words spoken directly to me that he was in command. I already knew that. Seeing tanks and guns and grenades and stockpiles of ammunition sealed his performance. His last stop on his "power tour" was a dormitory building on the base. He ordered a soldier on post outside to go in and bring out "Private Crusher."

The big white boy soldier came running out, then straightened himself as soon as he saw the General seated in the Hummer. He saluted and then approached with permission. He leaned in on the driver's side and asked what he could do for the General.

"Take a look at this guy. You think you could take him for a few rounds?" the General asked him.

He glanced over at me. "That's why they call me 'The Crusher,'" he said.

They laughed. I didn't. Easily I'd fight him. I'm not militarily trained. But these guys weren't street fighters, didn't come straight out of Rikers, and probably would never survive if they did.

"What do you say, son?" the General asked me.

"Anytime," I said solemnly.

"Whoa, let's go! Let's ring in the bloody New Year," the Crusher said.

"Not tonight," the General intervened. "He's got other things to do tonight. I just swung by so you could see your next challenge and get prepared."

"I'm the champ that whooped that big boy over in 'Little Siberia,' General. I'm already prepared." This guy was excited, hyped up like he just shot up steroids.

"You're dismissed, Private," the General said. Crusher left in an instant.

"I grabbed that guy out of the jaws of Little Siberia. You know where that is?" the General asked me as he did a 180 and drove off the base.

"Nah," I said.

"That's the prison where you were supposed to go last night. Dannemora, maximum security, Clinton Correctional Facility, a place where the worst sons of bitches in the region are housed and conquered, but never corrected." He was looking straight ahead. So was I. "Just remember that during our negotiation," he said suddenly.

"Negotiation," I repeated, really to myself.

"The one you and I are about to have," he said. We rode in silence after those words. My mind was heavy. There were too many X-factors. I needed to line up my thoughts before the negotiation. I began to do so for my own good. His daughter is my wife. I won her hand in marriage from him fair and square. He hadn't faltered on his debt to me, or on his word, although I always felt his reluctance, his presence, and his attempt to continue to control her from afar. That may have been annoying, but it wasn't terrible or evil, I told myself. His daughter loves me, I know. She will follow me wherever I go, and whatever choices I make. Even if she disagrees with me, she will yield and give way. Only in an instance where something conflicts with her faith would she fight and resist. I never go against her faith. Her faith is my faith. On the one hand, I have the General by the neck because I have his daughter. But why should our marriage be a problem to him? Is it only her conversion to Islam that he finds so disturbing? And now that it is clear that his daughter will be Muslim whether I'm dead or alive, he had to realize that he can't get her to roll back to whatever it was they used to believe in or do as a way of life. What does he want from his daughter? What does he want from me?

In a chess game, both opponents have the comfort of knowing how each piece can and can't move. Both the black knight and the white knight are limited to the same options. And that goes for the king, queen, rooks, and bishops also. Life, however, isn't like that. It's random, hostile, and impulsive. You can't sleep on any man, because no man is a game piece. The weakest and most frightened man might do the most unexpected, deadliest, and horrific thing.

He obviously wants me to attend some academy in Switzerland, I thought further. That's what I had gathered as I sat in complete silence at the dinner table. My objective was only to listen and consume an expensive meal in an expensive restaurant where the prices were not printed on the menu. Was that his method of separating his daughter and me by distance? Or, did he and his sister Aunt Tasha and their whole family believe that if I didn't start racking up the degrees the way they had, that I needed to be cut out from Chiasa and their family, like a cancer? Or was it worse? Is my Islamic lifestyle so unacceptable to them that they needed to see me humiliated in order to feel comfortable around me, and comfortable around Chiasa? Is this some deep-seated jealousy?

True, I had knocked out a guy at their family barbeque in the Vineyard. But he deserved it. A friend to Xavier, he had tried to kick it to my first wife, asking her to dance and touching her hand after she said no, to coax her to accept his offer. I dropped him. Had to let them all know that both women belonged to me by marriage and choice, theirs and mine. *I love Chiasa, true. She is your relative, true. But still don't fuck with my first wife, because I love her, true.* They thought that I was cocky, even though I had cooperated and showed up to Clementine Moody's all-male family breakfast very early that same morning, to squash the beef between Marcus and me. I was quiet and humble. I shook hands with Marcus even though he had tried to stab me in the back before and had actually stabbed me in my chest, inches above my heart. But at the late afternoon big blowout barbeque, male and female, family and friends and Vineyard neighbors gathered. Soon as I arrived with my beautiful Umma, covered in her summer-light sparkling fabrics, and my two beautifully modest wives and little sister, I felt all eyes on me. The men watched me, thinking I was too brazen. It felt like my everyday lifestyle and my wives were getting them green with envy and red with fury, while they fronted it off, glancing and gossiping while flashing fake smiles. I remember. Marcus had Chiasa captivated by his fireworks, a suitcase filled with stink bombs, firecrackers, nigger chasers, sparklers, M80s, and other holiday explosives. I was chilling in the shade, sipping a lemonade when I saw the dude looking, then approaching Akemi as she stood watching the dance steps intently, and admiring the art of the gathering.

They think I'm violent. I think they're uncivilized. They think they are higher-ups. I think they are spiritual lows. If they could separate me from my women, and infiltrate their minds, they would.

But, because my women are loyal, there was absolutely nothing they could do to break it. It was sad and funny to me. Their women of all ages, from very young to senior elders, were at that big barbeque event, most uncovered and nearly naked. Why focus on my wives, covered and true?

So my standing with my second wife's family before my lockup was left on shaky grounds.

But now, I was faced with a larger dilemma. The General might have gotten me freed at his daughter's demand. But if he got me out and off without me becoming a fugitive on the run, or the "most wanted," I understood that I owed him . . . something. Even though I did not ask him to do it, could have served out my time and come home in a year and a half. At the same time, if I am free, now, without doing the rest of my time, of course I got to be grateful. My praise goes to Allah, of course, but in the physical world, I paid my debts fair and square as well. What about all the men I left behind at Rikers? What about the ones who were waiting for me to drop a line and let them know my whereabouts? What about the handful of people who would be following up to check on me, like my lawyer and Santiaga, who would wait for news of my release, and Ditch, who was also sent to "Little Siberia"? What about DeQuan at Greenhaven and his newsletter that kept all of us aware and connected, and DeSean at Sing-Sing.

My second wife had been asked three questions by her father. According to her manuscript, he had asked her, "Do you understand that he murdered a man and how serious a crime that is?" And he asked her, "Why should I go out of my way to bring him home before he serves his time with the other convicted murderers and criminals?"

Chiasa, clever and swift, had replied softly, "And how many men have you killed, Daddy? Shall we count them? Or, are there too many to count? And doesn't it matter that he was defending his sister? Or, would it have been better if he was killing for pay? Just obeying orders because it was his occupation, and without any other real consideration or right reason? Daddy, I'll bet there are bodies buried beneath every medal on your chest. Aren't there? But if you were somewhere suffering, like I feel my husband is suffering, it would be unbearable to me. Same as I have waited for you my whole life, I can wait for my husband. But the thought of the element that he is in, and the conditions that he's enduring, is unbearable for me. And of course he is different than almost all of the men he might be locked up with. He is my husband. When I met him, he had already made twenty thousand more prayers than me. Before I met him, I had never made even one. He had already fasted for nine Ramadans. Now, he has fasted for eleven. He is so good and so beautiful. He is better than me. He loves and lives for his family and he loves me a whole heap, maybe more than you do. He would do anything for me, even give up his life. Won't you do what I ask of you?"

"He has another wife," the General had reminded her. As I read, it felt like it was his last desperate attempt to alter her allegiance to me.

"Yes, she is his wife and she is my wife, too."

I doubted that the General had read her manuscript. Now that I think about it, though, perhaps he was aware of its existence. Perhaps she had used it with the accuracy and precision of her knives and hit the bull right in his eye, so to speak. Perhaps she had threatened him with it. After a lifetime of his not being photographed, and under the protection of his family to keep everything concerning him private, he must have wanted to stop the autobiography of the General's young daughter from being published. Maybe it pushed him to the point that at the threat of losing his daughter's loyalty, he felt the shame of abandoning Marcus, his son. Maybe I was somehow ruining his "do-over."

The off-road vehicle rode rugged off road. We maneuvered over ice and rocks and sticks and even veered around a massive elk. After a bit of a journey, we arrived at a miniature oddly shaped log cabin in the wilderness. There was a Jeep already parked there below the towering trees. Again, I had no idea what was going on. He climbed out of the Hummer. I followed. I observed that the tiny place had a weird chimney. It was just a pipe popping out through its roof. The smoke was pouring upwards and then dispersed by the intensity of the cold air.

A woman, maybe about twenty-two years young, opened the door and stood in the doorway. She wore a colorful kimono, with no socks or stockings or anything to shield her from the cold. As we entered, I realized that she was wet but seemed unfazed by the intermingling of two extremely different temperatures. She rushed us into the warmth. "Happy New Year!" she said enthusiastically, and in a manner and a tone that led me to believe this was not her first meeting with the General.

The cabin ceiling was so low, the General, who stood six foot eight, had only two inches remaining above his head. I also was strangely close to the ceiling. She was not.

"I'll take your coats. You may hang your clothes right there." She pointed out a row of metal hooks lodged in the wall. We both removed our coats and suit jackets. I was following his lead. He began unbuttoning his dress shirt and removing it as well. I paused.

"Come on, son. When in Rome, do as the Romans. When in Alaska, do as the Eskimos; when in Buffalo, do as the Buffalos." He chuckled. "This place is a *muk'ee*, an Alaskan-style steam bath. You've had a hard run for a long time. You'll need this to extract all that filth from your skin." Even though we were not in Alaska, the General seemed to like Alaskan things. I noted that fact and the possibility that he is either currently stationed there, or had been stationed there for some extended period of time. Maybe that's why he was at ease in the Buffalo freeze. He was down to only his boxers and about to come out of those. I adjusted my mind. I moved it right past my recent past and beyond the jail and perversities that I never knew or considered existed before going to jail and observing. I settled my mind way back in the Sudan, in a memory of my southern Sudanese grandfather. He was a huge black-skinned man, same as the General. Grandfather was blacker than black, and shaded even deeper than the General, who was surely black too. In the Sudan men washed side by side at times, in the flesh. It was natural and clean, there with no suspicions or threats or even a remote thought of anything else.

Fully naked now, both of us men, the General and me, duck-walked to pass through the door that led to the next room, which was only five feet in height. The floor and the ceiling and the walls were all made of wood. We eased out of our duck squat and sat on a long wooden bench facing a wooden stove that was percolating. The metal pipe that sat in the middle of it ran all the way out through an opening in the roof and was so hot it was turning red. In this room, both of our heads were touching the ceiling.

"Is it too hot for you, son?" he asked me. I didn't say anything. I was adjusting, breathing in the moist heat. I felt it swirling in my lungs and was breathing it back out as all of my pores were opening. I knew he was using that statement to have a double or triple meaning. I knew he was trying to break me, get me under his wing and control, not kill me. But I'm from the desert. I'm from the Sudan, land of the blacks, home of the original pyramids even before Egypt, which was previously known as Kemet, the land of the black-skinned pharaohs, and the region of the prophets Moses, Jesus, and Mohammed, peace be upon them, for those who don't truly know.

"When it gets too hot for you, lie down," he said. "I got this place reserved for two hours. You should be good, clean, smoked, and steamed by then." He laughed, and the deepness of his voice echoed.

Crouched there on the bench, sweat pushing out of our pores and glazing our faces and bodies and even soaking our toes, he said, "Let's begin our negotiation."

"Let's do that," I responded. Even I was eager. I wanted the information, the verdict, and the conclusion. I'd rather be beside his daughter, nude and moist and wet.

"You realize that you are not in the same position as you were before when you won, and I allowed you to leave Asia with my sixteen-year-old daughter," he said.

"Right," I agreed, purposely brief.

"You realize that you committed a serious crime, murder, and you are a convict."

"I was in the middle of serving my time for that conviction when your people came locked and loaded and interrupted." He turned and looked at me hard and grimaced.

"Ungrateful. You should be glad my people came and 'interrupted' you. Or did you grow accustomed to living like a beast?"

"I'm not confirmed that you have rescued me. You may have sunk me into a deeper legal problem. Convince me. While you're at it, please tell me exactly what you want." He was quiet. As the steam rose, shrouding his face, he looked like a gorilla in the mist. At the same time, he resembled my father—his looks, not his content or his style.

"Son, call it what you like. But it is what it is. Since you have no negotiation etiquette, I'll give you the harsh bottom line. You are a prisoner of war. Do you know what that means? In this war between you and me, you've lost this battle. You know the rules of war, son? When you lose, you lose something of great value, something precious to you. The best outcome for a loser is that he becomes a hostage, a servant, a slave, or a dead man." He pulled a thick string that caused a bell to ring, then moved off the bench and lay out flat on the floor. The swinging door that separated the steam room from the dressing room pushed open. The blond-haired, blue-eyed young white woman walked in, completely nude and carrying a bucket filled with some fluid. She used a wooden bowl to scoop the liquid and began pouring it all over the General's body from head to toe. It was water. From his grunting out his relief and pleasure, I knew it was cool to cold water to lessen the intensity of the steam heat.

"Lay down, son. You gotta learn when to lay down," he said. "The wrong timing or the wrong decision could leave you out of breath." As she poured water on him, her eyes were trained on me. I turned from her gaze. I had already seen it all vividly, her plump titties and poked out nipples. Her bald pussy lips and thighs and feet. *She's a trick*, I said to myself. His spoonful of sugar to force down the bad-tasting medicine he was trying to feed me. She left.

"You were purchased, son. A private corporation purchased your sentence and your servitude. Now, they own you." The door swung back open. The woman reentered the room with two large paper cups filled with water. She handed one to me and placed the other beside him.

"If you lie down, I'd gladly soak you in some cool water," she said to me with her eyes and lips.

"That's enough," the General said to her. She turned and left in an instant, leaving the door in the open position, causing cool air to rush in and lessen the heat. I drank the water. Then my mind was ready.

"I agree. When a man loses a war he becomes a prisoner or a slave. I wasn't at war with you, though. We both have someone precious in common. The war I was in I won in a sense, because I did what had to be done. I lost in a sense because I got locked up. But I looked at it as me paying the blood price for my actions. My debt to the prison system was three years. That's in writing. I did seventeen months. I have nineteen months, roughly a year and a half, remaining on my debt to the prison system. If a company purchased that debt, which is something I never heard of, I would owe that company one year and nine months of my time," I said. Then I rang the bell and lay down.

"Good, now you're negotiating," he said. The naked girl reappeared and began pouring the cool water over me from head to toe. It was a relaxing feeling in a tense time. She left.

"Your debt was one year and nine months, 'without incident,'" he said.

"Incident?" I repeated.

"When your sponsors who purchased you went to pick you up, I'm told they encountered an accident. I'm not accusing you of causing the accident. I wasn't there. I didn't see it. But whatever the case, the Department of Corrections lost two men and a truck. That's a little messy. Your sponsor's team *contacted me*, not the local police or prison authorities. In less than thirty minutes, I deployed my team to clean up the scene. That increased your debt," he said, calm and sly.

"I'm a businessman," I said. "I have capital. Talk to me. How much did it cost you, sir, the helicopter ride?" We both sat up. He looked like he wanted knock my head off. The woman came back to refill the drinking water. I was already tired of her.

"It's a holiday, son. Our accountant is adding it up," he said, pleased with himself. The woman got on her knees and began dipping her sponge in the cold water bowl, and wiping and patting the General down. When she was done, she left. "That wasn't the only mess I had to clean up. There was the matter of cleaning up your identity, separating you from 'Jordan Mann.' Making sure he's the convict and you are not. That took time, burned up some of my connections, caused me to use up some favors that were owed to me, and I had to do some favors that I never intended to do as well."

"Are you saying wthat legally I'm free, not a fugitive or even a convict?"

"I see you look skeptical." He chuckled. "Right now, there's a Jordan Mann serving your sentence. He arrived at Clinton last night same time you were scheduled to arrive, wearing your clothes, doing your time in your place." My mind raced, although the heat and moisture in the air did slow my thoughts some. Was the prisoner walking downhill escorted by the guard the one who was doing time in my place?

"What about the fact that they already had my blood and urine and fingerprints?" I asked swiftly. "His profile won't match up with mine," I added.

"That's the expensive cleanup job that I've been alluding to. That increased my special services and your debt. But those services I already made happen. Although it is not a simple matter to delete one man's records and data, and alter another man's records and data, my efforts were a success. It turns out that you are going to live well as long as you follow the General's orders and pay the General what you owe him."

"How much is that?" I asked. "Tell it to me straight."

"Five painless years. You go to the school in Switzerland for one and a half years, full time, in fact overtime including summers. Graduate, and then you serve the remaining three-and-a-half years under contract," he said, scheming.

"Under contract as what?"

"A member of a secret mercenary army, the Elite Global Organization of Soldiers. You won't have to wear the uniform you hate so much. It's a private company. I own it. You will not be a part of the United States military. But you will be under my management and command. I'll contract you out to elite customers and move you to countries all around the world. You'll be highly paid. And when your time is up, you walk away," he said, clapping his hands once and splattering the water in his palms.

"I'd rather . . ." I began saying, and he interrupted.

Now I saw and understood the reason why him and me were naked in a strange steam bath. He needed to have this unexpected, strange, and "classified" conversation in a place where it couldn't be overheard, recorded, filmed, or reported on. Not only because of me and the murder I had committed and been convicted of, but because of the moves he had already taken, that I never requested and that he was now responsible for.

Teacher Karim Ali had given us a clear definition of the word criminal. He said a criminal is a person, network or institution, business, or system that violates and operates and participates in activities outside of the established laws of the legitimate government or recognized governing body of a city, state, country, or territory. According to Teacher Karim's definition, me taking the murder of Lance Polite into my own hands was criminal. At the same time, that definition meant that the General is a criminal, and the U.S. military is criminal too. Perhaps that was the reason Ricky Santiaga said "There is no such thing as a bad man." Because of the system we live in, we all fit the criminal definition perfectly. The only way out of that truth it seemed, was to change the system, completely.

But I am a Muslim man. I believe there are good and bad men, no matter what the situation. Islam is my belief and my way. I thought all these men, including myself, would be better, live better, and do better if Islam were the rules of law. It's a faith, and the guidelines are clear. And men can work and earn, live and love, and protect what any right thinking man wants to protect: his family. In order to do so though, men would have to gain a discipline and lose something also. Men would have to sacrifice some vices and habits and occupations that do more harm than good. Humble ourselves and lose something to gain something much better and much greater.

"Think about it before you speak, son. I'll give you twenty-four hours to make your choice."

"And what if I just buy back my freedom, pay you the debt back in cash or gold?" I proposed.

"Not possible. In this instance the time is worth more than any money you could put together and that I would accept."

"So are you saying that I don't have the option to serve out my sentence and be done with this?" I asked just to be clear.

"I told you, you are already serving your sentence and then some."

"And then some," I repeated.

"Yeah, right about now, Jordan Mann is seated in the hole and under close scrutiny and investigation. What else could he be? There are two corrections officers who died transporting him to prison," the General said, which translated in my ear as "checkmate."

"What about that man?" I asked.

"Who?"

"The one serving the time as Jordan Mann."

"Don't worry about him. He's a slave, a prisoner of war paying down his debt, which has nothing to do with you," the General said firmly. "If he wasn't paying it at Clinton, he would be paying it elsewhere in another not-so-nice place. In the prison system, son, you are just a body, a number. You're human waste."

"But, he's not me," I said, really at a loss for words.

"If he causes any mess, he could easily be eliminated in a sudden prison fight. If he interrupts big business, that will be his fate. He is whoever I say he is. Listen, son, when I was your age, I ran into some troubles. I figured out that there were only two sides in this world, simple. There's the winners and the losers and they're both heavily armed. I figured out that what makes the winners the winners is that they have authority, a license to hold, a license to kill . . . and get away with it. So you decide which team you want to be a part of, the winners or the losers. If you're stubborn or stupid, if you swim against the tide or go against the grain, you'll have no support. You'll have opened up a can of snakes, and at least one of them will eat you." He gritted his teeth.

"Take your time. You have twenty-four hours," he threatened, politely.

I had voices streaming through my thoughts: my own voice, the voices of my father and grandfather, Teacher Karim Ali's voice, Santiaga's, DeQuan's, and the voice of that girl who gave that speech in the jail. Seated in the back of the Hummer, on impulse, I did what she recommended. "Check the label," she had said. I pulled down the black jumper I wore this afternoon. I flipped the collar and checked the label. It had the letters *HWM* embossed on it. The snorkel had the same label and letters, as did the boots. I smiled. When I was on the yacht with Clementine Moody, he had handed me a note on a small notepad embossed with the capital letters *HWM.* Long before, my wife had told me that no one knew what her uncle actually did for a living. They only knew what he'd done in the past. Knitting the facts together, the tiniest sloppy mistakes that paid and powerful men are bound to make because no man is perfect, I got it. Clementine Moody was either the owner of HWM or their highly placed and paid consultant.

"What does *HWM* stand for?" I asked, suddenly breaking the silence of the ride to wherever was the General's next destination.

"Human Waste Management, they are your sponsors. How did you know?" he asked. "That's classified information."

"Their logo is stamped on this uniform they gave me last night, and the coat and the boots," I said.

"They're an up-and-coming powerhouse corporation. The privatization of every service available in the world is on the horizon, including the privatization of prisons and the military and even the privatizing of the individual. That's why I am in the lineup, son. I'm going to remain working high up in the military mainstream, and meanwhile, I'm investing, building and betting on the dark horse. Same as I figured out when I was young, exactly who had the authority to hold and fire their weapons. After a long career, I realized that the 'endless military budget,' of trillions of dollars—I needed a cut of that, not just great benefits and a paycheck. I had put in the work and the time. I had traveled the entire range of the globe, every nook and cranny. I had introduced kings and queens and corporate heads and politicians and military higher-ups and even presidents and prime ministers to each other. Through my efforts and introductions, I had created many multi-million-dollar financial business marriages. But, only through owning my own company could I get the cut I deserved. I chose what I know, the military. The creation of a global private army." He watched me through the rearview to measure his impact. "You know, son, the dark horse will win." He chuckled. He sounded like Slaughter to me.

"The HWM corp, is it owned by a black man?" I asked.

"Yes, but he's extremely private. He uses his vice president with dexterity. He's the owner. The VP is 'the face.' The owner is a good guy, though. I've known him for years." Then I knew. The General and his brother-in-law had each formed their own corporations and they were feeding one another. Moody had come from the hospital industry, while the General was from the military. The two biggest hustles in the world had joined hands secretly. So secretly that now they were buying and selling humans, their body parts in individual pieces, or their bodies in whole. The American prisons were their playgrounds that stored the inventory known as "human waste." The entire globe was their marketplace. They were even buying what Allah had gifted each of us in varying degrees, our time on Earth. Furthermore, the learned Clementine Moody had the balls to name his business Human Waste Management. I had gotten that feeling from him when I was riding on his yacht. He believed he could do more with people's lives and deaths than people could do for themselves. And he believed that people who were not pursuing Ivy League degrees and the status he achieved were actually "waste."

"I'll come for your decision tomorrow at eighteen hundred hours," the General said when he dropped me back at the lone stone house in the cold wilderness. It was almost ten p.m.

Now the lights were on in the house. I saw a man moving through the lighted curtain.

*This is life*, I said to myself. *You can't kill every immoral man*, I cautioned myself. *But if there's a man in there with my wife, he's a dead man.*

I walked around to the side of the house, sure that whoever was there heard the Hummer roll up over the ice. I heard the door open and feet crushing snow as he stepped out. I walked around front so swiftly he was startled. Before I could snap his neck I saw his face. It was Marcus.

Seated in her attic bedroom, purposely in the dark, I was behind a wooden pillar and the beam of moonlight. I waited. He told me she would soon come. I told him not to mention that I was here. I wanted to send him out and away. But, I did realize that would be too cruel due to the cold isolated location. Aside from that, he seemed less crazy than before. I'm sure it was the outcome of being in the atmosphere and presence of my lovely wife, his sister, who he had missed out on when he was young. He also told me that he had been working for her, managing her New York vending business. "She needed me to deal with the men," he said proudly. I smiled.

*Turns out he works for me.* But I knew he didn't need to hear that. I let it go.

I heard a vehicle roll up. I didn't look. She always saw too much. I didn't want to give myself away by appearing in the window or peering through the curtains before I could feel and see her true reaction. I smiled. She is eighteen now. Had her license, was driving now. Then I heard voices two flights down but couldn't distinguish their words. She didn't run right up. So I guess he kept his word and didn't tell her I was here.

Half an hour later, I heard her approaching slowly. It was strange because she was usually so swift. When she finally appeared, she was carrying something on her back. I stood still as a statue. She turned to pull out a dresser drawer and I saw my baby on her back. *Alhamdulillah*! My racing heart was beating now like a war drum. So loud I thought she could hear it. She placed our baby in the drawer after laying a blanket inside of it. She bent over and gently laid the drawer on the floor at the top of her cot. She began to undress. On her blouse a pendant of gold wings glistened. *Badass, she had even become a pilot.* Her hair was still wild beneath her *hijab*. She removed it. It was thick and braided into only two braids, even longer than before. Giving birth had made it grow. I had missed watching all of that happen. Her sculpted shoulders were still exquisite and her back a diamond cut. Her waist was still tiny ballerina and her butt African lovely. *Still training, she had made that happen. She must still be shooting her bows and arrows.* Her arms were lean and tight. She turned around and leaned back against her dresser. Her milk and honey breasts and hips more beautiful than heaven.

"If you only knew," she said softly, and tears fell from her smokey-gray eyes, "you wouldn't tease me by staring from over there. Come over here and love me."

# ACKNOWLEDGMENTS

This time around I'd like to acknowledge the people, the book readers and book buyers. Please accept my deep appreciation to each and every one of you.

Specifically, I'd like to thank every single youth and student who has taken it upon him or herself to ask for, find, and buy my novels even when your teachers have either refused or failed to assign or provide them to you.

Also, I'd like to thank those teachers, principals, and school districts courageous enough to order and buy my books because they are concerned about storytelling that connects to and improves the lives and realities of their student population.

Deep appreciation to every librarian who has ordered enough copies of my books to serve their communities. To the financially poor girls and boys who can only afford to check my books out at the library. That used to be me!!!

I'd like to send a heartfelt thank-you to the prison population, those who have purchased, passed around, shared and discussed my novel in order to create a new understanding and better lives for themselves.

Last, but never the least, I'd like to thank every father and mother who have handed the Midnight novels to their sons and daughters in hopes that they might make better choices and lead better lives than WE ever did.

Books offer knowledge that make it possible for us to break the negative cycles that we all have become too comfortable accepting.

*Love,*
*Sister Souljah*

**YOU CAN GET IN TOUCH WITH SISTER SOULJAH:**

**Email:** souljahworkshard@gmail.com

**Mail:** Sister Souljah
Souljah Story Inc.
208 East 51st Street, 2270
New York, New York 10022

**Turn the page**

**to enjoy an excerpt**

**from Sister Souljah's novel**

**LIFE AFTER DEATH:**

**Winter Santiaga is back.**

After a nasty breakup of any couple, the war begins. I knew bitches who keyed their ex's ride, or punctured his tires, or banged in his rims with a hammer. I knew bitches who beat the new bitch's ass who their man had replaced them with. Or even choked her, stabbed her, shot her, or mercked her. I knew even live-er bitches who, instead of killing his new bitch, killed him. I knew bitches who ran up his credit cards, crashed his car, cut up his clothes, pawned his jewels, and even burnt down his house. But when a man and woman used to be lovers, living together, working together, eating together, showering and fucking together, and one betrays the other, betrayal makes the matter more meaner than murder. 'Cause you can just kill someone if you want to, no matter who you are. No matter where they hide. They bound to resurface eventually. Let down their guard eventually, and that's precisely when they can get got. But ex-lovers, where one betrayed the other, sold him or her out, flipped on 'em, or was way-worser, like working as an undercover police, spying and telling on her or his lover, murder ain't good enough get back. A betrayed nigga or bitch wants to be the one who delivers the hurt, witnesses the pain and the torture and the downfall of the lover who is the traitor.

I know. Bullet was the main one who betrayed me. He's at the top of my payback list. He was my nigga for many months before I got arrested. Yeah, he was a hustler. I fucking loved that. His fuck game was strong. I loved that too. Once he and I first hooked up,

I never fucked around with no other nigga but him. I'm a loyal bitch. Loyalty runs through the Santiaga blood. But he never fully acknowledged my loyalty to him. He never gave his loyalty to me. It wasn't about me thinking, expecting, or believing that he was out fucking some random bitches while we was together. He didn't cause me to feel or think that he was. It was that he . . . I don't know. He loved me with his mind and body but never gave me his heart. He treated me like a suspect who was bound to turn on him or turn him in. I wasn't. I'm the one bitch that wouldn't . . . ever. Santiagas are born snitch-free.

Bullet put our Manhattan condo in my name, and he made every purchase for both of us in my name. Back then, at the time, I thought that meant he loved me. Of course I did, he provided. In turn, I covered for him. Held his coke, concealed his weapons, and carried his cash here and there quietly whenever he told me to. I was trying to earn my way up and also into his heart. I thought we should be on some Bonnie-and-Clyde shit. But fuck Bonnie and Clyde. We should have been on some Winter-and-Bullet shit, handling our business, styling while stacking our chips, eating and fucking, chilling and staying together.

Turned out he put everything in my name not for love or for providing for a top bitch and daughter of legendary hustler and entrepreneur Ricky Santiaga. Instead Bullet was on some Brooklyn scheming. He made it so that if everything or anything went wrong, he could drop all the legalities and blame onto me without losing any street credibility because it wasn't like he actually snitched on me. He simply left a paper trail and documentation all in my name that told the fictitious story of me being the hustler and him being blameless, unarrestable, and scot-free. On the day

ing me the condo or even for taking me on his big business run to Virginia. I was down for him. I wanted to go. I didn't like being left out of the business or the action. It's that that nigga Bullet didn't come for me. He didn't add a dime to my legal defense. He didn't send one of his men to make sure I had all that I needed. He didn't put one cent on my commissary. He didn't write me one letter, slip me one kite from his peoples on lock. He didn't check for me, and to me, that meant he never loved me. That's why he's on my payback list. He betrayed me. I never betrayed him, not even once.

So I understand this little sixteen-year-young-looking one, oddly named Ubs, who is tight and at war with her ex. He seemed more my age than hers. But I know that once a bitch blossoms, gets curves and titties and hungry between the thighs, whether she's twelve, thirteen, or sixteen, whether or not the law says she's a minor, she is bound to hunt and chase down a man she chooses for herself. A young sexy bitch, I know, can make it impossible for even an older guy to resist her powers, no matter who he is. He could be handsome or ugly, paid or broke, married or single, hustler or preacher, politician or teacher, doctor or lawyer, or even a goddamn judge. I accept that. As long as it's not the other way around, some old guy hunting, chasing, and cornering her young ass. Fucking and raping are never ever the same thing. He says she betrayed him. He says she's the police. She seemed too young to be anybody's police. And in the I guess seconds I had seen her, she didn't seem like a cop. But I ain't from down here. I don't know how shit goes 'round here. Everything is unexpected. It's like I'm stuck in the world of the unseen and unknown and can't control or predict the action.

But now I am not alone down here. Of course I choose him. He

of my arrest that led to my conviction as a drug dealer sentenced to serve fifteen years on a mandatory minimum, which at the time I had never even heard of, my nigga Bullet had a car rented in my name. In the rental car was me and the product. I was 'bout to ride round trip to Virginia on a run with him, a big and necessary business move.

Simone, who for some reason can't get the fuck out of my mind or life or death story, saw me sitting there on our Brooklyn block in the rental waiting on Bullet. I didn't see her, though. Simone had bullshit beef with me that she swore was real. So soon as she saw me that day, it was on. Bitch threw a brick through the rental window. Bitch dragged me out the car swinging. We thumped. My nigga Bullet saw the rah-rah from a distance. He started rushing over. He fired one shot in the air to cause the commotion to break. Seeing him boosted my confidence, but the gunshot distracted me from keeping my eyes on her. Simone took advantage and sliced my face. Bullet held my bleeding face in his hands. He sat me back in the rental car. He tossed the gun beneath the seat. He walked around to the driver's side. I was relieved that he had rescued me.

But the furious fight and the gunshot drew out the cops. They cops swooped in, and Bullet, instead of jumping into the rental car and speeding away, walked off calmly as though he never intended to get in the car with me at all. I was arrested in the rental car that was in my name, with the weight stuffed inside teddy bears, and the weapon tossed beneath the seat. They cuffed and jailed and grilled and investigated me. They asked me for names or just one big name. I gave them nothing. I rejected their bullshit tricks and game. The name is Santiaga, royalty not snitches. I wasn't mad at Bullet for being a hustler, obviously. I wasn't mad at him for rent-

chose me in the first place. He was the greatest sex I ever had. The wildest feeling I ever felt. He was the only man who ever caused me to let go of Midnight, who *never fucked me at all.* I like a man who *gives a bitch what she wants*. A man who *doesn't make a bitch feel lonely.* Wife number five! Oh hell no. That would never, ever be me.

My new nigga is my forever nigga, from now until the real lights-out. Even though he only fucked me once on the same night we met, I was able to exist inside of that fucking memory. And unlike Bullet, who left me because I was cut and bleeding and would obviously wear a scar, and who set me up to take the fall, or didn't set me up but reacted only to secure himself, my forever nigga is different.